The Citadel
and
The Keys of the Kingdom

[two complete novels]

A. J. CRONIN

The Citadel

and

The Keys of the Kingdom

[two complete novels]

BOSTON

LITTLE, BROWN AND COMPANY

The Citadel

BOOK I

1

LATE one October afternoon in the year 1921, a shabby young man gazed with fixed intensity through the window of a third-class compartment in the almost empty train labouring up the Penowell Valley from Swansea. All that day Manson had travelled from the North, changing at Carlisle and Shrewsbury, yet the final stage of his tedious journey to South Wales found him strung to a still greater excitement by the prospects of his post, the first of his medical career, in this strange, disfigured country.

Outside, a heavy rainstorm came blinding down between the mountains which rose on either side of the single railway track. The mountain tops were hidden in a grey waste of sky, but their sides, scarred by ore workings, fell black and desolate, blemished by great heaps of slag on which a few dirty sheep wandered in vain hope of pasture. No bush, no blade of vegetation was visible. The trees, seen in the fading light, were gaunt and stunted spectres. At a bend of the line the red glare of a foundry flashed into sight, illuminating a score of workmen stripped to the waist, their torsos straining, arms upraised to strike. Though the scene was swiftly lost behind the huddled top gear of a mine, a sense of power persisted, tense and vivid. Manson drew a long breath. He felt an answering surge of effort, a sudden overwhelming exhilaration springing from the hope and promise of the future.

Darkness had fallen, emphasizing the strangeness and remoteness of the scene when, half an hour later, the engine panted into Blaenelly, the end township of the Valley, and the terminus of the line. He had arrived at last. Gripping his bag, Manson leaped from the train and walked quickly down the platform, searching eagerly for some sign of welcome. At the station exit, beneath a wind-blown lamp, a yellow-faced old man in a square hat and a long nightshirt of a mackintosh stood waiting. He inspected Manson with a jaundiced eye and his voice, when it came, was reluctant.

"You Doctor Page's new assistant?"

"That's right. Manson. Andrew Manson is the name."

"Huh! Mine's Thomas; 'Old Thomas' they mostly call me, dang 'em! I got the gig here. Set in—unless you'd rayther swim."

Manson slung his bag up and climbed into the battered gig behind a tall, angular black horse. Thomas followed, took the reins and addressed the horse.

"Hue-up, Taffy!" he said.

They drove off through the town, which, though Andrew tried keenly to discern its outline, presented in the slashing rain no more than a blurred huddle of low grey houses ranged beneath the high and ever-present mountains. For several minutes the old groom did not speak, but continued to dart pessimistic glances at Andrew from beneath the dripping brim of his hat. He bore no resemblance to the smart coachman of a successful doctor, but was, on the contrary, wizened and slovenly, and all the time he gave off a peculiar yet powerful odour of stale cooking-fat.

At last he said: "Only jest got your parchment, eh?"

Andrew nodded.

"I knowed it." Old Thomas spat. His triumph made him more gravely communicative. "Last assistant went ten days ago. Mostly they don't stop."

"Why?" Despite his nervousness, Andrew smiled.

"Work's too hard for one thing, I reckon."

"And for another?"

"You'll find out!" A moment later, as a guide might indicate a fine cathedral, Thomas lifted his whip and pointed to the end of a row of houses where, from a small lighted doorway, a cloud of steam was emerging. "See that! That there's the missus and my chip petato shop. We fry twice a week. Wet fish." A secret amusement twitched his long upper lip. "Reckon you might want to know, shortly."

Here the main street ended and, turning up a short uneven side road, they boggled across a piece of waste ground, and entered the narrow drive of a house which stood isolated from the adjacent rows behind three monkey-puzzle trees. On the gate was the name BRYNGOWER.

"This is us," said Thomas, pulling up the horse.

Andrew descended. The next minute, while he was gathering himself for the ordeal of his entrance, the front door was flung open and he was in the lighted hall being welcomed effusively by a short, plump, smiling woman of about forty with a shining face and bright bold twinkling eyes.

"Well! Well! This must be Doctor Manson. Come in, my dee-ar, come in. I'm Doctor's wife, Mrs. Page. I do hope you didn't have a tryin' journey. I *am* pleased to see you. I been out my mind, nearly, since that last awful feller we had left us. You ought to have seen him. He was a waster if ever I met one, I can tell you. Oh! But never mind. It's all right now you're here. Come along, I'll show you to your room myself."

Upstairs, Andrew's room was a small camsiled apartment with a brass bed, a yellow varnished chest of drawers, and a bamboo table bearing a basin and ewer.

Glancing round it, while her black button eyes searched his face, he said with anxious politeness: "This looks very comfortable, Mrs. Page."

"Yes, indeed." She smiled and patted his shoulder maternally. "You'll do famous here, my dee-ar. You treat me right and I'll treat you right. I can't say fairer nor that, can I? Now come along before you're a minute older and meet Doctor." She paused, her gaze still questioning his, her tone striving to be off-hand. "I don't know if I said so in my letter but, as a matter of fact —Doctor 'asn't been too well, lately."

Andrew looked at her in sudden surprise.

"Oh, it's nothing much," she went on quickly, before he could speak. "He's been laid up a few weeks. But he'll soon be all right. Make no mistake about that."

Perplexed, Andrew followed her to the end of the passage, where she threw open a door, exclaiming blithely:—

"Here's Doctor Manson, Edward—our new assistant. He's come to say 'ow do."

As Andrew went into the room, a long fustily furnished bedroom with chenille curtains closely drawn and a small fire burning in the grate, Edward Page turned slowly upon the bed, seeming to do so by a great effort. He was a big, bony man of perhaps sixty with harshly lined features and tired, luminous eyes. His whole expression was stamped with suffering and a kind of weary patience. And there was something more. The light of the oil lamp, falling across the pillow, revealed one half of his face expressionless and waxen. The left side of his body was equally paralyzed and his left hand, which lay upon the patchwork counterpane, was contracted to a shiny cone.

Observing these signs of a severe and far from recent stroke, Andrew was conscious of a sudden shock of dismay. There was an odd silence.

"I hope you'll like it here," Doctor Page remarked at length, speaking slowly and with difficulty, slurring his words a little. "I hope you'll find the practice won't be too much for you. You're very young."

"I'm twenty-four, sir," Andrew answered awkwardly. "I know this is the first job I've had, and all that—but I'm not afraid of work."

"There, now!" Mrs. Page beamed. "Didn't I tell you, Edward, we'd be lucky with our next one?"

An even deeper immobility settled on Page's face. He gazed at Andrew. Then his interest seemed to fade.

He said in a tired voice: "I hope you'll stay."

"My goodness gracious!" cried Mrs. Page. "What a thing to say!" She turned to Andrew, smilingly and apologetic. "It's only because he's a morsel down to-day. But he'll soon be up and doing again. Won't you, ducky?" Bending, she kissed her husband heartily. "There now! I'll send your supper up by Annie whenever we've 'ad ours."

Page did not answer. The stony look on his one-sided face made his mouth seem twisted. His good hand strayed to the book that lay on the table beside his bed. Andrew saw that it was entitled *The Wild Birds of Europe*. Even before the paralyzed man began to read he felt himself dismissed.

As Andrew went down to supper his thoughts were painfully confused. He had applied for this assistantship in answer to an advertisement in the *Lancet*. Yet in the correspondence, conducted at this end by Mrs. Page, which had led to his securing the post, there had been no mention whatsoever of Doctor Page's illness. But Page was ill; there could be no question of the gravity of the cerebral hæmorrhage which had incapacitated him. It would be months before he was fit for work, if, indeed, he were ever fit for work again.

With an effort Andrew put the puzzle from his mind. He was young, strong, and had no objection to the extra work in which Page's illness might involve him. Indeed, in his enthusiasm, he yearned for an avalanche of calls.

"You're lucky, my dee-ar," remarked Mrs. Page brightly as she bustled into the dining room. "You can have your bit of snap straight off to-night. No surgery. Dai Jenkins done it."

"Dai Jenkins?"

"He's our dispenser," Mrs. Page threw out casually. "A handy little feller. An' willin' too. 'Doc' Jenkins some folks even call him, though of course he's not to be compared in the same breath with Doctor Page. He's done the surgery and visits also, these last ten days."

Andrew stared at her in fresh concern. All that he had been told, all the warnings he had received regarding the questionable ways of practice in these remote Welsh Valleys, flashed into his recollection. Again it cost him an effort to be silent.

Mrs. Page sat at the head of the table with her back to the fire. When she had wedged herself comfortably into her chair with a cushion she sighed in pleasant anticipation and tinkled the little cowbell in front of her. A middle-aged servant with a pale, well-scrubbed face brought in the supper, stealing a glance at Andrew as she entered.

"Come along, Annie," cried Mrs. Page, buttering a wedge of soft bread and stuffing it in her mouth. "This is Doctor Manson."

Annie did not answer. She served Andrew in a contained, silent fashion with a thin slice of cold boiled brisket. For Mrs. Page, however, there was a hot beefsteak and onions with a pint bottle of oatmeal stout. As the doctor's wife lifted the cover from her special dish and cut into the juicy meat, her teeth watering in expectation, she explained:—

"I didn't have much lunch, Doctor. Besides, I got to watch my diet. It's the blood. I have to take a drop of porter for the blood."

Andrew chewed his stringy brisket and drank cold water determinedly. After a momentary indignation his main difficulty lay with his own sense of humour. Her pretence of invalidism was so blatant he had to struggle to conquer a wild impulse to laugh.

During the meal Mrs. Page ate freely but said little. At length, sopping up the gravy with her bread, she finished her steak, smacked her lips over the last of the stout, and lay back in her chair, breathing a trifle heavily, her round little cheeks flushed and shiny. Now she seemed disposed to linger at table, inclined to confidences—perhaps trying, in her own bold way, to sum Manson up.

Studying him, she saw a spare and gawky youngster, dark, rather tensely drawn, with high cheekbones, a fine jaw and blue eyes. These eyes, when he raised them, were, despite the nervous tensity of his brow, extraordinarily steady and inquiring. Although Blodwen Page knew nothing of it, she was looking at a Celtic type. Though she admitted the vigour and alert intelligence in Andrew's face, what pleased her most of all was his acceptance, without demur, of that scanty cut from the three-days-old heel of brisket. She reflected that, though he looked hungry, he might not be hard to feed.

"I'm sure we'll get on famous, you and me," she again declared genially, picking her teeth with a hairpin. "I do need a bit o' luck for a change." Mellowed, she told him of her troubles, and sketched a vague outline of the practice and its position. "It's been awful, my dee-ar. You don't know. What with Doctor Page's illness, wicked bad assistants, nothin' comin' in and everythin' goin' out—well! you wouldn't believe it! And the job I've 'ad to keep the manager and mine officials sweet—it's them the practice money comes through—what there is of it," she added hurriedly. "You see, the way they work things in Blaenelly is like this: the Company has three doctors on its list, though mind you Doctor Page is far and away the cleverest doctor of the lot. And besides—the time he's been 'ere! Nearly thirty years and more; that's something, I should think! Well, then, these doctors can have as many assistants as they like,—Doctor Page has you, and Doctor Lewis has a would-be feller called Denny,—but the assistants don't ever get on the Company's list. Anyway, as I was sayin', the Company deducts so much from every man's wages they employ at the mines and the quarries, and pays that out to the listed doctors according to 'ow many of the men signs on with them."

She broke off under the strain of her illiteracy and an overloaded stomach.

"I think I see how the system works, Mrs. Page."

"Well, then!" She heaved out her jolly laugh. "You don't have to bother about it no more. All you got to remember is that you're workin' for Doctor Page. That's the main thing, Doctor. Just remember you're workin' for Doctor Page and you and poor little me'll get on a treat."

It seemed to Manson, silent and observant, that she tried at the same time to excite his pity and to establish her authority over him, all beneath that manner of breezy affability. Perhaps she felt she had unbent too far. With a glance at the clock, she straightened herself, restored the hairpin to her greasy black hair. Then she rose. Her voice was different, almost peremptory.

"By the way, there's a call for Number 7 Glydar Place. It come in the back of five o'clock. You better do it straight away."

2

ANDREW went out to the call immediately, with a queer sensation, almost of relief. He was glad of the opportunity to disentangle himself from the curious and conflicting emotions stirred up by his arrival at Bryngower. Already he had a glimmer of a suspicion as to how matters stood and of how he would be made use of by Blodwen Page to run the practice for his disabled principal. It was a strange situation, and very different from any romantic picture which his fancy might have painted. Yet, after all, his work was the important thing; beside it all else was trivial. He longed to begin it. Insensibly he hastened his pace, taut with anticipation, exulting in the realization—this, this was his first case.

It was still raining when he crossed the smeary blackness of the waste land and struck along Chapel Street in the direction vaguely indicated by Mrs. Page. Darkly, as he traversed it, the town took shape before him. Shops and chapels—Zion, Capel, Hebron, Bethel, Bethesda; he passed a round dozen of them—then the big Co-operative Stores, and a branch of the Western Counties Bank, all lining the main thoroughfare, lying deep in the bed of the Valley. The sense of being buried, far down in this cleft of the mountains, was singularly oppressive. There were few people about. At right angles, reaching up a short distance on either side of Chapel Street, were rows and rows of blue-roofed workers' houses. And, beyond, at the head of the gorge, beneath a glow that spread like a great fan into the opaque sky, the Blaenelly Hæmatite Mine and Ore Works.

He reached 7 Glydar Place, knocked breathlessly upon the door, and was at once admitted to the kitchen, where, in the recessed bed, the patient lay. She was a young woman, wife of a steel puddler named Williams, and as he approached the bedside with a fast-beating heart he felt, overwhelmingly, the significance of this, the real starting-point of his life. How often had he envisaged it as, in a crowd of students, he had watched a demonstration in Professor Lamplough's wards! Now there was no sustaining crowd, no easy exposition. He was alone, confronted by a case which he must diagnose and treat unaided. All at once, with a quick pang, he was conscious of his nervousness, his inexperience, his complete unpreparedness, for such a task.

While the husband stood by in the cramped, ill-lit stone-floored room, Andrew Manson examined the patient with scrupulous care. There was no doubt about it, she was ill. She complained that her head ached intolerably. Temperature, pulse, tongue, they all spoke of trouble, serious trouble. What was it? Andrew asked himself that question with a strained intensity as he went over her again. His first case. Oh, he knew that he was overanxious! But suppose he made an error, a frightful blunder? And worse—suppose he found himself unable to make a diagnosis? He had missed nothing. Nothing. Yet he still found himself struggling towards some solution of the problem, striving to group the symptoms under the heading of some recognized disease. At last, aware that he could protract his investigation no longer, he straightened himself slowly, folding up his stethoscope, fumbling for words.

"Did she have a chill?" he asked, his eyes upon the floor.

"Yes, indeed," Williams answered eagerly. He had looked scared during the prolonged examination. "Three, four days ago. I made sure it was a chill, Doctor."

Andrew nodded, attempting painfully to generate a confidence he did not feel. He muttered, "We'll soon have her right. Come to the surgery in half an hour. I'll give you a bottle of medicine."

He took his leave of them and with his head down, thinking desperately, he trudged back to the surgery, a ramshackle wooden erection standing at the entrance to Page's drive. Inside, he lit the gas and began to pace backwards and forwards beside the blue and green bottles on the dusty shelves, racking his brains, groping in the darkness. There was nothing symptomatic. It must, yes, it must be a chill. But in his heart he knew that it was not a chill. He groaned in exasperation, dismayed and angry at his own inadequacy. He was forced, unwillingly, to temporize. Professor Lamplough, when confronted by obscurity in his wards, had a neat little ticket, which he tactfully applied: P.U.O.—pyrexia of unknown origin—it was noncommittal and exact, and it had such an admirable scientific sound!

Unhappily, Andrew took a six-ounce bottle from the recess beneath the dispensary counter and began with a frown of concentration to compound an antipyretic mixture. Spirits of nitre, salicylate of sodium—where the dickens was the soda sal.? Oh, there it was! He tried to cheer himself by reflecting that they were all splendid, all excellent drugs, bound to get the temperature down, certain to do good. Professor Lamplough had often declared there was no drug so generally valuable as salicylate of sodium.

He had just finished his compounding and with a mild sense of achievement was writing the label when the surgery bell went *ping*, the outer door swung open, and a short, powerfully thickset red-faced man of thirty strolled in, followed by a dog. There was a silence while the black-and-tan mongrel squatted on its muddy haunches, and the man—who wore an old velveteen suit, pit stockings, and hobnail boots, with a sodden oilskin cape over his shoulders—looked Andrew up and down. His voice, when it came, was politely ironic and annoyingly well-bred.

"I saw a light in your window as I was passing. Thought I'd look in to welcome you. I'm Denny, assistant to the esteemed Doctor Lewis, L.S.A. That, in case you haven't met it, is the Licentiate of the Society of Apothecaries, the highest qualification known to God and man."

Andrew stared back doubtfully. Philip Denny lit a cigarette from a crumpled paper packet, threw the match on the floor, and strolled forward insolently. He picked up the bottle of medicine, read the address, the directions, uncorked it, sniffed it, recorked it and put it down, his morose red face turning blandly complimentary.

"Splendid! You've begun the good work already! One tablespoon every three hours. God Almighty! It's reassuring to meet the dear old mumbojummery. But, Doctor, why not three times a day? Don't you realize, Doctor, that in strict orthodoxy the tablespoonfuls should pass down the œsophagus three times a day?" He paused, becoming, with his assumed air of confidence, more blandly offensive than ever. "Now tell me, Doctor, what's in it? Spirit of nitre, by the smell. Wonderful stuff, sweet spirit of nitre. Wonderful, wonderful, my dear Doctor! Carminative, stimulant, diuretic, and you can swill it by the tubful. Don't you remember what it says in the little red book? When in doubt give spirit of nitre—or is it *pot. iod.*? Tut! Tut! I seem to have forgotten some of my essentials."

Again there was a silence in the wooden shed, broken only by the drumming of the rain upon the tin roof. Suddenly Denny laughed, a mocking appreciation of the blank expression on Andrew's face.

He said derisively: "Science apart, Doctor, you might satisfy my curiosity. Why have you come here?"

By this time Andrew's temper was rising rapidly. He answered grimly: "My idea was to turn Blaenelly into a health resort—a sort of spa, you know."

Again Denny laughed. His laugh was an insult, which made Andrew long to hit him.

"Witty, witty, my dear Doctor. The true Scots steam-roller humour. Unfortunately I can't recommend the water here as being ideally suited for a spa. As to the medical gentlemen—my dear Doctor, in this Valley they're the rag, tag, and bobtail of a glorious, a truly noble profession."

"Including yourself?"

"Precisely!" Denny nodded. He was silent a moment, contemplating Andrew from beneath his sandy eyebrows. Then he dropped his mocking irony; his ugly features turned morose again. His tone, though bitter, was serious.

"Look here, Manson! I realize you're just passing through on your way to Harley Street, but in the meantime there are one or two things about this place you ought to know. You won't find it conforms to the best traditions of romantic practice. There's no hospital, no ambulance, no X rays, no anything. If you want to operate you use the kitchen table. You wash up afterwards at the scullery bosh. The sanitation won't bear looking at. In a dry summer the kids die like flies with infantile cholera. Page, your boss, was a damn good old doctor, but he's finished now, bitched by Blodwen, and'll never do a hand's turn again. Lewis, my owner, is a tight little money-chasing midwife. Bramwell, the Silver King, knows nothing but a few sentimental recitations and the Songs of Solomon. As for myself, I'd better anticipate the gay tidings—I drink like a fish. Oh! and Jenkins, your tame druggist, does a thriving trade, on the side, in little lead pills for female ills. I think that's about all. Come, Hawkins, we'll go." He called the mongrel and moved heavily towards the door. There he paused, his eyes ranging again from the bottle on the counter to Manson. His tone was flat, quite uninterested. "By the way, I should look out for enteric in Glydar Place, if I were you. Some of these cases aren't exactly typical."

Ping! went the door again. Before Andrew could answer, Doctor Philip Denny and Hawkins disappeared into the wet darkness.

3

IT was not his lumpy flock mattress which caused Andrew to sleep badly that night, but growing anxiety about the case in Glydar Place. Was it enteric? Denny's parting remark had started a fresh train of doubt and misgiving in his already uncertain mind. Dreading that he had overlooked some vital symptom, he restrained himself with difficulty from rising and revisiting the case at an unearthly hour of the morning. Indeed, as he tossed and turned through the long restless night, he came to ask himself if he knew anything of medicine at all.

Manson's nature was extraordinarily intense. Probably he derived this from his mother, a Highland woman who, in her childhood, had watched the northern lights leap through the frosted sky from her home in Ullapool. His father, John Manson, a small Fifeshire farmer, had been solid, painstaking, and steady. He had never made a success of the land, and when he was killed in the Yeomanry in the last year of the War, he had left the affairs of the little steading in a sad muddle. For twelve months Jessie Manson had struggled to run the farm as a dairy, even driving the float upon the milkround herself when she felt Andrew was too busy with his books to do so. Then the cough which she had unsuspectingly endured for a period of years turned worse and suddenly she surrendered to the lung complaint which ravages that soft-skinned, dark-haired type.

At eighteen Andrew found himself alone, a first-year student at St. Andrews University, carrying a scholarship worth forty pounds a year, but otherwise penniless. His salvation had been the Glen Endowment, that typically Scottish foundation, which in the naïve terminology of the late Sir Andrew Glen "invites deserving and necessitous students of the baptismal name of Andrew to apply for loans not exceeding fifty pounds a year for five years provided they are conscientiously prepared to reimburse such loans whenever they have qualified."

The Glen Endowment, coupled with some gay starvation, had sent Andrew through the remainder of his course at St. Andrews, then on to the Medical Schools in the city of Dundee. And gratitude to the Endowment, allied to an inconvenient honesty, had sent him hurrying down to South Wales—where newly qualified assistants could command the highest remuneration—to a salary of two hundred and fifty pounds a year, when in his heart he would have preferred a clinical appointment at the Edinburgh Royal and an honorarium of one tenth that sum.

And now he was in Blaenelly, rising, shaving, dressing, all in a haze of worry over his first patient. He ate his breakfast quickly, then ran up to his room again. There he opened his bag and took out a small blue leather case. He opened the case and gazed earnestly at the medal inside—the Hunter Gold Medal, awarded annually at St. Andrews to the best student in clinical medicine. He, Andrew Manson, had won it. He prized it beyond everything, had come to regard it as his talisman, his inspiration for the future. But this morning he viewed it less with pride than with a queer, secret entreaty, as though trying to restore his confidence in himself. Then he hurried out for the morning surgery.

Dai Jenkins was already in the wooden shanty when Andrew reached it, running water from the tap into a large earthenware pipkin. He was a quick little whippet of a man with purple-veined, hollow cheeks, eyes that went everywhere at once, and the tightest pair of trousers on his thin legs that Andrew had ever seen.

He greeted Manson ingratiatingly:—

"You don't have to be so early, Doctor. I can do the repeat mixtures and the certificates before you come in. Mrs. Page had a rubber stamp made with Doctor's signature when he was taken bad."

"Thanks," Andrew answered. "I'd rather see the cases myself." He paused, shaken momentarily from his anxiety by the dispenser's procedure. "What's the idea?"

Jenkins winked. "Tastes better out of here. We know what good old *aqua* means, eh, Doctor, *bach*? But the patients don't. I'd look a proper fool too, wouldn't I, them standin' there watchin' me fillin' up their bottles out the tap."

Plainly the little dispenser wished to be communicative, but here a loud voice rang out from the back door of the house forty yards away.

"Jenkins! *Jenkins!* I want you—*this minnit.*"

Jenkins jumped like an overtrained dog at the crack of the ring-master's whip. He quavered: "Excuse me, Doctor. There's Mrs. Page callin' me. I'll . . . I'll have to run."

Fortunately there were few people at the morning surgery, which was over at half-past ten, and Andrew, presented with a list of visits by Jenkins, set out at once with Thomas in the gig. With an almost painful expectancy he told the old groom to drive direct to 7 Glydar Place.

Twenty minutes later he came out of Number 7, pale, with his lips tightly compressed and an odd expression on his face. He went two doors down, into Number 11, which was also on his list. From Number 11 he crossed the street to Number 18. From Number 18 he went round the corner to Radnor Place, where two further cases were marked by Jenkins as having been seen the day before. Altogether, within the space of an hour, he made seven such calls in the immediate vicinity. Five of them, including Number 7 Glydar Place, which was now showing a typical rash, were clear cases of enteric. For the last ten days Jenkins had been treating them with chalk and opium. Now, whatever his own bungling efforts of the previous night had been, Andrew realized with a shiver of apprehension that he had an outbreak of typhoid fever on his hands.

The remainder of his round he accomplished as quickly as possible in a state dithering towards panic. At lunch, during which Mrs. Page dealt exclusively with a nicely browned sweetbread, which she explained merrily, "I ordered it for Doctor Page but he don't seem to fancy it somehow," he brooded upon the problem in frozen silence. He saw that he would get little information and no help from Mrs. Page. He decided he must speak to Doctor Page himself.

But when he went up to the doctor's room the curtains were drawn and Edward lay prostrate with a pressure headache, his forehead deeply flushed and furrowed by pain. Though he motioned his visitor to sit with him a little Andrew felt it would be cruelty to thrust this trouble upon him at present.

As he rose to go, after remaining seated by the bedside for a few minutes, he had to confine himself to asking: "Doctor Page, if we get an infectious case, what's the best thing to do?"

There was a pause. Page replied with closed eyes, not moving, as though the mere act of speech were enough to aggravate his migraine.

"It's always been difficult. We've no hospital, let alone an isolation ward. If you should run into anything very nasty ring up Griffiths at Toniglan. That's fifteen miles down the Valley. He's the District Medical Officer." Another pause, longer than before. "But I'm afraid he's not very helpful."

Reinforced by this information, Andrew hastened down to the hall and rang up Toniglan. While he stood with the receiver to his ear he saw Annie, the servant, looking at him through the kitchen door.

"Hello! Hello! Is that Doctor Griffiths of Toniglan?" He got through at last.

A man's voice answered very guardedly. "Who wants him?"

"This is Manson of Blaenelly. Doctor Page's assistant." Andrew's tone was overpitched. "I've got five cases of typhoid up here. I want Doctor Griffiths to come up immediately."

There was the barest pause, then with a rush the reply came back in a singsong intonation, very Welsh and apologetic. "I'm powerful sorry, Doctor, indeed I am, but Doctor Griffiths has gone to Swansea. Important official business."

"When will he be back?" shouted Manson. The line was bad.

"Indeed, Doctor, I couldn't say for certain."

"But, listen . . ."

There was a click at the far end. Very quietly the other had rung off. Manson swore out loud with nervous violence. "Damn it, I believe that was Griffiths himself."

He rang the number again, failed to get a connection. Yet, persisting doggedly, he was about to ring again when, turning, he found that Annie had advanced into the hall, her hands folded upon her apron, her eyes contemplating him soberly. She was a woman of perhaps forty-five, very clean and tidy, with a grave, enduring placidity of expression.

"I couldn't help but hear, Doctor," she said. "You'll never find Doctor Griffiths in Toniglan this hour of day. He do go to the golf at Swansea afternoons mostly."

He answered angrily, swallowing a lump that hung in his throat.

"But I think that was him I spoke to."

"Maybe." She smiled faintly. "When he don't go to Swansea I've 'eard tell he do say 'e 'ave gone." She considered him with tranquil friendliness before turning away. "I wouldn't waste my time on him if I was you."

Andrew replaced the receiver with a deepening sense of indignation and distress. Cursing, he went out and visited his cases once more. When he got back it was time for evening surgery. For an hour and a half he sat in the little back-shop cubicle which was the consulting room, wrestling with a packed surgery until the walls sweated and the place was choked with the steam of damp bodies. Miners with beat knees, cut fingers, nystagmus, chronic arthritis. Their wives, too, and their children with coughs, colds, sprains—all the minor ailments of humanity. Normally he would have enjoyed it, welcomed the quiet appraising scrutiny of these dark, sallow-skinned people with whom he felt he was on probation. But now, obsessed by the major issue, his head reeled with the impact of these trifling complaints. Yet all the time he was reaching his decision, thinking, as he wrote prescriptions, sounded chests and offered words of advice, "It was he who put me on to the thing. I hate him. Yes, I loathe him—superior devil—like hell. But I can't help that; I'll have to go to him."

At half-past nine, when the last patient had left the surgery, he came out of his den with resolution in his eyes.

"Jenkins, where does Doctor Denny live?"

The little dispenser, hastily bolting the outer door for fear another straggler might come in, turned with a look of horror on his face that was almost comic.

"You aren't goin' to have anything to do with that feller, Doctor? Mrs. Page—she don't like him."

Andrew asked grimly: "Why doesn't Mrs. Page like him?"

"For the same reason everybody don't. 'E's been so damn rude to her." Jenkins paused then; reading Manson's look he added, reluctantly, "Oh, well, if you 'ave to know, it's with Mrs. Seager he stops, Number 49 Chapel Street."

Out again. He had been going the whole day long, yet any tiredness he might have felt was lost in a sense of responsibility, the burden of those cases pressing, pressing urgently upon his shoulders. His main feeling was one of relief when, on reaching Chapel Street, he found that Denny was at his lodgings. The landlady showed him in.

If Denny was surprised to see him he concealed it. He merely asked, after a prolonged and aggravating stare, "Well! Killed anybody yet?"

Still standing in the doorway of the warm untidy sitting-room, Andrew reddened. But, making a great effort, he conquered his temper and his pride.

He said abruptly: "You were right. It was enteric. I ought to be shot for not recognizing it. I've got five cases. I'm not exactly overjoyed at having to come here. But I don't know the ropes. I rang the M.O., and couldn't get a word out of him. I've come to ask your advice."

Denny, half-slewed round in his chair by the fire, listening, pipe in mouth, at last made a grudging gesture.

"You'd better come in." With sudden irritation: "Oh! and for God's sake take a chair. Don't stand there like a Presbyterian parson about to forbid the banns. Have a drink? No! I thought you wouldn't."

Though Andrew stiffly complied with the request, seating himself and even, defensively, lighting a cigarette, Denny seemed in no hurry. He sat prodding the dog Hawkins with the toe of his burst slipper.

But at length, when Manson had finished his cigarette, Denny said with a jerk of his head: "Take a look at that, if you like!"

On the table indicated a microscope stood,—a fine Zeiss,—and some slides. Andrew focussed a slide, then slid round the oil-immersion and immediately picked up the rod-shaped clusters of the bacteria.

"It's very clumsily done, of course," Denny said quickly and cynically, as though forestalling criticism. "Practically botched, in fact. I'm no lab. merchant, thank God! If anything, I'm a surgeon. But you've got to be jack-of-all-trades under our bloody system. There's no mistake, though, even to the naked eye. I cooked them on agar in my oven."

"You've got cases too?" Andrew asked with tense interest.

"Four! All in the same area as yours." He paused. "And these bugs come from the well in Glydar Place."

Andrew gazed at him, alert, burning to ask a dozen questions, realizing something of the genuineness of the other man's work, and, beyond everything, overjoyed that he had been shown the focus of the epidemic.

"You see," Denny resumed with that same cold and bitter irony, "paratyphoid is more or less endemic here. But one day soon, very soon, we're going to have a pretty little blaze-up. It's the main sewer that's to blame. It leaks like the devil, and seeps into half the low wells at the bottom of the town. I've hammered at Griffiths about it till I'm tired. He's a lazy, evasive, incompetent, pious swine. Last time I rang him I said I'd knock his block off next time I met him. Probably that's why he welshed on you to-day."

"It's a damned shame," Andrew burst out, forgetting himself in a sudden rush of indignation.

Denny shrugged his shoulders. "He's afraid to ask the Council for anything in case they dock his wretched salary to pay for it."

There was a silence. Andrew had a warm desire that the conversation might continue. Despite his hostility towards Denny, he found a strange stimulus in the other's pessimism, in his scepticism, his cold and measured cynicism. Yet now he had no pretext on which to prolong his stay. He got up from his seat at the table and moved towards the door, concealing his feelings, striving to express a formal gratitude, to give some indications of his relief.

"I'm much obliged for the information. You've let me see how I stand. I was worried about the origin, thought I might be dealing with a carrier; but since you've localized it to the well it's a lot simpler. From now on every drop of water in Glydar Place is going to be boiled."

Denny rose also. He growled: "It's Griffiths who ought to be boiled." Then, with a return of his satiric humour: "Now, no touching thanks, Doctor, if you please. We shall probably have to endure a little more of each other before this thing is finished. Come and see me any time you can bear it. We don't have much social life in this neighbourhood." He glanced at the dog and concluded rudely: "Even a Scots doctor would be welcome. Isn't that so, Sir John?"

Sir John Hawkins flogged the rug with his tail, his pink tongue lolling derisively at Manson.

Yet, going home via Glydar Place, where he left strict instructions regarding the water supply, Andrew realized that he did not detest Denny so much as he had thought.

4

ANDREW threw himself into the enteric campaign with all the fire of his impetuous and ardent nature. He loved his work and he counted himself fortunate to have such an opportunity so early in his career. During these first weeks he slaved joyfully. He had all the ordinary routine of the practice on his hands, yet somehow he got through with it, then turned exultantly to his typhoid cases.

Perhaps he was lucky in this, his first assault. As the end of the month drew near, all his enteric patients were doing well and he seemed to have confined the outbreak. When he thought of his precautions, so rigidly enforced—the boiling of the water, the disinfection and isolation, the carbolic-soaked sheet on every door, the pounds of chloride of lime he had ordered to Mrs. Page's account and himself shot down the Glydar drains, he exclaimed in elation: "It's working. I don't deserve it. But by God! I'm *doing* it!" He took a secret, detestable delight in the fact that his cases were mending quicker than Denny's.

Denny still puzzled, exasperated him. They naturally saw each other often because of the proximity of their cases. It pleased Denny to exert the full force of his irony upon the work which they were doing. He referred to Manson and himself as "grimly battling with the epidemic" and savoured the cliché with vindictive relish. But for all his satire, his sneers of "Don't forget, Doctor, we're upholding the honour of a truly glorious profession," he went close to his patients, sat on their beds, laid his hands upon them, spent hours in their sickrooms.

At times Andrew came near to liking him for a flash of shy, self-conscious simplicity, then the whole thing would be shattered by a morose and sneering word. Hurt and baffled, Andrew turned one day in the hope of enlightenment to the *Medical Directory*. It was a five-year-old copy on Doctor Page's shelf; but it held some startling information. It showed Philip Denny as an honours scholar of Cambridge and Guy's, an M.S. of England, holding—at that date— a practice with an honorary surgical appointment in the ducal town of Leeborough.

Then, on the tenth day of November, Denny unexpectedly rang him up.

"Manson! I'd like to see you. Can you come to my place at three o'clock? It's important."

"Very well. I'll be there."

Andrew went into lunch thoughtfully. As he ate the cottage pie that was his portion he felt Blodwen Page's eye fastened on him in a bright and over-bearing stare.

"Who was that on the phone? So it was Denny, eh? You don't have to go around with that feller. He's no use at all."

He faced her coldly. "On the contrary, I've found him a great deal of use."

"Go on with you, Doctor!" As usual, when opposed, Blodwen sparked out spitefully. "He's reg'lar quee-ar. Mostly he don't give medicine at all. Why, when Megan Rhys Morgan, what's had to have medicine all her life, went to him, he told her to walk two mile up the mountain every day and stop boggin' herself with hogwash. These was his very words. She came to us after, I can tell you, and has had bottles and bottles of splendid medicine from Jenkins ever since. Oh! he's a low insultin' devil. 'E's got a wife somewhere by all accounts. Not livin' with him. See! Mostly he's drunk also. You leave him alone, Doctor, and remember you're workin' for Doctor Page."

As she flung the familiar injunction at his head Andrew felt a quick rush of anger sweep over him. He was doing his utmost to please her; yet there seemed no limit to her demands. Her attitude, whether of suspicion or jollity, seemed always designed to get the last ounce out of him and to give as little as possible in return. His first month's pay was already three days overdue, perhaps an oversight upon her part, yet one which had worried and annoyed him considerably. At the sight of her there, greasily buxom, tight with good living, sitting in judgment upon Denny, his feelings got the better of him.

He said with sudden heat: "I'd be more likely to remember that I'm working for Doctor Page if I had my month's salary, Mrs. Page."

She reddened so quickly that he was sure the matter lay in the forefront of her mind. Then she tossed her head defiantly. "You shall have it. The idea!"

For the rest of the meal she sat in a huff, not looking at him, as though he had insulted her. But after lunch, when she called him into the sitting-room, her mood was affable, smiling, merry.

"Here's your money then, Doctor. Sit down and be friendly. We can't get along if we don't pull together proper."

She herself was seated in the green plush armchair, and in her pudgy lap were twenty pound notes and her black leather purse. Taking up the notes she began to count them slowly into Manson's hand—"One, two, three, four!" As she approached the end of the bundle she went slower and slower, her sly black eyes twinkling ingratiatingly, and when she came to eighteen she stopped altogether and gave a self-commiserating little gasp.

"Dear, oh dear, Doctor, it's a lot of money in these hard times. What d'you say? Give and take's always been my motto. Shall I keep the odd two for luck?"

He simply kept silent. The situation created by her meanness was abominable. He knew that the practice was paying her handsomely.

For a full minute she sat there, searching his face; then, finding no response but a stony blankness, with a peevish gesture she slapped over the rest of the notes and said sharply: "See you earn it, then!"

She rose abruptly and made to quit the room, but Andrew stopped her before she reached the door.

"Just a moment, Mrs. Page." There was nervous determination in his voice.

Hateful though this might be, he was determined not to let her, or her cupidity, get the better of him. "You've only given me twenty pounds, which works out at two hundred and forty a year, whereas we both definitely agreed that my salary should be two-fifty. You owe me another sixteen shillings and eightpence, Mrs. Page."

She went dead-white with temper and disappointment.

"So!" she panted. "You're goin' to let the silver come between us. I always heard the Scotch was mean. And now I know it. Here! Take your dirty shillin's, and your coppers too."

She counted out the money from her bulging purse, her fingers trembling, her eyes snapping at him. Then, with a final glare, she bounced out and slammed the door.

Andrew left the house smouldering with anger. Her taunt had stung him more deeply because he felt it to be unfair. Couldn't she see that it was not the paltry sum which was at stake but the whole principle of justice? Besides, apart from any high-sounding morality, he had an inborn trait: a Northern resolution never, while he breathed, to allow anyone to make a fool of him.

Only when he had reached the post office, bought a registered envelope, and posted the twenty pounds to the Glen Endowment—he kept the silver as pocket money for himself—did he feel better. Standing on the steps of the post office, he saw Doctor Bramwell approaching and his expression lightened further.

Bramwell came slowly, his large feet pressing down the pavement majestically, his seedy black figure erect, uncut white hair sweeping over the back of his soiled collar, eyes fixed on the book he held at arm's length. When he reached Andrew, whom he had seen from halfway down the street, he gave a theatrical start of recognition.

"Ah! Manson, my boy! I was so immersed, I almost missed you!"

Andrew smiled. He was already on friendly terms with Doctor Bramwell, who, unlike Lewis, the other "listed" doctor, had given him a cordial welcome on his arrival. Bramwell's practice was not extensive, and did not permit him the luxury of an assistant, but he had a grand manner, and some attitudes worthy of a great healer.

He closed his book, studiously marking the place with one dirty forefinger, then thrust his free hand picturesquely into the breast of his faded coat. He was so operatic he seemed hardly real. But there he was, in the main street of Blaenelly. No wonder Denny had named him "the Silver King."

"And how, my dear boy, are you liking our little community? As I told you when you called upon my dear wife and myself at The Retreat, it isn't so bad as it might appear at first sight. We have our talent, our culture. My dear wife and I do our best to foster it. We carry the torch, Manson, even in the wilderness. You must come to us one evening. Do you sing?"

Andrew had an awful feeling that he must laugh.

Bramwell was continuing with unction:—

"Of course, we have all heard of your work with the enteric cases. Blaenelly is proud of you, my dear boy. I only wish the chance had come my way. If there is any emergency in which I can be of service to you, call upon me!"

A sense of compunction—who was he that he should be amused by the older man?—prompted Andrew to reply:—

"As a matter of fact, Doctor Bramwell, I've got a really interesting secondary mediastinitis in one of my cases, very unusual. You may care to see it with me if you're free."

"Yes?" queried Bramwell with a slight fall in his enthusiasm. "I don't wish to trouble you."

"It's just round the corner," Andrew said hospitably. "And I've got half an hour to spare before I meet Doctor Denny. We'll be there in a second."

Bramwell hesitated, looked for a minute as though he might refuse, then made a damped gesture of assent. They walked down to Glydar Place and went in to see the patient.

The case was, as Manson had inferred, one of unusual interest, involving a rare instance of persistence of the thymus gland. He was genuinely proud to have diagnosed it and he experienced a warm sense of communicative ardour as he invited Bramwell to share the thrill of his discovery.

But Doctor Bramwell, despite his protestations, seemed unattracted by the opportunity. He followed Andrew into the room haltingly, breathing through his nose, and in ladylike fashion approached the bed. Here he drew up and, at a safe range, made a cursory investigation. Nor was he disposed to linger. Only when they left the house, and he had inhaled a long breath of the pure fresh air, did his normal eloquence return. He glowed towards Andrew.

"I'm glad to have seen your case with you my boy, firstly because I feel it part of a doctor's calling never to shrink from the danger of infection, and secondly because I rejoice in the chance of scientific advancement. *Believe it or not, this is the best case of inflammation of the pancreas I have ever seen!*"

He shook hands and hurried off, leaving Andrew utterly nonplussed. The pancreas, thought Andrew dazedly. It was no mere slip of the tongue which had caused Bramwell to make that crass error. His entire conduct at the case betrayed his ignorance. He simply did not know. Andrew rubbed his brow. To think that a qualified practitioner, in whose hands lay the lives of hundreds of human beings, did not know the difference between the pancreas and the thymus, when one lay in the belly and the other in the chest—why, it was nothing short of staggering!

He walked slowly up the street towards Denny's lodgings, realizing once again how his whole orderly conception of the practice of medicine was toppling about him. He knew himself to be raw, inadequately trained, quite capable of making mistakes through his inexperience. But Bramwell was not inexperienced and because of that his ignorance was inexcusable. Unconsciously Andrew's thoughts returned to Denny, who never failed in his derision towards this profession to which they belonged. Denny at first had aggravated him intensely by his weary contention that all over Britain there were thousands of incompetent doctors distinguished for nothing but their sheer stupidity and an acquired capacity for bluffing their patients. Now he began to question if there were not some truth in what Denny said. He determined to reopen the argument this afternoon.

But when he entered Denny's room, he saw immediately that the occasion was not one for academic discussion. Philip received him in morose silence with a gloomy eye and a darkened forehead.

Then, after a moment, he said: "Young Jones died this morning at seven o'clock. Perforation." He spoke quietly, with a still, cold fury. "And I have two new enterics in Ystrad Row."

Andrew dropped his eyes, sympathizing, yet hardly knowing what to say.

"Don't look so smug about it," Denny went on bitterly. "It's sweet for you to see my cases go wrong and yours recover. But it won't be so pretty when that cursed sewer leaks your way."

"No, no! Honestly, I'm sorry," Andrew said impulsively. "We'll have to do something about it. We must write to the Ministry of Health."

"We could write a dozen letters," Philip answered, with grim restraint. "And all we'd get would be a doddering commissioner down here in six months' time. No! I've thought it all out. There's only one way to make them build a new sewer."

"How?"

"Blow up the old one!"

For a second Andrew wondered if Denny had taken leave of his senses. Then he perceived something of the other's hard intention. He stared at him in consternation. Try as he might to reconstruct his changing ideas, Denny seemed fated to demolish them.

Manson muttered: "There'll be a heap of trouble—if it's found out."

Denny glanced up arrogantly.

"You needn't come in with me, if you don't want to."

"Oh, I'm coming in with you," Andrew answered slowly. "But God only knows why!"

All that afternoon Manson went about his work fretfully regretting the promise he had given. He was a madman, this Denny, who would, sooner or later, involve him in serious trouble. It was a dreadful thing that he now proposed, a breach of the law which, if discovered, would bring them into the police court and might even cause them to be scored off the Medical Register. A tremor of sheer horror passed over Andrew at the thought of his beautiful career, stretching so shiningly before him, suddenly cut short, ruined. He cursed Philip violently, swore inwardly, a dozen times, that he would not go.

Yet, for some strange and complex reason, he would not, could not draw back.

At eleven o'clock that night Denny and he started out in company with the mongrel Hawkins for the end of Chapel Street. It was very dark with a gusty wind and a fine spatter of rain which blew into their faces at the street corners. Denny had made his plan and timed it carefully. The late shift at the mine

had gone in an hour ago. A few lads hung about old Thomas' fish shop at
the top end, but otherwise the street was deserted.

The two men and the dog moved quietly. In the pocket of his heavy overcoat, Denny had six sticks of dynamite especially stolen for him that afternoon
from the powder shed at the quarry by Tom Seager, his landlady's son. Andrew carried six cocoa tins, each with a hole bored in the lid, an electric torch,
and a length of fuse. Slouching along, coat collar turned up, one eye directed
apprehensively across his shoulder, his mind a whirl of conflicting emotions,
he gave only the curtest answers to Denny's brief remarks. He wondered
grimly what Lamplough—bland professor of the orthodox—would think of
him, involved in this outrageous nocturnal adventure.

Immediately above Glydar Place they reached the main manhole of the
sewer, a rusty iron cover set in rotten concrete, and there they set to work.
The gangrenous cover had not been disturbed for years but, after a struggle,
they prised it up. Then Andrew shone the torch discreetly into the odorous
depths, where on the crumbled stonework a dirty stream flowed slimily.

"Pretty, isn't it?" Denny rasped. "Take a look at the cracks in that pointing.
Take a *last* look, Manson."

No more was said. Inexplicably, Andrew's mood had changed and he was
conscious now of a wild upswing of elation, a determination equal to Denny's
own. People were dying of this festering abomination, and petty officialdom
had done nothing. It was not the moment for the bedside manner and a
niggling bottle of physic!

They began to deal swiftly with the cocoa tins, slipping a stick of dynamite
in each. Fuses of graduated lengths were cut and attached. A match flared
in the darkness, startling in its harsh illumination of Denny's pale hard face,
his own shaking hands. Then the first fuse spluttered. One by one the live
cocoa tins were floated down the sluggish current, those with the longest fuses
going first.

Andrew could not see clearly. His heart was thudding with excitement. It
might not be orthodox medicine, but it was the best moment he had ever
known.

As the last tin went in with its short fuse fizzing, Hawkins took it into his
head to hunt a rat. There was a breathless interlude, filled with the yapping
of the dog and the fearful possibilities of an explosion beneath their feet,
while they chased and captured him. Then the manhole cover was flung back
and they raced frantically thirty yards up the street.

They had barely reached the corner of Radnor Place and stopped to look
round when *bang!* the first can went off.

"By God!" Andrew gasped, exultantly. "We've done it, Denny!" He had a
sense of comradeship with the other man, he wanted to grip him by the hand,
to shout aloud.

Then swiftly, beautifully, the muffled explosions followed: two, three, four,
five, and the last a glorious detonation that must have been at least a quarter
of a mile down the Valley.

"There!" said Denny in a suppressed voice, as though all the secret bitterness of his life escaped into that single word. "That's the end of one bit of rottenness!"

He had barely spoken before the commotion broke. Doors and windows were flung open, shedding light upon the darkened roadway. People ran out of their houses. In a minute the street was thronged. At first the cry went up that it was an explosion at the mine. But this was quickly contradicted—the sounds had come from down the Valley. Arguments arose, and shouted speculations. A party of men set out with lanterns to explore. The hubbub and confusion made the night ring. Under cover of the darkness and the noise, Denny and Manson started to dodge home by the back ways. There was a singing triumph in Andrew's blood.

Before eight o'clock next morning Doctor Griffiths arrived upon the scene by car—fat, veal-faced, and verging upon panic, summoned from his warm bed with much blasphemy by Councillor Glyn Morgan. Griffiths might refuse to answer the calls of the local doctors, but there was no denying the angry command of Glyn Morgan. And, indeed, Glyn Morgan had cause for anger. The Councillor's new villa, half a mile down the Valley, had, overnight, become surrounded by a moat of more than mediæval squalor.

For half an hour the Councillor, supported by his adherents, Hamar Davies and Deawn Roberts, told the Medical Officer, in voices audible to many, exactly what they thought of him.

At the end of it, wiping his forehead, Griffiths tottered over to Denny who, with Manson, stood amongst the interested and edified crowd. Andrew had a sudden qualm at the approach of the Health Officer. A troubled night had left him less elated. In the cold light of morning, abashed by the havoc of the torn-up road, he was again uncomfortable, nervously perturbed.

But Griffiths was in no condition to be suspicious.

"Man, man," he quavered to Philip, "we'll have to get that new sewer for you straight off now."

Denny's face remained expressionless.

"I warned you about that months ago," he said frigidly. "Don't you remember?"

"Yes, yes, indeed! But how was I to guess the wretched thing would blow up this way? It's a mystery to me how it all happened."

Denny looked at him coolly.

"Where's your knowledge of public health, Doctor? Don't you know these sewer gasses are highly inflammable?"

The construction of the new sewer was begun on the following Monday.

5

It was three months later, and a fine March afternoon. The promise of spring scented the soft breeze blowing across the mountains where vague streaks of green defied the dominating, heaped, and quarried ugliness. Under the crisp blue sky even Blaenelly was beautiful.

As he went out to pay a call, which had just come in, at 3 Riskin Street, Andrew felt his heart quicken to the day. Gradually he was becoming acclimatized to this strange town,—primitive and isolated, entombed by the mountains, with no places of amusement, not even a cinema, nothing but its grim mine, its quarries and ore works, its string of chapels and bleak rows of houses,—a queer and silently contained community.

And the people, they also were strange; yet Andrew, though he saw them so alien to himself, could not but feel stirrings of affection towards them. With the exception of the tradesfolk, the preachers, and a few professional people, they were all directly in the employment of the Company. At the end and beginning of each shift, the quiet streets would suddenly awake, re-echoing to steel-shod footfalls, unexpectedly alive with an army of marching figures. The clothing, boots, hands, even the faces of those from the hæmatite mine, bore a bright red powdering of ore dust. The quarrymen wore moleskins with pads and gartered knees. The puddlers were conspicuous in their trousers of blue twill.

They spoke little, and much of what they said was in the Welsh tongue. They had the air, in their self-contained aloofness, of being a race apart. Yet they were a kindly people. Their enjoyments were simple, and were found usually in their own homes, in the chapel halls, on the foreshortened Rugby football ground at the top of the town. Their prevailing passion was, perhaps, a love of music—not the cheap melodies of the moment, but stern, classical music. It was not uncommon for Andrew, walking at night along the rows, to hear the sound of a piano coming from one of these poor homes, a Beethoven sonata or a Chopin prelude, beautifully played, floating through the still air, rising to these inscrutable mountains and beyond.

The position in regard to Doctor Page's practice was now clear to Andrew. Edward Page would never see another patient again. But the men did not like to "go off" Page, who had served them faithfully for over thirty years. And the bold Blodwen, by uniting bluff and cajolery towards Watkins, the mine manager, through whom the workmen's medical contributions were paid, had succeeded in keeping Page on the Company's list, and was in consequence receiving a handsome income—perhaps one sixth of which she paid out to Manson, who did all the work.

Andrew was profoundly sorry for Edward Page. Edward, a gentle, simple soul, had married plump, trim, pert little Blodwen—not knowing what lay behind those dancing sloe-black eyes—out of an Aberystwyth tea-room. Now, broken and bedridden, he was at her mercy, subjected to a treatment which combined blandishment with a kind of jolly bullying. It was not that Blodwen did not love him. She was, in some extraordinary fashion, fond of Edward. He, Doctor Page, was hers. Coming into the room while Andrew sat with the sick man, she would advance, smiling apparently, yet with a queer jealous sense of exclusion, exclaiming: "Hey! What are you two talkin' about?"

It was impossible not to love Edward Page, he had so manifestly the spiritual qualities of sacrifice and unselfishness. He would lie there, helpless in bed, a worn-out man, submissive to all the blustering attentions of this bold, dark-faced, impatient woman who was his wife, the victim of her greediness, her persistent and shameless importunity.

There was no need for him to remain in Blaenelly, and he longed to get away to a warmer, kindlier place. Once, when Andrew asked, "Is there anything you'd like, sir?" he had sighed: "I'd like to get out of here, my boy. I've been reading about that island—Capri—they're going to make a bird sanctuary there." Then he had turned his face sideways on the pillow. The longing in his voice was very sad.

The children irritated him. He never spoke of the practice except to say occasionally in a spent voice: "I daresay I didn't know a great deal. Yet I did my best." But he would spend hours lying absolutely still, watching his window sill where Annie every morning devotedly placed crumbs, bacon rind, and grated coconut. On Sunday forenoons an old miner, Enoch Davies, came in, very stiff in his rusty black suit and celluloid dickey, to sit with Page. The two men watched the birds in silence.

On one occasion Andrew met Enoch stamping excitedly downstairs.

"Man alive," burst out the old miner, "we've had a rare fine mornin'! Two bluetits playin' pretty as you please on the sill for the best part of an hour."

Enoch was Page's only friend. He had great influence with the miners. He swore staunchly that not a man would come off the doctor's list so long as he drew breath. He little knew how great a disservice his loyalty was to poor Edward Page.

Another frequent visitor to the house was the manager of the Western Counties Bank, Aneurin Rees, a long dry bald-headed man whom Andrew at first sight distrusted. Rees was a highly respected townsman who never by any chance met anyone's eye. He came to spend a perfunctory five minutes with Doctor Page, and was then closeted for an hour at a time with Mrs. Page. These interviews were perfectly moral. The question under discussion was money. Andrew judged that Blodwen had a great deal of it invested in her own name and that under the admirable direction of Aneurin Rees she was from time to time shrewdly increasing her holdings. Money, at this period, held no significance for Andrew. It was enough that he was regularly paying off his obligation to the Endowment. He had a few shillings in his pocket for cigarettes. Beyond that he had his work.

Now, more than ever, he appreciated how much his clinical work meant to him. It existed, the knowledge, as a warm ever-present inner consciousness which was like a fire at which he warmed himself when he was tired, depressed, perplexed. Lately, indeed, even stranger perplexities had formed and were moving more strongly than before within him. Medically, he had begun to think for himself. Perhaps Denny, with his radical destructive outlook, was mainly responsible for this. Denny's codex was literally the opposite of everything which Manson had been taught. Condensed and framed, it might well have hung, textlike, above his bed: "I do not believe."

Turned out to pattern by his medical school, Manson had faced the future with a well-bound textbook confidence. He had acquired a smattering of physics, chemistry, and biology—at least he had slit up and studied the earthworm. Thereafter he had been dogmatically fed upon the accepted doctrines. He knew all the diseases, with their tabulated symptoms, and the remedies thereof. Take gout, for instance. You could cure it with colchicum. He could still see Professor Lamplough blandly purring to his class, "*Vinum colchici*, gentlemen, twenty to thirty minimum doses, an absolute specific in gout." But was it? That was the question he now asked himself. A month ago he had tried colchicum, pushing it to the limit in a genuine case of "poor man's" gout—a severe and painful case. The result had been dismal failure.

And what about half, three quarters of the other "remedies" in the pharmacopœia? This time he heard the voice of Doctor Eliot, lecturer on *Materia Medica*: "And now, gentlemen, we pass to *elemi*—a concrete resinous exudation, the botanical source of which is undetermined, but is probably *Canarium commune*, chiefly imported from Manila; employed in ointment form, one in five, an admirable stimulant and disinfectant to sores and issues."

Rubbish! Yes, absolute rubbish. He knew that now. Had Eliot ever tried *Unguentum elemi*? He was convinced that Eliot had not. All of that erudite information came out of a book; and that, in its turn, came out of another book; and so on, right back, probably to the Middle Ages. The word "issues," now dead as mutton, confirmed this view.

Denny had sneered at him, that first night, for naïvely compounding a bottle of medicine: Denny always sneered at the medicine compounders, the medicine swillers. Denny held that only half a dozen drugs were any use, the rest he cynically classed as "muck." It was something, that view of Denny's, to wrestle with in the night—a shattering thought, the ramifications of which Andrew could as yet only vaguely comprehend.

At this point in his reflections he arrived at Riskin Street and entered Number 3. Here he found the patient to be a small boy of nine years of age, named Joey Howells, who was exhibiting a mild, seasonal attack of measles. The case was of little consequence; yet, because of the circumstances of the household, which was a poor one, it promised inconvenience to Joey's mother. Howells himself, a day labourer at the quarries, had been laid up three months with pleurisy, for which no compensation was payable; and now Mrs. Howells, a delicate woman, already run off her feet attending to one invalid in addition to her work of cleaning Bethesda Chapel, was called upon to make provision for another.

At the end of his visit, as Andrew stood talking to her at the door of her house, he remarked with regret:—

"You have your hands full. It's a pity you must keep Idris home from school." Idris was Joey's younger brother.

Mrs. Howells raised her head quickly. She was a resigned little woman with shiny red hands and work-swollen finger-knuckles.

"But Miss Barlow said I needn't have him back."

In spite of his sympathy Andrew felt a throb of annoyance.

"Oh?" he inquired. "And who is Miss Barlow?"

"She's the teacher at Bank Street School," said the unsuspecting Mrs. Howells. "She come round to see me this morning. And seein' how hard put I was, she's let little Idris stop on in her class. Goodness knows what I'd have done if I'd had him fallin' over me as well!"

Andrew had a sharp impulse to tell her that she must obey his instructions and not those of a meddling schoolmistress. However, he saw well enough that Mrs. Howells was not to blame. For the moment he made no comment, but as he took his leave and came down Riskin Street his face wore a resentful frown. He hated interference, especially with his work, and beyond everything he hated interfering women. The more he thought of it the angrier he became. It was a distinct contravention of the regulations to keep Idris at school when Joey, his brother, was suffering from measles.

He decided suddenly to call upon this officious Miss Barlow and have the matter out with her.

Five minutes later he ascended the incline of Bank Street, walked into the school, and, having inquired his way of the janitor, found himself outside the classroom of Standard I. He knocked at the door, entered.

It was a large detached room, well-ventilated, with a fire burning at one end. All the children were under seven and, as it was the afternoon break when he entered, each was having a glass of milk—part of an assistance scheme introduced by the local branch of the M.W.U. His eyes fell upon the mistress at once. She was busy writing out sums upon the blackboard, her back towards him, and she did not immediately observe him. But suddenly she turned round.

She was so different from the intrusive female of his indignant fancy that he hesitated. Or perhaps it was the surprise in her brown eyes which made him immediately ill at ease.

He flushed and said: "Are you Miss Barlow?"

"Yes." She was a slight figure in a brown tweed skirt, woollen stockings, and small stout shoes. His own age, he guessed; no, younger—about twenty-two. She inspected him, a little doubtful, faintly smiling, as though, weary of infantile arithmetic, she welcomed distraction on this fine spring day. "Aren't you Doctor Page's new assistant?"

"That's hardly the point," he answered stiffly; "though, as a matter of fact, I am Doctor Manson. I believe you have a contact here: Idris Howells. You know his brother has measles."

There was a pause. Her eyes, though questioning now, were persistently friendly.

Brushing back untidy hair she answered: "Yes, I know."

Her failure to take his visit seriously was sending his temper up again.

"Don't you realize it's quite against the rules to have him here?"

At his tone her colour rose and she lost her air of comradeship. He could not help thinking how clear and fresh her skin was, with a tiny brown mole, exactly the colour of her eyes, high on her right cheek. She was very fragile in her white blouse, and ridiculously young. Now she was breathing rather quickly, yet she spoke slowly:—

"Mrs. Howells was at her wits' end. Most of the children here have had measles. Those that haven't are sure to get it sooner or later. If Idris had stopped off, he'd have missed his milk, which is doing him such a lot of good."

"It isn't a question of his milk," he snapped. "He ought to be isolated."

She answered stubbornly. "I have got him isolated—in a kind of way. If you don't believe me, look for yourself."

He followed her glance. Idris, aged five, at a little desk all by himself near the fire, was looking extraordinarily pleased with life. His pale blue eyes goggled contentedly over the rim of his milk mug.

The sight infuriated Andrew. He laughed contemptuously, offensively.

"That may be your idea of isolation. I'm afraid it isn't mine. You must send that child home at once."

Tiny points of light glinted in her eyes.

"Doesn't it occur to you that I'm the mistress of this class? You may be able to order people about in more exalted spheres. But here it's my word that counts."

He glared at her, with raging dignity.

"You're breaking the law! You can't keep him here. If you do, I'll have to report you."

A short silence followed. He could see her hand tighten on the chalk she held. That sign of her emotion added to his anger against her—yes, against himself.

She said disdainfully: "Then you had better report me. Or have me arrested. I've no doubt it will give you immense satisfaction."

Furious, he did not answer, feeling himself in an utterly false position. He tried to rally himself, raising his eyes, attempting to beat down hers, which now sparkled frostily towards him. For an instant they faced each other, so close he could see the soft beating in her neck, the gleam of her teeth between her parted lips.

Then she said: "There's nothing more, is there?" She swung round tensely to the class. "Stand up children, and say: 'Good morning, Doctor Manson. Thank you for coming.'"

There was a clatter of chairs as the infants rose and chanted her ironic bidding. His ears were burning as she escorted him to the door. He had an exasperating sense of discomfiture, and added to it the wretched suspicion that he had behaved badly in losing his temper while she had so admirably controlled hers. He sought for a crushing phrase, some final intimidating repartee. But before that came the door closed quietly in his face.

6

MANSON, after a furious evening during which he composed and tore up three vitriolic letters to the Medical Officer of Health, tried to forget about the episode. His sense of humour, momentarily lost in the vicinity of Bank Street, made him impatient with himself because of his display of petty feeling. Following a sharp struggle with his stiff Scots pride, he decided he had been wrong, he could not dream of reporting the case, least of all to the ineffable Griffiths. Yet, though he made the attempt, he could not so easily dismiss Christine Barlow from his mind.

It was absurd that a juvenile schoolmistress should so insistently occupy his thoughts or that he should be concerned by what she might think of him. He told himself it was a stupid case of injured pride. He knew that he was shy and awkward with women. Yet no amount of logic could alter the fact that he was now restless and a little irritable. At unguarded moments, as for example when he was falling off to sleep, the scene in the classroom would flash back to him with renewed vividness and he would find himself frowning in the darkness. He still saw her, crushing the chalk, her brown eyes warm with indignation. There were three small pearly buttons on the front of her blouse. Her figure was thin and agile, with a firm economy of line which spoke to him of much hard running and dauntless skipping in her childhood. He did not ask himself if she were pretty. It was enough that she stood, spare and living, before the screen of his sight. And his heart would turn unwillingly, with a kind of sweet oppression which he had never known before.

A fortnight later he was walking down Chapel Street in a fit of abstraction when he almost bumped into Mrs. Bramwell at the corner of Station Road. He would have gone on without recognizing her. She, however, stopped at once, and hailed him, dazzling him with her smile.

"Why, Doctor Manson! The very man I'm looking for. I'm giving one of my little social evenings to-night. You'll come, won't you?"

Gladys Bramwell was a corn-haired lady of thirty-five, showily dressed, with a full figure, baby-blue eyes and girlish ways. Gladys described herself romantically as a man's woman. The gossips of Blaenelly used another word. Doctor Bramwell doted upon her, and it was rumoured that only his blind fondness prevented him from observing her more than skittish preoccupation with Doctor Gabell, the "coloured" doctor from Toniglan.

As Andrew scanned her, he sought hurriedly for an evasion.

"I'm afraid, Mrs. Bramwell, I can't possibly get away to-night."

"But you must, silly. I've got such nice people coming. Mr. and Mrs. Watkins from the mine and," a conscious smile escaped her, "Doctor Gabell from Toniglan—oh, and I almost forgot, the little schoolteacher, Christine Barlow."

A shiver passed over Manson.

He smiled foolishly.

"Why, of course I'll come, Mrs. Bramwell. Thank you very much for asking me." He managed to sustain her conversation for a few moments until she departed. But for the remainder of the day he could think of nothing but the fact that he was going to see Christine Barlow again.

Mrs. Bramwell's "evening" began at nine o'clock, the late hour being chosen out of consideration for the medical gentlemen who might be detained at their surgeries. It was, in fact, quarter-past nine when Andrew finished his last consultation. Hurriedly, he splashed himself in the surgery sink, tugged back his hair with the broken comb, and hastened to The Retreat. He reached the house—which, belying its idyllic name, was a small brick dwelling in the middle of the town—to find that he was the last arrival. Mrs. Bramwell, chiding him brightly, led the way, followed by her five guests and her husband, into supper.

It was a cold meal, spread out on paper doilies on the fumed-oak table. Mrs. Bramwell prided herself upon being a hostess, something of a leader in style in Blaenelly, which permitted her to shock public opinion by "doing herself up," and her idea of "making things go" was to talk and laugh a great deal. She always implied that her background, before her marriage to Doctor Bramwell, had been one of excessive luxury.

To-night, as they sat down, she glittered: "Now! Has everybody got what they want?"

Andrew, breathless from his haste, was at first deeply embarrassed. For a full ten minutes he dared not look at Christine. He kept his eyes lowered, overpoweringly conscious of her sitting at the far end of the table between Doctor Gabell—a dark-complexioned dandy in spats, striped trousers, and pearl pin—and Mr. Watkins, the elderly scrubby-headed mine manager who, in his blunt fashion, was making much of her. At last, driven by a laughing allusion from Watkins,—"Are ye still my Yorkshire lass, Miss Christine?"—Andrew lifted his head jealously, looked at her, found her so intimately there, in a soft grey dress with white at the neck and cuffs, that he was stricken and withdrew his eyes lest she should read them.

Defensively, scarcely knowing what he said, he began to devote himself to his neighbour, Mrs. Watkins, a little wisp of a woman who had brought her knitting.

For the remainder of the meal he endured the anguish of talking to one person when he longed to talk to another.

He could have sighed with relief when Doctor Bramwell, presiding at the top of the table, viewed the cleared plates benevolently and made a Napoleonic gesture.

"I think, my dear, we have all finished. Shall we adjourn to the drawing-room?"

In the drawing-room, when the guests were variously disposed,—chiefly upon the three-piece suite,—it was plain that music was expected in the order of the evening. Bramwell beamed fondly on his wife and led her to the piano.

"What shall we oblige with first to-night, my love?" Humming, he fingered amongst the music on the stand.

" 'Temple Bells'," Gabell suggested. "I never get tired of that one, Mrs. Bramwell."

Seating herself on the revolving music-stool, Mrs. Bramwell played and sang while her husband, one hand behind his back, the other advanced as in the motion of snuff-taking, stood beside her and deftly turned the sheets. Gladys had a full contralto voice, bringing all her deep notes up from her bosom with a lifting motion of her chin. After the Love Lyrics she gave them "Wandering By" and "Just a Girl."

There was generous applause. Bramwell murmured absently, in a pleased undertone: "She's in fine voice to-night."

Doctor Gabell was then persuaded to his feet. Fiddling with his ring, smoothing his well-oiled but still traitorous hair, the olive-skinned buck bowed affectedly towards his hostess, and, clasping his hands well in front of him, bellowed fruitily "Love in Sweet Seville." Then, as an encore, he gave "Toreador."

"You sing these songs about Spain with real go, Doctor Gabell," commented the kindly Mrs. Watkins.

"It's my Spanish blood, I suppose," laughed Gabell modestly, as he resumed his seat.

Andrew saw an impish glint in Watkins' eye. The old mine manager, a true Welshman, knew music, had last winter helped his men to produce one of Verdi's more obscure operas, and now, dormant behind his pipe, was enjoying himself enigmatically. Andrew could not help thinking that it must afford Watkins deep amusement to observe these strangers to his native town affecting to dispense culture in the shape of worthless, sentimental ditties. When Christine smilingly refused to perform, Watkins turned to her with a twitch to his lips.

"You're like me, I reckon, my dear. Too fond of the piano to play it."

Then the high light of the evening shone. Doctor Bramwell took the centre of the stage. Clearing his throat, he struck out one foot, threw back his head, placed his hand histrionically inside his coat. He announced: "Ladies and gentlemen—'The Fallen Star. A Musical Monologue.'" At the piano, Gladys started to vamp a sympathetic accompaniment, and Bramwell began.

The recitation, which dealt with the pathetic vicissitudes of a once-famous actress now come to dire poverty, was glutinous with sentiment, and Bramwell gave it with soulful anguish. When the drama rose Gladys pressed bass chords. When the pathos oozed she tinkled on the treble. As the climax came, Bramwell drew himself up, his voice breaking on the final line, "There she was"— A pause—"starving in the gutter . . ." A long pause. "Only a fallen star!"

Little Mrs. Watkins, her knitting fallen to the floor, turned damp eyes towards him.

"Poor thing, poor thing! Oh, Doctor Bramwell, you always do that most beautiful."

The arrival of the claret-cup created a diversion. By this time it was after eleven o'clock, and, on the tacit understanding that anything following Bramwell's effort would be sheer anticlimax, the party prepared to break up. There were laughter, polite expressions of thanks, and a movement towards the hall. As Andrew pulled on his coat, he reflected miserably that he had not exchanged a word with Christine all night.

Outside, he stood at the gate. He felt that he must speak to her. The thought of the long wasted evening, in which he had meant so easily, so pleasantly, to put things right between them, weighed on him like lead. Though she had not seemed to look at him, she had been there, near him, in the same room, and he had kept his eyes doltishly upon his boots. "Oh, Lord!" he thought wretchedly, "I'm worse than the fallen star. I'd better get home and go to bed."

But he did not. He remained there, his pulse racing suddenly as she came down the steps and walked towards him, alone.

He gathered all his strength and stammered: "Miss Barlow— May I see you home?"

"I'm afraid—" She paused. "I've promised to wait for Mr. and Mrs. Watkins."

His heart sank. He felt like turning away, a beaten dog. Yet something still held him. His face was pale, but his chin had a firm line. The words came tumbling one upon another with a rush.

"I only want to say that I'm sorry about the Howells affair. I came round to give a cheap exhibition of authority. I ought to be kicked—hard. What you did about the kid was splendid. I admire you for it. After all, it's better to observe the spirit than the letter of the law. Sorry to bother you with all this, but I had to say it. Good night!"

He could not see her face. Nor did he wait for her answer. He swung round and walked down the road. For the first time in many days he felt happy.

7

THE half-yearly return of the practice had come in from the Company offices, giving Mrs. Page matter for serious reflection and another topic to discuss with Aneurin Rees, the bank manager. For the first time in eighteen months the figures showed an upward jump. There were over seventy more men on "Doctor Page's list" than there had been before Manson's arrival.

Delighted with the increase in her cheque, Blodwen nevertheless nursed a most disturbing thought. At mealtimes Andrew caught her unguardedly fixing him with an inquiring, suspicious stare.

On the Wednesday following Mrs. Bramwell's social evening, Blodwen came bustling into lunch with a great display of gaiety.

"I declare!" she remarked. "I just been thinkin'. It's near on four months since you been here, Doctor. And you 'aven't done too bad, neither. I'm not complainin'. Mind you, it isn't like Doctor Page himself. Oh, dear, no! Mr. Watkins was only sayin' the other day how they was all lookin' forward to Doctor Page comin' back. Doctor Page is so clever, says Mr. Watkins to me, we wouldn't never dream of havin' anybody in his place."

She laid herself out to describe, in picturesque detail, the extraordinary skill and ability of her husband. "You wouldn't believe it," she exclaimed, widening her eyes. "There's nothing he can't do or hasn't done. Operations! You ought to have seen them. Let me tell you this, Doctor, once he took a man's brains out and put them back again. Yes! look at me if you like, Doctor Page scraped these brains and put them back again."

She lay back in her chair and gazed at him, trying to read the effect of her words. Then she smiled confidently.

"There'll be great rejoicings in Blaenelly when Doctor Page gets back to work. And it'll be soon, too. In the summer, says I to Mr. Watkins, in the summer Doctor Page will be back."

Returning from his afternoon round towards the end of the same week, Andrew was shocked to find Edward huddled in a chair by the front porch, fully dressed, a rug over his knees and a cap stuck rakishly on his shaking head. A sharp wind was blowing and the gleam of April sunshine which bathed the tragic figure was pale and cold.

"There, now," cried Mrs. Page, bustling triumphantly towards Manson from the porch. "You see, don't you? Doctor's *up!* I've just telephoned Mr. Watkins to tell him Doctor's better. He'll soon be back at work, won't you, ducky?"

Andrew felt the blood rush to his brow.

"Who got him down here?"

"I did," said Blodwen defiantly; "and why not? He's my husband. And he's better."

"He's not fit to be up, and you know it." Andrew threw the words at her in a low tone. "Do as I tell you. Help me get him back to bed at once."

"Yes, yes," Edward said feebly. "Get me back to bed. I'm cold. I'm not right. I—I don't feel well." And to Manson's distress the sick man began to whimper.

Instantly Blodwen was in floods of tears beside him.

Down on her knees she flopped, her arms around him, contrite, slobbering: "There, there now, ducky. You shall go back to bed, poor lamb. Blodwen'll do it for you. Blodwen'll take care of you. Blodwen loves you, ducky."

She smacked wet kisses on his stiff cheek.

Half an hour later, with Edward upstairs and comfortable again, Andrew came to the kitchen, raging.

Annie was now a genuine friend: many a confidence they had exchanged in this same kitchen and many an apple and currant griddlecake the quietly contained middle-aged woman had slipped out of the larder for him when rations were extra tight. Sometimes, indeed, as a last resort, she would run down to Thomas' for a double fish supper and they would banquet sumptuously by candlelight at the scullery table.

Annie had been at Pages' for nearly twenty years. She had many relations in Blaenelly, all tidy folk, and her only reason for remaining so long in service was her devotion to Doctor Page.

"Give me my tea in here, Annie," Andrew now declared. "I can't stand any more of Blodwen at the moment."

He was in the kitchen before he realized that Annie had visitors—her sister Olwen and Olwen's husband, Emrys Hughes. He had met them several times before. Emrys was a shot-firer in the Blaenelly High Levels, a solid good-natured man with pale, thickened features.

As Manson, seeing them, hesitated, Olwen, a spry dark-eyed young woman, took an impulsive breath.

"Don't mind us, Doctor, if you want your tea. As a matter of fact, we were just talkin' about you when you came in."

"Yes?"

"Yes, indeed!" Olwen darted a glance at her sister. "It's no use your lookin' at me that way, Annie, I'll speak what's in my mind. All the men are talkin', Doctor Manson, about how they haven't had such a good young doctor as you for years, about how you take trouble to examine them, and all. You can ask Emrys if you don't believe me. And they're fair mad about how Mrs. Page is puttin' on them. They say you ought to 'ave the practice by rights. And she's 'eard that talk, mind you; that's why she got poor old Doctor Page up this afternoon. Pretendin' he was better, indeed, poor old feller!"

When he had finished his tea Andrew withdrew. Olwen's downright speech made him feel ill at ease. Yet it was flattering to be told that the people of Blaenelly liked him. And he took it as an especial tribute when, a few days later, Joe Morgan, a foreman driller at the hæmatite mine, came to see him with his wife.

The Morgans were a middle-aged couple, not well-off, but highly thought of in the district; they had been married for nearly twenty years. Andrew had heard that they were leaving shortly for South Africa, where Morgan had the promise of work in the Johannesburg mines. It was not unusual for good drillers to be tempted out to the gold mines on the Rand, where the drill work was similar and the pay much better. Yet no one was more surprised than Andrew when Morgan, seated in the little surgery with his wife, self-consciously explained the purpose of their visit.

"Well, sir, we have done it, at last, it seems. The missus here is goin' to have a baby. After nineteen year, mark you. We are plain delighted, man. And we've decided to put off our leavin' till after the event. For we've been thinkin' about doctors like, and we come to the conclusion that you're the one we must have to handle the case. It means a lot to us, Doctor. It'll be a hard job too, I fancy. Missus here is forty-three. Yes, indeed. But there, now, we know you'll give us every satisfaction."

Andrew entered up the case with a warm sense of having been honoured. It was a strange emotion, clear and without material origin, which in his present state was doubly comforting. Lately he had felt lost, completely des-

olate. Extraordinary currents were moving within him, disturbing and painful. There were times when his heart held a strange dull ache which, as a
mature bachelor of medicine, he had hitherto believed impossible.

He had never before thought seriously of love. At the University he had
been too poor, too badly dressed and far too intent on getting through his
examinations to come much in contact with the other sex. At St. Andrews
one had to be a blood, like his friend and classmate Freddie Hampton, to
move in that circle which danced and held parties and exhibited the social
graces. All this had been denied him. He had really belonged—his friendship
with Hampton apart—to that crowd of outsiders who turned up their coat
collars, swotted, smoked, and took their occasional recreation not at the
Union but in a downtown billiard saloon.

It is true that the inevitable romantic images had presented themselves
to him. Because of his poverty these were usually projected against a lavishly
wealthy background. But now, in Blaenelly, he stared through the window
of the ramshackle surgery, his clouded eyes fastened upon the dirty slag-heap
of the ore works, longing with all his heart for the skimpy junior mistress of
a council school. The bathos of it made him want to laugh.

He had always prided himself on being practical, upon his strong infusion
of native caution; and he attempted, violently and with determined self-
interest, to argue himself out of his emotion. He tried, coldly and logically,
to examine her defects. She was not beautiful, her figure was too small and
thin. She had that mole upon her cheek, and a slight crinkling, visible when
she smiled, in her upper lip. In addition she probably detested him.

He told himself angrily that he was utterly ill-advised to give way to his
feelings in this weak fashion. He had dedicated himself to his work. He was
still only an assistant. What kind of doctor was he, to form, at the very outset
of his career, an attachment which must hamper her future and was even
now seriously interfering with his work?

In the effort to take himself in hand, he created loopholes of distraction.
Deluding himself that he was missing the old associations of St. Andrews, he
wrote a long letter to Freddie Hampton, who had lately gone down to a hospital appointment in London. He fell back, a great deal, upon Denny. But
Philip, though sometimes friendly, was more often cold, suspicious, with the
bitterness of a man whom life has hurt.

Try as he would Andrew could not get Christine out of his mind, nor
that tormenting yearning for her from his heart. He had not seen her since
his outburst at the front gate of The Retreat. What did she think of him?
Did she ever think of him? It was so long since he had seen her, despite an
eager scanning of Bank Street when he passed it, that he despaired of seeing
her at all.

Then, on the afternoon of Saturday, May 25, when he had almost given
up hope, he received a note which ran as follows:—

Dear Doctor Manson,

Mr. and Mrs. Watkins are coming to supper with me to-morrow, Sunday evening. If you have nothing better to do, would you care to come too? Half-past seven.

Sincerely,
CHRISTINE BARLOW

He gave a cry which brought Annie hurrying from the scullery.

"Eh, Doctor, *bach*,"—reprovingly,—"sometimes you do act sil-ly."

"I have, Annie," he answered, still overcome. "But I—I seem to have got off with it. Listen, Annie, dear. Will you press my trousers for me before to-morrow? I'll sling them outside my door to-night when I go to bed."

On the following evening which, being Sunday, left him free of the evening surgery, he presented himself in tremulous expectation at the house of Mrs. Herbert, with whom Christine lodged, near the Institute. He was early and he knew it, but he could not wait a moment longer.

It was Christine herself who opened the door for him, her face welcoming, smiling towards him.

Yes, she was smiling, actually smiling. And he had felt that she disliked him! He was so overwhelmed he could barely speak.

"It's been a lovely day, hasn't it?" he mumbled as he followed her into her sitting-room.

"Lovely," she agreed. "And I had such a grand walk this afternoon. Right out beyond Pandy. I actually found some celandines."

They sat down. It was on his tongue to inquire nervously if she enjoyed walking, but he nipped the gauche futility in time.

"Mrs. Watkins has just sent word," she remarked. "She and her husband will be a little late. He's had to go down to the office. You don't mind waiting a few minutes on them?"

Mind! A few minutes! He could have laughed out of sheer happiness. If only she knew how he had waited all those days, how wonderful it was to be here with her. Surreptitiously, he looked about him. Her sitting-room, furnished with her own things, was different from any room he had entered in Blaenelly. It held neither plush nor horsehair nor Axminster, nor any of those shiny satin cushions which conspicuously adorned Mrs. Bramwell's drawing-room. The floorboards were stained and polished, with a plain brown rug before the open fireplace. The furniture was so unobtrusive he scarcely noticed it. In the centre of the table, set for supper, was a plain white dish in which floated, like masses of tiny water lilies, the celandines she had gathered. The effect was simple and beautiful. On the window sill stood a wooden confectionery box, now filled with earth, from which thin green seedlings were sprouting. Above the mantelpiece was a most peculiar picture, which showed nothing more than a child's small wooden chair, painted red and, he thought, extremely badly drawn.

She must have noticed the surprise with which he viewed it. She smiled with infectious amusement.

"I hope you don't think it's the original!"

Embarrassed, he did not know what to say. The expression of her personality through the room, the conviction that she knew things which were beyond him, confounded him. Yet his interest was so awakened he forgot his awkwardness, escaped from the stupid banalities of remarks about the weather. He began to ask her about herself.

She answered him simply. She was from Yorkshire. Her mother had died when she was fifteen. Her father had then been under-manager at one of the big Bramwell Main Collieries. Her only brother, John, had been trained in the same colliery as a mining engineer. Five years later, when she was nineteen and her Normal course completed, her father had been appointed manager of the Porth Pit twenty miles down the Valley. She and her brother had come to South Wales with him, she to keep the house, John to assist his father. Six months after their arrival, there had been an explosion in the Porth Pit. John had been underground, killed instantly. Her father, hearing of the disaster, had immediately gone down, only to be met by a rush of black damp. A week later his body and John's were brought out together.

When she concluded there was a silence.

"I'm sorry," Andrew said in a sympathetic voice.

"People were kind to me," she said soberly. "Mr. and Mrs. Watkins especially. I got this job at school here." She paused, her face lighting up again. "I'm like you, though. I'm still strange here. It takes a long time to get used to the Valleys."

He looked at her, searching for something which would even faintly express his feeling for her, a remark which might tactfully dispose of the past and hopefully open out the future.

"It's easy to feel cut off down here, lonely. I know. I do often. I often feel I want someone to talk to."

She smiled. "What do you want to talk about?"

He reddened, with a sense that she had cornered him. "Oh, my work, I suppose." He halted, then felt obliged to explain himself. "I seem just to be blundering about, running into one problem after another."

"Do you mean you have difficult cases?"

"It isn't that." He hesitated, went on. "I came down here full of formulæ, the things that everybody believes, or pretends to believe. That swollen joints mean rheumatism . . . That rheumatism means salicylate . . . You know, the orthodox things! Well, I'm finding out that some of them are all wrong. Take medicine, too . . . It seems to me that some of it does more harm than good. It's the system. A patient comes into the surgery. He expects his 'bottle of medicine.' And he gets it, even if it's only burnt sugar, soda bicarb. and good old *aqua*. That's why the prescription is written in Latin—so he won't understand it. It isn't right. It isn't scientific. And another thing: It seems to me that too many doctors treat disease empirically—that's to say, they treat the symptoms individually. They don't bother to combine the symptoms in their own mind and puzzle out the diagnosis. They say—very quick, because they're usually in a rush—'Ah! headache—try this powder!' Or 'You're anæmic, you must have some iron.' Instead of asking themselves what is *causing* the headache or the anæmia—" He broke off sharply. "Oh! I'm sorry! I'm boring you!"

"No, no," she said quickly. "It's awfully interesting."

"I'm just beginning, just feeling my way," he went on tempestuously, thrilled by her interest. "But I do honestly think, even from what I've seen, that the textbooks I was brought up on have too many old-fashioned conservative ideas in them. Remedies that are no use, symptoms that were shoved in by somebody in the Middle Ages. You might say it doesn't matter to the average G.P. But why should the general practitioner be no more than a poultice mixer or a medicine slinger? It's time science was brought into the front line. A lot of people think that science lies in the bottom of a test tube. I don't. I believe that the outlying G.P.'s have all the opportunities to *see* things, and a better chance to observe the first symptoms of new disease, than they have at any of the hospitals. By the time a case gets to hospital it's usually past the early stages."

She was about to answer quickly when the doorbell rang. She rose, suppressing her remark, saying instead, with her faint smile:—

"I hope you won't forget your promise to talk of this another time."

Watkins and his wife came in, apologizing for being late. And almost at once they sat down to supper.

It was a very different meal from that cold collation which had last brought them together. There was veal cooked in a casserole, and there were potatoes mashed with butter, followed by new rhubarb tart with cream, then cheese and coffee. Though plain, every dish was good and there was plenty of it.

After the skimpy meals served to him by Blodwen, it was a great treat to Andrew to find hot appetizing food before him. He sighed: "You're lucky in your landlady, Miss Barlow. She's a marvellous cook!"

Watkins, who had been observing Andrew's trencherwork with a quizzical eye, suddenly laughed out loud.

"That's a good one." He turned to his wife. "Did you hear him, Mother? He says old Mrs. Herbert's a marvellous cook!"

Christine coloured slightly.

"Don't pay any attention to him," she said to Andrew. "It's the nicest compliment I've ever had—because you didn't mean it as such. As it happens, I cooked the supper. I have the run of Mrs. Herbert's kitchen. I like doing for myself. And I'm used to it."

Her remark served to make the mine manager more jovially boisterous. He was quite changed from the taciturn individual who had stoically endured the entertainment at Mrs. Bramwell's. Blunt and likeably common, he enjoyed his supper, smacked his lips over the tart, put his elbows on the table, told stories which made them laugh.

The evening passed quickly. When Andrew looked at his watch he saw to

his amazement that it was nearly eleven o'clock. And he had promised to pay
a late visit to a case in Blaina Place before half-past ten!

As he rose, regretfully, to take his leave, Christine accompanied him to the
door. In the narrow passage his arm touched her side. A pang of sweetness
went over him. She was so different from anyone he had ever known, with
her quietness, her fragility, her dark intelligent eyes. Heaven forgive him for
daring to have thought her skimpy!

Breathing quickly, he mumbled: "I can't thank you enough for asking me
to-night. Please can I see you again? I don't always talk shop. Would you—
Christine, would you come to the Toniglan cinema with me, sometime?"

Her eyes smiled up at him, for the first time faintly provocative.

"You try asking me."

A long silent minute on the doorstep under the high stars . . . The dew-
scented air was cool on his hot cheek. Her breath came sweetly towards him.
He longed to kiss her. Fumblingly he pressed her hand, turned, clattered
down the path and was on his way home with dancing thoughts, walking on
air along that dizzy path which millions have tritely followed and still believed themselves unique, rapturously predestined, eternally blessed. Oh, she
was a wonderful girl! How well she had understood his meaning when he
spoke of his difficulties in practice! She was clever, far cleverer than he. What
a marvellous cook, too! And he had called her Christine!

8

THOUGH Christine now occupied his mind more than ever, the whole complexion of his thoughts was altered. He no longer felt despondent, but happy,
elated, hopeful. And this change of outlook was immediately reflected in his
work. He was young enough to create in fancy a constant situation wherein
she observed him at his cases, watched his careful methods, his scrupulous
examinations, commended him for the searching accuracy of his diagnosis.
Any temptation to scamp a visit, to reach a conclusion without first sounding
the patient's chest, was met by the instant thought: "Lord, no! What would
she think of me if I did that?"

More than once he found Denny's eye upon him, satirical, comprehensive.
But he did not care. In his intense, idealistic way he linked Christine with
his ambitions, made her unconsciously an extra incentive in the great assault
upon the unknown.

He admitted to himself that he still knew practically nothing. Yet he was
teaching himself to think for himself, to look behind the obvious in an effort
to find the proximate cause. Never before had he felt himself so powerfully
attracted to the scientific ideal. He prayed that he might never become slovenly or mercenary, never jump to conclusions, never come to write "the mixture as before." He wanted to find out, to be scientific, to be worthy of
Christine.

In the face of this ingenuous eagerness it seemed a pity that his work in
the practice should suddenly and uniformly turn dull. He wanted to scale

mountains. Yet for the next few weeks he was presented by a series of in-significant molehills. His cases were trivial, supremely uninteresting, a banal run of sprains, cut fingers, colds in the head. The climax came when he was called two miles down the Valley by an old woman who asked him, peering yellow-faced from beneath her flannel mutch, to cut her corns.

He felt foolish, chafed at his lack of opportunity, longed for whirlwind and tempest.

He began to question his own faith, to wonder if it were really possible for a doctor in this out-of-the-way place to be anything more than a petty, common hack. And then, at the lowest ebb of all, came an incident which sent the mercury of his belief soaring once again towards the skies.

Towards the end of the last week in June, as he came over the station bridge, he encountered Doctor Bramwell. The Silver King was slipping out of the side door of the Railway Inn, stealthily wiping his upper lip with the back of his hand. He had the habit, when Gladys departed, gay and dressed in her best, upon her enigmatic "shopping" expeditions to Toniglan, of sooth-ing himself unobtrusively with a pint or two of beer.

A trifle discomfited at being seen by Andrew, he nevertheless carried off the situation with a flourish.

"Ah, Manson! Glad to see you. I just had a call to Pritchard."

Pritchard was the proprietor of the Railway Inn—and Andrew had seen him five minutes ago, taking his bull terrier for a walk. But he allowed the opportunity to pass. He had an affection for the Silver King, whose high-flown language and mock heroics were offset in a very human way by his timidity, and the holes in his socks which the gay Gladys forgot to darn.

As they walked up the street together they began to talk shop. Bramwell was always ready to discuss his cases and now, with an air of gravity, he told Andrew that Emrys Hughes, Annie's brother-in-law, was on his hands. Emrys, he said, had been acting strangely lately, getting into trouble at the mine, losing his memory. He had turned quarrelsome and violent.

"I don't like it, Manson," Bramwell nodded sagely. "I've seen mental trou-ble before. And this looks uncommonly like it."

Andrew expressed his concern. He had always thought Hughes a stolid and agreeable fellow. He recollected that Annie had looked worried lately and when questioned had implied vaguely—for despite her proclivity for gossip she was reticent upon family affairs—that she was anxious about her brother-in-law. When he parted from Bramwell he ventured the hope that the case might quickly take a turn for the better.

But on the following Friday, at six o'clock in the morning, he was awakened by a knocking on his bedroom door. It was Annie, fully dressed and very red about the eyes, offering him a note.

Andrew tore open the envelope. It was a message from Doctor Bramwell:—

Come round at once. I want you to help certify a dangerous lunatic.

Annie struggled with her tears.

"It's Emrys, Doctor, *bach*. A dreadful thing has happened. I do hope you'll come down quick, like."

Andrew threw on his things in three minutes. Accompanying him down the road, Annie told him as best she could about Emrys. He had been ill and unlike himself for three weeks, but during the night he had turned violent, and gone clean out of his mind. He had set upon his wife with a bread-knife. Olwen had just managed to escape by running into the street in her nightgown. The sensational story was sufficiently distressing as Annie brokenly related it, hurrying beside him in the grey light of morning, and there seemed little he could add, by way of consolation, to alter it. They reached the Hughes's house. In the front room Andrew found Doctor Bramwell, unshaven, without his collar and tie, wearing a serious air, seated at the table, pen in hand. Before him was a bluish paper form, half filled in.

"Ah, Manson! Good of you to come so quickly. A bad business this. But it won't keep you long."

"What's up?"

"Hughes has gone mad. I think I mentioned to you a week ago I was afraid of it. Well! I was right. Acute mania." Bramwell rolled the words over his tongue with tragic grandeur. "Acute homicidal mania. We'll have to get him into Pontynewdd straight away. That means two signatures on the certificate, mine and yours—the relatives wanted me to call you in. You know the procedure, don't you?"

"Yes." Andrew nodded. "What's your evidence?"

Bramwell began, clearing his throat, to read what he had written upon the form. It was a full, flowing account of certain of Hughes's actions during the previous week, all of them conclusive of mental derangement. At the end of it Bramwell raised his head. "Clear evidence, I think!"

"It sounds pretty bad," Andrew answered slowly. "Well! I'll take a look at him."

"Thanks, Manson. You'll find me here when you're finished." And he began to add further particulars to the form.

Emrys Hughes was in bed, and seated beside him—in case restraint should be necessary—were two of his mates from the mine. Standing by the foot of the bed was Olwen, her pale face, ordinarily so pert and lively, now ravaged by weeping. Her attitude was so overwrought, the atmosphere of the room so dim and tense, that Andrew had a momentary thrill of coldness, almost of fear.

He went over to Emrys, and at first he hardly recognized him. The change was not gross; it was Emrys true enough, but a blurred and altered Emrys, his features coarsened in some subtle way. His face seemed swollen, the nostrils thickened, the skin waxy, except for a faint reddish patch that spread across the nose. His whole appearance was heavy, apathetic. Andrew spoke to him. He muttered an unintelligible reply. Then, clenching his hands, he came out with a tirade of aggressive nonsense, which, added to Bramwell's account, made the case for his removal only too conclusive.

A silence followed. Andrew felt that he ought to be convinced. Yet, in-explicably, he was not satisfied. Why, why, he kept asking himself, *why* should Hughes talk like this? Supposing the man had gone out of his mind, what was the cause of it all? He had always been a happy, contented man—no worries, easygoing, amicable. Why, without apparent reason, had he changed to *this*?

There must be a reason, Manson thought doggedly; symptoms don't just happen of themselves. Staring at the swollen features before him, puzzling, puzzling for some solution of the conundrum, he instinctively reached out and touched the swollen face, noting subconsciously, as he did so, that the pressure of his finger left no dent in the œdematous cheek.

All at once, electrically, a terminal vibrated in his brain. Why didn't the swelling pit on pressure? Because—now it was his heart which jumped!—be-cause it was not true œdema, but myxœdema. He had it, by God, he *had* it! No, no, he must not rush. Firmly, he caught hold of himself. He must not be a plunger, wildly leaping to conclusions. He must go cautiously, slowly, be sure!

Curbing himself, he lifted Emrys' hand. Yes, the skin was dry and rough, the fingers slightly thickened at the ends. Temperature—it was subnormal. Methodically he finished the examination, fighting back each successive wave of elation. Every sign and every symptom—they fitted as superbly as a com-plex jigsaw puzzle. The clumsy speech, dry skin, spatulate fingers, the swollen inelastic face, the defective memory, slow mentation, the attacks of irrita-bility culminating in an outburst of homicidal violence. Oh! the triumph of the completed picture was sublime.

Rising, he went down to the parlour, where Doctor Bramwell, standing on the hearthrug with his back to the fire, greeted him:—

"Well? Satisfied? The pen's on the table."

"Look here, Bramwell—" Andrew kept his eyes averted, battling to keep im-petuous triumph from his voice. "I don't think we ought to certify Hughes."

"Eh, what?" Gradually the blankness left Bramwell's face. He exclaimed in hurt astonishment: "But the man's out of his mind!"

"That's not my view," Andrew answered in a level tone, still stopping down his excitement, his elation. It was not enough that he had diagnosed the case. He must handle Bramwell gently, try not to antagonize him. "In my opinion Hughes is only sick in mind because he's sick in body. I feel that he's suffering from thyroid deficiency—an absolutely straight case of myxœ-dema."

Bramwell stared at Andrew glassily. Now, indeed, he was dumbfounded. He made several efforts to speak—a queer sound, like snow falling off a roof.

"After all," Andrew went on persuasively, his eyes on the hearthrug, "Pontynewdd is such a sink of a place. Once Hughes gets in there he'll never get out. And if he does he'll carry the stigma of it all his life. Suppose we try pushing thyroid into him first?"

"Why, Doctor," Bramwell quavered, "I don't see—"

"Think of the credit for you," Andrew cut in quickly. "If you should get him well again. Don't you think it's worth it? Come on now, I'll call in Mrs. Hughes. She's crying her eyes out because she thinks Emrys is going away. You can explain we're going to try a new treatment."

Before Bramwell could protest Andrew went out of the room. A few minutes later, when he came back with Mrs. Hughes, the Silver King had recovered himself. Planted on the hearthrug he informed Olwen in his best manner "that there might still be a ray of hope" while, behind his back, Andrew made a neat tight ball of the certificate and threw it in the fire. Then he went out to telephone to Cardiff for thyroid.

There was a period of quivering anxiety, several days of agonized suspense, before Hughes began to respond to the treatment. But once it had started, that response was magical. Emrys was out of bed in a fortnight, and back at his work at the end of two months. He came round one evening to the surgery at Bryngower, lean and active, accompanied by the smiling Olwen, to tell Andrew he had never felt better in his life.

Olwen said:—

"We owe everything to you, Doctor. We want to change over to you from Bramwell. Emrys was on his list before I married him. He's just a silly old woman. He'd have had my Emrys in the—well, you know what—if it hadn't been for you and all you've done for us."

"You *can't* change, Olwen," Andrew answered. "It would spoil everything." He dropped his professional gravity and broke into genuine youthful glee. "If you even try to—I'll come after you with that breadknife."

Bramwell, meeting Andrew in the street, remarked airily:—

"Hello, Manson! You've seen Hughes about, I suppose. Ha! They're both very grateful. I flatter myself I've never had a better case."

Annie said:—

"That ol' Bramwell, struttin' about the town like he was some-bod-ee. He don't know nothing. And his wife, bah! She can't keep her servants no time."

Mrs. Page said:—

"Doctor, don't forget you're workin' for Doctor Page."

Denny's comment was:—

"Manson! At present you're too conceited to live with. You're going to make a most hell of a bloomer. Soon. Very soon."

But Andrew, hurrying to Christine full of the triumph of the scientific method, kept everything he had to say for her.

9

In July of that year the Annual Conference of the British Medical Union was held in Cardiff. The Union, to which, as Professor Lamplough always informed his students in his final address, every reputable medical man ought to belong, was famous for its Annual Conferences. Splendidly organized, these Conferences offered sporting, social, and scientific enjoyments to members and their families, reduced terms at all but the best hotels, free charabanc trips to any ruined Abbey in the neighbourhood, a memento art brochure, souvenir diaries from the leading Surgical Appliance Makers and Drug Houses, and pumproom facilities at the nearest spa. The previous year, at the end of the week's festivity, generous free sample boxes of Non-Adipo Biscuits had been sent to each doctor and his wife.

Andrew was not a member of the Union, since the five-guinea subscription was, as yet, beyond his means, but he viewed it a little enviously from a distance. Its effect was to make him feel isolated and out of touch in Blaenelly. Photographs in the local newspapers of an array of doctors receiving addresses of welcome on a beflagged platform, driving off at the first tee of the Penarth Golf Course, flocking upon the steamer for a sea trip to Weston-super-Mare, served to intensify his sense of exclusion.

But midway through the week a letter arrived bearing the address of a Cardiff hotel which caused Andrew a more pleasurable sensation. It was from his friend Freddie Hampton. Freddie, as might be expected, was attending the Conference, and he asked Manson to run down and see him. He suggested Saturday, for dinner.

Andrew showed the letter to Christine. It was instinctive now for him to take her into his confidence. Since that evening, nearly two months before, when he had gone round to supper, he was more than ever in love. Now that he could see her frequently, and be reassured by her evident pleasure in these meetings, he was happier than ever he had been in his life before. Perhaps it was Christine who had this stabilizing effect upon him. She was a very practical little person, perfectly direct and entirely without coquetry. Often he would join her in a state of worry or irritation and come away soothed and tranquillized. She had a way of listening to what he had to say, quietly, then of making some comment which was usually apropos or amusing. She had a lively sense of humour. And she never flattered him.

Occasionally, despite her calmness, they had great arguments, for she had a mind of her own. She told him, with a smile, that her argumentativeness came from a Scottish grandmother. Perhaps her independent spirit came from that source too. He often felt that she had great courage, which touched him, made him long to protect her. She was really quite alone in the world except for an invalid aunt in Bridlington.

When it was fine on Saturday or Sunday afternoons they took long walks along the Pandy Road. Once they had gone to see a film, Chaplin in "The Gold Rush," and again to Toniglan, at her suggestion, to an orchestral concert. But most of all he enjoyed the evenings when Mrs. Watkins was visiting her and he was able to enjoy the intimacy of her companionship in her own sitting-room. It was then that most of their discussions took place, with Mrs. Watkins—knitting placidly yet primly resolved to make her wool last out the session—no more than a respectable buffer state between them.

Now, with this visit to Cardiff in prospect, he wished her to accompany him. Bank Street School broke up for the summer holidays at the end of the week, and she was going to Bridlington to spend her vacation with her aunt.

He felt that some special celebration was needed before she took her leave.

When she had read the letter he said, impulsively:—

"Will you come with me? It's only an hour and a half in the train. I'll get Blodwen to unchain me on Saturday evening. We might manage to see something of the Conference. And in any case I'd like you to meet Hampton."

She nodded.

"I'd love to come."

Excited by her acceptance, he had no intention of being baulked by Mrs. Page. Before he approached her upon the matter he placed a conspicuous notice in the surgery window:—

CLOSED SATURDAY EVENING

He went into the house gaily.

"Mrs. Page! According to my reading of the Sweated Medical Assistants Act, I'm entitled to one half-day off a year. I'd like mine on Saturday. I'm going to Cardiff."

"Now look you here, Doctor!" She bristled at his demand, thinking that he was very full of himself, uppish; but after staring at him suspiciously, she grudgingly declared: "Oh, well—you can go, I suppose." A sudden idea struck her. Her eye cleared. She smacked her lips. "Anyhow, I'll have you bring me some pastries from Parry's. There's nothing I fancy better nor Parry's pastries."

On Saturday, at half-past four, Christine and Andrew took the train for Cardiff. Andrew was in high spirits, boisterous, hailing porter and booking clerk by their first names. With a smile he looked across at Christine, seated on the opposite seat. She wore a navy blue coat and skirt which intensified her usual air of trimness. Her black shoes were very neat. Her eyes, like her whole appearance, conveyed a sense of appreciation of the expedition. They were shining.

At the sight of her there, a wave of tenderness came over him, and a fresh sense of desire. It was all very well, he thought, this comradeship of theirs. But he wanted more than that. He wanted to take her in his arms, to feel her, warm and breathing, close to him.

Involuntarily he said, "I'll be lost without you—when you're away this summer."

Her cheek coloured slightly. She looked out of the window.

He asked impulsively, "Shouldn't I have said that?"

"I'm glad you said it, anyway," she answered, without looking round.

It was on his tongue to tell her that he loved her, to ask her, in spite of the ridiculous insecurity of his position, if she would marry him. He saw, with sudden lucid insight, that this was the only, the inevitable solution for them. But something, an intuition that the moment was not apt, restrained him. He decided he would speak to her in the train coming home.

Meanwhile he went on, rather breathlessly:—

"We ought to have a grand time this evening. Hampton's a good chap. He was rather a blade at the Royal. He's a smart lad. I remember once,"—his eyes became reminiscent,—"there was a charity matinee in Dundee for the hospitals. All the stars were appearing, you know, regular artistes, at the Lyceum. Hanged if Hampton didn't go on and give a turn, sang and danced, and by George! he brought the house down!"

"He sounds more like a matinee idol than a doctor," she said, smiling.

"Now don't be highbrow, Chris! You'll like Freddie."

The train ran into Cardiff at quarter-past six, and they made directly for the Palace Hotel. Hampton had promised to meet them there at half-past, but he had not arrived when they entered the lounge.

They stood together watching the scene. The place was crowded with doctors and their wives, talking, laughing, generating immense cordiality. Friendly invitations flew back and forth.

"Doctor! You and Mrs. Smith must sit next to us to-night."

"Hey! Doctor! How about these theatre tickets?"

There was a great deal of excited coming and going, and gentlemen with red tabs in their buttonholes sped importantly across the tessellated floor with papers in their hands. In the alcove opposite an official kept up a booming monotone: "Section of O-tology and Laryn-gology *this* way please." Above a passage leading to the Annex was the notice: MEDICAL EXHIBITION. There were also palms and a string orchestra.

"Pretty social, eh?" Andrew remarked, feeling that they were rather outlawed by the general hilarity. "And Freddie's late as usual, hang him. Let's take a look round the Exhibition."

They walked interestedly around the Exhibition. Andrew soon found his hands full of elegant literature. He showed one of the leaflets to Christine with a smile. *Doctor! Is your surgery empty? We can show you how to fill it!* Also there were nineteen folders, all different, offering the newest sedatives and analgesics.

"It looks like the latest trend in medicine is dope," he remarked, frowning.

At the last stand, on their way out, a young man tactfully engaged them, producing a shiny watchlike contraption.

"Doctor! I think you'd be interested in our new indexometer. It has a multiplicity of uses, is absolutely up to the minute, creates an admirable impression by the bedside, and the price is only two guineas. Allow me, Doctor! You see, on the front, an index of incubation periods. One turn of the dial, and you find the period of infectivity. Inside," he clicked open the back of the case, "you have an excellent hæmoglobin colour index, while on the back in tabulated form—"

"My grandfather had one of these," Andrew interrupted him firmly. "But he gave it away."

Christine was smiling as they came back through the alcove again.

"Poor man," she said, "nobody ever dared laugh at his lovely meter before!"

At that moment, as they re-entered the lounge, Freddie Hampton arrived, leaping from his taxi and entering the hotel with a page boy carrying his golf clubs behind him. He saw them at once and advanced with a wide and winning smile.

"Hello! Hello! Here you are! Sorry I'm late. I had my tie to play off in the Lister Cup. I never saw such luck as that fellow had! Well, well! It's good to see you again, Andrew. Still the same old Manson. Ha! Ha! Why don't you buy yourself a new hat, my boy!" He clapped Andrew on the back, affectionate, hail fellow well met, his glance smilingly including Christine. "Introduce me, stick in the mud! What are you dreaming about?"

They sat down at one of the round tables. Hampton decided they must all have a drink. With a crack of his fingers he had a waiter running for them. Then, over the sherry, he told them all about his golf match, how he was absolutely set to win when his opponent had started sinking his mashie shots at every hole.

Fresh-complexioned, with blond brilliantine-plastered hair, a nicely cut suit, and black opal links in his projecting cuffs, Freddie was a well-turned-out figure, not good-looking—his features were very ordinary—but good-natured, smart. He looked a trifle conceited perhaps; yet, when he exerted himself, he had an attractive way. He made friends with ease, in spite of which, at the University, Doctor Muir, pathologist and cynic, had once glumly addressed him in the presence of the class: "You know nothing, Mr. Hampton. Your balloon-like mind is entirely filled with egotistical gas. But you're never at a loss. If you are successful in cribbing your way through the nursery games known here as examinations, I prophesy for you a great and shining future."

They went into the grillroom for dinner, since none of them was dressed, though Freddie informed them he would have to get into tails later in the evening. There was a dance, a confounded nuisance, but he must show up at it.

Having nonchalantly ordered from a menu gone wildly medical—*potage Pasteur, sole Madame Curie, tournedos à la Conférence Médicale*—he began recalling the old days with dramatic ardour.

"I'd never have thought, then," he ended with a shake of his head, "that old Manson would have buried himself in the South Wales Valleys!"

"Do you think he's quite buried?" Christine asked, and her smile was rather forced. There was a pause. Freddie surveyed the crowded grillroom, grinned at Andrew.

"What do you think of the Conference?"

"I suppose," Andrew answered doubtfully, "it's a useful way of keeping up-to-date."

"Up-to-date, my uncle! I haven't been to one of their ruddy sectional meetings all week. No, no, old man, it's the contacts you make that matter, the fellows you meet, mix up with. You've no idea the really influential people I've got in with this week. That's why I'm here. When I get back to town, I'll ring them up, go out and play golf with them. Later on—you mark my words—that means business."

"I don't quite follow you, Freddie," Manson said.

"Why, it's as simple as falling off a log. I'm holding down an appointment in the meantime, but I've got my eye on a nice little room up West where a smart little brass plate with FREDDIE HAMPTON, M.B. on it would look dashed well. When the plate does go up these fellows, my pals, will send me cases. You know how it happens. Reciprocity. You scratch my back and I'll scratch yours." Freddie took a slow, appreciative sip of hock. He went on: "And apart from that it pays to push in with the small suburban fellows. Sometimes they can send you stuff. Why, in a year or two, you old dog, you'll be sending patients up to me in town from your stick in the mud Blaen—whatever you call it."

Christine glanced quickly at Hampton, made as if to speak, then checked herself. She kept her eyes fastened upon her plate.

"And now tell me about yourself, Manson, old son," Freddie continued, smiling. "What's been happening to you?"

"Oh, nothing out of the ordinary. I consult in a wooden surgery, average thirty visits a day—mostly miners and their families."

"Doesn't sound too good to me." Freddie shook his head again, condolingly.

"I enjoy it," Andrew said mildly.

Christine interposed, "And you get in some real work."

"Yes, I did have one rather interesting case lately," Andrew reflected. "As a matter of fact I sent a note of it to the *Journal*."

He gave Hampton a short account of the case of Emrys Hughes. Though Freddie made a great show of interested listening, his eyes kept rolling round the room.

"That was pretty good," he remarked when Manson concluded. "I thought you only got goitre in Switzerland or somewhere. Anyhow, I hope you socked in a whacking good bill. And that reminds me. A fellow was telling me to-day the best way to handle this fee question . . ." He was off again, full of a scheme, which someone had suggested to him, for the cash payment of all fees. They had reached the end of the dinner before his voluble dissertation was over. He rose, flinging down his napkin.

"Let's have coffee outside. We'll finish our powwow in the lounge."

At quarter to ten, his cigar burned down, his stock of stories temporarily exhausted, Freddie yawned slightly and looked at his platinum wrist-watch.

But Christine was before him. She glanced at Andrew brightly, sat up straight and remarked: "Isn't it almost our train time?"

Manson was about to protest that they had another half-hour yet when Freddie said: "And I suppose I must think about this confounded dance. I can't let the party I'm going with down."

He accompanied them to the swing doors, taking prolonged and affectionate farewell of them both.

"Well, old man," he murmured with a final shake of the hand and a confidential pat on the shoulder, "when I put the little plate up in the West End I'll remember to send you a card."

Out in the warm evening air Andrew and Christine walked along Park

Street in silence. Vaguely, he was conscious that the evening had not been the success he had anticipated, that it had, at least, fallen short of Christine's expectations. He waited for her to speak, but she did not.

At last, diffidently, he said: "It was pretty dull for you, I'm afraid, listening to all these old hospital yarns."

"No," she answered. "I didn't find that dull in the least."

There was a pause.

He asked: "Didn't you like Hampton?"

"Not a great deal." She turned, losing her restraint, her eyes sparking with honest indignation. "The idea of him, sitting there, all evening, with his waxed hair and his cheap smile, patronizing you."

"Patronizing me?" he echoed in amazement.

She nodded hotly.

"It was unbearable. 'A fellow was telling me the best way to handle the fee question.' Just after you'd told him about your wonderful case! Calling it a goitre, too. Even I know it was exactly the opposite. And that remark about your sending him patients—" her lip curled, "it was simply superb." She finished quite fiercely: "Oh! I could hardly stand it, the way he put himself above you."

"I don't think he put himself above me," reasoned Andrew, puzzled. He paused. "I admit he seemed rather full of himself to-night. May have been a mood. He's the best-natured fellow you could hope to meet. We were great friends at College. We had digs together."

"Probably he found you useful to him," Christine said, with unusual bitterness. "Got you to help him with his work."

He protested unhappily: "Now, don't be mean, Chris."

"It's you," she flared, bright tears of vexation in her eyes. "You must be blind not to see the kind of person he is. And he's ruined our little expedition. It was lovely till he arrived and started talking about himself. And there was a wonderful concert at the Victoria Hall we could have gone to. But we've missed it, we're too late for anything—though he's just in time for his idiotic dance!"

They trudged towards the station some distance apart. It was the first time he had seen Christine angry. And he was angry too: angry at himself, at Hampton—yes, at Christine. Yet she was right when she said that the evening had not been a success. Now, in fact, secretly observing her pale constrained face, he felt it had been a dismal failure.

They entered the station. Suddenly, as they made their way towards the Up platform, Andrew caught sight of two people on the other side. He recognized them at once: Mrs. Bramwell and Doctor Gabell. At that moment the Down train came in, a local which ran out to the seaside at Porthcawl. Gabell and Mrs. Bramwell entered the Porthcawl train together, smiling at one another. The whistle blew. The train steamed off.

Andrew experienced a sudden sensation of distress. He glanced quickly at Christine, hoping she had not observed the incident. Only that morning he had encountered Bramwell—who, commenting on the fineness of the day, had rubbed his bony hands with satisfaction, remarking that his wife was going to spend the week end with her mother at Shrewsbury.

Andrew stood with his head bent, silent. He was so much in love that the scene he had just witnessed, with all its implications, hurt him like a physical pain. He felt slightly sick. It had only wanted this conclusion to make the day thoroughly depressing. His mood seemed to undergo a complete revulsion. A shadow had fallen on his joyfulness. He longed with all his soul to have a long quiet talk with Christine, to open his heart to her, to straighten out their stupid little disagreement. He longed, above everything, to be quite alone with her. But the Up Valley train, when it came in, was overcrowded. They had to be content with a compartment packed with miners, loudly discussing the City football match.

It was late when they reached Blaenelly, and Christine looked very tired. He was convinced that she had seen Mrs. Bramwell and Gabell. He could not possibly speak to her now. There was nothing for it but to see her to Mrs. Herbert's and unhappily bid her good night.

10

THOUGH it was nearly midnight when Andrew reached Bryngower, he found Joe Morgan waiting on him, walking up and down with short steps between the closed surgery and the entrance to the house. At the sight of him the burly driller's face expressed relief.

"Eh, Doctor, I'm glad to see you. I been back and forward here this last hour. The missus wants ye—before time, too."

Andrew, abruptly recalled from the contemplation of his own affairs, told Morgan to wait. He went into the house for his bag, then together they set out for Number 12 Blaina Terrace. The night air was cool and deep with quiet mystery. Usually so perceptive, Andrew now felt dull and listless. He had no premonition that this night call would prove unusual, still less that it would influence his whole future in Blaenelly.

The two men walked in silence until they reached the door of Number 12, then Joe drew up short.

"I'll not come in," he said, and his voice showed signs of strain. "But, man, I know ye'll do well for us."

Inside, a narrow stair led up to a small bedroom, clean but poorly furnished, and lit only by an oil lamp. Here Mrs. Morgan's mother, a tall grey-haired woman of nearly seventy, and the stout elderly midwife waited beside the patient, watching Andrew's expression as he moved about the room.

"Let me make you a cup of tea, Doctor, *bach*," said the former quickly, after a few moments.

Andrew smiled faintly. He saw that the old woman, wise in experience, realized there must be a period of waiting, that she was afraid he would leave the case, saying he would return later.

"Don't fret, Mother. I'll not run away."

Down in the kitchen he drank the tea which she gave him. Overwrought as he was, he knew he could not snatch even an hour's sleep if he went home. He knew, too, that the case here would demand all his attention. A queer lethargy of spirit came upon him. He decided to remain until everything was over.

An hour later he went upstairs again, noted the progress made, came down once more, sat by the kitchen fire. It was still, except for the rustle of a cinder in the grate and the slow tick-tock of the wall clock. No, there was another sound—the beat of Morgan's footsteps as he paced in the street outside. The old woman opposite him sat in her black dress, quite motionless, her eyes strangely alive and wise, probing, never leaving his face.

His thoughts were heavy, muddled. The episode he had witnessed at Cardiff station still obsessed him morbidly. He thought of Bramwell, foolishly devoted to a woman who deceived him sordidly, of Edward Page, bound to the shrewish Blodwen, of Denny, living unhappily, apart from his wife. His reason told him that all these marriages were dismal failures. It was a conclusion which, in his present state, made him wince. He wished to consider marriage as an idyllic state; yes, he could not otherwise consider it with the image of Christine before him. Her eyes, shining towards him, admitted no other conclusion. It was the conflict between his level, doubting mind and his overflowing heart which left him resentful and confused. He let his chin sink upon his chest, stretched out his legs, stared broodingly into the fire. He remained like this so long, and his thoughts were so filled with Christine, that he started when the old woman opposite suddenly addressed him. Her meditation had pursued a different course.

"Susan said not to give her the chloroform if it would harm the baby. She's awful set upon this child, Doctor, *bach*." Her old eyes warmed at a sudden thought. She added in a low tone: "Ay, we all are, I fancy."

He collected himself with an effort.

"It won't do any harm, the anæsthetic," he said kindly. "They'll be all right."

Here the nurse's voice was heard calling from the top landing. Andrew glanced at the clock, which now showed half-past three. He rose and went up to the bedroom. He perceived that he might now begin his work.

An hour elapsed. It was a long, harsh struggle. Then, as the first streaks of dawn strayed past the broken edges of the blind, the child was born, lifeless.

As he gazed at the still form a shiver of horror passed over Andrew. After all that he had promised! His face, heated with his own exertions, chilled suddenly. He hesitated, torn between his desire to attempt to resuscitate the child, and his obligation towards the mother, who was herself in a desperate state. The dilemma was so urgent he did not solve it consciously. Blindly, instinctively, he gave the child to the nurse and turned his attention to Susan Morgan, who now lay collapsed, almost pulseless, and not yet out of the ether, upon her side. His haste was desperate, a frantic race against her ebbing strength. It took him only an instant to smash a glass ampule and inject

pituitrin. Then he flung down the hypodermic syringe and working unsparingly to restore the flaccid woman. After a few minutes of feverish effort, her
heart strengthened; he saw that he might safely leave her. He swung round, in
his shirt sleeves, his hair sticking to his damp brow.

"Where's the child?"

The midwife made a frightened gesture. She had placed it beneath the bed.

In a flash Andrew knelt down. Fishing amongst the sodden newspapers
below the bed, he pulled out the child. A boy, perfectly formed. The limp
warm body was white and soft as tallow. The cord, hastily slashed, lay like a
broken stem. The skin was of a lovely texture, smooth and tender. The head
lolled on the thin neck. The limbs seemed boneless.

Still kneeling, Andrew stared at the child with a haggard frown. The whiteness meant only one thing: asphyxia pallida, and his mind, unnaturally tense,
raced back to a case he once had seen in the Samaritan, to the treatment that
had been used. Instantly he was on his feet.

"Get me hot water and cold water," he threw out to the nurse. "And
basins too. Quick! Quick!"

"But, Doctor—" she faltered, her eyes on the pallid body of the child.

"*Quick!*" he shouted.

Snatching a blanket he laid the child upon it and began the special method
of respiration. The basins arrived, the ewer, the big iron kettle. Frantically he
splashed cold water into one basin; into the other he mixed water as hot as his
hand could bear. Then, like some crazy juggler, he hurried the child between
the two, now plunging it into the icy, now into the steaming bath.

Fifteen minutes passed. Sweat was now running into Andrew's eyes, blinding him. One of his sleeves hung down, dripping. His breath came pantingly.
But no breath came from the lax body of the child.

A desperate sense of defeat pressed on him, a raging hopelessness. He felt
the midwife watching him in stark consternation, while there, pressed back
against the wall where she had all the time remained,—her hand pressed to
her throat, uttering no sound, her eyes burning upon him,—was the old
woman. He remembered her longing for a grandchild, as great as had been her
daughter's longing for this child. All dashed away now; futile, beyond
remedy . . .

The floor was now a draggled mess. Stumbling over a sopping towel, Andrew almost dropped the child, which was now wet and slippery in his hands,
like a strange white fish.

"For mercy's sake, Doctor," whimpered the midwife. "It's stillborn."

Andrew did not heed her. Beaten, despairing, having laboured in vain for
half an hour, he still persisted in one last effort, rubbing the child with a
rough towel, crushing and releasing the little chest with both his hands, trying
to get breath into that limp body.

And then, as by a miracle, the pigmy chest, which his hands enclosed, gave
a short convulsive heave. Another . . . And another . . . Andrew turned
giddy. The sense of life, springing beneath his fingers after all that unavailing

striving, was so exquisite it almost made him faint. He redoubled his efforts feverishly. The child was gasping now, deeper and deeper. A bubble of mucus came from one tiny nostril, a joyful iridescent bubble. The limbs were no longer boneless. The head no longer lay back spinelessly. The blanched skin was slowly turning pink. Then, exquisitely, came the child's cry.

"Dear Father in Heaven," the nurse sobbed hysterically, "it's come—it's come alive."

Andrew handed her the child. He felt weak and dazed. About him the room lay in a shuddering litter: blankets, towels, basins, soiled instruments, the hypodermic syringe impaled by its point in the linoleum, the ewer knocked over, the kettle on its side in a puddle of water. Upon the huddled bed the mother still dreamed her way quietly through the anæsthetic. The old woman still stood against the wall. But her hands were together, her lips moved without sound. She was praying.

Mechanically Andrew wrung out his sleeve, pulled on his jacket.

"I'll fetch my bag later, Nurse."

He went downstairs, through the kitchen into the scullery. His lips were dry. At the scullery he took a long drink of water. He reached for his hat and coat.

Outside he found Joe standing on the pavement with a tense, expectant face.

"All right, Joe," he said thickly. "Both all right."

It was quite light. Nearly five o'clock. A few miners were already in the streets: the first of the night shift moving out. As Andrew walked with them, spent and slow, his footfalls echoing with the others under the morning sky, he kept thinking blindly, oblivious to all other work he had done in Blaenelly: "I've done something; oh, God! I've done something real at last."

11

AFTER a shave and a bath—thanks to Annie there was always plenty of boiling water in the tap—he felt less tired. But Mrs. Page, finding his bed unslept in, was facetiously sarcastic at the breakfast table, the more so as he received her shafts in silence.

"Ha! You lookin' bit of a wreck this mornin', Doctor. Bit dark under the eyes like! Didn't get back from Swansea till this mornin', eh? And forgot my pastries from Parry's too, like. Been out on the tiles, my boy? Tee-hee! You can't deceive *me*! I thought you was too good to be true. You're all the same, you assistants. I never found one yet that didn't drink or go wrong some'ow!"

After morning surgery and his forenoon round, Andrew dropped in to see his case. It had just gone half-past twelve as he turned up Blaina Place. There were little knots of women talking at their open doorways, and as he passed they stopped talking to smile and give him a friendly "Good morning." Approaching Number 12 he fancied he saw a face at the window. And it was so. They had been waiting on him. The instant he placed his foot on the newly pipe-clayed doorstep, the door was swung open and the old woman, beaming unbelievably all over her wrinkled face, made him welcome to the house.

Indeed, she was so eager to make much of him she could barely frame the words. She asked him to come first for some refreshment to the parlour. When he refused, she fluttered:—

"All right, all right, Doctor, *bach*. It's as *you* say. Maybe you'll have time, though, on your way down for a drop of elderberry wine and a morsel of cake." She patted him upstairs with tremulous old hands.

He entered the bedroom. The little room, lately a shambles, had been scoured and polished until it shone. All his instruments, beautifully arranged, gleamed upon the varnished deal dresser. His bag had been carefully rubbed with goose-grease, the snib catches cleaned with metal polish, so that they were as silver. The bed had been changed, spread with fresh linen; and there, upon it, was the mother, her plain middle-aged face gazing in dumb happiness towards him, the babe sucking quiet and warm at her full breast.

"Ay!" The stout midwife rose from her seat by the bedside, unmasking a battery of smiles. "They do look all right now, don't they, Doctor, *bach*? They don't know the trouble they gave us. They don't *care*, either, do they?"

Moistening her lips, her soft eyes warmly inarticulate, Susan Morgan tried to stammer out her gratitude.

"Ay, you may well say," nodded the midwife, extracting the last ounce of credit from the situation. "An' don't you forget, my gal, you wouldn't never have another at your age. It was this time or *never*, so far as you was concerned!"

"We know that, Mrs. Jones," interrupted the old woman meaningly, from the door. "We know we do owe everything here to *Doctor*."

"Has my Joe been to see you yet, Doctor?" asked the mother timidly. "No? Well he's comin', you may be sure. He's fair overjoyed. He was only sayin' though. Doctor, that's the thing we will miss when we're in South Africa, not havin' you to 'tend to us."

Leaving the house, duly fortified with seedcake and homemade elderberry wine,—it would have broken the old woman's heart had he refused to drink her grandson's health,—Andrew continued on his round with a queer warmth round his heart. "They couldn't have made more of me," he thought self-consciously, "if I'd been the King of England." This case became somehow the antidote to that scene he had witnessed upon Cardiff platform. There was something to be said for marriage and the family life, when it brought such happiness as filled the Morgan home.

A fortnight later, when Andrew had paid his last visit at Number 12, Joe Morgan came round to see him. Joe's manner was solemnly portentous. And, having laboured long with words, he said explosively:—

"Dang it all, Doctor, *bach*, I'm no hand at talkin'. Money can't repay what you done for us. But all the same the missus and I want to make you this little present."

Impulsively, he handed over a slip to Andrew. It was an order on the Building Society, made out for five guineas.

Andrew stared at the cheque. The Morgans were, in the local idiom, tidy folk; but they were far from being well-off. This amount, on the eve of their departure, with expenses of transit to be faced, must represent a great sacrifice, a noble generosity.

Touched, Andrew said: "I can't take this, Joe, lad."

"You must take it," Joe said with grave insistence, his hand closing over Andrew's, "or Missus and me'll be mortal offended. It's a present for yourself. It's not for Doctor Page. He's had my money now for years and years, and we've never troubled him but this once. He's *well* paid. This is a present—for *yourself*—Doctor, *bach*. You understand."

"Yes, I understand, Joe," Andrew nodded, smiling.

He folded the order, placed it in his waistcoat pocket and for a few days forgot about it. Then, the following Tuesday, passing the Western Counties Bank, he paused, reflected a moment, and went in. As Mrs. Page always paid him in notes, which he forwarded by registered letter to the Endowment offices, he had never had occasion to deal through the bank. But now, with a comfortable recollection of his own substance, he decided to open a deposit account with Joe's gift.

At the grating he endorsed the order, filled in some forms, and handed them to the young cashier, remarking with a smile: "It's not much, but it's a start anyhow."

Meanwhile he had been conscious of Aneurin Rees hovering in the background, watching him. And, as he turned to go, the long-headed manager came forward to the counter. In his hands he held the order. Smoothing it gently, he glanced sideways across his spectacles.

"Afternoon, Doctor Manson. How are you?" Pause . . . Sucking his breath in over his yellow teeth . . . "Eh—you want this paid into your new account?"

"Yes." Manson spoke in some surprise. "Is it too small an amount to open with?"

"Oh, no, no, Doctor. 'Tisn't the amount, like. We're very glad to have the business." Rees hesitated, scrutinizing the order; then, raising his small suspicious eyes to Andrew's face: "Eh—you want it in your *own* name?"

"Why—certainly."

"All right, all right, Doctor." His expression broke suddenly into a watery smile. "I only wondered, like. Wanted to make sure. What lovely weather we're havin' for the time of year. Good day to you, Doctor Manson. Go-od day!"

Manson came out of the bank puzzled, asking himself what that bald, buttoned-up devil meant. It was some days before he found an answer to the question.

12

CHRISTINE had left on her vacation more than a week before. He had been so occupied by the Morgan case that he had not succeeded in seeing her for more than a few moments, on the day of her departure. He had not spoken to her. But now that she was gone he longed for her with all his heart.

The summer was exceptionally trying in the town. The green vestiges of spring had long been withered to a dirty yellow. The mountains wore a febrile air, and when the daily shot-firing from the mines or quarries re-echoed on the still spent air they seemed to enclose the valley in a dome of burnished sound. The men came out from the mine with the ore dust smeared upon their faces like rust. Children played listlessly. Old Thomas, the groom, had been taken with jaundice and Andrew was compelled to make his rounds on foot. As he slogged through the baking streets he thought of Christine. What was she doing? Was she thinking of him, perhaps, a little? And what of the future, her prospects, their chance of happiness together?

And then, quite unexpectedly, he received a message from Watkins asking him to call at the Company offices.

The mine manager received him in agreeable fashion, invited him to sit down, pushed over the packet of cigarettes on his desk.

"Look here, Doctor," he said in a friendly tone, "I've been wantin' to talk to you for some time—and we better get it over afore I make up my annual return." He paused to pick a yellow shred of tobacco off his tongue. "There's been a number of the lads at me, Emrys Hughes and Ed Williams are the leadin' spirits, askin' me to put you up for the Company's list."

Andrew straightened in his chair, pervaded by a swift glow of satisfaction, of excitement.

"You mean—arrange for me to take over Doctor Page's practice?"

"Why, no, not exactly, Doctor," Watkins said slowly. "You see the position is difficult. I've got to watch how I handle my labour question 'ere. I can't put Doctor Page off the list; there's a number of the men wouldn't have *that*. What I was meanin', in the best interests of yourself, was to squeeze you, quiet like, on to the Company's list; then them that wanted to slip away from Doctor Page to yourself could easily manage it."

The eagerness faded from Andrew's expression. He frowned, his figure still braced.

"But surely you see I couldn't do that? I came here as Page's assistant. If I set up in opposition—no decent doctor could do a thing like that!"

"There isn't any other way."

"Why don't you let me take over the practice?" Andrew said urgently. "I'd willingly pay something for it, out of receipts—that's another way."

Watkins shook his head bluntly.

"Blodwen won't 'ave it. I've put it up to her afore. She knows she's in a strong position. Nearly all the older men here, like Enoch Davies for instance, are on Page's side. They believe he'll come back. I'd have a strike on my hands if I even tried to shift him." He paused. "Take till to-morrow to think it over, Doctor. I send the new list to Swansea Head Office then. Once it's gone in we can't do anything for another twelve months."

Andrew stared at the floor a moment, then slowly made a gesture of negation. His hopes, so high a minute ago, were now dashed completely to the ground.

"What's the use? I couldn't do it—if I thought it over for weeks."

It cost him a bitter pang to reach this decision, and to maintain it in the face of Watkins's partiality towards him. Yet there was no escaping the fact that he had gained his introduction to Blaenelly as Doctor Page's assistant. To set up against his principal, even in the exceptional circumstances of the case, was quite unthinkable. Suppose Page did, by some chance, resume active practice—how well he would look, fighting the old man for patients! No, no. He could not, and would not, accept.

Nevertheless, for the rest of the day he was sadly cast-down, resentful of Blodwen's barefaced extortion, aware that he was caught in an impossible position, wishing the offer had not been made to him at all. In the evening, about eight o'clock, he went dejectedly to call on Denny. He had not seen him for some time, and he felt that a talk with Philip, perhaps some reassurance that he had acted correctly, would do him good. He reached Philip's lodgings about half-past eight, and, as was now his custom, walked into the house without knocking. He entered the sitting-room.

Philip lay on the sofa. At first, in the fading light, Manson thought that he was resting after a hard day's work. But Philip had done no work that day. He sprawled there on his back, breathing heavily, his arm flung across his face. He was dead-drunk.

Andrew turned to find the landlady at his elbow, watching him sideways, her eyes concerned, apprehensive.

"I heard you come in, Doctor. He's been like this all day. He's eaten nothing. I can't do a thing with him."

Andrew simply did not know what to say. He stood staring at Philip's senseless face, recollecting that first cynical remark, uttered in the surgery on the night of his arrival.

"It's ten months now since he had his last bout," the landlady went on. "And he don't touch it in between. But when he do begin he goes at it wicked. I can tell you it's more nor awkward, with Doctor Lewis bein' away on holiday. It looks like I must wire him."

"Send Tom up," Andrew said at last. "And we'll get him into bed."

With the help of the landlady's son, a young miner who seemed to regard the matter as something of a joke, they got Philip undressed and into his pyjamas. Then they carried him, dull and heavy as a sack, through to the bedroom.

"The main thing is to see that he doesn't get any more of it, you understand. Turn the key in the door if necessary," Andrew addressed the landlady as they came back into the sitting-room. "And now—you'd better let me have to-day's list of calls."

From the child's slate hanging in the hall he copied out the visits which Philip should have made that day. He went out. By hurrying round he could get most of them done before eleven.

Next morning, immediately after surgery, he went round to the lodgings. The landlady met him, wringing her hands.

"I don't know where he's got it. I 'aven't done it, I've only done my best for him."

Philip was drunker than before, heavy, insensible. After prolonged shakings and an effort to restore him with strong coffee, which in the end was upset and spilled all over the bed, Andrew took the list of calls again. Cursing the heat, the flies, Thomas' jaundice, and Denny, he again did double work that day.

In the late afternoon he came back, tired out, angrily resolved to get Denny sober. This time he found him astride one of the chairs in his pyjamas, still drunk, delivering a long address to Tom and Mrs. Seager. As Andrew entered Denny stopped short and gave him a lowering, derisive stare. He spoke thickly.

"Ha! The Good Samaritan. I understand you've done my round for me. Extremely noble. But why should you? Why should that blasted Lewis clear out and leave us to do the work?"

"I can't say." Andrew's patience was wearing thin. "All I know is it would be easier if you did your bit of it."

"I'm a surgeon. I'm not a blasted general practitioner—G.P. Huh! What does that mean? D'you ever ask yourself? You didn't? Well, I'll tell you. It's the last and most ster—stereotyped anachronism, the worst, the stupidest system ever created by God-made man. Dear old G.P.! And dear old B.P.!— that's the British Public. Ha! Ha!" He laughed derisively. "They made him. They love him. They weep over him." He swayed in his seat, his inflamed eye again bitter and morose, lecturing them drunkenly. "What can the poor devil do about it? Your G.P.—your dear old quack of all trades! Maybe it's twenty years since he qualified. How can he know medicine and obstetrics and bacteriology and all the modern scientific advances, and surgery as well? Oh, yes! Oh, yes! Don't forget the surgery! Occasionally he tries a little operation at the cottage hospital. Ha! Ha!" Again the sardonic amusement. "Say a mastoid. Two hours and a half by the clock. When he finds pus he's a saviour of humanity. When he doesn't, they bury the patient." His voice rose. He was angry, wildly, drunkenly angry. "Damn it to hell, Manson. It's been going on for hundreds of years. Don't they ever want to *change* the system? What's the use? What's the *use*? I ask you. Give me another whisky. We're all cracked. And it seems I'm drunk as well."

There was silence for a few moments; then, suppressing his irritation, Andrew said: "Oughtn't you to get back to bed now? Come on, we'll help you."

"Let me alone," said Denny sullenly. "Don't use your blasted bedside manner on me. I've used it plenty in my time. I know it too well." He rose abruptly, staggering, and, taking Mrs. Seager by the shoulder, he thrust her into the chair. Then, swaying on his feet, his manner a savage assumption of bland suavity, he addressed the frightened woman. "And how are you to-day, my dear lady? A leetle better, I fancy. A little more strength in the pulse. Sleep well? Ha! Hum! Then we must prescribe a leetle sedative."

There was, in the ludicrous scene, a strange, alarming note—the stocky, unshaven, pyjama-clad figure of Philip aping the society physician, swaying in servile deference before the shrinking miner's wife. Tom gave a nervous gulp of laughter. In a flash Denny turned on him and violently cuffed his ears.

"That's right! Laugh! Laugh your blasted head off. But I spent five years of my life doing that. God! When I think of it I could die." He glared at them, seized a vase that stood on the mantelpiece, and dashed it hard upon the floor. The next instant the companion piece was in his hands and he sent it shattering against the wall. He started forward, red destruction in his eye.

"For mercy's sake," whimpered Mrs. Seager. "Stop him, stop him—"

Andrew and Tom Seager flung themselves on Philip, who struggled with the wild intractability of intoxication. Then, perversely, he suddenly relaxed and was sentimental, fuddled.

"Manson," he drooled, hanging on Andrew's shoulder, "you're a good chap. I love you better than a brother. You and I—if we stuck together we could save the whole bloody medical profession."

He stood, his gaze wandering, lost. Then his head drooped. His body sagged. He allowed Andrew to help him to the next room and into bed. As his head rolled over on the pillow he made a last maudlin request:—

"Promise me one thing, Manson! For Christ's sake, don't marry a lady!"

Next morning he was drunker than ever. Andrew gave it up. He half-suspected young Seager of smuggling in the liquor, though the lad, when confronted, swore, pale-faced, that he had nothing to do with it.

All that week Andrew struggled through Denny's calls in addition to his own. On Sunday, after lunch, he visited the Chapel Street lodgings. Philip was up, shaved, dressed, and immaculate in his appearance; also, though drawn and shaky, cold sober.

"I understand you've been doing my work for me, Manson." Gone was the intimacy of these last few days. His manner was constrained, icily stiff.

"It was nothing," Andrew answered clumsily.

"On the contrary, it must have put you to a great deal of trouble."

Denny's attitude was so objectionable that Andrew flushed. Not a word of gratitude, he thought; nothing but that stiff, hidebound arrogance.

"If you do want to know the truth," he blurted out, "it put me to a hell of a lot of trouble!"

"You may take it from me something will be done about it."

"What do you think I am?" Andrew answered hotly. "Some damned cabby that expects a tip from you? If it hadn't been for me, Mrs. Seager would have wired Doctor Lewis and you'd have been thrown out on your neck. You're a supercilious, half-baked snob. And what you need is a damned good punch on the jaw."

Denny lit a cigarette, his fingers shaking so violently he could barely hold the match.

He sneered: "Nice of you to choose this moment to offer physical combat. True Scottish tact. Some other time I may oblige you."

"Oh, shut your bloody mouth!" said Andrew. "Here's your list of calls. Those with a cross should be seen on Monday."

He flung out of the house in a fury. Damn it, he raged, wincing, what kind of man is he to behave like God Almighty! It's as if he had done *me* the favour, *allowing* me to do his work!

But, on the way home, his resentment slowly cooled. He was genuinely fond of Philip, and he had by now a better insight into his complex nature: shy, inordinately sensitive, vulnerable. It was this alone which made him secrete a shell of hardness round himself. The memory of his recent bout, of how he had exposed himself during it, must even now be causing him excruciating torture.

Again Andrew was struck by the paradox of this clever man, using Blaenelly as a bolt-hole from convention. As a surgeon, Philip was exceptionally gifted. Andrew, administering the anæsthetic, had seen him perform a resection of the gall bladder on the kitchen table of a miner's house, the sweat dripping from his red face and hairy forearms, a model of swiftness and accuracy. It was possible to make allowances for a man who did such work.

Nevertheless, when Andrew reached home he still smarted from his impact with Philip's coldness. And so, as he came through the front door and hung his hat on the stand, he was scarcely in the mood to hear Mrs. Page's voice exclaiming:—

"Is that you, Doctor? Doctor Manson! I want you!"

Andrew ignored her call. Turning, he prepared to go upstairs to his own room. But as he placed his hand on the banister Blodwen's voice came again, sharper, louder.

"Doctor! Doctor Manson! I *want* you."

Andrew swung round, to see Mrs. Page sail out of the sitting-room, her face unusually pale, her black eyes sparking with some violent emotion. She came up to him.

"Are you deaf? Didn't you 'ear me say I *wanted* you?"

"What is it, Mrs. Page?" he asked irritably.

"What is it, indeed!" She could scarcely breathe. "I like that. You askin' me! It's me that wants to ask you somethin', my fine Doctor Manson!"

"What, then?" Andrew snapped.

The shortness of his manner seemed to excite her beyond endurance.

"It's *this*. Yes, my smart young gentleman! Maybe you'll be kind enough to explain this." From her pudgy bosom she produced a slip of paper and, without relinquishing it, fluttered it menacingly before his eyes. He saw it was Joe Morgan's cheque. Then, raising his head, he saw Rees behind Blodwen, skulking in the doorway of the sitting-room.

"Ay, you may well look!" Blodwen went on. "I see you recognize it. But you better tell us quick how you come to bank that money for yourself, when it's Doctor Page's money and you know it."

Andrew felt the blood rise behind his ears in quick surging waves.

"It's mine. Joe Morgan made me a present of it."

"A *present!* Ho! Ho! I like that. He's not 'ere now to deny it."

He answered between his shut teeth.

"You can write to him if you doubt my word."

"I've more to do than write letters all over the place." Losing the last of her restraint she shouted: "I do doubt your word. You think you're a wise one. Huh! Comin' down here and thinkin' you can get the practice into your own hands when you should be workin' for Doctor Page! But this shows what you are, all right. You're a thief, that's what you are, a common thief."

She spat the word at him, half-turning for support to Rees—who, in the doorway, was making sounds of expostulation in his throat, his face sallower than usual. Andrew, indeed, saw Rees as the instigator of the whole affair, dallying a few days in indecision, then scurrying to Blodwen with the story. His hands clenched fiercely. He came down the two bottom steps and advanced towards them, his eyes fixed on Rees's thin bloodless mouth with threatening intensity. He was livid with rage and thirsting for battle.

"Mrs. Page," he said, in a laboured tone, "you've made a charge against me. Unless you take it back and apologize within two minutes, I'll sue you for damages for defamation of character. The source of your information will come out in Court. I've no doubt Mr. Rees's board of governors will be interested to hear how he discloses his official business."

"I—I only did my duty," stuttered the bank manager, his complexion turning muddier than before.

"I'm waiting, Mrs. Page." The words came with a rush, choking him. "And if you don't hurry up, I'll give your bank manager the worst hiding he's ever had in his life."

She saw she had gone too far—had said more, far more than she had intended. His threat, his ominous attitude, frightened her. It was almost possible to follow her swift reflection: *Damages! Heavy damages! Oh, Lord, they might take a lot o' money off 'er!*

She choked, swallowed, stammered: "I—I take it back. I apologize."

It was almost comic, the plump little termagant so suddenly and unexpectedly subdued. But Andrew found it singularly humourless. He realized, all at once, with a great flood of bitterness, that he had reached the limit of his endurance. He could not put up with this nagging, importunate creature any longer. He took a quick deep breath. He forgot everything but his loathing of her. There was a wild and savage joy in letting himself go.

"Mrs. Page, there are just one or two things I want to tell you. In the first place I know for a fact that you are making one thousand, five hundred pounds a year because of the work which I do for you here. Out of this you pay me a miserable two hundred and fifty, and in addition you've done your best to starve me. It may interest you to know, also, that last week a deputation of the men approached the manager, who invited me to put my name on the Company's list. It may further interest you to know that on ethical grounds—which you couldn't possibly know anything about—I definitely refused. And now, Mrs. Page, I'm so absolutely sick of you, I couldn't stay on.

You're a mean, guzzling, mercenary bitch. In fact, you're a pathological case. I give you a month's notice here and now."

She gaped at him, her little button eyes nearly bursting from her head. Then suddenly she shrilled:—

"No, you don't. No, you don't. It's all lies. You couldn't get near the Company's list. And you're *sacked*, that's what you are. No assistant 'as ever given me notice in his life. The idea, the impudence, the insolence, talkin' to me like that. I said it first. You're sacked, you are, that's what you are, sacked, sacked, sacked—"

The outburst was loud, hysterical, degrading. And at the height of it, there was an interruption. Upstairs, the door of Edward's room swung slowly open and, a moment later, Edward himself appeared, a strange gaunt figure, his wasted shanks showing beneath his nightshirt.

So strange and unexpected was this apparition that Mrs. Page stopped dead in the middle of a word. From the hall she gazed upwards, as also did Rees and Andrew, while the sick man, dragging his paralyzed leg behind him, came slowly, painfully, to the topmost stair.

"Can't I have a little peace?" His voice, though agitated, was stern. "What's the matter?"

Blodwen took another gulp, launched into a tearful diatribe against Manson. She concluded: "And so—and so I gave him his notice."

Manson did not contradict her version of the case.

"You mean he's going?" Edward asked, trembling all over with agitation and the exertion of keeping himself upright.

"Yes, Edward." She sniffed. "Any'ow, you'll soon be back."

There was a silence. Edward abandoned all that he wished to say. His eyes dwelt on Andrew in mute apology, moved to Rees, passed quickly on to Blodwen, then came to rest sorrowfully on nothing at all. A look of hopelessness yet of dignity formed upon his stiff face.

"No," he said at last. "I'll never be back. You know that—all of you."

He said nothing more. Turning slowly, holding on to the wall, he dragged his way back into his room. The door closed without sound.

13

REMEMBERING the joy, the pure elation which the Morgan case had given him and which, with a few ugly words, Blodwen Page had turned to something sordid, Andrew brooded angrily, wondering if he should not take the matter further, write to Joe Morgan, demand something more than a mere apology. But he dismissed the idea as one worthy of Blodwen.

In the end he picked out the most useless charity in the district and in a mood of determined bitterness posted five guineas to the home and asked them to send the receipt to Aneurin Rees. After that he felt better. But he wished he might have seen Rees reading that receipt.

And now, realizing that his work must terminate here at the end of a month, he began immediately to look for another position, combing the back pages of the *Lancet*, applying for everything which seemed suitable. There were numerous advertisements inserted in the "Assistants Wanted" column. He sent in good applications, copies of his testimonials and even, as was frequently requested, photographs of himself. But at the end of the first week, and again at the conclusion of the second, he had received not a single answer to his applications. He was disappointed and astounded.

Then Denny offered him the explanation in one terse phrase: "You've been in Blaenelly."

It dawned upon Andrew, with a pang of dismay, that his having been in practice in this remote Welsh mining town condemned him. No one wanted assistants from "the Valleys"—they had a reputation.

When a fortnight of his notice had expired Andrew really began to worry. What on earth was he to do? He still owed over fifty pounds to the Glen Endowment. They would allow him to suspend payments, of course. But apart from that, if he could not find another job, how was he to live? He had two or three pounds in ready cash, no more. He had no equipment, no reserves. He had not even bought himself a new suit since coming to Blaenelly, and his present garments had been shabby enough when he arrived. He had moments of sheer terror when he saw himself sinking to destitution.

Surrounded by difficulties and uncertainty, he longed for Christine. Letters were no use; he had no talent for expressing himself on paper; anything he could write would undoubtedly convey a wrong impression. Yet she was not returning to Blaenelly until the first week in September. He turned a fretful, hungry eye upon the calendar, counting the days that intervened. There were still twelve of them to run. He felt, with growing despondency, that they might as well be past, for all the prospect which they held for him.

On the evening of the thirtieth of August, three weeks after Manson had given Mrs. Page his notice and at about the time he had begun, from stark necessity, to entertain the idea of trying for a dispenser's post, he was walking dispiritedly along Chapel Street when he met Denny. They had remained on terms of slightly strained civility during the past few weeks, and Andrew was surprised when the other man stopped him.

Knocking out his pipe on the heel of his boot, Philip inspected it as though it demanded all his attention.

"I'm rather sorry you're going, Manson. It's made quite a difference, your being here." He hesitated. "I heard this afternoon that the Aberalaw Medical Aid Society are looking for a new assistant. Aberalaw—that's just thirty miles across the Valleys. It's quite a decent Society, as these things go. I believe the head doctor—Llewellyn—is a useful man. And as it's a Valley town, they can't very well object to a Valley man. Why don't you try?"

Andrew gazed at him doubtfully. His expectations had recently been raised so high and dashed so hopelessly that he had lost all faith in his ability to succeed.

"Well, yes," he agreed slowly. "If that's the case, I may as well try."

A few minutes later he walked home, through the now heavy rain, to apply for the post.

On the sixth of September there took place a full meeting of the Committee of the Aberalaw Medical Aid Society for the purpose of selecting a successor to Doctor Leslie, who had recently resigned in order to take up an appointment on a Malay rubber plantation. Seven candidates had applied for the position and all seven candidates had been asked to attend.

It was a perfect summer afternoon and the time, by the big Co-operative Stores clock, was close on four o'clock. Prowling up and down on the pavement outside the Medical Aid offices in Aberalaw Square, darting anxious glances at the six other candidates, Andrew nervously awaited the first stroke of the hour. Now that his foreboding had proved incorrect and he was here, actually being considered for the post, he longed with all his heart to be successful.

From what he had seen of it he liked Aberalaw. Standing at the extreme end of the Gethely Valley, the town was less in the Valley than on top of it. High, bracing, considerably larger than Blaenelly,—nearly twenty thousand inhabitants was his guess,—with good streets and shops, two cinemas, and a sense of spaciousness conveyed by green fields on its outskirts, Aberalaw appeared to Andrew, after the sweltering confines of the Penelly ravine, as a perfect paradise.

"But I'll never get it," he fretted as he paced up and down—never, never, *never*. No, he couldn't be so lucky! All the other candidates looked far more likely to be successful than himself, better turned-out, more confident. Doctor Edwards, especially, radiated confidence. Andrew found himself hating Edwards, a stoutish, prosperous, middle-aged man who had freely intimated, in the general conversation a moment ago in the office doorway, that he had just sold his own practice down the Valley in order to "apply" for this position. Damn him, grated Andrew inwardly; he wouldn't have sold out of a safe berth if he hadn't been sure of this one!

Up and down, up and down, head bent, hands thrust in his pockets. What would Christine think of him if he failed? She was returning to Blaenelly either to-day or to-morrow—in her letter she had not been quite sure. Bank Street School reopened on the following Monday. Though he had written her no word of his application here failure would mean his meeting her gloomily, or worse, with a fictitious brightness, at that very moment when he wished, above everything in the world, to stand well with her, to win her quiet, intimate, exciting smile!

Four o'clock at last. As he turned towards the entrance a fine saloon motor car swept silently into the Square and drew up at the offices. From the back seat a short, dapper man emerged, smiling briskly, affably, yet with a sort of careless assurance, at the candidates. Before mounting the stairs he recognized Edwards, nodding casually.

"How do, Edwards." Then, aside: "It'll be all right, I fancy."

"Thank you, thank you ever so, Doctor Llewellyn," breathed Edwards with tremendous deference.

"Finish!" said Andrew to himself bitterly.

Upstairs, the waiting-room was small, bare, and sour-smelling, situated at the end of a short passage leading to the committee room. Andrew was the third to go in for interview. He entered the big committee room with nervous doggedness. If the post was already promised he was not going to cringe for it. He took the seat offered him with a blank expression.

About thirty miners filled the room, seated, and all of them smoking, gazing at him with blunt but not unfriendly curiosity. At the small side table was a pale, quiet man with a sensitive, intelligent face who looked, from his blue pitted features, as if he had once been a miner. He was Owen, the secretary. Lounging on the edge of the table, smiling good-naturedly at Andrew, was Doctor Llewellyn.

The interview began. Owen, in a quiet voice, explained the conditions of the post.

"It's like this, you see, Doctor. Under our scheme, the workers in Aberalaw —there are two anthracite mines here, a steel works, and one coal mine in the district—pay over a certain amount to the Society out of their wages every week. Out of this the Society administers the necessary medical services, provides a nice little hospital, surgeries, medicines, splints, *et cetera*. In addition, the Society engages doctors,—Doctor Llewellyn, the head physician and surgeon, and four assistants, together with a surgeon dentist,—and pays them a capitation fee—so much per head, according to the number on their list. I believe Doctor Leslie was making something like five hundred pounds a year when he left us." He paused. "Altogether, we find it a good scheme." There was a mutter of approval from the thirty committee men. Owen raised his head and faced them. "And now, gentlemen, have you any questions to ask?"

They began to fire questions at Andrew. He tried to answer calmly, without exaggeration, truly. Once he made a point.

"Do you speak Welsh, Doctor?" This from a persistent, youngish miner by the name of Chenkin.

"No," said Andrew. "I was brought up on the Gaelic."

"A lot o' good that would be 'ere!"

"I've always found it useful for swearing at my patients," said Andrew coolly, and a laugh went up against Chenkin.

It was over at last. "Thank you very much, Doctor Manson," Owen said. And Andrew was out again in the sour little waiting-room, feeling as if he had been buffeted by heavy seas, watching the rest of the candidates go in.

Edwards, the last man called, was absent a long, a very long time. He came out smiling broadly, his look plainly saying: "Sorry for you, fellows. This is in my pocket."

Then followed an interminable wait. But at last the door of the committee room opened and out of the smoke-swirling depths came Owen the secretary, a paper in his hand. His eyes, searching, rested finally with real friendliness upon Andrew.

"Would you come in a minute, Doctor Manson? The Committee would like to see you again."

Pale-lipped, his heart pounding in his side, Andrew followed the secretary back into the committee room. It couldn't be—no, no, it couldn't be that they were interested in him.

Back in the prisoner's chair again he found smiles and encouraging nods thrown in his direction. Doctor Llewellyn, however, was not looking at him.

Owen, spokesman of the meeting, commenced:—

"Doctor Manson, we may as well be frank with you. The Committee is in some doubt. The Committee, in fact, on Doctor Llewellyn's advice, had a strong bias in favour of another candidate, who has considerable knowledge of practice in the Gethely Valley."

"'E's too bloody fat, that Edwards," came an interruption from a grizzled member at the back. "I'd like to see 'im climb to the houses on Mardy Hill!"

Andrew was too tense to smile. Breathlessly, he waited on Owen's words.

"But to-day," the secretary went on, "I must say that the Committee have been very taken with you. The Committee—as Tom Kettles poetically expressed it a minute ago—want young, active men."

Laughter, with cries of "'Ear! 'Ear!" and "Good old Tom!"

"Moreover, Doctor Manson," continued Owen, "I must tell you that the Committee have been exceedin'ly struck by two testimonials, I might even say testimonials *unsolicited* by yourself, which makes them of more value in the eyes of the Committee and which reached us by post only this mornin'. These are from two practitioners in your own town, I mean Blaenelly. One is a Doctor Denny, who has the M.S., a very high degree, as Doctor Llewellyn, who should know, admits. The other, enclosed with Doctor Denny's, is signed by Doctor Page, whose assistant I believe you now are. Well, Doctor Manson, the Committee has experience of testimonials, and these two refer to your good self in such genuine terms that the Committee has been much impressed."

Andrew bit his lip, his eye lowered, aware for the first time of this generous thing that Denny had done for him.

"There is just one difficulty, Doctor Manson." Owen paused, diffidently moving the ruler on his table. "While the Committee is now unanimously disposed in your favour, this position with its—responsibilities—is more or less one for a married man. You see, apart from the fact that the men prefer a married doctor when it comes to attendin' their families, there's a house, Vale View, and a good house too, that goes with the position. It wouldn't —no, it wouldn't be very suitable for a single man."

A tumultuous silence. Andrew drew a tense breath, his thoughts focussed, a bright white light, upon the image of Christine. They were all, even Doctor Llewellyn, looking at him, awaiting his answer. Without thinking, entirely independent of his own volition, he spoke. He heard himself declaring calmly:—

"As a matter of fact, gentlemen, I'm engaged to someone in Blaenelly. I've —I've just been waiting on a suitable appointment—such as this—to get married."

Owen slapped down the ruler in satisfaction. There was approval, signified by a tapping of heavy boots.

And the irrepressible Kettles exclaimed: "Good enough, lad! Aberalaw's a rare fine place for an 'oneymoon!"

"I take it you're agreed then, gentlemen?" Owen's voice rose above the noise. "Doctor Manson is unanimously appointed?"

There was a vigorous murmur of assent. Andrew experienced a wild thrill of triumph.

"When can you take up your duties, Doctor Manson? The earlier the better, so far as the Committee is concerned."

"I could start the beginning of next week," Manson answered. Then he turned cold as he thought: "Suppose Christine won't have me. Suppose I lose her, and this wonderful job as well."

"That's settled then. Thank you, Doctor Manson. I'm sure the Committee wishes you—and Mrs. Manson that's to be—every success in your new appointment."

Applause. They were all congratulating him now, the members, Llewellyn, and, with a very cordial clasp, Owen. Then he was out in the waiting-room, trying not to show his elation, trying to appear unconscious of Edwards' incredulous, crestfallen face.

But it was no use, no use at all. As he walked from the Square to the station his heart swelled with excited victory. His step was quick and springy. On his right, as he strode down the hill, was a small green public park with a fountain and a bandstand. Think of it! A bandstand—when the only elevation, the only feature of the landscape in Blaenelly was a slag-heap! Look at that cinema over there, too; those fine big shops; the hard good road—not a rocky mountain track—under his feet! And hadn't Owen said something about a hospital too, a "nice little" hospital? Ah! Thinking of what the hospital would mean to his work, Andrew drew a deep, excited breath. He hurled himself into an empty compartment in the train for Cardiff. And as it bore him thither he exulted wildly.

14

THOUGH the distance was not great across the mountains, the railway journey from Aberalaw to Blaenelly was circuitous. The Down train stopped at every station, the Penelly Valley train into which he changed at Cardiff would not, simply would not go fast enough. Manson's mood had altered now. Sunk in the corner seat, chafing, burning to be back, his thoughts tormented him.

For the first time he saw how selfish he had been, these last few months, in considering only his side of the case. All his doubts about marriage, his hesitation in speaking to her, had centred on his own feelings and had preconceived the fact that she would take him. But suppose he had made a frightful mistake? Suppose Christine did not love him? He saw himself, rejected, dismally writing a letter to the Committee telling them that "owing to circumstances over which he had no control" he could not accept the position.

He saw her now, vividly before him. How well he knew her, that faint inquiring smile, the way in which she rested her hand against her chin, the steady candour in her dark brown eyes. A pang of longing shot through him. Dear Christine! If he had to forgo her he did not care what happened to him.

At nine o'clock the train crawled into Blaenelly. In a flash he was out on the platform and moving up Railway Road. Though he did not expect Christine until the morning, there was just the chance that she might already have arrived. Into Chapel Street . . . Round the corner of the Institute . . . A light in the front room of her lodgings sent a pang of expectation through him. Telling himself that he must contain himself, that it was probably only her landlady preparing the room, he swept into the house, burst into the sitting-room.

Yes! it was Christine. She was kneeling over some books in the corner, arranging them on the lowest shelf. Finished, she had begun to tidy up the string and paper which lay beside her on the floor. Her suitcase with her jacket and hat upon it lay in a chair. He saw she had not long returned.

"Christine!"

She swung round, still kneeling, a strand of hair fallen over her brow, then with a little cry of surprise and pleasure she rose.

"Andrew! How nice of you to come round."

Advancing towards him, her face alight, she held out her hand. But he took both her hands in his and held them tightly. He gazed down at her. He loved her especially in that skirt and blouse which she was wearing. It somehow increased her slightness, the tender sweetness of her youthfulness. Again his heart was throbbing.

"Chris! I've got to tell you something."

Concern swept into her eyes. She studied his pale and travel-grimed face with real anxiety.

She said quickly: "What has happened? Is it more trouble with Mrs. Page? Are you going away?"

He shook his head, enslaving her small hands more tightly in his.

And then, all at once, he broke out:—

"Christine! I've got a job, the most wonderful job. At Aberalaw. I was up seeing the Committee to-day. Five hundred a year, and a house. A house, Christine! Oh, darling—Christine—could you—would you marry me?"

She went very pale. Her eyes were lustrous in her pale face. Her breath seemed to catch in her throat.

She said faintly: "And I thought—I thought it was bad news you were going to tell me."

"No, no!"—impulsively. "It's the most marvellous news, darling. Oh! if you'd just seen the place. All open and clean, with green fields and decent shops and roads and a Park and—oh, Christine, actually a hospital! If only you'll marry me, darling, we can start there straight away."

Her lips were soft, trembling.

But her eyes smiled, smiled with that strange and shining lustre towards him.

"Is this because of Aberalaw, or because of me?"

"It's you, Chris. Oh, you know I love you; but then—perhaps you don't love me."

She gave a little sound in her throat, came towards him so that her head was buried in his breast.

As his arms went round her she said brokenly:—

"Oh, darling, darling. I've loved you ever since—" smiling through her happy tears—"oh, ever since I saw you walk into that stupid classroom."

BOOK II

1

GWILLIAM JOHN LOSSIN's decrepit motor van banged and boiled its way up the mountain road. Behind, an old tarpaulin drooped over the ruined tailboard, the rusted number-plate, the oil lamp that was never lit, dragging a smooth pattern in the dust. At the sides, the loose wings flapped and clattered to the rhythm of the ancient engine. And in front, jammed gaily in the driving seat with Gwilliam John, were Doctor Manson and his wife.

They had been married that morning. This was their bridal carriage. Underneath the tarpaulin were Christine's few pieces of furniture, a kitchen table bought secondhand in Blaenelly for twenty shillings, several new pots and pans, and their suitcases. Since they were without pride they had decided that the best, the cheapest way to bring this grand summation of their worldly goods, and themselves, to Aberalaw was in Gwilliam John's pantechnicon.

The day was bright, with a fresh breeze blowing, burnishing the blue sky. They had laughed and cracked jokes with Gwilliam John, who obliged occasionally with his special rendering of Handel's "Largo" upon the motor horn. They had stopped at the solitary inn high on the mountain at Ruthin Pass, to make Gwilliam John toast them in Rhymney beer. Gwilliam John, a scatter-brained little man with a squint, toasted them several times and then had a drop o' gin on his own account. Thereafter their career down Ruthin—with its two hairpin bends edging a sheer precipice of five hundred feet—had been demonic.

At last they crested the final rise and coasted down into Aberalaw. It was a moment tinged with ecstasy. The town lay before them with its long and undulating lines of roofs reaching up and down the Valley, its shops, churches, and offices clustered at the upper end and, at the lower, its mines and oreworks, the chimneys smoking steadily, the squat condenser belching clouds of steam—and all, all spangled by the midday sun.

"Look! Chris, look!" Andrew whispered, pressing her arm tightly. He had all the eagerness of the cicerone. "It's a fine place, isn't it? There's the Square up there. We've come in the back way. And look! No more oil lamps, darling. There's the gasworks. I wonder where our house is."

They stopped a passing miner, and were soon directed to Vale View, which lay, he told them, in this very road, on the fringe of the town. Another minute and they were there.

"Well!" said Christine. "It's—it's nice, isn't it?"

"Yes, darling. It looks—it looks a lovely house."

"By Gor!" Gwilliam John said, shoving his cap to the back of his head. "That's a rum-lookin' shop!"

Vale View was, indeed, an extraordinary edifice, at first sight something between a Swiss châlet and a Highland shooting-box, with a great profusion of little gables; the whole rough-cast, and standing in a half-acre of desolate garden choked with weeds and nettles, through which a stream tumbled over a variety of tin cans, to be surmounted midway in its course by a mouldering rustic bridge. Though they were not then aware of it, Vale View was their first introduction to the diverse power, the variegated omniscience, of the Committee—who, in the boom year of 1919, when contributions were rolling in, had said largely that they would build a house, a fine house that would do the Committee credit, something stylish, a "reglar smarter." Every member of that Committee had had his own positive idea as to what a reglar smarter should be. There were thirty members. Vale View was the result.

Whatever their impression of the outside, however, the new owners were speedily comforted within. The house was sound, well-floored, and cleanly papered. But the number of rooms was alarming. They both perceived instantly, though neither of them mentioned it, that Christine's few pieces would barely furnish two of these apartments.

"Let's see, darling," Chris said, counting practically on her fingers as they stood in the hall after their first breathless tour. "I make it a dining-room, drawing-room, and library, oh, or morning-room—whatever we like to call it—downstairs; and five bedrooms upstairs."

"That's right," Andrew smiled. "No wonder they wanted a married man!" His smile faded to compunction. "Honestly, Chris, I feel rotten about this—me, without a bean, using your nice furniture, like I was sponging on you, taking everything for granted, dragging you over here at a minute's notice—hardly giving them time to get your deputy into the school! I'm a selfish ass. I ought to have come over first and got the place decently ready for you."

"Andrew Manson! If you'd dared to leave me behind!"

"Anyhow I'm going to do something about it," he frowned at her doggedly. "Now listen, Chris—"

She interrupted with a smile.

"I think, darling, I'm going to make you an omelette—according to Madame Poulard. At least, the cookery book's idea of it."

Cut off at the outset of his declamation, his mouth open, he stared at her. Then gradually his frown vanished. Smiling again he followed her into the kitchen. He could not bear her out of his sight. Their footsteps made the empty house sound like a cathedral.

The omelette—Gwilliam John had been sent for the eggs before he took his departure—came out of the pan hot, savoury, and a delicate yellow. They ate it sitting together on the edge of the kitchen table. He exclaimed vigorously:—

"By God!—Sorry, darling; forgot I was a reformed character. By Jove! You *can* cook! That calendar they've left doesn't look bad on the wall. Fills it up nicely. And I like the picture on it—these roses. Is there a little more omelette? Who was Poulard? Sounds like a hen. Thanks, darling. Gosh! You don't know how keen I am to get started. There ought to be opportunities here. *Big* opportunities!" He broke off suddenly, his eyes resting on a varnished wooden case which stood beside their baggage in the corner. "I say, Chris! What's that?"

"Oh, that!" She made her voice sound casual. "That's a wedding present—from Denny!"

"Denny!" His face changed. Philip had been stiff and off-hand when he had charged down upon him to thank him for his help in getting the new job and to tell him he was marrying Christine. This morning he had not even come to see them off. It had hurt Andrew, made him feel that Denny was too complex, too incomprehensible to remain his friend. He advanced slowly, rather suspiciously, to the case; thinking, probably an old boot inside—that was Denny's idea of humour. He opened the case.

Then he gave a gasp of sheer delight. Inside was Denny's microscope, the exquisite Zeiss, and a note: "I don't really need this, I told you I was a saw-bones. Good luck."

There was nothing to be said. Thoughtful, almost subdued, Andrew finished his omelette, his eye fixed all the time upon the microscope. Then, reverently, he took it up and, accompanied by Christine, went into the room behind the dining-room. He placed the microscope solemnly in the middle of the bare floor.

"This isn't the library, Chris—or the morning-room or the study or anything like that. Thanks to our good friend, Philip Denny, I hereby christen it the Lab."

He had just kissed her, to make the ceremony really effective, when the phone rang—a persistent shrilling which, coming from the empty hall, was singularly startling. They gazed at each other questioningly, excitedly.

"Perhaps it's a call, Chris! Think of it! My first Aberalaw case."

He dashed into the hall.

It was not a case, however, but Doctor Llewellyn, telephoning his welcome from his home at the other end of the town. His voice came over the wire, distinct and urbane, so that Chris, on her toes at Andrew's shoulder, could hear the conversation perfectly.

"Hel-*lo*, Manson. How are you? Don't fret, now; it isn't work this time. I only wanted to be the first to welcome you and your missus to Aberalaw."

"Thanks; thanks, Doctor Llewellyn. It's awfully good of you. I don't mind if it is work, though?"

"Tut! Tut! Wouldn't dream of it till you get straight," Llewellyn gushed. "And look here, if you're not doing anything to-night come over and have dinner with us, you and your missus, no formality, half-past seven, we'll be delighted to see you both. Then you and I can have a chat. That's settled, then. Good-by, in the meantime."

Andrew put down the receiver, his expression deeply gratified.

"Wasn't that deeent of him, Chris? Asking us over bang off like that! The head doctor, mind you! He's a well-qualified man, too, I can tell you. I looked him up. London hospital—M.D., F.R.C.S., and the D.P.H. Think of it—all these star degrees! And he sounded so friendly. Believe me, Mrs. Manson, we're going to make a big hit here."

Slipping his arm round her waist, he began jubilantly to waltz her round the hall.

2

THAT night, at seven o'clock, they set out through the brisk and busy streets for Doctor Llewellyn's house, Glynmawr. It was a stimulating walk. Andrew viewed his new fellow townsmen with enthusiasm.

"See that man coming, Christine? Quick! That fellow coughing over there."

"Yes, dear—but why—?"

"Oh, nothing!"—nonchalantly. "Only, he's probably going to be my patient."

They had no difficulty in finding Glynmawr, a solid villa with well-tended grounds, for Doctor Llewellyn's beautiful car stood outside and Doctor Llewellyn's beautifully polished plate, his qualifications displayed in small chaste letters, was bolted to the wrought-iron gate. Suddenly nervous, in the face of such distinction, they rang the bell and were shown in.

Doctor Llewellyn came out of the drawing-room to meet them, more dapper than ever in frock coat and stiff gold-linked cuffs, his expression beamingly cordial.

"Well, well! This is splendid. Delighted to meet you, Mrs. Manson. Hope you'll like Aberalaw. It's not a bad little place, I can tell you. Come along in here. Mrs. Llewellyn'll be down in a minute."

Mrs. Llewellyn arrived immediately, as beaming as her husband. She was a reddish-haired woman of about forty-five, with a palish freckled face; and, having greeted Manson, she turned towards Christine with an affectionate gasp.

"Oh, my de-ar, you lovely little thing! I declare I've lost my heart to you already. I must kiss you. I must. You don't mind, my dear, do you?"

Without pausing, she embraced Christine, then held her at arm's length, still viewing her glowingly. At the end of the passage a gong sounded. They went in to dinner.

It was an excellent meal—tomato soup, two roast fowls with stuffing and sausages, sultana pudding. Doctor and Mrs. Llewellyn talked smilingly to their guests.

"You'll soon get the hang of things, Manson," Llewellyn was saying. "Yes, indeed. I'll help you all I can. By the way, I'm glad that feller Edwards didn't get himself appointed. I couldn't have stuck him at any price, though I did half-promise I'd put a word in for him. What was I sayin'? Oh, yes! Well, you'll be at the West Surgery—that's your end—with old Doctor Urquhart—he's a card I can tell you—and Gadge the dispenser. Up here at the East Surgery we've got Doctor Medley and Doctor Oxborrow. Oh! They're all good chaps. You'll like them. Do you play golf? We might run out sometimes to the Fernley Course—that's only nine miles down the Valley. Of course I have a lot to do here. Yes, yes, indeed. Myself, I don't bother about the surgeries. I have the hospital on my hands, I do the compensation cases for the Company, I'm Medical Officer for the town, I have the gasworks appointment, I'm surgeon to the workhouse, and public vaccinator as well. I do all the approved Society examinations, with a good deal of County Court work. Oh! and I'm coroner, too. And besides," a gleam escaped his guileless eye, "I do a goodish bit of private practice odd times."

"It's a full list," Manson said.

Llewellyn beamed. "We got to make ends meet, Doctor Manson. That little car you saw outside cost a little matter of twelve hundred pounds. As for —oh, well, never mind. There's no reason why you shouldn't make a good livin' here. Say a round three to four hundred for yourself, if you work hard and watch your *p*'s and *q*'s." He paused—confidential, humidly sincere. "There's just one thing I think I ought to put you up to. It's been all settled and agreed amongst the assistant doctors that they each pay me a fifth of their incomes." He went on quickly, guilelessly: "That's because I see their cases for them. When they get worried they have me in. It's worked very well for them, I may tell you."

Andrew glanced up in some surprise. "Doesn't that come under the Medical Aid Scheme?"

"Well, not exactly," Llewellyn said, corrugating his brow. "It was all gone into and arranged by the doctors themselves a long time ago."

"But—?"

"Doctor Manson!" Mrs. Llewellyn was calling him sweetly from her end of the table. "I'm just telling your dear little wife we must see a lot of each other. She must come to tea sometime. You'll spare her to me, won't you, Doctor? And sometime she must run down to Cardiff with me in the car. That'll be nice, won't it, my de-ar?"

"Of course," Llewellyn proceeded glossily, "where you'll score—Leslie, that's the feller that was here before you, was a slack devil. Oh, he was a rotten doctor, nearly as bad as old Edwards. He couldn't give a decent anæsthetic anyhow! You're a good anæsthetist, I hope, Doctor? When I have a big case, especially my private cases, I must have a good anæsthetic. But, bless my soul! We'll not talk about that at present. Why, you've hardly started; it isn't fair to bother you."

"Idris!" cried Mrs. Llewellyn to her husband with a kind of delighted sensationalism. "They were only *mar*ried this morning! Mrs. Manson just told me. She's a little bride! Why, would you believe it, the dear innocents!"

"Well, well, well, now!" beamed Llewellyn.

Mrs. Llewellyn patted Christine's hand. "My poor lamb! To think of the work you'll have getting straight in that stupid Vale View! I must come sometime and give you a hand."

Manson reddened slightly, collecting his scattered wits. He felt as though Christine and he had somehow become moulded into a soft little ball, played back and forth, with deft ease, between Doctor and Mrs. Llewellyn. However he judged the last remark propitious.

"Doctor Llewellyn," he said, with nervous resolution, "it's quite true what Mrs. Llewellyn says. I was wondering—I hate asking it—but could I have a couple of days off to take my wife to London to see about furnishings for our house and—and one or two other things?"

He saw Christine's eyes widen in surprise. But Llewellyn was graciously nodding his head.

"Why not? Why not? Once you start it won't be so easy to get off. You take to-morrow and the next day, Doctor Manson. You see! That's where I'm useful to you. I can help the assistants a lot. I'll speak to the Committee for you."

Andrew would not have minded speaking to the Committee, to Owen, himself. But he let the matter pass.

They drank their coffee in the drawing-room from, as Mrs. Llewellyn pointed out, "hand-painted" cups. Llewellyn offered cigarettes from his gold cigarette case.

"Take a look at that, Doctor Manson. There's a present for you! Grateful patient! Heavy, isn't it? Worth twenty pounds if it's worth a penny."

Towards ten o'clock Doctor Llewellyn looked at his fine half-hunter watch —actually he beamed at the watch, for he could contemplate even inanimate objects, particularly when they belonged to him, with that bland cordiality which was especially his own. For a moment Manson thought he was going into intimate details about the watch.

But instead he remarked: "I've got to go to the hospital. Gastro-duodenal I did this morning. How about runnin' round with me in the car and taking a look at it?"

Andrew sat up eagerly. "Why, I'd love to, Doctor Llewellyn."

Since Christine was included in the invitation also, they said good night to Mrs. Llewellyn, who waved them tender farewells from the front door, and stepped into the waiting car, which moved with silent elegance along the main street, then up the incline to the left.

"Powerful headlights, aren't they?" Llewellyn remarked, switching them on for their benefit. "Luxite! They're an extra. I had them fitted specially."

"Luxite!" said Christine suddenly, in a meek voice. "Surely they're very expensive, Doctor?"

"You bet they were," Llewellyn nodded emphatically, appreciative of the question. "Cost me every penny of thirty pounds."

Andrew, hugging himself, dared not meet his wife's eye.

"Here we are, then," said Llewellyn two minutes later. "This is my spiritual home."

The hospital was a red brick building, well-constructed and approached by a gravel drive flanked with laurel bushes. Immediately they entered Andrew's eyes lit up. Though small, the place was modern, beautifully equipped. As Llewellyn showed them round the theatre, the X-ray room, the splintroom, the two fine airy wards, Andrew kept thinking exultantly, this is perfect, perfect—what a difference from Blaenelly! God! I'll get my cases well, in here!

They picked up the matron on their travels, a tall, raw-boned woman who ignored Christine, greeted Andrew without enthusiasm, then melted into adoration before Llewellyn.

"We get pretty well all we want here, don't we, Matron?" Llewellyn said. "We just speak to the Committee. Yes, yes, they're not a bad lot, take them all in all. How's my gastro-enterostomy, Matron?"

"Very comfortable, Doctor Llewellyn," murmured the matron.

"Good! I'll see it in a minute!" He escorted Christine and Andrew back again to the vestibule.

"Yes, I do admit, Manson, I'm rather proud of this place. I regard it as my own. Can't blame me, either. You'll find your own way home, won't you? And look here, when you get back on Wednesday, ring me up. I might want you for an anæsthetic."

Walking down the road together they kept silence for a while; then Christine took Andrew's arm.

"Well?" she inquired.

He could feel her smiling in the darkness.

"I like him," he said quickly. "I like him a lot. Did you spot the matron, too—as if she was going to kiss the hem of his garment. But by Jove! That's a marvellous little hospital. It was a good dinner they gave us, too. They're not mean. Only—oh! I don't know—why should we pay him a fifth of our salary? It doesn't sound fair, or even ethical! And somehow—I feel as if I'd been smoothed and petted and told to be a good boy."

"You were a very good boy to ask for these two days. But really, darling— how can we do it? We've no money to buy furniture with—yet?"

"You wait and see," he answered cryptically.

The lights of the town lay behind now, and an odd silence fell between them as they approached Vale View. The touch of her hand upon his arm was precious to him. A great wave of love swept over him. He thought of her, married off-hand in a mining village, dragged in a derelict lorry across the mountains, dumped into a half-empty house where their wedding couch must be her own single bed—and sustaining these hardships and makeshifts with courage and a smiling tenderness. She loved him, trusted him, believed in him. A great determination swelled in him. He would repay it, he would show her, by his work, that her faith in him was justified.

They crossed the wooden bridge. The murmur of the stream, its littered banks hidden by the soft darkness of night, was sweet in their ears. He took the key from his pocket, the key of their house, and fitted it in the lock.

In the hall it was almost dark. When he had closed the door he turned to where she waited for him. Her face was faintly luminous, her slight figure expectant yet defenceless. He put his arm round her gently. He whispered, strangely:—

"What's your name, darling?"

"Christine," she answered wondering.

"Christine what?"

"Christine Manson." Her breath came quickly, quickly, and was warm upon his lips.

3

THE following afternoon their train drew into Paddington Station. Adventurously, yet conscious of their inexperience in the face of this great city which neither of them had seen before, Andrew and Christine descended to the platform.

"Do you see him?" Andrew asked anxiously.

"Perhaps he'll be at the barrier," Christine suggested.

They were looking for the Man with the Catalogue.

On the journey down Andrew had explained, in detail, the beauty, simplicity, and extraordinary foresight of his scheme; of how, realizing their needs even before they left Blaenelly, he had placed himself in touch with the Regency Plenishing Company and Depositaries, of London, E. It wasn't a colossal establishment, the Regency—none of your department store nonsense —but a decent, privately owned emporium which specialized in hire purchase. He had the recent letter from the proprietor in his pocket. Why, in point of fact . . .

"Ah!" he now exclaimed with satisfaction. "There he is!"

A seedy little man in a shiny blue suit and a bowler hat, holding a large green catalogue like a Sunday School prize, seemed, by some obscure feat of telepathy, to single them out from the crowd of travellers. He sidled towards them.

"Doctor Manson, sir? And Mrs. Manson?" Deferentially raising his hat: "I represent the Regency. We had your telegram this morning, sir. I have the car waiting. May I offer you a cigar?"

As they drove through the strange, traffic-laden streets, Andrew betrayed perhaps the faintest glimmer of disquiet, the corner of one eye on the presentation cigar, still unlighted, in his hand.

He grunted: "We're doing a lot of driving about in cars these days. But this must be all right. They guarantee everything, including free transport to and from the station, *also* our railway fares."

Yet, despite this assurance, their transit along bewilderingly complex and often mean thoroughfares was perceptibly anxious. At length, however, they were there. It was a showier establishment than either of them had expected, and there was a good deal of plate glass and shiny brass about the frontage. The door of the car was opened for them; they were bowed into the Regency Emporium.

Again they were expected, made royally welcome by an elderly salesman in a frock coat and high collar, who with his striking air of probity bore some resemblance to the late Prince Albert.

"This way, sir. This way, madam. Very happy to serve a medical gentleman, Doctor Manson. You'd be surprised the number of 'Arley Street specialists I've had the honour of attending to. The testimonials I've 'ad from them! And now, Doctor, what would you be requiring?"

He began to show them furniture, padding up and down the aisles of the emporium with a stately tread. He named prices that were inconveniently large. He used the words "Tudor," "Jacobean," and "Looez Sez." And what he showed them was fumed and varnished rubbish.

Christine bit her lip and her worried look increased. She willed with all her strength that Andrew would not be deceived, that he would not burden their home with this awful stuff.

"Darling," she whispered swiftly, when Prince Albert's back was turned, "no good—no good at all."

A barely perceptible tightening of his lips was her answer. They inspected a few more pieces. Then quietly, but with surprising rudeness, Andrew addressed the salesman.

"Look here, you! We've come a long way to buy furniture. I said *furniture*. Not this kind of junk." Violently with his thumb he pressed the front of an adjoining wardrobe, which, being of plywood, caved in with an ominous cracking.

The salesman almost collapsed. This, his expression said, simply cannot be true.

"But, Doctor," he gulped, "I've been showing you and your lady the best in the 'ouse."

"Then show us the worst," Andrew raged. "Show us old secondhand stuff—so long as it's *real!*"

A pause. Then, muttering under his breath, "The guv'ner'll give me what for, if I don't sell you!" the salesman padded disconsolately away. He did not return. Four minutes later, a short red-faced common man came bustling towards them.

He shot out: "What d'you want?"

"Good secondhand furniture—cheap!"

The short man fired a hard glance at Andrew. Without further speech he spun round and led them to a trade lift at the back, which, when manipulated, dropped them to a large chilly basement, crammed to the ceiling with secondhand goods.

For an hour Christine probed amongst the dust and cobwebs, finding a stout chest here, a good plain table there, a small upholstered easy chair beneath a pile of sacking, while Andrew, following behind, wrangled long and stubbornly with the short man over prices.

Their list was complete at last, and Christine, her face smudged but happy, pressed Andrew's hand with a thrilling sense of triumph as they ascended in the lift.

"Just what we wanted," she whispered.

The red-faced man took them to the office, where, laying down his order book on the proprietor's desk with the air of a man who has laboured to do his best, he said: "That's the lot then, Mr. Isaacs."

Mr. Isaacs caressed his nose. His eyes, liquid against his sallow skin, were sorrowful as he studied the order book.

"I'm afraid we can't give you E.P. terms on this, Doctor Manson. You see, it's all secondhand goods." A deprecating shrug. "We don't do our business like that."

Christine turned pale. But Andrew, grimly insistent, sat down upon a chair like a man who meant to stay.

"Oh, yes, you do, Mr. Isaacs. At least it says so in your letter. Printed in black and white on the top of your notepaper. 'New and secondhand furniture supplied on easy terms.'"

There was a pause. The red-faced man, bending over Mr. Isaacs, made rapid mutterings accompanied by gesticulations in his ear. Christine plainly caught impolite words which testified to the toughness of her husband's fibre, the power of his racial persistence.

"Well, Doctor Manson," smiled Mr. Isaacs, with an effort. "You shall have your way. Don't say the Regency wasn't good to you. And don't forget to tell your patients. All about how well you were treated here . . . Smith! Make out that bill on the H.P. sheet and see that Doctor Manson has a copy posted to him first thing to-morrow morning!"

"Thank you, Mr. Isaacs."

Another pause. Mr. Isaacs said, by way of closing the interview: "That's right, then, that's right. The goods will reach you on Friday."

Christine made to leave the office. But Andrew still remained fast to his chair. He said slowly: "And now, Mr. Isaacs? What about our railway fares?"

It was as if a bomb had exploded into the office. Smith, the red-faced man, looked as though his veins would burst.

"My God, Doctor Manson!" exclaimed Isaacs. "What d'you mean? We can't do business like that. Fair's fair, but I ain't a camel! *Railway fares!*"

Inexorably Andrew produced his pocketbook. His voice, though it wavered slightly, was measured.

"I have a letter here, Mr. Isaacs, in which you say in plain black and white that you will pay customers' railway fares from England and Wales on orders over fifty pounds."

"But I tell you," Isaacs expostulated wildly, "you only bought fifty-five pounds' worth of goods—and all secondhand stuff—"

"In your letter, Mr. Isaacs—"

"Never mind my letter." Isaacs threw up his hands. "Never mind anything. The deal's off. I never had a customer like you in all my life! We're used to nice young married people which we can talk to. First you insult my Mr.

Clapp, then my Mr. Smith can't do nothing with you, then you come here breakin' my heart with talk of *railway fares*. We can't do business, Doctor Manson. You can go try if you can do better somewhere else!"

Christine, in a panic, glanced at Andrew, her eyes holding a desperate appeal. She felt that all was lost. This terrible husband of hers had thrown away all the benefits he had so hardly won. But Andrew, appearing not to see her even, was dourly folding up his pocketbook and placing it in his pocket.

"Very well, then, Mr. Isaacs. We'll say good afternoon to you. But I'm telling you—this won't make very good hearing to all my patients and their friends. I have a large practice. And this is bound to get round. How you brought us up to London, promising to pay our fares, and when we—"

"Stop! Stop!" Isaacs wailed in something like a frenzy. "How much was your fares? Pay them, Mr. Smith! Pay them, pay them, *pay* them. Only don't say the Regency didn't ever do what it promised. *There* now! Are you satisfied?"

"Thank you, Mr. Isaacs. We're very satisfied. We'll expect delivery on Friday. Good afternoon, Mr. Isaacs."

Gravely, Manson shook him by the hand and, taking Christine's arm, hastened her to the door. Outside, the antique limousine which had brought them was waiting and, as though he had given the largest order in the history of the Regency, Andrew exclaimed:—

"Take us to the Museum Hotel, driver!"

They were off immediately, without interference, swinging out of the East End in the direction of Bloomsbury. And Christine, tensely clutching Andrew's arm, allowed herself gradually to relax.

"Oh, darling," she whispered. "You managed that wonderfully. Just when I thought—"

He shook his head, his jaw still stubbornly set.

"They didn't want trouble, that crowd. I had their promise, their *written promise*—" He swung round to her, his eyes burning. "It wasn't these idiotic fares, darling. You know that. It was the principle of the thing. People ought to keep their word. It put my back up too, the way they were waiting for us, you could see it a mile away—here's a couple of greenhorns—easy money— Oh, and that cigar they dumped on me too, the whole thing reeked of swindle."

"We managed to get what we wanted, anyhow," she murmured tactfully.

He nodded. He was too strung-up, too seething with indignation, to see the humour of it then. But in their room at the Museum the comic side became apparent. As he lit a cigarette and stretched himself on the bed, watching her as she tidied her hair, he suddenly began to laugh. He laughed so much that he set her laughing too.

"That look on old Isaacs' face—" he wheezed, his ribs aching. "It was—it was screamingly funny."

"When you," she gasped weakly, "when you asked him for the fares!"

"'Business,' he said, 'we can't do business—'" He went off into another paroxysm. "'Am I a camel,' he said. Oh, lord!—a *camel*—"

"Yes, darling." Comb in hand, tears running down her cheeks, she turned to him, scarcely able to articulate. "But the funniest thing—to me—was the way you kept saying 'I've got it here in black and white' when I—when I—oh, dear!—*when I knew all the time you'd left the letter on the mantelpiece at home.*"

He sat up, staring at her, then flung himself down with a yell of laughter. He rolled about, stuffing the pillow into his mouth, helpless, out of all control, while she clung to the dressing table, shaking, sore with laughter, begging him, deliriously, to stop or she would expire.

Later, when they had managed to compose themselves, they went to the theatre. Since he gave her free choice, she selected "Saint Joan." All her life, she told him, she had wanted to see a play by Shaw.

Seated beside her in the crowded pit he was less engaged by the play—too historical, he told her afterwards, who does this fellow Shaw think he is, anyway?—than by the faint flush upon her eager, entranced face. Their first visit to the theatre together. . . . Well, it wouldn't be the last by a long way. His eyes wandered round the full house. They would be back here again some day—not in the pit, in one of those boxes there. He would see to it; he would show them all a thing or two! Christine would wear a low-necked evening dress, people would look at him, nudge each other; that's Manson—you know, that doctor who did that marvellous work on lungs. . . . He pulled himself up sharply, rather sheepishly, and bought Christine an ice cream at the interval.

Afterwards he was reckless in the princely manner. Outside the theatre they found themselves completely lost, baffled by the lights, the buses, the teeming crowds. Peremptorily Andrew held up his hand. Safely ensconced, being driven to their hotel, they thought themselves, blissfully, pioneers in discovering the privacy afforded by a London taxi.

4

AFTER London the breeze of Aberalaw was crisp and cool. Walking down from Vale View on Thursday morning to commence his duties, Andrew felt it strike invigoratingly on his cheek. A tingling exhilaration filled him. He saw his work stretching out before him here, work well and cleanly done, work always guided by his principle, the scientific method.

The West Surgery, which lay not more than four hundred yards from his house, was a high vaulted building, white-tiled and with a vague air of sanitation. Its main and central portion was the waiting-room. At the bottom end, cut off from the waiting-room by a sliding hatch, was the dispensary. At the top were two consulting rooms, one bearing the name of Doctor Urquhart and the other, freshly painted, the mysteriously arresting name, DOCTOR MANSON.

It gave Andrew a thrill of pleasure to see himself identified, already, with his room, which though not large had a good desk and a sound leather couch for examinations. He was flattered too by the number of people waiting on him—such a crowd, in fact, that he thought it better to begin work immediately without first making himself known, as he had intended, to Doctor Urquhart and the dispenser, Gadge.

Seating himself, he signed for his first case to come in. This was a man who asked simply for a certificate—adding, as a kind of afterthought, "Beat knee." Andrew examined him, found him suffering from beat knee, gave him the certificate of incapacity for work.

The second case came in. He also demanded his certificate: nystagmus. The third case: certificate, bronchitis. The fourth case: certificate, beat elbow.

Andrew got up, anxious to know where he stood. These certificative examinations took a great deal of time.

He went to his door and asked: "How many more men for certificates? Will they stand up, please?"

There were perhaps forty men waiting outside. They all stood up. Andrew reflected quickly. It would take him the best part of the day to examine them all properly—an impossible situation. Reluctantly, he made up his mind to defer the more exacting examinations until another time.

Even so, it was half-past ten when he got through his last case. Then, as he glanced up, there stamped into his room a medium-sized, oldish man with a brick-red face and a small pugnacious grey imperial. He stooped slightly, so that his head had a forward, belligerent thrust. He wore cord breeches, gaiters, and a tweed jacket, the side pockets stuffed to bursting-point with pipe, handkerchief, an apple, a gum-elastic catheter. About him hung the odour of drugs, carbolic, and strong tobacco. Andrew knew before he spoke that it was Doctor Urquhart.

"Dammit to hell, man," said Urquhart without a handshake or a word of introduction, "where were ye these last two days? I've had to lump your work for ye. Never mind, never mind! We'll say no more about it. Thank God ye look sound in mind an' limb now ye have arrived. Do ye smoke a pipe?"

"I do."

"Thank God for that also! Can ye play the fiddle?"

"No."

"Neither can I—but I can make them bonny. I collect china too. They've had my name in a book. I'll show ye some day when ye come ben my house. It's just at the side of the surgery, ye'll have observed. And now, come away and meet Gadge. He's a miserable devil. But he knows his incompatibles."

Andrew followed Urquhart through the waiting-room into the dispensary, where Gadge greeted him with a gloomy nod. He was a long, lean, cadaverous man with a bald head streaked with jet black hair and drooping whiskers of the same colour. He wore a short alpaca jacket, green with age and the stains of drugs, which showed his bony wrists and death's door shoulder blades. His air was sad, caustic, tired; his attitude that of the most disillusioned man in the whole universe. As Andrew entered he was serving his last client, flinging a box of pills through the hatch as though it were rat poison. "Take it or leave it," he seemed to say. "You've got to die in any case!"

"Well," said Urquhart spryly, when he had effected the introduction. "Ye've met Gadge and ye know the worst. I warn ye he believes in nothing except maybe castor oil and Charles Bradlaugh. Now—is there anything I can tell ye?"

"I'm worried about the number of certificates I had to sign. Some of these chaps this morning looked to me quite capable of work."

"Ay, ay. Leslie let them pile up on him anyhow. His idea of examining a patient was to take his pulse for exactly five seconds by the clock. He didn't mind a docken."

Andrew answered quickly: "What can anyone think of a doctor who hands out certificates like cigarette coupons?"

Urquhart darted a glance at him. He said bluntly:—

"Be careful how you go. They're liable not to like it if you sign them off."

For the first and last time that morning Gadge made gloomy interjection.

"That's because there's nothing wrong wi' half o' them, ruddy scrim-shankers!"

All that day as he went on his visits Andrew worried about these certifi-cates. His round was not easy, for he did not know the neighbourhood, the streets were unfamiliar, and more than once he had to go back and cover the same ground twice. His district, moreover, or the greater part of it, lay on the side of that Mardy Hill to which Tom Kettles had referred, and this meant stiff climbing between one row of houses and the next.

Before afternoon his cogitation had forced him to an unpleasant decision. He could not, on any account, give a slack certificate. He went down to his evening surgery with an anxious yet determined line fixed between his brows.

The crowd, if anything, was larger than at the morning surgery. And the first patient to enter was a great lump of a man, rolling in fat, who smelled strongly of beer and looked as if he had never done a full day's work in his life. He was about fifty and had small pig eyes which blinked down at Andrew.

"Certificate," he said, without minding his manners.

"What for?" Andrew asked.

" 'Stagmus." He held out his hand. "The name's Chenkin. Ben Chenkin."

The tone alone caused Andrew to look at Chenkin with quick resentment. Even from a cursory inspection he felt convinced that Chenkin had no nys-tagmus. He was well aware, apart from Gadge's hint, that some of these old pitmen "swung the lead on 'stagmus," drawing compensation money to which they were not entitled for years on end. However, he had brought his oph-thalmoscope with him this evening. He would soon make sure. He rose from his seat.

"Take your things off."

This time it was Chenkin who asked: "What for?"

"I'm going to examine you."

Ben Chenkin's jaw dropped. He had not been examined, so far as he could remember, in the whole of Doctor Leslie's seven years of office. Unwillingly, sulkily, he pulled off his jacket, his muffler, his red-and-blue-striped shirt, revealing a hairy torso swathed in adiposity.

Andrew made a long and thorough examination, particularly of the eyes, searching both retinæ carefully with his tiny electric bulb.

Then, sharply, he said: "Dress up, Chenkin." He sat down and, taking his pen, he began to write out a certificate.

"Ha!" sneered old Ben. "I thought you'd let us 'ave it."

"Next, please," Andrew called out.

Chenkin almost snatched the pink slip from Andrew's hand. Then he strode triumphantly from the surgery.

Five minutes later he was back, his face livid, bellowing like a bull, thrusting his way between the men seated waiting on the benches.

"Look what he's done on us! Let us in, will ye? Hey! What's the meanin' of this?"

He flourished the certificate in Andrew's face.

Andrew affected to read the slip. It said, in his own handwriting:—

This is to certify that Ben Chenkin is suffering from the effects of over-indulgence in malt liquors but is perfectly fit to work.

Signed: A. Manson, M.B.

"Well?" he asked.

"'Stagmus," shouted Chenkin. "Certificate for 'stagmus. You can't play the bloody fool on us. Fifteen year us got 'stagmus!"

"You haven't got it now," Andrew said.

A crowd had gathered round the open door. He was conscious of Urquhart's head popping out curiously from the other room, of Gadge inspecting the tumult with relish through his hatch.

"For the last time—are ye going to give us 'stagmus certificate?" Chenkin bawled.

Andrew lost his temper.

"No, I'm not," he shouted back. "And get out of here before I put you out."

Ben's stomach heaved. He looked as if he might wipe the floor with Andrew. Then his eyes dropped; he turned and, muttering profane threats, walked out of the surgery.

The minute he was gone Gadge came out of the dispensary and shuffled across to Andrew. He rubbed his hands with melancholy delight.

"You know who that was you just knocked off? Ben Chenkin. His son's a big man on the Committee."

5

THE sensation of the Chenkin case was enormous; it hummed round Manson's district in a flash. Some people said it was "a good job"—a few went so far as "a damned good job"—that Ben had been pulled up in his swindling and signed fit for work. But the majority were on Ben's side. All the "compo cases"—those drawing compensation money for disabilities—were especially bitter against the new doctor. As he went on his rounds Andrew was conscious of black looks directed towards him. And at night, in the surgery, he had to face an even worse manifestation of unpopularity.

Although nominally every assistant was allotted a district, the workmen in that district had still the right of free choice of doctor. Each man had a card and by demanding that card and handing it to another doctor he could effect a change. It was this ignominy which now began for Andrew. Every night that week men whom he had never seen dropped into his surgery—some who were disinclined for the personal encounter even sent their wives—to say, without looking at him: "If you don't mind, Doctor, I'll 'ave my card."

The wretchedness, the humiliation of rising to extract these cards from the box on his desk was intolerable. And every card he gave away meant ten shillings subtracted from his salary.

On Saturday night Urquhart invited him into his house. The old man, who had gone about all week with an air of self-justification on his choleric features, began by exhibiting the treasures of his forty years of practice. He had perhaps a score of yellow violins, all made by himself, hung up on his walls, but these were as nothing compared with the choice perfection of his collection of old English china.

It was a superb collection—Spode, Wedgwood, Crown Derby, and, best of all, old Swansea—they were all there. His plates and mugs, his bowls, cups, and jugs—they filled every room in the house and overflowed into the bathroom where it was possible for Urquhart, when making his toilet, to survey with pride an original willow pattern tea service.

China was, in fact, the passion of Urquhart's life, and he was an old and cunning master in the gentle art of acquiring it. Whenever he saw a "nice bit" —his own phrase—in a patient's house he would call and call with unwearying attention, meanwhile fixing his eye, with a kind of wistful persistence, upon the coveted piece; until at last in desperation the good woman of the house would exclaim: "Doctor, you seem awful struck on that bit. I can't see but what I'm goin' to let you 'ave it!"

Thereupon Urquhart would make a virtuous protest; then, bearing his trophy, wrapped up in newspaper, he would dance home in triumph and place it tenderly on his shelves.

The old man passed, in the town, as a character. He gave his age as sixty but was probably over seventy, and possibly near to eighty. Tough as whalebone, his sole vehicle shoe leather, he covered incredible distances, swore murderously at his patients, and could yet be tender as a woman; lived by himself—since the death of his wife eleven years before—and existed almost entirely upon tinned soup.

This evening, having proudly displayed his collection, he suddenly remarked to Andrew with an injured air:—

"Dammit, man! I don't want any of your patients. I've got enough of my own. But what can I do if they come pestering me? They can't all go to the East Surgery; it's too far away."

Andrew reddened. There was nothing that he could say.

"You want to be more careful, man," Urquhart went on in an altered tone. "Oh, I know, I know. You want to tear down the walls of Babylon—I was young myself once. But all the same, go slow, go easy, look before you leap! Good night. My compliments to your wife."

With Urquhart's words sounding in his ear, Andrew made every effort to steer a cautious course. But, even so, a greater disaster immediately overtook him.

On the Monday following he went to the house of Thomas Evans in Cefen Row. Evans, a hewer at the Aberalaw colliery, had upset a kettle of boiling water over his left arm. It was a serious scald, covering a large area and particularly bad in the region of the elbow. When Andrew arrived he found that the District Nurse, who had been in the Row at the time of the accident, had dressed the scald with carron oil and had then continued on her round.

Andrew examined the arm, carefully suppressing his horror of the filthy dressing. Out of the corner of his eye he observed the carron oil bottle, corked with a plug of newspaper, holding a dirty whitish liquid, in which he could almost see bacteria seething in shoals.

"Nurse Lloyd done it pretty good, eh, Doctor?" said Evans nervously. He was a dark-eyed, highly strung youngster and his wife, who stood near, closely observing Andrew, was nervous too and not unlike him in appearance.

"A beautiful dressing," Andrew said with a great show of enthusiasm. "I've rarely seen a neater one. Only a first dressing, of course. Now I think we'll try some picric."

He knew that if he did not quickly use the antiseptic the arm would almost certainly become infected. And then, he thought, heaven help that elbow joint!

They watched him dubiously while, with scrupulous gentleness, he cleansed the arm and slipped on a moist picric dressing.

"There now," he exclaimed. "Doesn't that feel easier?"

"I don't know as how it does," Evans said. "Are you sure it's goin' to be all right, Doctor?"

"Positive!" Andrew smiled reassuringly. "You must leave this to Nurse and me."

Before he left the house he wrote a short note to the District Nurse, taking extra pains to be tactful, considerate of her feelings, wise. He thanked her for her splendid emergency treatment and asked her, as a measure against possible sepsis, if she would mind continuing with the picric dressings. He sealed the envelope carefully.

Next morning, when he arrived at the house, his picric dressings had been thrown in the fire and the arm was redressed with carron oil. Waiting upon him, prepared for battle, was the District Nurse.

"What's all this about, I'd like to know? Isn't my work good enough for you, Doctor Manson?" She was a broad, middle-aged woman with untidy iron-grey hair and a harassed, over-wrought face. She could barely speak for the heaving of her bosom.

Andrew's heart sank. But he took a rigid grip upon himself. He forced a smile.

"Come now, Nurse Lloyd, don't misunderstand me. Suppose we talk this over together in the front room."

The nurse bridled, swept her eye to where Evans and his wife, who clutched a little girl of three to her skirts, were listening wide-eyed and alarmed.

"No, indeed, we'll talk it over here. I got nothing to hide. My conscience is clear. Born and brought up in Aberalaw I was; went to school here; married here; 'ad children here; lost my 'usband here; and worked here twenty year as District Nurse. And nobody ever told me not to use carron oil on a burn or scald."

"Now listen, Nurse," Andrew pleaded. "Carron oil is all right in its way, perhaps. But there's a great danger of contracture here." He stiffened up her elbow by way of illustration. "That's why I want you to try my dressing."

"Never 'eard of the stuff. Old Doctor Urquhart don't use it. And that's what I told Mr. Evans. I don't hold with newfangled ideas of somebody that's been here no more nor a week!"

Andrew's lips were dry. He felt shaky and ill at the thought of further trouble, of all the repercussions of this scene; for the nurse, going from house to house, and talking her mind in all of them, was a person with whom it was dangerous to quarrel. But he could not, he dared not, risk his patient with that antiquated treatment.

He said in a low voice: "If you won't do the dressing, Nurse, I'll come in morning and evening and do it myself."

"You can then, for all I care," Nurse Lloyd declared, moisture flashing to her eyes. "And I 'ope Tom Evans lives through it."

The next minute she had flounced out of the house.

In dead silence Andrew removed the dressing once again. He spent nearly half an hour patiently bathing and attending to the damaged arm. When he left the house he promised to return at nine o'clock that night.

That same evening, as he entered his consulting-room, the first person to enter was Mrs. Evans, her face white, her dark frightened eyes avoiding his.

"I'm sure, Doctor," she stammered, "I do hate to trouble you; but can I have Tom's card?"

A wave of hopelessness passed over Andrew. He rose without a word, searched for Tom Evans' card, handed it to her.

"You understand, Doctor, you—you won't be callin' any more!"

He said unsteadily: "I understand, Mrs. Evans." Then as she made for the door he asked—he had to ask—the question: "Is the carron oil on again?"

She gulped, nodded, and was gone.

After surgery, Andrew, who usually tore home at top speed, made the passage to Vale View wearily. A triumph, he thought bitterly, for the scientific method! And again, am I honest or am I simply clumsy? Clumsy and stupid, stupid and clumsy!

He was very silent during supper. But afterwards, in the sitting-room, now comfortably furnished, while they sat together on the couch before the cheerful fire, he laid his head close to her soft young breasts.

"Oh, darling," he groaned, "I've made an awful muddle of our start!"

As she soothed him, gently stroking his brow, he felt tears smarting behind his eyes.

6

WINTER set in early and unexpectedly with a heavy fall of snow. Though it was only mid-October, Aberalaw lay so high that hard and bitter frosts gripped the town almost before the leaves had fallen from the trees. The snow came silently through the night, soft drifting flakes, and Christine and Andrew woke to a great glittering whiteness. A herd of mountain ponies had come through a gap in the broken wooden palings at the side of the house and were gathered round the back door. Upon the wide uplands, stretches of rough grass land all around Aberalaw, these dark wild little creatures roamed in large numbers, starting away at the approach of man. But in snowy weather, hunger drove them down to the outskirts of the town.

All winter Christine fed the ponies. At first they backed from her, shy and stumbling, but in the end they came to eat from her hand. One especially became her friend, the smallest of them all, a black, tangle-maned, roguish-eyed creature, no larger than a Shetland, whom they named Darkie.

The ponies would eat any kind of food, scraps of loaf, potato and apple rinds, even orange peel. Once, in fun, Andrew offered Darkie an empty matchbox. Darkie munched it down, then licked his lips, like a gourmet eating pâté.

Though they were so poor, though they had to bear many things, Christine and Andrew knew happiness. Andrew had only pence to jingle in his pockets, but the Endowment debt was almost settled and the furniture instalments were being paid. Christine, for all her fragility and look of inexperience, had the attribute of the Yorkshire woman: she was a housewife. With the help only of a young girl named Jenny, a miner's daughter from the Row behind who came daily for a few shillings each week, she kept the house shining. Although four of its rooms remained unfurnished, and discreetly locked, she made Vale View a home. When Andrew came in tired, almost defeated by a long day, she would have a hot meal on the table which quickly restored him.

The work of the practice was desperately hard—not, alas! because he had many patients, but because of the snow, the difficult "climbs" to the high parts of his district, the long distances between his calls. When it thawed and the roads turned to slush, before freezing hard again at night, the going was heavy and difficult. He came in so often with sodden trouser-ends that

Christine bought him a pair of leggings. At night when he sank into a chair exhausted she would kneel and take off these leggings, then his heavy boots, before handing him his slippers. It was not an act of service but of love.

The people remained suspicious, difficult. All Chenkin's relations—and they were numerous, since intermarriage was common in the Valleys—had become welded into a hostile unit. Nurse Lloyd was openly and bitterly his enemy, and would run him down as she sat drinking tea in the houses which she visited, listened to by a knot of women from the Row.

In addition he had to contend with an ever-increasing irritation. Doctor Llewellyn was using him for anæsthetics far oftener than he judged fair. Andrew hated giving anæsthetics—it was mechanical work which demanded a specialized type of mind, a slow and measured temperament which he certainly did not possess. He did not in the least object to serving his own patients. But when he found himself requisitioned three days a week for cases he had never seen before, he began to feel that he was shouldering a burden which belonged to someone else. Yet he simply dared not risk a protest, for fear of losing his job.

One day in November, however, Christine noticed that something unusual had upset him. He came in that evening without hailing her gaily and, though he made pretence of unconcern, she loved him too well not to detect, from the deepened line between his eyes and a score of other minute signs, that he had received an unexpected blow.

She made no comment during supper, and afterwards she began to busy herself with some sewing beside the fire.

He sat beside her, biting on his pipe; then all at once he declared:—

"I hate grousing, Chris! And I hate bothering you. God knows I try to keep things to myself!"

This, considering that he poured his heart out to her every night, was highly diverting. But Christine did not smile as he continued:—

"You know the hospital, darling. You remember going over it our first night. Remember how I loved it and raved about opportunities and chances of doing fine work there, and everything? I thought a lot about that, didn't I, darling? I had great ideas about our little Aberalaw Hospital?"

"Yes, I know you did."

He said stonily:—

"I needn't have deluded myself. It isn't the Aberalaw Hospital. It's Llewellyn's Hospital."

She was silent, her eyes concerned, waiting for him to explain.

"I had a case this morning, Chris!" He spoke quickly now, at white heat. "You'll note that I say *had!*—a really early apical pneumonia, in one of the anthracite drillers, too. I've told you often how terribly interested I am in their lung conditions. I'm positive there's a big field for research work there. I thought to myself: Here's my first case for hospital—genuine chance for charting and scientific recording. I rang up Llewellyn, asked him to see the case with me, so that I could get it into the ward."

He stopped to take a swift breath, then rushed on:—

"Well! Down came Llewellyn, limousine and all. Nice as you please, and damned thorough in his examination. He knows his work inside-out, mind you; he's an absolute topnotch man. He confirmed the diagnosis, after pointing out one or two things I'd missed, and absolutely agreed to take the case into hospital there and then. I began to thank him, saying how much I would appreciate coming into the ward and having such good facilities for this particular case." He paused again, his jaw set. "Llewellyn gave me a look at that, Chris, very friendly and nice. 'You needn't bother about coming up, Manson,' he said, '*I'll* look after him now. We couldn't have you assistants clattering around the wards'—he took a look at my leggings—'in your hobnail boots.'" Andrew broke off with a choking exclamation. "Oh! What's the use going over what he said? It all boils down to this: I can go tramping into miners' kitchens, in my sopping raincoat and dirty boots, examining my cases in a bad light, treating them in bad conditions, but when it comes to the hospital—ah! I'm only wanted there to give the ether!"

He was interrupted by the ringing of the telephone. Gazing at him with sympathy she rose, after a moment, to answer it. He could hear her speaking in the hall. Then, very hesitatingly, she returned.

"It's Doctor Llewellyn on the phone. I'm—I'm terribly sorry, darling. He wants you to-morrow at eleven for—for an anæsthetic."

He did not answer, but remained with his head bowed despondently between his clenched fists.

"What shall I tell him, darling?" Christine murmured anxiously.

"Tell him to go to hell!" he shouted; then, passing his hand across his brow: "No, no. Tell him I'll be there at eleven." He smiled bitterly. "At eleven *sharp.*"

When she came back she brought him a cup of hot coffee—one of her effectual devices for combating his moods of depression.

As he drank it he smiled at her wryly.

"I'm so dashed happy here with you, Chris. If only the work would go right. Oh! I admit there's nothing personal or unusual in Llewellyn's keeping me out of the wards. It's the same in London, in all the big hospitals everywhere. It's the system. But why should it be, Chris? Why should a doctor be dragged off his case when it goes into hospital? He loses the case as completely as if he'd lost the patient. It's part of our damn Specialist-G.P. system, and it's wrong, all wrong! Lord! why am I lecturing you, though? As if we hadn't enough worries of our own. When I think how I started here! What I was going to do! And instead—one thing after another—all gone wrong!"

But at the end of the week he had an unexpected visitor. Quite late, when he and Christine were upon the point of going upstairs, the doorbell rang. It was Owen, the secretary to the Society.

Andrew paled. He saw the secretary's visit as the most ominous event of all, the climax of these struggling unsuccessful months. Did the Committee want him to resign? Was he to be sacked, thrown out with Christine into the street, a wretched failure? His heart contracted as he gazed at the secretary's thin, diffident face, then suddenly expanded with relief and joy as Owen produced a yellow card.

"I'm sorry to call so late, Doctor Manson, but I've been detained late at the office; I didn't have time to look in at the surgery. I was wondering if you would care to have my medical card. It's strange, in a way, me being secretary to the Society, that I haven't ever bothered to fix up. The last time I visited a doctor I was down in Cardiff. But now, if you'll have me, I'd greatly appreciate to be on your list."

Andrew could scarcely speak. He had handed over so many of these cards, wincing as he did so, that now to receive one, and from the secretary himself, was overwhelming.

"Thank you, Mr. Owen. I'll—I'll be delighted to have you."

Christine, standing in the hall, was quick to interpose.

"Won't you come in, Mr. Owen? Please."

Protesting that he was disturbing them, the secretary seemed nevertheless willing to be persuaded into the sitting-room. Seated in an armchair, his eyes fixed reflectively upon the fire, he had an air of extraordinary tranquillity. Though in his dress and speech he seemed no different from an ordinary working man, he had the contemplative stillness, the almost transparent complexion, of the ascetic. He appeared for some moments to be arranging his thoughts. Then he said:—

"I'm glad to have the opportunity of talking to you, Doctor. Don't be downhearted if you're havin' a bit of a setback to begin with, like! They're a little stiff, the folks here, but they're all right at heart. They'll come, after a bit, they'll come!"

Before Andrew could intervene he continued:—

"You haven't heard of Tom Evans, like? No? His arm has turned out very bad. Ay, that stuff you warned them against did exactly what you was afraid of. His elbow's gone all stiff and crooked, he can't use it, he's lost his job at the pit over it. Ay, and since it was at home he scalded himself, he don't get a penny piece of compo."

Andrew muttered an expression of regret. He had no rancour against Evans, merely a sense of sadness at the futility of this case which had so needlessly gone wrong.

Owen was again silent, then in his quiet voice he began to tell them about his own early struggles, of how he had worked underground as a boy of fourteen, attended night school and gradually "improved himself," learned typing and shorthand, and finally secured the secretaryship of the Society.

Andrew could see that Owen's whole life was dedicated to improving the lot of the men. He loved his work in the Society because it was an expression of his ideal. But he wanted more than mere medical services. He wanted better housing, better sanitation, better and safer conditions, not only for the miners, but for their dependents. He quoted the maternity mortality rate amongst miners' wives, the infantile mortality rate. He had all the figures, all the facts at his finger-ends.

But, besides talking, he listened. He smiled when Andrew related his experience with the sewer in the typhoid epidemic at Blaenelly. He showed a deeper interest in the view that the anthracite workers were more liable to lung troubles than other underground workers.

Stimulated by Owen's presence, Andrew launched into this subject with great ardour. He had been struck, as the result of many painstaking examinations, by the large percentage of the anthracite miners who suffered from insidious forms of lung disease. In Blaenelly many of the drillers who came to him complaining of a cough or "a bit of phlegm in the tubes" were in reality incipient or even open cases of pulmonary tuberculosis. And he was finding the same thing here. He had begun to ask himself if there was not some direct connection between the occupation and the disease.

"You see what I mean?" he exclaimed eagerly. "These men are working in dust all day, bad stone dust in the hard headings—their lungs get choked with it. Now I have my suspicion that it's injurious. The drillers, for instance, who get most of it—they seem to develop trouble more frequently than, say, the hauliers. Oh! I may be on the wrong track. But I don't think so! And what excites me so much is—oh, well! it's a line of investigation nobody has covered much. There's no mention in the Home Office list of any such industrial disease. When these men are laid up they don't get a penny piece of compensation!"

Roused, Owen bent forward, a vivid animation kindling his pale face.

"My goodness, Doctor. You're really talkin'! I never heard anything so important for a long time."

They fell into a lively discussion of the question. It was late when the secretary rose to go. Apologizing for having stayed so long, he pressed Andrew wholeheartedly to proceed with his investigation, promising him all the help in his power.

As the front door closed behind Owen, he left a warm impression of sincerity. And Andrew thought, as at the Committee meeting when he had been given the appointment: "That man is my friend."

7

THE news that the secretary had lodged his card with Andrew spread quickly through the district, and did something to arrest the run of the new doctor's unpopularity.

Apart from this material gain both Christine and he felt better for Owen's visit. So far, the social life of the town had completely passed them by. Though Christine never spoke of it there were moments during Andrew's long absences upon his rounds when she felt her loneliness. The wives of the higher officials of the Company were too conscious of their own importance to call upon the wives of medical aid assistants. Mrs. Llewellyn, who had promised undying affection, and delightful little motor trips to Cardiff, left

cards when Christine was out and was not heard of again. While the wives of
Doctors Medley and Oxborrow of the East Surgery—the former a faded white
rabbit of a woman, the latter a stringy zealot who talked West African missions for one hour by the secondhand Regency clock—had proved singularly
uninspiring. There seemed, indeed, to be no sense of unity or social intercourse amongst the medical assistants or their wives. They were indifferent,
unresistant, and even downtrodden in the attitude they presented to the
town.

One December afternoon, when Andrew was returning to Vale View by
the back road which led along the brow of the hill, he saw approaching a
lanky yet erect young man of his own age whom he recognized at once as
Richard Vaughan. His first impulse was to cross to the other side to avoid
the oncoming figure. And then, doggedly, came the thought: "Why should I?
I don't care a damn who he is!"

With his eyes averted, he prepared to trudge past Vaughan—when, to his
surprise, he heard himself addressed in a friendly, half-humorous tone.

"Hello! You're the chap who put Ben Chenkin back to work, aren't you?"

Andrew stopped, his gaze lifting warily, his expression saying: "What of it?
I didn't do it for you." Though he answered civilly enough, he told himself
he was not prepared to be patronized even by the son of Edwin Vaughan.
The Vaughans were the virtual owners of the Aberalaw Company; they drew
all the royalties from the adjacent pits, were rich, exclusive, unapproachable.
Now that old Edwin had retired to an estate near Brecon, Richard, the only
son, had taken over the managing directorship of the Company. Recently
married, he had built himself a large modern house overlooking the town.

Now, considering Andrew and tugging at his spare moustache, Vaughan
said:—

"I'd have enjoyed seeing old Ben's face."

"I didn't find it particularly amusing."

Vaughan's lip twitched behind his hand at the stiff Scots pride.

He said easily: "You're by way of being our nearest neighbours. My missus
—she's been away in Switzerland these last weeks—will be calling on yours,
now that you're settled in."

"Thanks!" Andrew said curtly, walking on.

At tea that night he related the incident sardonically to Christine.

"What was his idea? Tell me that! I've seen him pass Llewellyn in the
street and barely throw him a nod. Perhaps he thought he'd mug me into
sending a few more men back to work at his dashed mines!"

"Now, don't, Andrew," Christine protested. "That's one thing about you!
You're suspicious, frightfully suspicious of people."

"Think I would be suspicious of him. Stuck up blighter, rolling in money,
old school tie under his ugly phiz—'My missus'—been yodelling on the Alps
while you pigged it on Mardy Hill—'will be calling on yours'! Huh! I can *see*
her looking near us, darling! And if she does,"—he was suddenly fierce,—"take
jolly good care you don't let her patronize you."

Chris answered—more shortly than he had ever heard her in all the tenderness of those first months—"I think I know how to behave."

Despite Andrew's premonitions Mrs. Vaughan did call upon Christine and remained, apparently, much longer than the bare period demanded by convention. When Andrew came in that evening he found Christine gay, slightly flushed, with every appearance of having enjoyed herself. She was reticent to his ironic probings but admitted that the occasion had been a success.

He mocked her. "I suppose you had out the family silver, the best china, the gold-plated samovar. Oh! and a cake from Parry's."

"No. We had bread and butter," she answered equably, "and the brown teapot."

He raised his brows derisively.

"And she liked it?"

"I hope so!"

Something rankled queerly in Andrew after this conversation, an emotion which, had he tried, he could not quite have analyzed. Ten days later when Mrs. Vaughan rang him up and asked Christine and him to dinner he was shaken. Christine was in the kitchen at the time baking a cake, and he answered the phone himself.

"I'm sorry," he said. "I'm afraid it's impossible. I have surgery till nearly nine every evening."

"But not on Sunday, surely!" Her voice was light, charming. "Come to supper next Sunday. That's settled, then. We'll expect you!"

He stormed in to Christine.

"These dashed high-blown friends of yours have raked us in to supper. We can't go! I've got a positive conviction I'm having a midder case next Sunday evening!"

"Now you listen to me, Andrew Manson!" Her eyes had sparkled at the invitation, but nevertheless she lectured him severely. "You've got to stop being silly. We're poor, and everybody knows it. You wear old clothes and I do the cooking. But that doesn't matter. You're a doctor and a good doctor, too; and I'm your wife." Her expression relaxed momentarily. "Are you listening to me? Yes; it may surprise you, but I have my marriage lines tucked away in my bottom drawer. The Vaughans have got a lot of money, but that's just a detail beside the fact that they're kind and charming and intelligent people. We're marvellously happy together here, darling; but we must have friends. Why shouldn't we be friendly with them if they'll let us? Now don't you be ashamed of being poor. Forget about money and position and everything, and learn to take people for what they really are!"

"Oh, well—" he said grudgingly.

He went, on Sunday, expressionless and with apparent docility, merely using the corner of his mouth to remark, as they walked up the well-laid-out drive beside a new hard tennis court: "Probably won't let us in, seeing I haven't got on a fish-and-soup."

Contrary to his expectation, they were well received. Vaughan's bony, ugly face smiled hospitably over a silver canister which, for a reason unexplained, he shook heartily. Mrs. Vaughan greeted them with effortless simplicity. There were two other guests, Professor and Mrs. Challis, who were staying over the week end with the Vaughans.

Over the first cocktail he had ever dealt with in his life Andrew took stock of the long fawn-carpeted room with its flowers, books, strangely beautiful old furniture. Christine was talking lightheartedly with Vaughan and his wife and Mrs. Challis, an elderly woman with humorous wrinkles around her eyes. Feeling isolated and conspicuous, Andrew gingerly approached Challis who, despite a large white beard, was successfully and cheerfully dispatching his third short drink.

"Will some bright young physician kindly undertake an investigation," he smiled at Andrew, "as to the exact function of the olive in the Martini? Mind you I warn you beforehand—I have my suspicions. But what do you think, Doctor?"

"Why—" Andrew stammered. "I—I hardly know—"

"My theory!" Challis took pity on him. "A conspiracy of bartenders and inhospitable fellows like our friend Vaughan. An exploitation of the law of Archimedes." He blinked rapidly under his black bushy brows. "By the simple action of displacement they hope to save the gin!"

Andrew could not smile for thinking of his own awkwardness. He had no social graces and he had never been in so grand a house in all his life. He did not know what to do with his empty glass, his cigarette ash, his own—actually his own hands! He was glad when they went into supper. But here again he felt himself at a disadvantage.

It was a simple but beautifully set-out meal—hot bouillon, followed by a chicken salad, all white breast and heart of lettuce and strange delicate flavours.

Andrew was next to Mrs. Vaughan. "Your wife is charming, Doctor Manson," she quietly remarked as they sat down. She was a tall, thin, elegant girl, very delicate in her appearance, not in the least pretty but with wide intelligent eyes and a manner of distinguished ease. Her mouth had a kind of upturned crookedness, a mobility which somehow conveyed a sense of wit and breeding.

She began to talk to him about his work, saying that her husband had heard of his thoroughness on more than one occasion. She tried kindly to draw him out, asking, in an interested fashion, how he felt the conditions of practice could be improved in the district.

"Well—I don't know—" clumsily spilling some soup—"I suppose—I'd like to see more scientific methods used."

Stiff and tongue-tied upon his favourite subject,—with which he had entranced Christine for hours,—he kept his eyes upon his plate until, to his relief, Mrs. Vaughan slipped into conversation with Challis, on her other side.

Challis—presently revealed as Professor of Metallurgy at Cardiff, lecturer on the same subject at London University, and a member of the exalted Mines

Fatigue Board—was a gay and gusty talker. He talked with his body, his hands, his beard, arguing, laughing, exploding, gurgling, meanwhile throwing great quantities of food and drink into himself like a stoker deliriously raising steam. But his talk was good; and the rest of the table seemed to like it.

Andrew, however, refused to admit the value of the conversation; he listened grudgingly as it turned to music, to the qualities of Bach, and then, by one of Challis' prodigious leaps, to Russian literature. He heard mentioned the names of Tolstoy, Chekhov, Turgenev, Pushkin with his teeth on edge.

Tripe, he raged to himself, all unimportant tripe. Who does this old beaver think he is? I'd like to see him tackle a tracheotomy, say, in a black kitchen in Cefen Row. He wouldn't get far with his Pushkin there!

Christine, however, was enjoying herself thoroughly. Glaring sideways, Andrew saw her smiling at Challis, heard her take her part in the discussion. She made no pretence, she was perfectly natural. Once or twice she referred to her council schoolroom in Bank Street. It amazed him how well she stood up to the professor, how quickly, unselfconsciously she made her points. He began to see his wife as for the first time, and in a strange new light. Seems to know all about these Russian bugs, he grated inwardly; funny she never talks to me about them! And later, as Challis approvingly patted Christine on the hand: Can't old Bird's-nest keep his paws to himself? Hasn't he got a wife of his *own*?

Once or twice he caught Christine's eyes offering him a bright interchange of intimacy, and several times she diverted the conversation in his direction.

"My husband is very interested in the anthracite workers, Professor Challis. He's started a line of investigation. On dust inhalation."

"Yes, yes," puffed Challis, turning an interested glance on Manson.

"Isn't that so, darling?" Christine encouraged. "You were telling me all about it the other night."

"Oh, I don't know," Andrew growled. "There's probably nothing in it. I haven't enough data yet. Perhaps this T.B. doesn't come from the dust at all."

He was furious with himself, of course. Perhaps this man Challis might have helped him, not that he would have asked him for assistance, yet the fact that he was connected with the Mines Fatigue Board certainly seemed to offer a wonderful opportunity. For some incomprehensible reason his anger became directed towards Christine.

As they walked home towards Vale View at the end of the evening he was jealously silent. And in the same silence he preceded her to the bedroom.

While they undressed, usually a communicative and informal proceeding when, with his braces hanging and a toothbrush in his hand, he would dilate upon the doings of the day, he kept his gaze studiously averted.

When Christine pleaded, "We did have a nice time, didn't we, darling?" he answered with great politeness, "Oh! An excellent time!" In bed he kept well to the edge, away from her, resisting the slight movement which he felt her make towards him, with a long and heavy snore.

Next morning the same sense of constraint persisted between them. He went about his work sulking, stupidly unlike himself. About five o'clock in the afternoon, while they were having tea, a ring came to the front door. It was the Vaughan chauffeur with a pile of books and a great bunch of pheasant's eye narcissi laid on top of them.

"From Mrs. Vaughan, madam," he said smiling, touching his peaked cap as he retreated.

Christine returned to the sitting-room with heaped arms and a glowing face.

"Look, darling," she cried excitedly. "Isn't that too kind? The whole of Trollope loaned me by Mrs. Vaughan. I've always wanted to read him right through! And such lovely—lovely flowers."

He stood up stiffly, sneering: "Very pretty! Books and flowers from the lady of the manor! You've got to have them, I suppose, to help you to endure living with me! I'm too *dull* for you. I'm not one of those flash talkers that you seemed to like so much last night. I don't know the Russian for boloney! I'm just one of these bloody ordinary medical aid assistants!"

"Andrew!" All the colour had gone out of her face. "How can you?"

"It's true, isn't it? I could see while I was gawking my way through that blasted supper. I've got eyes in my head. You're sick of me already. I'm only fit for slogging round in the slush, turning over dirty blankets, collecting fleas. I'm too much of a lout for your taste now!"

Her eyes were dark and pitiful in her pale face. But she said steadily: "How can you talk like that? It's because you *are* yourself that I love you. And I'll never love anybody else."

"Sounds like it," he snarled, and banged out of the room.

For five minutes he skulked in the kitchen, tramping up and down, biting his lip. Then all at once he turned, dashed back to the sitting-room, where she stood, her head bent forlornly, staring into the fire. He took her fiercely in his arms.

"Chris, darling!" he cried, in hot repentance. "Darling, darling! I'm sorry! For heaven's sake forgive me. I didn't mean a word of it. I'm just a crazy, jealous fool. I adore you!"

They clung to each other wildly, closely. The scent of the narcissi was in the air.

"Don't you know," she sobbed, "that I'd just die without you!"

Afterwards, as she sat with her cheek pressed against his, he said sheepishly, reaching forward for a book:—

"Who is this chap Trollope anyway? Will you teach me, darling? I'm just an ignorant hog!"

8

THE winter passed. He had now the added incentive of his work on dust inhalation which he had begun by planning and conducting a systematic examination of every anthracite worker upon his list. Their evenings together were even happier than before. Christine helped him to transcribe his notes, working before the fine coal fire—it was one advantage of the district that they never lacked an abundance of cheap coal—when he came home from his late surgery. Often they had long talks in which the extent of her knowledge, though she never obtruded it, and her acquaintance with books, astounded him. He began, moreover, to discern in her a fineness of instinct, an intuition which made her judgment of literature, of music, and especially of people, uncannily correct.

"Hang it all," he would tease her. "I'm just getting to know my wife. In case you're getting swelled head we'll take half an hour off and I'll beat you at piquet." They had learned the game from the Vaughans.

As the days lengthened, without speaking of it to him, she began on the wilderness that was the garden. Jenny, the maid, had a great-uncle,—she was proud of the unique relationship,—an elderly, disabled miner who for tenpence an hour became Christine's assistant. Manson, crossing the dilapidated bridge, found them down by the stream-bed one March afternoon, starting an assault on the rusty salmon-tins that lay there.

"Hey, you below!" he shouted from the bridge. "What are you doing? Spoiling my fishing?"

She answered his gibes with a brisk nod:—

"You wait and see."

In a few weeks she had grubbed out the weeds and cleared the neglected paths. The bed of the stream was clean, its edges were cut and trimmed. A new rockery, made from loose stones lying about, stood at the foot of the glen. Vaughan's gardener, John Roberts, kept coming over, bringing bulbs and cuttings, offering advice. With real triumph she led Andrew by the arm to view the first daffodil.

Then, on the last Sunday in March, without warning, Denny came over to visit them. They fell upon him with open arms, belaboured him with their delighted welcome. To see the squat figure, that red sandy-browed face again, gave Manson a rare pleasure. When they had shown him round, fed him on their best, and thrust him into their softest chair, they eagerly demanded news.

"Page is gone," Philip announced. "Yes, the poor chap died a month ago. Another hæmorrhage. And a good thing too!" He drew on his pipe, the familiar cynicism puckering his eyes. "Blodwen and your friend Rees seem all set for matrimony."

"A golden wedding from the start," Andrew said with unusual bitterness. "Poor Edward!"

"Page was a fine fellow. A good old G.P.," Denny reflected. "You know I hate the very sound of those fatal letters and all that they stand for. But Page let them down lightly."

There was a pause while they thought of Edward Page, who had longed for Capri with its birds and sunshine through all those drudging years amidst the slag-heaps of Blaenelly.

"And how about you, Philip?" Andrew asked at last.

"Oh, I don't know! I'm getting restless." Denny smiled drily. "Blaenelly hasn't seemed quite the same since you people cleared out. I think I'll take a trip abroad somewhere. Ship's surgeon, maybe—if some cheap cargo boat will have me."

Andrew was silent, distressed once again by the thought of this clever man, this really talented surgeon, wasting his life, deliberately, with a kind of self-inflicted sadism. Yet was Denny really wasting his life? Christine and he had often spoken of Philip, trying to solve the enigma of his career. Vaguely they knew that he had married a woman, socially his superior, who had tried to mould him to the demands of a county practice where there was no credit in operating well four days of the week if one did not hunt the other three. After five years of effort on Denny's part she had rewarded him by leaving him, quite casually, for another man. It was no wonder that Denny had fled to the backwoods, despising convention and hating orthodoxy. Perhaps, one day, he would return to civilization.

They talked all afternoon and Philip waited till the last train. He was interested in Andrew's account of the conditions of practice in Aberalaw. As Andrew came, indignantly, to the question of Llewellyn's percentage deducted from the assistants' salaries, Denny said, with an odd smile:—

"I can't see you sitting down under that for long!"

When Philip had gone Andrew became gradually aware, as the days passed, of a gap, an odd vacancy existing in his work. In Blaenelly with Philip near him he had always been aware of a common bond, a definite purpose shared between them. But in Aberalaw he had no such bond, felt no such purpose amongst his fellow doctors.

Doctor Urquhart, his colleague in the West Surgery, was, for all his fiery humour, a kindly man. Yet he was old, rather automatic, and absolutely without inspiration. Though long experience enabled him, as he put it, to smell pneumonia the moment he "put his nose in" the sickroom, though he was deft in his application of splints and plasters and an adept in the cruciform treatment of boils, though occasionally he delighted to prove that he could perform some small operation, he was, nevertheless, in many directions, shatteringly antiquated. He stood out plainly, in Andrew's view, as Denny's "good old type" of family doctor—shrewd, painstaking, experienced, a doctor sentimentalized by his patients and by the public at large, who had not opened a medical book for twenty years and was almost dangerously out-of-date. Though Andrew was always eager to start discussions with Urquhart, the old man had little time for "shop." When his day's work was over he would drink his tinned soup,—tomato was his favourite,—sandpaper his new violin, inspect his old china, then clump off to the Masonic Club to play draughts and smoke.

The two assistants at the East Surgery were equally unencouraging. Doctor Medley, the elder of the two, a man of nearly fifty, with a clever sensitive face, was unhappily almost stone deaf. But for this affliction, which for some reason the vulgar always found amusing, Charles Medley would have been a very long way from an assistantship in the mining Valleys. He was, like Andrew, essentially a physician. As a diagnostician he was remarkable. But when his patients spoke to him he could not hear a word. Of course, he was a practiced lip-reader. Yet he was timid, for he often made laughable mistakes. It was quite painful to see his harassed eyes fastened, in a kind of desperate inquiry, upon the moving lips of the person speaking to him. Because he was so fearful of making a grave error he never prescribed anything but the smallest doses of any drug. He was not well off, for he had met with trouble and expense over his grown-up family, and like his faded wife he had become an ineffectual, strangely pathetic being who went in dread of Doctor Llewellyn and the Committee lest he should be suddenly dismissed.

The other assistant, Doctor Oxborrow, was a very different character from poor Medley and Andrew did not like him nearly so well. Oxborrow was a large pasty man with pudgy fingers and a jerky heartiness. Andrew often felt that with more blood in him Oxborrow would have made an admirable bookmaker. As it was Oxborrow, accompanied by his wife, who played the portable harmonium, betook himself on Saturday afternoons to the near-by town of Fernley—etiquette precluding his appearing in Aberalaw—and there, in the Market, he would set up his little carpet-covered stand and hold an open-air religious meeting. Oxborrow was an evangelist. As an idealist, a believer in a supreme quickening force in life, Andrew could have admired this fervour. But Oxborrow, alas! was embarrassingly emotional. He wept unexpectedly and prayed even more disconcertingly. Once when confronted by a difficult confinement which defeated his own straining skill, he plumped suddenly upon his knees beside the bed and, blubbering, implored God to work a miracle upon the poor woman. Urquhart, who detested Oxborrow, told Andrew of this incident, for it was Urquhart who, arriving, had got upon the bed in his boots, and successfully delivered the patient with high forceps.

The more Andrew considered his fellow assistants and the system under which they worked the more he desired to bring them together. As it was they had no unity, no sense of co-operation, and little friendliness amongst themselves. They were simply set up, one against the other, in the ordinary competitive way existing in general practice all over the country, each trying to secure as many patients for himself as he could. Downright suspicion and bad feeling were often the result. Andrew had seen Urquhart, for instance, when a patient of Oxborrow's transferred his card to him, take the half-finished bottle of medicine from the man's hand in the surgery, uncork it, smell it with contempt, and explode: "So *this* is what Oxborrow's been givin' ye! Damn it to hell! He's been slowly poisonin' ye!"

Meanwhile, in the face of this diversity, Doctor Llewellyn was quietly taking his cut from each assistant's pay cheque. Andrew burned under it, longed to create a different arrangement, to institute a new and better understanding which would enable the assistants to stand together—without subsidizing Llewellyn. But his own difficulties, the sense of his own newness to the place, and above all the mistakes he had made at the start in his own district, caused him to be cautious.

It was not until he met Con Boland that he decided to make the great attempt.

9

ONE day early in April Andrew discovered a cavity in a back tooth and went, in consequence, upon an afternoon of the following week, in search of the Society's dentist. He had not yet met Boland and did not know his hours of consultation. When he reached the Square, where Boland's little surgery stood, he found the door closed and, pinned upon it, this red-inked notice: *Gone to Extraction. If Urgent Apply at House.*

On a moment's reflection Andrew decided that since he was here, he might at least call to make an appointment; so, having inquired the way from one of the group of youths lounging outside the Valley Ice Cream Saloon, he set out for the dentist's house.

This was a small semidetached villa on the upper outskirts of the East side of the town. As Andrew walked up the untidy path to the front door he heard a loud hammering and, glancing through the wide-open doors of a dilapidated wooden shed situated at the side of the house, he saw a red-haired rangy man in his shirt sleeves, violently attacking the dismembered body of a car with a hammer. At the same time the man caught sight of him.

"Hello!" he said.

"Hello!" Andrew answered a trifle warily.

"What are ye after?"

"I want to make an appointment with the dentist. I'm Doctor Manson."

"Come in," said the man, hospitably waving the hammer.

He was Boland.

Andrew entered the wooden shed, which was littered with portions of an incredibly old motor car. In the middle stood the chassis, supported on wooden egg-boxes, and actually presenting the evidence of having been sawn in half. Andrew glanced from this extraordinary spectacle of engineering to Boland.

"Is this the extraction?"

"It is," Con agreed. "When I'm inclined to be slack in the surgery I just up to my garage and put a little bit in on my car."

Apart from his brogue, which was thick enough to be cut with a knife, he used the words "garage," meaning the falling down shed, and "car," as applied to the fallen-down vehicle, with an accent of unmistakable pride.

"You wouldn't believe what I'm doing now," he went on; "that's to say, unless you're mechanical-minded like myself. I've had her five year this little car of mine and, mind ye, she was three year old when I got her. Ye mightn't believe seeing her *sthripped* but she goes like a hare. But she's small, Manson, she's small by the size of my family now. So I'm in the process of extendin' her. I've cut her, ye see, right across her middle, and that's where I'll slip in a good two feet of insertion. Wait till ye see her finished,

Manson!" He reached for his jacket. "She'll be long enough to take a regiment. Come away now, to the surgery, and I'll fix your tooth."

At the surgery, which was almost as untidy as the garage and, it must be confessed, equally dirty, Con filled the tooth, talking all the time. Con talked so much and so violently that his bushy red moustache was always dewed with beads of moisture. His shock of chestnut hair, which badly needed cutting, kept getting into Andrew's eyes, as he bent over, using the amalgam filling which he had tucked under his oily fingernail. He had not bothered to wash his hands—that was a trifle with Con!

He was a careless, impetuous, good-natured, generous fellow. The more Andrew knew Con, the more he was utterly captivated by his humour, simplicity, wildness, and improvidence. Con, who had been six years in Aberalaw, had not a penny to his name. Yet he extracted a vast amount of fun from life. He was mad on "mechanics," was always making gadgets, and he idolized his motor car. The fact that Con should possess a motor car was in itself a joke. But Con loved jokes, even when they were against himself. He told Andrew of the occasion when, called to extract the decayed molar of an important Committee man, he had gone to the patient's house with, as he imagined, his forceps in his pocket—only to find himself reaching for the tooth with a six-inch spanner.

The filling completed, Con threw his instruments into a jelly jar containing Lysol, which was his light-hearted notion of asepsis, and demanded that Andrew should return to the house with him to tea.

"Come on, now," he insisted hospitably. "You've got to meet the family. And we're just in time. It's five o'clock."

Con's family were, in fact, in the process of having tea when they arrived, but were obviously too accustomed to Con's eccentricities to be disturbed by his bringing in a stranger. In the warm, disordered room Mrs. Boland sat at the head of the table with the baby at her breast. Next came Mary, fifteen, quiet, shy—"the only dark-haired one and her dad's favourite" was Con's introduction—who was already earning a decent wage as a clerk to Joe Larkins, the bookmaker, in the Square. Beside Mary was Terence, twelve, then three other younger children sprawling about, crying out to be taken notice of by their father.

There existed about this family, except perhaps for the shyly conscious Mary, a careless gaiety which entranced Andrew. The room itself spoke with a gorgeous brogue. Above the fireplace, beneath the coloured picture of Pope Pius X which bore a strip of palm, the baby's napkins were drying. The canary's cage, uncleaned but bursting with song, stood on the dresser beside Mrs. Boland's rolled-up stays—she had previously removed them in the cause of comfort—and a split bag of puppy biscuits. Six bottles of stout, newly in from the grocer, were upon the chest of drawers, also Terence's flute. And in the corner were broken toys, odd boots, one rusty skate, a Japanese parasol, two slightly battered prayer-books and a copy of *Photo-Bits*.

But, as he drank his tea, Andrew was most fascinated by Mrs. Boland—he simply could not keep his eyes from her. Pale, dreamy, unperturbed, she sat silently imbibing endless cups of black boiled tea while the children squabbled about her and the baby openly drew his nourishment from her generous fount. She smiled and nodded, cut bread for the children, poured out the tea, drank and gave suck, all with a kind of abstracted placidity, as though years of din, dirt, drabness—and Con's ebullience—had in the end exalted her to a plane of heavenly lunacy where she was isolated and immune.

He almost upset his cup when she addressed him, gazing over the top of his head, her voice meek, apologetic.

"I meant to call on Mrs. Manson, Doctor. But I was so busy—"

"In the name of God!" Con rolled with laughter. "Busy, indeed! She hadn't a new dress—that's what she means. I had the money laid by—but damn it all, Terence or one of them had to have new boots. Never mind, Mother, wait till I get the car lengthened and we'll whirl ye up in style." He turned to Andrew with perfect naturalness. "We're hard up, Manson. It's the devil! We've plenty of grub, thank God, but sometimes we're not so fancy with the duds. They're a stingy lot on the Committee. And of course the big chief gets his whack!"

"Who?" Andrew asked, astonished.

"Llewellyn! He takes his fifth from me as well as you."

"But what on earth for?"

"Oh! he sees a case or two for me occasionally. He's taken a couple of dentigerous cysts out for me in the last six years. And he's the X-ray expert when that's needed. But it's a bugger." The family had bundled out to play in the kitchen, so Con could speak freely. "Him and his big saloon. The damn thing's all paint. Let me inform ye, Manson, once I was comin' up Mardy Hill behind him in my own little bus when I make up my mind to step on the gas. Bejasus! Ye should have seen his face when I give him my dust."

"Look here, Boland," Andrew said quickly. "This business of Llewellyn's cut is a shocking imposition. Why don't we fight it?"

"Eh?"

"Why don't we fight it?" Andrew repeated in a louder voice. Even as he spoke he felt his blood rise. "It's a damned injustice. Here are we hard up, trying to make our way— Listen, Boland, you're the very man I've been wanting to meet. Will you stand in with me on this? We'll get hold of the other assistants. Make a big united effort—"

A slow gleam irradiated Con's eye.

"Ye mean, ye want to go after Llewellyn?"

"I do."

Con impressively extended his hand.

"Manson my boy," he declared momentously. "We're together from the start."

Andrew raced home to Christine full of eagerness, thirsting for the fight. "Chris! Chris! I've found a gem of a chap. A redheaded dentist—quite mad

—yes, like me, I knew you'd say that. But listen, darling, we're going to start a revolution." He laughed excitedly. "Oh! Lord! If old man Llewellyn only knew what was in store for him!"

He did not require her caution to go carefully. He was determined to proceed with discernment in everything he did. He began, therefore, the following day, by calling upon Owen.

The secretary was interested and emphatic. He told Andrew that the agreement in question was a voluntary one between the head doctor and his assistants. The whole thing lay outside the jurisdiction of the Committee.

"You see, Doctor Manson," Owen concluded, "Doctor Llewellyn is a very clever, well-qualified man. We count ourselves fortunate to have him. But he has a handsome remuneration from the Society for acting as our Medical Superintendent. It is you assistant doctors who think he ought to have more—"

"Do we hell," thought Andrew. He went away satisfied, rang up Oxborrow and Medley, made them agree to come to his house that evening. Urquhart and Boland had already promised to be there. He knew, from past conversations, that every one of the four loathed losing a fifth of his salary. Once he had them together the thing was done.

His next step was to speak to Llewellyn. He had decided, on reflection, that it would be underhand not to make some disclosure of his intention beforehand. That afternoon he was at the hospital giving an anæsthetic. As he watched Llewellyn go through with the operation, a long and complicated abdominal case, he could not repress a feeling of admiration. Owen's remark was absolutely true: Llewellyn was amazingly clever, not only clever but versatile. He was the exception, the unique instance, which—Denny would have contended—proved the rule. Nothing came amiss to him, nothing floored him. From public health administration, every bylaw of which he knew by heart, to the latest radiological technique, the whole range of his multifarious duties found Llewellyn blandly expert and prepared.

After the operation, while Llewellyn was washing up, Andrew went up to him, jerkily tugging off his gown.

"Excuse me for mentioning it, Doctor Llewellyn—but I couldn't help noticing the way you handled that tumour, it was awfully fine."

Llewellyn's dull skin tinged with gratification. He beamed affably.

"Glad you think so, Manson. Come to speak of it, you're improvin' nicely with your anæsthetics."

"No, no," Andrew muttered. "I'll never be much good at that."

There was a pause. Llewellyn went on soaping his hands equably. Andrew, at his elbow, cleared his throat nervously. Now that the moment had come he found it almost impossible to speak. But he managed to blurt out:—

"Look here, Doctor Llewellyn. It's only right to tell you—all we assistants think our salary percentage payments to you unfair. It's an awkward thing to have to say, but I—I'm going to propose they are done away with. We've got a meeting at my house to-night. I'd rather you knew that now, than afterwards. I—I want you to feel I'm at least honest about it."

Before Llewellyn could reply, and without looking at his face, Andrew swung round and left the theatre. How badly he had said it! Yet anyway, he *had* said it. When they sent him their ultimatum, Llewellyn could not accuse him of stabbing him in the back.

The meeting at Vale View was fixed for nine o'clock that evening. Andrew put out some bottled beer and asked Christine to prepare sandwiches. When she had done this, she slipped on her coat and went round to Vaughans' for an hour. Strung with anticipation, Andrew stumped up and down the hall, striving to collect his ideas. And presently the others arrived—Boland first, Urquhart next, Oxborrow and Medley together.

In the sitting-room, pouring beer and proffering sandwiches, Andrew tried to initiate a cordial note. Since he almost disliked him, he addressed Doctor Oxborrow first.

"Help yourself, Oxborrow! Plenty more in the cellar."

"Thanks, Manson." The evangelist's voice was chill. "I don't touch alcohol in any shape or form. It's against my principles."

"In the name of God!" Con said, out of the froth on his moustache.

As a beginning it was not auspicious. Medley, munching sandwiches, kept his eyes all the time on the alert, his face wearing the stony anxiety of the deaf. Already the beer was increasing Urquhart's natural belligerence; after glaring steadily at Oxborrow for some minutes he suddenly shot out:—

"Now I find myself in your company, *Doctor* Oxborrow, maybe you'll find it convenient to explain how Tudor Evans, Seventeen Glyn Terrace, came off *my* list onto *yours.*"

"I don't remember the case," said Oxborrow, pressing his finger tips together aloofly.

"But I do!" Urquhart exploded. "It was one of the cases you stole from me, Your Medical Reverence! And what's more—"

"Gentlemen!" cried Andrew in a panic. "Please, *please!* How can we ever do anything if we quarrel amongst ourselves? Remember what we're here for."

"What *are* we here for?" Oxborrow said womanishly. "I ought to be at a case."

Andrew, standing on the hearthrug, his expression taut and earnest, took a grab at the slippery situation.

"This is the way of it, then, gentlemen!" He drew a deep breath. "I'm the youngest man here and I'm not long in this practice but I—I hope you'll excuse all that! Perhaps it's because I am new that I get a fresh look at things—things you've been putting up with too long. It seems to me in the first place that our system here is all wrong. We just go hacking and muddling through in the antediluvian way, like we were ordinary town and country G.P.'s, fighting each other, not members of the same Medical Society with wonderful opportunities for working together! Every doctor I've met swears that practice is a dog's life. He'll tell you he drudges on, run off his feet, never a minute to himself, no time for meals, always on call! *Why* is that? It's because there's *no attempt at organization in our profession*. Take just one example of what I mean—though I could give you dozens. Night calls! You know how we all go to bed at night, dreading we'll be wakened and called out. We have rotten nights because we *may* be called out. Suppose we knew we *couldn't* be called out. Suppose we arranged, for a start, a co-operative system of night work. One doctor taking all night calls for one week, and then *going* free of all night calls for the rest of that month, while the others take their turn. Wouldn't that be splendid! Think how fresh you'd be for your day's work—"

He broke off, observing their blank faces.

"Wouldn't work," Urquhart snapped. "Dammit to hell! I'd sooner stay up every night of the month than trust old Oxborrow with one of my cases. Hee! Hee! When *he* borrows he doesn't pay back."

Andrew interposed feverishly:—

"We'll leave that, then—anyway, till another meeting—seeing that we're not agreed on it. But there's one thing we are agreed on. And that's why we're here. This percentage we pay to Doctor Llewellyn." He paused. They were all looking at him now, touched in their pockets, interested. "We've all agreed it's unjust. I've spoken to Owen about it. He says it has nothing to do with the Committee but is a matter for adjustment between the doctors."

"That's right," threw out Urquhart. "I remember when it was fixed. A matter of nine year ago. We had two rank Jonahs of assistants then. One at the East Surgery and one at my end. They gave Llewellyn a lot of trouble over their cases. So one fine day he called us all together and said it wasn't goin' to be worth his while unless we could make some arrangement with him. That's the way it started. And that's the way it's gone on."

"But his salary from the Committee already covers *all* his work in the Society. And he simply rakes in the shekels from his other appointments. He's rolling in it!"

"I know, I know," said Urquhart testily. "But, mind you, Manson, he's damn useful to us, is the same Llewellyn. And he knows it. If he chose to cut up rough we'd be in a pretty poor way."

"Why should *we* pay him?" Andrew kept on inexorably.

"Hear! Hear!" interjected Con, refilling his glass.

Oxborrow cast one glance at the dentist.

"If I may be allowed to get a word in . . . I agree with Doctor Manson in that it is unjust for us to have our salaries deducted. But the fact is— Doctor Llewellyn is a man of high standing, excellently qualified, who gives great distinction to the Society. And besides he goes out of his way to take our bad cases off our hands."

Andrew stared at the other.

"Do you *want* your bad cases off your hands?"

"Of course," said Oxborrow pettishly. "Who doesn't?"

"I don't," Andrew shouted. "I want to keep them, see them through!"

"Oxborrow's right," Medley muttered unexpectedly. "It's the first rule of medical practice, Manson. You'll realize it when you're older. Get rid of the bad stuff, get rid of it, rid of it."

"But damn it all!" Andrew protested hotly.

The discussion continued, in circles, for three quarters of an hour.

At the end of that time Andrew, very heated, chanced to exclaim: "We've got to put this through. D'you hear me, we've simply *got* to. Llewellyn knows we're after him. I told him this afternoon."

"What?" The exclamation came from Oxborrow, Urquhart, even from Medley.

"Do you mean to say, Doctor, you *told* Doctor Llewellyn—" Half-rising, Oxborrow bent his startled gaze on Andrew.

"Of course I did! He's got to know sometime. Don't you see, we've only got to stand together, show a united front and *we're bound to win!*"

"Dammit to hell!" Urquhart was livid. "You've got a nerve! You don't know what influence Llewellyn has! He's got a finger in everything! We'll be lucky if we're not all sacked. Think of *me* trying to find another pitch at my time of life." He bullocked his way towards the door. "You're a good fellow, Manson. But you're too *young*. Good *night*."

Medley had already risen hurriedly to his feet. The look in his eyes said he was going straight to his telephone to tell Doctor Llewellyn apologetically that he, Llewellyn, was a superb doctor and he, Medley, could hear him perfectly. Oxborrow was on his heels. In two minutes the room was clear of all but Con, Andrew, and the remainder of the beer.

They finished the beverage in silence. Then Andrew remembered that there were six more bottles in the larder. They finished these six bottles. Then they began to talk. They said things touching the origin, parentage, and moral character of Oxborrow, Medley, and Urquhart. They dwelt especially upon Oxborrow and Oxborrow's harmonium. They did not observe Christine come in and go upstairs. They talked together soulfully, as brothers shamefully betrayed.

Next morning Andrew marched on his rounds with a splitting headache and a scowl. In the Square he passed Llewellyn in his car. As Andrew lifted his head in shamed defiance Llewellyn beamed at him.

10

FOR a week Andrew went about chafing under his defeat, bitterly cast-down. On Sunday morning, usually devoted to long and peaceful repose, he suddenly broke loose.

"It isn't the money, Chris! It's the principle of the thing! When I think of it—it drives me crazy. Why can't I let it slip? Why don't I like Llewellyn? At least why do I like him one minute and hate him the next? Tell me honestly, Chris. Why don't I sit at his feet? Am I jealous? What is it?"

Her answer staggered him. "Yes, I think you are jealous!"

"What?"

"Don't break my eardrums, dear. You asked me to tell you honestly. You're jealous, frightfully jealous. And why shouldn't you be? I don't want to be married to a saint. There's enough cleaning in this house already without you setting up a halo."

"Go on," he growled. "Give me all my faults when you're about it. Suspicious! Jealous! You've been at me before! Oh, and I'm too *young*, I suppose. Octogenarian Urquhart rammed that in my teeth the other day!"

A pause during which he waited for her to continue the argument. Then, irritably, "Why should I be jealous of Llewellyn?"

"Because he's frightfully good at his work, knows so much, and well— chiefly because he has all these first-class qualifications."

"While I have a scrubby little M.B. from a Scots University! God Almighty! Now I know what you really think of me." Furious, he flung out of bed and began to walk about the room in his pyjamas. "What do qualifications matter anyway? Pure damn swank! It's method, clinical ability that counts. I don't believe all the tripe they serve up in textbooks. I believe in what I hear through the ends of my stethoscope! And in case you don't know it, I hear plenty. I'm beginning to find out real things in my anthracite investigation. Perhaps I'll surprise you one fine day, my lady! Damn it all! It's a fine state of affairs when a man wakes up on Sunday morning and his wife tells him he knows *nothing!*"

Sitting up in bed, she took her manicure set and began to do her nails, waiting till he had finished.

"I didn't say all that, Andrew." Her reasonableness aggravated him the more. "It's just—darling, you're not going to be an assistant *all* your life. You want people to listen to you, pay attention to your work, your ideas—oh, you understand what I mean. If you had a really fine degree—an M.D. or—or the M.R.C.P.—it would stand you in good stead."

"The M.R.C.P.!" he echoed blankly. Then: "So she's been thinking it out all by her little self. The M.R.C.P.—huh!—take *that* from a mining practice!" His satire should have overwhelmed her. "Don't you understand they only give that to the crowned heads of Europe?"

He banged the door and went into the bathroom to shave. Five minutes later he was back again, one half of his chin shaved, the other lathered. He was penitent, excited.

"Do you *think* I could do it, Chris? You're absolutely right. We need a few pips on the good old name plate so we can hold our own up! But the M.R.C.P.—it's the most difficult medical exam. in the whole shoot. It's—it's *murder!* Still—I believe . . . Wait and I'll get the particulars—"

Breaking off, he dashed downstairs for the *Medical Directory*. When he returned with it his face had fallen to acute dejection.

"Sunk!" he muttered dismally. "Right bang off. I *told* you it was an impossible exam. There's a preliminary paper in languages. Four languages: Latin, French, Greek, German—and two of them are compulsory, before you can even *sit* the cursed thing. I don't know languages. All the Latin I know is dog lingo: *mist. alba—mitte decem.* As for French—"

She did not answer. There was a silence while he stood at the window gloomily considering the empty view. At last he turned, frowning, worrying, unable to leave the bone alone.

"Why shouldn't I—*damn* it all, Chris—why shouldn't I learn these languages *for* the exam.?"

Her manicure things spread themselves upon the floor as she jumped out of bed and hugged him.

"Oh, I did want you to say that, my dear! That's the real *you.* I could—I could help you, perhaps. Don't forget your old woman's a retired schoolmarm!"

They made plans excitedly all day. They bundled Trollope, Chekhov, and Dostoievski into the spare bedroom. They cleared the sitting-room for action. And that evening he went to school with her. The next evening, and the next . . .

Sometimes Andrew felt the sublime bathos of it, heard from afar off the mocking laughter of the gods. Sitting over the hard table with his wife, in this remote Welsh mining town, muttering after her *caput—capitis,* or *Madame, est-il possible que* . . . , wading through declensions, irregular verbs, reading aloud from *Tacitus* and a patriotic reader they had picked up, *Pro Patria—*he would jerk back suddenly in his chair, morbidly conscious.

"If Llewellyn could see us here—wouldn't he grin? And to think this is only the beginning, that I've got all the medical stuff after!"

Towards the end of the following month, parcels of books began to arrive periodically at Vale View from the London branch of the International Medical Library. Andrew began to read where, at college, he had left off. He discovered, quickly, how early he had left off. He discovered and was swamped by the therapeutic advance of biochemistry. He discovered renal thresholds, blood ureas, basal metabolism, and the fallibility of the albumen test. As this keystone of his student's days fell from him he groaned aloud.

"Chris! I know nothing. And this stuff is killing me!"

He had to contend with the work of his practice, he had only the long nights in which to study. Sustained by black coffee and a wet towel round his head he battled on, reading into the early hours of the morning. When he fell into bed, exhausted, often he could not sleep. And sometimes when he slept he would awake, sweating from a nightmare, his head ablaze with terms, formulæ, and some drivelling imbecility of his halting French.

He smoked to excess, lost weight, became thinner in the face. But Chris was there, constantly, silently there, permitting him to talk, to draw diagrams, to explain, in tongue-twisting nomenclature, the extraordinary, the astounding, the fascinating selective action of the kidney tubules. She also permitted him to shout, to gesticulate, and, as his nerves grew more ragged, to hurl abuse at her.

At eleven o'clock as she brought him fresh coffee he became liable to snarl:—

"Why can't you leave me alone? What's this slush for, anyway? Caffein— it's only a rotten drug. You know I'm killing myself, don't you? And it's all for you. You're hard! You're damnably hard. You're like a female turnkey, marching in and out with skilly! I'll never get this blasted thing. There are hundreds of fellows trying to get it from the West End of London, from the big hospitals, and me!—from Aberalaw—ha! ha!" His laughter was hysterical. "From the dear old Medical Aid Society! Oh, God! I'm so tired and I know they'll have me out to-night for that confinement in Cefen Row, and . . ."

She was a better soldier than he. She had a quality of balance which steadied them through every crisis. She also had a temper, but she controlled it. She made sacrifices, refused all invitations from the Vaughans, stopped going to the orchestral concerts in the Temperance Hall. No matter how badly they had slept she was always up early, neatly dressed, ready with his breakfast when he came dragging down, unshaven, the first cigarette of the day already between his lips.

Suddenly, when he had been working six months, her aunt in Bridlington took ill with phlebitis and wrote asking her to come North. Handing him the letter she declared immediately that it was impossible for her to leave him.

But he, bunched sulkily over his bacon and egg, growled out:—

"I wish you'd go, Chris! Studying this way, I'd get on better without you. We've been getting on each other's nerves lately. Sorry—but it seems the best thing to do."

She went, unwillingly, at the end of the week. Before she had been gone twenty-four hours he found out his mistake. It was agony without her. Jenny, though working to carefully prepared instructions, was a perpetual aggrava- tion. But it was not Jenny's cooking, or the lukewarm coffee, or the badly made bed. It was Christine's absence: knowing she was not in the house, being unable to call out to her, missing her. He found himself gazing dully at his books, losing hours, while he thought of her.

At the end of a fortnight she wired that she was returning. He dropped everything and prepared to receive her. Nothing was too good, too spectacu- lar for the celebration of their reunion. Her wire had not given him much time; but he thought rapidly, then sped to the town on a mission of ex- travagance. He bought first a bunch of roses. In Kendrick's, the fishmonger's, he was lucky to find a lobster, fresh in that morning. He seized it quickly, lest Mrs. Vaughan—for whom Kendrick primarily intended all such delicacies— should ring up and forestall him. Then he bought ice in quantity, called at the greengrocer's for salad, and finally, with trepidation, ordered one bottle of Moselle which Lampert, the grocer in the Square, assured him was "sound."

After tea he told Jenny she might go, for already he could feel her youthful eye fastened inquisitively upon him. He then set to work and lovingly composed a lobster salad. The zinc bucket from the scullery, filled with ice, made an excellent wine pail. The flowers presented an unexpected difficulty, for Jenny had locked up the cupboard under the stairs where all the vases were kept and, to all intents, hidden the key. But he surmounted even this obstruction, placing half the roses in the water jug and the remainder in the toothbrush holder from the toilet set upstairs. This struck quite a note of variety.

At last his preparations were complete—the flowers, the food, the wine upon the ice; his eye surveyed the scene with shining intensity. After surgery, at half-past nine, he raced to meet her train at the Upper Station.

It was like falling in love all over again—fresh, wonderful. Tenderly, he escorted her to the love feast. The evening was hot and still. The moon shone in upon them. He forgot about the intricacies of basal metabolism. He told her they might be in Provence, or some place like that, in a great castle by a lake. He told her she was a sweet, exquisite child. He told her he had been a brute to her but that for the rest of his life he would be a carpet —not red, since she interjected her objection to that colour—on which she might tread. He told her much more than that.

By the end of the week he was telling her to fetch his slippers.

August arrived, dusty and scorching. With the finish of his reading in sight, he was confronted with the necessity of brushing up his practical work, particularly histology—an apparently insuperable difficulty in his present situation. It was Christine who thought of Professor Challis and his position at Cardiff University. When Andrew wrote to him, Challis immediately replied stating, with verbosity, that he would rejoice to use his influence with the Department of Pathology. Manson, he said, would find Doctor Glyn-Jones a first-rate fellow. He concluded with a carolling inquiry for Christine.

"I've got to hand it to you, Chris! It does mean something to have friends. And I very nearly stuck away from meeting Challis that night at Vaughans'! Decent old bouncer! But all the same, I hate asking favours. And what's this about sending tender regards to you?"

In the middle of that month a secondhand Red Indian motorcycle—a low, wickedly unprofessional machine, advertised as "too fast" for its previous owner—made its appearance at Vale View. There were, in the slackness of summer, three afternoon hours which Andrew might reasonably regard as his own. Every day, immediately after lunch, a red streak went roaring down the Valley in the direction of Cardiff, thirty miles away. And every day, towards five o'clock, a slightly dustier red streak, moving in the opposite direction, made a target of Vale View.

These sixty miles in the broiling heat, with an hour's work at Glyn-Jones' specimens and slides sandwiched midway—often he used the microscope with hands which still shook from the handle-bars' vibration—made heavy going of the next few weeks. For Christine it was the most anxious part of the whole lunatic adventure to see him depart with a swift crackling exhaust, to wait anxiously for the first faint beat of his return, fearing all the time that something must happen to him, bent to the metal of that satanic machine.

Though he was so rushed he found a moment occasionally to bring her strawberries from Cardiff. They saved these till after his surgery. At tea he was always parched from the dust and red-eyed, wondering gloomily if his duodenum had not dropped off at that last pothole in Trecoed, asking himself if he could possibly manage, before the surgery, these two calls which had come in during his absence.

But the final journey was made at last. Glyn-Jones had nothing more to show him. He knew every slide and every single specimen by heart. All that remained was to enter his name and send up the heavy entrance fees for the examination.

On the fifteenth of October Andrew set out alone for London. Christine saw him to the station. Now that the actual event was so close at hand, a queer calmness had settled upon him. All his striving, his frenzied efforts, his almost hysterical outbursts, seemed far away and done with. His brain was inactive, almost dull. He felt that he knew nothing.

Yet, on the following day, when he began the written part of the examination which was held at the College of Physicians, he found himself answering the papers with a blind automatism. He wrote and wrote, never looking at the clock, filling sheet after sheet, until his head reeled.

He had taken a room at the Museum Hotel, where Christine and he had stayed on their first visit to London. Here it was extremely cheap. But the food was vile, adding the final touch to his upset digestion required to produce a bad attack of dyspepsia. He was compelled to restrict his diet to hot malted milk. A tumblerful in an A.B.C. tea-room in the Strand was his lunch. Between his papers he lived in a kind of daze. He did not dream of going to a place of amusement. He scarcely saw the people in the streets. Occasionally, to clear his head, he took a ride on the top of an omnibus.

After the written papers, the practical and *viva voce* part of the examination began; and Andrew found himself dreading this more than anything which had gone before. There were perhaps twenty other candidates, all of them men older than himself, and all with an unmistakable air of assurance and position. The candidate placed next to him, for instance, a man named Harrison whom he had once or twice spoken to, had an Oxford B.Ch., an outpatient appointment at St. John's and a consulting-room in Brook Street. When Andrew compared Harrison's charming manners and obvious standing with his own provincial awkwardness he felt his chances of favourably impressing the examiners to be small indeed.

His practical, at the South London Hospital, went, he thought, well enough. His case was one of bronchiectasis in a young boy of fourteen, which, since he knew lungs so intimately, was a piece of good fortune. He felt he had written a good report. But when it came to the *viva voce* his luck seemed to change completely. The *viva* procedure at the College of Physicians had its peculiarities. On two successive days each candidate was questioned, in turn, by two separate examiners. If at the end of the first session the candidate was found inadequate he was handed a polite note telling him he need not return on the following day. Faced with the imminence of this fatal missive, Andrew found to his horror that he had drawn as his first examiner a man he had heard Harrison speak of with apprehension, Doctor Maurice Gadsby.

Gadsby was a spare, undersized man with a ragged black moustache and small mean eyes. Recently elected to his Fellowship, he had none of the tolerance of the older examiners, but seemed to set out deliberately to fail the candidates who came before him. He considered Andrew with a supercilious lift to his brows and placed before him six slides. Five of these slides Andrew named correctly, but the sixth he could not name. It was on this slide that Gadsby concentrated. For five minutes he harassed Andrew on this section,—which, it appeared, was the ovum of an obscure West African parasite,—then idly, without interest, he passed him on to the next examiner, Sir Robert Abbey.

Andrew rose and crossed the room with a pale face and a heavily beating heart. All the lassitude, the inertia he had experienced at the beginning of the week was gone now. He had an almost desperate desire to succeed. But he was convinced that Gadsby would fail him. He raised his eyes to find Robert Abbey contemplating him with a friendly, half-humorous smile.

"What's the matter?" said Abbey unexpectedly.

"Nothing, sir," Andrew stammered. "I think I've done rather badly with Doctor Gadsby—that's all."

"Never mind about that. Have a look at these specimens. Then just say anything you think about them." Abbey smiled encouragingly. He was a cleanshaven, ruddy-complexioned man of about sixty-five with a high forehead and a long humorous upper lip. Though Abbey was now perhaps the third most distinguished physician in Europe, he had known hardship and bitter struggles in his earlier days when, coming from his native Leeds, with only a provincial reputation to sustain him, he had encountered prejudice and opposition in London. As he gazed, without seeming to do so, at Andrew, observing his ill-cut suit, the soft collar and shirt, the cheap, ill-knotted tie, and above all, the look of strained intensity upon his serious face, the days of his own provincial youth came back to him. Instinctively his heart went out to this unusual candidate, and his eye, ranging down the list before him, noted with satisfaction that his markings, particularly in the recent practical, were above pass level.

Meanwhile Andrew, with his eyes fixed upon the glass jars before him, had been stumbling unhappily through his commentary upon the specimens.

"Good," Abbey said suddenly. He took up a specimen—it was an aneurism of the ascending aorta—and began in a friendly manner to question Andrew. His questions, from being simple, gradually became wider and more searching in their scope, until finally they came to bear upon a recent specific treatment by the induction of malaria. But Andrew, opening out under Abbey's sympathetic manner, answered well.

Finally, as he put down the specimen, Abbey remarked:—

"Do you know anything of the history of aneurism?"

"Ambroise Paré," Andrew answered, and Abbey had already begun his approving nod, "is presumed to have first discovered the condition."

Abbey's face expressed surprise.

"Why 'presumed,' Doctor Manson? Paré did discover aneurism."

Andrew reddened, then turned pale as he plunged on:—

"Well, sir, that's what the textbooks say. You'll find it in every book—I myself took the trouble to verify that it was in six." A quick breath. "But I happened to be reading Celsus, brushing up my Latin,—which needed brushing up, sir,—when I definitely came across the word *aneurismus*. Celsus knew aneurism. He described it in full. And that was a matter of thirteen centuries before Paré!"

There was a silence. Andrew raised his eyes, prepared for kindly satire. Abbey was looking at him with a queer expression on his ruddy face.

"Doctor Manson," he said at length, "you are the first candidate in this examination hall who has ever told me something original, something true, and something which I did not know. I congratulate you."

Andrew turned scarlet again.

"Just tell me one thing more—as a matter of personal curiosity," Abbey concluded. "What do you regard as the main principle—the, shall I say the basic idea—which you keep before you when you are exercising the practice of your profession?"

There was a pause while Andrew reflected desperately. At length, feeling he was spoiling all the good effect he had created, he blurted out:—

"I suppose—I suppose I keep telling myself never to take anything for granted."

"Thank you, Doctor Manson."

As Andrew left the room Abbey reached for his pen. He felt young again, and suspiciously sentimental. He thought: "If he'd told me he went about trying to heal people, trying to help suffering humanity, I'd have flunked him out of sheer damned disappointment." As it was, Abbey traced the unheard-of maximum, 100, opposite the name of Andrew Manson. Indeed, could Abbey have "got away with it"—his own eloquent reflection—that figure would have been doubled.

A few minutes later Andrew went downstairs with the other candidates. At the foot of the stairs beside his leather-hooded cave a liveried porter stood with a little pile of envelopes before him. As the candidates went past he handed an envelope to each of them. Harrison, walking out next to Andrew, tore his open quickly. His expression altered; he said quietly, "It would appear I'm not wanted to-morrow." Then, forcing a smile, "How about you?" Andrew's fingers were shaking. He could barely read. Dazedly he heard Harrison congratulate him. His chances were still alive. He walked down to the A.B.C. and treated himself to a malted milk. He thought tensely, "If I don't get through now, after all this, I'll—I'll walk in front of a bus."

The next day passed grindingly. Barely half the original candidates remained and it was rumoured that out of these another half would go. Andrew had no idea whether he was doing well or badly: he knew only that his head ached abominably, that his feet were icy, his inside void.

At last it was over. At four o'clock in the afternoon Andrew came out of the cloakroom, spent and melancholy, pulling on his coat. Then he became aware of Abbey standing before the big open fire in the hall. He made to pass. But Abbey, for some reason, was holding out his hand, smiling, speaking to him, telling him—telling him that he was through.

Dear God, he had done it! He had *done* it! He was alive again, gloriously alive, his headache gone, all his weariness forgotten. As he dashed down to the nearest post office his heart sang wildly, madly. He was through, he had done it, not from the West End of London, but from an outlandish mining town. His whole being was a surging exultation. It hadn't been for nothing after all: these long nights, these mad dashes down to Cardiff, these racking hours of study. On he sped, bumping and cannoning through the crowds, missing the wheels of taxis and omnibuses, his eyes shining—racing, racing to wire news of the miracle to Christine.

11

WHEN the train got in, half an hour late, it was nearly midnight. All the way up the Valley the engine had been battling against a high head wind and at Aberalaw, as Andrew stepped out on the platform, the force of the hurricane almost bowled him off his feet. The station was deserted. The young poplars planted in line at its entrance bent like bows, whistling and shivering at every blast. Overhead the stars were polished to a high glitter.

Andrew started along Station Road, his body braced, his mind exhilarated by the batter of the wind. Full of his success, his contact with the great, the sophisticated medical world, his ears ringing with Sir Robert Abbey's words, he could not reach Christine fast enough to tell her joyously everything, everything which had taken place. His telegram would have given her the good news; but now he wished to pour out in detail the full exciting story.

As he swung, head down, into Talgarth Street he was conscious, suddenly, of a man running. The man came behind him, labouring heavily, the noisy clatter of his boots upon the pavement so lost in the gale he seemed a phantom figure. Instinctively Andrew stopped. As the man drew near he recognized him: Frank Davis, an ambulance man of Anthracite Sinking Number Three, who had been one of his first-aid class the previous spring. At the same moment Davis saw him.

"I was comin' for you, Doctor. Comin' for you to your house. This wind's knocked the wires all to smash." A gust tore the rest of his words away.

"What's wrong?" shouted Andrew.

"There's been a fall-down at Number Three." Davis cupped his hands close to Manson's ear. "A lad got buried there, almost. They don't seem to be able to shift him. Sam Bevan; he's on your list. Better look sharp, Doctor, and get to him."

Andrew took a few steps down the road with Davis; then a sudden reflection brought him up short.

"I've got to have my bag," he bawled to Davis. "You go up to my house and fetch it for me. I'll go on to Number Three." He added: "And Frank! Tell my missus where I've gone."

He was at Sinking Number Three in four minutes, blown there, across the railway siding and along Roath Lane, by the following wind. In the rescue room he found the under-manager and three men waiting on him. At the sight of him the under-manager's worried expression lifted slightly.

"Glad to see you, Doctor. We're all to bits with the storm. And we've had a nasty fall on top of it. Nobody killed, thank God, but one of the lads pinned by his arm. We can't shift him an inch. And the roof's rotten."

They went to the winding shaft, two of the men carrying a stretcher with splints strapped to it and the third a wooden box of first-aid material. As they entered the cage another figure came bundling across the yard. It was Davis, panting, with the bag.

"You've been quick, Frank," Manson said as Davis squatted beside him in the cage.

Davis simply nodded; he could not speak. There was a clang, an instant's suspense, and the cage dropped and rocketed to the bottom. They all got out, moving in single file, the under-manager first, then Andrew, Davis,—still clutching the bag,—then the three men.

Andrew had been underground before; he was used to the high vaulted caverns of the Blaenelly mines, great dark resounding caves, deep down in the earth where the mineral had been gouged and blasted from its bed. But this sinking, Number Three, was an old one with a long and tortuous haulage-way leading to the workings. The haulage was less a passage than a low-roofed burrow, dripping and clammy, through which they crawled, often on their hands and knees for nearly half a mile. Suddenly the light borne by the under-manager stopped just ahead of Andrew, who then knew that they were there.

Slowly, he crept forward. Three men, cramped together on their bellies in a dead end, were doing their best to revive another man who lay in a huddled attitude, his body slewed sideways, one shoulder pointing backwards, lost seemingly in the mass of fallen rock around him. Tools lay scattered behind the men, two overturned bait cans, stripped-off jackets.

"Well then, lads?" asked the under-manager in a low voice.

"We can't shift him, nohow." The man who spoke turned a sweat-grimed face. "We tried everything."

"Don't try," said the under-manager with a quick look at the roof. "Here's the doctor. Get back a bit, lads, and give us room. Get back a tidy bit if I were you."

The three men pulled themselves back from the dead end and Andrew, when they had squeezed their way past him, went forward. As he did so, in one brief moment, there flashed through his head a memory of his recent examination, its advanced biochemistry, high-sounding terminology, scientific phrases. It had not covered such a contingency as this.

Sam Bevan was quite conscious. But his features were haggard beneath their powdering of dust. Weakly, he tried to smile to Manson.

"Looks like you're goin' to 'ave some amb'lance practice on me proper!" Bevan had been a member of that same first-aid class, and had often been requisitioned for bandage practice.

Andrew reached forward. By the light of the under-manager's lamp, thrust across his shoulder, he ran his hands over the injured man. The whole of Bevan's body was free except his left forearm, which lay beneath the fall, so pressed and mangled under that enormous weight of rock that it held him immovably a prisoner.

Andrew saw instantly that the only way to free Bevan was to amputate the forearm. And Bevan, straining his pain-tormented eyes, read that decision the moment it was made.

"Go on, then, Doctor," he muttered. "Only get me out of here quick."

"Don't worry, Sam," Andrew said. "I'm going to send you to sleep now. When you wake up you'll be in bed."

Stretched flat in a puddle of muck under the two-foot roof he slipped off his coat, folded it, and slipped it under Bevan's head. He rolled up his sleeves and asked for his bag.

The under-manager handed forward the bag and as he did so he whispered in Andrew's ear:—

"For God's sake, hurry, Doctor. We'll have this roof down on us before we know where we are."

Andrew opened the bag. Immediately he smelt the reek of chloroform. Almost before he thrust his hand into the dark interior and felt the jagged edge of broken glass he knew what had occurred. Frank Davis, in his haste to reach the mine, had dropped the bag. The chloroform bottle was broken, its contents irretrievably spilled. A shiver passed over Andrew. He had no time to send up to the surface. And he had no anæsthetic.

For perhaps thirty seconds he remained paralyzed. Then automatically he felt for his hypodermic, charged it, gave Bevan a maximum of morphine. He could not linger for the full effect. Tipping his bag sideways so that the instruments were ready to his hand he again bent over Bevan. He said, as he tightened the tourniquet:—

"Shut your eyes, Sam!"

The light was dim and the shadows moved with flickering confusion. At the first incision Bevan groaned between his shut teeth. He groaned again. Then, mercifully, when the knife grated upon the bone, he fainted.

A cold perspiration broke on Andrew's brow as he clipped the artery forceps on spurting, mangled flesh. He could not see what he was doing. He felt suffocated here, in this rat-hole, deep down beneath the surface of the ground, lying in the mud. No anæsthesia, no theatre, no row of nurses to run to do his bidding. He wasn't a surgeon. He was guddling hopelessly. He would never get through. The roof would crash upon them all.

Behind him the hurried breathing of the under-manager . . . A slow drip of water falling cold upon his neck . . . His fingers, working feverishly, stained and warm . . . The grating of the saw . . . The voice of Sir Robert Abbey, a long way off: "The opportunity for scientific practice . . ." Oh, God! would he never get through?

At last. He almost sobbed with relief. He slipped a pad of gauze on the bloodied stump. Stumbling to his knees he said:—

"Take him out."

Fifty yards back, in a clearing in the haulage-way, with space to stand up and four lamps round him, he finished the job. Here it was easier. He tidied up, ligatured, drenched the wound with antiseptic. A tube now. Then a couple of holding-sutures. Bevan remained unconscious. But his pulse, though thin, was steady. Andrew drew his hand across his forehead. Finished.

"Go steady with the stretcher. Wrap these blankets round him. We'll want hot bottles whenever we get out."

The slow procession, bent double in the low places, began to sway up the shadows of the haulage. They had not gone sixty paces when a low rumbling subsidence echoed in the darkness down behind them. It was like the last low rumble of a train entering a tunnel. The under-manager did not turn round. He merely said to Andrew with a quiet grimness:—

"That's it. The rest of the roof."

The journey out-bye took close upon an hour. They had to edge the stretcher sideways at the bad places. Andrew could not tell how long they had been under. But at length they came to the shaft bottom.

Up, up they shot, out of the depths. The keen bite of the wind met them, as they stepped out of the cage. With a kind of ecstasy Andrew drew a long breath.

He stood at the foot of the steps, holding on to the guard-rail. It was still dark, but in the mine yard they had hung a big naphtha flare which hissed and leaped with many tongues. Around the flare he saw a small crowd of waiting figures. There were women amongst them, with shawls about their heads.

Suddenly, as the stretcher moved slowly past them, Andrew heard his name called wildly and the next instant Christine's arms were about his neck. Sobbing hysterically she clung to him. Bareheaded, with only a coat above her nightdress, her bare feet thrust into leather shoes, she was a waiflike figure in the gusty darkness.

"What's wrong?" he asked, startled, trying to disengage her arms so that he might see her face.

But she would not let him go. Clinging to him frantically like a drowning woman she said brokenly:—

"They told us the roof was down—that you wouldn't—wouldn't come out."

Her skin was blue, her teeth chattering with cold. He carried her into the fire of the rescue-room, ashamed, yet deeply touched. There was hot cocoa in the rescue-room. They drank from the same scalding cup. It was a long time before either of them remembered about his grand new degree.

12

THE rescue of Sam Bevan was commonplace to a town which had known, in the past, the agony and horror of major mine disasters. Yet in his own district it did Andrew a vast amount of good. Had he returned with the bare success of London behind him he would have earned merely an extra sneer for "more newfangled nonsense." As it was, he received nods and even smiles from people who had never seemed to look at him before. The real extent of a doctor's popularity in Aberalaw could be gauged by his passage down the Rows. And where Andrew had hitherto been met by a line of tight-shut doors he now found them open, the off-shift men smoking in their shirt sleeves ready for a word with him, the women ready to "call him in," as he went by, the children greeting him smilingly by name.

Old Gus Parry, head driller in Number Two and doyen of the West district, summed up the new current of opinion for his mates as he gazed after Andrew's retreating figure.

"Eh, lads! 'E's a bookish chap no doubt. But he can do the real stuff, like, when it's wanted."

Cards began to come back to Andrew, gradually at first and, when it was seen that he did not abuse his returned renegades, with a sudden rush. Owen was pleased at the increase in Andrew's list. Meeting Andrew in the Square one day he smiled: "Didn't I tell you, now?"

Llewellyn had affected great delight at the result of the examination. He congratulated Andrew effusively upon the phone, then blandly raked him in for double duty at the theatre.

"By the way," he remarked, beaming, at the end of the long and ether-ridden session, "did you tell the examiners you were an assistant in a medical aid scheme?"

"I mentioned your name to them, Doctor Llewellyn," Andrew answered sweetly. "And that made it quite all right."

Oxborrow and Medley of the East Surgery took no notice of Andrew's success. But Urquhart was genuinely glad, though his comment took the form of vituperative explosion.

"Dammit to hell, Manson! What d'you think you're doin'? Trying to put my eye out?"

By way of complimenting his distinguished colleague he asked him in consultation to a case of pneumonia he was then attending and demanded to know the prognosis.

"She'll recover," Andrew said, and he gave scientific reasons.

Urquhart shook his old head dubiously.

He said: "I never heard tell of your polyvalent sera or your antibodies or your international units. But she was a Powell before her marriage and when the Powells get a swollen belly with their pneumonias they die before the eighth day. I know that family backwards. She's got a swollen belly, hasn't she?"

The old man went about with an air of sombre triumph over the scientific method when his patient died on the seventh day.

Denny, now abroad, knew nothing of the new degree. But a final and somewhat unexpected congratulation came in a long letter from Freddie Hampton. Freddie had seen the results in the *Lancet*, chided Andrew on his success, invited him to London, and then detailed his own exciting triumphs in Queen Anne Street where, as he had predicted that night at Cardiff, his neat brass plate now shone.

"It's a shame the way we've lost touch with Freddie," Manson declared. "I must write to him oftener. I've a feeling we shall run into him again. Nice letter, isn't it?"

"Yes, very nice," Christine answered drily. "But most of it seems to be about himself."

With the approach of Christmas the weather turned colder—crisp frosty days and still, starry nights. The iron hard roads rang under Andrew's feet. The clear air was like an exhilarating wine. Already shaping in his mind was the next step which he would take in his great assault on the problem of dust inhalation. His findings amongst his own patients had raised his hopes high, and now he had obtained permission from Vaughan to extend the field of his investigation by making a systematic examination of all the workers in the three anthracite sinkings—a marvellous opportunity. He planned to use the pit workers and surfacemen as controls. He would begin at the start of the New Year.

On Christmas Eve he returned from the surgery to Vale View with an extraordinary sense of spiritual anticipation and physical well-being. As he walked up the road it was impossible to escape the signs of the impending festival. The miners made much of Christmas here. For the past week the front room in each house had been locked against the children, festooned with paper streamers; toys were hidden in the drawers of the chest, and a steady accumulation of good things to eat—cake, oranges, sweet sugar biscuits, all bought with the club money paid out at this time of year—was laid upon the table.

Christine had made her own decorations of holly and mistletoe in gay expectation. But to-night as he came into the house he saw at once an extra excitement upon her face.

"Don't say a word," she said quickly, holding out her hand. "Not a single word! Just shut your eyes and come with me!"

He allowed her to lead him into the kitchen. There, on the table, lay a number of parcels, clumsily made up, some merely wrapped in newspaper, but each with a little note attached. In a flash he realized that they were presents from his patients. Some of the gifts were not wrapped up at all.

"Look, Andrew!" Christine cried. "A goose! And two ducks! And a lovely iced cake! And a bottle of elderberry wine! Isn't it kind of them? Isn't it wonderful they should want to give them to you?"

He simply could not speak. It overwhelmed him, this kindly evidence that the people of his district had at last begun to appreciate, to like him. With Christine at his shoulder he read the notes, the handwriting laboured and illiterate, some scrawled in pencil upon old envelopes turned inside out. "Your grateful patient at 3 Cefen Row"; "With thanks from Mrs. Williams"; one lopsided gem from Sam Bevan, "Thanks for getting me out for Christmas Doctor *bach*"—so they went on.

"We must keep these, darling," Christine said in a low voice. "I'll put them away upstairs."

When he had recovered his normal loquacity—a glass of homemade elderberry assisted him—he paced up and down the kitchen while Christine stuffed the goose. He raved beautifully:—

"That's how fees should be paid, Chris. No money, no damned bills, no capitation fee, no guinea-grabbing. Payment in kind. You understand me, don't you, darling? You get your patient right, he sends you something that he has made, produced. Coal if you like, a sack of potatoes from his garden, eggs maybe if he keeps hens—see my point? Then you'd have an ethical ideal! By the way, that Mrs. Williams who sent us the ducks—Leslie had her guzzling pills and physic for five stricken years before I cured her gastric ulcer with five weeks' diet. Where was I? Oh, yes! Don't you see? If every doctor was to eliminate the question of *gain* the whole system would be purer—"

"Yes, dear. Would you mind handing me the currants? Top shelf in the cupboard!"

"Damn it all, woman, why don't you listen? Gosh! That stuffing's going to taste good."

Next morning, Christmas Day, came fine and clear. Tallyn Beacons in the blue distance were pearly, with a white icing of snow. After a few morning consultations, with the pleasant prospect of no surgery in the evening, Andrew went on his round. He had a short list. Dinners were cooking in all the little houses and his own was cooking at home. He did not tire of the Christmas greetings he gave and received, all along the Rows. He could not help contrasting this present cheerfulness with his bleak passage up those same streets only a year ago.

Perhaps it was this thought which made him draw up, with an odd hesitation in his eyes, outside Number 18 Cefen Row. Of all his patients, apart from Chenkin, whom he did not want, the only one who had not come back to him was Tom Evans. To-day, when he was so unusually stirred, perhaps unduly exalted by a sense of the brotherhood of man, he had a sudden impulse to approach Evans and wish him a merry Christmas.

Knocking once, he opened the front door and walked through to the back kitchen. Here he paused, quite taken aback. The kitchen was very bare, almost empty, and in the grate there burned only a spark of fire. Seated before this, on a broken-backed wooden chair, with his crooked arm bent out like a wing, was Tom Evans. The droop of his shoulders was dispirited, hopeless. On his knee sat his little girl, four years of age. They were gazing, both of them, in silent contemplation, at a branch of fir planted in an old bucket. Upon this diminutive Christmas tree, which Evans had walked two miles over the mountain to procure, were three tiny tallow candles, as yet unlighted. And beneath it lay the family's Christmas treat—three small oranges.

Suddenly Evans turned and caught sight of Andrew. He started, and a slow flush of shame and resentment spread over his face. Andrew sensed that it was agony for him to be found—out of work, half his furniture pawned, crippled—by the doctor whose advice he had rejected.

Andrew had known, of course, that Evans was down on his luck, but he had not suspected anything so pitiful as this. He felt upset and uncomfortable, he wanted to turn and go away. At that moment Mrs. Evans came into the kitchen through the back door with a paper bag under her arm. She was so startled at the sight of Andrew that she dropped the paper bag, which fell to the stone floor and burst open—revealing two beef faggots, the cheapest meat that Aberalaw provided. The child, glancing at her mother's face, began suddenly to cry.

"What's like the matter, sir?" Mrs. Evans ventured at last, her hand pressed against her side. "He hasn't done anything?"

Andrew gritted his teeth together. He was so moved and surprised by this scene he had stumbled upon, only one course would satisfy him.

"Mrs. Evans!" He kept his eyes stiffly upon the floor. "I know there was a bit of a misunderstanding between your Tom and me. But it's Christmas—and—oh, well, I want—" he broke down lamely—"I mean, I'd be awfully pleased if the three of you would come round and help us eat our Christmas dinner."

"But, Doctor—" she wavered.

"You be quiet, lass," Evans interrupted her fiercely. "We're not goin' out to no dinner. If faggots is all we *can* have, it's all we *will* have. We don't want any bloody charity from nobody."

"What are you talking about?" Andrew exclaimed in dismay. "I'm asking you as a friend."

"Ah! you're all the same!" Evans answered wretchedly. "Once you get a man down, all you can do is fling some grub in his face. Keep your bloody dinner. We don't want it."

"Now, Tom—" Mrs. Evans protested weakly.

Andrew turned towards her, distressed, yet still determined to carry out his intention.

"You persuade him, Mrs. Evans. I'll be really upset now, if you don't come. Half-past one. We'll expect you."

Before any of them could say another word he swung round and left the house.

Christine made no comment when he blurted out what he had done. The Vaughans would probably have come to them to-day but for the fact that they had gone to Switzerland for the skiing. And now he had asked an unemployed miner and his family! These were his thoughts as he stood with his back to the fire watching her lay the extra places.

"You're cross, Chris?" he said at last.

"I thought I married Doctor Manson," she answered a trifle brusquely. "Not Doctor Bernardo. Really, darling, you're an incorrigible sentimentalist!"

The Evanses arrived exactly upon time, washed and brushed, desperately ill at ease, proud and frightened. Andrew, striving nervously to generate hospitality, had a dreadful premonition that Christine was right, that the entertainment would be a dismal failure. Evans, with a queer look at Andrew, proved to be clumsy at the table because of his bad arm. His wife was obliged to break and to butter his roll for him. And then, by good fortune, as Andrew was using the cruet, the top fell off the pepper caster and the entire half-ounce of white pepper shot into his soup. There was a hollow silence; then Agnes, the little girl, gave a sudden delighted giggle. Panic-stricken, the mother bent to rebuke her, when the sight of Andrew's face restrained her. The next minute they were all laughing.

Free of his dread of being patronized, Evans revealed himself a human being, a staunch Rugby football supporter and a great music lover. He had gone to Cardigan three years before, to sing at the Eisteddfod there. Proud to show his knowledge he discussed with Christine the oratorios of Elgar, while Agnes pulled crackers with Andrew.

Later, Christine drew Mrs. Evans and the little girl into the other room. When they were left alone, a strange silence fell between Andrew and Evans. A common thought was uppermost in the mind of each, yet neither knew how to broach it.

Finally with a kind of desperation Andrew said: "I'm sorry about that arm of yours, Tom. I know you've lost your work underground over the head of it. Don't think I'm trying to crow over you or anything like that. I'm just damned sorry."

"You're not any sorrier than I am," Evans said.

There was a pause, then Andrew resumed:—

"I wonder if you'd let me speak to Mr. Vaughan about you. Shut me up if you think I'm interfering—but I've got a little bit of influence with him and I feel sure I could get you a job on the surface—timekeeper—or something—"

He broke off, not daring to look at Evans. This time the silence was prolonged. At length Andrew raised his eyes, only to lower them again immediately. Tears were running down Evans' cheek, his entire body was shaking with his effort not to give way. But it was no use. He laid his good arm on the table, buried his head in it.

Andrew got up and crossed to the window where he remained for a few minutes. At the end of that time Evans had collected himself. He said nothing, absolutely nothing, and his eyes avoided Andrew's with a dumb reticence more significant than speech.

At half-past three the Evans family departed in a mood contrasting cheerfully with the constraint of their arrival. Christine and Andrew went into the sitting-room.

"You know, Chris," Andrew philosophized, "all that poor fellow's trouble— his stiff elbow I mean—isn't *his* fault. He distrusted me because I was new. He couldn't be expected to know about that damn carron oil. But friend Oxborrow—who accepted his card—*he* should have known. Ignorance, ignorance, pure damned ignorance. There ought to be a law to make doctors keep up-to-date. It's all the fault of our rotten system. There ought to be compulsory post-graduate classes—to be taken every five years—"

"Darling!" protested Christine, smiling at him from the sofa. "I've put up with your philanthropy all day. I've watched your wings sprouting like an archangel's. Don't give me the Harveian Oration on top of it! Come and sit by me here; I had a really important reason for wanting us to be alone to-day."

"Yes?"—doubtfully; then, indignantly: "You're not complaining, I hope. I thought I had behaved pretty decently. After all—Christmas Day—"

She laughed silently.

"Oh, my dear, you're just too lovely. Another minute there'll be a snowstorm and you'll take out the St. Bernards—muffled to the throat—to bring in somebody off the mountain—late, late at night."

"I know somebody who came down to Number Three Sinking—late, late at night," he grunted in retaliation; "and she wasn't muffled either."

"Sit here." She stretched out her arm. "I want to tell you something."

He went over to seat himself beside her, when suddenly there came the loud braying of a Klaxon from outside.

"*Krr-krr-krr-ki-ki-ki-krr.*"

"Damn!" said Christine concisely. Only one motor horn in Aberalaw could sound like that. It belonged to Con Boland.

"Don't you want them?" Andrew asked in some surprise. "Con half-said they'd be round for tea."

"Oh, well!" Christine said, rising and accompanying him to the door.

They advanced to meet the Bolands, who sat opposite the front gate in the reconstructed motor car—Con upright at the wheel in a bowler hat and enormous new gauntlets, with Mary and Terence beside him; the three other children tucked around Mrs. Boland, who bore the infant in her arms, in the rear, all packed, despite the elongation of the vehicle, like herrings in a tin.

Suddenly the horn began again: "*Krr-krr-krr-krr—*" Con had inadvertently pushed the button in switching off and now it was jammed. The Klaxon would not stop. "*Krr-krr-krr—*" it went, while Con fumbled and swore, and windows went up in the Row opposite, and Mrs. Boland sat with a remote expression on her face, unperturbed, holding the baby dreamily.

"In the name of God," Con cried, his moustache bristling along the dashboard. "I'm wastin' juice. What's happened? Am I short-circuited or what?"

"It's the button, Father," Mary told him calmly. She took her little fingernail and edged it out. The racket ceased.

"Ah! That's better," Con sighed. "How are you, Manson, my boy? How d'you like the old car now? I've lengthened her a good two feet. Isn't she grand? Mind you, there's still a little bother with the gearbox. We didn't quite take the hill in our stride, as ye might say!"

"We only stuck a few minutes, Father," interposed Mary.

"Ah! never mind," said Con. "I'll soon have that right when I sthrip her again. How are ye, Mrs. Manson? Here we all are, to wish ye a merry Christmas and take our tea off ye!"

"Come in, Con," Christine smiled. "I like your gloves!"

"Christmas present from the wife," Con answered, admiring the flapping gauntlets. "Army Surplus. Would ye believe they were still dishin' them out? Ah! What's gone wrong with this door?"

Unable to open the door he threw his long legs over it, climbed out, helped the children and his wife from the back, surveyed the car,—fondly removing a lump of mud from the windscreen,—then tore himself away to follow the others to Vale View.

They had a cheerful tea party. Con was in high spirits, full of his creation— "You'll not know her when she has a lick of paint." Mrs. Boland abstractedly drank six cups of strong black tea. The children began upon the chocolate biscuits and ended with a fight for the last piece of bread. They cleared every plate upon the table.

After tea, while Mary had gone to wash the dishes,—she insisted that Christine looked tired,—Andrew detached the baby from Mrs. Boland and played with it on the hearthrug before the fire. It was the fattest baby he had ever seen, a Rubens infant, with enormous solemn eyes and pads of plumpness upon its limbs. It tried repeatedly to poke a finger into his eye. Every time it failed a look of solemn wonder came upon its face. Christine sat with her hands in her lap, doing nothing—watching him playing with the baby.

But Con and his family could not stay long. Outside the light was fading and Con, worried about his "juice," had doubts which he did not choose to express concerning the functioning of his lamps.

When they rose to go, he delivered the invitation: "Come out and see us start."

Again Andrew and Christine stood at the gate while Con packed the car with his offspring. After a couple of swings the engine obeyed and Con, with a triumphant nod towards them, pulled on his gauntlets and adjusted his derby to a more rakish tilt. Then he heaved himself proudly into the driving seat.

At that moment Con's union broke and the car, with a groan, collapsed. Bearing the entire Boland family, the overextended vehicle sank slowly to the ground like some beast of burden perishing from sheer exhaustion. Before the bedazzled eyes of Andrew and Christine, the wheels splayed outwards. There was the sound of pieces dropping off, a vomit of tools shot from the locker; then the body of the car came to rest, dismembered, on street level. One minute there was a car, and the next a fun-fair gondola. In the forepart was Con clutching the wheel, in the aft part his wife, clutching the baby.

Mrs. Boland's mouth had dropped wide open, her dreamy eyes well fixed upon eternity. The stupefaction on Con's face, at his sudden loss of elevation, was irresistible.

Andew and Christine gave out a shriek of laughter. Once they began they could not stop. They laughed till they were weak.

"In the name of God," Con said, rubbing his head and picking himself up. Observing that none of the children were hurt, that Mrs. Boland remained, pale but undisturbed, in her seat, he considered the wreckage, pondering dazedly. "Sabotage," he declared at last, glaring at the windows opposite as a solution struck him. "Some of them devils in the Rows has tampered with her." Then his face brightened. He took the helpless Andrew by the arm and pointed with melancholy pride to the crumpled bonnet, beneath which the engine still feebly emitted a few convulsive beats. "See that, Manson! She's still runnin'."

Somehow they dragged the remains into the back yard of Vale View. In due course the Boland family went home on foot.

"What a day!" Andrew exclaimed when they had secured peace for themselves at last. "I'll never forget that look on Con's face as long as I live."

They were silent for a moment; then, turning to her, he asked: "You did enjoy your Christmas?"

She replied oddly: "I enjoyed seeing you play with Baby Boland."

He glanced at her.

"Why?"

She did not look at him. "I've been trying to tell you all day. Oh, can't you guess, darling? I don't think you're such a smart physician after all."

13

SPRING once more . . . And early summer . . . The garden at Vale View was a patch of tender colours which the miners often stopped to admire on their way back from their shift. Chiefly these colours came from flowering shrubs which Christine had planted the previous autumn, for now Andrew would allow her to do no heavy work at all.

"You've *made* the place!" he told her, with authority. "Now *sit* in it."

Her favourite seat was at the end of the little glen where, beside a tiny watersplash, she could hear the soothing converse of the stream. An overhanging willow offered protection from the rows of houses above. The difficulty with the rest of the garden of Vale View was that they had only to sit outside the porch for all the front windows of the Rows to be tenanted and the murmur to go round: "Eh! There's nice! Come an' 'ave a look, Fan-ee! Doctor and his missus are havin' bit of sun, like!" Once indeed, in their early days, when Andrew slipped his arm round Christine's waist as they stretched by the bank of the stream, he had seen the gleam of focussed glass from old Glyn Joseph's parlour. "Damn it!" Andrew had realized hotly. "The old dog—he's got his telescope on us!"

But beneath the willow they were completely screened and here Andrew defined his policy.

"You see, Chris,"—fidgeting with his thermometer; it had just occurred to him in a passion of precaution to take her temperature,—"we've got to keep calm. It's not as if we were—oh! well—*ordinary* people. After all you're a doctor's wife and I'm—I'm a doctor. I've seen this happen hundreds, at least scores of times before. It's a very *ordinary affair*. A phenomenon of nature, survival of the race, all that sort of thing, see! Now don't misunderstand me, darling, it's *wonderful* for us, of course. The fact is I'd begun to ask myself if you weren't too slight, too much of a kid ever to—oh, well, I'm *delighted*. But we're not going to get sentimental. Slushy, I mean. No, no! Let's leave that sort of thing to Mr. and Mrs. Smith. It would be rather idiotic, wouldn't it, for me, a doctor, to start—oh, say to start mooning over those little things you're knitting or crocheting, or whatever it is? No! I just look at them and grunt: 'Hope they'll be warm enough!' And all this junk about what colour of eyes she—er—it will have, and what sort of rosy future we'll give her— that's right off the map!" He paused, frowning; then gradually a reflective smile broke over his face. "I say, though, Chris! I wonder if it *will* be a girl!"

She laughed till the tears ran down her cheeks. She laughed so hard that he sat up, concerned.

"Now stop it, Chris! You'll—you might bring on something."

"Oh, my dear," she wiped her eyes. "As a sentimental idealist I adore you. As a hard-boiled cynic—well! I wouldn't have you in the house!"

He did not quite know what she meant. But he knew he was being scientific and restrained. In the afternoons when he felt she ought to have some exercise he took her for walks in the Public Park, climbing to the uplands being severely forbidden. In the Park they strolled about, listened to the band, watched the miners' children who came to picnic there with bottles of liquorice water and sherbet suckers.

Early one May morning as they lay in bed he became aware, through his light sleep, of a faint movement. He awoke, again conscious of that gentle thrusting, the first movement of the child within Christine. He held himself rigid, scarcely daring to believe, suffocated by a rush of feeling, of ecstasy. Oh, hell! he thought a moment later, perhaps I'm just a Smith after all. I suppose that's why they make the rule a medico can't attend his own wife.

The following week he felt it time to speak to Doctor Llewellyn who, from the outset, they had both decided must undertake the case. Llewellyn, when Andrew rang him, was pleased and flattered. He came down at once, made a preliminary examination, then chatted to Andrew in the sitting-room:—

"I'm glad to help you, Manson—" accepting a cigarette. "I always felt you didn't like me enough to ask me to do this for you. Believe me, I'll do my best. By the way, it's pretty stifling in Aberalaw at present. Don't you think your little missus ought to have a change of air while she can?"

"What's happening to me?" Andrew asked himself when Llewellyn had gone. "I like that man! He was decent, damned decent. He's got sympathy and tact. He's a wizard at his work. And twelve months ago I was trying to cut his throat. I'm just a stiff, jealous, clumsy Highland stot!"

Christine did not wish to go away, but he was gently insistent.

"I know you don't want to leave me, Chris! But it's for the best. We've got to think of—oh! everything. Would you rather have the seaside? Or maybe you'd like to go up North to your aunt. Dash it all, I can afford to send you, Chris. We're pretty well off now!"

They had paid off the Glen Endowment and the last of the furniture instalments and now they had nearly one hundred pounds saved in the bank. But she was not thinking of this when, pressing his hand, she answered steadily:—

"Yes! We're pretty well off, Andrew."

Since she must go, she decided to visit her aunt in Bridlington and a week later he saw her off at the Upper Station with a long hug and a basket of fruit to sustain her on the journey.

He missed her more than he could have believed; their comradeship had become such a part of his life. Their talks, discussions, squabbles, their silences together, the way in which he would call to her whenever he entered the house and wait, his ear cocked, for her cheery answer—he came to see how much these meant to him. Without her, their bedroom became a strange room in a hotel. His meals, conscientiously served by Jenny according to the programme written out by Christine, were arid snatches behind a propped-up book.

Wandering round the garden she had made, he was struck, suddenly, by the dilapidated condition of the bridge. It offended him, seemed an insult to his absent Christine. He had several times spoken to the Committee about this, telling them the bridge was falling to pieces, but they were always hard to move when it came to repairing the assistants' houses. Now, however, in an access of sentiment, he rang up the office and pressed the point strenuously. Owen had gone away upon a few days' leave, but the clerk assured Andrew that the matter had already been passed by the Committee and referred to Richards the builder. It was only because Richards was busy with another contract that the work had not been put in hand.

In the evenings he betook himself to Boland, twice to the Vaughans who made him remain for bridge, and once, greatly to his surprise, he found himself playing golf with Llewellyn. He wrote letters to Hampton and to Denny, who was journeying to Tampico as the surgeon of a tanker. His correspondence with Christine was a model of illuminating restraint. But he sought distraction, chiefly, in his work.

His clinical examinations at the anthracite sinkings were, by this time, well under way. He could not hasten them, since, apart from the demands of his own patients, his opportunity for examining the men came as they went to the mine-head baths at the end of the shift and it was impossible to keep them hanging about for any length of time when they wanted to get home for their dinners. He got through, on an average, two examinations a day;

yet already the results were adding further to his excitement. He saw, without jumping to any immediate conclusion, that the incidence of pulmonary trouble amongst the anthracite workers was positively in excess of that existing in the other underground workers in the coal mines.

Though he distrusted textbooks, in self-defence, since he had no wish to find afterwards that he had merely put his feet in footprints made by others, he went through the literature on the subject. Its paucity astounded him. Few investigators seemed to have concerned themselves greatly with the pulmonary occupational diseases. Zenker had introduced a high-sounding term, "pneumonokoniosis," embracing three forms of fibrosis of the lung due to dust inhalation. Anthracosis, of course, the black infiltration of the lungs met with in coal miners, had long been known and was held by Goldman in Germany and Trotter in England to be harmless. There were a few treatises on the prevalence of lung trouble in makers of millstones, particularly the French millstones, and in knife and axe grinders—"grinder's rot"—and stonecutters. There was evidence, mostly conflicting, from South Africa upon that red rag of Rand labour troubles, gold-miners' phthisis, which was undoubtedly due to dust inhalation. It was recorded also that workers in flax and in cotton, and grain shovellers, were subject to chronic changes in the lungs. But beyond that, nothing!

Andrew drew back from his reading with excitement in his eyes. He felt himself upon the track of something definitely unexplored. He thought of the vast numbers of underground workers in the great anthracite mines, the looseness of the legislation upon the disabilities from which they suffered, the enormous social importance of this line of investigation. What a chance, what a wonderful chance! A cold sweat broke over him at the sudden thought that someone might forestall him. But he thrust this from him. Striding up and down the sitting-room before the dead fire long after midnight, he suddenly seized Christine's photograph from the mantelshelf.

"Chris! I really believe I'm going to *do* something!"

In the card-index he bought for the purpose he carefully began to classify the results of his examinations. Though he never considered this, his clinical skill was now quite brilliant. There, in the changing room, the men stood before him, stripped to the waist, and with his fingers, his stethoscope, he plumbed uncannily the hidden pathology of those living lungs: a fibroid spot here, the next an emphysema, then a chronic bronchitis—deprecatingly admitted as "a bit of a cough." Carefully he localized the lesions upon the diagrams printed on the back of every card.

At the same time he took sputum samples from each man and, working till two and three in the morning at Denny's microscope, tabulated his findings on the cards. He found that most of these samples of muco-pus—locally described by the men as "white-spit"—contained bright angular particles of silica. He was amazed at the number of alveolar cells present, at the frequency with which he came upon the tubercule bacillus. But it was the presence, almost constant, of crystalline silicon, in the alveolar cells, the phagocytes, everywhere, which riveted his attention. He could not escape the thrilling idea that the changes in the lungs, perhaps even the coincident infections, were fundamentally dependent on this factor.

This was the extent of his advance when Christine returned at the end of June and flung her arms round his neck.

"It's so good to be back. Yes, I enjoyed myself; but oh! I don't know—and you look pale, darling! I don't believe Jenny's been feeding you!"

Her holiday had done her good, she was well and her cheeks had a fine bloom upon them. But she was concerned about him, his lack of appetite, his perpetual fumbling for a cigarette.

She asked him seriously:—

"How long is this special work going to take?"

"I don't know." It was the day after her return, a wet day, and he was unexpectedly moody. "It might take a year, it might take five."

"Well, listen to me. I'm not reforming you, one in the family is enough; but don't you think, since it's going on so long as that, you'll have to work systematically, keep regular hours, not stay up late and kill yourself?"

"There's nothing the matter with me."

But in some things she had a peculiar insistence. She got Jenny to scrub out the floor of the Lab., brought in an armchair and a rug. It was a room cool on these hot nights and the pine boards had a sweet resinous smell which mingled with the pungent ethereal scent of the reagents he used. Here she would sit, sewing and knitting, while he worked at the table. Bent over the microscope, he quite forgot about her, but she was there; and at eleven o'clock every night she got up.

"Time for bed!"

"Oh, I say!"—blinking at her nearsightedly over the eyepiece. "You go up, Chris! I'll follow you in a minute."

"Andrew Manson, if you think I'm going up to bed alone, *in my condition*—"

This last phrase had become a comic byword in the household. They both used it, indiscriminately, facetiously, as a clincher to all their arguments. He could not resist it. With a laugh he would rise, stretch himself, swing round his lenses, put the slides away.

Towards the end of July a sharp outbreak of chicken pox made him busy in the practice, and on the third of August he had an especially heavy list which kept him out from morning surgery until well after three o'clock. As he came up the road, tired, ready for that combination of lunch and tea which would be his meal, he saw Doctor Llewellyn's car at the gate of Vale View.

The implication of that static object caused him to start suddenly and to hasten, his heart beating rapidly with anticipation, towards his house. He ran up the porch steps, threw open the front door and there, in the hall, he found Llewellyn.

Gazing at the other man with nervous eagerness he stammered: "Hello, Llewellyn. I—I didn't expect to see you here so soon."

"No," Llewellyn answered.

Andrew smiled. "Well?" In his excitement he could find no better words, but the question in his bright face was plain enough.

Llewellyn did not smile. After the faintest pause he said: "Come in here a minute, my dear chap." And he drew Andrew into the sitting-room. "We've been trying to find you, on your rounds, all morning."

Llewellyn's manner, his hesitation, the strange sympathy in his voice, shot a wave of coldness over Andrew.

He faltered: "Is anything wrong?"

Llewellyn looked through the window, his glance travelling towards the bridge, as if searching for the best, the kindest explanation. Andrew could bear it no longer. He could scarcely breathe, his breast was filled with a stifling agony of suspense.

"Manson," Llewellyn said gently, "this morning, as your wife was going over the bridge—one of the rotten planks gave way. *She's* all right now, quite all right; but I'm afraid—"

He understood even before Llewellyn finished. A great pulse of anguish beat within him.

"You might like to know," Llewellyn went on, in a tone of quiet compassion, "that we did everything. I came at once, brought Matron from the hospital, we've been here all day—"

There was a bar of silence. A sob broke in Andrew's throat, another, then another. He covered his eyes with his hand.

"Please, my dear fellow—" Llewellyn entreated—"who could help an accident like that? I beg of you—go up and console your wife."

His head lowered, holding to the banister, Andrew went upstairs. Outside the door of the bedroom he paused, scarcely breathing; then, stumblingly, he went in.

14

By the year 1927 Doctor Manson of Aberalaw had a somewhat unusual reputation. His practice was not prodigious—numerically his list had not greatly increased since those first nervous days of his arrival in the town. But everyone upon that list had a convincing belief in him. He used few drugs—indeed, he had the incredible habit of advising his patients against medicine —but when he did use them he prescribed in shattering style. It was no uncommon sight to see Gadge drooping across the waiting-room with a prescription in his hand.

"What's all this, Doctor Manson! *Sixty* grain doses of KBr. for Evan Jones! And the Pharmacopœia says *five*."

"So does Aunt Kate's dream-book! Go ahead with sixty, Gadge. You know you'd really enjoy knocking off Evan Jones."

But Evan Jones, epileptic, was not knocked off. Instead he was seen, a week later, his fits lessened, taking walks in the Public Park.

The Committee ought to have cherished Doctor Manson tenderly, because his drug bill—despite explosive incidents—was less than half that of any other assistant. But alas! Manson cost the Committee three times as much in other directions, and often there was war because of it. He used vaccines and sera for instance, ruinous things which, as Ed Chenkin heatedly declared, none of them had ever heard of. When Owen, defending, instanced that winter month when Manson, using Bordet and Gengou vaccine, had arrested a raging epidemic of whooping cough in his district when all over the rest of the town children were going down of it, Ed Chenkin countered: "How do we know this newfangled thing did it? Why! When I tackled 'im myself, he said nobody could be *sure!*"

While Manson had many loyal friends, he also had enemies. There were those on the Committee who had never completely forgiven him for his outburst, those agonized words hurled at them, over that matter of the bridge, as they sat in full session three years before. They sympathized, of course, with Mrs. Manson and himself in their bereavement, but they could not hold themselves responsible. The Committee never did things in a hurry; Owen was then on holiday, and Len Richards, who had been given the job, was busy at the time with the new houses in Powis Street. It was preposterous to blame them.

As time went on Andrew had many heartburnings with the Committee, for he had a stubborn desire for his own way which the Committee did not like. In addition there was a certain clerical bias against him. Though his wife went to church, he was never seen there,—Doctor Oxborrow had been the first to point this out,—and he was reported to have laughed at the doctrine of total immersion. He had, moreover, a deadly enemy amongst "the chapel" folk—no less a person than the Reverend Edwal Parry, pastor of Sinai.

In the spring of 1926 the good Edwal, newly married, had sidled, late, into Manson's surgery with an air thoroughly Christian, yet ingratiatingly man of the world.

"How are you, Doctor Manson! I just happened to be passing. As a rule I attend with Doctor Oxborrow, he's one of my flock you know, and he's handy at the East Surgery also. But you're a very up-to-date doctor by all accounts and purposes. You're in the way of knowin' everything that's new. And I'd be glad—mind you I'll pay you a nice little fee too—if you could advise me." Edwal masked a faint priestly blush by show of worldly candour. "You see the wife and I don't want any children for a while yet anyhow, my stipend bein' what it is, like . . ."

Manson considered the minister of Sinai in a cold distaste. He said carefully:—

"Don't you realize there are people with a quarter of your stipend who would give their right hand to have children? What did you get married for?" His anger rose to a sudden white heat. "Get out—quick—you—you dirty little man of God!"

With a queer twist to his face Parry had slunk out. Perhaps Andrew had spoken too violently. But then Christine, since that fatal stumble, would never have children, and they both desired them with all their hearts.

Walking home from a call on this, the fifteenth of May, 1927, Andrew was inclined to ask himself why he and Christine had remained in Aberalaw since the death of their child. The answer was plain enough: his work on dust inhalation. It had absorbed him, fascinated him, bound him to the mines.

As he reviewed what he had done, considering the difficulties he had been obliged to face, he wondered that he had not taken longer to complete his findings. Those first examinations he had made—how far removed they seemed in time—yes, and in technique.

After he had made a complete clinical survey of the pulmonary conditions of all the workmen in the district and tabulated his findings, he had plain evidence of the marked preponderance of lung diseases amongst the anthracite workers. For example, he found that ninety per cent. of his cases of fibrosed lung came from the anthracite mines. He found also that the death rate from lung troubles amongst the older anthracite miners was nearly three times that of miners employed in all coal mines. He drew up a series of tables indicating the ratio-incidence of pulmonary disease, amongst the various grades of anthracite workmen.

Next, he set out to show that the silica dust he had found in his examinations of sputum was actually present in the anthracite headings. Not only did he demonstrate this conclusively, but, by exposing glass slides smeared with Canada balsam for varying periods in different parts of the mine, he obtained figures of the varying dust concentrations, figures which rose sharply during blasting and drilling.

He now had a series of exciting equations correlating excessive atmosphere concentrations of silica dust with excessive incidence of pulmonary disease. But this was not enough. He had actually to *prove* that the dust was harmful, that it was destructive to lung tissue and not merely an innocuous accessory after the fact. It was necessary for him to conduct a series of pathological experiments upon guinea pigs, to study the action of the silica dust upon their lungs.

Here, though his excitement rose, his real troubles began. He already had the spare room, the Lab. It was easy to procure a few guinea pigs. And the equipment required for his experiments was simple. But though his ingenuity was considerable he was not, and never would be, a pathologist. Awareness of this fact made him angry, more resolved than ever. He swore at a system which compelled him to work alone; and pressed Christine to his service, teaching her to cut and prepare sections, the mechanics of the trade which, in no time at all, she did better than he.

Next he constructed, very simply, a dust chamber in which for certain hours of the day the animals were exposed to concentrations of the dust, others being unexposed—the controls. It was exasperating work, demanding more patience than he possessed. Twice his small electric fan broke down. At a critical stage of the experiment he bungled his system of controls and was forced to begin all over again. But, in spite of mistakes and delays, he got his specimens, proving, in progressive stages, the deterioration of the lung and induction of fibrosis from the dust.

He drew a long breath of satisfaction, stopped scolding Christine and, for a few days, was fit to live with. Then another idea struck him and he was off again.

All his investigations had been conducted on the supposition that the damage to the lung was produced in response to mechanical destruction by the hard sharp silicate crystals inhaled. But now, suddenly, he asked himself if there was not some chemical action beyond the mere physical irritation of the particles. He was not a chemist but he was, by this time, too deeply immersed to allow himself to be defeated. He devised a fresh series of experiments.

He procured colloidal silica and injected it under the skin of one of his animals. The result was an abscess. Similar abscesses could, he found, be induced by the injection of aqueous solutions of amorphous silica, which was, physically, a nonirritant; while, in triumphant conclusion, he found that the injection of a mechanically irritating substance, such as particles of carbon, produced no abscess at all. The silica dust *was* chemically active.

He was now almost out of his mind with excitement and delight. He had done even more than he had set out to do. Feverishly he collected his data, drew up in compact form the results of his three years' work. He had decided, months ago, not only to publish his investigation but to send it in as his thesis for the degree of M.D. When the typescript came back from Cardiff, neatly bound in a pale blue folder, he read it exultantly, went out with Christine to post it, then slumped into a backwash of despair.

He felt worn-out and inert. He became aware, more vividly than ever, that he was no laboratory worker, that the best, the most valuable part of his work was that first phase of clinical research. He recollected, with a pang of compunction, how often he had raged at poor Christine. For days he was dispirited and listless. And yet, through it all, there were shining moments when he knew he had accomplished something after all.

15

THAT May afternoon, when Andrew reached home, his mood of preoccupation, this oddly negative phase which had persisted since the dispatch of his thesis, caused him to miss the look of distress upon Christine's face. He greeted her absent-mindedly, went upstairs to wash, then came down to tea.

When he had finished, however, and lit a cigarette, he suddenly observed her expression. He asked, as he reached out for the evening paper:—

"Why? What's the matter?"

She appeared to examine her teaspoon for a moment.

"We had some visitors to-day—or rather I had—when you were out this afternoon."

"Oh? Who were they?"

"A deputation from the Committee, five of them, including Ed Chenkin, and escorted by Parry—you know, the Sinai minister—and a man Davies."

An odd silence fell. He took a long pull at his cigarette, lowered the paper to gaze at her.

"What did they want?"

She met his scrutiny for the first time, fully revealing the vexation and anxiety in her eyes. She spoke hurriedly.

"They came about four o'clock—asked for you. I told them you were out. Then Parry said it didn't matter, they wanted to come in. Of course I was quite taken aback. I didn't know whether they wanted to wait for you, or what. Then Ed Chenkin said it was the Committee's house, that they represented the Committee and that in the name of the Committee they could and would come in." She paused, drew a quick breath. "I didn't budge an inch. I was angry—upset. But I managed to ask them *why* they wished to come in. Parry took it up then. He said it had come to his ears, and the ears of the Committee, in fact it was all over the town, that you were performing experiments on animals—vivisection, he had the cheek to call it. And because of that they had come to look at your workroom and brought Mr. Davies, the Prevention of Cruelty to Animals man, along with them."

Andrew had not moved, nor had his eyes left her face.

"Go on, dear," he said quietly.

"Well, I tried to stop them, but it was no use. They just pushed past, the seven of them, through the hall and into the Lab. Whenever they saw the guinea pigs Parry let out a howl—'Oh, the poor dumb creatures!' And Chenkin pointed to the stain on the boards—where I dropped the fuscine bottle, you remember, dear—and shouted out: ''Ave a look at that, *blood!*' They prowled round everything, went through our beautiful sections, the microtome, everything. Then Parry said, 'I'm not leavin' those poor suffering creatures to be tortured any more. I'd rather have them put out of their pain than that.' He took the bag Davies had with him and shoved them all into it. I tried to tell him there was no question of suffering, or vivisection, or any such rubbish. And in any case that those five guinea pigs were not going to be used for experiments, that we were going to give them to the Boland children, and to little Agnes Evans, for pets. But they simply wouldn't listen to me. And then they—they went away."

There was a silence. Andrew's face was now deeply flushed. He sat up.

"I never heard such rank impertinence in all my life. It—it's damnable you had to put up with it, Chris! But I'll make them pay for it!"

He reflected a minute, then started towards the hall to use the telephone. But just as he reached it the instrument rang. He snatched it from the hook.

"Hullo!" he said angrily, then his voice altered slightly. Owen was on the other end of the line. "Yes, it's Manson speaking. Look here, Owen—"

"I know, I know, Doctor," Owen interrupted Andrew quickly. "I've been trying to get in touch with you all afternoon. Now listen. No, no, don't interrupt me. We got to keep our heads over this. We're up against a nasty bit o' business, Doctor. Don't say any more on the telephone. I'm comin' down to see you now."

Andrew went back to Christine.

"What does he mean?" he fumed, when he had told her of the conversation. "Anyone would think we were to blame."

They waited for Owen's arrival, Andrew striding up and down in a passion of impatience and indignation, Chris sitting at her sewing with disquieted eyes.

Owen came. But there was nothing reassuring in his face.

Before Andrew could speak he said:—

"Doctor, did you have a licence?"

"A what?" Andrew stared at him. "What kind of licence?"

Owen's face now seemed more troubled. "You've got to have a licence from the Home Office for experimental work on animals. You knew that, didn't you?"

"But damn it all!" Manson protested hotly, "I'm not a pathologist; I never will be. And I'm not running a laboratory. I only wanted to do a few simple experiments to tie up with my clinical work. We didn't have more than a dozen animals altogether—did we, Chris?"

Owen's eyes were averted. "You ought to have had that licence, Doctor. There's a section of the Committee are tryin' to play you up pretty bad over this!" He went on quickly. "You see, Doctor, a chap like you, that's doin' pioneer work, who's honest enough to speak his mind, he's bound to —well, anyhow, it's only right you should know there's a section here that's dyin' to put a knife in you. But there now! It'll be all right. There'll be a regular old shindy with the Committee; you'll have to come before them, like. But you've had your troubles with them before. You'll come out on top again."

Andrew stormed. "I'll bring a counteraction. I'll sue them for—for illegal entry. No, damn it, I'll sue them for stealing my guinea pigs. I want them back, anyway."

A pale amusement twitched Owen's face. "You can't have them back, Doctor. Reverend Parry and Ed Chenkin they allowed they'd have to put them out their misery. In the cause of 'umanity they drowned them with their own hands."

Sorrowfully, Owen went away. And the following evening Andrew received a summons to appear before the Committee in one week's time.

Meanwhile the case had flared into prominence like a petrol blaze. Nothing so exciting, so scandalous, so savouring of the black arts had startled Aberalaw since Trevor Day, the solicitor, was suspected of killing his wife with arsenic. Sides were taken, violent factions formed. From his rostrum at Sinai, Edwal Parry thundered the punishment meted out, in this life and the hereafter, to those who tortured animals and little children. At the other end of the town, Reverend David Walpole, chubby minister of the Established Church, to whom Parry was as pig to good Mohammedan, bleated of progress and the feud between the Liberal Church of God and Science. Even the women were aroused to action. Miss Myfanwy Bensusan, local president of the Welsh Ladies' Endeavour League, spoke to a crowded meeting in the Temperance Hall. It is true that Andrew had once offended Myfanwy by failing to take the chair at the W.L.E. Annual Rally. But her motives, otherwise, were unquestionably pure. After the meeting and on subsequent evenings, young lady members of the League—normally active in the streets only upon flag days—could be seen distributing gruesome antivivisection folders, each bearing an illustration of a partially disembowelled dog.

On Wednesday night Con Boland rang up with a joyous tale.

"How are ye, Manson, boy? Keepin' the old chin up? Good enough! I was thinking ye might be interested—our Mary was comin' home this evening from Larkins' when one of them simperin' flag sellers stopped her with a pamphlet—these cruelty falderals they've been shovin' around against ye. Do ye know—ha! ha!— Do ye know what the bold Mary did? She up with the pamphlet and tore it into bits. Then she up with her hand, boxed the flag-sellin' female's ears, tugged the hat off her head, and said—ha! ha!—what do you think our Mary said? 'If it's cruelty you're after,' says she—ha! ha!—'If it's cruelty you're after—*I'll give ye it!*' "

Physical combat was offered by others as loyal as Mary.

Though Andrew's district was solidly behind him, round the East Surgery there was a block of contrary opinion. Fights broke out in the pubs between Andrew's supporters and his enemies. Frank Davis came to the surgery on Thursday night, slightly battered, to inform Andrew that he had "knocked the block off two of Oxborrow's patients for saying as 'ow our man was a bloody butcher!"

Thereafter Doctor Oxborrow passed Andrew with a bouncing tread and eyes fixed a long way off. He was known to be working openly with the Reverend Parry against his undesirable colleague. Urquhart came back from the Masonic Club with the meaty Christian's comments, of which perhaps the choicest was: "Why should any doctor have to murder God's living creatures?"

Urquhart had few remarks to make himself. But once, squinting across at Andrew's constrained, tense face, he declared:—

"Dammit to hell! When I was your age I'd have enjoyed a scrap like this, too. But now—oh, dammit! I suppose I'm getting old."

Andrew could not help thinking that Urquhart misjudged him. He was far from enjoying the "scrap." He felt tired, irritable, worried. He asked himself fretfully if he was to spend all his life running his head into stone walls. Yet, although his vitality was low, he had a desperate desire to justify himself, to be openly vindicated before the squabbling town.

The week passed at last, and on Saturday afternoon the Committee assembled for what was specified in the agenda as "the disciplinary examination" of Doctor Manson. There was not a vacant place in the Committee room, and outside in the Square groups of people were hanging about as

Andrew entered the offices and walked up the narrow stairs. He felt his heart bumping rapidly. He had told himself he must be calm and steeled. Instead, as he took his seat on that same chair which as a candidate he had occupied five years before, he was stiff, dry-lipped, nervous.

The proceedings began—not with prayer, as might have been expected from the sanctimony with which the opposition had conducted their campaign— but with a fiery speech from Ed Chenkin.

"I'm going to put the full facts of this case," said Chenkin, jumping up, "before my fellow members of this Committee." He proceeded, in a loud, illiterate speech to enumerate the complaints: Doctor Manson had no right to do this work. It was work done in the Committee's time, work done when he was being paid for doing the *Committee's* work, and work done on the Committee's property. Also it was vivisection, or near neighbour to it. And it was all done without the necessary permit, a very serious offence in the eye of the law!

Here Owen intervened swiftly:—

"As regards that last point, I must advise the Committee that if they report Doctor Manson's failure to secure this permit any subsequent action taken would involve the Medical Aid Society as a whole."

"What th'ell d'you mean?" Chenkin asked.

"As he is our assistant," Owen held, "we are legally responsible for Doctor Manson!"

There was a murmur of assent at this, and cries of: "Owen's right! We don't want any trouble on the Society. Keep it amongst ourselves."

"Never mind the bloody permit, then," bawled Chenkin, still upon his feet. "There's enough in the other charges to hang anybody."

"Hear! Hear!" called out someone at the back. "What about all them times he sneaked off to Cardiff on his motor bike—that summer three years back?"

"He don't give medicine," came the voice of Len Richards. "You can wait an hour outside his surgery and not get your bottle filled."

"Order! Order!" Chenkin shouted. When he had stilled them he proceeded to his final peroration. "All these complaints are bad enough! They show that Doctor Manson 'as never been a satisfactory servant to the Medical Aid. Besides which I might add that he don't give proper certificates to the men. But we got to keep our minds on the main item. Here we have an assistant that the whole town's up against for what ought by rights to be a police case, a man who has turned our property into a slaughter 'ouse —I swear by the Almighty, fellow members, I saw the blood on the floor with my own eyes—a man who's nothing but an experimenter and a crank. I ask you, fellow members, if you're goin' to stand it. No! say I. No! say you. Fellow members, I know you are with me one and all, when I say that here and now we demand Doctor Manson's resignation."

Chenkin glanced round at his friends and sat down amidst loud applause.

"Perhaps you'll allow Doctor Manson to state his case," Owen said palely, and turned to Andrew.

There was a silence. Andrew sat still for a moment. The situation was worse, even, than he had imagined. Put not your trust in Committees, he thought bitterly. Were these the same men who had smiled at him approvingly when they gave him the appointment? His heart burned. He would not, simply would not resign. He got to his feet. He was no speaker and he knew that he was no speaker. But he was angry now, his nervousness lost in a swelling indignation at the ignorance, the intolerant stupidity of Chenkin's accusation, and the acclamation with which the others had received it.

He began:—

"No one seems to have said anything about the animals Ed Chenkin drowned. That was cruelty if you like—useless cruelty. What I've been doing wasn't that! Why do you men take white mice and canaries down the mine? To test for black damp—you all know that. And when these mice get finished by a whiff of gas—do you call that cruelty? No you don't. You realize that these animals have been used to save men's lives, perhaps your *own* lives.

"That's what I've been trying to do for you! I've been working on these lung diseases that you get from the dust in the mine headings. You all know that you get chest trouble and that when you *do* get it you don't get compensation. For these last three years I've spent nearly every minute of my spare time on this inhalation problem. I've found out something which might improve your working conditions, give you a fairer deal, keep you in health —better than that stinking bottle of medicine Len Richards was talking about would have done! What if I did use a dozen guinea pigs? Don't you think it was worth it?

"You don't believe me, perhaps. You're prejudiced enough to think I would lie to you. Maybe you still think I've been wasting my time, *your* time as you call it, in a lot of cranky experiments." He was so worked up he forgot his stern resolution not to be dramatic. Diving into his breast pocket he produced the letter he had received earlier in the week. "But this'll show you what other people think of it, people who are qualified to judge."

He walked across to Owen and handed him the letter. It was an intimation from the Clerk of the Senate at St. Andrews that, for his thesis on Dust Inhalation, he had been awarded his M.D.

Owen read the crested, blue-typed letter with a sudden brightening of his face. Thereafter it was passed slowly from hand to hand.

It annoyed Andrew to observe the effect created by the Senate's communication. Although he was so desperately anxious to prove his case, he almost regretted his impulse in producing it. If they could not take his word without some sort of official bolstering they must be heavily prejudiced against him. Letter or no letter, he felt moodily, they were bent on making an example of him.

He was relieved when, after a few further remarks, Owen said:—

"Perhaps you'll leave us now, Doctor, please."

Waiting outside, while they voted on his case, he kicked his heels, simmering with exasperation. It was a wonderful ideal, this group of working men controlling the medical services of the community for the benefit of their fellow workers. But it was only an ideal. They were too biased, too unintelligent, ever to administer such a scheme progressively. It was perpetual labour for Owen to drag them along the road with him. And he had the conviction that, on this occasion, even Owen's good will would not save him.

But the secretary, when Andrew went in again, was smiling, briskly rubbing his hands. Others on the Committee were regarding him more favourably, at least without hostility.

And Owen immediately stood up and said:—

"I'm glad to tell you, Doctor Manson—I may even say that personally I'm delighted to tell you—that the Committee have decided by a majority to ask you to remain."

He had won, he had carried them after all. But the knowledge, after one swift throb of satisfaction, gave him no elation. There was a pause. They obviously expected him to express his relief, his gratitude. But he could not. He felt tired of the whole distorted business, of the Committee, Aberalaw, medicine, silica dust, guinea pigs and himself.

At last he said:—

"Thank you, Mr. Owen. I'm glad, after all I've tried to do here, that the Committee don't wish me to go. But, I'm sorry, I can't wait on in Aberalaw any longer. I give the Committee a month's notice from to-day." He spoke without feeling; then he spun round and walked out of the room.

There was a dead silence. Ed Chenkin was the quickest to recover himself.

"Good riddance," he called half-heartedly after Manson.

Then Owen startled them all with the first burst of anger he had ever shown in that Committee room.

"Shut your senseless mouth, Ed Chenkin." He flung down his ruler with intimidating violence. "We have lost the best man we ever had."

16

ANDREW woke up in the middle of that night groaning:—

"Am I a fool, Chris? Chucking away our living—a sound job? After all, I *was* getting a few private patients lately. And Llewellyn has been pretty decent. Did I tell you? He half-promised to let me consult at the hospital. And the Committee,—they aren't a bad lot when you cut out the Chenkin crowd, —I believe in time when Llewellyn retired they might have made me head doctor in his place."

She comforted him, quiet, reasonable, lying beside him in the darkness.

"You don't really want us to stay in a Welsh mining practice all our lives, my dear. We've been happy here, but it's time for us to move on."

"But listen, Chris," he worried, "we haven't enough to buy a practice yet. We ought to have collected some more money before we hoofed it."

She answered sleepily: "What has money got to do with it? Besides we're going to spend all we've got—almost—on a real holiday. Do you realize you've hardly been away from these old mines for nearly four years?"

Her spirit infected him. Next morning the world seemed a gay and careless place. At breakfast, which he ate with new relish, he declared:—

"You're not a bad old girl, Chris. Instead of getting up on the platform and telling me you expect Big Things of me now, that it's time for me to go out and make my mark in the world, you just—"

She was not listening to him. Irrelevantly she protested:—

"Really, dear, I wish you wouldn't bunch the paper so! I thought it was only women did that. How do you expect me to read my gardening column?"

"Don't read it." On his way to the door he kissed her, smiling. "Think about me."

He felt adventurous, prepared to take his chance with life. Besides, the cautious side of him could not avoid glancing at the assets side of his balance sheet. He had his M.R.C.P., an honours M.D., and over three hundred pounds in the bank. With all this behind them surely they would not starve.

It was well that their intention stood firm. A revulsion of sentiment had swept upon the town. Now that he was going of his own free will, everybody wished him to remain.

The climax came a week after the meeting, when Owen unsuccessfully headed a deputation to Vale View to ask Andrew to reconsider his decision. Thereafter the feeling against Ed Chenkin swelled to the verge of violence. He was booed in the Rows. Twice he was played home from the mine by the penny whistle band, an ignominy usually reserved by the workmen for a blackleg.

In the face of all these local reverberations it was strange how lightly his thesis appeared to have shaken the outer world. It had gained him his M.D. It had been printed in the *Journal of Industrial Health* in England, and published as a brochure in the United States by the Association of American Hygiene. But beyond that, it earned him exactly three letters.

The first was from a firm in Brick Lane E.C. informing him that samples were being forwarded to him of their Pulmo-Syrup, the infallible lung specific for which they had hundreds of testimonials including several from prominent physicians. They hoped he would recommend Pulmo-Syrup amongst the miners in his practice. Pulmo-Syrup, they added, also cured rheumatism.

The second was from Professor Challis, an enthusiastic letter of congratulation and appreciation which ended by asking if Andrew could not call at the Institute in Cardiff sometime that week. In a P.S. Challis added: *Try and come Thursday*. But Andrew, in the hurry of these last few days, was unable to keep that appointment. Indeed, he mislaid the letter and for the time being forgot to answer it.

The third letter he did immediately answer, he was so genuinely thrilled to receive it. It was an unusual, stimulating communication which had crossed the Atlantic from Oregon. Andrew read and re-read the typewritten sheets, then took them in excitement to Christine.

"This is rather decent, Chris!—this American letter—it's from a fellow called Stillman, Richard Stillman of Oregon—you've probably never heard of him, but I have—it's full of the most exact appreciation of my Inhalation stuff. More, much more than Challis—damn it, I should have answered his letter! This chap has absolutely understood what I was after, in fact he quietly puts me right on one or two points. Apparently the active destructive ingredient in my silicon is serecite. I hadn't enough chemistry to get to that. But it's a marvellous letter, congratulatory; and from Stillman!"

"Yes?" She peeped inquiringly. "Is he some doctor out there?"

"No, that's the amazing thing. He's a physicist, really. But he runs a clinic for disorders of the lungs, near Portland, Oregon. Look, it's on the notepaper. Some of them don't recognize him yet, but he's as big a man as Sphalinger in his own way. I'll tell you about him when we've time."

He showed how much he thought of Stillman's letter by sitting down to answer it on the spot.

They were now overwhelmed by preparations for their holiday, by arrangements for storing their furniture in Cardiff—the most convenient centre—and by the doleful processes of leave-taking. Their departure from Blaenelly had been abrupt, a heroic cleavage. But here they suffered much lingering sentiment. They were entertained by the Vaughans, the Bolands, even by the Llewellyns. Andrew developed "farewell-dyspepsia," symptomatic of these parting banquets. When the actual day arrived Jenny, in tears, told them—to their consternation—that they were to be given a "platform send-off!"

At the last moment, on top of this unsettling information, Vaughan came hastening round.

"Sorry to harass you people again. But look here, Manson, what have you been doing to Challis? I've just had a letter from the old boy. Your paper has sent him quite gaga—and incidentally, at least so I understand, the Metalliferous Board as well. Anyway he's asked me to get in touch with you. He wants you to see him in London without fail; says it's extremely important."

Andrew answered a trifle peevishly.

"We're going on holiday, man. The first real holiday we've had for years. How *can* I see him?"

"Let's have your address then. He'll obviously want to write to you."

Andrew glanced uncertainly at Christine. They had meant to keep their destination a secret, so that they should be free from all worries, correspondence, interference. But he gave Vaughan the information.

Then they were hurrying to the station, engulfed by the crowd from the district who waited there, shaken by the hand, shouted at, patted on the back, embraced, and finally hustled into their compartment of the moving train. As they steamed off their friends, massed on the platform, began lustily to sing "Men of Harlech."

"My God!" Andrew said, trying out his numb fingers. "That was the last straw." But his eyes were glistening, and a minute later he added, "I wouldn't have had us miss it for anything, Chris. Aren't people *decent*? And to think that a month ago half the town was after my blood! You can't get away from the fact—life's damn funny." He gazed at her humorously as she sat beside him. "And this, Mrs. Manson, though you are now an old woman, is your second honeymoon!"

They reached Southampton that evening, took their berths in the cross-channel steamer. Next morning they saw the sun rise behind St. Malo, and an hour later Brittany received them.

The wheat was ripening, the cherry trees were heavy with fruit, goats strayed on the flowering pastures. It had been Christine's idea to come here, to get close to the real France—not its picture galleries or palaces, not historic ruins or monuments, nothing which the tourist's guidebook insisted that they should see.

They reached Val André. Their little hotel was within sound of the sea, within scent of the meadows. Their bedroom had plain scrubbed boards and their morning coffee came to them steaming in thick blue bowls. They lazed the whole day long.

"Oh, Lord!" Andrew kept repeating. "Isn't this wonderful, darling? I never, never never want to look a lobar pneumonia in the face again." They drank cider, ate *langoustes*, shrimps, pastries, and whiteheart cherries. In the evenings Andrew played billiards with the proprietor on the antique octagonal table. Sometimes he only lost by fifty in the hundred.

It was lovely, wonderful, exquisite—the adjectives were Andrew's—all but the cigarettes, he would add.

A whole blissful month slipped past. And then, more frequently, and with unceasing restlessness, Andrew began to finger the unopened letter, now stained by cherry juice and chocolate, which had remained in his jacket for the past fortnight.

"Go on," Christine urged, at last, one morning. "We've kept our word! Open it."

He slit up the envelope studiously, read the letter lying upon his back in the sunlight, sat up slowly, then read it again. In silence he passed it over to Christine.

The letter was from Professor Challis. It stated that, as the direct result of his researches into dust inhalation, the C.M.M.F.B.—Coal Mines and Metalliferous Fatigue Board—had decided to open up the whole question with a view to reporting to the Parliamentary Committee. A whole-time medical officer was, for this purpose, to be appointed by the Board. And the Board on the strength of his recent investigations unanimously and without hesitation offered the appointment to him.

When she had read it, she looked at him happily.

"Didn't I tell you something would turn up?" She smiled. "Isn't it splendid?"

He was throwing stones quickly, nervously at a lobster pot on the beach.

"It's clinical work," he reflected aloud. "Couldn't be anything else. They *know* I'm a clinician."

She observed him with a deepening smile.

"Of course, darling, you remember our bargain: Six weeks here as a minimum, doing nothing, lying still. You won't let this interrupt our holiday?"

"No, no!"—looking at his watch. "We'll finish our holiday, but—anyhow—" he jumped up and gaily pulled her to her feet—"it won't do us any harm to run down to the telegraph office. And I wonder—I wonder if they've got a timetable there."

BOOK III

1

THE Coal and Metalliferous Mines Fatigue Board—usually abbreviated to M.F.B.—was housed in a large impressive grey stone building on the Embankment, not far from Westminster Gardens, conveniently situated near the Board of Trade and the Mines Department,—both of which alternately forgot about, and fought fiercely for, a proprietary interest in the Board.

On the fourteenth of August, a fresh bright morning, in bustling health and immense spirits, Andrew ran up the steps of the building, the look in his eye that of a man about to conquer London.

"I'm the new Medical Officer," he told the commissionaire in the Office of Works uniform.

"Yes, sir, yes, sir," said the commissionaire, with a fatherly air. It was gratifying to Andrew that he seemed to be expected. "You'll want to see our Mr. Gill. Jones! Take our new doctor up to Mr. Gill's room."

The lift rose slowly, revealing green tiled corridors and many floors, on which the Office of Works uniform was again sedately visible. Then Andrew was ushered into a large, sunny room where he found himself shaking hands with Mr. Gill, who rose from his desk and put down his copy of the *Times* to welcome him.

"I'm a little late in getting in," Andrew declared with vigour. "Sorry! We just got back from France yesterday—but I'm absolutely ready to start."

"That's nice!" Gill was a jolly little man, in gold-rimmed glasses, a near-clerical collar, dark blue suit, dark blue tie held in place with a flat gold ring. He looked on Andrew with prim approval.

"Please sit down! Will you have a cup of tea, or a glass of hot milk? I usually have one about eleven. And yes—yes, it's nearly that now—"

"Oh, well—" said Andrew, hesitating; then, brightening: "Perhaps you can tell me about the work while we—"

Five minutes later the Office of Works uniform brought in a nice cup of tea and a glass of hot milk.

"I think you'll find that right, Mr. Gill. It 'as boiled, Mr. Gill."

"Thank you, Stevens." When Stevens had gone Gill turned to Andrew with a smile. "You'll find him a useful chap. He makes delicious hot buttered toast. It's rather awkward here—to get really first-class messengers. We're bits and pieces of all departments—Home Office, Mines Depart.,

Board of Trade—I myself," Gill coughed with mild pride, "am from the Admiralty."

While Andrew sipped his boiled milk and chafed for information about his job, Gill pleasantly discussed the weather, Brittany, the Civil Service pension scheme, and the efficacy of Pasteurization. Then, rising, he led Andrew to his room.

This also was a warmly carpeted, restful, sunny room with a superb view of the river. A large bluebottle was making drowsy nostalgic noises against the windowpane.

"I chose this for you," said Gill pleasantly. "Took a little bit of arrangement. There's an open coal fireplace, you'll see—nice for the winter. I—I hope you like it?"

"Why—it's a marvellous room, but—"

"Now I'll introduce you to your secretary, Miss Mason." Gill tapped, threw open a communicating door, revealing Miss Mason, a nice, elderly girl, neat and composed, seated at a small desk. Rising, Miss Mason put down her *Times.*

"Good morning, Miss Mason."

"Good morning, Mr. Gill."

"Miss Mason, this is Doctor Manson."

"Good morning, Doctor Manson."

Andrew's head reeled slightly under the impact of these salutations, but he collected himself, joined in the conversation.

Five minutes later, as Gill stole pleasantly away, he remarked to Andrew, encouragingly:—

"I'll send you along some files."

The files arrived, borne tenderly by Stevens. In addition to his talents as toastmaker and dairyman, Stevens was the best file-bearer in the building. Every hour he entered Andrew's office, with cradled documents which he placed lovingly upon the desk of the japanned tin marked IN, while his eye, searching eagerly, besought something to take away from the tin marked OUT. It quite broke Stevens' heart when the OUT tin was empty. In this lamentable contingency he slunk away, defeated.

Lost, bewildered, irritated, Andrew raced through the files—minutes of past meetings of the M.F.B., dull, stodgy, unimportant. Then he turned urgently to Miss Mason. But Miss Mason—who came, she explained, from the Home Office Frozen Meat Investigation Department—proved a restricted source of enlightenment. She told him that the hours were from ten o'clock till four. She told him of the office hockey team—"the ladies' eleven of course, Doctor Manson"—of which she was vice-captain. She asked him if he would care to have her copy of the *Times.* Her gaze entreated him to be calm.

But Andrew was not calm. Fresh from his holiday, longing to work, he began to weave a pattern on the Office of Works' carpet. He gazed chafingly at the brisk river scene where tugs fussed about and long lines of coal barges went spattering against the tide. Then he strode down to Gill.

"When do I start?"

Gill jumped at the abruptness of the question.

"My dear fellow, you quite startled me. I thought I'd given you enough files to last you for a month." He looked at his watch. "Come along—it's time we had lunch."

Over his steamed sole, Gill tactfully explained, while Andrew battled with a chump chop, that the next meeting of the Board did not, and could not, take place until September the eighteenth; that Professor Challis was in Norway, Doctor Maurice Gadsby in Scotland, Sir William Dewar, Chairman of the Board, in Germany, and his own immediate chief, Mr. Blades, at Frinton with his family.

Andrew went back to Christine that evening with his thoughts in a maze. Their furniture was still in storage and, so that they might have time to look round and find a proper home, they had taken for a month a small furnished flat in Earl's Court.

"Could you believe it, Chris! They're not even *ready* for me. I've got a whole month to drink milk in, and read the *Times*, and initial files—oh! and have long intimate hockey talks with old girl Mason."

"If you don't mind, you'll confine your talks to your own old girl. Oh, really, darling, it's lovely here—after Aberalaw. I had a little expedition this afternoon, down to Chelsea. I found out where Carlyle's house is, and the Tate Gallery. Oh! I planned such lovely things for us to do. You can take a penny steamboat up to Kew. Think of the Gardens, darling. And next month Kreisler at the Albert Hall. Oh, and we must see the Memorial, to find out why everyone laughs at it. And there's a play on from the New York Theatre Guild; and wouldn't it be lovely if I could meet you someday for lunch?" She reached out a small vibrant hand. He had rarely seen her so excited. "Darling! Let's go out and have a meal. There's a Russian restaurant along this street. It looks *good*. Then, if you're not too tired, we might—"

"Here!" he protested as she led him to the door. "I thought you were supposed to be the matter-of-fact member of this family. But believe me, Chris, after my first day's 'toil' I could do with a lively evening."

Next morning he read every file on his desk, initialled them, and was ranging about his room by eleven o'clock. But soon the cage became too small to hold him and he set out, with violence, to explore the building. It proved uninteresting as a morgue without bodies until, reaching the top storey, he suddenly found himself in a long room, half-fitted as a laboratory, where, seated on a box which had once held sulphur, was a young man in a long dirty white coat, disconsolately trimming his fingernails, while his cigarette made yellower the nicotine stain upon his upper lip.

"Hello!" Andrew said.

A moment's pause, then the other answered uninterestedly:—

"If you've lost your way, the lift is the third on the right."

Andrew propped himself against the test bench and picked a cigarette from his packet. He asked:—

"Don't you serve tea here?"

For the first time the young man raised his head, jet-black and glossily brushed, singularly at variance with the upturned collar of his soiled coat.

"Only to the white mice," he answered with interest. "The tea leaves are particularly nourishing for them."

Andrew laughed, perhaps because the jester was five years younger than himself. He explained:—

"My name's Manson."

"I feared as much. So you've come to join the forgotten men." A pause. "I'm Doctor Hope! At least I used to think I was Hope. Now I am definitely Hope deferred."

"What are you doing here?"

"God only knows—and Billy Buttons—that's Dewar! Some of the time I sit here and think. But most of the time I sit. Occasionally they send me chunks of decomposed miners and ask me the cause of the explosion."

"And do you tell them?" Andrew inquired politely.

"No," Hope said rudely. "I fart!"

They both felt better after that extreme vulgarity and went out to lunch together. Going out to lunch, Doctor Hope explained, was the sole function of the day which enabled him to cling to reason. Hope explained other things to Manson. He was a Backhouse Research Scholar from Cambridge, *via* Birmingham, which probably—he grinned—accounted for his frequent lapses of good taste. He had been loaned to the Metalliferous Board through the pestering application of Professor Dewar. He had nothing to do but sheer mechanics, a routine which any lab. attendant could have tackled. He implied that he was surely going mad through indolence and the inertia of the Board, which he now referred to tersely as Maniac's Delight. It was typical of most of the research work in the country: controlled by a quorum of eminent mugs who were too engrossed by their own particular theories and too busy squabbling amongst themselves to shove the waggon in any one definite direction. Hope was pulled this way and that, told what to do instead of being allowed to do what he wished, and so interrupted he was never six months on the same job.

He gave Andrew thumbnail sketches of the council of Maniac's Delight. Sir William Dewar, the doddering but indomitable nonagenarian Chairman, he alluded to as "Billy Buttons" because of Sir William's propensity for leaving certain essential fastenings unlatched. Old Billy Buttons was chairman of almost every scientific committee in England, Hope told Andrew. In addition he gave those riotously popular wireless talks: Science for the Children.

Then there was Professor Whinney, aptly known to his students as the Nag; Challis, who wasn't bad when he forgot to dramatize himself as Rabelais Pasteur Challis; and Doctor Maurice Gadsby.

"Do you know Gadsby?" Hope asked.

"I've met the gentleman." Andrew related his examination experience.

"That's our Maurice," said Hope bitterly. "And he's such a damned little thruster. He's into everything. He'll stick himself into a Royal Apothecary-ship one of these days. He's a clever little beast all right. But he's not inter-ested in research. He's only interested in himself." Hope laughed suddenly. "Robert Abbey has a good one about Gadsby. Gadsby wanted to get into the Rump-steak Club—that's one of those dining-out affairs that occur in London, and a pretty decent one, as it happens! Well, Abbey, who's an obliging pot, promised to do his best for Gadsby, though God knows why. Anyhow a week later Gadsby met Abbey. 'Am I in?' he asked. 'No,' Abbey said, 'You're not.' 'Good God,' blusters Gadsby. 'You don't mean I was blackballed.' 'Black-balled,' Abbey said. 'Listen, Gadsby! *Have you ever seen a plate of caviar?'* " Hope lay back and howled with laughter. A moment later he added: "Abbey happens to be on our Board as well. He's a white man. But he's got too much savvy to come often."

This was the first of many lunches which Andrew and Hope took together. Hope, despite his undergraduate humour and a natural tendency to flippancy, was well endowed with brains. His irreverence had a wholesome ring. Andrew felt that he might one day do something. Indeed, in his serious moments, Hope often exposed his eagerness to get back to the real work he had planned for himself, on the isolation of gastric enzymes.

Occasionally Gill came to lunch with them. Hope's phrase for Gill was characteristic: "a good little egg." Though veneered by his thirty years in the Civil Service—he had worked his way from boy clerk to principal—Gill was human underneath. In the office he functioned like a well oiled, easy-moving little machine. He arrived from Sunbury by the same train every morning, returned, unless he was "detained," by the same train every night. He had, in Sunbury, a wife and three daughters, and a small garden where he grew roses. He was superficially so true to type he might have stood as the perfect pattern of smug suburbia. Yet there existed, beneath, a real Gill who loved Yarmouth in winter and always spent his holiday there in December; who had a queer Bible, which he knew almost by heart, in a book named Hadji Baba; who—for fifteen years a fellow of the Society—was quite fatuously de-voted to the penguins in the zoo.

Upon one occasion Christine made a fourth at this table. Gill surpassed himself in upholding the civility of the service. Even Hope behaved with admirable gentility. He confided to Andrew that he was a less likely candi-date for the strait-jacket since meeting Mrs. Manson.

The days slipped past. While Andrew waited for the meeting of the Board, Christine and he discovered London. They took the steamboat trip to Rich-mond. They chanced upon a theatre named the Old Vic. They came to know the windy flutter of Hampstead Heath, the fascination of a coffee stall at midnight. They walked in the Row and rowed on the Serpentine. They solved the delusion of Soho. When they no longer had occasion to study the Under-ground maps before entrusting themselves to the Tube, they began to feel that they were Londoners.

2

THE afternoon of September the eighteenth brought the M.F.B. council together, and to Andrew, at last. Sitting beside Gill and Hope, conscious of the
latter's flippant glances upon him, Andrew watched the members roll in
to the long gilt-corniced Board room: Whinney, Doctor Lancelot Dodd-
Canterbury, Challis, Sir Robert Abbey, Gadsby, and finally Billy Buttons Dewar himself.

Before Dewar's entry Abbey and Challis had spoken to Andrew—Abbey a
quiet word, the professor an airy gush of graciousness—congratulating him
upon his appointment. And when Dewar came in he veered upon Gill, exclaiming in his peculiar high-pitched voice:—

"Where is our new Medical Officer, Mr. Gill? Where is Doctor Manson?"

Andrew stood up, confounded at Dewar's appearance, which transcended
even Hope's description. Billy was short, bowed, and hairy. He wore old
clothes, his waistcoat much dropped upon, his greenish overcoat bulging with
papers, pamphlets and the memoranda of a dozen different societies. There
was no excuse for Billy, for he had much money and daughters, one of them
married to a millionaire peer, but he looked now, and he always looked, like
a neglected old baboon.

"There was a Manson at Queens with me in eighteen-eighty," he squeaked
benevolently, by way of greeting.

"This is he, sir," murmured Hope, to whom the temptation was irresistible.

Billy heard him. "How would *you* know, Doctor Hope?" he squinted ur-
banely over the steel rimmed pince-nez on the end of his nose. "You weren't
even in swaddling clothes then. Hee! Hee! Hee! Hee!"

He flapped away, chuckling, to his place at the head of the table. None of
his colleagues, who were already seated, took any notice of him. Part of the
technique of this Board was a proud unawareness of one's neighbours. But
this did not dismay Billy. Pulling a wad of papers from his pocket he took
a drink of water from the carafe, picked up the little hammer in front of
him and hit the table a resounding thwack.

"Gentlemen, gentlemen! Mr. Gill will now read the minutes."

Gill, who acted as secretary to the Board, rapidly intoned the minutes of
the last meeting, while Billy, giving to this chanting no attention whatsoever,
alternately pawed amongst his papers and let his eye twinkle benevolently
down the board towards Andrew whom he still vaguely associated with the
Manson of Queens, 1880.

At last Gill finished. Billy immediately wielded the hammer.

"Gentlemen! We are particularly happy to have our new Medical Officer
with us to-day. I remember, as recently as nineteen hundred and four, I emphasized the need of a permanent clinician who should be attached to the
Board as a solid adjuvant to the pathologists whom we occasionally *filch*, gentlemen—Hee! Hee!—whom we occasionally filch from the Backhouse Research. And I say this with all respect to our young friend Hope, on whose

charity—Hee! Hee!—on whose charity we have been so largely dependent. Now I well remember as recently as eighteen eighty-nine . . ."

Sir Robert Abbey interposed:—

"I'm sure, sir, the other members of the Board wish to join you whole-heartedly in congratulating Doctor Manson on his silicosis paper. If I may say so, I felt this to be a particularly patient and original piece of clinical research, and one which, as the Board well knows, may have the most far-reaching effects upon our industrial legislation."

"Hear, hear," boomed Challis, supporting his protégé.

"That is what I was about to say, Robert," said Billy peevishly. To him Abbey was still a young man, a student almost, whose interruptions demanded mild reproof. "When we decided at our last meeting that this investigation must be pursued, Doctor Manson's name immediately suggested itself to me. He has opened up this question and he must be given every opportunity to pursue it. We wish him, gentlemen,"—this being for Andrew's benefit he twinkled at him bushily along the table,—"to visit all the anthracite mines in the country, and possibly later we may extend this to all the coal mines. Also we wish him to have every opportunity for clinical examination of the miners in the industry. We will afford him every facility—including the skilled bacteriological services of our young friend Doctor Hope. In short, gentlemen, there is nothing we will *not* do to ensure that our new medical officer presses this all-important matter of dust inhalation to its ultimate scientific and administrative conclusion."

Andrew drew one quick and furtive breath. It was splendid, splendid—better than he had ever hoped. They were going to give him a free hand, back him up with their immense authority, turn him loose on clinical research. They were angels, all of them, and Billy was Gabriel himself.

"But, gentlemen," Billy suddenly piped, shuffling himself a new deal from his coat pockets, "*before* Doctor Manson goes on with this problem, before we can feel ourselves at liberty to allow him to concentrate his efforts upon it, there is another and more pressing matter which I feel he ought to take up."

A pause. Andrew felt his heart contract, and it began slowly to sink as Billy continued:—

"Doctor Bigsby of the Board of Trade has been pointing out to me the alarming discrepancy in the specifications of industrial first-aid equipments. There is, of course, a definition under the existing Act, but it is elastic and unsatisfactory. There are no precise standards, for example, as to the size and weave of bandages, the length, material, and type of splints. Now, gentlemen, this is an important matter and one which directly concerns this Board. I feel very strongly that our Medical Officer should conduct a thorough investigation and submit a report upon it before he begins upon the problem of inhalation."

Silence. Andrew glanced desperately round the table. Dodd-Canterbury, with his legs outstretched, had his eyes on the ceiling. Gadsby was drawing diagrams upon his blotter, Whinney frowning, Challis inflating his chest for speech.

But it was Abbey who said:—

"Surely, Sir William, this is matter either for the Board of Trade or the Mines Department."

"We are at the disposal of each of these bodies," squeaked Billy. "We are—Hee! Hee!—the orphan child of both."

"Yes, I know. But after all this—this bandage question is comparatively trivial, and Doctor Manson . . ."

"I assure you, Robert, it is far from trivial. There will be a question in the House presently. I had that from Lord Ungar only yesterday."

"Ah!" Gadsby said, lifting his ears. "If Ungar is keen, we have no choice." Gadsby could toady with deceptive brusqueness, and Ungar was a man he wished particularly to please.

Andrew felt driven to intervene.

"Excuse me, Sir William," he stumbled; "I—I understood I was going to do clinical work here. For a month I have been kicking about in my office, and now if I'm to . . ."

He broke off, looking round at them. It was Abbey who helped him.

"Doctor Manson's point is very just. For four years he's been working patiently at his own subject and now, having offered him every facility to expand it, we propose sending him out to count bandages."

"If Doctor Manson has been patient for four years, Robert," Billy squeaked, "he can be patient a little longer. Hee! Hee!"

"True, true," boomed Challis. "He'll be free for silicosis eventually."

Whinney cleared his throat. "Now," Hope muttered to Andrew, "the Nag is about to neigh."

"Gentlemen," Whinney said, "for a long time I have been asking this Board to investigate the question of muscular fatigue in relation to steam heat—a subject which, as you know, interests me deeply, and which, I venture to say, you have hitherto not given the consideration it so richly merits. Now it appears to me that, if Doctor Manson is going to be diverted from the question of inhalation, it would be an admirable opportunity to pursue this all-important question of muscular fatigue . . ."

Gadsby looked at his watch: "I have an appointment in Harley Street in exactly thirty-five minutes."

Whinney turned angrily to Gadsby. Co-Professor Challis supported him with a gusty: "Intolerable impertinence."

Tumult seemed about to break.

But Billy's urbane yellow face peered from behind its whiskers at the meeting. He was not disturbed. He had handled such meetings for forty years. He knew they detested him and wanted him to go. But he was not going—he was never going. His vast cranium was filled with problems, data, agenda, obscure formulæ, equations; with physiology and chemistry; with facts and figments of research—a vaulted incalculable sepulchre, haunted by phantoms

of decerebrated cats, illumined by polarized light and all rosy-hued by the
great remembrance that when he was a boy, Lister had patted him upon the
head.

He declared guilelessly:—

"I must tell you, gentlemen, I have already as good as promised Lord Ungar
and Doctor Bigsby that we shall assist them in their difficulty. Six months
ought to suffice, Doctor Manson. Perhaps a little longer. It will not be uninteresting. It will bring you into contact with people and things, young man.
You remember Lavoisier's remark concerning the drop of water! Hee! Hee!
And now, touching Doctor Hope's pathological examination of the specimen
from Wendover Colliery in July last . . ."

At four o'clock, when it was all over, Andrew threshed the matter out with
Gill and Hope in Gill's room. The effect of this Board, and perhaps of his
increasing years, was to implant in him the beginnings of restraint. He neither
raved nor furiously split his infinitives but contented himself merely with
stabbing a neat pattern with a Government pen upon a Government desk.

"It won't be so bad," Gill consoled. "It means travelling all over the country, I know, but that can be rather pleasant. You might even take Mrs. Manson with you. There's Buxton now—that's a centre for all the Derbyshire
coalfield. And at the end of six months you can begin your anthracite work."

"He'll never get the chance," Hope grinned. "He's a bandage counter—for
life!"

Andrew picked up his hat. "The trouble with you, Hope, is—you're too
young."

He went home to Christine. And the following Monday, since she resolutely refused to miss the gay adventure, they bought a secondhand Morris
for sixty pounds and started out together upon the Great First Aid Investigation. It is to be admitted they were happy as the car sped up the highway to
the North, and Andrew, having given a simian impersonation of Billy Buttons
steering the car with his feet, remarked:—

"Anyway! Never mind what Lavoisier said to the drop of water in eighteen
thirty-two. We're together, Chris!"

The work was imbecile. It consisted of the inspection of the first-aid materials kept at different collieries throughout the country: splints, bandages,
cotton wool, antiseptics, tourniquets and the rest. At the good collieries the
equipment was good; and at poor collieries the equipment was poor. Underground inspection was no novelty to Andrew. He made hundreds of underground inspections, crawling miles along haulage-ways to the coal face, to
view a box of bandages carefully planted there half an hour beforehand.

At small pits in hardy Yorkshire he overheard under-managers whisper
aside:—

"Run down, Geordie, and tell Alex to go to the chemist's . . ." then:
"Have a chair, Doctor, we'll be ready for ye in a minute!" In Nottingham
he comforted temperance ambulance men by telling them cold tea was a superior stimulant to brandy. Elsewhere, he swore by whisky. But mostly he

did the work with alarming conscientiousness. He and Christine found rooms in a convenient centre. Thereafter he combed the district in the car. While he inspected Christine sat and knitted at a distance. They had adventures, usually with landladies. They made friends, chiefly among the mining inspectors. Andrew was not surprised that his mission provoked these hardheaded, hardfisted citizens to senseless laughter. It is to be regretted that he laughed with them.

And then, in March, they returned to London, resold the car for only ten pounds less than they had paid for it, and Andrew set about writing his report. He had made up his mind to give the Board value for its money, to offer them statistics by the tubful, pages of tables, charts, and divisional graphs showing how the bandage curve rose as the splint curve fell. He was determined, he told Christine, to show them how well he had done the work and how excellently they had all wasted their time.

At the end of the month when he had rushed a rough draft through to Gill, he was surprised to receive a summons from Doctor Bigsby of the Board of Trade.

"He's delighted with your report," Gill fluttered, as he escorted Andrew along Whitehall. "I shouldn't have let the cat out. But there it is—it's a lucky start for you, my dear fellow. You've no idea how important Bigsby is. He's got the whole factory administration in his pocket!"

It took them some time to reach Doctor Bigsby. They had to sit with their hats in two anterooms before gaining admission to the final chamber. But there was Doctor Bigsby, at last, thickset and cordial, with a dark grey suit and darker grey spats, double-breasted waistcoat and a bustling efficiency.

"Sit down, gentlemen. This report of yours, Manson. I've seen the draft and though it's early to speak I must say I like the look of it. Highly scientific. Excellent graphing. That's what we want in this department. Now as we're out to standardize equipment in factories and mines you ought to know my views. First of all I see you recommend a three-inch bandage as the major bandage of the specification. Now, I prefer the two-and-a-half-inch. You'll agree there, won't you?"

Andrew was irritated; it may have been the spats.

"Personally, so far as the mines are concerned, I think the bigger the bandage the better. But I don't think it makes a hell of a lot of difference!"

"Eh? What?" Reddening behind the ears. "No *difference?*"

"Not a bit."

"But don't you see—don't you realize—the whole principle of standardization is involved? If we suggest two-and-a-half-inch and you recommend three-inch there may be enormous difficulty."

"Then I'll recommend three-inch," Andrew said coolly.

Doctor Bigsby's hackles rose, it was possible to see them rising.

"Your attitude is difficult to understand. We've been working for years towards the two-and-a-half-inch bandage. Why . . . Don't you know how much this *matters* . . . ?"

"Yes, I know!" Andrew equally lost his temper. "Have you ever been underground? I have. I've done a bloody operation, lying on my guts in a puddle of water, with one safety lamp and no headroom. And I tell you straight, any finicky half-inch difference in your bandage doesn't matter a tinker's curse."

He passed out of the building more swiftly than he had entered, followed by Gill, who wrung his hands and lamented the fracas all the way to the Embankment.

When he got back Andrew stood in his room, sternly regarding the traffic on the river, the bustling streets, the buses running, trams clanging over bridges, the movement of human people, all the pulsing vivid flow of life.

"I don't belong to this outfit in here," he thought with a surge of impatience. "I should be out there—out there!"

Abbey had given up attending the Board meetings. And Challis had disheartened Manson, even to the point of panic, by taking him to lunch the week before and warning him that Whinney was lobbying hard, would try to put him on to his muscular fatigue investigation before the silicosis question was touched.

Andrew reflected, with a despairing pretence at humour: "If *that* happens, on top of the bandages, I might as well take a reader's ticket for the British Museum."

Walking home from the Embankment he found himself peering enviously at the brass plates bolted on area railings outside the houses of doctors. He would stop, watch a patient mount to the door, ring the bell, be admitted—then, walking moodily on, he would visualize the ensuing scene, the interrogations, the swift production of stethoscope, the whole thrilling science of diagnosis. He was a doctor, too, wasn't he? At least, once upon a time . . .

Towards the end of May, in this frame of mind, he was walking up Oakley Street about five in the evening when he suddenly saw a crowd of people gathered round a man lying on the pavement. In the gutter alongside was a shattered bicycle and, almost on top of it, a drunkenly arrested motor lorry.

Five seconds later Andrew was in the middle of the crowd, observing the injured man, who, attended by a kneeling policeman, was bleeding from a deep wound in the groin.

"Here! Let me through. I'm a doctor."

The policeman, striving unsuccessfully to fix a tourniquet, turned a flustered face.

"I can't stop the bleeding, Doctor. It's too high up."

Andrew saw that it was impossible to tourniquet. The wound was too high up in the iliac vessel, and the man was bleeding to death.

"Get up," he said to the policeman. "Put him flat on his back." Then, making his right arm rigid, he leaned over and thrust his fist hard into the man's belly over the descending aorta. The whole weight of his body, thus transmitted to the great vessel, immediately arrested the hæmorrhage. The policeman removed his helmet and wiped his forehead. Five minutes later the ambulance arrived. Andrew went with it.

Next morning Andrew rang up the hospital. The house surgeon answered brusquely, after the fashion of his kind:—

"Yes, yes, he's comfortable. Doing well. Who wants to know?"

"Oh," mumbled Andrew from the public phone box, "nobody."

And that, he thought bitterly, was exactly what he was: nobody, doing nothing, getting nowhere. He endured it till the end of the week, then quietly, without fuss, he handed in his resignation to Gill for transmission to the Board.

Gill was upset, yet admitted that a premonition of this sad event had troubled him. He made a neat little speech which concluded:—

"After all, my dear fellow, I have realized that your place is—well, if I may borrow a wartime comparison—not at the base but—er—in the front line with the—er—troops."

Hope said:—

"Don't listen to the rose-cultivating penguin fancier! You're lucky. And I'll be after you if I keep my reason—as soon as my three years are up!"

Andrew heard nothing about the Board's activities on the question of dust inhalation until months later when Lord Ungar raised the question dramatically in the House, quoting freely from medical evidence afforded him by Doctor Maurice Gadsby.

Gadsby was acclaimed by the Press as a Humanitarian and a Great Physician. And silicosis was, in that year, scheduled as an industrial disease.

BOOK IV

1

THEY began their search for a practice. It was a jagged business—wild peaks of expectation followed by wilder plunges of despair. Stung by a consciousness of three successive failures—at least so he construed his departures from Blaenelly, Aberalaw, and the M.F.B.—Andrew longed to vindicate himself at last. But their total capital, increased by stringent saving during the last months of salaried security, was no more than six hundred pounds. Though they haunted the medical agencies and reached for every opportunity offered in the columns of the *Lancet*, it appeared that this sum was scarcely adequate as purchase money for a London practice.

They never forgot their first interview. Doctor Brent, of Cadogan Gardens, was retiring, and he offered a nice nucleus practice, suitable for a well-qualified gentleman. It seemed, on the face of it, an admirable chance. An extravagant taxi—for fear that someone speedier might snatch the plum—rushed them to Doctor Brent, whom they found to be a white-haired, pleasant, almost demure little man.

"Yes," Doctor Brent said modestly. "It's a pretty good pitch. Nice house, too. I want only seven thousand pounds for the lease. There's forty years to run, and the ground rent's only three hundred a year. As to the practice—I thought the usual—two years' premium for cash, eh, Doctor Manson?"

"Quite!" Andrew nodded gravely. "You'd give a long introduction, too? Thank you, Doctor Brent. We'll consider it."

They considered it over threepenny cups of tea in the Brompton Road Lyons.

"Seven thousand—for the lease!" Andrew gave a short laugh. He thrust his hat back from his corrugated brow, stuck his elbows on the marble table. "It's pretty damnable, Chris! The way these old fellows hang on with their back teeth. And you can't prise them loose unless you've got money. Isn't that an indictment of our system? But rotten as it is, I'll accept it. You wait! I'm going to attend to this money question from now on."

"I hope not," she smiled. "We've been moderately happy without it."

He grunted. "You won't say that when we start to sing in the streets. Check, miss, please."

Because of his M.D., M.R.C.P., he wanted a non-panel, non-dispensing practice. He wanted to be free of the tyranny of the card system. But as the weeks went on he wanted anything, anything that offered him a chance. He inspected practices in Tulse Hill, Islington, and Brixton, and one—the surgery had a hole in the roof—in Camden Town. He went to the length of debating with Hope—who assured him that on his capital it was suicide—the plan of taking a house and setting out his plate on chance.

And then, after two months, when they had reached the point of desperation, all at once Heaven relented and allowed old Doctor Foy to die, painlessly, in Paddington. Doctor Foy's obituary notice, four lines in the *Medical Journal*, caught Andrew's eye. They went, their enthusiasm all spent, to Number 9 Chesborough Terrace. They saw the house, a tall, leaden-hued sepulchre with a surgery at the side and a brick garage behind. They saw the books, which indicated that Doctor Foy had made perhaps five hundred pounds a year, mainly from consultations, with medicine, at the rate of three and six. They saw the widow, who assured them timidly that Doctor Foy's practice was sound and had once been excellent with many "good patients" coming to the "front door." They thanked her and left without enthusiasm.

"And yet I don't know," Andrew worried. "It's full of disadvantages. I hate the dispensing. It's a baddish locality. D'you notice all those moth-eaten boarding houses next door? But it's on the *fringe* of a decent neighbourhood. And a corner situation. And a main street. And near enough our price. One and a half years' purchase—and it was decent of her to say she'd fling in the old man's consulting room and surgery furniture as well—and all ready to step into—that's the advantage of a death vacancy. What do you say, Chris? It's now or never. Shall we chance it?"

Christine's eyes rested upon him doubtfully. For her, the novelty of London had worn off. She loved the country and now, in these drab surroundings, she longed for it with all her heart. Yet he was so set upon a London practice she could not bring herself to try, even, to persuade him from it.

She nodded slowly. "If you want to, Andrew."

The next day he offered Mrs. Foy's solicitors six hundred pounds in place of the seven hundred and fifty demanded. The offer was accepted, the cheque written. On Saturday, the tenth of October, they moved their furniture from storage and entered into possession of their new home.

It was Sunday before they extracted themselves from the frantic eruption of straw and sacking and wondered shakily how they stood. Andrew took advantage of the moment to launch one of those lectures, rare yet odious, which made him sound like a deacon of a nonconformist chapel.

"We are properly up against it here, Chris. We've paid out every stiver we've got. We've got to live on what we earn. Heaven only knows what that'll be. But we've got to do it. You've got to spruce things up, Chris, economize—"

To his dismay she burst into tears, standing palely there in the large, gloomy, dirty-ceilinged, and as yet uncarpeted, front room.

"For mercy's sake!" she sobbed. "Leave me alone. Economize. Don't I always economize for you? Do I cost you *anything*?"

"Chris!" he exclaimed aghast.

She flung herself frantically against him. "It's this house! I didn't realize. That basement, the stairs, the *dirt*—"

"But hang it all, it's the practice that really matters!"

"We might have had a little country practice, somewhere."

"Yes! With roses round the cottage door. Damn it all . . ."

In the end he apologized for his sermon. Then they went, his arm still round her waist, to fry eggs in the condemned basement. There he tried to cheer her by pretending that it was not a basement but a section of the Paddington Tunnel through which trains would at any minute pass. She smiled wanly at his attempted humour, but she was in reality looking at the broken scullery sink.

Next morning, at nine o'clock sharp—he decided: I must not be early or they will think I'm too eager!—he opened his surgery. His heart was beating with excitement and a greater, far greater expectation than on that almost-forgotten morning when he took the first surgery of all at Blaenelly.

Half-past nine came. He waited anxiously. Since the little surgery, which had its own door to the side street, was attached by a short passage to the house, he could equally control his consulting room—the main room on the ground floor, not badly equipped with Doctor Foy's desk, a couch, and a cabinet—to which the "good" patients, by Mrs. Foy's account, were admitted through the front door of the house. He had, in fact, a double net cast out. Tense as any fisherman, he waited for what that double cast might bring.

Yet it brought nothing, nothing! It was nearly eleven o'clock now and still no patient had arrived. The group of taxi drivers standing by their cabs at the rank opposite talked equably together. His plate shone on the door, beneath Doctor Foy's old battered one.

Suddenly, when he had almost abandoned hope, the bell on the surgery door tinkled sharply and an old woman in a shawl came in. Chronic bronchitis—he saw it, before she spoke, in every rheumy wheeze. Tenderly, tenderly he seated and sounded her. She was an old patient of Doctor Foy's. He talked to her. In the tiny cubbyhole of a dispensary, a mere lair halfway down the passage between the surgery and the consulting room, he made up her physic. He returned with it. And then, without question, as he prepared, tremblingly, to ask her for it, she handed him the fee, three and six.

The thrill of that moment—the joy, the sheer relief of these silver coins there in the palm of his hand—was unbelievable. It felt like the first money he had ever earned in his life. He closed the surgery, ran to Christine, thrust the coins upon her.

"First patient, Chris. It mightn't be a bad old practice after all. Anyhow, this buys us our lunch!"

He had no visits to make, for the old doctor had been dead nearly three weeks now, and no locum had kept the practice going in the interval. He must wait till the calls came in. Meanwhile, aware from her mood that Christine wished to wrestle with her domestic worries in solitude, he occupied the forenoon by walking round the district, prospecting, viewing the peeling

houses, the long succession of drab private hotels, the sooted, grimly arbo-
rescent squares, the narrow mews converted into garages; then, at a sudden
turn of North Street, a squalid patch of slum—pawnshops, hawkers' barrows,
pubs, shop windows showing patent medicines, devices in gaudy rubber.

He admitted to himself that the district had come down in the world since
those days when carriages had spun to the yellow-painted porticoes. It was
dingy and soiled, yet there were signs of new life springing up amidst the
fungus—a new block of flats in course of erection, some good shops and offices
and, at the end of Gladstone Place, the famous Laurier's. Even he, who knew
nothing of women's fashions, had heard of Laurier's, and it did not require
the long line of elegant motor cars standing outside the windowless, immaculately white-stoned building to convince him that the little he knew of its
exclusiveness was true. He felt it strange that Laurier's should stand incon-
gruously amongst these faded terraces. Yet there it was, indubitable as that
policeman opposite.

In the afternoon he completed his inaugural tour by calling upon the doctors in the immediate vicinity. Altogether he made eight such calls. Only
three of them made any deep impression on him—Doctor Ince of Gladstone
Place, a young man; Reeder, at the end of Alexandra Street; and at the corner
of Royal Crescent an elderly Scotsman named McLean.

But the way in which they all said: "Oh! It's poor old Foy's practice you've
taken on," somehow depressed him. Why that "on"? he thought, a trifle angrily. He told himself that in six months' time they would change their manner. Though Manson was thirty now, and knew the value of restraint, he still
hated condescension as a cat hates water.

That night in the surgery there were three patients, two of whom paid him
the three and sixpenny fee. The third promised to return and settle up on
Saturday. He had, in his first day's practice, earned the sum of ten and six.

But the following day he took nothing at all. And the day after, only seven
shillings. Thursday was a good day; Friday just saved from being blank; and
on Saturday, after an empty morning, he took seventeen and six at the evening
surgery, though the patient to whom he had given credit on Monday failed
to keep his promise to return and pay.

On Sunday, though he made no comment to Christine, Andrew morbidly
reviewed the week. Had he made a horrible mistake in taking this derelict
practice, in sinking all their savings in this tomblike house? What was *wrong*
with him? He was thirty; yes, over thirty. He had an M.D., honours, and the
M.R.C.P. He had clinical ability, and a fine piece of clinical research work
to his credit. Yet here he was, taking barely enough three and sixpences to
keep them in bread. It's the system, he thought savagely, it's *senile*. There
ought to be some better scheme, a chance for everybody; say—oh, say State
control! Then he groaned, remembering Doctor Bigsby and the M.F.B. No,
damn it, that's hopeless; bureaucracy, chokes individual effort—it would suf-
focate me. I must succeed; damn it all, I *will* succeed!

Never before had the financial side of practice so obtruded itself upon him.

And no subtler method of converting him to materialism could have been devised than those genuine pangs of appetite—the euphemism was his own—which he carried with him many days of the week.

About a hundred yards down the main bus route stood a small delicatessen shop kept by a fat little woman, a naturalized German, who called herself Smith but who, from her broken speech and insistent *s*'s, was obviously Schmidt. It was typically Continental, this little place of Frau Schmidt's, its narrow marble counter loaded with soused herrings, olives in jars, sauerkraut, several kinds of *wurst*, pastries, salami, and a delicious kind of cheese named Libtauer. Also it had the virtue of being very cheap. Since money was so scarce at 9 Chesborough Terrace and the cooking stove a choked and antique ruin, Andrew and Christine dealt a great deal with Frau Schmidt. On good days they had hot Frankfurters and "apfelstrudel"; on bad they would lunch on a soused herring and baked potatoes. Often at night they would drop into Frau Schmidt's, after scanning her display through the steamed window with a selective eye, and come away with something savoury in a string bag.

Frau Schmidt soon got to know them. She developed an especial liking for Christine. Her larded, pastry-cook's face would wrinkle up, almost closing her eyes, beneath her high dome of blonde hair, as she smiled and nodded to Andrew:—

"You will be all right. You will succeed. You have a good wife. She iss small, like me. But she iss good. Chust wait—I will send you patients!"

Almost at once, the winter was upon them and fogs hung about the streets, always intensified, it seemed, by the smoke from the great railway station near by. They made light of it, they pretended their struggles were amusing, but never in all their years at Aberalaw had they known such hardship.

Christine did her utmost with their chill barracks. She whitewashed the ceilings, made new curtains for the waiting room. She repapered their bedroom. By painting the panels black and gold, she transformed the senile folding doors which disfigured the first floor drawing-room.

Most of his calls, infrequent though these were, took him to the boarding houses of the neighbourhood. It was difficult to collect the fees from such patients—many of them were seedy, even doubtful characters, and adept in the art of bilking. He tried to make himself agreeable to the gaunt females who kept these establishments. He made conversation in gloomy hallways. He would say, "I'd no idea it was so cold! I should have brought my coat," or "It's awkward getting about. My car's laid up for the moment."

He struck up a friendship with the policeman who usually took point duty at the busy traffic crossing outside Frau Schmidt's delicatessen. Donald Struthers was the policeman's name, and there was kinship between them from the start, for Struthers, like Andrew, came from Fife. He promised, in his own style, to do what he could do to help his compatriot, remarking with a grim facetiousness:—

"If ever anybody gets run down and killed here, Doctor, I'll be sure and fetch them along to ye."

One afternoon, about a month after their arrival, when Andrew got home—he had been calling on the chemists of the district, inquiring brightly for a special 10cc. Voss syringe which he knew none of them would keep in stock, then, casually introducing himself as the new and vigorous practitioner of Chesborough Terrace—Christine's expression appraised him of some excitement.

"There's a patient in the consulting room," she breathed. "She came by the front door."

His face brightened. This was the first "good" patient who had come to him. Perhaps it was the beginning of better things. Preparing himself, he walked briskly into the consulting room.

"Good afternoon! What can I do for you?"

"Good afternoon, Doctor. Mrs. Smith recommended me."

She rose from her chair to shake hands with him. She was plump, good-natured, thickly made up, with a short fur jacket and a large handbag. He saw at once that she was one of the street-women who frequented the district.

"Yes?" he inquired, his expectation sinking a little.

"Oh, Doctor," she smiled diffidently. "My friend just give me a nice pair of gold earrings. And Mrs. Smith—I am customer there—she said you would pierce my ears for me? My friend, he's very anxious I don't get done with a dirty needle or something, Doctor."

He took a long steadying breath. Had it actually come to this? He said:—

"Yes, I'll pierce your ears for you."

He did this carefully, sterilizing the needle, spraying her lobes with ethyl chloride, even fitting the gold rings in for her.

"Oh, Doctor, that's lovely"—peering in the mirror of her handbag. "And I never felt a thing. My friend'll be pleased. How much, Doctor?"

The statutory fee for Foy's "good" patients, mythical though they might be, was seven and six. He mentioned this sum.

She produced a ten-shilling note from her bag. She thought him a kind, distinguished, and very handsome gentleman—she always liked them dark, somehow—and she also thought, as she accepted her change, that he looked hungry.

When she had gone he did not wear holes in the carpet, as he would once have done, raving that he, too, had prostituted himself by this petty, servile act. He was conscious of a strange humility. Holding the crumpled note, he went to the window, watching her disappear down the street, swaying her hips, swinging her handbag, proudly wearing her new earrings.

2

THROUGH the rigours of the battle he hungered for medical friendship. He had gone to a meeting of the local medical association without enjoying himself greatly. Denny was still abroad. Finding Tampico to his liking Philip had remained there, taking a post as surgeon to the New Century Oil Company. For the present, at least, he was lost to Andrew. While Hope, on a mission

to Cumberland, was—as he phrased it in his rudely coloured postcard—counting corpuscles for Maniac's Delight.

Many times Andrew was taken by the impulse to get in touch with Freddie
Hampton; but always, though he often got as far as the phone book, the
reflection that he was still unsuccessful—not properly settled, he told himself
—restrained him. Freddie was still in Queen Anne Street, though he had
moved to a different number. Andrew found himself wondering more and
more how Freddie had got on, recollecting the old adventures of their student
days, until suddenly he found the compulsion too strong for him. He did ring
Hampton.

"You've probably forgotten all about me," he grunted, half-prepared for a
snub. "This is Manson—Andrew Manson. I'm in practice here in Paddington."

"Manson! Forgotten you! You old warhorse!" Freddie was lyrical on the
other end of the line. "Good lord, man! *Why* haven't you rung me?"

"Oh, we've barely got settled," Andrew smiled into the receiver, warmed
by Freddie's gush. "And before—on that Board job—we were rushing all over
England. I'm married now, you know."

"So am I! Look here, old man, we've got to get together again. Soon! I can't
get over it. You, here, in London. Marvellous! Where's my book— Look here,
how about next Thursday? Can you come to dinner then? Yes, yes. That's
great. So long then, old man, in the meantime I'll have my wife drop yours a
line."

Christine seemed lacking in enthusiasm when he told her of the invitation.

"You go, Andrew," she suggested after a pause.

"Oh! that's nonsense! Freddie wants you to meet his wife. I know you
don't care about him much, but there'll be other people there, other doctors
probably. We may get a new slant on things there, dear. Besides, we've had
no fun lately. Black tie, he said. Lucky I bought myself that dinner jacket for
the Newcastle mines do. But what about you, Chris? You ought to have
something to wear."

"I ought to have a new gas cooker," she answered a trifle grimly.

These last weeks had taken toll of her. She had lost a little of that freshness
which had always been her greatest charm. And sometimes, as just now, her
tone was short and jaded.

But on Thursday night, when they started out for Queen Anne Street, he
could not help thinking how sweet she looked in the dress—yes, it was the
white dress she had bought for that Newcastle dinner, altered in some way
which made it seem newer, smarter. Her hair was done in a new style too,
closer to her head, so that it lay darkly about her pale brow. He noticed this as
she tied his bow for him, meant to tell her how nice it was, then forgot, in the
sudden fear that they would be late.

They were not late, however, but early, so early that an awkward three
minutes elapsed before Freddie came gaily in, both hands outstretched,
apologizing and greeting them in the same breath, telling them he had just
come in from hospital, that his wife would be down in a second, offering

drinks, pounding Andrew on the back, bidding them be seated. Freddie had put on weight since that evening at Cardiff, there was heavy prosperity in the pink roll of flesh on the back of his neck, but his small eyes still glistened and not a single yellow plastered hair was out of its place. He was so well-groomed that he shone.

"Believe me!"—he elevated his glass—"it's wonderful to see you people again. This time we've got to keep it up. How do you like my place here, old man? Didn't I tell you at that dinner—and *what* a dinner!—I bet we'll do better to-night—that I'd do it? I've got the whole house here, of course—not just rooms; bought the freehold last year. And did it cost money?" He patted his tie approvingly. "No need to advertise the fact, of course, even if I am successful. But I don't mind you knowing, old man."

It looked an expensive background, there was no doubt: smooth modern furniture, deepset fireplace, a baby grand player-piano with artificial magnolia blossoms shaped from mother-of-pearl in a big white vase.

Andrew was preparing to voice admiration when Mrs. Hampton entered, tall, cool, with dark hair parted in the middle and clothes extraordinarily different from Christine's.

"Come along, my dear." Freddie greeted her with affection, even with deference, and darted to pour and offer her a glass of sherry. She had time negligently to wave away the glass before the other guests—Mr. and Mrs. Charles Ivory, Doctor and Mrs. Paul Freedman—were announced. Introductions followed, with much talk and laughter amongst the Ivorys, the Freedmans and the Hamptons. Then they went in—not too soon—to dinner.

The table appointments were rich and superfine. They closely resembled a costly display, complete with candelabra, which Andrew had seen in the window of Labin and Benn, the famous Regent Street jewellers. The food was unrecognizable as meat or fish, yet it tasted extremely well. And there was champagne. After two glasses Andrew felt more confident. He began to talk to Mrs. Ivory, who sat on his left, a slender woman in black with an extraordinary amount of jewellery around her neck and large protruding blue eyes which she turned upon him from time to time with an almost babyish stare.

Her husband was Charles Ivory, the surgeon—she laughed in answer to his question; she thought everyone knew Charles. They lived in New Cavendish Street round the corner, the whole house was theirs. It was nice being near Freddie and his wife. Charles and Freddie and Paul Freedman were all such good friends, all members of the Sackville Club. She was surprised when he admitted he was not a member. She thought everyone was a member of the Sackville.

Deserted, he turned to Mrs. Freedman on his other side, finding her softer, friendlier, with a pretty, almost oriental bloom. He encouraged her to talk of her husband also. He said to himself: "I want to *know* about these fellows, they're so damned prosperous and smart."

Paul, said Mrs. Freedman, was a physician, and though they had a flat in Portland Place, Paul's rooms were in Harley Street. He had a wonderful practice—she spoke too fondly to be bragging—chiefly at the Plaza Hotel; he must know the big new Plaza, overlooking the Park. Why, at lunchtime the Grill Room was crammed with celebrities. Paul was practically the official doctor for the Plaza Hotel. So many wealthy Americans and film stars and—she broke off smiling—oh, everybody came to the Plaza, which made it rather wonderful for Paul.

Andrew liked Mrs. Freedman. He let her run on until Mrs. Hampton rose, when he jumped up gallantly to draw back her chair.

"Cigar, Manson?" Freddie asked him with a knowledgeable air when the ladies had gone. "You'll find these pretty sound. And I advise you not to miss this brandy. Eighteen ninety-four. Absolutely no nonsense about it."

With his cigar going and a drain of brandy in the wide-bellied glass before him, Andrew drew his chair nearer to the others. It was this he had really been looking forward to, a close, lively medical palaver—straight cut shop, and nothing else. He hoped Hampton and his friends would talk. They did.

"By the way," Freddie said, "I ordered myself one of these new Iradium lamps to-day at Glickert's. Pretty stiff. Something around eighty guineas. But it's worth it."

"M'yes," said Freedman thoughtfully. He was slight, dark-eyed, with a clever Jewish face. "It ought to pay for its keep."

Andrew took an argumentative grip of his cigar.

"I don't think much of these lamps, you know. Did you see Abbey's paper in the *Journal* on bogus Heliotherapy? These Iradiums have got absolutely no infrared content."

Freddie stared, then laughed.

"They've got a hell of a lot of three-guinea content. Besides, they bronze nicely."

"Mind you, Freddie," Freedman cut in, "I'm not in favour of expensive apparatus. It's got to be paid for before you show a profit. Besides, it dates, loses its vogue. Honestly, old chap, you'll find nothing to beat the good old hypo."

"*You* certainly use it," said Hampton.

Ivory joined in. He was bulky, older than the others, with a pale, shaven jowl, and the easy style of a man about town.

"Talking of that, I booked a course of injections to-day. Twelve. You know, manganese. And I tell you what I did. And I think it pays these days. I said to the fellow—I said, 'Look here, you're a businessman. This course is going to cost you fifty guineas, but if you care to pay me now and be done with it I'll make it forty-five.' He wrote me the cheque there and then."

"Ruddy old poacher," Freddie expostulated. "I thought you were a surgeon."

"I am," Ivory nodded. "Doing a curettage at Sherrington's to-morrow."

"Love's labour lost," Freedman muttered absently to his cigar; then, returning to his original thought: "There's no getting away from it, though. Basically, it's interesting. In good class practice oral administration is definitely demoded. If I prescribed—oh, say an Omnipon powder, at the Plaza, it wouldn't cut one guinea's worth of ice. But if you give the same thing hypodermically, swabbing up the skin, sterilizing and all the rest of the game, your patient thinks, scientifically, that you are the cat's pyjamas!"

Hampton declared vigorously:—

"It's a damn good job for the medical profession that oral administration is off the map in the West End. Take Charlie's case here, as an example. Suppose he'd prescribed manganese—or manganese and iron, the good old bottle of physic—probably just as much use to the patient—all he knocks out of it is three guineas. Instead of that he splits the medicine into twelve ampules, and gets fifty—sorry, Charlie, I mean forty-five."

"Less twelve shillings," murmured Freedman gently. "The price of the ampules."

Andrew's head rocked. Here was an argument in favour of the abolition of the medicine bottle which staggered him with its novelty. He took another swig of brandy to steady himself.

"That's another point," reflected Freedman. "They don't know how little these things cost. Whenever a patient sees a row of ampules on your desk she thinks instinctively, 'Heavens! this is going to mean money!'"

"You'll observe," Hampton winked at Andrew, "how Freedman's parsing of the good word patient is usually feminine. By the way, Paul, I heard about that shoot yesterday. Dummett's willing to make up a syndicate if you, Charles, and I will go in with him."

For the next ten minutes they talked of shooting, golf,—which they played on various expensive courses around London,—and cars,—Ivory was having a special body built to his instructions on a new three-and-a-half-litre Rex,—while Andrew listened and smoked his cigar and drank his brandy. They all drank a deal of brandy. Andrew felt, a trifle muzzily, that they were extraordinarily good fellows. They did not exclude him from their conversation, but always managed to make him feel by a word or a look that he was with them. Somehow they made him forget that he had eaten a soused herring for his luncheon. And as they stood up Ivory clapped him on the shoulder.

"I must send you a card, Manson. It'd be a real pleasure to see a case with you—any time."

Back in the drawing-room the atmosphere seemed, by contrast, formal; but Freddie, in tremendous spirits, more shining than ever, hands in his pockets, linen spotlessly agleam, decided that the evening was still young, that they must finish it altogether at the Embassy.

"I'm afraid—" Christine threw a pale glance at Andrew—"we ought to be going."

"Nonsense, darling!" Andrew smiled roseately. "We couldn't dream of breaking up the party!"

At the Embassy, Freddie was obviously popular. He and his party were bowed and smiled to a table against the wall. There was more champagne.

There was dancing. These fellows do themselves well, thought Andrew mistily, expansively.

"Oh! tha's a—tha's a splen'id tune they're playing—I won-woner if Chris would like t'dance."

In the taxi, returning at last to Chesborough Terrace, he proclaimed happily:—

"First-rate chaps these, Chris! 'Sbeen a wonderful evening, hasn't it?"

She answered in a thin, steady voice:—

"It's been a hateful evening!"

"Eh—what?"

"I like Denny and Hope as—oh—as your medical friends, Andrew; not these, these flashy—"

He broke in. "But look here, Chris— Wha's wrong with—"

"Oh! Couldn't you see?" she answered in an icy fury. "It was everything. The food, the furniture, the way they talked—money, money all the time. Perhaps you didn't see the way she looked at my dress, Mrs. Hampton I mean. You could see her *realizing* that she spends more on one beauty treatment than I do on clothes in a whole year. It was almost funny in the drawing-room when she found out what a nobody I was. She of course is the daughter of Whitton—the whisky Whitton! You can't guess what it was like—the conversation—before you came in. Smart Set gossip, who's week-ending with whom, what the hairdresser told her, the latest society abortion, not one word of anything *decent*. Why! She actually hinted that she was "sweet on"— as she put it—the dance-band leader at the Plaza."

The sarcasm in her tone was diabolic. Mistaking it for jealousy, he babbled:—

"I'll make money for you, Chris. I'll buy you plenty of expensive clothes."

"I don't want money," she said tautly. "And I hate expensive clothes."

"But—darling!" Tipsily he reached for her.

"Don't!" Her voice struck him. "I love you, Andrew. But not when you're drunk."

He subsided in his corner, fuddled, furious. It was the first time she had ever repulsed him.

"All right, my girl," he muttered. "If that's the way of it."

He paid the taxi, let himself into the house before her. Then without a word he marched up to the spare bedroom. Everything seemed squalid and dismal after the luxury he had just quitted. The electric switch would not work properly—the whole house was imperfectly wired.

"Damn it," he thought as he flung himself into bed. "I'm going to get out of this hole. I'll show her. I *will* make money. What *can* you do without it?"

Until now, in all their married life, they had never slept apart.

3

AT breakfast next morning Christine behaved as though the whole episode were forgotten. He could see that she was trying to be especially nice to him.

This gratified him and made him sulkier than ever. A woman, he reflected,—pretending absorption in the morning paper,—has got to be shown her place occasionally. But after he had grunted a few surly replies Christine suddenly stopped being nice to him and retired within herself, sitting at the table with compressed lips, not looking at him, waiting till he should finish the meal. Stubborn little devil, he thought, rising and walking out of the room; I'll show her!

His first action in his consulting room was to take down the *Medical Directory*. He was both curious and eager to have more precise information of his friends of the previous evening. Quickly he turned the pages, taking Freddie first. Yes, there it was—Frederick Hampton, Queen Anne Street, M.B., Ch.B., assistant to outpatients, Walthamwood.

Andrew's brows drew into a frown of perplexity. Freddie had talked a great deal last night about the hospital appointment—nothing like a hospital appointment for helping a fellow in the West End, he had said, gives the patients confidence to know he's a visiting physician. Yet surely this wasn't it: a poor-law institution—and at Walthamwood, one of the newer outer suburbs? There couldn't be a mistake, though, this was the current directory, he had bought it only a month ago.

More slowly, Andrew looked up Ivory and Freedman, then he rested the big red book on his knees, his expression puzzled, oddly reflective. Paul Freedman was, like Freddie, an M.B. but without Freddie's distinction. Freedman had no visiting appointment. And Ivory? Mr. Charles Ivory of New Cavendish Street had no surgical qualification but the lowest, the M.R.C.S., and no hospital appointment whatsoever. His record indicated a certain amount of experience in wartime and pensions hospitals. Beyond that—nothing.

Extremely thoughtful now, Andrew rose and put the book on its shelf, then his face drew into a sudden resolution. There was no comparison between his own qualifications and those of the prosperous fellows he had dined with last night. What they could do he could do also. Better. Despite Christine's outburst, he was more determined than ever to make a success of himself. But first he must get himself attached, not to Walthamwood or any such poor-law make-believe, but to one of the London hospitals. Yes! a real hospital—that must be his immediate objective. But how?

For three days he brooded, then he went shakily to Sir Robert Abbey. It was the most difficult task in the world for him to ask a favour, particularly as Abbey received him with such twinkling kindness.

"Well! How is our express bandage enumerator? Aren't you ashamed to look me in the eye? I'm told Doctor Bigsby has developed hypertension. Know anything about that? What is it you want, an argument with me, or a seat on the Board?"

"Well, no, Sir Robert. I was wondering—that's to say—could you help me, Sir Robert, to find an outpatients hospital appointment?"

"Hmm! That's much more difficult than the Board. Do you know how many young fellows there are walking the Embankment? All waiting on honorary appointments. You ought really to be going on with your lung work too —and that narrows the field."

"Well—I—I suppose—"

"The Victoria Chest Hospital. That's your target. One of our oldest London Hospitals. Suppose I make some inquiries. Oh! I don't promise anything, but I'll keep my eye scientifically open."

Abbey made him stay to tea. At four o'clock, unvaryingly, he had a ritual of drinking two cups of China tea in his consulting room, no milk or sugar, and nothing to eat. It was a special tea which tasted of orange blossoms. Abbey kept the conversation flowing easily on diverse topics, from Khang Hsi saucerless cups to the Pirquet reaction; then, as he showed Andrew to the door, he said:—

"Still quarrelling with the textbooks? Don't give that up. And don't—even if I do get you into the Victoria—for the love of Galen!—don't develop a bedside manner." His eyes twinkled. "That's what has ruined me."

Andrew went home treading the clouds. He was so pleased he neglected to maintain his dignity with Christine. He blurted out:—

"I've been to Abbey. He's going to try and fix me up at the Victoria Chest! That practically gives me a consultant's standing." The gladness in her eyes made him suddenly feel shamefaced, small. "I've been pretty difficult lately, Chris! We haven't been getting on too well, I suppose. Let's—oh! let's make it up, darling."

She ran to him, protesting it had all been her fault. Then, for some strange reason, it appeared entirely to be his. Only a small segment of his mind retained the fixed intention of confounding her, at some early date, by the greatness of his material success.

He flung himself into his work with renewed vigour, feeling that something fortunate would surely turn up soon. Meanwhile there was no doubt that his practice was increasing. It was not, he told himself, the class of practice he wanted, these three-and-sixpenny consultations and five-shilling visits. Yet it was genuine practice. The people who came to him or called him out were far too poor to dream of troubling the doctor unless they were really ill. Thus he met diphtheria in queer stuffy rooms above converted stables, rheumatic fever in damp servants' basements, pneumonia in the attics of lodging houses. He fought disease in that most tragic room of all: the single apartment where some elderly man or woman lived alone, forgotten by friends and relatives, cooking poor meals on a gas ring, neglected, unkempt, forsaken. There were many such cases. He came across the father of a well-known actress—whose name shone in bright lights in Shaftesbury Avenue—an old man of seventy, paralyzed, living in filthy squalor. He visited an elderly gentlewoman, gaunt, ludicrous, and starving, who could show him her photograph in her Court presentation dress, tell him of the days when she had driven down these same streets in her own carriage. In the middle of the night he pulled back to life—and afterwards hated himself for it—a wretched creature, penniless and desperate, who had preferred the gas oven to the workhouse.

Many of his cases were urgent—surgical emergencies which cried aloud for immediate admission to hospital. And here Andrew encountered his greatest difficulty. It was the hardest thing in the world to secure admission, even for the worst, the most dangerous case. These emergencies had a way of happening late at night. Returning, coat and jacket over his pyjamas, a scarf round his neck, hat still on the back of his head, he would hang over the telephone, ringing one hospital after another, entreating, imploring, threatening; but he always met with the same refusal, the curt, often insolent: "Doctor Who? Who? No, no! Sorry! We're full up!"

He went to Christine, livid, blaspheming.

"They're not full up. They've plenty of beds at St. John's for their own men. If they don't know you they freeze you stiff. I'd like to wring that last young pup's neck! Isn't it *hell*, Chris? Here am I with this strangulated hernia and I can't get a bed. Oh! I suppose some of them *are* full up. And this is London! This is the heart of the bloody British Empire. This is our voluntary hospital system. And some banqueting bastard of a philanthropist got up the other day and said it was the most marvellous in the world. It means the workhouse again for the poor devil. Filling in forms— What do you earn? What's your religion? and was your mother born in wedlock?—and him with peritonitis! Oh, well! Be a good sort, Chris, and get the relieving officer on the phone for me."

Whatever his difficulties, no matter if he railed against the dirt and poverty which he often had to combat, she always had the same reply:—

"It's *real* work anyway. And that seems to me to make all the difference."

"Not enough to keep the bugs off me," he growled, going up to the bath to shake himself free.

She laughed; for she was back again to her old happiness. Though the fight had been formidable, she had at last subdued the house. Sometimes it would attempt to rear its head and strike at her, but in the main it lay clean, furbished, obedient to her eye. She had her new gas cooker, new shades for the lamps; she had the loose chair-covers freshly cleaned. And her stair-rods shone like a guardsman's buttons. After weeks of worry with servants who, in this district, preferred to work in the boarding houses because of the tips they earned there, Christine had chanced on Mrs. Bennett, a widow of forty, clean and hardworking, who, because of her daughter, a child of seven, had found it almost impossible to secure a "living in" position. Together Mrs. Bennett and Christine had attacked the basement. Now the former railway tunnel was a comfortable bed-sitting-room, with a highly floral wallpaper, furniture brought from "the barrows" and painted cream by Christine, where Mrs. Bennett and little Florrie—now departing regularly with her satchel to Paddington School—felt themselves secure. In return for this security and comfort—after months of straitened uncertainty—Mrs. Bennett could not do enough to prove her worth.

The early spring flowers which made the waiting-room so bright reflected the happiness of Christine's house. She bought them at the street market for a few pence, as she went on her round of morning shopping. Many of the hawkers in Mussleburgh Road knew her. It was possible to buy fruit and fish and vegetables cheaply there. She ought to have been more conscious of her standing as the wife of a professional man; but alas! she was not, and she often brought her purchases back in her neat string bag, stopping at Frau Schmidt's on the way back for a few minutes' conversation and a wedge of the Libtauer cheese which Andrew liked so well.

Frequently, in the afternoons, she walked round the Serpentine. The chestnut trees were breaking into green and the waterfowl went scurrying across the wind-ruffled water. It was a good substitute for the open countryside which she had always loved so much.

Sometimes in the evening Andrew would glance at her in that oddly jealous manner which meant that he was cross because the day had gone past without his noticing her.

"What have you been up to all day while I've been busy? If I ever do get a car you'll have to drive the damn thing. That'll keep you close to me."

He was still waiting for those "good" patients who did not come, longing to hear from Abbey about the appointment, fretful because their evening at Queen Anne Street had produced no subsequent opportunity. Secretly he was cut that he had seen nothing of Hampton or his friends since then.

In this condition he sat in his surgery one evening towards the end of April. It was nearly nine o'clock and he was about to close up, when a young woman entered.

She gazed at him uncertainly.

"I didn't know whether to come this way—or by the front door."

"It's exactly the same," he smiled sourly. "Except that it's half-price this end. Come along. What is it?"

"I don't mind paying the full fee." She came forward with a peculiar earnestness and sat down on the rexine-covered chair. She was about twenty-eight, he judged, stockily built, dressed in dark olive-green, with bunchy legs and a large plain serious face. To look at her was to have the instinctive thought: No nonsense here!

He relented, saying: "Don't let's talk about the fee! Tell me your trouble."

"Well, Doctor!" She still seemed to wish, gravely, to establish herself. "It was Mrs. Smith—in the little provision shop—who recommended me to come to you. I've known her a long time, I work at Laurier's, quite near. My name is Cramb. But I must tell you I've been to a great many doctors round here." She pulled off her gloves. "It's my hands."

He looked at her hands, the palms of which were covered by a reddish dermatitis, rather like psoriasis. But it was not psoriasis, the edges were not serpiginous. With sudden interest he took up a magnifying glass and peered more closely. Meanwhile she went on talking in her earnest, convincing voice.

"I can't tell you what a disadvantage this is to me in my work. I'd give anything to get rid of it. I've tried every kind of ointment under the sun. But none of them seem to be the slightest use."

"No! They wouldn't." He put down the glass, feeling all the thrill of an obscure yet positive diagnosis. "This is rather an uncommon skin condition, Miss Cramb. It's no good treating it locally. It's due to a blood condition and the only way to get rid of it is by dieting."

"No medicine?" Her earnestness gave way to doubt. "No one ever told me that before."

"I'm telling you now." He laughed and, taking his pad, drew out a diet for her, adding also a list of foods which she must absolutely avoid.

She accepted it hesitatingly. "Well! Of course I'll try it, Doctor. I'd try *anything*." Meticulously she paid him his fee, lingered as though still dubious, then went away. He immediately forgot her.

Ten days later she returned, coming this time by the front door, and entering the consulting room with such an expression of suppressed fervour that he could barely keep from smiling.

"Would you like to see my hands, Doctor?"

"Yes." Now he did smile. "I hope you don't regret the diet."

"Regret it!" She surrendered her hands to him in a passion of gratitude. "Look! Completely cured. Not a single spot on them. You don't know how much it means to me—I can't tell you—such cleverness—"

"That's all right," he said lightly. "It's my job to know these things. You run away and don't worry. Keep off those foods I told you about and you'll never have it again."

She rose.

"And now let me pay you, Doctor?"

"You've already paid me." He was conscious of a mild æsthetic thrill. Right gladly would he have taken another three and six, or even seven and six, from her, but the temptation to dramatize the triumph of his skill proved irresistible.

"But, Doctor—" Unwillingly she allowed herself to be escorted to the door, where she paused for the final earnestness. "Perhaps I'll be able to show my gratitude some other way?"

Gazing at her upturned moon face, a ribald thought crossed his mind. But he merely nodded and closed the door upon her. Again he forgot about her. He was tired, already half-regretful at refusing the fee, and, in any case, he had little thought of what any shopgirl might do for him.

But here at least he did not know Miss Cramb. Moreover, he quite overlooked a possibility, emphasized by Æsop, which as a bad philosophizer he ought to have remembered.

4

MARTHA CRAMB was known as "the Halfback" to the "juniors" at Laurier's. Sturdy, unattractive, sexless, she seemed a strange person to be one of the senior assistants in this unique shop which dealt luxuriously in smart gowns, exquisite undergarments, and furs so rich their prices mounted to hundreds of pounds. Yet the Halfback was an admirable saleswoman, highly valued by her clients. The fact was that Laurier's, in its pride, employed a special system, each "Senior" collecting her own especial clients, a little group of the Laurier customers whom she served exclusively, studied, "dressed" and for whom she "laid aside" things when the new models came in. The relationship was intimate, often existed over many years, and was one to which the Halfback in her earnest sincerity was particularly suited.

She was the daughter of a Kettering solicitor. Many of the Laurier girls were daughters of small professional men in the provinces and outer suburbs. It was esteemed an honour to be allowed to enter Laurier's, to wear the dark green dress which was the uniform of the establishment. Sweated employment and the bad "living-in" conditions which ordinary shop assistants were sometimes made to endure simply did not exist at Laurier's, where the girls were admirably fed and housed and chaperoned. Mr. Winch, the only male buyer in the shop, especially saw to it that they were chaperoned. He particularly esteemed the Halfback, and often held sedate conference with her. He was a pink motherly old gentleman who had been in millinery for forty years. His thumb was worn flat from appraising material, his back permanently cricked in deferential greeting. Maternal though he might be, Mr. Winch, to the stranger entering Laurier's, exhibited the only trousers in a vast and frothy sea of femininity. He had an unsympathetic eye for those husbands who came with their wives to inspect the mannequins. He knew Royalty. He was almost as great an institution as Laurier's.

The incident of Miss Cramb's cure caused a mild sensation amongst the staff at Laurier's. And the immediate result was that from sheer curiosity a number of the Juniors dropped in to Andrew's surgery with mild complaints. Giggling, they told each other that they wanted to see "what the Halfback's doctor was like!"

Gradually however, more and more of the Laurier girls began to come to the surgery at Chesborough Terrace. All the girls were insurance patients. They were compelled by law to be "on the panel," but, with true Laurier arrogance, they repudiated the scheme. By the end of May it was not uncommon for half a dozen of them to be waiting in the surgery—very smart, modelled upon their customers, lipsticked, young. The result was a marked improvement in the surgery receipts. Also a laughing remark by Christine:—

"What *are* you doing with that beauty chorus, darling? Sure they haven't mistaken this for the stage door?"

But Miss Cramb's throbbing gratitude—oh, the ecstasy of those healed hands!—was only beginning to express itself. Hitherto Doctor McLean, safe and elderly, of Royal Crescent, had been regarded as the semi-official doctor of Laurier's, called upon when emergency demanded—as, for instance, when Miss Twig of the Tailoring burned herself badly with a hot iron. But Doctor McLean was on the verge of retiring, and his partner and immediate successor, Doctor Benton, was neither safe nor elderly. Indeed, more than once, Doctor Benton's ankle-roving eye and too tender solicitude for the prettier Juniors had caused Mr. Winch pinkly to frown. Miss Cramb and Mr. Winch discussed these matters at their little conferences together, Mr. Winch nodding gravely with hands clasped behind his back, as Miss Cramb dwelled upon Benton's inadequacy and the presence of another professional man at Chesborough Terrace, strict and ungaudy, who achieved brilliance without sacrifice to Thaïs. Nothing was settled, Mr. Winch always took his time, but there was a portentous gleam in his eye as he swam away to greet a duchess.

In the first week of June, when Andrew had already come to feel shame for his earlier contempt of her, still another manifestation of Miss Cramb's good offices fell in burning fire upon his head.

He received a letter, very neat and precise—no such informality as a phone call, he afterwards learned, would have befitted the writer—asking him to call on Tuesday, the following forenoon, as near eleven o'clock as possible, at 9 Park Gardens, to see Miss Winifred Everett.

Closing his surgery early, he left, with a rising sense of anticipation, to make this visit. It was the first time he had been called out of the drab neighbourhood which had, up till now, contained his practice. Park Gardens was a handsome block of flats, not altogether modern, but large and substantial, with a fine view of Hyde Park. He rang the bell of Number 9, expectant and tense, with the odd conviction that this was his chance at last.

An elderly servant showed him in. The room was spacious, with old furniture, books and flowers, reminding him of Mrs. Vaughan's drawing room. The moment he entered it he felt that his premonition was correct. He swung round as Miss Everett entered, finding her glance, level and composed, fixed appraisingly upon him.

She was a well-made woman of about fifty, dark-haired and sallow-skinned, severely dressed, with an air of complete assurance. She began immediately, in a measured tone:—

"I have lost my doctor—unfortunately—for I had great faith in him. My Miss Cramb recommended you. She's a very faithful creature and I trust her. I've looked you up. You're well-qualified." She paused, quite openly inspecting him, weighing him up. She had the look of a woman well-fed, well-taken-care-of, who would not allow a finger near her without due inspection of the cuticle. Then, guardedly, "I think perhaps you might suit. I usually have a course of injections at this time of year. I'm subject to hay fever. You know all about hay fever, I presume?"

"Yes," he answered. "Which injections do you have?"

She mentioned the name of a well-known preparation. "My old doctor put me on that. I have great faith in it."

"Oh, that!" Nettled at her manner, he was on the point of telling her that the faithful remedy of her faithful doctor was worthless, that it had achieved its popularity through skilful advertising on the part of the firm who produced it and the absence of pollen in most English summers. But with an effort he restrained himself. There was a struggle between all that he believed and all he wished to have. He thought defiantly: If I let this chance slip, after all these months, I'm a fool.

He said, "I think I can give you the injection as well as anyone."

"Very well. And now about your fees. I never paid Doctor Sinclair more than one guinea a visit. May I take it that you will continue this arrangement?"

A guinea a visit—it was three times the largest fee he had ever earned! And more important still, it represented his first step into the superior class of practice he had coveted all these months. Again he stifled the quick protest of his convictions. What did it matter if the injections were useless? That was her look-out, not his. He was sick of failure, tired of being a three-and-sixpenny hack. He wanted to get on, succeed. And he would succeed at all costs.

He came again the following day at eleven o'clock sharp. She had warned him, in her severe way, against being late. She did not wish her forenoon walk interfered with. He gave her the first injection. And thereafter he called twice a week, continuing the treatment.

He was punctual, precise as she, and he never presumed. It was almost amusing the way in which she gradually thawed to him. She was a queer person, Winifred Everett, and a most decided personality. Though she was rich—her father had been a large manufacturer of cutlery in Sheffield and all the money that she had inherited from him was safely invested in the funds—she set herself out to get the utmost value from every penny. It was not meanness but rather an odd kind of egoism. She made herself the centre of her universe, took the utmost care of her body, which was still white and fine, went in for all sorts of treatments which she felt would benefit her. She must have everything of the best. She ate sparingly, but only the finest food. When on his sixth visit she unbent to offer him a glass of sherry, he observed that it was Amontillado of the year 1819. Her clothes came from Laurier's. Her bed linen was the finest he had ever seen. And yet, with all this, she never, according to her lights, wasted a farthing. Not for the life of him could he imagine Miss Everett flinging a half-crown to a taximan without first carefully looking at the meter.

He ought to have loathed her, yet strangely he did not. She had developed her selfishness to the point of a philosophy. And she was so eminently sensible. She exactly reminded him of a woman in an old Dutch picture, a Ter Borch which Christine and he had once seen. She had the same large body, the same smooth-textured skin, the same forbidding yet pleasure-loving mouth.

When she saw that he was, in her own phrase, really going to suit her, she became much less reserved. It was an unwritten law with her that the doctor's visit should last twenty minutes, otherwise she felt she had not had the value of it. But by the end of a month he was extending this to half an hour. They talked together. He told her of his desire for success. She approved it. Her range of conversation was limited. But the range of her relations was unlimited, and it was of them, mostly, that she talked. She spoke to him frequently of her niece, named Catharine Sutton, who lived in Derbyshire and who often came to town since her husband, Captain Sutton, was M.P. for Barnwell.

"Doctor Sinclair used to look after them," she remarked in a noncommittal voice. "I don't see why you shouldn't now."

On his last visit she gave him another glass of her Amontillado and, very pleasantly, she said:—

"I hate bills coming in. Please let me settle up now." She handed him a folded cheque for twelve guineas. "Of course, I shall have you in again soon. I usually have an anticoryza vaccine in the winter."

She actually accompanied him to the door of the flat and there she stood for a moment, her face drily illumined, the nearest approach to a smile he had ever seen there. But it passed quickly and, gazing at him forbiddingly, she said:—

"Will you take the advice of a woman old enough to be your mother? Go to a good tailor. Go to Captain Sutton's tailor—Rogers, in Conduit Street. You've told me how much you wish to succeed. You never will, in that suit."

He strode down the road cursing her, the hot indignity still burning on his brow, cursing her in his old impassioned style. Interfering old bitch! What business was it of hers! What right had she to tell him how he should dress? Did she take him for a *lapdog*? That was the worst of compromise, of truckling to convention. His Paddington patients paid him only three and six, yet they did not ask him to be a tailor's dummy. In future he would confine himself to them and call his soul his own!

But somehow that mood passed. It was perfectly true that he had never taken the slightest interest in his clothes, a suit off the peg had always served him excellently, covered him, kept him warm without elegance. Christine, too, though she was always so neat, never bothered about clothes. She was happiest in a tweed skirt and a woollen jumper she had knitted herself.

Surreptitiously he took stock of himself: his nondescript, worsted, un-creased trousers, mud-spattered at the selvedge. Hang it all, he thought testily, she's perfectly right. How can I attract first-class patients if I look like this? Why didn't Christine tell me? It was *her* job; not old lady Winnie's. What was that name she gave me—Rogers of Conduit Street? Hell! I'm likely to go there!

He had recovered his spirits when he reached home. He flourished the cheque under Christine's nose.

"See that, my good woman! Remember when I came running in with that first wretched three and a bender from the surgery? Bah! That's what I say to it now—bah! This is real money, gen-u-ine fees, like a first-rate M.D., M.R.C.P. ought to be earning. Twelve guineas for talking nicely to Winnie the Pooh, and innocuously inoculating her with Glickert's Eptone."

"What's that?" she asked smiling; then suddenly she was doubtful. "Isn't that the stuff I've heard you run down so much?"

His face altered, he frowned at her, completely at a loss. She had made the one remark he did not wish to hear. All at once he felt angry, not with himself, but with her.

"Blast it, Chris! You're *never* satisfied!" He turned and banged out of the room. For the rest of that day he was in a sulky humour. But next day he cheered up. He went then to Rogers, in Conduit Street.

5

HE was self-conscious as a schoolboy when, a fortnight later, he came down in one of his two new suits. It was a dark double-breasted grey, worn, on Rogers' suggestion, with a wing collar and a dark bow tie which picked up the shade of the grey. There was not the shadow of a doubt, the Conduit Street tailor knew his job; and the mention of Captain Sutton's name had made him do it thoroughly.

This morning, as it fell out, Christine was not looking her best. She had a slight sore throat and had wound her old scarf protectively around her throat and head. She was pouring his coffee when the radiance of his presence burst upon her. For a moment she was too staggered to speak.

"Why Andrew!" she gasped. "You look wonderful. Are you going anywhere?"

"Going anywhere? I'm going on my rounds, my work, of course!" Being self-conscious made him almost snappy. "Well! Do you like it?"

"Yes," she said, not quickly enough to please him. "It's—it's frightfully smart—but," she smiled, "somehow it doesn't quite seem *you!*"

"You'd rather keep me looking like a tramp, I suppose."

She was silent, her hand, raising her cup, suddenly contracted so that the knuckles showed white. Ah! he thought, I got her there. He finished breakfast and entered the consulting room.

Five minutes later she followed him there, scarf still round her throat, her eyes hesitant, pleading.

"Darling," she said, "please don't misunderstand me! I'm delighted to see you in a new suit. I want you to have everything, everything that's best for you. I'm sorry I said that a moment ago; but you see—I'm accustomed to you—oh! it's awfully hard to explain—but I've always identified you as—now *please* don't misunderstand me—as someone who doesn't give a hang about how he looks or how people think he looks. You remember that Epstein head we saw. That it wouldn't have looked quite the same if—oh!—if it had been trimmed and polished up?"

He answered abruptly.

"I'm not an Epstein head."

She made no reply. Lately, he had been difficult to reason with and, hurt at this misunderstanding, she did not know what to say. Still hesitating, she turned away.

Three weeks later, when Miss Everett's niece came to spend a few weeks in London, he was rewarded for his wise observance of the elder lady's hint. On a pretext Miss Everett summoned him to Park Gardens, where she scanned him with severe approval. He could almost see her passing him as a fit candidate for her recommendation. On the following day he received a call from Mrs. Sutton who, since the condition ran, apparently, in the family, wished the same hay-fever treatment as her aunt. This time he had no compunction about injecting the useless eptone of the useful Messrs. Glickert. He made an excellent impression upon Mrs. Sutton. And before the end of that same month he was called to a friend of Miss Everett's who also occupied a flat in Park Gardens.

Andrew was highly diverted with himself. He was winning, winning, winning. In his straining eagerness for success he forgot how contrary was his progress to all that he had hitherto believed. His vanity was touched. He felt alert and confident. He did not pause to reflect that this rolling snowball of his high-class practice had been started, in the first place, by a fat little German woman behind the counter of a ham-and-beef shop near that vulgar Mussleburgh Market. Indeed, almost before he had time to reflect at all, the snowball took a further downhill roll—another and more exciting opportunity was offered to his grasp.

One afternoon in June, the zero hour between two o'clock and four, when nothing of consequence normally occurred, he was sitting in the consulting room, totalling his receipts for the past month, when suddenly the phone rang. Three seconds and he was at the instrument.

"Yes, yes! This is Doctor Manson speaking."

A voice, anguished and palpitant, came back to him.

"Oh, Doctor Manson! I'm relieved to find you in. This is Mr. Winch! Mr. Winch of Laurier's. We've had a slight mishap to one of our customers. Could you come? Could you come at once?"

"I'll be there in four minutes." Andrew clicked back the receiver and sprang for his hat. A 33 bus, hurtling outside, solidly sustained his impetuous leap. In four minutes and a half he was inside the revolving doors of Laurier's, met by an anxious Miss Cramb, and escorted over swimming surfaces of green-piled carpet, past long gilt mirrors and satinwood panelling against which, as if by chance, there could be seen one small hat on its stand, a lacy scarf, an ermine evening wrap.

As they hastened, with rapid earnestness, Miss Cramb explained:—

"It's Miss le Roy, Doctor Manson. One of our customers. Not mine, thank goodness, she's always giving trouble. But, Doctor Manson, you see I spoke to Mr. Winch about you—"

"Thanks!"—brusquely—he could still on occasion be brusque. "What's happened?"

"She seems—oh, Doctor Manson—she seems to have had a fit in the fitting-room!"

At the head of the broad staircase she surrendered him to Mr. Winch, pinkly agitated, who fluttered:—

"This way, Doctor—this way—I hope you can do something. It's most dreadfully unfortunate—"

Into the fitting-room,—warm, exquisitely carpeted in a lighter shade of green, with gilt-and-green-panelled walls,—a crowd of twittering girls, a gilt chair upturned, a towel thrown down, a spilled glass of water, pandemonium

. . . And there, the centre of it all, Miss le Roy, the woman in the fit. She lay on the floor, rigid, with spasmodic clutchings of her hands and sudden stiffenings of her feet. From time to time a straining, intimidating crowing broke from her tense throat.

As Andrew entered with Mr. Winch one of the older assistants in the group burst into tears.

"It wasn't my fault," she sobbed. "I only pointed out to Miss le Roy it was the design she chose herself—"

"Oh, dear. Oh, dear," muttered Mr. Winch. "This is dreadful, dreadful. Shall I—shall I ring for the ambulance?"

"No, not yet," Andrew said in a peculiar tone. He bent down beside Miss le Roy. She was very young, about twenty-four, with blue eyes and washed-out silky hair all tumbled under her askew hat. Her rigidity, her convulsive spasms were increasing.

On the other side of her knelt another woman, with dark concerned eyes, apparently her friend. "Oh, Toppy, Toppy," she kept murmuring.

"Please clear the room," said Andrew suddenly. "I'd like everyone out but—" his eye fell upon the dark young woman—"but this lady here."

The girls went, a trifle unwillingly—it had been pleasurable diversion assisting at Miss le Roy's fit. Miss Cramb, even Mr. Winch, removed themselves from the room. The moment they had gone the convulsions became terrifying.

"This is an extremely serious case," Andrew said, speaking very distinctly. Miss le Roy's eyeballs rolled towards him. "Get me a chair, please."

The fallen chair was righted, in the centre of the room, by the other woman. Then slowly and with great sympathy, supporting her by the armpits, Andrew helped the convulsed Miss le Roy upright into the chair. He held her head erect.

"There," he said with greater sympathy. Then, taking the flat of his hand, he hit her a resounding smack upon the cheek. It was his most courageous action for many months, and remained so—alas!—for many months to come.

Miss le Roy stopped crowing, the spasm ceased, her rolling eyeballs righted themselves. She gazed at him in pained, in infantile bewilderment. Before she could relapse he took his hand again and struck her on the other cheek. Smack! The anguish in Miss le Roy's face was ludicrous. She dithered, seemed about to crow again, and then began, gently, to cry.

Turning to her friend she wept: "Darling, I want to go home."

Andrew gazed apologetically at the dark young woman, who now regarded him with restrained yet singular interest.

"Sorry," he muttered. "It was the only way. Bad hysteria—carpopedal spasms. She might have harmed herself—I hadn't an anæsthetic or anything. And anyway—it worked."

"Yes, it worked."

"Let her cry this out," Andrew said. "Good safety-valve. She'll be all right in a few minutes."

"Wait though—" quickly. "You must see her home."

"Very well," Andrew said, in his busiest professional tone.

In five minutes' time Toppy le Roy was able to make good her face, a lengthy operation punctuated by a few desultory sobs.

"I don't look too foul, do I, darling?" she inquired of her friend. Of Andrew she took no notice whatsoever.

They left the fitting-room thereafter, and their progress through the long showroom was sheer sensation. Wonder and relief left Mr. Winch almost speechless. He did not know, he would never know how this had come about, how the writhing paralytic had been made to walk. He followed, babbling deferential words. As Andrew passed through the main entrance behind the two women he wrung him fervently with a spongy hand.

The taxi took them along Bayswater Road in the direction of Marble Arch. There was not even pretence of speech. Miss le Roy was sulking now, like a spoiled child who has been punished, and she was still jumpy—from time to time, her hands and the muscles of her face gave slight involuntary twitches. She was, now that she could be seen more normally, very thin and almost pretty in a scrawny little way. Her clothes were beautiful yet, despite them, she seemed to Andrew exactly like a young pulled chicken, through which traces of electric current periodically passed. He was himself nervous, conscious of the awkward situation, yet determined in his own interests to take advantage of it to the full.

The taxi rounded the Marble Arch, ran alongside Hyde Park, and, wheeling to the left, they drew up before a house in Green Street. Then, almost immediately, they were inside. The house took Andrew's breath away; he had never imagined anything so luxurious—the wide soft-pinewood hall, the cabinet gorgeous with jade, the strange single painting set in a costly panel, the reddish-gold lacquer chairs, the wide settees, the skin-thin faded rugs.

Toppy le Roy flung herself down on a satin cushioned sofa, still ignoring Andrew, and tugged off her little hat which she flung on the floor.

"Press the bell, darling, I must have a drink. Thank God, Father isn't home."

Quickly, a manservant brought cocktails. When he had gone Toppy's friend considered Andrew thoughtfully—almost, but not quite, smiling.

"I think we ought to explain ourselves to you, Doctor. It's all been rather hurried. I'm Mrs. Lawrence. Toppy here—Miss le Roy—had rather a row over a dress she's having specially designed for the Arts Charity Ball and—well! she's been doing too much lately, she's a very nervy little person—and the long and the short of it is that although Toppy's very cross with you we're frightfully indebted to you for getting us back here. And I'm going to have another cocktail."

"Me too," said Toppy peevishly. "That bloody Laurier woman. I'll tell Father to ring up and get her sacked! Oh, no I won't!" As she tilted her second cocktail a smile of gratification slowly overspread her face. "I did give them something to think about, though, didn't I, Frances! I simply went *wild!*

That look on old Mamma Winch's face was too, too funny." Her scraggy little frame shook with laughter. She met Andrew's eyes without ill-will. "Go on, Doctor. Laugh! It was priceless."

"No, I don't think it was so amusing." He spoke quickly, anxious to explain himself, establish his position, convince her she was ill. "You really had a bad attack. I'm sorry I had to treat you as I did. If I'd had an anæsthetic I'd have given you that. Much less—less annoying for you. And please don't imagine that I think you tried to bring on that attack. Hysteria—well, that's what it was—is a definite syndrome. People oughtn't to be unsympathetic about it. It's a condition of the nervous system. You see, you're extremely run-down, Miss le Roy, all your reflexes are on edge; you're in a very nervous state."

"That's perfectly true," Frances Lawrence nodded. "You've been doing far too much lately, Toppy."

"Would you really have given me chloroform?" Toppy asked Andrew in childish wonder. "That would have been fun."

"But seriously, Toppy," Mrs. Lawrence said, "I wish you'd take yourself up."

"You sound like Father," Toppy said, losing her good humour.

There was a pause. Andrew had finished his cocktail. He put the glass down on the carved pine mantelpiece behind him. There seemed nothing more for him to do.

"Well!" he said effectively, "I must get on with my work. Please take my advice, Miss le Roy. Have a light meal, go to bed, and—since I cannot be of any further service to you—call in your own doctor to-morrow. Good-by."

Mrs. Lawrence accompanied him into the hall, her manner so unhurried that he was obliged to restrain the busy briskness of his exit. She was tall and slim, with rather high shoulders and a small elegant head. In her dark, beautifully waved hair a few iron-grey strands gave her a curious distinction. Yet she was quite young; not more than twenty-seven, he was sure. Despite her height she had fine bones; her wrists especially were small and fine; indeed, her whole figure seemed flexible, exquisitely tempered, like a fencer's. She gave him her hand, her greenish hazel eyes fixed upon him in that faint, friendly, unhurried smile.

"I only wished to tell you how I admired your new line of treatment." Her lips twitched. "Don't give it up on any account. I foresee you making it a crashing success."

Walking down Green Street to pick up a bus he saw to his amazement that it was nearly five o'clock. He had spent three hours in the company of these two women. He ought to be able to charge a really big fee for that! And yet, despite this elevating thought—so symptomatic of his brave new outlook—he felt confused, strangely dissatisfied. Had he really made the most of his chance? Mrs. Lawrence had seemed to like him. But you never could tell with people like that. What a marvellous house, too!

Suddenly he gritted his teeth in angry exasperation. Not only had he omitted to leave his card; he had forgotten even to tell them who he was. As he took his seat in the crowded bus beside an old workman in soiled overalls he blamed himself bitterly for missing a golden opportunity.

<h1 style="text-align:center">6</h1>

THE following morning, at quarter-past eleven, as he was on the point of taking his departure on a round of cheap visits centred about the Mussel-burgh Market, the telephone rang. A manservant's voice, gravely solicitous, purred at him.

"Doctor Manson, sir! Ah! Miss le Roy wishes to know, sir, what time you will be calling on her to-day. Ah! Excuse me sir, hold on—Mrs. Lawrence will speak to you herself."

Andrew hung on, with a quick throbbing excitement, while Mrs. Lawrence talked to him in friendly fashion, explaining that they were expecting him to call, without fail.

As he came away from the phone he told himself exultantly that he hadn't missed the opportunity yesterday; he hadn't—no, he hadn't missed it after all.

He dropped all his other calls, urgent or otherwise, and went straight to the house in Green Street. And here, for the first time, he met Joseph le Roy. He found Le Roy impatiently awaiting him in the jade-bedizened hall, a bald thickset figure, downright and bejowled, who abused his cigar like a man who has no time to lose. In one second his eyes bored into Andrew, a swift surgical operation which ended to his satisfaction. He then spoke forcibly in a colonial tongue.

"See here, doc, I'm in a hurry. Mrs. Lawrence had a hell of a bother track-ing you down this morning. I understand you're a clever young fellow and you don't stand any nonsense. You're married too, aren't you? That's good. Now you take my girl in hand. Get her right, get her strong, get all this damn hysteria out of her system. Don't spare anything. I can pay. Good-by."

Joseph le Roy was a New Zealander. And despite his money, his Green Street house, and his exotic little Toppy, it was not difficult to believe the truth—that his great-grandfather was one Michael Cleary, an illiterate farm hand on the lands around Greymouth Harbour, who was known colloquially to his fellow "scrubbies" as Leary. Joseph le Roy had certainly faced up to life as Joe Leary, a boy whose first job was that of "milker" on the great Greymouth farms. But Joe was born, as he said himself, to milk more than cows. And thirty years later, in the top-floor office of the first Auckland sky-scraper, it was Joseph le Roy who put his signature to the deal unifying the Island dairy farms into a great dried milk combine.

It was a magic scheme—the Cremogen Combine. At this time dried milk goods were unknown, commercially unorganized. It was Le Roy who saw their possibility, who led their attack on the world market, advertising them as God-given nourishment for infants and invalids. The cream of the achieve-ment lay, not in Joe's products, but in his own rich audacity. The surplus skim milk, which had been poured down the drain or given to the pigs in hundreds of New Zealand farms, was now sold in the cities of the world, in Joe's neat brightly papered tins, as Cremogen, Cremax, and Cremefat, at three times the price of pure fresh milk.

Co-director in the Le Roy Combine, and manager of the English interests, was Jack Lawrence, who had been, illogically enough, a Guards officer before he went into business in the city. Yet it was more than the bare association of commerce which drew Mrs. Lawrence and Toppy together. Frances, rich in her own right and far more at home in the smart society of London than Toppy—who occasionally betrayed her brushwood antecedents—had an amused affection for the *enfant gâté*. When Andrew went upstairs after his interview with Le Roy she was waiting for him outside Toppy's room.

Indeed, on subsequent days Frances Lawrence was usually present at the time of his visit, helping him with his exciting, wilful patient, ready to see an improvement in Toppy, insistent that she continue with the treatment, asking when they might expect his next call.

Grateful to Mrs. Lawrence, he was still diffident enough to feel it strange that this patrician, self-admittedly selective person whom, before he came to see her photographs in the illustrated weeklies, he knew to be exclusive, should have even this mild interest in him. Her wide and rather sulky mouth usually expressed hostility towards people who were not her intimates, yet for some reason she was never hostile to him. He had an extraordinary desire, greater than curiosity, to fathom her character, her personality. He seemed to know nothing of the real Mrs. Lawrence. It was a delight to watch the controlled actions of her limbs, as she moved about the room. She was always at ease, watchful in everything she did, with a mind behind her friendly guarded eyes, despite the graceful casualness of her speech.

He hardly realized that the suggestion was hers, yet—though he said nothing to Christine, who still contentedly balanced her housekeeping budget in shillings and pence—he began to ask himself impatiently how any doctor could develop a high-class practice without a smart car? It was ridiculous to think of him stepping along Green Street, carrying his own bag, with dust on his shoes, facing the slightly superior manservant, without a car. He had the brick garage at the back of his house, which would considerably reduce the cost of upkeep, and there were firms who specialized in supplying cars to doctors, admirable firms who did not mind graciously deferring the terms of payment.

Three weeks later a brown folding-roof coupé, brand new and darkly glittering, drew up at 9 Chesborough Terrace. Easing himself from the driving seat, Andrew ran up the stairs of his house.

"Christine!" he called out, trying to suppress the gloating excitement in his voice. "Christine! Come and see something!"

He had meant to stagger her. And he succeeded.

"Goodness!" She clutched his arm. "Is it *ours*? Oh! what a beauty!"

"Isn't she? Look *out*, dear, don't handle the paintwork! It's—it's liable to mark the varnish!" He smiled at her in quite his old way. "Pretty good surprise, eh, Chris? Me getting it and licencing it and everything and never saying a word to you. Step in, lady, and I'll demonstrate. She goes like a bird."

She could not admire the little car enough as he took her, bare-headed, on an easy spin round the Square. Four minutes later they were back, standing on the pavement, while he still feasted his eyes upon the treasure. Their moments of intimacy, of understanding and happiness together, were so rare now that she was loath to relinquish this one.

She murmured: "It'll be so easy for you to get about now, dear." Then again, diffidently: "And if we could get out a little bit into the country, say on Sundays, into the woods—oh, it would be *wonderful*."

"Of course," he answered absently. "But it's really for the practice. We can't go gadding about, getting mud all over it!" He was thinking of the effect this dashing little coupé would have upon his patients.

The main effect, however, was beyond his expectation. On Thursday of the following week, as he came out of the heavy glass and iron-grilled door of Number 17a Green Street, he ran straight into Freddie Hampton.

"Hello, Hampton," he said casually. He could not repress a thrill of satisfaction at the sight of Hampton's face. At first Hampton had barely recognized him, and as he did so, his expression, falling through various degrees of surprise, was still frankly nonplussed.

"Why, hello!" said Freddie. "What are you doing here?"

"Patient," Andrew answered, jerking his head backwards in the direction of Number 17a. "I've got Joe le Roy's daughter on my hands."

"Joe le Roy!"

That exclamation alone was worth a lot to Manson. He put a proprietary hand on the door of his beautiful new coupé.

"Which way are you going? Can I drop you anywhere?"

Freddie revived himself quickly. He was seldom at a loss, and never for any length of time. Indeed, in thirty seconds, his opinion of Manson, his whole idea of Manson's usefulness to him, had undergone a swift and unexpected revolution.

"Yes," he smiled companionably. "I was going along to Bentinck Street— to Ida Sherrington's Home. Walking to keep the old figure down. But I'll step in with you."

There was a pause for a few minutes while they ran across Bond Street. Hampton was thinking hard. He had welcomed Andrew effusively to London because he hoped Manson's practice might occasionally provide him with a three-guinea consultation at Queen Anne Street. But now the change in his old classmate, the car, and above all the mention of Joe le Roy—the name had for him infinitely more worldly significance than it had for Andrew— showed him his mistake. There were Manson's ideal qualifications, too—useful, extremely useful. Looking astutely ahead, Freddie saw a better, an altogether more profitable basis for co-operation between Andrew and himself. He would go carefully of course, for Manson was a touchy, uncertain devil.

He said:—

"Why don't you come in with me and meet Ida? She's a useful person to know, though she keeps the worst nursing home in London. Oh! I don't know! She's probably as good as the rest of them. And she certainly charges more."

"Yes?"

"Come in with me and see my patient. She's harmless—old Mrs. Raeburn. Ivory and I are doing a few tests on her. You're strong on lungs, aren't you? Come along and examine her chest. It'll please her enormously. And it'll be five guineas for you."

"What! You mean . . . ? But what's the matter with her chest?"

"Nothing much," Freddie smiled. "Don't look so stricken! She's probably got a touch of senile bronchitis! And she'd love to see you! That's how we do it here. Ivory and Freedman and I. You really ought to be in on it, Manson. We won't talk about it now—yes, round that first corner there!—but it would amaze you how it works out."

Andrew drew up the car at the house indicated by Hampton, an ordinary town dwelling-house, tall and narrow, which had obviously never been intended for its present purpose. Indeed, gazing at the busy street, along which the traffic racketed and hooted, it was difficult to imagine how any sick person could find peace here. It looked precisely the place to provoke rather than to cure a nervous breakdown. Andrew mentioned this to Hampton as they mounted the steps to the front door.

"I know, my dear fellow," Freddie agreed with ready cordiality. "But they're all the same. This little bit of the West End is jammed with them. You see, we must have them convenient to ourselves." He grinned. "Ideal if they were out somewhere quiet, but—for instance—what surgeon would drive ten miles every day to see his case for five minutes? Oh! You'll get to know about our little West End sick bays in due course." He drew up in the narrow hall into which they passed. "They've all got three smells, you observe—anæsthetics, cooking, and excreta—logical sequence—forgive me, old man! And now meet Ida."

With the air of a man who knows his way about, he led the way into a constricted office on the ground floor, where a little woman in a mauve uniform and a stiff white headdress sat at a small desk.

"Morning, Ida," Freddie exclaimed between flattery and familiarity. "Doing your sums?"

She raised her eyes, saw him, and smiled good-naturedly. She was short, stout, and extremely full-blooded. But her bright red face was so thickly covered with powder that the result was a mauve complexion almost the colour of her uniform. She had a look of coarse bustling vitality, of knowing humour, of pluck. Her teeth were false and ill-fitting. Her hair was grizzled. Somehow, it was easy to suspect her of a strong vocabulary, to imagine her performing admirably as the keeper of a second-rate night club.

Yet Ida Sherrington's nursing home was the most fashionable in London.

Half the peerage had been to Ida; and society women, racing men, famous barristers, and diplomats. You had only to pick up the morning paper to read that yet another bright young person famous on stage or screen had left her appendix safely in Ida's motherly hands. She dressed all her nurses in a delicate shade of mauve, paid her wine butler two hundred pounds and her chef twice that sum a year. The prices which she charged her patients were fantastic. Forty guineas for a room each week was not an uncommon figure. And on top of that came extras, the chemist's bill—often a matter of pounds—the special night nurse, the theatre fee. But when argued with, Ida had one answer which she often adorned with a free and easy adjective. She had her own worries, with cuts and percentages to be paid out, and often she felt it was she who was being bled.

Ida had a soft side for the younger members of the profession and she greeted Manson agreeably as Freddie babbled:—

"Take a good look at him. He'll soon be sending you so many patients you'll overflow into the Plaza Hotel."

"The Plaza overflows into me." Ida nodded her headdress meaningly.

"Ha! Ha!" Freddie laughed. "That's pretty good—I must tell old Freedman that one. Paul'll appreciate it. Come on Manson. We'll go up top."

The cramped lift, just wide enough to hold a wheeled stretcher diagonally, took them to the fourth floor. The passage was narrow; trays stood outside the doors, and vases of flowers wilting in the hot atmosphere. They went into Mrs. Raeburn's room.

She was a woman of over sixty, propped up on her pillows, expectant of the doctor's visit, holding in her hand a slip of paper on which she had written certain symptoms experienced during the night, together with questions which she wished to ask. Andrew placed her unerringly as the elderly hypochondriac, Charcot's *malade au petit morceau de papier*.

Seated on the bed, Freddie talked to her, felt her pulse—no more—listened to her and gaily reassured her. He told her Mr. Ivory would be calling with the results of some highly scientific tests in the afternoon. He asked her to allow his colleague, Doctor Manson, whose speciality was lungs, to examine her chest. Mrs. Raeburn was flattered. She enjoyed it all very much. It emerged that she had been in Hampton's hands for two years. She was wealthy, without relatives, and spent her time equally between exclusive private hotels and West End nursing homes.

"Lord!" Freddie exclaimed as they left the room. "You've no idea what a gold mine that old woman has been to us. We've taken nuggets out of her."

Andrew did not answer. The atmosphere of this place slightly sickened him. There was nothing wrong with the old lady's lungs, and only her touching look of gratitude towards Freddie saved the matter from being downright dishonest. He tried to convince himself. Why should he be such a stickler? He would never make a success of himself if he continued intolerant, opinionative. And Freddie had meant it kindly, giving him the chance to examine this patient.

He shook hands amicably enough with Hampton before stepping into his coupé. And at the end of the month, when he received a neatly written cheque from Mrs. Raeburn—with her best thanks—for five guineas, he was able to laugh at his silly scruples. He enjoyed receiving cheques now, and to his extreme satisfaction more and more of them were coming his way.

7

THE practice, which had shown a promising increase, now began a rapid, almost electrifying expansion in all directions, the effect of which was to sweep Andrew more swiftly with the stream. In a sense he was the victim of his own intensity. He had always been poor. In the past, his obstinate individualism had brought him nothing but defeat. Now he could justify himself with the amazing proofs of his material success.

Shortly after his emergency call to Laurier's he had a highly gratifying interview with Mr. Winch, and thereafter more of the Laurier Juniors, and even some of the Seniors, came to consult him. They came chiefly for trivial complaints, yet once the girls had visited him it was strange how frequently they reappeared—his manner was so kind, so cheering, so brisk. His surgery receipts soared. Soon he managed to have the front of the house repainted, and with the help of one of those firms of surgical outfitters—all of them burning to assist young practitioners to enlarge their incomes—he was able to refurnish his surgery and consulting room with a new couch, a padded swing chair, a dinky rubber tyred trolley, and sundry elegantly scientific cabinets in white enamel and glass.

The manifest prosperity of the freshly cream-painted house, of his car, of this glitteringly modern equipment, soon traversed the neighbourhood, bringing back many of the "good" patients who had consulted Doctor Foy in the past but had gradually dropped off when the old doctor and his consulting room became progressively dingy.

The days of waiting, of hanging about, were finished for Andrew. At the evening surgeries it was as much as he could do to keep going—the front bell purring, the surgery door *pinging*, patients waiting for him back and front, causing him to dash between the surgery and the consulting room. The next step came inevitably. He was forced to evolve a scheme to save his time.

"Listen, Chris," he said one morning. "I've just struck on something that's going to help me a lot in these rush hours. You know—when I've seen a patient in the surgery I come back into the house to make up the medicine. Takes me five minutes usually. And it's a shocking waste of time—when I might be using it to polish off one of the 'good' patients waiting to see me in the consulting room. Well, d'you get my scheme? From now on, you're my dispenser!"

She looked at him with a startled contraction of her brows.

"But I don't know anything about making up medicine."

He smiled reassuringly.

"That's all right, dear. I've prepared a couple of nice stock mixtures. All you have to do is fill the bottles, label and wrap them."

"But—" Christine's perplexity showed in her eyes. "Oh, I want to help you Andrew, only—do you really believe—"

"Don't you see I've *got* to?" His gaze avoided hers. He drank the rest of his coffee irritably. "I know I used to talk a lot of hot air about medicine at Aberalaw. All theories! I'm—I'm a practical physician now. Besides, all these Laurier girls are anæmic. A good iron mixture won't do them any harm."

Before she could answer the sound of the surgery bell had pulled him away.

In the old days she would have argued, taken a firm stand. But now, sadly, she reflected on the reversal of their earlier relationship. She no longer influenced, guided him. It was he who drove ahead.

She began to stand in the cubbyhole of the dispensary during those hectic surgery periods, waiting for his tense exclamation, in his rapid transit between "good" and surgery patients—"Iron!" or "Alba!" or "Carminative!" or sometimes, when she would protest that the iron mixture had run out, a strung-up, significant bark: "Anything! Damn it! *Anything at all!*"

Often the surgery was not over until half-past nine. Then they made up the book, Doctor Foy's heavy ledger, which had only been half used when they took over the practice.

"My God! What a day, Chris!" he gloated. "D'you remember that first measly three and six I took, like a shaky schoolboy? Well, to-day—to-day, we took over eight pounds *cash*."

He tucked the money, heavy piles of silver and a few notes, into the little Afrikander tobacco sack which Doctor Foy had used as his moneybag, and locked it in the middle drawer of the desk. As with the ledger, he kept on using this old bag in order to continue his luck.

Now, indeed, he forgot all about his early doubts and praised his acumen in taking over the practice.

"We've got it absolutely gilt-edged every way, Chris," he exulted. "A paying surgery and a sound middle-class connection. And on top of that I'm building up a first-rate consultant practice on my own. You just watch where we're going."

On the first of October he was able to tell her to refurnish the house. After his morning surgery he said—with impressive casualness, his new manner:—

"I'd like you to go up West to-day, Chris. Go to Hudson's—or to Ostley's if you like it better. Go to the best place. And get all the new furniture you want. Get a couple of new bedroom suites, drawing-room suite, get *everything*."

She glanced at him in silence as he lit a cigarette, smiling.

"That's one of the joys of making money, being able to give you everything you want. Don't think I'm mean. Lord, no! You've been a little brick,

Chris, the whole way through our bad times. Now we're just beginning to enjoy our good times."

"By ordering expensive shiny furniture and—and hair-stuffed three-piece suites from Ostley's."

He missed the bitterness in her tone. He laughed.

"That's right, dear. It's high time we got rid of our old Regency junk."

Tears sprang to her eyes. She flashed:—

"You didn't think it was junk at Aberalaw. And it isn't, either. Oh! those were real days, those were happy days!"

With a choking sob she spun round and left the room.

He stared after her in blank surprise. Her moods had been queer recently —uncertain and depressed, with sudden bursts of incomprehensible bitterness. He sensed that they were drifting away from each other, losing that mysterious unity, that hidden bond of comradeship which had always existed between them. Well! It was not his fault. He was doing his best, his utmost. He thought angrily, my getting on means nothing to her, nothing. But he could not dwell upon the unreasonableness, the injustice of her behaviour. He had a full list of calls before him and, since it was Tuesday, his usual visit to the bank.

Twice a week, regularly, he dropped in at the bank to make payments into his account, for he knew it was unwise to let cash accumulate in his desk. He could not but contrast these pleasant visits with his experience in Blaenelly when, as a down-at-heel assistant, he had been humiliated by Aneurin Rees. Here Mr. Wade, the manager, always gave him a warmly deferential smile and often an invitation to smoke a cigarette in his private room.

"If I may say so, Doctor, without being personal, you're doing remarkably nicely. Round here we can do with a go-ahead doctor, who's just got the right amount of conservatism. Like yourself, Doctor, if I may say so. Now these Southern Railway Guaranteed we were discussing the other day . . ."

Wade's deference was merely one instance of the general upswing of opinion. He now found the other doctors of the district giving him a friendly salute as their coupés went past his own. At the autumn divisional meeting of the Medical Association, in that same room where, on his first appearance, he had been made to feel himself a pariah, he was welcomed, made much of, given a cigar by Doctor Ferrie, vice president of the division.

"Glad to see you with us, Doctor," fussed little red-faced Ferrie. "Did you approve of my speech? We've got to hold out for our fees. On night calls especially, I am taking a firm stand. The other night I was knocked up by a boy—a mere child of twelve, if you please. 'Come round quick Doctor,' he blubbers. 'Father's at work and my mother's taken awful bad.' You *know* that 2 A.M. conversation. And I'd never seen the kid in my life before. 'My dear boy,' says I, 'your mother's no patient of mine! Away and fetch me my half guinea and *then* I'll come.' Of course he never came back. I tell you, Doctor, this district is *terrible* . . ."

On the week after the divisional meeting Mrs. Lawrence rang him up. He always enjoyed the graceful inconsequence of her telephone conversations, but to-day, after mentioning that her husband was fishing in Ireland, that she might possibly be going later to join him there, she asked him, dropping out her invitation as though it were of no importance, to luncheon on the following Friday.

"Toppy'll be there. And one or two people—less dull, I think, than one usually meets. It might do you some good, perhaps, to know them."

He hung up the receiver between satisfaction and an odd irritation. In his heart he was piqued that Christine had not been invited too. Then, gradually, he came to see that it was not a social but really a business occasion. He must get about and make contacts, particularly amongst the class of people who would be present at this luncheon. And, in any case, Christine need know nothing at all of the affair. When Friday came he told her that he had a luncheon engagement with Hampton and jumped into his car, relieved. He forgot that he was an extremely bad liar.

Frances Lawrence's house was in Knightsbridge, in a quiet street, between Hans Place and Wilton Crescent. Though it had not the splendour of the Le Roy mansion, its restrained taste conveyed an equal sense of opulence. Andrew was late in arriving and most of the guests were already there: Toppy; Rosa Keane the novelist; Sir Dudley Rumbold-Blane, M.D., F.R.C.P., famous physician and member of the board of Cremo Products; Nicol Watson, traveller and anthropologist, and several others of less alarming distinction.

He found himself at table beside a Mrs. Thornton, who lived, she told him, in Leicestershire, and who came up periodically to Brown's Hotel for a short season in town. Though he was now able calmly to sustain the ordeal of introductions, he was glad to regain his assurance under cover of her chatter, a maternal account of a foot injury received at hockey by her daughter Sybil, a schoolgirl at Roedean.

Giving one ear to Mrs. Thornton, who took his mute listening for interest, he still managed to hear something of the suave and witty conversation around him—Rosa Keane's acid pleasantries, Watson's fascinatingly graceful account of an expedition he had recently made through the Paraguayan interior. He admired also the ease with which Frances kept the talk moving, at the same time sustaining the measured pedantry of Sir Rumbold, who sat beside her. Once or twice he felt her eyes upon him, half-smiling, interrogative.

"Of course," Watson concluded his narrative with a deprecatory smile, "easily one's most devastating experience was to come home and run straight into an attack of influenza."

"Ha!" said Sir Rumbold. "So you've been a victim too." By the device of clearing his throat and placing his pince-nez upon his richly endowed nose, he gained the attention of the table. Sir Rumbold was at home in this position—for many years now the attention of the great British Public had been focussed upon him. It was Sir Rumbold who, a quarter of a century before, had staggered humanity by the declaration that a certain portion of man's intestine was not only useless but definitely harmful. Hundreds of people had rushed straight away to have the dangerous section removed and, though Sir Rumbold was not himself amongst this number, the fame of the operation, which the surgeons named the Rumbold-Blane excision, established his reputation as a dietician. Since then he had kept well to the front, successfully introducing to the nation bran food, Yourghout, and the lactic acid bacillus. Later he invented the Rumbold-Blane Mastication, and now, in addition to his activities on many company boards, he wrote the menus for the famous Railey chain of restaurants: *Come, Ladies and Gentlemen, Let Sir Rumbold-Blane, M.D., F.R.C.P., Help You Choose Your Calories!* Many were the muttered grumbles amongst more legitimate healers that Sir Rumbold should have been scored off the *Register* years ago: to which the answer manifestly was—what would the *Register* be without Sir Rumbold?

He now said, glancing paternally at Frances:—

"One of the most interesting features of this recent epidemic has been the spectacular therapeutic effect of Cremogen. I had occasion to say the same thing at our Company meeting last week. We have—aha!—no cure for influenza. And in the absence of cure, the only way to resist its murderous invasion is to develop a high state of resistance, a vital defence of the body against the inroads of the disease. I happened to say, I flatter myself rather aptly, that we had proved incontestably, not on guinea pigs—aha! aha!—like our laboratory friends—but on *human beings*, the phenomenal power of Cremogen in organizing and energizing the vital antagonism of the body."

Watson turned to Andrew with his odd smile. "What do you think of Cremo productions, Doctor?"

Caught unawares, Andrew found himself saying:—

"It's as good a way of taking skim milk as any other."

Rosa Keane, with a swift approving side-glance, was unkind enough to laugh. Frances was smiling too. Hurriedly, Sir Rumbold passed to a description of his recent visit, as a guest of the Northern Medical Union, to the Trossachs.

Otherwise the luncheon was harmonious. Andrew eventually found himself joining freely in the conversation. Before he took his leave from her drawing-room Frances had a word with him.

"You really do shine," she murmured, "out of the consulting room. Mrs. Thornton hasn't been able to drink her coffee for telling me about you. I have a strange presentiment that you've bagged her—is that the phrase?—as a patient."

With that remark ringing in his ear, he went home feeling that he was much the better, and Christine none the worse, for the adventure.

On the following morning, however, at half-past ten, he had an unpleasant shock.

Freddie Hampton rang him to inquire briskly: "Enjoy your lunch yesterday? How did I know? Why, you old dog, haven't you seen this morning's *Tribune?*"

Dismayed, Andrew went directly into the waiting-room, where the papers were laid out when Christine and he had finished with them. For the second time he went through the *Tribune*, one of the better-known pictorial dailies. Suddenly he started. How had he missed it before? There, on a page devoted to society gossip, was a photograph of Frances Lawrence with a paragraph describing her luncheon party of the day before, his name amongst the guests.

With a chagrined face he slipped the sheet from the others, crushed it into a ball, flung it in the fire. Then he realized that Christine had already read the paper. He frowned in an access of vexation. Though he felt sure that she had not seen this confounded paragraph, he went scowling into his consulting room.

But Christine had seen the paragraph. And, after a momentary bewilderment, the hurt of it struck her to the heart. Why had he not told her? Why? Why? She would not have minded his going to this stupid lunch. She tried to reassure herself—it was all too trivial to cause her such anxiety and pain. But she saw, with a dull ache, that its implications were not trivial.

When he went out on his round she attempted to go on with her work in the house. But she could not. She wandered into his consulting room, from there into his surgery, with the same heavy oppression in her breast. She began in a desultory fashion to dust the surgery. Beside the desk lay his old medical bag, the first he had ever possessed, which he had used at Blaenelly, carrying it along the Rows, using it in his emergency calls down the mine. She touched it with a strange tenderness. He had a new bag now, a finer one. It was part of this new, this finer practice which he was striving after so feverishly, and which, deep in her heart, she so distrusted. She knew it was useless to attempt to speak to him about her misgivings on his behalf. He was so touchy now—the sign of his own conflict—a word from her would set him off, instantly provoke a quarrel. She must do her best in other ways.

It was Saturday forenoon and she had promised to take Florrie with her when she set out to do her shopping. Florrie was a bright little girl and Christine had become attached to her. She could hear her waiting now, at the head of the basement stairs, sent up by her mother, very clean and wearing a fresh frock, in a state of great preparedness. They often went out together like this on a Saturday.

She felt better in the open air with the child holding her hand, walking down the Market, talking to her friends amongst the hawkers, buying fruit, flowers, trying to think of something especially nice to please Andrew.

Yet the wound was still open. Why, why had he not told her? And why had she not been there? She recollected that first occasion at Aberalaw, when they had gone to the Vaughans and it had taken all her efforts to drag him with her. How different was the position now! Was she to blame? Had she changed, withdrawn into herself, become in some way antisocial? She did not think so. She still liked meeting and knowing people, irrespective of who or what they were. Her friendship with Mrs. Vaughan still persisted in their regular exchange of letters.

But actually, though she felt hurt and slighted, her main concern was less for herself than for him. She knew that rich people could be ill as well as poor, that it was possible for him to be as fine a doctor in Green Street, Mayfair, as in Cefen Row, Aberalaw. She did not demand the persistence of such heroic effects as leggings and his old Red Indian motorcycle. Yet she did feel with all her soul that in those days his idealism had been pure and wonderful, illuminating both their lives with a clear white flame. Now the flame had turned yellower and the globe of the lamp was smudged.

As she went into Frau Schmidt's she tried to erase the lines of worry from her brow. Nevertheless she found the woman looking at her sharply.

And presently Frau Schmidt grumbled: "You don't eat enough, my dear! You don't look as you should! And you haf a fine car now and money and everything. Look! I will make you taste this. It iss good!"

The long thin knife in her hand, she cut a slice of her famous boiled ham and made Christine eat a soft bread sandwich. At the same time Florrie was provided with an iced pastry. Frau Schmidt kept talking all the time.

"And now you want some Libtauer. Herr Doctor—he has eaten pounds of my cheese and he never grows tired of it. Some day I will ask him to write me a testimonial to put in my window. This is the cheese what has made me famous . . ."

Chuckling, Frau Schmidt ran on until they left her.

Outside, Christine and Florrie stood on the kerb waiting for the policeman on duty—it was their old friend Struthers—to signal them across. Christine kept a restraining hand on the impulsive Florrie's arm.

"You must always watch out for the traffic here," she cautioned. "What would your mother say if you were to get run over?"

Florrie, her mouth stuffed with the end of her pastry, considered this an excellent joke.

They were home at last and Christine began to undo the wrappings from her purchases. As she moved about the front room, putting the bronze chrysanthemums she had bought into a vase, she felt sad again.

Suddenly the telephone rang.

She went to answer it, her face still, her lips slightly drooping. For perhaps five minutes she was absent. When she returned her expression was transfigured. Her eyes were bright, excited. From time to time she glanced out of the window, eager for Andrew's return, her despondency forgotten in the good news she had received, news which was so important to him; yes, important to both of them. She had a happy conviction that nothing could have been more propitious. No better antidote to the poison of a facile success could ever have been decreed. And it was such an advance, such a real step up for him as well. Eagerly she went to the window again.

When he arrived she could not contain herself to wait but ran to meet him in the hall.

"Andrew! I've got a message for you from Sir Robert Abbey. He's just been on the telephone."

"Yes?" His face, which had drawn into sudden compunction at the sight of her, cleared.

"Yes! He rang up himself, wanted to speak to you. I told him who I was —oh! he was terribly nice—oh!—oh! I'm telling you so badly. Darling! You're to be appointed to outpatients at the Victoria Hospital—immediately!"

His eyes filled slowly with excited realization.

"Why—that's good news, Chris."

"Isn't it, isn't it," she cried, delighted. "Your own work again—chances for research—everything you wanted on the Fatigue Board and didn't get!" She put her arms round his neck and hugged him.

He looked down at her, indescribably touched by her love, her generous unselfishness. He had a momentary pang.

"What a good soul you are, Chris! And—and what a lout I am!"

8

Upon the fourteenth of the following month, Andrew began his duties in the outpatients department of the Victoria Chest Hospital. His days were Tuesdays and Thursdays, the hours from three until five o'clock in the afternoon. It was exactly like his old surgery days in Aberalaw, except that now all the cases which came to him were specialized lung and bronchial conditions. And he was, of course, to his great and secret pride, no longer a medical aid assistant but an honorary physician in one of the oldest and most famous hospitals in London.

The Victoria Hospital was unquestionably old. Situated in Battersea in a network of mean streets close to the Thames, it seldom caught, even in summer, more than a stray gleam of sunshine; while in winter its balconies, onto which the patients' beds were intended to be wheeled, were more often than not blanketed in river fog. Upon the gloomy, dilapidated façade was a great placard in red and white, which seemed obvious and redundant: Victoria Hospital is Falling Down.

The outpatients department, where Andrew found himself, was, in part, a relic of the eighteenth century. Indeed, a pestle and mortar used by Doctor Lintel Hodges, honorary physician to the same section of the hospital from 1761 to 1793, was proudly exhibited in a glass case in the entrance hall. The untiled walls were painted a peculiar shade of dark chocolate, the uneven passages, though scrupulously clean, were so ill-ventilated that they sweated, and throughout all the rooms there hung the musty odour of sheer old age.

On his first day, he went round with Doctor Eustace Thoroughgood, the Senior Honorary, an elderly, pleasantly precise man of fifty, well under the middle height, with a small grey imperial and a kindly manner, rather like an agreeable churchwarden. Doctor Thoroughgood had his own wards in the hospital and under the existing system, a survival of old tradition—in which he was interestingly erudite—he was "responsible" for Andrew and for Doctor Milligan, the other Junior Honorary.

After their tour of the hospital he took Andrew to the long basement common room where, although it was barely four o'clock, the lights were already on. A fine fire blazed in the steel grate and on the linenfold walls there hung portraits of distinguished physicians to the hospital—Doctor Lintel Hodges, very pursy in his wig, in the place of honour above the mantelpiece. It was a perfect survival of a venerable and spacious past, and from the delicate dilation of his nostrils Doctor Thoroughgood—bachelor and churchwarden though he was—loved it as his own child.

They had a pleasant tea and much hot buttered toast with the other members of the staff. Andrew thought the house physicians very likeable youngsters. Yet as he noted their deference to Doctor Thoroughgood and himself he could not refrain from smiling at the recollection of his clashes with other "insolent pups," not so many months ago, in the frequent struggles to get his patients into hospital.

Seated next to him was a young man, Doctor Vallance, who had spent twelve months studying under the Mayo Brothers in the United States. Andrew and he began to talk about the famous Clinic and its system; then Andrew, with sudden interest, asked him if he had heard of Stillman while he was in America.

"Yes, of course," said Vallance. "They think a lot of him out there. He has no diploma of course, but the State has recognized him, making an exception in his case because of his accomplishments. He gets the most amazing results."

"Have you seen his clinic?"

"No," Vallance shook his head. "I didn't get as far as Oregon."

Andrew paused for a moment, wondering if he should speak. "I believe it's a most remarkable place," he said at length. "I happen to have been in touch with Stillman over a period of years—he first wrote me about a paper of mine published by the Association of American Hygiene. I've seen photographs and details of his clinic. One couldn't wish for a more ideal place to treat one's cases. High up, in the centre of a pine wood; isolated; glassed balconies, a special air-conditioning system to ensure perfect purity and constant temperature in winter . . ." Andrew broke off, deprecating his own enthusiasm, for a break in the general conversation made everything he said audible to the entire table. "When one thinks of our conditions in London, it seems an unattainable ideal."

Doctor Thoroughgood smiled with dry asperity.

"Our London physicians have always managed to get along very well in these same London conditions, Doctor Manson. We may not have the exotic devices of which you speak. But I venture to suggest that our solid, well-tried methods—though less spectacular—bring equally satisfactory and probably more lasting results."

Andrew, keeping his eyes lowered, did not answer. He felt that as a new member of the staff he had been indiscreet in voicing his opinion so openly. And Doctor Thoroughgood, to show that he had intended no snub, went on very pleasantly to turn the conversation. He talked about the art of cupping. This history of medicine had long been his special hobby and he had a mass of information on the subject of the surgeon-barbers of ancient London.

As they rose he declared agreeably to Andrew:—

"I actually have an authentic set of cups. I must show you them one day. It really is a shame cupping has gone out. It was—still is—an admirable way of inducing counterirritation."

Beyond that first slight breeze, Doctor Thoroughgood set himself out to be a sympathetic and helpful colleague. He was a sound physician, an almost unerring diagnostician, and he was always glad to have Andrew round his wards. But in treatment, his tidy mind resented the intrusion of the new. He would have nothing to do with tuberculin, holding that its therapeutic value was still completely unproved. He was chary of using pneumothorax and his percentage of inductions was the lowest in the hospital. He was, however, extremely liberal in the matter of cod-liver oil and malt. He prescribed it for all his patients.

Andrew forgot about Thoroughgood in beginning his own work. It was wonderful, he told himself, after months of waiting, to find himself starting again. He gave, at the outset, quite a good imitation of his old ardour and enthusiasm.

Inevitably his past work on the tubercular lesions induced by dust inhalation had brought him forward to the consideration of pulmonary tuberculosis as a whole. He planned vaguely, in conjunction with the Pirquet test, to investigate the earliest physical signs of the primary lesion. He had a wealth of material available in the undernourished children brought by their mothers in the hope of benefiting by Doctor Thoroughgood's well-known liberality with extract of malt.

And yet, though he tried very hard to convince himself, his heart was not in the work. He could not recapture the spontaneous enthusiasm of his inhalation investigations. He had far too much upon his mind, too many important cases in his practice, to be able to concentrate upon obscure signs which might not even exist. No one knew better than he how long it took to examine a case properly. And he was always in a hurry. This argument was unanswerable. Soon he fell into an attitude of admirable logic—humanly speaking, he simply could not do it.

The poor people who came to the dispensary did not demand much of him. His predecessor had, it appeared, been something of a bully, and so long as he prescribed generously and made an occasional joke his popularity was never in doubt. He got on, well, too, with Doctor Milligan, his opposite number, and it was not long before he found himself adopting Milligan's method of dealing with the regular patients. He would have them up, in a bunch, to his desk at the beginning of dispensary, and rapidly initial their cards. As he scribbled *Rep. Mixt.*—"the mixture as before"—he had no time to recollect how he had once derided this classic phrase. He was well on the way to being an admirable honorary physician.

9

Six weeks after he had taken over at the Victoria, as he sat at breakfast with Christine, he opened a letter which bore the Marseilles postmark. Gazing at it unbelievingly for a moment, he gave a sudden exclamation:—

"It's from Denny! He's sick of Mexico at last! Coming back to settle down, he says—I'll believe that when I see it! But Lord! It'll be good to see him again. How long has he been away? It seems ages. Have you got the paper there, Chris? Look up when the *Oreta* gets in."

She was as pleased as he at the unexpected news, but for a rather different reason. There was a strong maternal strain in Christine, a queer Calvinistic protectiveness towards her husband. She had always recognized that Denny, and indeed, in a lesser degree, Hope, exerted a beneficial effect upon him. Now, especially, when he seemed changing, she was more anxiously alert. No sooner had this letter arrived than her mind was at work planning a meeting which would bring these three together.

The day before the *Oreta* was due at Tilbury she broached the matter.

"I wonder if you'd mind, Andrew—I thought I might give a little dinner next week—just for you and Denny and Hope."

He gazed at her in some surprise. In view of the vague undercurrent of constraint between them, it was strange to hear her talk of entertaining.

He answered:—

"Hope's probably at Cambridge. And Denny and I might as well go out somewhere." Then, seeing her face, he relented quickly. "Oh! All right. Make it Sunday though, that's the best night for all of us."

On the following Sunday Denny arrived, stockier and more brick-red of face and neck than ever. He looked older, seemed less morose, more contented, in his manner. Yet he was the same Denny, his greeting to them being:—

"This is a very grand house. Sure I haven't made a mistake?" Half-turning gravely to Christine: "This well-dressed gentleman *is* Doctor Manson, isn't he? If I'd known I'd have brought him a canary."

Seated, a moment later, he refused a drink.

"No! I'm a regular lime-juicer now. Strange as it may seem, I'm going to set to and get a real pull on the collar. I've had about enough of the wide and starry sky. Best way to get to like this blamed country is to go abroad."

Andrew considered him with affectionate reproof.

"You really ought to settle down, you know, Philip," he said. "After all you're on the right side of forty. And with your talents—"

Denny shot him an odd glance from beneath his brows.

"Don't be so smug, Professor. I may still show you a few tricks one of these days."

He told them he had been lucky enough to be appointed Surgical Registrar of the South Hertfordshire Infirmary, three hundred a year and all found. He did not consider it a permanency, of course, but there was a considerable amount of operative work to be done there and he would be able to refresh his surgical technique. After that he would see what could be done.

"Don't know how they gave me the job," he argued. "It must be another case of mistaken identity."

"No," said Andrew rather stolidly, "it's your M.S., Philip. A first-class degree like that will get you anywhere."

"What have you been doing to him?" Denny groaned. "He don't sound like the bloke what blew up that sewer with me."

At this point Hope arrived. He had not met Denny before. But five minutes was enough for them to understand one another. At the end of that time, as they went in to dinner, they were agreeably united in being rude to Manson.

"Of course, Hope," Philip sadly remarked as he unfolded his napkin, "you needn't expect much food here. Oh, no! I've known these people a long time. Knew the Professor before he turned into a woolly West-Ender. They were thrown out of their last home for starving their guinea pigs."

"I usually carry a rasher in my pocket," said Hope. "It's a habit I acquired from Billy Buttons on the last Kitchenguenga expedition. But unfortunately I'm out of eggs. Mother's hens are not laying at the moment."

There was more of this as the meal went on,—Hope's facetiousness seemed especially provoked by Denny's presence,—but gradually they settled down to talk. Denny related some of his experiences in the Southern States—he had one or two Negro stories which made Christine laugh—and Hope detailed for them the latest activities of the Board. Whinney had at last succeeded in steering his long-contemplated muscular fatigue experiments into action.

"That's what I'm doing now," Hope gloomed. "But thank heaven my scholarship has only another nine months to run. Then I'm going to *do* something. I'm tired of working out other people's ideas, having old men stand over me." His tone dropped into ribald mimicry. " 'How much sarcolactic acid did you find for me this time, Mr. Hope?' I want to do something for myself. I wish to God I had a little lab. of my own!"

Then, as Christine had hoped, the talk became violently medical. After dinner,—despite Denny's melancholy prognostication, they had stripped a brace of ducks,—when coffee was brought in, she pleaded to remain. And though Hope assured her that the language would not be ladylike she sat, her elbows on the table, chin upon her hands, listening silently, forgotten, her eyes fixed earnestly on Andrew's face.

At first he had appeared stiff and reserved. Though it was a joy to see Philip again he had the feeling that his old friend was a little casual towards his success, unappreciative, even mildly derisive. After all, he had done pretty well for himself, hadn't he? And what had Denny—yes, what had Denny done? When Hope had chipped in with his attempts of humour he had almost told them, pretty sharply, to stop being funny at his expense.

Yet now that they were talking shop he was drawn into it, unconsciously.

Momentarily, whether he wished it or not, he caught the infection from the other two and, with not a bad copy of his old rapture, he made himself heard.

They were discussing hospitals, which caused him suddenly to express himself upon the whole hospital system.

"The way I look at it is this." He took a long breath of smoke—it was not now a cheap Virginian cigarette but a cigar, from the box which he had, braving the devil in Denny's eye, self-consciously produced. "The whole lay-out is obsolete. Mind you, I wouldn't for anything have you think I'm knocking my own hospital. I love it down there at the Victoria and I can tell you we do great work. But it's the system. Nobody but the good old apathetic B.P. would put up with it—like our roads, for instance, a hopeless out-of-date chaos. The Victoria is falling down. So is St. John's; half the hospitals in London are shrieking that they're falling down! And what are we doing about it? Collecting pennies. Getting a few quid out of the advertisement hoardings we stick up on our frontage. *Brown's Beer Is Best.* Isn't that sweet? At the Victoria, if we're lucky, in ten years' time we'll start to build a new wing, or a nurses' home—incidentally you should see where the nurses *sleep!* But what's the use of patching up the old carcass? What *is* the use of a lung hospital in the centre of a noisy foggy city like London—damn it all, it's like taking a pneumonia down a coal mine. And it's the same with most of the other hospitals, *and* the nursing homes too. They're bang in the middle of roaring traffic, foundations shaken by the Underground; even the patients' beds rattle when the buses go past. If I went in there, *healthy*, I'd want ten grains of barbitone every night to get to sleep. Think of patients lying in that racket after a serious abdominal, or running a temperature of a hundred and four with meningitis!"

"Well, what's the remedy?" Philip lifted an eyebrow in that new irritating fashion. "A joint hospital board with you as director in chief?"

"Don't be an ass, Denny," Andrew answered irritably. "Decentralization is the remedy. No, that isn't just a word out of a book, it's the result of all that I've gone through since I came to London. Why shouldn't our big hospitals stand in a green belt outside London, say fifteen miles outside? Take a place like Benham, for instance, only ten miles out, where there's still green country, fresh air, quiet. Don't think there would be any transportation difficulties. The tube—and why not a specially run hospital service—one straight, silent line?—could take you out to Benham in exactly eighteen minutes. Considering that it takes our fastest ambulance forty minutes on the average to bring in an emergency, that sounds to me an improvement. You might say if we moved the hospitals we'd denude each area of its medical services. That's rot! The dispensary stops in the area, the hospital moves out. And while we're talking about it, this question of area service is just one large hopeless muddle. When I came here at first, I found here in *West* London that the only place I could get in my patient was the *East* London Hospital.

Down at the Victoria too, we get patients from all over the shop—Kensington, Ealing, Muswell Hill. There's no attempt to delimit special areas—everything comes pouring in to the centre of the city. I'm telling you fellows straight, the confusion is often unbelievable. And what's being done? Zero, absolute zero. We just drag on in the old, old way, rattling tin boxes, holding flag days, making appeals, letting students clown for pennies in fancy dress. One thing about these new European countries—they get things *done*. Lord, if I had my way I'd raze the Victoria flat and have a new Chest Hospital setting out at Benham with a straight line of communication. And by God! I'd show a rise in our recovery rate!"

This was merely by way of introduction. The crescendo of discussion rose.

Philip got on to his old contention—the folly of asking the general practitioner to pull everything out of the one black bag, the stupidity of making him carry every case on his shoulders until that delightful moment when, for five guineas, some specialist he had never seen before drove up to tell him it was too late to carry anything at all.

Hope, without mildness or restraint, expressed the case of the young bacteriologist, sandwiched between commercialism and conservatism—on the one hand, the bland firm of chemists who would pay him a wage to make proprietary articles, on the other a Board of blithering dotards.

"Can you imagine," Hope hissed, "the Marx brothers sitting in a rickety motor car with four independent steering wheels and an unlimited supply of motor horns? That's us at the M.F.B."

They did not stop until after twelve o'clock and then, unexpectedly, they found sandwiches and coffee before them on the table.

"Oh I say, Mrs. Manson," Hope protested with a politeness which showed that, in Denny's gibe, he was a Nice Young Man at Heart. "We must have bored you stiff. Funny how hungry talking makes one. I'll suggest that to Whinney as a new line of investigation—effect upon the gastric secretions of hot-air fatigue. Ha! Ha! That's a perfect Nag-ism!"

When Hope had gone, with fervent protestations that he had enjoyed the evening, Denny remained a few minutes longer, exacting the privilege of his older friendship. Then, Andrew having left the room to ring for a taxi, Philip apologetically brought out a small, very beautiful Spanish shawl.

"The Professor will probably slay me," he said. "But this is for you. Don't tell him till I'm safely out of the way." He arrested her gratitude, always for him the most embarrassing emotion. "Extraordinary how all these shawls come from China. They're not really Spanish. I got that one via Shanghai."

A silence fell. They could hear Andrew coming back from the telephone in the hall.

Denny got up, his kind, wrinkled eyes avoiding hers.

"I wouldn't worry too much about him, you know." He smiled. "But we must try, mustn't we, to get him back to Blaenelly standards?"

10

AT the beginning of the Easter school holidays Andrew received a note from
Mrs. Thornton asking him to call at Brown's Hotel to see her daughter. She
told him briefly, in the letter, that Sybil's foot had not improved and, since
she had been much struck by his interest at Mrs. Lawrence's, she was anxious to have his advice. Flattered by this tribute to his personality, he made
the visit promptly.

The condition which he found upon examination was perfectly simple. Yet
it was one which demanded an early operation. He straightened himself, with
a smile to the solid, bare-legged Sybil now seated upon the edge of the bed,
pulling on her long black stocking, and explained this to Mrs. Thornton.

"The bone has thickened. Might develop into a hammer toe, if it's left
untreated. I suggest you have it seen to at once."

"That's what the school doctor said." Mrs. Thornton was not surprised.
"We are really prepared. Sybil can go into a home here. But—well! I've got
confidence in you, Doctor. And I want you to undertake all the arrangements.
Whom do you suggest should do it?"

The direct question placed Andrew in a dilemma. His work being almost
entirely medical he had met many of the leading physicians, yet he knew
none of the London surgeons.

Suddenly he thought of Ivory. He said pleasantly:—

"Mr. Ivory might do this for us—if he's available."

Mrs. Thornton had heard of Mr. Ivory. Of course! Wasn't he the surgeon
who had been in all the newspapers the month before through having flown
to Cairo to attend a case of sunstroke? An extremely well-known man! She
thought it an admirable suggestion that he should undertake her daughter's
case. Her only stipulation was that Sybil should go to Miss Sherrington's
Home. So many of her friends had been there she could not think of letting
her go anywhere else.

Andrew went home and rang up Ivory, with all the hesitation of a man
making a preliminary approach. But Ivory's manner—friendly, confident,
charming—reassured him. They arranged to see the case together on the following day; and Ivory asserted that, though he knew Ida to be bunged up to
the attics, he could persuade her to make room for Miss Thornton should
this be necessary.

Next morning, when Ivory had agreed emphatically in Mrs. Thornton's
presence with all that Andrew had said—adding that immediate operation
was imperative—Sybil was transferred to Miss Sherrington's Home; and two
days later, giving her time to settle down, the operation was performed.

Andrew was there. Ivory insisted that he be present, in the most genuine
and friendly fashion imaginable.

The operation was not difficult,—indeed in his Blaenelly days Andrew
would have tackled it himself,—and Ivory, though he seemed disinclined to
speed, accomplished it with imposing competence. He made a strong cool

figure in his big white gown, above which his face showed firm, massive, dominant-jawed. No one more completely resembled the popular conception of the great surgeon than Charles Ivory. He had the fine supple hands with which popular fiction always endows the hero of the operating theatre. In his handsomeness and assurance he was dramatically impressive. Andrew, who had himself slipped on a gown, watched him from the other side of the table with grudging respect.

A fortnight later, when Sybil Thornton had left the home, Ivory asked him to lunch at the Sackville Club. It was a pleasant meal. Ivory was a perfect conversationalist, easy and entertaining, with a fund of up-to-the-minute gossip, which somehow placed his companion on the same intimate, man-of-the-world footing as himself. The high dining-room of the Sackville, with its Adam ceilings and rock-crystal chandeliers, was full of famous—Ivory named them "amusing"—people. Andrew found the experience flattering, as no doubt Ivory intended it to be.

"You must let me put your name up at the next meeting," the surgeon remarked. "You'd find a lot of friends here, Freddie, Paul, myself—by the way, Jackie Lawrence is a member. Interesting marriage that; they're perfectly good friends, and they each go their own way! Honestly, I'd love to put you up. I've rather felt, you know, that you've just been a shade suspicious of me, old fellow. Your Scottish caution, eh? As you know I don't visit any of the hospitals. That's because I prefer to free-lance. Besides, my dear boy, I'm too *busy*. Some of these hospital fogies don't have one private case a month. I average ten a week! By the by, we'll be hearing from the Thorntons presently. You leave all that to me. They're first-class people. And incidentally, while I speak of it, don't you think Sybil ought to have her tonsils seen to? Did you look at them?"

"No—no, I didn't."

"Oh, you ought to have done, my boy. Absolutely pocketed, no end of septic absorption. I took the liberty—hope you don't mind—of saying we might do them for her when the warm weather comes in."

On his way home Andrew could not help reflecting what a charming fellow Ivory had turned out to be—actually, he ought to be grateful to Hampton for the introduction. This case had passed off superbly. The Thorntons were particularly pleased. Surely there could be no better criterion.

Three weeks later, as he sat at tea with Christine, the afternoon post brought him a letter from Ivory.

My dear Manson,—

Mrs. Thornton has just come nicely to scratch. As I am sending the anæsthetist his bit I may as well send you yours—for assisting me so splendidly at the operation. Sybil will be coming to see you at the end of this term. You remember those tonsils I mentioned. Mrs. Thornton is delighted.—

Ever cordially yours,—

C.I.

Enclosed was a cheque for twenty guineas.

Andrew stared at the cheque in astonishment,—he had done nothing to assist Ivory at the operation,—then gradually the warm feeling which money always gave him now stole round his heart. With a complacent smile he handed over the letter and the cheque for Christine's inspection.

"Damned decent of Ivory, isn't it, Chris? I bet we'll have a record in our receipts this month."

"But I don't understand." Her expression was perplexed. "Is this your bill to Mrs. Thornton?"

"No—silly," he chuckled. "It's a little extra—merely for the time I gave up to the operation."

"You mean Mr. Ivory is giving you part of his fee."

He flushed, suddenly up in arms.

"Good lord, no! That's absolutely forbidden. We wouldn't dream of that. Don't you see I earned this fee for assisting, for being *there*, just as the anæsthetist earned his fee for giving the anæsthetic. Ivory sends it all in with his bill. And I'll bet it was a bumper."

She laid the cheque upon the table, subdued, unhappy.

"It seems a great deal of money."

"Well, why not?" He closed the argument in a blaze of indignation. "The Thorntons are tremendously rich. This is probably no more to them than three and six to one of our surgery patients."

When he had gone, her eyes remained fastened upon the cheque with strained apprehension. She had not realized that he had associated himself professionally with Ivory. Suddenly all her former uneasiness swept back over her. That evening with Denny and Hope might never have taken place for all its effect upon him. How fond he now was, how terribly fond, of money. His work at the Victoria seemed not to matter beside this devouring desire for material success. Even in the surgery she had observed that he was using more and more stock mixtures, prescribing for people who had nothing wrong with them, urging them to call and call again. The worried look deepened upon her face, making it pinched and small, as she sat there, confronted by Charles Ivory's cheque. Tears welled slowly to her eyes. She must speak to him, oh, she must, she must.

That evening, after surgery, she approached him diffidently. "Andrew, would you do something to please me? Would you take me out to the country on Sunday in the car? You promised me when you got it. And of course—all winter we haven't been able to go."

He glanced at her queerly.

"Well—Oh, all right!"

Sunday came fine, as she had hoped, a soft spring day. By eleven o'clock he had done what visits were essential and with a rug and a picnic basket in the back of the car they set off. Christine's spirits lifted as they ran across Hammersmith Bridge and took the Kingston By-Pass for Surrey. Soon they were through Dorking, turning to the right on the road to Shere. It was so long since they had been together in the country that the sweetness of it, the vivid green of the fields, the purple of the budding elms, the golden dust of drooping catkins, the paler yellow of primroses clumped beneath a bank, suffused her being, intoxicating her.

"Don't drive so fast, dear," she murmured in a tone softer than she had used for weeks. "It's so lovely here." He seemed intent upon passing every car upon the road.

Towards one o'clock they reached Shere. The village, with its few red-roofed cottages and its stream quietly wandering amongst the watercress beds, was as yet untroubled by the rush of summer tourists. They reached the wooded hill beyond, and parked the car near one of the close-turfed bridle-paths. There, in the little clearing where they spread the rug, was a singing solitude which belonged only to them and to the birds.

They ate their sandwiches in the sunshine, drank the coffee from the thermos. Around them, in the alder clumps, the primroses grew in great profusion. Christine longed to gather them, to bury her face in their cool softness. Andrew lay with half-closed eyes, his head resting near her. A sweet tranquillity settled upon the dark uneasiness of her soul. If their life together could always be like this!

His drowsy gaze had for some moments been resting on the car. Suddenly he said:—

"Not a bad old bus, is she, Chris? I mean, for what she cost us. But we shall want a new one at the Show."

She stirred—her disquiet renewed by this fresh instance of his restless striving.

"But we haven't had her any time! She seems to me all that we could wish for."

"Hum! She's sluggish. Didn't you notice how that Buick kept ahead of us? I want one of these new Vitesse saloons."

"But why?"

"Why not? We can afford it. We're getting on, you know, Chris. Yes!" He lit a cigarette and turned to her with every sign of satisfaction. "In case you may not be aware of the fact, my dear little schoolmarm from Blaenelly, we are rapidly getting rich."

She did not answer his smile. She felt her body, peaceful and warm in the sunshine, chill suddenly. She began to pick at a tuft of grass, to twine it foolishly with a tassel of the rugs. She said slowly:—

"Dear, do we really want to be rich? I know I don't. Why all this talk about money? When we had scarcely any we were—oh! we were deliriously happy. We never talked of it, then. But now we never talk of anything else."

He smiled again, in a superior manner.

"After years of tramping about in slush, eating sausage and soused herrings, taking dog's abuse from pigheaded committees, and attending miners' wives in dirty back bedrooms, I propose, for a change, to ameliorate our lot. Any objections?"

"Don't make a joke of it, darling. You usen't to talk that way. Oh! Don't you see, don't you see, you're falling a victim to the very system you used to run down, the thing you used to hate?" Her face was pitiful in its agitation. "Don't you remember how you used to speak of life, that it was an attack on the unknown, an assault uphill—as though you had to take some castle that you knew was there, but couldn't see, on the top—"

He muttered uncomfortably:—

"Oh! I was young then—foolish. That was just romantic talk. You look round; you'll see that everybody's doing the same thing—getting together as much as they can! It's the only thing to do."

She took a shaky breath. She knew that she must speak now or not at all.

"Darling! It isn't the only thing. Please listen to me. Please! I've been so unhappy at this—the change in you. Denny saw it too. It's dragging us away from one another. You're not the Andrew Manson I married. Oh! If only you'd be as you used to be!"

"What have I done?" he protested irritably. "Do I beat you, do I get drunk, do I commit murder? Give me one example of my *crimes*."

Desperately, she replied:—

"It isn't the obvious things; it's your whole attitude, darling. Take that cheque Ivory sent you, for instance. It's a small matter, on the surface perhaps, but underneath—oh, if you take it underneath it's cheap and grasping and dishonest."

She felt him stiffen; then he sat up, offended, glaring at her.

"For God's sake! Why bring that up again? What's wrong with my taking it?"

"Can't you see?" All the accumulated emotion of the past months overwhelmed her, stifling her arguments, causing her suddenly to burst into tears. She cried hysterically: "For God's sake, darling. Don't, don't sell yourself!"

He ground his teeth, furious with her. He spoke slowly, with cutting deliberation.

"For the last time, I warn you to stop making a neurotic fool of yourself. Can't you try to be a help to me, instead of a hindrance, nagging me every minute of the day?"

"I haven't nagged you," she sobbed. "I've wanted to speak before, but I haven't."

"Then don't." He lost his temper and suddenly shouted: "Do you hear me? *Don't*. It's some complex you've got. You talk as if I was some kind of dirty crook. I only want to get on. And if I want money it's only as a means to an end. People judge you by what you are, what you have. If you're one of the have-nots you get ordered about. Well, I've had enough of that in my time. In future I'm going to do the ordering. Now do you understand? Don't even mention this damned nonsense to me again."

"All right, all right," she wept. "I won't. But I tell you—some day you'll be sorry."

The excursion was ruined for them, and most of all for her. Though she dried her eyes and gathered a large bunch of primroses, though they spent another hour on the sunny slope and stopped on the way down at the *Lavender Lady* for tea, though they spoke, in apparent amity, of ordinary things, all the rapture of the day was dead. Her face, as they drove through the early darkness, was pale and stiff.

His anger turned gradually to indignation. Why should Chris of all people set upon him? Other women, and charming women too, were enthusiastic at his rapid rise.

A few days later Frances Lawrence rang him up. She had been away, spending the winter at Jamaica—he had several times in the past two months had letters from the Myrtle Bank Hotel; but now she was back, eager to see her friends, radiating the sunshine she had absorbed. She told him gaily she wanted him to see her before she lost her sunburn.

He went round to tea. As she had implied, she was beautifully tanned, her hands and slender wrists, her spare interrogative face, strained as a faun's. The pleasure of seeing her again was intensified extraordinarily by the welcome in her eyes, those eyes which were indifferent to so many persons and which were, with their high points of light, so friendly to him.

Yes, they talked as old friends. She told him of her trip, of the coral gardens, the fishes seen through the glass-bottomed boats, of the heavenly climate. He gave her, in return, an account of his progress.

Perhaps some indication of his thoughts crept into his words, for she answered lightly: "You're frightfully solemn and disgracefully prosy. That's what happens to you when I'm away. No! Frankly I think it's because you're doing too much. *Must* you keep on with all this surgery work? For my part I should have thought it time for you to take a room up West—Wimpole Street or Welbeck Street for instance—and do your consulting there."

At this point her husband entered, tall, lounging, mannered. He nodded to Andrew, whom he now knew fairly well—they had once or twice played bridge at the Sackville Club—and gracefully accepted a cup of tea.

Though he protested cheerfully that he would not for anything disturb them, Lawrence's entrance interrupted the serious turn of the conversation. They began to discuss, with considerable amusement, the latest junketing of Rumbold-Blane.

But half an hour later, as Andrew drove back to Chesborough Terrace Mrs. Lawrence's suggestion firmly occupied his mind. Why shouldn't he take a consulting room in Welbeck Street? The time was clearly ripe for it. He wouldn't give up anything of his Paddington practice—the surgery was far too profitable a concern to abandon lightly. But he could easily combine it with a room up West, use the better address for his correspondence, have the heading on his notepaper, his bills.

The thought sparkled within him, nerved him to greater conquest. What a good sort Frances was, just as helpful as Miss Everett and infinitely more charming, more exciting! Yet he was on excellent terms with her husband.

He could meet his eye steadily. He needn't come skulking out of the house like some low boudoir hound. Oh! friendship was a great thing!

Without saying anything to Christine, he began to look for a convenient consulting room up West. And when he found one, about a month later, it gave him great satisfaction to declare, in assumed indifference, over the morning paper:—

"By the way—you might care to know—I've taken a place in Welbeck Street now. I shall use it for my better-class consultations."

11

The room at Number 57a Welbeck Street gave Andrew a new surge of triumph. I'm there, he secretly exulted, I'm there at last! Though not large, the room was well lit by a bay window and situated on the ground floor, a distinct advantage, since most patients hated to climb stairs. Moreover, although he shared the waiting-room with several other consultants whose neat plates shone beside his own on the front door, this consulting room was exclusively his own.

On the nineteenth of April, when the lease was signed, Hampton accompanied him as he went round to take possession. Freddie had proved extraordinarily helpful in all the preliminaries and had found him a useful nurse, a friend of the woman whom he employed at Queen Anne Street. Nurse Sharp was not beautiful. She was middle-aged, with a sour, vaguely ill-used yet capable expression. Freddie explained Nurse Sharp concisely:—

"The last thing a fellow wants is a pretty nurse. You know what I mean, old man. Fun is fun. But business is business. And you can't combine the two. We none of us are in this for our health. As a damned hardheaded fellow, you'll appreciate that. As a matter of fact I've got a notion you and I are going to come pretty close together now you've moved alongside me."

While Freddie and he stood discussing the arrangement of the room Mrs. Lawrence unexpectedly appeared. She had been passing and came in, gaily, to investigate his choice. She had an attractive way of turning up casually, of never appearing to obtrude herself. To-day she was especially charming in a black coat and skirt with a necklet of rich brown fur about her throat. She did not stay long but she had ideas, suggestions for decoration, for the window hangings and the curtains behind his desk, far more tasteful than the crude plannings Freddie and he had arranged.

Bereft of her vivacious presence the room was suddenly empty.

Freddie gushed: "You're a lucky devil, if ever I met one. She's a nice thing." He grinned enviously. "What did Gladstone say in eighteen ninety about the surest way to advance a man's career?"

"I don't know what you're driving at."

Nevertheless when his room was finished he had to agree with Freddie, and with Frances, who arrived to view her complete scheme, that it struck exactly the right note—advanced yet professionally correct. Consultations in these surroundings made three guineas seem a right and reasonable fee.

He had not many patients at the start. But by dint of writing politely to every doctor who sent cases to him at the Chest Hospital—letters relating, naturally, to these hospital cases and their symptoms—he soon had a network of filaments reaching out all over London which began to bring private patients to his door. He was a busy man these days, dashing in his new Vitesse saloon between Chesborough Terrace and the Victoria, between the Victoria and Welbeck Street, with a full round of visits in addition and always his packed surgery, often running as late as ten o'clock at night.

The tonic of success braced him for everything, tingled through his veins like a gorgeous elixir. He found time to run round to Rogers to order another three suits, then to a shirtmaker in Jermyn Street whom Hampton had recommended. His popularity at the hospital was increasing. True, he had less time to devote to his work in the outpatient department, but he told himself that what he sacrificed in time he made up in expertness. Even to his friends he developed a speedy brusqueness, rather taking, with his ready smile: "I must go, old fellow, simply rushed off my legs."

One Friday afternoon, five weeks after his installation at Welbeck Street, an elderly woman came to consult him about her throat. Her condition was no more than a simple laryngitis, but she was a querulous little person and she seemed anxious for a second opinion. Mildly injured in his pride, Andrew reflected to whom he should send her. It was ridiculous to think of her wasting the time of a man like Sir Robert Abbey. Suddenly his face cleared as he thought of Hampton round the corner. Freddie had been extremely kind to him lately. He might as well "pick up" the three guineas as some ungrateful stranger. Andrew sent her along with a note to Freddie.

Three quarters of an hour later she came back, in quite a different humour, soothed and apologetic, satisfied with herself, with Freddie and—most of all—with him.

"Excuse me for coming back, Doctor. I only wanted to thank you for the trouble you've taken with me. I saw Doctor Hampton and he confirmed everything you said. And he—he told me the prescription you gave me simply couldn't be improved on."

In June Sybil Thornton's tonsils came out. They were, to a certain extent, enlarged, and lately, in the *Journal,* suspicion had been thrown upon tonsillar absorption in its bearing upon the etiology of rheumatism. Ivory did the enucleation with tedious care.

"I prefer to go slow with these lymphoid tissues," he said to Andrew as they washed up. "I daresay you've seen people whip them out. *I* don't work that way."

When Andrew received his cheque from Ivory—again it came by post—Freddie was with him. They were frequently in and out of each other's consulting rooms. Hampton had promptly returned the ball by sending Andrew a nice gastritis in return for the laryngitis case. By this time, in fact, several patients had found their way, with notes, between Welbeck and Queen Anne Street.

"You know, Manson," Freddie now remarked, "I'm glad you've chucked your old dog-in-the-manger, holy-willy attitude. Even now, you know," he squinted across Andrew's shoulder at the cheque, "you're not getting all the juice out of the orange. You hang in with me, my lad, and you'll find your fruit more succulent."

Andrew had to laugh.

That evening, as he drove home, he was in an unusually lighthearted mood. Finding himself without cigarettes he drew up and dashed into a tobacconist's in Oxford Street. Here, as he came through the door, he suddenly observed a woman loitering at an adjacent window. It was Blodwen Page.

Though he recognized her at once, she was sadly altered from the bustling mistress of Bryngower. No longer stout, her figure had a listless droop, and the eye which she turned upon him when he addressed her was apathetic, cowed.

"It is Mrs. Page." He went up to her. "I ought to say Mrs. Rees now, I suppose. Don't you remember me? Doctor Manson."

She took him in, his well-dressed and prosperous air. She sighed: "I remember you, Doctor. I hope you're very well." Then, as though afraid to linger, she turned to where a few yards along the pavement a long bald-headed man impatiently awaited her. She concluded apprehensively, "I'll have to go now, Doctor. My husband's waiting."

Andrew observed her hurry off, saw Rees's thin lips shape themselves to the rebuke, "What d'you mean—keeping me waiting?" while she submissively bent her head. For an instant he was conscious of the bank manager's cold eye directed blankly upon himself. Then the pair moved off and were lost in the crowd.

Andrew could not get the picture out of his head. When he reached Chesborough Terrace and entered the front room he found Christine knitting there, with his tea—which she had rung for at the sound of his car—set out upon a tray. He glanced at her quickly, sounding her. He wanted to tell her of the incident, longed suddenly to end their period of strife.

But when he had accepted a cup of tea, and before he could speak, she said quietly:—

"Mrs. Lawrence rang you again this afternoon. No message."

"Oh!" He flushed. "How do you mean—again?"

"This is the fourth time she's rung you in a week."

"Well, what of it?"

"Nothing. I didn't say anything."

"It's how you look. Can I help it if she rings me?"

She was silent, her eyes downcast, upon her knitting. If he had known the tumult in that still breast he would not have lost his temper as he did.

"You would think I was a bigamist, the way you go on. She's a perfectly nice woman. Why, her husband is one of my best friends. They're charming people. They don't hang about looking like a sick pup. Oh, hell—"

He gulped down the rest of his tea and got up. Yet the moment he was out of the room he was sorry. He flung into the surgery, lit a cigarette, reflecting wretchedly that things were going from bad to worse between Christine and himself. And he did not want them to get worse. Their growing estrangement depressed and irritated him; it was the one dark cloud in the bright sky of his success.

Christine and he had been ideally happy in their married life. The unexpected meeting with Mrs. Page had brought back a rush of tender memories of his courtship in Blaenelly. He did not idolize his wife as he once had done, but he was—oh, damn it all!—he was *fond* of her. Perhaps he had hurt her once or twice lately. As he stood there he had a sudden desire to make up with her, to please, propitiate her. He thought hard. Suddenly his eyes brightened. He glanced at his watch, found that he had just half an hour before Laurier's closed. The next minute he was in his car and on his way to interview Miss Cramb.

Miss Cramb, when he mentioned what he desired, was immediately and fervently at his service. They fell into serious conversation together, then walked into the fur department where various "skins" were modelled for Doctor Manson. Miss Cramb stroked them with expert fingers, pointing out the lustre, the silvering, all that one should look for in this special pelt. Once or twice she disagreed gently with his views, earnestly indicating what was *quality* and what was not. In the end he made a selection which she cordially approved. Then she departed in search of Mr. Winch, and presently returned to state glowingly:—

"Mr. Winch says you're to have them *at cost*." No such word as "wholesale" had ever sullied the lips of a Laurier employee. "That brings them out at fifty-five pounds; and you can take it from me, Doctor, it's genuine value. They're beautiful skins, beautiful. Your wife will be proud to wear them."

On the following Saturday at eleven o'clock Andrew took the dark olive-green box, with the inimitable mark artistically scrawled upon its lid, and went into the drawing-room.

"Christine!" he called. "Here a moment!"

She was upstairs with Mrs. Bennett helping to make the beds, but she came at once, slightly out of breath, her eyes wondering a little at his summons.

"Look, dear!" Now that the climax approached he felt an almost suffocating awkwardness. "I bought you this. I know—I know we haven't been getting on so well lately. But this ought to show you—" He broke off and like a schoolboy, handed her the box.

She was very pale as she opened it. Her hands trembled upon the string. Then she gave a little overwhelmed cry:—

"What lovely, lovely furs!"

There, in the tissue paper, lay a double stole of silver fox, two exquisite skins shaped fashionably into one. Quickly he picked them up, smoothing them as Miss Cramb had done, his voice excited now.

"Do you like them, Chris? Try them on. The good old Halfback helped me choose them. They're absolutely first-class quality. Couldn't have better. And value too. You see that sheen on them and the silver marking on the back—that's what you want specially to look for!"

Tears were running down her cheeks. She turned to him quite wildly.

"You do love me, don't you, darling? That's all that matters to me in the world!"

Reassured at last, she tried on the furs. They were magnificent.

He could not admire them enough. He wanted to make the reconciliation complete. He smiled.

"Look here, Chris. We might as well have a little celebration while we're about it. We'll go out to lunch to-day. Meet me one o'clock at the Plaza Grill."

"Yes, darling," she half-questioned. "Only—I've got some shepherd's pie for lunch to-day—that you used to like so much."

"No, no." His laugh was gayer than it had been for months. "Don't be an old stay-at-home. One o'clock. Meet the dark handsome gentleman at the Plaza. You needn't wear a red carnation. He'll know you by the furs."

All morning he was in a mood of high satisfaction. Fool that he'd been!— neglecting Christine. All women liked to have attention paid to them, to be taken out, given a good time. The Plaza Grill was just the place—all London, or most of it that mattered, could be seen there between the hours of one and three.

Christine was late, an unusual occurrence which caused him to fret slightly, as he sat in the small lounge facing the glass partition, watching all the best tables become quickly occupied. He ordered himself a second Martini. It was twenty minutes past one when she came hurrying in, flustered by the noise, the people, the ornate flunkeys and the fact that, for the last half-hour, she had been standing in the wrong lounge.

"I'm so sorry, darling," she gasped. "I really did ask. I waited and waited. And then I found it was the restaurant lounge."

They were given a bad table wedged against a pillar beside the service. The place was grotesquely crowded, the tables so close together people seemed to be sitting on each other's laps. The waiters moved like contortionists. The heat was tropical. The din rose and fell like a transpontine college yell.

"Now, Chris, what would you like?" Andrew said determinedly.

"You order, darling," she answered faintly.

He ordered a rich, expensive lunch: caviar, *soupe prince de Galles, poulet riche*, asparagus, *fraises des bois* in syrup. Also a bottle of Liebfraumilch, 1929.

"We didn't know much about this in our Blaenelly days." He laughed, determined to make merry. "Nothing like doing ourselves well, old girl."

Nobly she tried to respond to his mood. She praised the caviar, made an heroic effort with the rich soup. She pretended interest when he pointed out Glen Roscoe, the cinema star, Marvis Yorke, an American woman celebrated for her six husbands, and other cosmopolitans equally distinguished. The smart vulgarity of the place was hateful to her. The men were overgroomed, smooth and oiled. Every woman visible to her was a blonde, dressed in black, smart, made-up, carelessly hard.

All at once Christine felt herself turn a little giddy. She began to lose her poise. Usually her manner was one of natural simplicity. But lately the strain upon her nerves had been great. She became conscious of the discrepancy between her new furs and her inexpensive dress. She felt other women staring at her. She knew she was as out of place here as a daisy in an orchid house.

"What's the matter?" he asked suddenly. "Aren't you enjoying yourself?"

"Yes, of course," she protested, wanly trying to smile. But her lips were stiff now. She could barely swallow, let alone taste, the heavily creamed chicken on her plate.

"You're not listening to a thing I say," he muttered resentfully. "You haven't even touched your wine. Damn it all, when a man takes his wife out—"

"Could I have a little water?" she asked feebly. She could have screamed. She didn't belong to a place like this. Her hair wasn't bleached, her face not made-up; no wonder even the waiters watched her now. Nervously she lifted an asparagus stalk. As she did so the head broke and fell, dripping with sauce, on the new fur.

The metallic blonde at the next table turned to her companion with a smile of amusement. Andrew saw that smile. He gave up the attempt at entertainment. The meal ended in a dreary silence.

They went home more drearily. Then he departed, summarily, to do his calls. They were wider apart than before. The pain in Christine's heart was intolerable. She began to lose faith in herself, to ask herself if she was really the right wife for him. That night she put her arms round his neck and kissed him, thanking him again for the furs and for taking her out.

"Glad you enjoyed it," he said flatly, and went to his own room.

12

At this point an event occurred which, for the time being, diverted Andrew's attention from his difficulties at home. He came upon a paragraph in the *Tribune*, which announced that Mr. Richard Stillman, the well-known health expert of Portland, Oregon, U.S.A., had arrived on the *Imperial* and was staying at Brooks Hotel.

In the old days he would have rushed excitedly to Christine with the paper in his hand: "Look here, Chris! Richard Stillman has come over. You remember—I corresponded with him all that time. I wonder if he'd see me—honestly, I'd love to meet him."

But now he had lost the habit of running to Christine. Instead he pondered maturely over the *Tribune*, glad that he could approach Stillman, not as a medical aid assistant, but with the standing of a Welbeck Street consultant.

Methodically he typed a letter recalling himself to the American and asking him to lunch at the Plaza Grill on Wednesday.

The following morning Stillman rang him up. His voice was quiet, friendly, alertly efficient.

"Glad to be talking to you, Doctor Manson. I'd be pleased for us to lunch. But don't let's make it the Plaza. I hate that place already. Why don't you come here and lunch with me?"

Andrew found Stillman in the sitting-room of his suite at Brooks, a quietly select hotel which put the racket of the Plaza to shame. It was a hot day, the morning had been a rush, and at the first sight of his host Andrew almost wished he had not come. The American was about fifty, small and slight, with a disproportionately large head and an undershot jaw. His complexion was a boyish pink-and-white, his light-coloured hair thin and parted in the middle. It was only when Andrew saw his eyes, pale, steady, and glacially blue, that he realized—almost felt the impact of—the driving force behind this insignificant frame.

"Hope you didn't mind coming here," said Richard Stillman in the quiet manner of one to whom many have been glad to come. "I know we Americans are supposed to like the Plaza." He smiled, revealing himself human. "But it's a lousy crowd that goes there." He paused. "And now I've seen you, let me really congratulate you on that splendid inhalation paper. You didn't mind my telling you about serecite? What have you been doing lately?"

They descended to the restaurant, where the head of many waiters gave Stillman his attention.

"How about you? I'm going to have orange juice," Stillman said then, promptly, without looking at the long French menu, "and two mutton cutlets with peas. Then coffee."

Andrew gave his order and turned with increasing respect to his companion. It was impossible to remain in Stillman's presence long without acknowledging the compelling interest of his personality. His history, which Andrew knew in outline, was in itself unique.

Richard Stillman came of an old Massachusetts family which had, for generations, been connected with the law, in Boston. But young Stillman, despite this continuity, evinced a strong desire to enter the medical profession, and at the age of eighteen at last persuaded his father to allow him to begin his studies at Harvard with that end in view. For three years he had followed the science curriculum at this University when his father died suddenly leaving Richard, his mother, and his only sister in unexpectedly poor circumstances.

At this point, when some means of support had to be found for the family, old John Stillman, Richard's grandfather, insisted that he attend a law school, following the family tradition. Arguments proved useless—the old man was implacable—and Richard was forced to take, not the medical degree he had hoped for, but a legal one. Then he entered the family offices in Boston and for four years devoted himself to the law.

It was, however, a half-hearted devotion. Bacteriology, in particular, microbiology, had fascinated him from his earliest student days, and in the attic of his Beacon Hill home he set up a small laboratory and devoted every spare moment to the pursuit of his passion. This attic was in fact the beginning of the Stillman Institute. Richard was no amateur. On the contrary he displayed not only the highest technical skill but an originality amounting almost to genius. And when, in the winter of 1908, his sister Mary, to whom he was much attached, died of rapid consumption, he began the concentration of his forces against the tubercule bacillus. He picked up the early work of Pierre Louis and Louis's American disciple, James Jackson, Jr. His examination of Laënnac's life work on auscultation brought him to the physiological study of the lungs. He invented a new type of stethoscope. He commenced, with the limited apparatus at his disposal, his first attempts to produce a blood serum.

In the year 1910, when old John Stillman died, Richard had at last succeeded in curing tuberculosis in guinea pigs. The results of this double event were immediate. Stillman's mother had all along sympathized with his scientific work. He needed little urging to dispose of the Boston law connection, and, with his inheritance from the old man's estate, to purchase a farm near Portland, Oregon, where he at once flung himself into the real business of his life.

So many valuable years had already been wasted he made no attempt to take a medical degree. He wanted progress, results. Soon he produced a serum from bay horses, succeeded with a bovine vaccine in the mass immunization of a herd of Jersey cows. At the same time he was applying the fundamental observations of Helmholtz and Willard Gibbs of Yale, and of later physicists like Bisaillon and Zinks, to the treatment of the damaged lung through immobilization. From this he launched straight into therapeutics.

His curative work at the new Institute soon brought him into prominence with triumphs greater than his laboratory victories. Many of his patients were ambulant consumptives, wandering from one sanatorium to another, reputably adjudged incurable. His success with these cases immediately earned for him disparagement, accusation, and the determined antagonism of the medical profession.

There now began for Stillman a different and more protracted struggle, the battle for recognition of his work. He had sunk every dollar he possessed in establishing his Institute and the cost of maintaining it was heavy. He hated publicity and resisted all inducements to commercialize his work. Often it seemed as though material difficulties, allied to the bitterness of the opposition, must submerge him. Yet Stillman with magnificent courage survived every crisis—even a national newspaper campaign conducted against him.

The era of misrepresentation passed, the storm of controversy subsided. Gradually Stillman won a grudging recognition from his opponents. In 1925 a Washington Commission visited and reported glowingly upon the work at the Institute. Stillman, now recognized, began to receive large donations from private individuals, from trust executives, and even from public bodies. These funds he devoted to the extension and perfection of his Institute, which became, with its superb equipment and situation, its herds of Jersey cattle and pure-bred Irish serum horses, a show place in the state of Oregon.

Though Stillman was not entirely free from enemies—in 1929, for instance, the grievances of a dismissed laboratory attendant set alight another flare of scandal—he had at least secured immunity to pursue his life work. Unchanged by success, he remained the same quiet and restrained personality who, nearly twenty-five years before, had grown his first cultures in the attic on Beacon Hill.

And now, seated in the restaurant of Brooks Hotel, he gazed across at Andrew with quiet friendliness.

"It's very pleasant," he said, "to be in England. I like your countryside. Our summers aren't so cool as this."

"I suppose you've come over on a lecture tour?" Andrew said.

Stillman smiled.

"No! I don't lecture now. Is it vanity to say that I let my results lecture for me? As a matter of fact I'm over here very quietly. It so happens your Mr. Cranston—I mean Herbert Cranston, who makes those marvellous little automobiles—came to me in America about a year back. He'd been a martyr to asthma all his life and I—well, at the Institute we managed to set him right. Ever since then he's been bothering me to come over and start a small clinic here on the lines of our place at Portland. Six months ago I agreed. We passed the plans and now the place—we're calling it Bellevue—is pretty near completion, out on the Chilterns near High Wycombe. I'm going to get it started, then I'll turn it over to Marland—one of my assistants. Frankly, I look upon it as an experiment, a very promising experiment with my methods, particularly from the climatic and racial angles. The financial aspect is unimportant!"

Andrew leaned forward.

"That sounds interesting. What are you specially concentrating on? I'd like to look over your place."

"You must come when we are ready. We shall have our radical asthma régime. Cranston wants that. And then I have particularly specified for a few early tuberculosis cases. I say a few because," he smiled, "mind you, I don't forget I am just a biophysicist who knows a little about the respiratory apparatus—but in America our difficulty is to keep ourselves from being swamped. What was I saying? Ah, yes. These early T.B.'s. This will interest you. I have a new method of inducing pneumothorax. It is really an advance."

"You mean the Emile-Weil?"

"No, no. Much better. Without the disadvantages of negative fluctuation." Stillman's face lighted up. "You appreciate the difficulty of the fixed bottle apparatus—that point when the intrapleural pressure balances the fluid pressure and the flow of gas ceases altogether? Now, at the Institute, we've devised an accessory pressure chamber—I'll show you when you come out—through which we can introduce gas at a decided negative pressure, right at the start."

"But what about gas embolism?" Andrew said quickly.

"We eliminate the risk entirely. Look! It's quite a dodge. By introducing a small bromoform manometer close to the needle we avoid rarefaction. A fluctuation of −14 c.m. provides only 1 c.c. of gas at the needle-joint. Incidentally our needle has a four-way adjustment that goes a little better than Sangman's."

Andrew, in spite of himself—and his honorary appointment at the Victoria —was impressed.

"Why," he said, "if that is so, you're going to diminish pleural shock right down to nothing. You know, Mr. Stillman—well, it seems strange, quite startling to me, that all this should have come from you. Oh! forgive me, I've said that badly, but you know what I mean—so many doctors, going on with the old apparatus—"

"My dear physician," Stillman answered with amusement in his eyes, "don't forget that Carson, the first man to urge pneumothorax, was only a physiological essayist!"

After that they plunged into technicalities. They discussed apicolysis and phrenicotomy. They argued over Brauer's four points, passed on to oleothorax and Bernon's work in France—massive intrapleural injections in tuberculous empyema. They ceased only when Stillman looked at his watch and realized, with an exclamation, that he was half an hour late for an appointment with Cranston.

Andrew left Brooks Hotel with a stimulated and exalted mind. But, on the heels of that, came a queer reaction of confusion, dissatisfaction with his own work. I let myself get carried away by that fellow, he told himself, annoyed.

He was not in a particularly amiable frame of mind when he arrived at Chesborough Terrace; yet, as he drew up opposite his house, he composed his features into a noncommittal mould. His relations with Christine had come to demand this blankness, for she now presented to him a face so acquiescent and expressionless he felt, however much he raged internally, that he must answer it in kind.

It seemed to him that she had retired within herself, fallen back upon an inner life where he could not penetrate. She read a great deal, wrote letters. Once or twice when he came in he found her playing with Florrie—childish games, played with coloured counters, which they bought at the Stores. She began also, with unobtrusive regularity, to go to church. And this exasperated him most of all.

At Blaenelly she had accompanied Mrs. Watkins every Sunday to the parish church and he had found no reason for complaint. But now, unsympathetic and estranged from her, he saw it only as a further slight upon himself, a gesture of pietism directed at his suffering head.

This evening as he entered the front room she was seated alone in the room with her elbows on the table, wearing the glasses she had recently taken to, a book before her, a small occupied figure like a scholar at her lesson. An angry swell of exclusion swept over him. Reaching over her shoulders he picked up the book which, too late, she attempted to conceal. And there, at the head of the page, he read: *The Gospel According to St. Luke.*

"Good God!" He was staggered, somehow furious. "Is this what you've come to? Taken to Bible-thumping now?"

"Why not? I used to read it before I met you."

"Oh, you did, eh?"

"Yes." A queer look of pain was in her eyes. "Possibly your Plaza friends wouldn't appreciate the fact. But it is at least good literature."

"Is that so! Well, let me tell you this, in case you don't know it—you're developing into a blasted neurotic woman!"

"Quite probably. That again is entirely my fault. But let me tell you this. I'd rather be a blasted neurotic woman and be spiritually alive than a blasted successful man—and spiritually dead!"

She broke off suddenly, biting her lip, forcing back her tears. With a great effort she took control of herself. Looking at him steadily, with pain in her eyes, she said, in a low contained voice:—

"Andrew! Don't you think it would be a good thing for us both if I went away for a little while? Mrs. Vaughan has written me, asking me to spend a fortnight or three weeks with her. They've taken a house at Newquay for the summer. Don't you think I ought to go?"

"Yes! Go! Damn it all! Go!"

He swung round and left her.

13

CHRISTINE's departure for Newquay was a relief, an exquisite emancipation—for three whole days. Then he began to brood, to wonder what she was doing and whether she was missing him, to fret jealously as to when she would return. Though he told himself he was now a free man, he had the same sense of incompleteness which had kept him from his work at Aberalaw when she had gone to Bridlington, leaving him to study for his examination.

Her image rose before him, not the fresh young features of that earlier Christine, but a paler, maturer face with cheeks faintly drawn and eyes short-sighted behind their round glasses. It was not a beautiful face but it had some enduring quality which haunted him.

He went out a great deal, played bridge with Ivory, Freddie, and Freedman at the club. Despite his reaction to their first meeting he frequently saw Stillman, who was moving between Brooks Hotel and the nearly completed clinic at Wycombe. He wrote asking Denny to meet him in London, but it was impossible at this early stage of his appointment for Philip to get to town. Hope was inaccessible in Cambridge.

Fitfully he tried to concentrate on his clinical research at the hospital. Impossible. He was too restless. With this same restless intensity he went over his investments with Wade, the bank manager. All satisfactory; all going well.

He began to thresh out a scheme for buying a freehold house in Welbeck Street—a heavy investment, but one which should prove highly profitable—of selling the Chesborough Terrace house, merely retaining the surgery at the side. One of the building societies would help him. He woke during the still hot nights, his mind seething with schemes, with his work in the practice, his nerves overwrought, missing Christine, his hand reaching automatically to his bedside table for a cigarette.

In the middle of it all he rang up Frances Lawrence.

"I'm all alone here at present. You wouldn't care to run out somewhere in the evening? It's so hot in London."

Her voice was collected, oddly soothing to him. "That would be frightfully nice. I was hoping somehow you might ring. Do you know Crossways? Flood-lit Elizabethan, I'm afraid. But the river is too perfect there."

The following evening he cleared his surgery in three quarters of an hour. Well before eight, he had picked her up at Knightsbridge and set the car in the direction of Chertsey.

They ran due west, through the flat market gardens outside Staines, into a great flood of sunset. She sat beside him, as he drove, saying little yet filling the car with her alien, charming presence. She wore a coat and skirt of some thin fawn material, a dark hat close to her small head. He was over-whelmingly conscious of her gracefulness, her perfect finish. Her ungloved hand, near to him, was curiously expressive of this quality—white, slender. Each long finger tipped by an exquisite scarlet oval. Fastidious.

Crossways, as she had implied, was an exquisite Elizabethan house set in perfect gardens on the Thames, with age-long topiary work and lovely formal lily ponds all outraged in the conversion from mansion to roadhouse by modern conveniences and an infamous jazz band. But although a fake lackey sprang to the car as they ran into the courtyard, already filled by expensive cars, the old bricks glowed behind the wistaria vine and the tall angled chim-neys clustered serenely against the sky.

They went into the restaurant. It was smart, full, with tables placed round a square of polished floor and a head waiter who might have been brother to the grand vizier of the Plaza. Andrew hated and feared head waiters. But that, he now discovered, was because he had never faced them with a woman like Frances. One swift glance and they were ministered, with reverence, to the finest table in the room—surrounded by a corps of servitors, one of whom unflicked Andrew's napkin and placed it holily upon his knees.

Frances wanted very little: a salad, toast melba, no wine, only iced water. Undisturbed, the head waiter seemed to see in this frugality a confirmation of her caste. Andrew realized with a sudden qualm of dismay that, had he walked into this sanctuary with Christine and ordered such a trivial repast, he would have been hounded forth upon the highway with scorn.

He recollected himself to find Frances smiling at him.

"Do you realize we've known each other for quite a period of time now? And this is the first occasion you have asked me to come out with you."

"Are you sorry?"

"Not noticeably so, I hope." Again the charming intimacy of her faintly smiling face elevated him, caused him to feel wittier, more at ease, of a superior status. It was no mere pretentiousness, no silly snobbishness. The stamp of her breeding was somehow extended until it caught up and included him. He was aware of people at the adjoining tables viewing them with interest, of masculine admiration to which she was calmly oblivious. He could not help visualizing the stimulus of a more constant association with her.

She said:—

"Would it flatter you too much if I told you I had put off a previous theatre engagement to come here? Nicol Watson—do you remember him? He was taking me to the Ballet—one of my favourites—what will you think of my infantile taste? Massine in *La Boutique Fantastique*."

"I remember Watson. And his ride through Paraguay. Clever fellow."

"He's frightfully nice."

"But you felt it would be too hot at the Ballet?"

She smiled without answering, took a cigarette from a flat enamel box on which was depicted in faded colours an exquisite Boucher miniature.

"Yes, I heard Watson was running after you," he persisted with sudden vehemence. "What does your husband think of that?"

Again she did not speak, merely lifting an eyebrow as if mildly deprecating some lack of subtlety.

After a moment she said:—

"Surely you understand? Jackie and I are the best of friends. But we each have our *own* friends. He's at Juan at present. But I don't ask him why." Then lightly, "Shall we dance—just once?"

They danced. She moved with that same extraordinary fascinating grace, light in his arms, impersonal.

"I'm not altogether good," he said when they returned. He was even falling into her idiom—gone, gone were the days when he would have grunted, "Damn it, Chris, I'm no hoofer."

Frances did not reply. That again he felt to be eminently characteristic of her. Another woman would have flattered, contradicted him, made him feel clumsy. Driven by a sudden impulsive curiosity he exclaimed:—

"Please tell me something. Why have you been so kind to me? Helping me the way you've done—all those months?"

She looked at him, faintly amused yet without evasion.

"You are extraordinarily attractive to women. And your greatest charm is that you do not realize it."

"No, but, really—" he protested, flushed; then he muttered, "I hope I'm some kind of a doctor as well."

She laughed, slowly fanning away the cigarette smoke with her hand. "You will not be convinced. Or I should not have told you. And of course you're an excellent doctor. We were talking of you only the other night at Green Street. Le Roy is getting a little tired of our company dietician. Poor Rumbold! He wouldn't have enjoyed hearing Le Roy bark, 'We must put the skids under Grandpa.' But Jackie agrees. They want someone younger, with more drive, on the board,—shall I use the cliché?—a coming man. Apparently they plan a big campaign in the medical journals, they want really to interest the profession—from the scientific angle, as Le Roy put it. And of course Rumbold is just a joke amongst his colleagues. But why am I talking like this? Such a waste of a night like this. Now don't frown as though you were about to assassinate me, or the waiter, or the band-leader—I wish you would actually, isn't he odious? You look exactly as you did that first day—when you came into the fitting-room—very haughty and proud and nervous—even a little ridiculous. And then—poor Toppy! By the ordinary convention it is *she* who should be here."

"I'm very glad she's not," he said with his eyes upon the table.

"Please don't think me banal. I couldn't bear that. We are fairly intelligent I hope—and we—well, I for one—just do not believe in the *grande passion*. Isn't the phrase enough? But I do think life is so much gayer if one has—a friend—to go a bit of the way with one." Her eyes showed high points of amusement again. "Now I sound completely Rossetti-ish, which is too frightful." She picked up her cigarette case. "And anyhow it's stuffy here and I want you to see the moon on the river."

He paid the bill and followed her through the long glass windows which an act of vandalism had inset in the fine old wall. On the balustered terrace the music of the dance band came faintly. Before them a wide avenue of turf led down to the river between dark borders of clipped yew. As she had said, there was a moon which splashed great shadows from the yews and glinted palely upon a group of archery targets standing on the bottom lawns. Beyond lay the silver sheen of water.

They strolled down to the river, seated themselves upon a bench that stood beside the verge. She took off her hat and gazed silently at the slowly moving current, its eternal murmur strangely blended with the muted hum of a high-powered car travelling at speed into the distance.

"What queer night sounds," she said. "The old and the new. And searchlights across the moon there. It's our age."

He kissed her. She gave no sign either way. Her lips were warm and dry. In a minute she said:—

"That was very sweet. And very badly done."

"I can do better," he mumbled, staring in front of him, not moving. He was awkward, without conviction, ashamed and nervous. Angrily he told himself that it was wonderful to be here on such a night with such a graceful, charming woman. He ought by all the canons of moonshine and the magazines to have swept her madly into his arms. As it was he became aware of his cramped position, of a desire to smoke, of the vinegar in the salad touching up his old indigestion.

And Christine's face in some unaccountable way was mirrored in the water before him, a jaded and rather harassed face, on her cheek a plaintive smudge of paint from the brush with which she had painted the heavy folding doors, when first they came to Chesborough Terrace. It worried and exasperated him. He was here, bound by the obligation of the circumstances. And he was a man, wasn't he—not a candidate for Voronoff? Defiantly, he kissed Frances again.

"I thought possibly you were taking another twelve months to make up your mind." Her eyes held that high affectionate amusement. "And now, don't you think we should go, Doctor? These night airs—aren't they rather treacherous to the Puritanical mind?"

He helped her to her feet and she retained his hand, holding it lightly as they walked to the car. He flung a shilling to the baroque retainer, started the engine for London. As he drove her silence was eloquently happy.

But he was not happy. He felt himself a hound and a fool. Hating himself, disappointed in his own reactions, he still dreaded the return to his sultry room, his restless solitary bed. His heart was cold, his brain a mass of tormenting thoughts. The recollection swept before him of the agonizing sweetness of his first love for Christine, the beating ecstasy of those early days at Blaenelly. He pushed it away from him furiously.

They were at her house and his mind still struggled with the problem. He got out of the car and opened the door for her. They stood together on the pavement while she opened her bag and took out her latchkey.

"You'll come up, won't you? I'm afraid the servants are in bed."

He hesitated, stammered.

"It's very late, isn't it?"

She did not seem to hear him but went up the few flagstone steps with her key in her hand. As he followed, sneaking after her, he had a fading vision of Christine's figure walking down the market, carrying her old string bag.

14

THREE days later Andrew sat in his Welbeck Street consulting room. It was a hot afternoon and, through the screen of his open window, there came the pestering drone of traffic, borne upon the exhausted air. He was tired, overworked, fearful of Christine's return at the end of the week, expectant yet nervous of every telephone ring, sweating under the task of coping with six three-guinea patients in the space of one hour, and the knowledge that he must rush his surgery to take Frances out to supper. He glanced up impatiently as Nurse Sharp entered, more than usual acrimony on her patchy features.

"There's a man called to see you, a dreadful person. He's not a patient and he says he's not a traveller. He's got no card. His name's Boland."

"Boland?" Andrew echoed blankly; then his face cleared suddenly. "Not Con Boland? Let him in, Nurse! Straightaway."

"But you have a patient waiting. And in ten minutes Mrs. Roberts—"

"Oh! never mind Mrs. Roberts!" he threw out irritably. "Do as I say."

Nurse Sharp flushed at his tone. It was on her tongue to tell him she was not used to being spoken to like that. She sniffed and went out with her head in the air. The next minute she showed Boland in.

"Why, Con!" said Andrew jumping up.

"Hello, hello, he*llo*," shouted Con, as he bounded forward with a broad and genial grin. It was the redheaded dentist himself, no different, as real and untidy in his oversize shiny blue suit and large brown boots as if he had that moment walked out of his wooden garage; a shade older perhaps, but with no less violence in the beaded brush of his red moustache, still undaunted, wild-haired, exclamatory. He pounded Andrew vehemently on the back. "In the name of God, Manson! It's great to see ye again. Ye're lookin' marvellous, marvellous. I'd have known ye in a million. Well! Well! To think of this now. It's a high-class place you have here and all." He turned his beaming gaze upon the acidulous Sharp, who stood watching scornfully. "This lady nurse of yours wasn't for lettin' me in till I told her I was a professional man, myself. It's the God's truth, Nurse. This swanky-lookin' fella ye work for was in the same wan-horse medical scheme as myself not so long ago. Up in Aberalaw. If ever ye're passin' that way, drop in on the missus and me and we'll give ye a cup of tea. Any friend of my old friend Manson is welcome as the day!"

Nurse Sharp gave him one look and walked out of the room. But it was wasted on Con, who gushed and bubbled with a pure and natural joy, swinging round to Andrew irrepressibly:—

"No beauty, eh, Manson, my boy? But a decent woman I'll be bound. Well, well, well! How are ye, now? How *are* ye?"

He refused to relinquish Andrew's hand, but pumped it up and down, grinning away in sheer delight.

It was a rare tonic to see Con again on this devitalizing day. When Andrew at last freed himself, he flung himself into his swing chair, feeling himself human again, shoving over the cigarettes to Con. Then Con, with one grubby thumb in an armhole, the other pressing the wet end of a freshly lit cigarette, sketched the reason of his coming.

"I had a bit of a holiday due to me, Manson, my boy, and a couple of matters to attend to, so the wife just told me to pack off and hit it. Ye see, I've been workin' on a sort of a spring invention for tightenin' up slack brakes. Off and on I've been devotin' the full candlepower of the old grey mather to th' idee. But devil take them, there's nobody'll look at the gadget! But never mind, never mind, we'll let it go. It's not important besides the other thing." Con cast his cigarette ash upon the carpet and his face took a more serious turn. "Listen, Manson, my boy! It's Mary—you'll remember Mary surely, for I can tell you she remembers you! She's been poorly lately—not up to the mark at all. We've had her to Llewellyn and devil the bit of good he's doin' her." Con grew heated suddenly; his voice was thick. "Damn it all, Manson, he's got the sauce to say she's got a touch of T.B.—as if that wasn't all finished and done with in the Boland family when her Uncle Dan went to the sanatorium fifteen years ago. Now look here, Manson, will ye do something for old friendship's sake? We knew ye're a big man now; sure ye're the talk of Aberalaw. Will ye take a look at Mary for us? Ye can't tell what confidence that girl has in you; we've got it ourselves—Mrs. B. and me—for that matter. That's why she says to me, she says, 'You go to Doctor Manson when you're in the way of meetin' him. And if he'll see the daughter sure we'll send her up any time that's likely to be convenient.' Now what do you say, Manson? If you're too busy ye've only got to say so and I can easy sling my hook."

Andrew's expression had turned concerned.

"Don't talk that way, Con. Can't you see how delighted I am to see you? And Mary, poor kid—you know I'll do everything I can for her, everything."

Unmindful of Nurse Sharp's significant inthrustings he squandered his precious time in conversation with Con until at last she could bear it no longer.

"You have five patients waiting now, Doctor Manson. And you're more than an hour behind your appointment times. I can't make any more excuses to them, I'm not used to treating patients this way."

Even then, he still clutched at Con, and accompanied him to the front door, pressing hospitality upon him.

"I'm not going to let you rush back home, Con. How long are you up for? Three or four days? That's fine! Where are you staying? The Westland —out Bayswater way! That's no good! Why don't you come and stop with me instead; you're near us already. And we've bag-loads of room. Christine'll be back on Friday. She'll be delighted to see you, Con, delighted. We can talk over old times together."

On the following day Con brought his bag round to Chesborough Terrace. After the evening surgery they went together to the second house of the Palladium Music Hall. It was amazing how good every turn seemed in Con's company. The dentist's ready laugh rang out, dismaying at first, then infecting the immediate vicinity. People twisted round to smile at Con in sympathy.

"In the name of God!" Con rolled in his seat. "D'y' see that fella? With the bicycle? D'y' mind the time, Manson—"

In the interval they stood in the bar, Con with his hat on the back of his head, froth on his moustache, brown boots, happily planted.

"I can't tell ye, Manson, my boy, what a treat this is for me. Sure you're kindness itself!"

In the face of Con's genial gratitude Andrew somehow felt himself a tarnished hypocrite.

Afterwards they had a steak and beer at the Cadero; then they returned, stirred up the fire in the front room and sat down to talk. They talked and smoked and drank further bottles of beer. Momentarily Andrew forgot the complexities of supercivilized existence. The straining tension of his practice, the prospect of his adoption by Le Roy, the chance of promotion at the

Victoria, the state of his investments, the soft-textured nicety of Frances Lawrence, the dread of an accusation in Christine's distant eyes—these all faded as Con bellowed:—

"D'you mind the time we fought Llewellyn? And Urquhart and the rest drew back on us—Urquhart's still goin' strong by the same token, sends his best regards—and then we set to, the both of us, and finished the beer?"

But the next day came. And it brought, inexorably, the moment of re-union with Christine. Andrew dragged the unsuspecting Con to the end of the platform, irritably aware of the inadequacy of his self-possession, realizing that Boland was his salvation. His heart was beating in painful expectation as the train steamed in. He knew one shattering moment of anguish and remorse at the sight of Christine's small familiar face advancing amongst the crowd of strangers, straining in expectation towards his own. Then he lost everything in the effort to achieve cordial unconcern.

"Hello, Chris! Thought you were never coming! Yes, you may well look at him. It's Con all right! Himself and no other! And not a day older. He's staying with us, Chris—we'll tell you all about it in the car. I've got it outside. Did you have a good time? Oh, look here! *Why* are you carrying your case?"

Swept away by the unexpectedness of this platform reception—when she had feared she might not be met at all—Christine lost her wan expression, and colour flowed back nervously into her cheeks. She also had been apprehensive, nervously keyed, longing for a new beginning. She felt almost hopeful now. Ensconced in the back of the car with Con she talked eagerly, stealing glances at Andrew's profile in the driving seat.

"Oh, it is good to be home." She took a long breath inside the front door of the house; then, quickly, wistfully, "You have missed me, Andrew?"

"I should think I have. We *all* have. Eh, Mrs. Bennett? Eh, Florrie? Con! What the devil are you doing with that luggage?"

He was out in a second, giving Con a hand, performing unnecessarily with suitcases. Then, before anything more could be done or said, he had to leave on his rounds. He insisted that they could expect him for tea.

As he slumped into the seat of his car he groaned:—

"Thank God that's over! She doesn't look a lot the better of the holiday. Oh, hell! I'm sure she didn't notice. And that's the main thing at present."

Though he was late in returning, his briskness, his cheerfulness were excessive. Con was enraptured with such spirits.

"In the name of God! Ye've more go in ye than ever ye had in the old days, Manson, my boy."

Once or twice he felt Christine's eye upon him, half-pleading for a sign, a look of understanding. He perceived that Mary's illness was distracting her—a conflicting anxiety. She explained, in an interval of conversation, that she had asked Con to wire Mary to come through at once, to-morrow if possible. She was worried about Mary. She hoped that something, or rather everything, would be done without delay.

It fell out better than Andrew had expected. Mary wired back that she would arrive on the following day before lunch, and Christine was fully occupied in preparing for her. The stir and excitement in the house masked even his hollow heartiness.

But when Mary appeared he suddenly became himself again. It was evident at first sight that she was not well. Grown in these intervening years to a lanky young woman, with a slight droop to her shoulders, she had that almost unnatural beauty of complexion which spoke an immediate warning to Andrew.

She was tired out by her journey and though she wished, in her pleasure at seeing them again, to sit up and continue talking, she was persuaded to bed about six o'clock. It was then that Andrew went up to auscultate her chest.

He remained upstairs for only fifteen minutes, but when he came down to Con and Christine in the drawing-room his expression was, for once, genuinely disturbed.

"I'm afraid there's no doubt about it. The left apex. Llewellyn was perfectly right, Con. But don't worry. It's in the primary stage. We can do something with it!"

"You mean," said Con, gloomily apprehensive, "you mean it can be cured?"

"Yes. I'd go so far as to say that. It means keeping an eye on her, constant observation, every care." He reflected, frowning deeply. "It seems to me, Con, that Aberalaw's about the worst place for her—always bad for early T.B. at home. Why don't you let me get her into the Victoria? I've got a pull with Doctor Thoroughgood. I'd get her into his ward for a certainty. I'd keep my eye on her."

"Manson!" Con exclaimed impressively. "That's one true act of friendship. If ye only knew the trust that girl of mine has in ye! If any man'll get her right it's yourself."

Andrew went immediately to telephone Thoroughgood. He returned in five minutes with the information that Mary could be admitted to the Victoria at the end of the week. Con brightened visibly and, his bounding optimism responding to the idea of the Chest Hospital, of Andrew's attention, and Thoroughgood's supervision, Mary was for him as good as cured.

The next two days were fully occupied. By Saturday afternoon when Mary was admitted and Con had boarded his train at Paddington, Andrew's self-possession was at last equal to the occasion. He was able to press Christine's arm, and exclaim lightly on his way to the surgery:—

"Nice to be together again, Chris! Lord! What a week it has been."

It sounded perfectly in key. But it was as well he did not see the look upon her face. She sat down in the room, alone, her head bent slightly, her hands in her lap, very still.

She had been so hopeful when first she came back. But now, within her, was the dreadful foreboding: *Dear God! When and how is this going to end?*

15

On and on rushed the spate of his success, a bursting dam sweeping him irresistibly forward in an ever-sounding, ever-swelling flood.

His association with Hampton and Ivory was now closer and more profitable than ever. Moreover, Freedman had asked him to deputize for him at the Plaza, while he flew to Le Touquet for seven days' golf, and, by way of acknowledgment, to split the fees. Usually it was Hampton who acted as Freedman's locum, but lately Andrew suspected a rift between these two.

How flattering for Andrew to discover that he could walk straight into the bedroom of a paroxysmal film star, sit on her satin sheets, palpate her sexless anatomy with sure hands, perhaps smoke a cigarette with her if he had time!

But even more flattering was the patronage of Joseph Le Roy. Twice in the last month he had lunched with Le Roy. He knew there were important ideas working in the other man's mind. At their last meeting Le Roy had tentatively remarked:—

"You know, Doc, I've been feeling my way with you. It's a pretty large thing I'm going on to, and I'll need a lot of clever medical advice. I don't want any more double-handed big hats—old Rumbold isn't worth his own calories, we're going to pin the crape on him right away! And I don't want a lot of so-called experts goin' into a huddle and pulling me round in circles. I want one level-headed medical adviser, and I'm beginning to think you're about it. You see, we've reached a wide section of the public with our products on a popular basis. But I honestly believe the time has come to expand our interests and go in for more scientific derivatives. Split up the milk components, electrify them, irradiate them, tabloid them. Cremo with vitamin B, Cremofax and lethecin for malnutrition, rickets, deficiency insomnia—you get me, Doc. And further, I believe if we tackle this on more orthodox professional lines we can enlist the help and sympathy of the whole medical profession, make every doctor, so to speak, a potential salesman. Now this means scientific advertising, Doc, scientific approach; and that's where I believe a young scientific doctor on the inside could help us all along the road. Now I want you to get me straight. This is all perfectly open and *scientific*. We are actually raising our own status. And when you consider the worthless extracts that doctors do recommend, like Marrobin C and Vegatog and Bonebran, why, I consider in elevating the general standard of health we are doing a great public service to the nation."

Andrew did not pause to consider that there was probably more vitamin value in one fresh green pea than in several tins of Cremofax. He was excited, not by the fee he would receive for acting on the board, but at the thought of Le Roy's interest.

It was Frances who told him how he might profit by Le Roy's spectacular market operations. Ah! it was pleasant to drop in to tea with her, to feel that this charming sophisticated woman had a special glance for him, a swift provoking smile of intimacy! Association with her gave him sophistication too, added assurance, a harder polish. Unconsciously he absorbed her philoso-phy. Under her guidance he was learning to cultivate the superficial niceties and let the deeper things go hang.

It was no longer an embarrassment to face Christine; he could come into his house quite naturally, following an hour spent with Frances. He did not stop to wonder at this astounding change. If he thought of it at all it was to argue that he did not love Mrs. Lawrence, that Christine knew nothing of it, that every man came to this particular *impasse* some time in his life. Why should he set himself up to be different?

By way of recompense he went out of his way to be nice to Christine, spoke to her with consideration, even discussed his plans with her. She was aware that he proposed to buy the Welbeck Street house next spring, that they would be leaving Chesborough Terrace whenever the arrangements were complete. She never argued with him now, never threw recriminations at his head, and if she had moods he never saw them. She seemed altogether pas-sive. Life moved too swiftly for him to pause long for reflection. The pace exhilarated him. He had a false sensation of strength. He felt vital, increasing in consequence, master of himself and of his destiny.

And then, out of high heaven, the bolt fell.

One evening the wife of a neighbouring petty tradesman came to his con-sulting room at Chesborough Terrace. She was Mrs. Vidler, a small sparrow of a woman, middle-aged, but bright-eyed and spry, a regular Londoner who had all her life never been further from Bow Bells than Margate. Andrew knew the Vidlers well; he had attended the little boy for some childish com-plaint when he first came to the district. In those early days, too, he had sent his shoes there to be mended, for the Vidlers, respectable, hard-working tradespeople, kept a double shop at the head of Paddington Street named, rather magnificently, "Renovations Ltd."—one half devoted to boot repairs and the other to the cleaning and pressing of wearing apparel. Harry Vidler himself might often be seen, a sturdy pale-faced man, collarless and in his shirt sleeves, with a last between his knees or, though he kept a couple of helpers, using a damping-board if work in the other department was urgent.

It was of Harry that Mrs. Vidler now spoke.

"Doctor," she said in her brisk way, "my husband isn't well. For weeks now he's been poorly. I've been at him and at him to come, but he wouldn't. Will you call to-morrow, Doctor? I'll keep him in bed."

Andrew promised that he would call.

Next morning he found Vidler in bed, giving a history of internal pain and growing stoutness. His girth had increased extraordinarily in these last few months and inevitably, like most patients who have enjoyed good health all their lives, he had several ways of accounting for it. He suggested that he had been taking a drop too much ale, or that perhaps his sedentary life was to blame.

But Andrew, after his investigation, was obliged to contradict these elucida-tions. He was convinced that the condition was cystic and, although not dangerous, it was one which demanded operative treatment. He did his best to reassure Vidler and his wife by explaining how a simple cyst such as this might develop internally and cause no end of inconvenience which would all disappear when it was removed. He had no doubt at all in his mind as to the upshot of the operation, and he proposed that Vidler should go into hospital at once.

Here, however, Mrs. Vidler held up her hands.

"No, sir, I won't have my Harry in a hospital!" She struggled to compose her agitation. "I've had a kind of feeling this was coming—the way he's been overworking in the business. But now it *as* come, thank God we're in a position as can deal with it. We're not well-off people, Doctor, as you know, but we 'ave got a little bit put by. And now's the time to use it. I won't have Harry go beggin' for subscribers' letters, and standin' in queues, and goin' into a public ward like he was a pauper."

"But, Mrs. Vidler, I can arrange—"

"No! You can get him in a private home, sir. There's plenty round about here. And you can get a private doctor to operate on him. I can promise you, sir, so long as I'm here, no public hospital shall 'ave Harry Vidler."

He saw that her mind was firmly made up. And indeed Vidler himself, since this unpleasant necessity had arisen, was of the same opinion as his wife. He wanted the best treatment that could be had.

That evening Andrew rang up Ivory. It was automatic now for him to turn to Ivory; the more so as, in this instance, he had to ask a favour.

"I'd like you to do something for me, Ivory. I've an abdominal here, that wants doing—decent hard-working people but not rich, you understand. There's nothing much in it for you, I'm afraid. But it would oblige me if you did it for—shall we say a third of the usual fee?"

Ivory was very gracious. Nothing would please him more than to do his friend Manson any service within his power. They discussed the case for several minutes and at the end of that discussion Andrew telephoned Mrs. Vidler.

"I've just been on to Mr. Charles Ivory, a West End surgeon who happens to be a particular friend of mine. He's coming to see your husband with me to-morrow, Mrs. Vidler, at eleven o'clock. That all right? And he says—are you there?—he says, Mrs. Vidler, that if the operation has to be undertaken he'll do it for thirty guineas. Considering that his usual fee would be a hundred guineas—perhaps more—I think we're not doing too badly."

"Yes, Doctor, yes." Her tone was worried, yet she made the effort to sound relieved. "It's very kind of you, I'm sure. I think we can manage that some'ow."

Next morning Ivory saw the case with Andrew and on the following day Harry Vidler moved into the Brunsland Nursing Home in Brunsland Square.

It was a clean, old-fashioned home not far from Chesborough Terrace, one of many in the district where the fees were moderate and the equipment scanty. Most of its patients were medical cases, hemiplegics, chronic cardiacs, bedridden old women with whom the main difficulty was the prevention of bedsores. Like every other home which Andrew had entered in London it had never been intended for its present purpose. There was no lift, and the operating theatre had once been a conservatory. But Miss Buxton, the proprietress, was a qualified Sister and a hard working woman. Whatever its defects, the Brunsland was spotlessly aseptic—and even to the furthest corner of its shining linoleumed floors.

The operation was fixed for Friday and, since Ivory could not come early, it was set for the unusually late hour of two o'clock.

Though Andrew was at Brunsland Square first, Ivory arrived punctually. He drove up with the anæsthetist and stood watching while his chauffeur carried in his large bag of instruments—so that nothing might interfere with his subsequent delicacy of touch. And, though he plainly thought little of the home, his manner remained as suave as ever. Within the space of ten minutes he had reassured Mrs. Vidler, who waited in the front room, made the conquest of Miss Buxton and her nurses; then, gowned and gloved in the little travesty of a theatre, he was imperturbably ready.

The patient walked in with determined cheerfulness, slipped off his dressing-gown, which one of the nurses then whipped away, and climbed upon the narrow table. Realizing that he must go through with the ordeal, Vidler had come to face it with courage. Before the anæsthetist placed the mask over his face he smiled at Andrew.

"I'll be better after this is over." The next moment he had closed his eyes and was almost eagerly drinking in deep draughts of ether. Miss Buxton removed the bandages. The iodined area was exposed, unnaturally tumescent, a glistening mound. Ivory commenced the operation.

He began with some spectacular deep injections into the lumbar muscles. "Combat shock," he threw out gravely to Andrew. "I always use it."

Then the real work began.

His medial incision was large, and immediately, almost ludicrously, the trouble was revealed. The cyst bobbed through the opening like a fully inflated wet rubber football. The justification of his diagnosis added, if anything, to Andrew's self-esteem. He reflected that Vidler would do nicely when detached from this uncomfortable accessory and with an eye on his next case he surreptitiously looked at his watch.

Meanwhile Ivory, in his masterly manner, was playing with the football, imperturbably trying to get his hands round it to its point of attachment and imperturbably failing. Every time he attempted to control it the ball slithered away from him. If he tried once he tried twenty times.

Andrew glanced irritably at Ivory, thinking, What is the man doing? There was not much space in the abdomen in which to work, but there was space enough. He had seen Llewellyn, Denny, a dozen others at his old hospital manipulate expertly with far less latitude. It was a surgeon's job to fiddle through cramped positions. Suddenly he realized that this was the first abdominal operation Ivory had ever done for him. Insensibly, he dropped his watch back into his pocket, drew nearer, rather rigidly, to the table.

Ivory was still straining to get behind the cyst, still calm, incisive, unruffled. Miss Buxton and a young nurse stood trustfully by, not knowing very much about anything. The anæsthetist, an elderly grizzled man, was stroking the end of the stoppered bottle contemplatively with his thumb. The atmosphere of the bare little glass-roofed theatre was flat, supremely uneventful. There was no high sense of tension or steam-heated drama, merely Ivory raising one shoulder, manœuvring with his gloved hands, trying to get behind the smooth rubber ball. But for some reason a sense of coldness fell on Andrew.

He found himself frowning, watching tensely. What was he dreading? There was nothing to be afraid of, nothing. It was a straightforward operation. In a few minutes it would be finished.

Ivory, with a faint smile, as of satisfaction, gave up the attempt to find the cyst's point of attachment. The young nurse gazed at him humbly as he asked for a knife. Ivory took the knife in slow motion. Probably never in his career had he looked more exactly like the great surgeon of fiction. Holding the knife, before Andrew knew what he was about, he made a generous puncture in the glistening wall of the cyst.

After that everything happened at once.

The cyst burst, exploding a great clot of venous blood into the air, vomiting its contents into the abdominal cavity. One second there was a round tight sphere, the next a flaccid purse of tissue lay in a mess of gurgling blood. Frantically Miss Buxton felt in the drum for swabs.

The anæsthetist sat up abruptly. The young nurse looked like fainting. Ivory said gravely:—

"Clamp, please."

A wave of horror swept over Andrew. He saw that Ivory, failing to reach the pedicle to ligature it, had blindly, wantonly, incised the cyst. And it was a hæmorrhagic cyst.

"Swab, please," Ivory said in his impassive voice. He was fiddling about in the mess, trying to clamp the pedicle, swabbing out the blood-filled cavity, packing, failing to control the hæmorrhage. Realization broke on Andrew in a blinding flash. He thought: God Almighty! He can't operate, he can't operate at all!

The anæsthetist, with his finger on the carotid, murmured in a gentle, apologetic voice: "I'm afraid—he seems to be going, Ivory."

Ivory, relinquishing the clamp, stuffed the belly cavity full of blooded gauze. He began to suture up his great incision.

There was no swelling now. Vidler's stomach had a caved-in, pallid, empty look, the reason being that Vidler was dead.

"Yes, he's gone now," said the anæsthetist finally.

Ivory put in his last stitch, clipped it methodically and turned to the instrument tray to lay down his scissors. Paralyzed, Andrew could not move. Miss Buxton, with a clay-coloured face, was automatically packing the hot bottles outside the blanket. By great force of will she seemed to collect herself. She went outside. The porter, unaware of what had happened, brought in the stretcher. Another minute and Harry Vidler's body was being carried upstairs to his bedroom.

Ivory spoke at last.

"Very unfortunate," he said in his collected voice as he stripped off his gown. "I imagine it was shock. Don't you think so, Gray?"

Gray, the anæsthetist, mumbled an answer. He was busy packing up his apparatus.

Still Andrew could not speak. Amidst the dazed welter of his emotion he suddenly remembered Mrs. Vidler, waiting downstairs. It seemed as if Ivory read that thought. He said: "Don't worry, Manson. I'll attend to the little woman. Come. I'll get it over for you now."

Instinctively, like a man unable to resist, Andrew found himself following Ivory down the stairs to the waiting-room. He was still stunned, weak with nausea, wholly incapable of telling Mrs. Vidler. It was Ivory who rose to the occasion, rose almost to the heights.

"My dear lady," he said, compassionate and upstanding, placing his hand gently on her shoulder, "I'm afraid—I'm afraid we have bad news for you."

She clasped her hands, in worn brown kid gloves, together. Terror and entreaty were mingled in her eyes.

"What?"

"Your poor husband, Mrs. Vidler, in spite of everything which we could do for him—"

She collapsed into the chair, her face ashen, her gloved hands still working together.

"Harry!" she whispered in a heartrending voice. Then again, "Harry!"

"I can only assure you," Ivory went on, sadly, "on behalf of Doctor Manson, Doctor Gray, Miss Buxton, and myself, that no power on earth could have saved him. And even if he had survived the operation . . ." He shrugged his shoulders significantly. She looked up at him, sensing his meaning, aware, even at this frightful moment, of his condescension, his goodness to her.

"That's the kindest thing you could have told me, Doctor." She spoke through her tears.

"I'll send down Sister to you. Do your best to bear up. And thank you, thank you for your courage."

He went out of the room and once again Andrew went with him. At the end of the hall was the empty office, the door of which stood open. Feeling for his cigarette case, Ivory walked into the office. There he lit a cigarette and took a long pull at it. His face was perhaps a trifle paler than usual but his jaw was firm, his hand steady, his nerve absolutely unshaken.

"Well, that's over," he reflected coolly. "I'm sorry, Manson. I didn't dream that cyst was hæmorrhagic. But these things happen in the best-regulated circles, you know."

It was a small room with the only chair pushed underneath the desk. Andrew sank down on the leather-covered club fender that surrounded the fireplace. He stared feverishly at the aspidistra in the yellowish green pot placed in the empty grate. He was sick, shattered, on the verge of a complete collapse. He could not escape the vision of Harry Vidler, walking unaided to the table—"I'll be better after this is over"—and then ten minutes later, sagging on the stretcher, a mutilated, butchered corpse. He gritted his teeth together, covered his eyes with his hand.

"Of course," Ivory inspected the end of his cigarette, "he didn't die on the table. I finished before that—which makes it all right. No necessity for an inquest."

Andrew raised his head. He was trembling, infuriated by the consciousness of his own weakness in this awful situation which Ivory had sustained with such cold-blooded nerve.

He said, in a kind of frenzy:—

"For Christ's sake stop talking. You know you killed him. You're not a surgeon. You never were; you never will be a surgeon. You're the worst botcher I've ever seen in all my life."

There was a silence. Ivory gave Andrew a pale, hard glance. "I don't recommend that line of talk, Manson."

"You don't?" A painful, hysterical sob shook Andrew. "I know you don't! But it's the truth. All the cases I've given you up till now have been child's play. But this—the first real case we've had— Oh, God! I should have known —I'm just as bad as you—"

"Pull yourself together, you hysterical fool. You'll be heard."

"What if I am?" Another weak burst of anger seized Andrew. He choked: "You know it's the truth as well as I do. You bungled so much—it was almost murder!"

For an instant it seemed as if Ivory would knock him senseless off the fender, a physical effort which, with his weight and strength, the older man could easily have accomplished. But with a great struggle he controlled himself. He said nothing, simply turned and walked out of the room. But there was an ugly look on his cold, hard face which spoke, icily, of unforgiving fury.

How long Andrew remained in the office, his forehead pressed against the cold marble of the mantelpiece, he did not know. But at last he rose, realizing dully that he had work which he must do. The dreadful shock of the calamity had caught him with the destructive violence of an explosive shell. It was as though he, also, were eviscerate and empty. Yet he still moved automatically, advancing as might a horribly wounded soldier, compelled by machine-like habit to perform the duties expected of him.

In this fashion he managed, somehow, to drag round his remaining visits. Then, with a leaden heart and an aching head, he came back home. It was late, nearly seven o'clock. He was just in time for his surgery and evening consultations.

His front waiting-room was full, his surgery packed to the door. Heavily, like a dying man, he took stock of them: his patients, gathered, despite the fine summer evening, to pay tribute to his manner, his personality. Mostly women, a great many of them Laurier's girls, people who had been coming to him for weeks, encouraged by his smile, his tact, his suggestion that they persevere with their medicine; the old gang, he thought numbly, the old game!

He dropped into his surgery swing chair, began with a mask-like face the usual evening rite.

"How are you? Yes, I think you're looking a shade better! Yes. Pulse has much more tone. The physic is doing you good. Hope it's not too nasty for you, my dear girl."

Out to the waiting Christine, handing her the empty bottle, forward along the passage to the consulting room, stringing out the same interrogative platitudes there, the same bogus sympathy; then back along the passage, picking up the full bottle, back into the surgery again. So it went on, this infernal circus of his own damnation.

It was a sultry night. He suffered abominably, but still he went on, half to torture himself and half in empty deadness because he could not stop. As he passed backwards and forwards in a daze of pain he kept asking himself: Where am I going? Where, in the name of God, am I going?

At last, later than usual, at quarter to ten, it was finished. He locked the outer door of the surgery, came through to the consulting room where, according to routine, Christine waited, ready to call out the lists, to help him make up the book.

For the first time in many weeks he really looked at her, gazed deeply into her face as, with lowered eyes, she studied the list in her hand. Piercing even his numbness, the change in her shocked him. Her expression was still and fixed, her mouth drooped. Though she did not look at him there was a mortal sadness in her eyes.

Seated at the desk before the heavy ledger he felt a frightful straining in his side. But his body, that outer covering of deadness, allowed nothing of that inner throbbing to escape. Before he could speak she had begun to call out the list.

On and on he went, marking the book, a cross for a visit, a circle for a consultation, marking the total of his iniquity.

When it was finished she asked, in a voice whose wincing satire he only then observed:—

"Well! How much to-day?"

He did not, could not answer. She left the room. He heard her go upstairs to her room, heard the quiet sound of her closing the door. He was alone: dry, stricken, bemused.

Where am I going? Where in the name of God am I going?

Suddenly his eyes fell upon the tobacco sack, full of money, bulging with his cash takings for the day. Another wave of hysteria swept over him. He took up the bag and flung it into the corner of the room. It fell with a dull and senseless sound.

He jumped up. He was stifling, he could not breathe.

Leaving the consulting room, he rushed into the little back yard of the house, a small well of darkness beneath the stars. Here he leaned weakly against the brick dividing-wall. He began, violently, to retch.

16

HE tossed restlessly in bed all through the night until, at six in the morning, he at last fell asleep. Awakening late he came down after nine o'clock, pale and heavy-eyed, to find that Christine had already breakfasted and gone out. Normally this would not have upset him. Now, with a pang of anguish, it made him feel how far they were apart.

When Mrs. Bennett brought him his nicely cooked bacon and egg he could not eat it, the muscles of his throat refused to work. He drank a cup of coffee; then, on an impulse, he mixed himself a stiff whisky-and-soda, drank that too. He then prepared to face the day.

Though the machine still held him, his movements were less automatic than before. A faint gleam, a haggard shaft of light had begun to penetrate his dazed uncertainty. He knew that he was on the verge of a great, a colossal breakdown. He knew also that if he once fell into that abyss he would never crawl out of it. Cautiously holding himself in, he opened the garage and took out his car. The effort made the sweat spring out on his palms.

His main purpose this morning was to reach the Victoria. He had made an appointment with Doctor Thoroughgood to see Mary Boland. That, at least, was an engagement he did not wish to miss. He drove slowly to the hospital. Actually he felt better in the car than when he walked—he was so used to driving that it had become automatic, reflex.

He reached the hospital, parked his car, went up to the ward. With a nod to Sister he passed along to Mary's bed, picking up her chart on the way. Then he sat down on the red blanketed edge of the bed, aware of her welcoming smile, of the big bunch of roses beside her, but all the while studying her chart. The chart was not satisfactory.

"Good morning," she said. "Aren't my flowers beautiful? Christine brought them yesterday."

He looked at her. No more flushed, but a little thinner than when she came in.

"Yes, they're nice flowers. How do you feel, Mary?"

"Oh! All right." Her eyes avoided his momentarily, then swept back full of warm confidence. "Anyway I know it won't be for long. You'll soon have me better."

The trust in her words and, above all, in her gaze, sent a great throb of pain through him. He thought: If anything goes wrong here it will be the final smash.

At that moment Doctor Thoroughgood arrived to make his round of the ward. As he came in, he saw Andrew, and at once advanced towards him.

"Morning, Manson," he said pleasantly. "Why? What's the matter? Are you ill?"

Andrew stood up.

"I'm quite well, thank you."

Doctor Thoroughgood gave him an odd glance; then he turned to Mary's bed.

"I'm glad you asked to see this case with me. Let's have the screens, Sister."

They spent ten minutes together examining Mary, then Thoroughgood went over to the alcove by the end window, where, though in full view of the ward, they could not be overheard.

"Well?" he said.

Out of the haze Andrew heard himself speak.

"I don't know how you feel, Doctor Thoroughgood, but it seems to me that the progress of this case isn't quite satisfactory."

"There are one or two features . . ." Thoroughgood pulled at his narrow little beard.

"It seems to me that there's some slight extension."

"Oh, I don't think so, Manson."

"The temperature is more erratic."

"'M, perhaps."

"Excuse me for suggesting it—I appreciate our relative positions perfectly, but this case means a great deal to me—under the circumstances would you not consider pneumothorax? You remember I was very anxious we should use it when Mary—when the case came in."

Thoroughgood glanced sideways at Manson. His face altered, set into stubborn lines.

"No, Manson. I'm afraid I don't see this as a case for induction. I didn't then, and I don't now."

There was a silence. Andrew could not utter another word. He knew Thoroughgood, his crotchety obstinacy. He felt spent, physically and morally, unable to pursue an argument which must be fruitless. He listened with an immobile face while Thoroughgood ran on, airing his own views about the case. When the other concluded and started to go round the remaining beds he went over to Mary, told her he would call again soon, and left the ward. Before he drove away from the hospital he asked the lodge porter to ring up his house to say he would not be in for lunch.

It was now not far off one o'clock. He was still distressed, wrapped in painful self-contemplation, and faint for want of food. Near Battersea Bridge he stopped outside a small cheap tea-room. Here he ordered coffee and some hot buttered toast. But he could only drink the coffee, his stomach revolted at the toast. He felt the waitress gazing at him curiously.

"Ain't it right?" she said. "I'll change it."

He shook his head, asked her for his check. As she wrote it he caught himself stupidly counting the shiny black buttons on her dress. Once, a long time ago, he had gazed at three pearly buttons in a Blaenelly schoolroom. Outside, a yellow glare hung oppressively above the river. As from a distance he remembered that he had two appointments this afternoon at Welbeck Street. He drove there slowly.

Nurse Sharp was in a bad temper, her usual humour when he asked her to come in on Saturdays. Yet she also inquired if he felt ill. Then, in a softer voice, for Doctor Hampton was a particular object of her regard, she told him that Freddie had rung him twice since lunchtime.

When she went out of the consulting room he sat at his desk staring straight in front of him. The first of his patients arrived at half-past two—a heart case, a young clerk from the Mines Department who had come to him through Gill, who was genuinely suffering from a valvular complaint. He found that he was spending a long time over this case, taking especial pains, detaining the young man earnestly while he carefully went over the details of the treatment.

At the end, as the other fumbled for his thin pocketbook he said quickly: "Please don't pay me now. Wait until I send your bill."

The thought that he would never send the bill, that he had lost his thirst for money and could once again despise it, comforted him strangely.

Then the second case came in, a woman of forty-five, Miss Basden, one of the most faithful of his followers. His heart sank at the sight of her. Rich, selfish, hypochondriacal, she was a younger, a more egotistic replica of that Mrs. Raeburn he had once seen with Hampton in Sherrington's home.

He listened wearily, his hand on his brow, while, smiling, she launched into an account of all that had happened to her constitution since her visit to him a few days before.

Suddenly he raised his head.

"Why do you come to me, Miss Basden?"

She broke off in the middle of a sentence, the pleased expression still fixed upon the upper part of her face, but her mouth dropping slowly open.

"Oh, I know I'm to blame," he said. "I told you to come. But there's nothing really wrong with you."

"Doctor Manson!" she gasped, unable to believe her ears.

It was quite true. He realized, with cruel insight, that all her symptoms were due to money. She had never done a day's work in her life, her body was soft, pampered, overfed. She did not sleep because she did not exercise her muscles. She did not even exercise her brain. She had nothing to do but cut coupons and think about her dividends and scold her maid and wonder what she, and her pet Pomeranian, would eat. If only she would walk out of his room and do something real; stop all the little pills and sedatives and hypnotics and cholagogues and every other kind of rubbish; give some of her money to the poor; help other people and stop thinking about herself! But she would never, never do that, it was useless even to demand it of her. She was spiritually dead and, God help him, so was he!

He said heavily:—

"I'm sorry I can't be of any further service to you, Miss Basden. I—I may be going away. But I've no doubt you'll find other doctors, round about here, who will be only too happy to pander to you."

She opened her mouth several times like a fish gasping for air. Then an expression of positive apprehension came upon her face. She was sure, quite sure, that he had gone out of his mind. She did not wait to reason with him. She rose, hastily gathering her belongings together, and hurried from the room.

He prepared to go home, shutting the drawers of his desk with an air of finality. But before he got up Nurse Sharp bounced into the room, smiling. "Doctor Hampton to see you! He's come round himself instead of telephoning."

The next minute Freddie was there, airily lighting a cigarette, flinging himself into a chair with an air of purpose in his eye. His tone had never been friendlier.

"Sorry to bother you on a Saturday, old man. But I knew you were here, so I brought round the old mountain to Mahomet. Now look here, Manson. I've heard all about the operation yesterday and I don't mind telling you I'm darn well glad. It's about high time you had an inside slant on dear friend Ivory."

Hampton's voice took on a sudden vicious twist. "I think you ought to know, old chap, that I've been rather falling out with Ivory and Freedman lately. They haven't been playing the game with me. We've been running a little pool together, and very profitable it was, but now I'm pretty well sure these two are twisting me out of some of my share. Besides which, I'm about sick of Ivory's bloody side. He's no surgeon. You're damned well right. He's nothing but a damned abortionist. You didn't know that, eh? Well, take it from me as gospel. There's a couple of nursing homes not one hundred miles from this house where they do nothing else—all very pretty and above-board of course—and Ivory's the head scraper! Freedman isn't much better. He's nothing but a sleek dope peddler and he isn't so smart as Ivory. One of these days he's going to get it in the neck from the D.D.A. Now you listen to me, old man, I'm speaking to you for your own good. I'd like you to know the whole inside story about these fellows because I want you to throw them over and come in with me. You've been too damn green. You haven't been getting your proper whack. Don't you know that when Ivory gets a hundred guineas for an operation he hands back fifty?—that's how he gets them, you see! And what has he been handing you? A measly fifteen or maybe twenty. It isn't good enough, Manson! And after this bit of botching yesterday I damn well wouldn't stand for it. Now I've said nothing to *them* yet, I'm too smart for that; but here's my scheme, old man: Let's ditch them altogether, you and me, and start a tight little partnership of our own. After all we were old pals at college, weren't we? I like you. I've always liked you. And I can show you a hell of a lot."

Freddie broke off to light another cigarette, then he smiled agreeably, expansively, exhibiting his possibilities as a potential partner. "You wouldn't believe the stunts I've pulled. D'you know my latest? Three-guineas-a-time injections—*of sterile water!* Patient came in one day for her vaccine; I'd forgotten to order the damn thing; so, rather than disappoint, pumped in the H_2O. She came back the next day to say she'd had a better reaction than from any of the others. So I went on. And why not? It all boils down to faith and the bottle of coloured water. Mind you I can plug the whole pharmacopœia into them when it's necessary. I'm not unprofessional—Lord, no! It's just that I'm wise, and if you and I really got together, Manson,—you with your degrees and me with my savvy,—we'd simply skim the pool. There's got to be two of us, you see. You want second opinions all the time. And I've got my eye on a smart young surgeon—hell of a lot better than Ivory! We might snaffle him later. Eventually we might even have our own nursing home. And *then* we'd be in Klondike."

Andrew remained motionless and stiff. He had no anger against Hampton, only a bitter loathing of himself. Nothing could have shown him more blastingly how he stood, what he had done, where he had been going, than this suggestion of Hampton's.

At last, seeing that some answer was demanded of him, he mumbled:—

"I can't go in with you, Freddie. I've—I've suddenly got sick of it. I think I'll chuck it here for a bit. There are too many jackals in this square mile of country. There's a lot of good men, trying to do good work, practising honestly, fairly, but the rest of them are just jackals. It's the jackals who give all these unnecessary injections, whip out tonsils and appendices that aren't doing any harm, play ball amongst one another with their patients, split fees, perform abortions, back up pseudoscientific remedies, chase the guineas all the time."

Hampton's face had slowly reddened.

"What the hell!" he spluttered. "What about yourself?"

"I know, Freddie," Andrew said heavily. "I'm just as bad. I don't want any ill-feeling between us. You used to be my best friend."

Hampton jumped up.

"Have you gone off your rocker, or what?"

"Perhaps. But I'm going to try and stop thinking of money and material success. That isn't the test of a good doctor. When a doctor earns five thousand a year he's not healthy. And why—why should a man try to make money out of suffering humanity?"

"You bloody fool," said Hampton distinctly. He swung round and went out of the room.

Again Andrew sat woodenly at his desk, alone, desolate. He got up at last and drove home. As he approached his house he was conscious of the rapid beating of his heart. It was now after six o'clock. The whole trend of his weary day seemed working upwards to its climax. His hand trembled violently as he turned his latchkey in the door.

Christine was in the front room. The sight of her pale still face sent a great shiver through him. He longed for her to ask, to show some concern as to how he had spent these hours away from her.

But she merely said, in that even noncommittal voice: "You've had a long day. Will you have some tea before the surgery?"

He answered: "There won't be any surgery to-night."

She glanced at him.

"But Saturday—it's your busiest night!"

His answer was to write out a notice stating that the surgery was closed to-night. He walked along the passage, pinned it upon the surgery door. His heart was now thumping so violently he felt that it must burst. When he returned along the passage she was in the consulting room, her face paler still, her eyes distraught.

"What is the matter?" she asked in a strange voice.

He looked at her. The anguish in his heart tore at him, broke through in a great rush that swept him beyond all control.

"Christine!" Everything within him went into that single word. Then he was at her feet, kneeling, weeping.

17

THEIR reconciliation was the most wonderful thing that had happened to them since they first fell in love. Next morning, which was Sunday, he lay beside her, as in those days at Aberalaw, talking, talking and, as though years had slipped from him, pouring out his heart to her. Outside the quiet of Sunday was in the air, the sound of bells, soothing and peaceful. But he was not peaceful.

"How did I come to do it?" he groaned restlessly. "Was I mad, Chris, or what? I can't believe it when I look back on it. Me—getting in with that crowd—after Denny, and Hope—God! I should be executed."

She soothed him. "It all happened with such a rush, dear. It would have swept anyone off his feet."

"No, but honestly, *Chris*. I feel like going off my head when I think about it. And what a hell of a time it must have been for you! Lord! it ought to be a *painful* execution!"

She smiled, actually smiled. It was the most marvellous experience to see her face stripped of that frozen blankness, tender, happy, solicitous of him. Oh! God, he thought: we're both *living* again.

"There's only one thing to be done," he brought his brows together determinedly. Despite his nervous brooding he felt strong now, freed from a haze of illusion, ready to act. "We've got to clear out of here. I'm in too deep, Chris, far too deep. I'd only be reminded at every turn of the fake stuff I'd been doing; yes, and maybe get pulled back. We can easily sell the practice. And oh! Chris, I've got a wonderful idea."

"Yes, darling?"

He relaxed his nervous frown to smile at her diffidently, tenderly.

"How long is it since you called me that? I like it. Yes, I know, I deserved it—oh, don't let me start thinking again, Chris! This idea, this scheme—it hit me when I woke up this morning. I was worrying all over again about Hampton having asked me to join up with his rotten team idea—then suddenly it struck me, why not a genuine team? It's the sort of thing they have amongst doctors in America—Stillman always cracks it up to me, even though he isn't a doctor himself—but we just don't seem to have gone in for it here much. You see, Chris, even in quite a small provincial town you could have a clinic, a little team of doctors, each doing his own stuff. Now listen, darling, instead of sticking in with Hampton and Ivory and Freedman why don't I get Denny and Hope together and form a genuine threesome? Denny does all the surgical work,—and you know how good he is!—I handle the medical side, and Hope is our bacteriologist! You see the benefit of that, we're each specializing in our own province and pooling our knowledge. Perhaps you remember all Denny's arguments—and mine too—about our hidebound G.P. system—how the general practitioner is made to stagger along, carrying everything on his shoulders, an impossibility? Group medicine is the answer to that, the perfect answer. It comes between state medicine and isolated, individual effort. The only reason we haven't had it here is because the big men like keeping everything in their own hands. But oh! wouldn't it be wonderful, dear, if we could form a little front-line unit, scientifically and—yes, let me say it—spiritually intact, a kind of pioneer force to try to break down prejudice, knock out the old fetishes, maybe start a complete revolution in our whole medical system?"

Her cheek pressed against the pillow, she gazed at him with shining eyes.

"It's like old times to hear you talk that way. I can't tell you how I love it. Oh! it's like beginning all over again. I am happy, darling, *happy*."

"I've got a lot to make up for," he reasoned sombrely. "I've been a fool. And worse." He pressed his brow with his hands. "I can't get poor Harry Vidler out of my head. And I won't, either, till I do something really to make up for it." He groaned suddenly. "I was to blame there, Chris, as much as Ivory. I can't help feeling I've got off too easily. It doesn't seem right that I should get away with it. But I'll work like hell, Chris. And I believe Denny and Hope will come in with me. You know their ideas. Denny's really dying to get back into the rough-and-tumble of a practice again. And Hope—if we give him a little lab., where he can do original stuff between making our sera—he'll follow us anywhere."

He jumped out of bed and began to pace up and down the room in his old impetuous style, torn between elation for the future and remorse for the past, turning things over in his head, worrying, hoping, planning.

"I've so much to settle up, Chris," he cried; "and one thing I must see about. Look, dear! When I've written some letters—and we've had lunch—how about taking a little run into the country with me?"

She looked at him questioningly.

"But if you're busy?"

"I'm not too busy for this. Honestly, Chris, I have a fearful weight on my mind over Mary Boland. She's not getting on well at the Victoria and I haven't taken near enough notice. Thoroughgood is most unsympathetic and he doesn't properly understand her case, at least not to my way of thinking. God! If anything happened to Mary after me making myself responsible to Con for her I would just about go crazy. It's an awful thing to say of one's own hospital, but she'll *never* recover at the Victoria. She ought to be out in the country, in the fresh air, in a good sanatorium."

"Yes?"

"That's why I want us to run out to Stillman's. Bellevue's the finest, the most marvellous little place you could ever hope to see. If only I could persuade him to take Mary in— Oh! I'd not only be satisfied, I'd feel I'd really done something worth while."

She said with decision:—

"We'll leave the minute you're ready."

When he had dressed he went downstairs, wrote a long letter to Denny and another to Hope. He had only three serious cases on his hands and on his way to visit them he posted the letters. Then, after a light meal, he and Christine set out for Wycombe.

The journey, despite the emotional tension persisting in his mind, was a happy one. More than ever it was borne upon him that happiness was an inner state, wholly spiritual, independent—whatever the cynics might say—of worldly possessions. All this time, when he had been striving and tearing after wealth and position and succeeding in every material sense, he had imagined himself happy. But he had not been happy. He had been existing in a kind of delirium, craving more after everything he got. Money, he thought bitterly, it was all for dirty money! First he had told himself he wanted to make a thousand pounds a year. When he reached that income he had immediately doubled it, and set that figure as his maximum. But that maximum, when achieved, found him dissatisfied. And so it had gone on. He wanted more and more. It would in the end have destroyed him.

He glanced sideways at Christine. How she must have suffered because of him! But now, if he had wished for any confirmation of the sanity of his decision, the sight of her altered glowing face was evidence enough. It was not now a pretty face, for there were marks of the wear and tear of life drawn upon it, a little dark of lines about the eyes, a faint hollowing of the cheeks which had once been firm and blooming. But it was a face which had always worn an aspect of serenity and truth. And this re-animation which kindled it was so bright and moving he felt a fresh pang of compunction strike deeply into him. He swore he would never again in all his life do anything to make her sad.

They reached Wycombe towards three o'clock, then took a side road uphill which led along the crest of the ridge past Lacey Green. The situation of Bellevue was superb, upon a little plateau which, though sheltered on the North, afforded an outlook over both valleys.

Stillman was cordial in his reception. He was a self-contained, undemonstrative little man seldom given to enthusiasm; yet he showed his pleasure in

Andrew's visit by demonstrating the full beauty and efficiency of his creation.

Bellevue was intentionally small, but of its perfection there could be no question. Two wings, angled to a southwestern exposure, were united by a central administrative section. Above the entrance hall and offices was a lavishly equipped treatment room, its south wall entirely of Vitaglass. All the windows were of this material, the heating and ventilating system the last word in modern efficiency. As Andrew walked round he could not help contrasting this ultra-modern perfection with the antique buildings, built a hundred years before, which served as many of the London hospitals, and with those old dwelling-houses, badly converted and ill-equipped, which masqueraded as nursing homes.

Afterwards, when he had shown them round, Stillman gave them tea. And here Andrew brought out his request with a rush.

"I hate asking you a favour, Mr. Stillman." Christine had to smile at the almost-forgotten formula. "But I wonder if you'd take in a case for me here? Early T.B. Probably requires pneumothorax. You see she's the daughter of a great friend of mine, a professional man—dentist—and she's not getting on where she is—"

Something like amusement gathered behind Stillman's pale blue eyes.

"You don't mean you're proposing to send me a case? Doctors don't send me cases here—though they do in America. You forget that here I'm a fake healer running a quack sanatorium, the kind that makes his patients walk barefooted in the dew before leading them in to a grated carrot breakfast!"

Andrew did not smile.

"I didn't ask you to pull my leg, Mr. Stillman. I'm dead-serious about this girl. I'm—I'm worried about her."

"But I'm afraid I am full up, my friend. In spite of the antipathy of your medical fraternity I have a waiting list as long as my arm. Strange!" Stillman did at last impassively smile. "People want me to cure them in spite of the doctors."

"Well!" Andrew muttered. Stillman's refusal was a great disappointment to him. "I was more or less banking on it. If we could have got Mary in here—oh! I'd have felt *relieved*. Why, you've got the finest treatment centre in England. I'm not trying to flatter you. I know! When I think of that old ward in the Victoria where she's lying now, listening to the cockroaches scramble behind the skirting—"

Stillman leaned forward and picked up a thin cucumber sandwich from the low table before them. He had a characteristic, almost finicky way of handling things as though he had just, with the utmost care, washed his hands and went in fear of soiling them.

"So! It's a little ironic comedy you are arranging. No, no, I mustn't talk that way, I see you are worried. And I will help you. Although you *are* a doctor I'll take your case." Stillman's lip twitched at the blank expression on Andrew's face. "You see, I'm broad-minded. I don't mind dealing with the profession when I'm obliged to. Why don't you smile? That's a joke. Never mind. Even if you've no sense of humour you're a darn sight more enlightened than most of the brethren. Let me see. I have no room vacant till next week. Wednesday, I think. Bring your case to me a week from Wednesday, and I promise you I'll do the best for her I can!"

Andrew's face reddened with gratitude.

"I—I can't thank you enough—I—"

"Then don't. And don't be so polite. I prefer you when you look like throwing things about. Mrs. Manson, does he ever throw the china at you? I have a great friend in America, he owns sixteen newspapers, and every time he gets in a temper he breaks a five-cent plate. Well, one day, it so happened . . ."

He went on to tell them a long, and, to Manson, quite pointless story.

But, driving home in the cool of the evening Andrew meditated to Christine:—

"That's one thing settled anyway, Chris—a big load off my mind. I'm positive it's the right place for Mary. He's a great chap is Stillman. I like him a lot. He's nothing to look at, but underneath he's just pressed steel. I wonder if ever we could have a clinic on these lines—miniature replica—Hope and Denny and me. That's a wild dream, eh? But you never know. And I've been thinking, if Denny and Hope do come in with me and we pitch out in the provinces—we might be near enough one of the coal fields for me to pick up my inhalation work again. What d'you think, Chris?"

By way of answer she leaned sideways and, greatly to the common danger on the public highway, she soundly kissed him.

18

Next morning he rose early, after a good night's rest. He felt tense, keyed for anything. Going straight to the telephone, he put the practice in the hands of Fulger and Turner, medical transfer agents, of Adam Street. Mr. Gerald Turner, present head of that old, established firm answered personally and, in response to Andrew's request, he came out promptly to Chesborough Terrace. After a scrutiny of the books lasting all that forenoon he assured him that he would have not the slightest difficulty in effecting a quick sale.

"Of course, we shall have to state a reason, Doctor, in our advertisements," said Mr. Turner gently tapping his teeth with his cased pencil. "Any purchaser is bound to ask himself, Why should any doctor give up a gold-mine like this? And excuse me for saying so, Doctor, it *is* a gold-mine. I've never seen such spot-cash receipts for many a day. Shall we say on account of ill-health?"

"No," said Andrew brusquely. "Tell them the truth. Say—" he checked himself. "Oh, say for personal reasons."

"Very well, Doctor." And Mr. Gerald Turner wrote, against his draft advertisement: "Relinquished from motives purely personal and unconnected with the practice."

Andrew concluded:—

"And remember, I don't want a fortune for this thing—only a good price. There's a lot of tame cats who mightn't follow the new man around."

At lunchtime Christine produced two telegrams which had come for him. He had asked both Denny and Hope to wire him in reply to the letters he had written the day before.

The first, from Denny, said simply:—

IMPRESSED. EXPECT ME TO-MORROW EVENING.

The second declared with typical flippancy:—

MUST I SPEND ALL MY LIFE WITH LUNATICS? FEATURE OF ENGLISH PROVINCIAL TOWNS PUBS STOCKS CATHEDRALS AND PIG MARKETS. DID YOU SAY LABORATORY? SIGNED INDIGNANT RATEPAYER.

After lunch Andrew ran down to the Victoria. It was not Doctor Thoroughgood's visiting hour, but that suited his purpose admirably. He wanted no fuss or unpleasantness, least of all did he wish to upset his senior who, for all his obstinacy and prim concern with the barber-surgeons of the past, had always treated him well.

Seated beside Mary's bed he explained privately to her what he wished to do.

"It was my fault to begin with." He patted her hand reassuringly. "I ought to have foreseen this wasn't quite the place for you. You'll find a difference when you get to Bellevue—a big difference, Mary. But they've been very kind to you here; there's no need to hurt anybody's feelings. You must just say you want to go out the fifteenth; discharge yourself. If you don't like to do it yourself I'll get Con to write and say he wants you out. They've so many people waiting for beds it'll be easy. Then on Wednesday I'll take you out myself by car to Bellevue. I'll have a nurse with me and everything. Nothing could be simpler—or better for you."

He returned home with a sense of something further accomplished, feeling that he was beginning to clear up the mess into which his life had fallen. That evening in his surgery he set himself sternly to weed out the chronics, ruthlessly to sacrifice his charm school. A dozen times in the course of an hour he declared firmly:—

"This must be your last visit. You've been coming a long time. You're quite better now. And it doesn't do to go on drinking medicine!"

It was amazing, at the end of it, how much lighter he felt. To be able to speak his mind, honestly and emphatically, was a luxury he had long denied himself. He went in to Christine with a step almost boyish.

"Now I feel less like a salesman for bath salts!" He groaned: "God! How can I talk that way? I'm forgetting what's happened—Vidler—everything I've done!"

It was then that the telephone rang. She went to answer it, and it seemed to him that she was a longish time absent and when she returned her expression was oddly strained.

"Someone wants you on the phone."

"Who . . . ?" All at once he realized that Frances Lawrence had called him up. There was a bar of silence in the room. Then, hurriedly, he said, "Tell her I'm not in. Tell her I've gone away. No, wait!" His expression strengthened, he took an abrupt movement forward. "I'll speak to her myself."

He came back in five minutes to find that she had seated herself with some work in her familiar corner where the light was good. He glanced at her covertly, then glanced away, walked to the window and stood there moodily looking out with his hands in his pockets. The quiet click of her knitting needles made him feel inordinately foolish, a sad and stupid dog, cringing home limp-tailed and bedraggled from some illicit foray. At last he could contain himself no longer.

Still with his back to her he said:—

"That's finished too. It may interest you to know it was only my stupid vanity—that and self-interest. I loved you all the time." Suddenly he ground out: "Damn it, Chris. It was all my fault. These people don't know any better, but I do. I'm getting out of this too easy—too easy. But let me tell you: While I was at the 'phone I rang up Le Roy; thought I might as well make one job of it. Cremo products won't be interested in me any more. I've wiped myself off their slate, too, Chris. And, God! I'll see that I stay off!"

She did not answer but the click of her needles made, in the silent room, a brisk and cheerful sound. He must have remained there a long time, his shamed eyes upon the movement of the street outside, upon the lights springing up through the summer darkness. When at length he turned, the invading dusk had crept into the room, but she still sat there, almost invisible in the shadowed chair, a small slight figure occupied with her knitting.

That night he woke up sweating and distressed, turning to her blindly, still anguished by the terrors of his dream.

"Where are you, Chris? I'm sorry. I'm truly sorry. I'll do my best to be decent to you in future." Then quieted, already half-asleep: "We'll take a holiday when we sell out here. God! my nerves are rotten—to think I once called you neurotic! And when we settle down, wherever it is, you'll have a garden, Chris. I know how you love it. Remember—remember at Vale View, Chris?"

Next morning he brought her home a great bunch of chrysanthemums. He strove with all his old intensity to show his affection for her, not by that showy generosity which she had hated—the thought of that Plaza luncheon still made him shiver!—but in small, considerate, almost forgotten ways.

At teatime when he came home with a special kind of sponge cake that she liked and on top of that silently brought in her house slippers from the cupboard at the end of the passage, she sat up in her chair, frowning, mildly protesting:—

"Don't, darling, don't—or I'm sure to suffer for it. Next week you'll be tearing your hair and kicking me round the house—like you used to in those old days."

"Chris!" he exclaimed, his face shocked, pained. "Can't you see that's all changed? From now on I'm going to make things up to you."

"All right, all right, my dear." Smiling she wiped her eyes. Then with a sudden tensity of which he had never suspected her, "I don't mind how it is, so long as we're *together*. I don't want you to run after me. All I ask is that you don't run after anybody else!"

That evening Denny arrived, as he had promised, for supper. He brought a message from Hope, who had rung him on the toll line from Cambridge, to say that he would be unable to get to London that evening.

"He said he was detained on business," Denny declared, knocking out his pipe. "But I strongly suspect friend Hope will shortly be taking unto himself a bride. Romantic business—the mating of a bacteriologist!"

"Did he say anything about my idea?" Andrew asked quickly.

"Yes, he's keen—not that it matters, we could just pocket him and take him along with us! And I'm keen too." Denny unfurled his napkin and helped himself to salad. "I can't imagine how a first-class scheme like this came out of your fool head. Especially when I fancied you'd tucked yourself up as a West End soap merchant. Tell me about it."

Andrew told him, fully, and with increasing emphasis. They began to discuss the scheme in its more practical details.

They suddenly realized how far they had progressed when Denny said:—

"My view is that we don't want to pick too large a town. Under twenty thousand inhabitants—that's ideal. We can make things hum there. Look at a map of the West Midlands. You'll find scores of industrial towns served by four or five doctors who are politely at each other's throats, where the good old M.D. drags out half a tonsil one morning and sludges Mist Alba the next. It's just there that we can demonstrate our idea of specialized co-operation. We won't buy ourselves in. We just so to speak arrive. Lord! I'd like to see their faces, Doctor Brown and Jones and Robinson, I mean. We'll have to stand wagonloads of abuse—incidentally, we may be lynched. Seriously, though, we want a central clinic—as you say—with Hope's lab. attached. We might even have a couple of beds upstairs. We won't be very grand at first —it means conversion rather than building, I suppose—but I've a feeling we'll take root." Suddenly aware of Christine's glistening eyes as she sat following their talk he smiled. "What do you think about it, ma'am? Crazy, isn't it?"

"Yes," she answered a trifle huskily. "But it's—it's the crazy things that matter."

"That's the word, Chris! By God! This does matter."

Andrew bounced the cutlery as he brought down his fist. "The scheme's good. But it's the ideal behind the scheme! A new interpretation of the Hippocratic oath; an absolute allegiance to the scientific ideal, no empiricism, no shoddy methods, no stock prescribing, no fee-snatching, no proprietary muck, no soft-soaping of hypochondriacs, no— Oh! for the Lord's sake, give me a drink! My vocal cords won't stand up to this, I ought to have a drum."

They talked on until one o'clock in the morning. Andrew's tense excitement was a stimulus felt even by the stoic Denny. His last train had long since departed. That night he occupied the spare room and as he hurried off after breakfast on the following day he promised to come to town again on the following Friday. Meanwhile he would see Hope and—final proof of his enthusiasm—buy a large-scale map of the West Midlands.

"It's on, Chris, it's on!" Andrew came back triumphant from the door. "Philip's as keen as mustard. He doesn't say much. But I *know*."

That same day they had the first inquiry for the practice. A prospective buyer arrived, and he was followed by others. Gerald Turner came in person with the more likely purchasers. He had a beautiful flow of elegant language which he even directed upon the architecture of the garage. On Monday, Doctor Noel Lowry called twice, alone in the morning and escorted by the agent in the afternoon. Thereafter Turner rang up Andrew, suavely confidential:—

"Doctor Lowry is interested, Doctor; *very* interested I may say. He's particularly anxious we don't sell till his wife has a chance to see the house. She's at the seaside with the children. She's coming up Wednesday."

This was the day on which Andrew had arranged to take Mary to Bellevue but he felt the matter could be left in Turner's hands. Everything had gone as he anticipated at the hospital. Mary was due to leave at two o'clock. He had fixed up with Nurse Sharp to accompany them in the car.

It was raining heavily as, at half-past one, he started off by driving to Welbeck Street to pick up Nurse Sharp. She was in a sulky humour, waiting but unwilling, when he reached Number 57a. Since he had told her he must dispense with her services at the end of the month her moods had been even more uncertain. She snapped an answer to his greeting and stepped into the car.

Fortunately he had no difficulty with Mary. He drew up as she came through the porter's lodge and the next moment she was in the back of the saloon with Nurse Sharp, warmly wrapped in a rug with a hot bottle at her feet. They had not gone far, however, before he began to wish he had not brought the sulky and suspicious nurse. It was evident that she considered the expedition far beyond the scope of her duties. He wondered how he had managed to put up with her so long.

At half-past three they reached Bellevue. The rain had now ceased, and a burst of sun came through the clouds as they ran up the drive. Mary leaned forward, her eyes fastened nervously, a little apprehensively, upon the place from which she had been led to expect so much.

Andrew found Stillman in the office. He was anxious to see the case with him at once, for the question of pneumothorax induction weighed heavily on his mind. He spoke of this as he smoked a cigarette and drank a cup of tea.

"Very well," Stillman nodded as he concluded. "We'll go up right now."

He led the way to Mary's room. She was now in bed, pale from her journey and still inclined to apprehensiveness, gazing at Nurse Sharp who stood at one end of the room folding up her dress. She gave a little start as Stillman came forward.

He examined her meticulously. His examination was an illumination to

Andrew, quiet, silent, absolutely precise. He had no bedside manner. He was not impressive. He did not, indeed, resemble a physician at work. He was like a business man engaged with the complications of an adding machine which has gone wrong. Although he used the stethoscope, most of his investigation was tactile, a palpation of the inter-rib and supra-clavicular spaces as if, through his smooth fingers, he could actually sense the condition of the living, breathing lung cells beneath.

When it was over he said nothing to Mary but took Andrew beyond the door.

"Pneumothorax," he said. "There's no question. That lung should have been collapsed weeks ago. I'm going to do it right away. Go back and tell her."

While he went off to see to the apparatus Andrew returned to the room and informed Mary of their decision. He spoke as lightly as he could, yet it was evident that the immediate prospect of the induction upset her further.

"You'll do it?" she asked in an uneasy tone. "Oh! I'd much rather you did it."

"It's nothing, Mary. You won't feel the slightest pain. I'll be here. I'll be helping him! I'll see that you're all right."

He had meant actually to leave the whole technique to Stillman. But as she was so nervous, so palpably depending upon him, and as, indeed, he felt himself responsible for her presence here he went to the treatment room and offered his assistance to Stillman.

Ten minutes later they were ready. When Mary was brought in he gave her the local anæsthesia. He then stood by the manometer, while Stillman skilfully inserted the needle, controlling the flow of sterile nitrogen gas into the pleura. The apparatus was exquisitely delicate and Stillman undoubtedly a master of the technique. He had an expert touch with the cannula, driving it deftly forward, his eye fixed upon the manometer for the final "snap" which announced perforation of the parietal pleura. He had his own method of deep manipulation to prevent the occurrence of surgical emphysema.

After an early phase of acute nervousness Mary's anxiety gradually faded. She submitted to the operation with increasing confidence and at the end she could smile at Andrew, completely relaxed. Back again in her room she said:—

"You were right. It was nothing. I don't feel as if you'd done anything at all."

"No?" He lifted an eyebrow; then laughed: "That's how it should be—no fuss, no sense of anything terrible happening to you—I wish every operation could go that way! But we've immobilized that lung of yours all the same. It'll have a rest now. And when it starts breathing again—believe me!—it will be healed."

Her glance rested upon him, then wandered round the pleasant room, through the window to the view of the valley beyond.

"I'm going to like it here, after all. He doesn't try to be nice—Mr. Stillman, I mean—but somehow you feel he is nice. Do you think I could have my tea?"

19

I⊤ was nearly seven o'clock when he left Bellevue. He had remained longer than he had anticipated, talking to Stillman on the lower verandah, enjoying the cool air and the quiet conversation of the other man. As he drove off he was pervaded by an extraordinary sense of placidity, of tranquility. He derived that benefit from Stillman, whose personality, with its repose, its indifference to the trivialities of life, reacted favourably upon his own impetuous disposition. Moreover he was now easy in his mind about Mary. He contrasted his previous hurried action, her summary dispatch into an out-of-date hospital, with all that he had done for her this afternoon. It had caused him inconvenience, a great deal of troublesome arrangement. It was quite unorthodox. Though he had not discussed the question of payment with Stillman, he realized that Con was in no position to meet the Bellevue fees and that, in consequence, the settlement of the bill would fall upon himself. But all this became as nothing beside the glowing sense of real achievement which pervaded him. For the first time in many months he felt that he had done something which, to his own belief, was worthy. It pervaded him warmly, a cherished thought, the beginning of his vindication.

He drove slowly, enjoying the quiet of the evening. Nurse Sharp once again sat in the back seat of the car but she had nothing to say and he, with his own thoughts, was almost unconscious of her. When they drew into London, however, he asked where he should drop her and, on her reply, drew up at Notting Hill Tube Station. He was glad to be rid of her. She was a good nurse but her nature was repressed and unhappy. She had never liked him. He decided to post her month's salary to her the next day. Then he would not see her again.

Strangely, his mood had altered as he came along Paddington Street. It always affected him to pass the Vidlers' shop. Out of the corner of his eye he saw it—Renovations Ltd. One of the assistants was pulling down the shutters. The simple action was so symbolic it sent a shiver through him. Subdued, he reached Chesborough Terrace and ran the car into his garage. He went into his house with a curious sadness pressing upon him.

Christine met him joyfully in the hall. Whatever his mood might be, hers was vivid with success. Her eyes were shining with her news.

"Sold!" she declared gaily. "Knocked down lock, stock, and basement. They waited and waited for you, darling—they've only just gone. Doctor and Mrs. Lowry, I mean. He got so agitated," she laughed, "because you weren't here for the surgery, that he set to and did it himself. Then I gave them supper. Then we made more conversation. I could almost see Mrs. Lowry deciding that you'd had a motor smash. Then I began to worry! But now you are here, dear! And it's all *right*. You've to meet him at Mr. Turner's office to-morrow at eleven to sign the contract. And . . . Oh! yes—he's given Mr. Turner a deposit."

He followed her into the front room, where the supper had been cleared from the table. He was pleased, naturally, that the practice should be sold, yet he could not, at present, summon any great show of elation.

"It is good, isn't it," Christine went on, "that it should all be settled up so quickly? I don't think he expects a very long introduction. Oh! I've been thinking so much before you came in. If only we could have a little holiday at Val André again, before we start work. . . . It was so lovely there, wasn't it, darling—and we had such a wonderful time . . ." She broke off, gazing at him. "Why, what's the matter, dear?"

"Oh, nothing," he smiled, sitting down. "I'm a little tired, I think. Probably because I missed my dinner—"

"What?" she exclaimed, aghast. "I was certain you'd had it at Bellevue, before you left." Her glance swept round. "And I've cleared everything away, and let Mrs. Bennett out to the pictures."

"It doesn't matter."

"But it *does*. No wonder you didn't jump when I told you about the practice. Now you just sit there one minute and I'll bring up a tray. Is there anything you'd especially like? I could heat up some soup—or make you some scrambled egg—or *what?*"

He considered.

"The egg, I think, Chris. Oh! but don't bother. Well, if you like, then—and perhaps a bit of cheese afterwards."

She was back in no time with a tray on which stood a plate of scrambled eggs, a glass of celery heart, bread, biscuits, butter and the cheese dish. She placed the tray upon the table. As he pulled in his chair she brought out a bottle of ale from the sideboard cupboard.

While he ate she watched him solicitously. She smiled.

"You know, dear, I've often thought—if we'd lived in Cefen Row, say a kitchen and one bedroom, we'd have fitted in perfectly. High life doesn't agree with us. Now I'm going to be a workingman's wife again I'm awfully happy."

He went on with his scrambled egg. The food was certainly making him feel better.

"You know, darling," she continued, placing her hands beneath her chin in her characteristic way, "I've thought such a lot these last few days. Before that my mind was stiff, somehow, all closed up. But since we're together—oh, since we're ourselves again everything has seemed so clear. It's only when you've got to fight for things that they really become worth while. When they just drop into your lap there's no satisfaction in them. Don't you remember those days at Aberalaw—they've been living, simply living in my mind all day—when we had to go through all those rough times together? Well! Now I feel that the same thing is starting for us all over again. It's our kind of life, darling. It's *us!* And oh! I'm so happy about it."

He glanced towards her.

"You're really happy, Chris?"

She kissed him lightly.

"Never happier in my life than I am at this moment."

There was a pause. He buttered a biscuit and lifted the lid of the dish to help himself to cheese. But there was anticlimax in the action which revealed, not his favourite Libtauer but no more than a barren end of cheddar, which Mrs. Bennett used for cooking. The instant she saw it Christine gave a self-reproachful cry.

"And I meant to call at Frau Schmidt's to-day!"

"Oh! it's all right, Chris."

"But it isn't all right." She whipped the dish away before he could help himself. "Here am I mooning like a sentimental schoolgirl, giving you no dinner at all—when you come in tired—starving you. Fine sort of working-man's wife I'd be!" She jumped up, her eye upon the clock. "I've just time to rush across for it now before she closes."

"Don't bother, Chris—"

"*Please*, darling." She silenced him gaily. "I *want* to do it. I want to—because you love Frau Schmidt's cheese and I—I love you."

She was out of the room before he could protest again. He heard her quick step in the hall, the light closing of the outer door. His eyes still were faintly smiling—it was so like her to do this. He buttered another biscuit, waiting for the arrival of the famous Libtauer, waiting for her return.

The house was very still: Florrie sleeping downstairs, he reflected, and Mrs. Bennett at the cinema. He was glad Mrs. Bennett was coming with them on their new venture. Stillman had been great this afternoon. Mary would be all right now, right as rain. Marvellous how the rain had cleared off this afternoon—beautiful it had been coming home through the country, so fresh and quiet. Thank God! Christine would soon have her garden again. He and Denny and Hope might get themselves lynched by the five doctors in Muddletown. But Chris would always have her garden!

He began absently to eat one of the buttered biscuits. He'd lose his appetite if she didn't hurry up. She must be talking to Frau Schmidt. Good old Frau; sending him his first cases. If he'd only gone on decently instead of—oh, well, that was finished with now, thank God! They were together again, Christine and he, happier than ever they had been. Wonderful to hear her say that a minute ago. He lit a cigarette.

Suddenly the doorbell rang violently. He glanced up, laid down his cigarette, went into the hall. But not before the bell had been wrenched again. He opened the front door.

Immediately he was conscious of the commotion outside, a crowd of people on the pavement, faces and heads interwoven with the darkness. But before he could resolve the mingling pattern, the policeman who had rung the bell loomed up before him. It was Struthers, his old Fife friend, the pointsman. What seemed strange about Struthers was the staring whiteness of his eyes.

"Doctor," he breathed with difficulty like a man who has been running. "Your wife's got hurted. She ran— Oh! God Almighty!—she ran right out the shop in front of the bus."

A great hand of ice enclosed him. Before he could speak the commotion was upon him. Suddenly, dreadfully, the hall was filled with people, Frau Schmidt weeping, a bus conductor, another policeman, strangers, all pressing in, forcing him back, into the consulting room. And then, through the crowd, carried by two men, the figure of his Christine. Her head drooped backwards upon the thin white arch of her neck. Still entwined by its string in the fingers of her left hand was the little parcel from Frau Schmidt. They laid her upon the high couch of his consulting room.

She was quite dead.

20

HE broke down completely and for days was out of his mind. Moments of lucidity there were when he became aware of Mrs. Bennett, of Denny, and, once or twice, of Hope. But for the most part he went through life, performed the actions demanded of him, in sheer automatism, his whole being concentrated deep within himself in one long nightmare of despair. His frayed-out nervous system intensified the agony of his loss by creating morbid fancies and terrors of remorse, from which he awoke, sweating, crying out in anguish.

Dimly he was conscious of the inquest, the drab informality of the coroner's court, of the evidence given so minutely, so unnecessarily by the witnesses. He stared fixedly at the squat figure of Frau Schmidt upon whose plump cheeks the tears kept rolling, rolling down.

"She was laughing, laughing all the time she came into my shop. Hurry, please—she kept on telling me—I don't want to keep my husband waiting—"

When he heard the coroner expressing sympathy with Doctor Manson in his sad bereavement he knew that it was over. He stood up mechanically, found himself walking upon grey pavements with Denny.

How the arrangements for the funeral were made he did not know, they all came mysteriously to pass without his knowledge. As he drove to Kensal Green his thoughts kept darting hither and thither, backwards through the years. In the dingy confines of the cemetery he remembered the wide and windswept uplands behind Vale View where the mountain ponies raced and reared their tangled manes. She had loved to walk there, to feel the breeze upon her cheeks. And now she was being laid in this grimy city graveyard.

That night in the stark torture of his neurosis he tried to drink himself insensible. But the whisky only seemed to goad him to fresh anger against himself. He paced up and down the room, late into the night, muttering aloud, drunkenly apostrophizing himself.

"You thought you could get away with it. You thought you *were* getting away with it. But by God! you weren't. Crime and punishment, crime and punishment! You're to blame for what happened to her. You've *got* to suffer." He walked the length of the street, hatless, swaying, to stare, wild-eyed at the blank shuttered windows of the Vidler shop. He came back muttering, through bitter maudlin tears, "God is not mocked! Chris said that once—God is not mocked, my friend."

He staggered upstairs, hesitated, went into her room, silent, cold, deserted. There on the dressing table lay her bag. He picked it up, pressed it against his cheeks, then fumblingly opened it. Some coppers and loose silver lay inside, a small handkerchief, a bill for groceries. And then, in the middle pocket he came upon some papers—a faded snapshot of himself taken at Blaenelly and —yes, he recognized them with a throbbing pang—those little notes he had received at Christmas from his patients at Aberalaw: *With grateful thanks*— she had treasured them all those years. A heavy sob broke from his breast. He fell on his knees by the bed in a passion of weeping.

Denny made no effort to stop his drinking. It seemed to him that Denny was about the house almost every day. It was not because of the practice, for Doctor Lowry was doing that now. Lowry was living out somewhere but coming in to consult and pick up the calls. He knew nothing, nothing whatever of what was going on, he did not wish to know. He kept out of Lowry's way. His nerves had gone to pieces. The sound of the doorbell made his heart palpitate madly. A sudden step made the sweat break out on the palms of his hands. He sat upstairs in his room with a rolled-up handkerchief between his fingers, wiping his sweating palms from time to time, staring at the fire, knowing that when night came he must face the spectre of insomnia.

This was his condition when Denny walked in one morning and said:—

"I'm free at last, thank God. Now we can go away."

There was no question of refusal, his power of resistance was completely gone. He did not even ask where they were going. In silent apathy he watched Denny pack a suitcase for him. Within an hour they were on their way to Paddington Station.

They travelled all afternoon through the southwest counties, changed at Newport and struck up through Monmouthshire. At Abergavenny they left the train and here, outside the station, Denny hired a car. As they drove out of the town across the River Usk and through the rich autumnal tinted countryside he said:—

"This is a small place I once used to come to—fishing. Llantony Abbey. I think it ought to suit."

They reached their destination, through a network of hazel-fringed lanes, at six o'clock. Round a square of close green turf lay the ruins of the Abbey, smooth grey stones, a few arches of the cloisters still upstanding. And adjoining was the guest house, built entirely from the fallen stones. Near at hand a small stream flowed with a constant soothing ripple. Wood smoke rose, straight and blue, into the quiet evening air.

Next morning Denny dragged Andrew out to walk. It was a crisp dry day but Andrew, sick from a sleepless night, his flabby muscles failing on the first hill, made to turn back when they had gone only a short way. Denny, however, was firm. He walked Andrew eight miles that first day and on the next he made it ten. By the end of the week they were walking twenty miles a day and Andrew, crawling up to his room at night, fell immediately into insensibility upon his bed.

There was no one to worry them at the Abbey. Only a few fishermen remained, for it was now close to the end of the trout season. They ate in the stone-flagged refectory at a long oak table before an open log fire. The food was plain and good.

During their walks they did not speak. Often they walked the whole day long with no more than a few words passing between them. At the beginning Andrew was quite unconscious of the countryside through which they tramped, but as the days passed the beauty of its woods and rivers, of its sweeping bracken-covered hills, penetrated gradually, imperceptibly through his numbed senses.

The progress of his recovery was not sensationally swift—yet by the end of the first month he was able to stand the fatigue of their long marches, eat and sleep normally, bathe in cold water every morning and face the future without cowering. He saw that no better place could have been chosen for his recovery than this isolated spot, no better routine than this Spartan, this monastic existence. When the first frost bit hard into the ground he felt the joy of it instinctively in his blood.

He began unexpectedly to talk. The topics of their discussion were inconsequential at the outset. His mind, like an athlete performing simple exercises before approaching greater feats, was guarded in its approach to life. But imperceptibly he learned from Denny the progress of events.

His practice had been sold to Doctor Lowry, not for the full amount which Turner had stipulated—since under the circumstances no introduction had been given—but for a figure near enough that sum. Hope had at last completed the full term of his scholarship and was now at his home in Birmingham. Denny also was free. He had given up his registrarship before coming to Llantony. The inference was so clear that Andrew suddenly lifted up his head.

"I ought to be fit for work at the beginning of the year."

Now they began to talk in earnest, and within a week his hard-faced listlessness was gone. He felt it strange and sad that the human mind should be capable of recovering from such a mortal blow as that which had struck him. Yet he could not help it, the recovery was there. Previously he had trudged with stoic indifference, a perfectly functioning machine. Now he breathed the sharp air with real vigour, switched at the bracken with his stick, took his correspondence out of Denny's hands, and cursed when the post did not bring the *Medical Journal*.

At night Denny and he pored over a large-scale map. With the help of an almanac they made a list of towns, weeded out that list, then narrowed their selection down to eight. Two of the towns were in Staffordshire, three in Northamptonshire, and three in Warwickshire.

On the following Monday Denny took his departure, and was away a week. During these seven days Andrew felt the rushing return of his old desire for work, his own work, the real work he could do with Hope and Denny. His impatience became colossal. On Saturday afternoon he walked all the way to

Abergavenny to meet the last train of the week. Returning, disappointed, to endure two further nights and one whole day of this intensifying delay, he found a small dark Ford drawn up at the guest house. He hurried through the door. There in the lamp-lit refectory, Denny and Hope sat at a ham-and-egg tea with whipped cream and tinned peaches on the sideboard.

That week end they had the place entirely to themselves. Philip's report, delivered at that richly composite meal, was a fiery prelude to the excitement of their discussions. Outside rain and hail battered on the windows. The weather had finally broken. It made no difference to them.

Two of the towns visited by Denny—Franton and Stanborough—were, in Hope's phrase, ripe for medical development. Both were solid semi-agricul-tural towns upon which recently a new industry had been grafted. Stan-borough had a freshly erected plant for the manufacture of motor engine bearings, Franton a large sugar-beet factory. Houses were springing up on the outskirts, the population increasing. But in each case the medical services had lagged behind. Franton had only a cottage hospital and Stanborough none at all. Emergency cases were sent to Coventry, fifteen miles away.

These bare details were enough to set them off like hounds upon a scent. But Denny had information even more stimulating. He produced a plan of Stanborough torn from an A.A. Midland Route itinerary. He remarked:—

"I regret to say I stole it from the hotel at Stanborough. Sounds like a good beginning for us there."

"Quick," impatiently declared the once facetious Hope, "what's this mark here?"

"That," Denny said, as they bent their heads over the plan, "is the market square—at least, that's what it amounts to, only for some reason they call it the Circle. It's bang in the centre of the town, high up, too, with a fine situation. You know the kind of thing, a ring of houses and shops and offices, half-residential, half old established businesses, rather a Georgian effect, with low windows and porticoes. The chief medico of the place—a whale of a fellow, I saw him, important red face and mutton chops; incidentally he employs two assistants—has his house in the Circle." Denny's tone was gently ironic. "Directly opposite, on the other side of the charming granite fountain in the middle of the Circle, are two empty houses, large rooms, sound floors, good frontage *and* for sale. It seems to me—"

"And to me," said Hope with a catch of his breath, "off-hand I should say there's nothing I should like better than a little lab. opposite that fountain."

They went on talking. Denny unfolded further details, interesting details.

"Of course," he concluded, "we are probably all quite mad. This idea has been brought to perfection in the big American cities by thorough organization and tremendous outlay. But here—in Stanborough! And we none of us have a lot of cash! We shall also probably fight like hell amongst ourselves. But somehow—"

"God help Old Mutton-Chops!" said Hope, rising and stretching himself.

On Sunday they took their plans a stage further, arranging that Hope should make a détour to include Stanborough on his way home on Monday. Denny and Andrew would arrive on Wednesday, meet him at the Stanborough Hotel, when one of them would make discreet inquiry at the local house-agent's.

With the prospect of a full day before him Hope left early next morning, dashing off in his Ford in a spatter of mud before the others had finished breakfast. The sky was still heavily overcast but the wind was high, a gusty exhilarating day. After breakfast Andrew went out by himself for an hour. It was good to feel fit again, with his work reaching out to him once more in the high adventure of the new clinic. He had not realized how much his scheme meant to him until now, quite suddenly, it was near fruition.

When he returned at eleven o'clock the post had come in, a pile of letters forwarded from London. He sat down at the table with a sense of anticipation to open them. Denny was beside the fire behind the morning paper.

His first letter was from Mary Boland. As he scanned the closely written sheets his face warmed to a smile. She began by sympathizing with him, hoping he had now recovered fully. Then briefly she told him about herself. She was better, infinitely better, almost well again. Her temperature had been normal for the last five weeks. She was up, taking graduated exercise. She had put on so much weight he would scarcely recognize her. She asked him if he could not come to see her. Mr. Stillman had returned to America for several months, leaving his assistant Mr. Marland in charge. She could not thank him sufficiently for having sent her to Bellevue.

Andrew laid down the letter, his expression still bright with the thought of Mary's recovery. Then, throwing aside a number of circulars and advertising literature, all in flimsy envelopes with halfpenny stamps, he picked up his next letter. This was a long official-looking envelope. He opened it, drew out the stiff sheet of notepaper within.

Then the smile left his face. He stared at the letter with disbelieving eyes. His pupils widened. He turned deadly pale. For a full minute he remained motionless—staring, staring at the letter.

"Denny," he said, in a low voice. "Look at this."

21

EIGHT weeks before, when Andrew set down Nurse Sharp at Notting Hill Station, she went on by tube to Oxford Circus and from there walked rapidly in the direction of Queen Anne Street. She had arranged with her friend Nurse Trent, who was Doctor Hampton's receptionist, to spend the evening at the Queen's Theatre where Louis Savory, whom they both adored, was appearing in "The Duchess Declares." But since it was now quarter-past eight and the performance began at eight forty-five the margin of time left for Nurse Sharp to call for her friend and be in the upper circle of the Queen's was narrow. Moreover, instead of having leisure for a nice hot meal at the Corner House as they had planned, they would be obliged to snatch a sandwich on the way down or perhaps do without altogether. Nurse Sharp's mood, as she thrust her way along Queen Anne Street, was that of a woman bitterly ill-used. As the events of the afternoon kept turning in her mind she seethed with indignation and resentment. Mounting the steps of Number 17c she hurriedly pressed the bell.

It was Nurse Trent who opened the door, her expression patiently reproachful. But before she could speak Nurse Sharp pressed her arm.

"My dear," she said, speaking rapidly, "I'm ever so sorry. But *what* a day I've had! I'll tell you later. Just let me pop in to leave my things. If I come as I am I think we can just do it."

At that moment, as the two nurses stood together in the passage, Hampton came down the stairs, groomed, shining, and in his evening clothes. Seeing them, he paused. Freddie could never resist an opportunity to demonstrate the charm of his personality. It was part of his technique, making people like him, getting the most out of them.

"Hello, Nurse Sharp!"—rather gaily, as he picked a cigarette from his gold case. "You look weary. And why are you both so late? Didn't I hear something from Nurse Trent about a theatre to-night?"

"Yes, Doctor," said Nurse Sharp. "But I—I was detained over one of Doctor Manson's cases."

"Oh?" Freddie's tone held just a hint of interrogation.

It was enough for Nurse Sharp. Rankling from her injustices, disliking Andrew and admiring Hampton, she suddenly let herself go.

"I've never had such a time in all my life, Doctor Hampton. Never. Taking a patient from the Victoria and sneaking her out to that Bellevue place, and Doctor Manson keeping me there all hours while he does a pneumothorax with an unqualified man . . ." She poured out the whole story of the afternoon, repressing her smarting tears of vexation with difficulty.

There was a silence when she concluded. Freddie's eyes held an odd expression.

"That was too bad, Nurse," he said at length. "But I hope you won't miss your theatre. Look, Nurse Trent—you must take a taxi and charge it to me. Put it on your expense sheet. Now if you'll excuse me, I must go."

"*There's* a gentleman," Nurse Sharp murmured, following him admiringly with her eyes. "Come, dear, get the taxi."

Freddie drove thoughtfully to the club. Since his quarrel with Andrew he had almost of necessity pocketed his pride and fallen back to a closer association with Freedman and Ivory. To-night, the three were dining together. And as they dined, Freddie, less in malice than from a desire to interest the other two, to pull himself up with them again, airily remarked:—

"Manson seems to be playing pretty parlour tricks since he left us. I hear he's started feeding patients to that Stillman fellow."

"What!" Ivory laid down his fork.

"And co-operating, I understand." Hampton sketched a graceful version of the story.

When he finished Ivory demanded with sudden harshness:—
"Is this true?"

"My dear fellow," Freddie answered in an aggrieved tone, "I had it from his own nurse not half an hour ago."

A pause followed. Ivory lowered his eyes and went on with his dinner. Yet beneath his calm he was conscious of a savage elation. He had never forgiven Manson for that final remark after the Vidler operation. Though he was not thin-skinned, Ivory had the sultry pride of a man who knows his own weakness and guards it jealously. He knew deep in his heart that he was an incompetent surgeon. But no one had ever told him with such cutting violence the full extent of his incompetence. He hated Manson for that bitter truth.

The others had been talking a few moments when he raised his head. His voice was impersonal.

"This nurse of Manson's—can you get her address?"

Freddie broke off, gazing at him across the table.

"Absolutely."

"It seems to me," Ivory reflected coolly, "that something ought to be done about this. Between you and me, Freddie, I never had much time for this Manson of yours, but that's neither here nor there. I'm thinking purely of the ethical aspect. Gadsby happened to be speaking to me about this Stillman only the other evening—we were guests at the Mayfly Dinner. He's getting into the papers—Stillman, I mean. Some ignorant jackass in Fleet Street has got together a list of alleged cures by Stillman, cases where doctors had failed; you know, the usual twaddle. Gadsby is pretty hot about it all. I believe Cranston was a patient of his at one time—before he ditched him for this quack. Now! Just what is going to happen if members of the profession are going to *support* this rank outsider? Gad! the more I think about it the less I like it. I'm going to get in touch with Gadsby straight off the handle. Waiter! Find out if Doctor Maurice Gadsby is in the Club. If not, have the porter ring up and find out if he's at his house."

Hampton, for once, looked uncomfortable about his collar. He had no rancour in his disposition and no ill-will towards Manson, whom, in his easy, egotistic fashion he had always liked.

He muttered: "Don't bring me into it."

"Don't be a fool, Freddie. Are we going to let that fellow sling mud at us and then get away with *this*?"

The waiter returned to say that Doctor Gadsby was at home. Ivory thanked him.

"I'm afraid this means the end of my bridge, you fellows. Unless Gadsby happens to be engaged."

But Gadsby was not engaged and later that evening Ivory called upon him. Though the two were not exactly friends, they were good enough acquaintances for the physician to produce his second best port and a reputable cigar. Whether or not Doctor Gadsby knew something of Ivory's reputation he was at least aware of the surgeon's social standing, which ranked high enough for Maurice Gadsby, aspirant to fashionable honours, to treat him with adequate goodfellowship.

When Ivory mentioned the object of his visit Gadsby had no need to assume interest. He leaned forward in his chair, his small eyes fastened upon Ivory, listening intently to the story.

"Well! I'm damned!" he exclaimed with unusual vehemence at the end of it. "I know this Manson. We had him for a short time on the M.F.B. and I assure you we were extremely relieved to see the end of him. A complete outsider; hasn't the manners of an errand boy. And do you actually mean to tell me that he took a case from the Victoria—it must have been one of Thoroughgood's cases, we'll hear what Thoroughgood has to say about *that* —and turned it over to Stillman?"

"More than that, he actually assisted Stillman at the operation."

"If that is true," Gadsby said, carefully, "the case is one for the G.M.C."

"Well—" Ivory hesitated becomingly. "That was precisely my own view. But I rather held back. You see I knew this fellow at one time rather better than you. I didn't really feel like lodging the complaint myself."

"I will lodge it," said Gadsby authoritatively. "If what you tell me is indeed a fact I will lodge it personally. I should consider myself failing in my duty if I did not take immediate action. The point at issue is a vital one, Ivory. This man Stillman is a menace, not so much to the public, as to the profession. I think I told you my experience of him the other night at dinner. He threatens our status, our training, our tradition. He threatens everything that we stand for. Our only remedy is to ostracize him. Then, sooner or later, he runs into disaster over the question of certification. Observe that, Ivory! Thank God! We have kept that in the hands of the profession. We alone can sign a death certificate. But if—mark you—if this fellow and others like him can secure professional collaboration, then we're lost. Fortunately the G.M.C. have always come down like a ton of bricks upon that sort of thing in the past. You remember the case of Jarvis, the manipulator, several years ago, when he got some cad of a doctor to anæsthetize for him. *He* was struck off, *instanter*. The more I think of that bounder Stillman the more I'm determined to make an example of this. If you'll excuse me one minute now I'll ring Thoroughgood. And then tomorrow I shall want to interrogate that nurse."

He rose and telephoned Doctor Thoroughgood. On the following day, in Doctor Thoroughgood's presence, he took a signed statement from Nurse Sharp. So conclusive was her testimony he immediately put himself in touch with his solicitors, Messrs. Boon and Everton of Bloomsbury Square. He detested Stillman, of course. But he had already a soothing premonition of the benefit likely to accrue to a public upholder of the medical morality.

When Andrew, oblivious, went to Llantony, the process raised against him was moving steadily upon its way. It is true that Freddie, coming, in dismay, on a paragraph reporting the inquest upon Christine's death, had telephoned

Ivory to try to stop the case. But by then it was too late. The complaint had been lodged.

Later the Penal Cases Committee considered that complaint and upon its authority a letter was dispatched summoning Andrew to attend the November meeting of the Council to answer the charge laid against him.

This was the letter which he now held in his hand, white with anxiety, confronted by the menace of its legal phrasing:—

That you, Andrew Manson, knowingly and wilfully, on August 15th, assisted one Richard Stillman, an unregistered person practicing in a department of medicine, and that you associated yourself in a professional capacity with him in carrying out such practice. And that in relation thereto you have been guilty of infamous conduct in a professional respect.

22

THE case was to be heard on November tenth and Andrew was in London a full week before that date. He was alone, for he had asked Hope and Denny to leave him entirely to himself. And he stayed, with a bitter, melancholy sentiment, at the Museum Hotel.

Though outwardly controlled, his state of mind was desperate. He swung between dark fits of bitterness and an emotional suspense which came not only from his doubts about the future but from the vivid remembrance of every past moment of his medical career. Six weeks ago this crisis would have found him still benumbed by the agony of Christine's death, heedless, uncaring. But now, recovered, eager and ready to begin work again, he felt the shock of it with cruel intensity.

He realized, with a heavy heart, that if all his reborn hopes were killed then he too might just as well be dead.

These and other painful thoughts perpetually thronged his brain, producing at times a state of bewildering confusion. He could not believe that he, Andrew Manson, was in this horrible situation, really facing the dreaded nightmare of every doctor. Why was he called before the Council? Why did they wish to strike him off the register? He had done nothing disgraceful. He was guilty of no felony, no misdemeanour. All that he had done was to cure Mary Boland of consumption.

His defence was in the hands of Horner and Co., of Lincoln's Inn Fields, a firm of solicitors Denny had strongly recommended to him. At first sight Thomas Horner was not impressive, a small red-faced man with gold-rimmed glasses and a fussy manner. Through some defect in his circulation he was subject to attacks of suffusion of his skin, which gave him a self-conscious air, a peculiarity that certainly did not serve to inspire confidence. Nevertheless Horner had decided views upon the conduct of the case. When Andrew, in his first burst of agonized indignation, had wished to rush to Sir Robert Abbey, his one influential friend in London, Horner had wryly pointed out that Abbey was a member of the Council. With equal disapproval the fussy little solicitor had vetoed Andrew's frantic plea that they cable Stillman to return immediately from America. They had all the evidence that Stillman could give them and the actual presence of the unqualified practitioner could serve only to exasperate the Council members. For the same reason Marland, now acting at Bellevue, must stay away.

Gradually Andrew began to see that the legal aspect of the case was utterly different from his own. His frenzied logic as, in Horner's office, he protested his innocence, caused the solicitor disapprovingly to wrinkle up his brow. At last Horner was forced to declare:—

"There is one thing I must beg of you, Doctor Manson,—*not* to express yourself in such terms during the hearing on Wednesday. I assure you nothing would be more fatal to our case."

Andrew stopped short, his hands clenched, his eyes burning.

"But I want them to know the *truth*. I want to show them that getting this girl cured was the best thing I'd done for years. After mucking about for months doing ordinary material practice I'd actually done something fine and that—*that's* what they're having me up for."

Horner's eyes, behind his glasses, were deeply concerned. In his vexation the blood rushed into his skin.

"Please, *please*, Doctor Manson. You don't *understand* the gravity of our position! I must take this opportunity to tell you frankly that at the *best* I consider our chances of—of success to be slender. Precedent is dead against us: Kent in nineteen nine, Louden in nineteen twelve, Foulger in nineteen nineteen; they were all deleted for unprofessional associations. And of course, in the famous Hexam case, in nineteen twenty-one, Hexam was struck off for administering a general anæsthetic for Jarvis the bonesetter. Now, what I wish to entreat of you is this—answer questions in the affirmative or negative or, failing that, as briefly as possible. For I solemnly warn you that if you launch into one of these digressions which you have recently been offering me we will unquestionably lose our case, and you will be struck off the register as sure as my name is Thomas Horner."

Andrew saw dimly that he must try to hold himself in check. Here he must, like a patient laid upon the table, submit to the formal operations of the Council. But it was difficult for him to reach that passive state. The mere idea that he must forgo all attempt at self-exoneration and dully answer "Yes" or "No" was more than he could bear.

On the evening of Tuesday, November ninth, when his febrile expectation of what the next day would bring had reached its zenith, he found himself unaccountably in Paddington, walking in the direction of the Vidlers' shop, driven by a strange subconscious impulse. Deeply buried in his mind lay the morbid, still unconquered fancy that all the calamity of these last months came in punishment for Harry Vidler's death. The inference was involuntary, unadmitted. Yet it was there, springing from the deep roots of his earliest belief. He was drawn irresistibly to Vidler's widow as though the mere sight of her might help him—give him, in some strange manner, appeasement from his suffering.

It was a wet dark night and there were few people in the streets. He had a sense of queer unreality, walking unrecognized in this district where he had been known so well. His own dark figure became a shadow amongst other phantoms, all hurrying, hurrying through the teeming rain. He reached the shop just before closing time, hesitated; then, as a customer came out, hurriedly he went in.

Mrs. Vidler was alone, behind the counter of the cleaning and pressing department, folding a woman's coat which had just been left with her. She wore a black skirt and an old blouse, dyed black, gaping a little at the neck. Her mourning made her somehow smaller. Suddenly she lifted her eyes and saw him.

"It's Doctor Manson," she exclaimed, her face lighting up. "How are you, Doctor?"

His answer came stiffly. He saw that she knew nothing of his present trouble. He remained standing in the doorway, rigid, gazing at her, the rain dripping slowly from his hat brim.

"Come in, Doctor. Why, you're drenched. It's a wicked night—"

He interrupted her, his voice strained, unreal.

"Mrs. Vidler, I've wanted to come and see you for a long time. I've often wondered how you were getting on."

"I'm managing, Doctor. Not so bad. I've a new young man in the cobbling. He's a good worker. But come in and let me give you a cup of tea."

He shook his head.

"I'm—I'm just passing." Then he went on, almost desperately. "You must miss Harry very much."

"Well, yes, I do. At least, at first I did. But it's wonderful,"—she even smiled at him,—"how you come to get used to things."

He said rapidly, confusedly:—

"I reproach myself—in a way. Oh! it all happened so suddenly for you, I've often felt you must blame me—"

"Blame you!" She shook her head. "How can you say such a thing, when you done everything, even to the home, and getting the finest surgeon—"

"But you see," he persisted huskily, a rigid coldness in all his body, "if you had done differently, perhaps if Harry had gone to hospital—"

"I wouldn't have had it any different, Doctor. My Harry had the best that money could give him. Why, even his funeral, I wish you could have seen it, the wreaths. As for *blaming* yourself—why, many's the time I've said in this shop Harry couldn't have had a better nor a kinder nor a cleverer doctor than yourself . . ."

As she went on talking he saw with a conclusive pang that, though he made open confession, she would never believe him. She had her illusion of Harry's peaceful, inevitable, costly passing. It would be cruelty to shake her from this pillar to which she clung so happily. He said, after a pause:—

"I'm very glad to have seen you again, Mrs. Vidler. As I've said, I wanted to look you up."

He broke off, shook hands with her, bade her good night and went out.

The encounter, far from reassuring or consoling him, served only to intensify his wretchedness. His mood underwent a complete revulsion. What had he expected? Forgiveness, in the best fictional tradition? Condemnation? He reflected bitterly that now she probably thought more highly of him than ever. As he tramped back through the sopping streets he had the sudden conviction that he must lose his case to-morrow. The conviction deepened to a terrifying certainty.

Not far from his hotel, in a quiet side street, he passed the open doorway of a church. Once again impulse caught him, caused him to stop, retrace his steps and enter. It was dark inside, empty and warm, as though a service had not long ended. He did not know what church it was, nor did he care. He simply sat down in the back seat of all and fixed his haggard gaze upon the dark enshrouded apse. He reflected that Christine in their estrangement had fallen back upon the thought of God. He had never been a churchgoer, but now here he was, in this unknown church. Tribulation brought people here, brought people to their senses, brought people to the thought of God.

There he sat, bowed, like a man resting at the end of a journey. His thoughts flowed outwards, not in any considered prayer, but winged with the longing of his soul. God! don't let me be struck off. Oh, God! don't let me be struck off. For perhaps half an hour he remained in this strange meditation, then he rose and went straight to his hotel.

Next morning, though he had slept heavily, he woke to an even greater sense of sick anxiety. As he dressed his hands trembled slightly. He blamed himself for having come to this hotel with its associations of his membership examination. The feeling he now experienced was exactly that pre-examination dread, intensified a hundredfold.

Downstairs he could eat no breakfast. The time of his case was eleven o'clock and Horner had asked him to be early. He estimated it would take him not more than twenty minutes to get to Hallam Street, and he fretted, in nervous pretence, with the newspapers in the hotel lounge until half-past ten. But when he started his taxi was caught in a long traffic jam due to an obstruction in Oxford Street. It was striking eleven when he reached the G.M.C. offices.

He hurried into the Council Chamber with only a disturbed impression of its size, of the high table where the Council sat with the President, Sir Jenner Halliday, in the chair. Seated at the far end were the participants in his own case, oddly like actors waiting for their cue. Horner was there; Mary Boland, accompanied by her father; Nurse Sharp, Doctor Thoroughgood, Mr. Boon, Ward Sister Myles—his glance travelled along the line of chairs. Then hastily he seated himself beside Horner.

"I thought I told you to be early," the solicitor said in an aggrieved tone. "This other case is almost over. With the Council it's fatal to be late."

Andrew made no answer. As Horner had said, the President was even now pronouncing judgment on the case before his own, an adverse judgment, erasure from the register. Andrew could not keep his eye from the doctor convicted of some drab misdemeanour, a seedy down-at-heel individual who looked as though he had struggled hard to make a living. His utterly hopeless expression, as he stood condemned by this august body of his fellows, sent a shiver over Andrew.

But he had no time for thought, for more than a passing wave of pity. The next minute his own case was called. His heart contracted as the proceedings began.

The charge was formally read through. Then Mr. George Boon, the prosecuting solicitor, rose to open. He was a thin, precise frock-coated figure, clean-shaven, with a wide black ribbon to his eyeglasses. His voice came deliberately.

"Mr. President, gentlemen, this case which you are about to consider has, I submit, nothing to do with any theory of medicine as defined under Section Twenty-eight of the Medical Act. On the contrary, it exhibits a clear-cut instance of professional association with an unregistered person, a tendency which, I may perhaps observe, the Council has recently had cause to deplore.

"The facts of the case are these. The patient, Mary Boland, suffering from apical phthisis, was admitted to the wards of Doctor Thoroughgood at the Victoria Chest Hospital on July the eighteenth. There she remained under the care of Doctor Thoroughgood until August the fifteenth, when she discharged herself on the pretext that she wished to return to her home. I say 'pretext' because, on the day of her discharge, instead of returning home, the patient was met at the lodge of the hospital by Doctor Manson, who immediately took her to an institution by the name of Bellevue which purports, I believe, to undertake the cure of pulmonary disorders.

"On arrival at this place, Bellevue, the patient was put to bed and examined by Doctor Manson in conjunction with the proprietor of the establishment, Mr. Richard Stillman, an unqualified person and—er—I understand, an alien. Upon examination, it was decided in consultation,—I particularly call the Council to mark that phrase,—in consultation, by Doctor Manson and Mr. Stillman, to operate upon the patient and to induce the condition of pneumothorax. Thereupon Doctor Manson administered the local anæsthetic and the induction was performed by Doctor Manson and Mr. Stillman.

"Now, gentlemen, having briefly outlined the case I propose with your permission to call further evidence. Doctor Eustace Thoroughgood, please."

Doctor Thoroughgood rose and came forward. Removing his eyeglasses, and holding them in readiness to emphasize his points, Boon began his interrogation.

"Doctor Thoroughgood, I have no wish to embarrass you. We are well aware of your reputation, I might say your eminence, as a consulting physician upon diseases of the lungs and I have no doubt you may be actuated by a sense of leniency towards your junior colleague; but, Doctor Thoroughgood, is it not the fact that on Saturday the morning of August the fourth, Doctor Manson pressed you to a consultation upon this patient Mary Boland?"

"Yes."

"And is it not also the fact that in the course of this consultation he pressed you to adopt a line of treatment which you thought to be unwise?"

"He wished me to perform A.P.T."

"Exactly! And in the best interests of the patient you refused?"

"I did."

"Was Doctor Manson's manner in any way peculiar when you refused?"

"Well—" Thoroughgood hesitated.

"Please, Doctor Thoroughgood! We respect your natural reluctance."

"He didn't seem altogether himself that morning. He seemed to disagree with my decision."

"Thank you, Doctor Thoroughgood. You had no reason to imagine that the patient was dissatisfied with her treatment at the hospital,—" at the mere idea a watery smile touched Boon's arid face,—"that she had any grounds for complaint against you or the staff?"

"None whatever. She always seemed well pleased, happy and contented."

"Thank you, Doctor Thoroughgood." Boon picked up his next paper. "And now, Ward Sister Myles, please."

Doctor Thoroughgood sat down. Ward Sister Myles came forward. Boon resumed:—

"Sister Myles, on the forenoon of Monday, August the sixth, the next day but one after this consultation between Doctor Thoroughgood and Doctor Manson, did Doctor Manson call to see the patient?"

"He did."

"Was it a usual hour for him to call?"

"No."

"Did he examine the patient?"

"No. We had no screens that morning. He just sat and talked with her."

"Exactly, Sister—a long and earnest conversation, if I may use the wording of your statutory declaration. But tell us, Sister, in your own words now, what took place immediately subsequent to Doctor Manson's departure."

"About half an hour after, Number Seventeen—that's to say, Mary Boland —said to me: 'Sister, I've been thinking things over and I've made up my mind to go. You've been very kind to me. But I want to leave a week from Wednesday.'"

Boon interrupted quickly.

"'A week from Wednesday.' Thank you, Sister. It was that point I wished to establish. That will be all at present."

Ward Sister Myles stepped back.

The solicitor made a politely satisfied gesture with his beribboned eye-glasses.

"And now—Nurse Sharp, please." A pause. "Nurse Sharp, you are in a position to bear out the statement relating to Doctor Manson's movements on the afternoon of Wednesday, August the fifteenth."

"Yes, I was there!"

"I gather from your tone, Nurse Sharp, that you were there unwillingly."

"When I found out where we were going and who this man Stillman was, not a doctor or anything, I was—"

"Shocked," Boon suggested.

"Yes, I was," shot out Nurse Sharp. "I've never had to do with anybody but proper doctors, real specialists, all my life."

"Exactly," Boon purred. "Now, Nurse Sharp, there is just one point which I wish you to make quite clear once again for the benefit of the Council. Did Doctor Manson actually co-operate with Mr. Stillman in—in performing this operation?"

"He did," Nurse Sharp answered vindictively.

At this point Abbey leaned forward and put a question suavely, through the President.

"Is it not the case, Nurse Sharp, that when the events in question took place you were under notice to Doctor Manson?"

Nurse Sharp reddened, violently, lost her composure and stammered: "Yes, I suppose so."

As she sat down a minute later Andrew was conscious of a faint spark of warmth—Abbey, at least, remained his friend.

Boon turned to the Council table, mildly aggrieved at the interruption.

"Mr. President, gentlemen, I might continue to call witnesses but I am too sensible of the value of the Council's time. Moreover, I submit that I have proved my case conclusively. There seems not the slightest doubt that the patient Mary Boland was removed, entirely through the connivance of Doctor Manson, from the care of an eminent specialist in one of the best hospitals in London to this questionable institute—which in itself constitutes a grave breach of professional conduct—and that there Doctor Manson deliberately associated himself with the unqualified proprietor of this institute in the performance of a dangerous operation, already stated to be contraindicated by Doctor Thoroughgood, the specialist ethically responsible for the case. Mr. President, gentlemen, here, I submit, we are not dealing, as might appear at first sight, with an isolated instance, an accidental misconduct, but with a planned, preconceived, and almost systematic infringement of the medical code."

Mr. Boon sat down, well-pleased, and began to polish his glasses. There was a moment's silence. Andrew kept his eyes firmly upon the floor. It had been torture for him to endure the biased presentation of the case. Bitterly he told himself that they were treating him like some hole-and-corner criminal. Then his solicitor came forward and prepared to address the Council.

As usual, Horner seemed flustered, his face was red, and he had difficulty in arranging his papers. Yet, strangely, this seemed to gain him the indulgence of the Council. The President said:—

"Yes, Mr. Horner?"

Horner cleared his throat.

"May it please you, Mr. President, gentlemen—I am not in dispute with the evidence brought by Mr. Boon. I have no wish to go behind the facts. But the manner of their interpretation gravely concerns us. There are, besides, certain additional points which throw a complexion upon the case much more favourable to my client.

"It has not yet been stated that Miss Boland was primarily Doctor Manson's patient, since she consulted him, previous to seeing Doctor Thoroughgood, on July the eleventh. Further, Doctor Manson was personally interested in the case. Miss Boland is the daughter of a close friend. Thus, all along, he regarded her as his own responsibility. We must frankly admit that Doctor Manson's action was completely misguided. But I suggest respectfully it was neither dishonourable nor malicious.

"We have heard of this slight difference of opinion over the question of treatment between Doctor Thoroughgood and Doctor Manson. Bearing in mind Doctor Manson's great interest in the case, it was not unnatural for him to wish to take it back into his own hands. Naturally, he wished to cause his senior colleague no distress. That, and nothing more, was the reason of the subterfuge upon which Mr. Boon has laid such stress." Here Horner paused, pulled out a handkerchief and coughed. He had the air of a man approaching a more difficult hurdle. "And now we come to the matter of association, of Mr. Stillman and Bellevue. I assume members of the Council are not ignorant of Mr. Stillman's name. Although unqualified, he enjoys a certain reputation and is even reported to have brought about certain obscure cures."

The President interrupted gravely:—

"Mr. Horner, what can you, a layman, know of these matters?"

"I agree, sir," Horner said hurriedly. "My real point is that Mr. Stillman would appear to be a man of character. It so happens that he introduced himself to Doctor Manson many years ago through a letter complimenting Doctor Manson upon some research work he had done upon the lungs. The two met later on a purely unprofessional footing when Mr. Stillman came here to establish his clinic. Thus, though it was ill-considered, it was not unnatural that Doctor Manson, seeking a place where he could himself give treatment to Miss Boland, should avail himself of the convenience offered him at Bellevue. My friend Mr. Boon has referred to Bellevue as a 'questionable' establishment. On that point I feel the Council might be interested to hear evidence. Miss Boland, please."

As Mary rose the scrutiny of the Council members fell upon her with marked curiosity. Though she was nervous and kept her gaze on Horner, not once glancing at Andrew, she seemed well, in normal health.

"Miss Boland," said Horner, "I want you to tell us frankly—did you find anything to complain of while you were a patient at Bellevue?"

"No! Quite the reverse." Andrew saw at once that she had been carefully instructed beforehand. Her answer came with guarded moderation.

"You suffered no ill effects?"

"On the contrary. I am better."

"In fact, the treatment carried out there was really the treatment Doctor Manson suggested for you at your first interview with him on—let me see— on July the eleventh."

"Yes."

"Is this relevant?" the President asked.

"I have finished with this witness, sir," Horner said quickly. As Mary sat down he threw out his hands towards the Council table in his deprecatory style. "What I am venturing to suggest, gentlemen, is that the treatment effected at Bellevue was in actuality Doctor Manson's treatment carried out— unethically perhaps—by other persons. There was, I contend, within the mean- ing of the act, no professional co-operation between Stillman and Doctor Manson. I should like to call Doctor Manson."

Andrew stood up, acutely conscious of his position, of every eye directed towards him. He was pale and drawn. A sense of cold emptiness lay in the pit of his stomach. He heard Horner address him.

"Doctor Manson, you received no financial gain in respect of this alleged co-operation with Mr. Stillman?"

"Not a penny."

"You had no ulterior motive, no base objective, in doing as you did?"

"No."

"You meant no reflection on your senior colleague, Doctor Thoroughgood?"

"No. We got on well together. It was just—our opinions did not coincide on this case."

"Exactly," Horner intervened rather hastily. "You can assure the Council, then, honestly and sincerely, that you had no intention of offending against the medical code, nor the remotest idea that your conduct was in any degree infamous."

"That is the absolute truth."

Horner suppressed a sigh of relief as, with a nod, he dismissed Andrew. Though he had felt himself obliged to produce this evidence he had feared his client's impetuosity. But now it was safely over, and he felt that, if his summing-up were brief, they might now possibly have a slender chance of success.

He said with a contrite air:—

"I have no wish to keep the Council further. I have tried to show that Doctor Manson made merely an unhappy mistake. I appeal, not only to the justice, but to the mercy of the Council. And I should like finally to draw the Council's attention to my client's attainments. His past history is one of which any man might be proud. We are all aware of cases in which brilliant men have been guilty of a single error, and, failing to secure mercy, their careers were eclipsed. I hope, and indeed I pray, that this case which you are about to judge may not be such as these."

The apology and humility in Horner's tone were quite admirable in their effect upon the Council. But almost at once Boon was on his feet again, craving the indulgence of the President.

.

"With your permission, sir, there are one or two questions I should like to put to Dr. Manson." He swung round, inviting Andrew to his feet by an upward movement of his eyeglasses.

"Doctor Manson, your last answer was scarcely clear to me. You say you had no knowledge that your conduct was in any degree infamous. Yet you *did* know that Mr. Stillman was not a qualified gentleman."

Andrew considered Boon from beneath his brows. The attitude of the finicky solicitor had, during the entire hearing, made him feel guilty of some disgraceful act. A slow spark kindled in the chilly void within him.

He said distinctly:—

"Yes, I knew he was not a doctor."

The little wintry smirk of satisfaction showed on Boon's face. He said goadingly:—

"I see. I see. Yet even that did not deter you."

"Even that didn't," echoed Andrew with sudden bitterness. He felt his control going. He took a long breath. "Mr. Boon, I've listened to you asking a great many questions. Will you allow me to ask you one? Have you heard of Louis Pasteur?"

"Yes," Boon was startled into the reply. "Who hasn't?"

"Exactly! Who hasn't? You are probably unaware of the fact, Mr. Boon, but perhaps you will allow me to tell you that Louis Pasteur, the greatest figure of all in scientific medicine, was *not* a doctor. Nor was Ehrlich—the man who gave medicine the best and most specific remedy in its entire history. Nor was Haffkine—who fought the plague in India better than any *qualified gentleman* has ever done. Nor was Metchnikoff, inferior only to Pasteur in his greatness. Forgive me for reminding you of these elementary facts, Mr. Boon. They may show you that every man fighting disease who hasn't got his name on the register isn't necessarily a knave or a fool."

Electric silence. Hitherto the proceedings had dragged along in an atmosphere of pompous dreariness, a musty staleness, like a secondhand law court. But now every member at the Council table sat erect; Abbey, in particular, had his eyes upon Andrew with a strange intentness. A moment passed.

Horner, with his hand before his face, groaned in dismay. Now, indeed, he knew the case was lost. Boon, though horribly discomfited, made an effort to recover himself.

"Yes, yes, these are illustrious names, we know. Surely you don't compare Stillman with them?"

"Why not?" Andrew rushed on in burning indignation. "They're only illustrious because they're dead. Virchow laughed at Koch in his lifetime—abused him! We don't abuse him now. We abuse men like Sphalinger and Stillman. There's another example for you—Sphalinger—a great and original scientific thinker. He's not a doctor. He has no medical degree. But he's done more for medicine than thousands of men *with* degrees, men who ride about in motor cars and charge their fees, free as air, while Sphalinger is opposed and disparaged and accused, allowed to spend his fortune in research and treatment, and then left to struggle on in poverty."

"Are we to take it," Boon managed a sneer, "that you have an equal admiration for Richard Stillman?"

"Yes. He's a great man, a man who has devoted his whole life to benefiting mankind. He's had to fight jealousy and prejudice, and misrepresentation, too. In his own country he has overcome it. But apparently not here. Yet I'm convinced that he's done more against tuberculosis than any man living in this country. He's outside the profession. Yes! But there are plenty inside it who have been running up against T.B. all their lives and have never done an atom of good in fighting it."

There was sensation in the long high room. Mary Boland's eyes, now fixed on Andrew, were shining between admiration and anxiety. Horner, slowly and sadly, was gathering his papers, slipping them into his leather case.

The President intervened.

"Do you realize what you are saying?"

"I do." Andrew gripped the back of his chair tensely, aware that he had been carried into grave indiscretion but determined to stand by his opinions. Breathing quickly, strung to breaking pitch, a queer kind of recklessness took hold of him. If they were going to strike him off, let him give them cause to do so.

He rushed on: "I've listened to the pleading that's been going on to-day on my behalf and all the time I've been asking myself what harm I've done. I don't want to work with quacks. I don't believe in bogus remedies. That's why I don't open half the highly scientific advertisements that come pouring into my letter box by every post. I know I am speaking more strongly than I should, but I can't help it. We're not nearly liberal enough. If we go on trying to make out that everything's wrong outside the profession and everything is right within, it means the death of scientific progress. We'll just turn into a tight little trade protection society. It's high time we started putting our own house in order, and I don't mean the superficial things either. Go to the beginning, think of the hopelessly inadequate training doctors get. When I qualified I was more of a menace to society than anything else. All I knew was the names of a few diseases and the drugs I was supposed to give for them. I couldn't even lock a pair of midwifery forceps. Anything I know I've learned since then. But how many doctors do learn anything beyond the ordinary rudiments they pick up in practice? They haven't got time, poor devils; they're rushed off their feet. That's where our whole organization is rotten. We ought to be arranged in scientific units. There ought to be compulsory post-graduate classes. There ought to be a great attempt to bring science into the front line, to do away with the old bottle-of-medicine idea, give every practitioner a chance to study, to co-operate in research. And what about commercialism? The useless guinea-chasing treatments, the unnecessary operations, the crowds of worthless pseudo-scientific proprietary preparations we use—isn't it time some of these were eliminated? The whole profession is far too intolerant and smug. Structurally, we're static. We never think of advancing, altering our system. We say we'll do things, and we don't. For years we've been bleating about the sweated conditions under which our nurses work, the wretched pittances we pay them. Well? They're still being sweated, still paid their pittances. That's just an example. What I really mean is deeper than that. We don't give our pioneers a chance. Doctor Hexam, the man who was brave enough to give anæsthetics for Jarvis, the manipulator, when he was beginning his work, got struck off the register. Ten years later when Jarvis had cured hundreds of cases which had baffled the best surgeons in London, when he had been given a knighthood, when all the 'best people' proclaimed him a genius, then we crawled back and gave him an honorary M.D. By that time Hexam was dead of a broken heart. I know I have made plenty of mistakes, and bad mistakes, in practice. And I regret them. But I made no mistake with Richard Stillman. And I don't regret what I did with him. All I ask you to do is to look at Mary Boland. She had apical phthisis when she went to Stillman. Now she's cured. If you want any justification of my infamous conduct here it is, in this room, before you."

Quite abruptly he ended and sat down. At the high Council table there was a queer light upon Abbey's face. Boon, still upon his feet, gazed at Manson with mixed feelings. Then, reflecting vengefully that he had at least given this upstart doctor enough rope to hang himself with, he bowed to the President and took his chair.

For a minute a peculiar silence filled the chamber, then the President made the customary declaration.

"I ask all strangers to withdraw."

Andrew went out with the rest. Now his recklessness was gone and his head, his whole body, was throbbing like an overtaxed machine. The atmosphere of the Council chamber stifled him. He could not endure the presence of Horner, Boland, Mary, and the other witnesses. He dreaded especially that melancholy reproach on the face of his solicitor. He knew he had behaved like a fool, a wretched declamatory fool. Now he saw his honesty as sheer madness. Yes, it was madness to attempt to harangue the Council as he had done. He ought to have been not a doctor but a stump orator in Hyde Park. Well! Soon he would cease to be a doctor. They would simply wipe him off the list.

He went into the cloakroom, desiring only to be alone, and sat on the edge of one of the washbasins, mechanically feeling for a cigarette. But the smoke was tasteless on his parched tongue and he crushed the cigarette beneath his heel. It was strange, despite the hard things, the true things he had said of the profession a few moments ago, how miserable he should feel at being cast out from it. He realized that he might find work with Stillman. But this was not the work he wanted. No! He wished to be with Denny and Hope, to develop his own bent, drive the spearhead of his scheme into the hide of apathy and conservatism. But all this must be done from within the profession; it could never, in England, never, never, be accomplished from outside. Now Denny and Hope must man the Trojan horse alone. A great wave of bitterness swept over him. The future stretched out before him desolately. He had already that most painful sense of all, the feeling of exclusion; and allied to it, the knowledge that he was finished, done for—this was the end.

The sound of people moving in the corridor brought him wearily to his feet. As he joined them and re-entered the Council Chamber, he told himself sternly that only one thing remained to him. He must not grovel. He prayed that he would give no sign of subservience, of weakness. With his eyes fixed firmly on the floor immediately before him, he saw no one, gave no glance towards the high table, remained passive, motionless. All the trivial sounds of the room re-echoed maddeningly about him—the scraping of chairs, the coughing, whispering, even the incredible sound of someone tapping idly with a pencil.

But suddenly there was silence. A spasm of rigidity took hold of Andrew. Now, he thought, now it is coming!

The President spoke. He spoke slowly, impressively.

"Andrew Manson, I have to inform you that the Council has given very careful consideration to the charge brought against you and to the evidence brought in support of it. The Council is of opinion that, despite the peculiar circumstances of the case and your own particularly unorthodox presentation of it, you were acting in good faith and were sincerely desirous of complying with the spirit of the law demanding a high standard of professional conduct. I have to inform you, accordingly, that the Council has not seen fit to direct the Registrar to erase your name."

For one dazed second he did not comprehend. Then a sudden shivering thrill passed over him. They had not struck him off. He was free, clear, vindicated.

He raised his head shakily towards the Council table. Of all the faces, strangely blurred, turned towards his own, the one he saw most distinctly was that of Robert Abbey. The understanding in Abbey's eyes distressed him even more. He knew, in one illuminating flash, that it was Abbey who had got him off.

Gone now was his pretence of indifference. He muttered feebly—and though he addressed the President it was to Abbey that he spoke:—

"Thank you, sir."

The President said: "That terminates the case."

Andrew stood up, instantly surrounded by his friends, by Con, Mary, the astounded Mr. Horner, by people he had never seen before, who now shook him warmly by the hand. Somehow he was in the street outside, still being beaten about the shoulders by Con, oddly reassured in his nervous confusion by the passing buses, the normal stream of traffic, recapturing every now and then, with a start of joy, the unbelievable ecstasy of his release.

He looked down unexpectedly to see Mary gazing up at him, her eyes still filled with tears.

"If they'd done anything to you—after all you've done for me I'd— Oh! I'd have killed that old President."

"In the name of God!" Con irrepressibly declared. "I don't know what ye were worrying about! The minute old Manson started to get goin'—sure, I knew he would knock the stuffing outa them."

Andrew smiled weakly, doubtfully, joyously.

The three reached the Museum Hotel after one o'clock. And there, waiting in the lounge, was Denny. He sauntered towards them, gravely smiling. Horner had telephoned the news.

But he had no comment to make. He merely said:—

"I'm hungry. But we can't feed here. Come along, all of you, and lunch with me."

They lunched at the Connaught Restaurant. Though no flicker of emotion crossed Philip's face, though he talked mainly of motor cars to Con, he made it a happy celebration.

Afterwards he said to Andrew:—

"Our train leaves at four o'clock. Hope's in Stanborough—at the hotel, waiting on us. We can get that property dirt cheap. I've got some shopping to do. But I'll meet you at Euston at ten to four!"

Andrew gazed at Denny, conscious of his friendship, of all that he owed him since the first moment of their meeting in the little Blaenelly surgery.

He said suddenly:—

"Supposing I'd been struck off?"

"You're not." Philip shook his head. "And I'll see to it that you never will be."

When Denny left to make his purchases Andrew accompanied Con and Mary to their train at Paddington. As they waited on the platform, rather silent now, he repeated the invitation he had already given them.

"You must come and see us at Stanborough."

"We will that," Con assured him. "In the spring—whenever I get the little bus tuned up."

When their train steamed out Andrew still had an hour to spare. But there was no doubt in his mind as to what he wished to do. Instinctively, he boarded a bus, and soon he was in Kensal Green. He entered the cemetery, stood a long time at Christine's grave, thinking of many things. It was a bright, fresh afternoon, with that crispness in the breeze which she had always loved. Above him, on the branch of a grimy tree, a sparrow chirped merrily.

When at last he turned away, hastening for fear he should be late, there in the sky before him a bank of cloud lay brightly, bearing the shape of battlements.

The Keys
of the Kingdom

TO MY FRIEND F. M.,
FOR TWENTY YEARS A MISSIONARY IN CHINA

CONTENTS

"And I will give to thee the keys
of the kingdom of heaven."
—Christ to Peter

I

BEGINNING OF THE END

1

LATE one afternoon in September 1938 old Father Francis Chisholm limped up the steep path from the church of St. Columba to his house upon the hill. He preferred this way, despite his infirmities, to the less arduous ascent of Mercat Wynd; and, having reached the narrow door of his walled-in garden, he paused with a kind of naïve triumph—recovering his breath, contemplating the view he had always loved.

Beneath him was the River Tweed, a great wide sweep of placid silver, tinted by the low saffron smudge of autumn sunset. Down the slope of the northern Scottish bank tumbled the town of Tweedside, its tiled roofs a crazy quilt of pink and yellow, masking the maze of cobbled streets. High stone ramparts still ringed this Border burgh, with captured Crimean cannon making perches for the gulls as they pecked at partan crabs. At the river's mouth a wraith lay upon the sand bar, misting the lines of drying nets, the masts of smacks inside the harbour pointing upwards, brittle and motionless. Inland, dusk was already creeping upon the still bronze woods of Derham, towards which, as he gazed, a lonely heron made laboured flight. The air was thin and clear, stringent with wood smoke and the tang of fallen apples, sharp with the hint of early frost.

With a contented sigh, Father Chisholm turned into his garden: a patch beside his pleasance upon the Hill of Brilliant Green Jade, but a pretty one, and, like all Scots gardens, productive, with a few fine fruit trees splayed on the mellow wall. The jargonelle espalier in the south corner was at its best. Since there was no sign of the tyrant Dougal, with a cautious glance towards the kitchen window he stole the finest pear from his own tree, slid it under his soutane. His yellow, wrinkled cheek was ripe with triumph as he hobbled —dot and carry—down the gravelled drive, leaning on his one indulgence, the new umbrella of Chisholm tartan which replaced his battered favourite of Pai-tan. And there, standing at the front porch, was the car.

His face puckered slowly. Though his memory was bad and his fits of absent-mindedness a perpetual embarrassment, he now recollected the vexation of the Bishop's letter, proposing, or rather announcing, this visit of his secretary Monsignor Sleeth. He hastened forward to welcome his guest.

Monsignor Sleeth was in the parlour, standing, dark, thin, distinguished, and not quite at ease, with his back to the empty fireplace—his youthful im-

patience heightened, his clerical dignity repelled, by the mean surroundings
in which he found himself. He had looked for a note of individuality: some
piece of porcelain perhaps, or lacquer, a souvenir from the East. But the
apartment was bare and nondescript, with poor linoleum, horsehair chairs
and a chipped mantelpiece on which, out of the corner of a disapproving eye,
he had already noted a spinning top beside an uncounted litter of collection
pennies. Yet he was resolved to be pleasant. Smoothing his frown, he stifled
Father Chisholm's apology with a gracious gesture.

"Your housekeeper has already shown me my room. I trust it will not
disturb you to have me here for a few days. What a superb afternoon it has
been. The colourings!—as I drove up from Tynecastle I almost fancied myself in dear San Morales." He gazed away, through the darkening window,
with a studied air.

The old man nearly smiled at the imprint of Father Tarrant and the Seminary—Sleeth's elegance, that bladelike look, even the hint of hardness in the
nostril, made him a perfect replica.

"I hope you'll be comfortable," he murmured. "We'll have our bite presently. I'm sorry I can't offer you dinner. Somehow we've just fallen to the
habit of a Scots high tea!"

Sleeth, head half-averted, nodded noncommittally. Indeed, at that moment, Miss Moffat entered and, having drawn the drab chenille curtains,
stealthily began to set the table. He could not but reflect, ironically, how
the neutral creature, darting him one frightened glance, matched the room.
Though it caused him a passing asperity to observe her lay places for three,
her presence enabled him to lead the conversation safely into generalities.

As the two priests sat down at table he was eulogizing the special marble
which the Bishop had brought from Carrara for the transept of the new
Tynecastle pro-cathedral. Helping himself with good appetite from the ashet
of ham, eggs and kidneys before him, he accepted a cup of tea poured from
the Britannia metal teapot. Then, busy buttering brown toast, he heard his
host remark mildly:—

"You won't mind if Andrew sups his porridge with us. Andrew—this is
Monsignor Sleeth!"

Sleeth raised his head abruptly. A boy about nine years of age had come
silently into the room and now, after an instant's indecision, when he stood
tugging at his blue jersey, his long pale face intense with nervousness, slipped
into his place, reaching mechanically for the milk jug. As he bent over his
plate a lock of dank brown hair—tribute to Miss Moffat's sponge—fell over
his ugly bony forehead. His eyes, of a remarkable blue, held a childish
prescience of crisis—they were so uneasy he dared not lift them up.

The Bishop's secretary relaxed his attitude, slowly resumed his meal. After
all, the moment was not opportune. Yet from time to time his stare travelled
covertly towards the boy.

"So you are Andrew!" Decency demanded speech, even a hint of benign-
ness. "And you go to school here?"

"Yes . . ."

"Come then! Let us see how much you know." Amiably enough, he propounded a few simple questions. The boy, flushed and inarticulate, too confused to think, betrayed humiliating ignorance.

Monsignor Sleeth's eyebrows lifted. "Dreadful," he thought. "Quite a gutter brat!"

He helped himself to another kidney—then suddenly became aware that while he trifled with the rich meats of the table the other two kept soberly to porridge. He flushed: this show of asceticism on the old man's part was insufferable affectation.

Perhaps Father Chisholm had a wry perception of that thought. He shook his head: "I went without good Scots oatmeal so many years I never miss it now I have the chance."

Sleeth received the remark in silence. Presently, with a hurried glance, out of his downcast muteness, Andrew begged permission to depart. Rising to say his grace, he knocked a spoon spinning with his elbow. His stiff boots made an uncouth scuffling towards the door.

Another pause. Then, having concluded his meal, Monsignor Sleeth rose easily and repossessed, without apparent purpose, the fleshless hearth-rug. With feet apart and hands clasped behind his back he considered, without seeming to do so, his aged colleague, who, still seated, had the curious air of waiting. Dear God, thought Sleeth, what a pitiable presentation of the priesthood—this shabby old man, with the stained soutane, soiled collar and sallow, desiccated skin! On one cheek was an ugly weal, a kind of cicatrix, which everted the lower eyelid, seemed to tug the head down and sideways. The impression was that of a permanent wry neck, counterpoising the lame and shortened leg. His eyes, usually lowered, took thus—on the rare occasions that he raised them—a penetrating obliqueness which was strangely disconcerting.

Sleeth cleared his throat. He judged it time for him to speak and, forcing a note of cordiality, he inquired: "How long have you been here, Father Chisholm?"

"Twelve months."

"Ah, yes. It was a kindly gesture of His Grace to send you—on your return —to your native parish."

"And his!"

Sleeth inclined his head suavely. "I was aware that His Grace shared with you the distinction of having been born here. Let me see . . . what age are you, Father? Nearly seventy is it not?"

Father Chisholm nodded, adding with gentle senile pride: "I am no older than Anselm Mealey."

Sleeth's frown at the familiarity melted into a half-pitying smile. "No doubt—but life has treated you rather differently. To be brief,—" he gathered himself up, firm, but not unkind,—"the Bishop and I both have the feeling that your long and faithful years should now be recompensed; that you should, in short, retire!"

There was a moment of strange quiet.

"But I have no wish to retire."

"It is a painful duty for me to come here"—Sleeth kept his gaze discreetly on the ceiling—"to investigate . . . and report to His Grace. But there are certain things which cannot be overlooked."

"What things?"

Sleeth moved irritably. "Six—ten—a dozen things! It isn't my place to enumerate your—your Oriental eccentricities!"

"I'm sorry." A slow spark kindled in the old man's eyes. "You must remember that I spent thirty-five years in China."

"Your parish affairs are in a hopeless muddle."

"Am I in debt?"

"How are we to know? No returns on your quarterly collections for six months." Sleeth's voice rose, he spoke a little faster. "Everything so . . . so unbusinesslike. . . . For instance when Bland's traveller presented his bill last month—three pounds for candles, and so forth—you paid him entirely in coppers!"

"That's how it comes to me." Father Chisholm viewed his visitor thoughtfully, as though he looked straight through him. "I've always been stupid about money. I've never had any, you see. . . . But after all . . . Do you think money so dreadfully important?"

To his annoyance Monsignor Sleeth found himself reddening. "It makes talk, Father." He rushed on. "And there is other talk. Some of your sermons . . . the advice you give . . . certain points of doctrine." He consulted a Morocco-covered notebook already in his palm. "They seem dangerously peculiar."

"Impossible!"

"On Whitsunday you told your congregation, 'Don't think heaven is in the sky . . . it's in the hollow of your hand . . . it's everywhere and anywhere.'" Sleeth frowned censoriously as he turned the pages. "And again . . . here is an incredible remark you made during Holy Week. 'Atheists may not all go to hell. I knew one who didn't. Hell is only for those who spit in the face of God!' And, good gracious, this atrocity: 'Christ was a perfect man, but Confucius had a better sense of humour!'" Another page was turned indignantly. "And this incredible incident . . . when one of your best parishioners, Mrs. Glendenning, who cannot of course help her extreme stoutness, came to you for spiritual guidance you looked at her and replied, 'Eat less. The gates of Paradise are narrow.' But why should I continue?" Decisively, Monsignor Sleeth closed the gilt-edged book. "To say the least, you seem to have lost your command of souls."

"But . . ." Calmly: "I don't want to command anyone's soul."

Sleeth's colour heightened disagreeably. He did not see himself in theological discussion with this shambling dotard.

"There remains the matter of this boy whom you have so misguidedly adopted."

"Who is to look after him—if I don't?"

"Our own Sisters at Ralstone. It is the finest orphanage in the diocese."

Again Father Chisholm raised his disconcerting eyes. "Would you have wished to spend your own childhood at that orphanage?"

"Need we be personal, Father? I've told you . . . even conceding the circumstances . . . the situation is highly irregular and must be ended. Besides . . ." He threw out his hands. "If you are going away—we must find some place for him."

"You seem determined to be rid of us. Am I to be entrusted to the Sisters too?"

"Of course not. You can go to the Aged Priests' Home at Clinton. It is a perfect haven of rest."

The old man actually laughed—a dry short laugh. "I'll have enough perfect rest when I'm dead. While I'm alive I don't want to be mixed up with a lot of aged priests. You may think it strange—but I never have been able to stand the clergy in bulk."

Sleeth's smile was pained and flustered. "I think nothing strange from you, Father. Forgive me, but to say the least of it . . . your reputation, even before you went to China . . . your whole life has been peculiar!"

There was a pause. Father Chisholm said in a quiet voice: "I shall render an account of my life to God."

The younger man dropped his eyelids with an unhappy sense of indiscretion. He had gone too far. Though his nature was cold he strove always to be just, even considerate. He had the grace to look uncomfortable. "Naturally I don't presume to be your judge—or your inquisitor. Nothing is decided yet. That is why I am here. We must see what the next few days bring forth." He stepped towards the door. "I am going to the church now. Please don't trouble. I know my way." His mouth creased into an unwilling smile. He went out.

Father Chisholm remained seated, motionless, at the table, his hand shading his eyes, as though thinking deeply. He felt crushed by this threat which had gathered, so suddenly, above the quiet of his hard-won retreat. His sense of resignation, long overtaxed, refused acceptance of it. All at once he felt empty and used-up, unwanted by God or man. A burning desolation filled his breast. Such a little thing; and yet so much. He wanted to cry out: My God, my God, why hast thou forsaken me? He rose heavily, and went upstairs.

In his attic above the spare room the boy Andrew was already in bed and asleep. He lay upon his side, one skinny arm crooked before him on the pillow, defensively. Watching him, Father Chisholm took the pear from his pocket and placed it on the clothes folded upon the cane-bottomed chair beside the bed. There seemed nothing more for him to do.

A faint breeze swayed the muslin curtains. He moved to the window and parted them. Stars were quivering in the frosty sky. Under these stars the span of his years reached out in all its ineptitude, built of his puny strivings, without form or nobility. It seemed such a short time since he had been a boy himself, running and laughing in this same town of Tweedside. His thoughts flew back. If there were any pattern in his life at all the first fateful stroke was surely drawn on that April Saturday sixty years ago when, out of untroubled happiness, so deep it passed unrecognized . . .

II

STRANGE VOCATION

1

THAT spring morning, at early breakfast in the snug dark kitchen, with the fire warm to his stockinged feet and the smell of kindling wood and hot oatcakes making him hungry, he was happy, despite the rain, because it was Saturday and the tide was right for salmon.

His mother finished her brisk stirring with the wooden spurtle, and placed the blue-ringed bowl of pease brose on the scrubbed table between his father and himself. He reached for his horn spoon, dipped in the bowl, then in the cup of buttermilk before him. He rolled his tongue over the smooth golden brose, made perfectly, without lumps or gritty unmixed meal.

His father, in worn blue jersey and darned fishing stockings, sat opposite, his big frame bowed, supping in silence, with quiet slow movements of his red hands. His mother shook the last batch of oat-cakes from the griddle, set them on their ends against the bowl, and sat down to her cup of tea. The yellow butter melted on the broken oat-cake which she took. There was silence and comradeship in the little kitchen, with the flames leaping across the bright fender and the pipe-clayed hearth. He was nine years of age and he was going to the bothy with his father.

There, he was known—he was Alex Chisholm's laddie, accepted by the men in their woollen jerseys and leather hip-boots with a quiet nod or, better still, a friendly silence. He had a dark secret glow of pride as he went out with them, the big flat cobble sweeping wide round the butt, the rowlocks creaking, the seine skilfully payed out by his father in the stern. Back on the butt, their tackets rasping the wet stones, the men huddled themselves low against the wind, some squatting with a yellowed sailcloth across their shoulders, others sucking warmth from a blackened inch-long clay. He stood with his father, apart. Alex Chisholm was the head man, the watcher of Tweed Fisheries Station No. 3. Together, not speaking, cut by the wind, they stood watching the far circle of corks dancing in the choppy back-lash where the river met the sea. Often the glare of sun upon the ripples made his head swim. But he would not, he could not blink. Missing even a single second might mean the missing of a dozen fish—so hard to come by, these days, that in distant Billingsgate they brought the Fisheries Company a good half-crown a pound. His father's tall figure, the head sunk a little on the shoulders, the profile keen beneath the old peaked cap, a fine blood whipped into the high cheekbones, had the same still unswerving tensity. At times, mingled exquisitely in his consciousness with the smell of wrack, the distant strike of the Burgess Clock, the cawing of the Derham rooks, the sense of this unspeaking comradeship drew moisture to the boy's already smarting eyes.

Suddenly his father shouted. Try as he might Francis could never win first sight of the dipping cork: not that tidal bobbing which sometimes caused him foolishly to start, but the slow downward tug which to long experience denoted the thrusting of a fish. At the quick high shout there was an instant clatter as the crew jumped to the windlass which hauled the net. Usage never staled that moment: though the men drew a poundage bonus on their catch, the thought of money did not stir them; this deep excitement sprang from far primeval roots. In came the net, slowly, dripping, flaked with kelp, the guide ropes squeaking on the wooden drum. A final heave, then, in the purse of the billowing seine, a molten flash, powerful, exquisite—salmon.

One memorable Saturday they had taken forty at a cast. The great shining things arched and fought, bursting through the net, slithering back to the river from the slippery butt. Francis flung himself forward with the others, desperately clutching at the precious escaping fish. They had picked him up, sequined with scales and soaked to the bone, a perfect monster locked in his embrace. Going home that evening, his hand inside his father's, their footfalls echoing in the smoky twilight, they had stopped, without comment, at Burley's in the High Street, to buy a pennyworth of cockles, the peppermint ones that were his special choice.

Their fellowship went further still. On Sundays, after mass, they took their rods and slipped secretly—lest they shock finer sensibilities—through the back ways of the Sabbath-stricken town, out into the verdant valley of the Whitadder. In his tin, packed with sawdust, were luscious maggots, picked the night before from Mealey's boneyard. Thereafter the day was heady with the sound of the stream, the scent of meadowsweet,—his father showing him the likely eddies,—the crimson-speckled trout wriggling on bleached shingle,—his father bent over a twig fire,—the crisp sweet goodness of the frizzled fish . . .

At other seasons they would go to gather blueberries, wood strawberries, or the wild yellow rasps which made good jam. It was a gala day when his mother accompanied them. His father knew all the best places and would take them deep into devious woods, to untouched cane-brakes of the juicy fruit.

When snow came and the ground was clamped by winter, they stalked between the frozen trees of Derham "policies," his breath a rime before him, his skin pricking for the keeper's whistle. He could hear his own heart beating as they cleared their snares, under the windows, almost, of the great house itself—then home, home with the heavy gamebag, his eyes smiling, his marrow melting to the thought of rabbit pie. His mother was a grand cook, a woman who earned—with her thrift, her knack of management and homely skill—the grudging panegyric of a Scots community: "Elizabeth Chisholm is a well-doing woman!"

Now, as he finished his brose, he became conscious that she was speaking, with a look across the breakfast table towards his father.

"You'll mind to be home early tonight, Alex, for the Burgess."

There was a pause. He could see that his father, preoccupied,—perhaps by the flooded river and the indifferent salmon season,—was caught unawares, recalled to the annual formality of the Burgess Concert which they must sustain that evening.

"You're set on going, woman?" With a faint smile.

She flushed slightly; Francis wondered why she should seem so queer. "It's one of the few things I look forward to in the year. After all, you are a Burgess of the town. It's . . . it's right for you to take your seat on the platform with your family and your friends."

His smile deepened, setting lines of kindness about his eyes—it was a smile Francis would have died to win. "Then it looks like we maun gang, Lisbeth." He had always disliked "the Burgess," as he disliked teacups, stiff collars, and his squeaky Sunday boots. But he did not dislike this woman who wanted him to go.

"I'm relying on you, Alex. You see," her voice, striving to be casual, sounded an odd note of relief, "I have asked Polly and Nora up from Tyne-castle—unfortunately it seems Ned cannot get away." She paused. "You'll have to send someone else to Ettal with the tallies."

He straightened with a quick look which seemed to see through her, right to the bottom of her tender subterfuge. At first, in his delight, Francis noticed nothing. His father's sister, now dead, had married Ned Bannon, proprietor of the Union Tavern in Tynecastle, a bustling city some sixty miles due South. Polly, Ned's sister, and Nora, his ten-year-old orphan niece, were not exactly close relations. Yet their visits could always be counted occasions of joy.

Suddenly he heard his father say in a quiet voice: "I'll have to go to Ettal all the same."

A sharp and throbbing silence. Francis saw that his mother had turned white.

"It isn't as if you had to. . . . Sam Mirlees, any of the men, would be glad to row up for you."

He did not answer, still gazing at her quietly, touched on his pride, his proud exclusiveness of race. Her agitation increased. She dropped all pretence of concealment, bent forward, placed nervous fingers upon his sleeve.

"To please me, Alex. You know what happened last time. Things are bad again there—awful bad, I hear."

He put his big hand over hers, warmly, reassuringly.

"You wouldn't have me run away, would you, woman?" He smiled and rose abruptly. "I'll go early and be back early . . . in plenty time for you, our daft friends, and your precious concert to the bargain."

Defeated, that strained look fixed upon her face, she watched him pull on his hip-boots. Francis, chilled and downcast, had a dreadful premonition of what must come. And indeed, when his father straightened it was towards him he turned, mildly, and with rare compunction.

"Come to think of it, boy, you'd better bide home today. Your mother could do with you about the house. There'll be plenty to see to before our visitors arrive."

Blind with disappointment, Francis made no protest. He felt his mother's arm tensely, detainingly about his shoulders.

His father stood a moment at the door, with that deep contained affection in his eyes, then he silently went out.

Though the rain ceased at noon the hours dragged dismally for Francis. While pretending not to see his mother's worried frown, he was racked by the full awareness of their situation. Here in this quiet burgh they were known for what they were—unmolested, even warily esteemed. But in Ettal, the market town four miles away where, at the Fisheries Head Office, his father, every month, was obliged to check the record of the catches, a different attitude prevailed. A hundred years before the Ettal moors had blossomed with the blood of Covenanters; and now the pendulum of oppression had relentlessly swung back. Under the leadership of the new Provost a furious religious persecution had recently arisen. Conventicles were formed, mass gatherings held in the Square, popular feelings whipped to frenzy. When the violence of the mob broke loose, the few Catholics in the town were hounded from their homes, while all others in the district received solemn warning not to show themselves upon the Ettal streets. His father's calm disregard of this threat had singled him for special execration. Last month there had been a fight in which the sturdy salmon-watcher had given good account of himself. Now, despite renewed menaces, and the careful plan to stay him, he was going again. . . . Francis flinched at his own thoughts and his small fists clenched violently. Why could not people let each other be? His father and his mother had not the same belief; yet they lived together, respecting each other, in perfect peace. His father was a good man, the best in the world . . . why should they want to do him harm? Like a blade thrust into the warmth of his life came a dread, a shrinking from that word "religion," a chill bewilderment that men could hate each other for worshipping the same God with different words.

Returning from the station at four o'clock, sombrely leaping the puddles to which Nora, his half-cousin, gaily dared him,—his mother walking with Aunt Polly, who came, dressed up and sedate, behind,—he felt the day oppressive with disaster. Nora's friskiness, the neatness of her new brown braided dress, her manifest delight in seeing him, proved but a wan diversion.

Stoically, he approached his home, the low neat greystone cottage, fronting the Cannelgate, behind a trim little green where in summer his father grew asters and begonias. There was evidence of his mother's passionate cleanliness in the shining brass knocker and the spotless doorstep. Behind the immaculately curtained windows three potted geraniums made a scarlet splash.

By this time, Nora was flushed, out of breath, her blue eyes sparkling with fun, in one of her moods of daring, impish gaiety. As they went round the side of the house to the back garden where, through his mother's arrangement, they were to play with Anselm Mealey until teatime, she bent close to Francis' ear so that her hair fell across her thin laughing face, and whispered in his ear. The puddles they had barely missed, the sappy moisture of the earth, prompted her ingenuity.

At first Francis would not listen—strangely, for Nora's presence stirred him usually to a shy swift eagerness. Standing small and reticent, he viewed her doubtfully.

"I know he will," she urged. "He always wants to play at being holy. Come on, Francis. Let's do it. Let's!"

A slow smile barely touched his sombre lips. Half-unwilling, he fetched a spade, a watering can, an old news sheet from the little toolshed at the garden end. Led by Nora, he dug a two-foot hole between the laurel bushes, watered it, then spread the paper over it. Nora artistically sprinkled the sheet with a coating of dry soil. They had barely replaced the spade when Anselm Mealey arrived, wearing a beautiful white sailor suit. Nora threw Francis a look of terrible joy.

"Hello, Anselm!" she welcomed brilliantly. "What a lovely new suit. We were waiting on you. What shall we play at?"

Anselm Mealey considered the question with agreeable condescension. He was a large boy for eleven, well-padded, with pink and white cheeks. His hair was fair and curly, his eyes were soulful. The only child of rich and devoted parents,—his father owned the profitable bone-meal works across the river,—he was already destined, by his own election and that of his pious mother, to enter Holywell, the famous Catholic college in Northern Scotland, to study for the priesthood. With Francis he served the altar at St. Columba's. Frequently he was to be found kneeling in church, his big eyes fervent with tears. Visiting nuns patted him on the head. He was acknowledged, with good reason, as a truly saintly boy.

"We'll have a procession," he said. "In honour of St. Julia. This is her feast day."

Nora clapped her hands. "Let's pretend her shrine is by the laurel bushes. Shall we dress up?"

"No." Anselm shook his head. "We're praying more than playing. But imagine I'm wearing a cope and bearing a jewelled monstrance. You're a white Carthusian Sister. And Francis, you're my acolyte. Now, are we all ready?"

A sudden qualm swept over Francis. He was not of the age to analyze his relationships; he only knew that, though Anselm claimed him fervently as his best friend, the other's gushing piety evoked in him a curious painful shame. Towards God he had a desperate reserve. It was a feeling he protected without knowing why, or what it was, like a tender nerve, deep within his body. When Anselm burningly declared in the Christian Doctrine class "I love and adore our Saviour from the bottom of my heart," Francis, fingering the marbles in his pocket, flushed a deep dark red, went home sullenly from school and broke a window.

Next morning when Anselm, already a seasoned sick-visitor, arrived at school with a cooked chicken, loftily proclaiming the object of his charity as Mother Paxton,—the old fishwife, sere with hypocrisy and cirrhosis of the liver, whose Saturday-night brawls made the Cannelgate a bedlam,—Francis, possessed, visited the cloakroom during class and opened the package, substituting for the delicious bird—which he consumed with his companions—the decayed head of a cod. Anselm's tears, and the curses of Meg Paxton, had later stirred in him a deep dark satisfaction.

Now, however, he hesitated, as if to offer the other boy an opportunity of escape. He said slowly: "Who'll go first?"

"Me, of course," Anselm gushed. He took up his position as leader. "Sing, Nora: Tantum Ergo."

In single file, at Nora's shrill pipe, the procession moved off. As they neared the laurel bushes Anselm raised his clasped hands to heaven. The next instant he stepped through the paper and squelched full-length in the mud.

For ten seconds no one moved. It was Anselm's howl as he struggled to get up that set Nora off. While Mealey blubbered clammily, "It's a sin, it's a sin!" she hopped about laughing, taunting wildly, "Fight, Anselm, fight. Why don't you hit Francis?"

"I won't, I won't," Anselm bawled. "I'll turn the other cheek."

He started to run home. Nora clung deliriously to Francis—helpless, choking, tears of laughter running down her cheeks. But Francis did not laugh. He stared in moody silence at the ground. Why had he stooped to such inanity while his father walked those hostile Ettal causeways? He was still silent as they went in to tea.

In the cosy front room, where the table was already set for the supreme rite of Scots hospitality, with the best china and all the electroplate the little household could muster, Francis' mother sat with Aunt Polly, her open rather earnest face a trifle flushed from the fire, her stocky figure showing an occasional stiffening towards the clock.

Now, after an uneasy day, shot equally with doubt and reassurance,—when she told herself how stupid were her fears,—her ears were tuned acutely for her husband's step: she was conscious of an overwhelming longing for him. The daughter of Daniel Glennie, a small and unsuccessful baker by profession, and by election an open-air preacher, leader of his own singular Christian brotherhood in Darrow, that shipbuilding town of incomparable drabness which lies some twenty miles from the city of Tynecastle, she had, at eighteen, during a week's holiday from the parental cake counter, fallen wildly in love with the young Tweedside fisher, Alexander Chisholm, and promptly married him.

In theory, the utter incompatibility of such a union foredoomed it. Reality had proved it a rare success. Chisholm was no fanatic: a quiet, easy-going type, he had no desire to influence his wife's belief. And she, on her side, sated with early piety, grounded by her peculiar father in a strange doctrine of universal tolerance, was not contentious.

Even when the first transports had subsided she knew a glowing happiness. He was, in her phrase, such a comfort about the place; neat, willing, never at a loss when it came to mending her wringer, drawing a fowl, clearing the bee-skeps of their honey. His asters were the best in Tweedside, his bantams never failed to take prizes at the show, the dovecot he had finished recently for Francis was a wonder of patient craftsmanship. There were moments, in the winter evenings when she sat knitting by the hearth, with Francis snug in bed, the wind whistling cosily around the little house, the kettle hissing on the hob, while her long raw-boned Alex padded the kitchen in his stocking feet, silently intent upon some handiwork, when she would turn to him with an odd, tender smile: "Man, I'm fond of you."

Nervously she glanced at the clock: yes, it was late, well past his usual time of homecoming. Outside a gathering of clouds was precipitating the darkness and again heavy raindrops splashed against the window-panes. Almost immediately Nora and Francis came in. She found herself avoiding her son's troubled eye.

"Well, children!" Aunt Polly summoned them to her chair and wisely apostrophized the air above their heads. "Did you have a good play? That's right. Have you washed your hands, Nora? You'll be looking forward to the concert tonight, Francis. I love a tune myself. God save us, girl, stand still. And don't forget your company manners, either, my lady—we're going to get our tea."

There was no disregarding this suggestion. With a hollow sensation of distress, intensified because she concealed it, Elizabeth rose.

"We won't wait on Alex any longer. We'll just begin." She forced a justifying smile. "He'll be in any moment now."

The tea was delicious, the scones and bannocks home-made, the preserves jelled by Elizabeth's own hands. But an air of strain lay heavily about the table. Aunt Polly made none of those dry remarks which usually gave Francis such secret joy, but sat erect, elbows drawn in, one finger crooked for her cup. A spinster, under forty, with a long, worn, agreeable face, somewhat odd in her attire, stately, composed, abstracted in her manner, she looked a model of conscious gentility, her lace handkerchief upon her lap, her nose humanly red from the hot tea, the bird in her hat brooding warmly over all.

"Come to think, Elizabeth—" She tactfully filled a pause. "They might have brought in the Mealey boy—Ned knows his father. A wonderful vocation, Anselm has." Without moving her head she touched Francis with her kindly omniscient eye. "We'll need to send you to Holywell too, young man. Elizabeth, you'd like to see your boy wag his head in a pulpit?"

"Not my only one."

"The Almighty likes the only ones." Aunt Polly spoke profoundly.

Elizabeth did not smile. Her son would be a great man, she was resolved, a famous lawyer, perhaps a surgeon; she could not bear to think of him as suffering the obscurity, the sorry hardships of the clerical life. Torn by her growing agitation she exclaimed: "I do wish Alex would come. It's . . . it's most inconsiderate. He'll keep us all late if he doesn't look sharp."

"Maybe he's not through with the tallies," Aunt Polly reflected considerately.

Elizabeth flushed painfully, out of all control. "He must be back at the bothy by now . . . he always goes there after Ettal." Desperately she tried to stem her fears. "I wouldn't wonder if he'd forgotten all about us. He's the most heedless man." She paused. "We'll give him five minutes. Another cup, Aunt Polly?"

But tea was over and could not be prolonged. There was an unhappy silence. What had happened to him? . . . Would he never, never come? Sick with anxiety, Elizabeth could restrain herself no longer. With a last glance, charged with open foreboding, towards the marble timepiece, she rose. "You'll excuse me, Aunt Polly, I'll have to run down, and see what's keeping him. I'll not be long."

Francis had suffered through these moments of suspense—haunted by the terror of a narrow wynd, heavy with darkness and surging faces and confusion, his father penned . . . fighting . . . falling under the crowd . . . the sickening crunch of his head upon the cobblestones. Unaccountably he found himself trembling. "Let me go, Mother," he said.

"Nonsense, boy." She smiled palely. "You stay and entertain our visitors."

Surprisingly, Aunt Polly shook her head. Hitherto she had betrayed no perception of the growing stress. Nor did she now. But with a penetrating staidness she remarked: "Take the boy with you, Elizabeth. Nora and I can manage fine."

There was a pause during which Francis pleaded with his eyes.

"All right . . . you can come."

His mother wrapped him in his thick coat; then, bundling into her plaid cape, she took his hand and stepped out of the warm bright room.

It was a streaming, pitch-dark night. The rain lathered the cobblestones, foamed down the gutters of the deserted streets. As they struggled up the Mercat Wynd past the distant Square and the blurred illumination of the Burgess Hall, new fear reached at Francis from the gusty blackness. He tried to combat it, setting his lips, matching his mother's increased pace with quivering determination.

Ten minutes later they crossed the river by the Border Bridge and picked their way along the waterlogged quay to Bothy No. 3. Here his mother halted, dismayed. The bothy was locked, deserted. She turned indecisively, then suddenly observed a faint beacon, vaporous in the rainy darkness, a mile up-river: Bothy No. 5, where Sam Mirlees, the underwatcher, made his lodging. Though Mirlees was an aimless, tippling fellow, he could surely give them news. She started off again, firmly, plodding across the sodden meadows, stumbling over unseen tussocks, fences, ditches. Francis, close at her side, could sense her apprehension, mounting with every step.

At last they reached the other bothy, a wooden shanty of tarred boards, stoutly planted on the riverbank, behind the high stone butt and a swathe of hanging nets. Francis could bear it no longer. Darting forward with throbbing breast, he threw open the door. Then, at the consummation of his day-long fear, he cried aloud in choking anguish, his pupils wide with shock. His father was there with Sam Mirlees, stretched on a bench, his face pale and bloodied, one arm bound up roughly in a sling, a great purple weal across his brow. Both men were in their jerseys and hip-boots, glasses and a mutchkin jar on the near-by table, a dirty crimsoned sponge beside the turbid water dipper, the hurricane swing lamp throwing a haggard yellow beam upon them, while beyond the indigo shadows crept, wavered in the mysterious corners and under the drumming roof.

His mother rushed forward, flung herself on her knees beside the bench. "Alex . . . Alex . . . are ye hurt?"

Though his eyes were muddled he smiled, or tried to, with his blenched and battered lips.

"No worse nor some that tried to hurt me, woman."

Tears sprang to her eyes, born of his wilfulness and her love for him, tears of rage against those who had brought him to this pass.

"When he came in he was near done," Mirlees interposed with a hazy gesture. "But I've stiffened him up with a dram or two."

She threw a blazing look at the other man: fuddled, as usual on Saturday night. She felt weak with anger that this sottish fool should have filled Alex up with drink on top of the dreadful hurt he had sustained. She saw that he had lost a great quantity of blood . . . she had nothing here to treat him with . . . she must get him away at once . . . at once. She murmured, tensely:—

"Could you manage home with me, Alex?"

"I think so, woman . . . if we take it slow."

She thought feverishly, battling her panic, her confusion. All her instinct was to move him to warmth, light and safety. She saw that his worst wound, a gash to the temple bone, had ceased to bleed. She swung round towards her son.

"Run back quick, Francis. Tell Polly to get ready for us. Then fetch the doctor to the house at once."

Francis, shivering as with ague, made a blind, convulsive gesture of understanding. With a last glance at his father he bent his head and set off frantically along the quay.

"Try, then, Alex . . . let me give you a hand." Bitterly dismissing Mirlees' offer of assistance which she knew to be worse than none, she helped her husband up. He swayed slowly, obediently to his feet. He was dreadfully shaky, hardly knew what he was doing. "I'll away then, Sam," he muttered, dizzily. "Good night to ye."

She bit her lip in a torment of uncertainty, yet persisted, led him out, met by the stinging sheets of rain. As the door shut behind them and he stood, unsteady, heedless of the weather, she was daunted by the prospect of that devious return, back through the mire of the fields with a helpless man in tow. But suddenly, as she hesitated, a thought illuminated her. Why had it not occurred to her before? If she took the short cut by the Tileworks Bridge she could save a mile at least, have him home and safe in bed within half an hour. She took his arm with fresh resolution. Pressing into the downpour, supporting him, she pointed their course up-river towards the bridge.

At first he did not apparently suspect her purpose, but suddenly, as the sound of rushing water struck his ear, he halted.

"Whatna way's this to come, Lisbeth? We cannot cross by the Tileworks with Tweed in such a spate."

"Hush, Alex . . . don't waste your strength by talking." She soothed him, helped him forward.

They came to the bridge, a narrow hanging span, fashioned of planks with a wire rope handrail, crossing the river at its narrowest, quite sound, though rarely used, since the Tileworks which it served had long ago shut down. As Elizabeth placed her foot upon the bridge, the blackness, the deafening near-ness of the water, caused a vague doubt, perhaps a premonition, to cross her mind. She paused, since there was not room for them to go abreast, peering back at his subdued and sodden figure, swept by a rush of strange maternal tenderness.

"Have ye got the handrail?"

"Ay, I have the handrail."

She saw plainly that the thick wire rope was in his big fist. Distracted, breathless and obsessed, she could not reason further. "Keep close to me, then." She turned and led on.

They began to cross the bridge. Halfway across his foot slid off a rain-slimed board. It would have mattered little another night. Tonight it mat-tered more, for the Tweed, in flood, had risen to the planking of the bridge. At once the racing current filled his thigh-boot. He struggled against the pull, the overpowering weight. But they had beaten the strength from him at Ettal. His other leg slipped, both boots were waterlogged, loaded as with lead.

At his cry she spun round with a scream and caught at him. As the river tore the handrail from his grip her arms enfolded him; she fought closely, desperately, for a deathless instant to sustain him. Then the sound and the darkness of the waters sucked them down.

All that night Francis waited for them. But they did not come. Next morn-ing they were found, clasped together, at low tide, in the quiet water near the sand bar.

2

ONE Thursday evening in September four years later, when Francis Chisholm ended his nightly tramp from Darrow Shipyard by veering wearily towards the blistered double headboard of Glennie's Bakery, he had reached a great decision. As he trudged down the floury passage dividing the bakehouse from the shop—his smallish figure oddly suppressed by an outsize suit of dungarees, his face grimy, beneath a man's cloth cap worn back to front—and went through the back door, placing his empty lunch pail on the scullery sink, his dark young eyes were smouldering with this purpose.

In the kitchen Malcom Glennie occupied the table—its soiled cover now, as always, littered with crockery—lolling on his elbow over *Locke's Conveyancing,* a lumpish pallid youth of seventeen, one hand massaging his oily black hair, sending showers of dandruff to his collar, the other attacking the sweetbread cooked for him by his mother on his return from the Armstrong College. As Francis took his supper from the oven—a twopenny pie and potatoes cremated there since noon—and cleared a place for himself, aware, through the torn opaque paper on the half-glazed partition door, of Mrs. Glennie serving a customer in the front shop, the son of the house threw him a glance of peevish disapproval. "Can't you make less noise when I'm studying? And God! What hands! Don't you ever wash before you eat?"

In stolid silence—his best defence—Francis picked up a knife and fork in his calloused, rivet-burned fingers.

The partition door clicked open and Mrs. Glennie solicitously scuffled in. "Are you done yet, Malcom dear? I have the nicest baked custard—just fresh eggs and milk—it won't do your indigestion a mite of harm."

He grumbled: "I've been gastric all day." Swallowing a deep bellyful of wind, he brought it back with an air of virtuous injury. "Listen to that!"

"It's the study, son, that does it." She hurried to the range. "But this'll keep your strength up . . . just try it . . . to please me."

He suffered her to remove his empty plate and to place a large dish of custard before him. As he slobbered it down she watched him tenderly, enjoying every mouthful he took, her raddled figure, in broken corsets and dowdy, gaping skirt, inclined towards him, her shrewish face with its long thin nose and pinched-in lips doting with maternal fondness.

She murmured, presently: "I'm glad you're back early tonight, son. Your father has a meeting."

"Oh, no!" Malcom reared himself, in startled annoyance. "At the Mission Hall?"

She shook her narrow head. "Open air. On the Green."

"We're not going?"

She answered with a strange, embittered vanity: "It's the only position your father ever gave us, Malcom. Until he fails at the preaching too, we'd better take it."

He protested heatedly. "You may like it, Mother. But it's damned awful for me, standing there, with Father Bible-banging, and the kids yelling 'Holy Dan.' It wasn't so bad when I was young, but now when I'm coming out for a solicitor!" He stopped short, sulkily, as the outer door opened and his father, Daniel Glennie, came gently into the room.

Holy Dan advanced to the table, absently cut himself a slice of cheese, poured a glass of milk and, still standing, began his simple meal. Changed from his working singlet, slacks and burst carpet slippers, he was still an insignificant and drooping figure in shiny black trousers, an old cut-away coat too tight and short for him, a celluloid dickey and a stringy black tie. His cuffs were of celluloid too, to save the washing; they were cracked; and his boots might have done with mending. He stooped slightly. His gaze, usually harassed, often ecstatically remote, was now thoughtful, kind, behind his steel-rimmed spectacles. As he chewed, he let it dwell in quiet consideration on Francis.

"You look tired, grandson. Have you had your dinner?"

Francis nodded. The room was brighter since the baker's entry. The eyes upon him now were like his mother's.

"There's a batch of cherry cakes I've just drawn. You can have one, if you've a mind to—on the oven rack."

At the senseless prodigality Mrs. Glennie sniffed: casting his goods about like this had made him twice a bankrupt, a failure. Her head inclined in greater resignation.

"When do you want to start? If we're going now I'll shut the shop."

He consulted his big silver watch with the yellow bone guard. "Ay, close up now, Mother, the Lord's work comes first. And besides—" sadly—"we'll have no more customers tonight."

While she pulled down the blinds on the fly-blown pastries he stood, detached, considering his address for tonight. Then he stirred. "Come, Malcom!" And to Francis: "Take care of yourself, grandson. Don't be late out your bed!"

Malcom, muttering beneath his breath, shut his book and picked up his hat. He sulkily followed his father out. Mrs. Glennie, pulling on tight black kid gloves, assumed her martyred "meeting" face. "Don't forget the dishes, now." She threw a meaning sickly smile at Francis. "It's a pity you're not coming with us!"

When they had gone he fought the inclination to lay his head upon the table. His new heroic resolution inflamed him, the thought of Willie Tulloch galvanized his tired limbs. Piling the greasy dishes into the scullery he began to wash them, rapidly probing his position, his brows tense, resentful.

The blight of enforced benefactions had lain upon him since that moment, before the funeral, when Daniel had raptly told Polly Bannon: "I'll take Elizabeth's boy. We are his only blood relations. He must come to us!"

Such rash benevolence alone would not have uprooted him. It took that later hateful scene when Mrs. Glennie, grasping at the small estate, money from his father's insurance and the sale of the furniture, had beaten down Polly's offer of guardianship, with intimidating invocations of the law.

This final acrimony had severed all contact with the Bannons—abruptly, painfully, as though he, indirectly, had been to blame: Polly, hurt and offended, yet with the air of having done her best, had undoubtedly erased him from her memory.

On his arrival at the baker's household, with all the attraction of a novelty, he was sent, a new satchel on his back, to the Darrow Academy: escorted by Malcom; straightened and brushed by Mrs. Glennie, who watched the departing scholars from the shop door with a vague proprietary air.

Alas! The philanthropic flush soon faded. Daniel Glennie was a saint, a gentle noble derided soul who passed out tracts of his own composition with his pies and every Saturday night paraded his van horse through the town with a big printed text on the beast's rump: *"Love thy neighbour as thyself."* But he lived in a heavenly dream, from which he periodically emerged, careworn, damp with sweat, to meet his creditors. Working unsparingly, with his head on Abraham's bosom and his feet in a tub of dough, he could not but forget his grandson's presence. When he remembered he would take the small boy by the hand to the back yard, with a bag of crumbs, to feed the sparrows.

Mean, shiftless yet avaricious, viewing with a self-commiserating eye her husband's progressive failure,—the sacking of the van man, of the shopgirl, the closing of one oven after another, the gradual decline to a meagre output of twopenny pies and farthing pastries,—Mrs. Glennie soon discovered in Francis an insufferable incubus. The attraction of the sum of seventy pounds she had acquired with him quickly faded, seemed dearly bought. Already wrung by a desperate economy, to her the cost of his clothing, his food, his schooling became a perpetual Calvary. She counted his mouthfuls resignedly. When his trousers wore out she "made down" an old green suit of Daniel's, a relic of her husband's youth, of such outlandish pattern and colour it provided derisive outcry in the streets, shrouded the boy's life in misery. Though Malcom's fees at the Academy were paid upon the nail she usually succeeded in forgetting Francis' until, trembling, pale with humiliation, having publicly been called as a defaulter before the class, he was forced to approach her. Then she would gasp, feign a heart attack by fumbling at her withered bosom, count out the shillings as though he drew away her very blood.

Though he bore it with stoic endurance the sense of being alone . . . alone . . . was terrible for the little boy. Demented with sorrow, he took long solitary walks, combing the sick country vainly for a stream in which to guddle trout. He would scan the outgoing ships, consumed with longing, stuffing his cap between his teeth to stifle his despair. Caught between conflicting creeds, he knew not where he stood; his bright and eager mind was dulled, his face turned sullen. His only happiness came on the nights that Malcom and Mrs. Glennie were from home, when he sat opposite Daniel by the kitchen fire watching the little baker turning the pages of his Bible, in perfect silence, with a look of ineffable joy.

Daniel's quiet but inflexible resolve not to interfere with the boy's religion —how could he, when he preached universal tolerance!—was an added, everpresent goad to Mrs. Glennie. To a "Christian" like herself, who was saved, this reminder of her daughter's folly was anathema. It made the neighbours talk.

The climax came at the end of eighteen months when Francis, with ungrateful cleverness, had the bad taste to beat Malcom in an essay competition open to the school. It was not to be endured. Weeks of nagging wore the baker down. He was on the verge of another failure. It was agreed that Francis' education was complete. Smiling archly for the first time in months, Mrs. Glennie assured him that now he was a little man, fit to contribute to the household, to take his coat off and prove the nobility of toil. He went to work in Darrow Shipyard as a rivet-boy, twelve years old, at three and six a week.

By quarter-past seven he had finished the dishes. With greater alacrity, he spruced himself before the inch of mirror and went out. It was still light, but the night air made him cough and turn up his jacket as he hurried into High Street, past the livery stable and the Darrow Spirit Vaults, reaching at length the doctor's shop on the corner, with its two bulbous red and green vials and its square brass plate: DR. SUTHERLAND TULLOCH: PHYSICIAN AND SURGEON. Francis' lips were parted, faintly, as he entered.

The shop was dim and aromatic with the smell of aloes, assafœtida and liquorice root. Shelves of dark green bottles filled one side and at the end three wooden steps gave access to the small back surgery where Dr. Tulloch held his consultations. Behind the long counter, wrapping physic on a marble slab spattered with red sealing wax, stood the doctor's eldest son, a sturdy freckled boy of sixteen with big hands, sandy colouring and a slow taciturn smile.

He smiled now, staunchly, as he greeted Francis. Then the two boys looked away, avoiding one other, each reluctant to view the affection in the other's eyes.

"I'm late, Willie!" Francis kept his gaze intently on the skirting of the counter.

"I was late myself . . . and I've to deliver these medicines for Father, bless him." Now that Willie had begun his medical curriculum at the Armstrong College, Dr. Tulloch had, with solemn facetiousness, accredited him his assistant.

There was a pause. Then the older boy threw a secret glance towards his friend.

"Have you decided?"

Francis' gaze was still downcast. He nodded broodingly, his lips set. "Yes."

"You're right, Francis." Approval flooded Willie's plain and stolid features. "I wouldn't have stood it so long."

"I wouldn't . . . either . . ." Francis mumbled, "except for . . . well . . . my grandfather and you." His thin young face, concealed and sombre, reddened deeply as the last words came out with a rush.

Flushing in sympathy, Willie muttered: "I found out the train for you.

There's a through leaves Alstead every Saturday at six-thirty-five . . . Quiet. Here's Dad." He broke off, with a warning glance, when the surgery door opened and Dr. Tulloch appeared, showing his last patient out. As the doctor returned towards the boys, a brusque, bristling dark-skinned figure in pepper-and-salt tweeds, his bushy hair and glossy whiskers seemed to spark with sheer vitality. For one who bore the awful reputation of the town's professed free-thinker, open adherent of Robert Ingersoll and Professor Darwin, he had a most disarming charm, and the look of one who would be useful in a sick-room. Because the hollows in Francis' cheeks made him grave, he cracked a frightful joke. "Well, my lad—that's another one killed off! Oh, he's not dead yet! Soon will be! Such a nice man too, leaves a large family." The boy's smile was too drawn to please him. He cocked his clear, challenging eye, mindful of his own troubled boyhood: "Cheer up, young housemaid's knee—it'll all be the same in a hundred years." Before Francis could reply the doctor laughed briefly, thrust his hard square hat on the back of his head and began pulling on his driving gloves. On his way out to his gig he called back: "Don't fail to bring him for supper, Will. Hot prussic acid served at nine!"

An hour later, with the physic delivered, the two boys made their way in unspeaking comradeship towards Willie's house, a large dilapidated villa facing the Green. As they talked in low voices of the daring promise of the day beyond tomorrow, Francis' spirits lifted. Life never seemed so hostile in Willie Tulloch's company. And yet, perversely, their friendship had begun in strife. After school, one day, larking down Castle Street with a dozen classmates, Willie's gaze had strayed to the Catholic church, ugly but inoffensive, beside the gasworks. "Come on," he shouted, in animal spirits. "I've got sixpence. Let's go in and get our sins forgiven!" Then, glancing round, he saw Francis in the group. He reddened with healthy shame. He had not meant the stupid jibe, which would have passed unheeded if Malcom Glennie had not pounced on it and fanned it skilfully into the occasion for a fight.

Incited by the rest, Francis and Willie fought a bloody indecisive battle on the Green. It was a good fight, rich in uncomplaining courage, and when the darkness stopped it, though neither was the victor, each had clearly had enough. But the spectators, with the cruelty of youth, refused to let the quarrel rest. On the next night, after school, the contestants were brought together, whetted with the taunt of cowardice and set to batter each other's already battered head. Again, bloody, spent, yet dogged, neither would concede the victory. Thus for a dreadful week they were matched, like game-cocks, to make sport for their baser fellows. The inhuman conflict, motiveless and endless, became, for each, a nightmare. Then, on the Saturday, the two met unexpectedly, face to face, alone. An agonizing moment followed, then the earth opened, the sky melted and each had an arm round the other's neck, Willie blubbering: "I don't want to fight you, I like ye, man!"—while

Francis, knuckling his purple eyes, wept back: "Willie, I like you best in the whole of Darrow!"

They were halfway across the Green, a public open space carpeted by dingy grass, with a forlorn bandstand in the centre, a rusty iron urinal at the far end and a few benches, mostly without backs, where pale-faced children played and loafers smoked and argued noisily, when suddenly Francis saw, with a tightening of his skin, that they must pass his grandfather's meeting. At the end farthest from the urinal a small red banner had been planted bearing the words in tarnished gilt: *"Peace on Earth to Men of Goodwill."* Opposite the banner stood a portable harmonium furnished with a camp-stool on which Mrs. Glennie sat, wearing her victim's air, with Malcom, glumly clasping a hymn-book, beside her. Between the banner and the harmonium on a low wooden stand, surrounded by some thirty persons, was Holy Dan.

As the boys drew up on the fringe of the gathering Daniel had finished his opening prayer and, with his uncovered head thrown back, was beginning his address. It was a gentle and beautiful plea. It expressed Daniel's burning conviction, bared his simple soul. His doctrine was based on brotherhood, the love of one another and of God. Man should help his fellow man, bring peace and goodwill to earth. If only he could lead humanity to that ideal! He had no quarrel with the churches but chastised them mildly: it was not the form which mattered but the fundamentals, humility and charity. Yes, and toler-ance! It was worthless to voice these sentiments if one did not practise them.

Francis had heard his grandfather speak before, and felt a throb of dogged sympathy for these views which made Holy Dan the laughing-stock of half the town. Now, edged by his wild intention, his heart swelled in understand-ing and affection, in longing for a world free of cruelty and hate. Suddenly, as he stood listening, he saw Joe Moir, the skip of his riveting squad at the Shipyard, sidle up the outskirts of the meeting. Accompanying Joe was the gang that hung about the Darrow Vaults, with an armament of bricks, de-cayed fruit, and oily waste thrown out from the boiler works. Moir was a ribald likeable giant, who, when drunk, gleefully pursued salvation rallies and other outdoor conclaves. He fingered a fistful of dripping waste and shouted: "Hey! Dan! Give us a song and dance!"

Francis' eyes dilated in his pale face. They were going to break up the meeting! He had a vision of Mrs. Glennie, clawing a ripe tomato from her splattered hair, of Malcom, with a greasy rag plastering his hateful face. His being exulted with a wild ecstatic joy.

Then he saw Daniel's face: still unconscious of the danger, lit by a strange intensity, every word throbbing, born of unquenchable sincerity, from the depths of his soul.

He started forward. Without knowing how, or why, he found himself at Moir's side, restraining his elbow, pleading breathlessly: "Don't Joe! Please don't! We're friends, aren't we?"

"Hell!" Moir glanced down, his boozy scowl melting to friendly recognition. "For Christ's sake, Francis!" Then, slowly, "I forgot he was your grandpa." A desperate pause. Then, commandingly, to his followers: "Come on lads, we'll go up to the Square and take it out on the Hallelujas!"

As they moved off the harmonium wheezed with life. No one but Willie Tulloch knew why the thunderbolt had not fallen.

A minute later, entering his house, he asked, baffled yet impressed: "Why did you, Francis?"

Francis answered shakily: "I don't know . . . There's something in what he says . . . I've had enough hating these last four years. My father and mother wouldn't have got drowned if people hadn't hated him . . ." He broke off, inarticulate, ashamed.

Silently, Willie led the way to the living room, which, after the outer dusk, glowed with light and sound and a prodigal untidy comfort. It was a long high maroon-papered chamber, asprawl with broken red plush furniture, the chairs castorless, the vases cracked and glued together, the bell pull tugged out, a litter of vials, labels, pillboxes on the mantelpiece and of toys, books and children upon the worn ink-stained Axminster. Though it was shockingly near nine o'clock none of the Tulloch family was abed. Willie's seven young brothers and sisters, Jean, Tom, Richard,—a list so complex even their father admitted to forgetting it,—were diversely occupied in reading, writing, drawing, scuffling and swallowing their supper of hot bread and milk while their mother Agnes Tulloch, a dreamy voluptuous woman with her hair half down and her bosom open, had picked the baby from his crib upon the hearth and, having removed its steaming napkin, now placidly refreshed the nuzzling bare-bottomed infant at her creamy, fire-lit breast.

She smiled her welcome, unperturbed, to Francis. "Here you are then, boys. Jean, set out more plates and spoons. Richard, leave Sophia alone. And Jean, dear, a fresh diaper for Sutherland from the line! Also see that the kettle's boiling for your father's toddy. What lovely weather we are having. Dr. Tulloch says there is much inflammation about though. Be seated, Francis. Thomas, didn't your father tell you to keep away from the others!" The doctor was always bringing home some disorder: measles one month, chicken-pox the next. Now Thomas, aged six, was the victim. His poll shorn and smelling of carbolic, he was happily disseminating ringworm through the tribe.

Squeezed on the crowded twanging sofa beside Jean, at fourteen the image of her mother, with the same creamy skin, the same placid smile, Francis supped his bread and milk flavoured with cinnamon. He was still upset from his recent outburst; there was an enormous lump inside his chest, his mind was a maze of confusion. Here was another problem for his aching brain. Why were these people so kind, happy, and contented? Reared by an impious rationalist to deny, or rather to ignore, the existence of their God, they were damned, hell fire already licked their feet.

At quarter-past nine the crunch of the dogcart's wheels was heard on the gravel. Dr. Tulloch strode in, a shout went up, he was at once the centre of an attacking mob. When the tumult stilled the doctor had bussed his wife heartily, was in his chair, a glass of toddy in his hand, slippers on his feet, the infant Sutherland goggling on his knee.

Catching Francis' eye, he raised his steaming tumbler in friendly satire. "Didn't I tell you there was poison going! Strong drink is raging—eh, Francis?"

Seeing his father in high humour, Willie was tempted to relate the story of the prayer meeting. The doctor slapped his thigh, smiling at Francis. "Good for you, my wee Roman Voltaire. I will disagree to the death with what you say and defend with my life your right to say it! Jean, stop making sheep's eyes at the poor laddie. I thought ye wanted to be a nurse! Ye'll have me a grandfather before I'm forty. Eh, well—" He sighed suddenly, toasting his wife. "We'll never get to heaven, woman—but at least we get our meat and drink."

Later, at the front door, Willie gripped Francis by the hand.

"Good luck . . . Write to me when you're there."

At five next morning, while all was still dark, the Shipyard hooter sounded, long and dolorous, over the cowering dreariness of Darrow. Half senseless with sleep, Francis tumbled out of bed and into his dungarees, stumbled downstairs. The frigid morning, pale yet murky, met him like a blow as he joined the march of silent shivering figures, hurrying with bent head and huddled shoulders towards the Shipyard gates.

Over the weighbridge, past the checker's window, inside the gates . . . Gaunt spectres of ships rose dimly in their stocks around him. Beside the half-formed skeleton of a new ironclad Joe Moir's squad was mustering: Joe and the assistant plater, the holders-on, the two other rivet-boys and himself.

He lit the charcoal fire, blew the bellows beneath the forge. Silently, unwillingly, as in a dream, the squad set itself to work. Moir lifted his sledge, the hammers rang, swelled and strengthened, throughout the Shipyard.

Holding the rivets, white-hot from the brazier, Francis shinned up the ladder and thrust them quickly through the bolt-holes in the frame, where they were hammered flat and tight, annealing the great sheets of metal which formed the ship's hull. The work was fierce: blistering by the brazier, freezing on the ladders. The men were paid by piece work. They wanted rivets fast, faster than the boys could give them. And the rivets must be heated to the proper incandescence. If they were not malleable the men threw them back at the boys. Up and down the ladder, to and from the fires, scorched, smoky, with inflamed eyes, panting, perspiring, Francis fed the platers all day long.

In afternoon the work went faster: the men seemed careless, straining every nerve, unsparing of their bodies. The closing hour passed in a swimming daze with ear drums tense for the final hooter.

At last, at last it sounded. What blessed relief! Francis stood still, moistening his cracked lips, deafened by the cessation of all sound. On the way home, grimed and sweaty, through his tiredness, he thought: Tomorrow . . .

tomorrow. That strange glitter returned to his eye, he squared his shoulders.

That night he took the wooden box down from its hiding place in the disused oven and changed his hoard of silver and coppers, saved with agonizing slowness, into half a sovereign. The golden coin, clutched deep in his trouser pocket, fevered him. With a queer, exalted flush he asked Mrs. Glennie for a needle and thread. She snubbed him, then threw him suddenly a veiled appraising glance.

"Wait! There's a reel in the top drawer—by that card of needles. You can take it." She watched him go out.

In the privacy of his bare and wretched room above the bakehouse he folded the coin in a square of paper, sewed it firm and tight inside the lining of his coat. He had a sense of glad security as he came down to give her back the thread.

The following day, Saturday, the Shipyard closed at twelve. The thought that he would never enter these gates again so elated him that at dinner he could scarcely eat; he felt his flushed restlessness more than enough to raise some sharp inquiry from Mrs. Glennie. To his relief she made no comment. As soon as he left the table, he edged out of the house, slipped down East Street, then fairly took to his heels.

Outside the town, he slipped into a brisk walk. His heart was singing within him. It was pathetic commonplace: the timeworn flight of all unhappy childhood. Yet for him it was the road to freedom. Once he was in Manchester he could find work at the cotton-mills, he was sure, doubly sure. He covered the fifteen miles to the railway Junction in four hours. It was striking six o'clock as he entered Alstead Station.

Seated under an oil lamp on the draughty deserted platform, he opened his penknife, cut the sewing on his jacket, removed the folded paper, took the shining coin from within. A porter appeared on the platform, some other passengers, then the booking office opened.

He took his place at the grille, demanded his ticket.

"Nine and six," the clerk said, punching the green cardboard slip into the machine.

Francis gasped with relief: he had not, after all, miscalculated the fare. He pushed his money through the grille.

There was a pause. "What's the game? I said nine and six."

"I gave you half a sovereign."

"Oh, you did! Try that again, young feller, and I'll have you run in!" The clerk indignantly flung the coin back at him.

It was not a half-sovereign but a bright new farthing.

In anguished stupor, Francis saw the train tear in, take up its freight, and go whistling into the night. Then his mind, groping dully, struck the heart of the enigma. The sewing, when he ripped it open, was not his own clumsy stitching but a close firm seam. In a withering flash he knew who had taken his money: Mrs. Glennie.

At half-past nine, outside the colliery village of Sanderston, in the dank wet mist which blurred his gig-lamps, a man in a dogcart almost ran down the solitary figure keeping the middle of the road. Only one person was likely to be driving in such a place on such a night. Dr. Tulloch, holding in his startled beast, peered downwards through the fog, his masterly invective suddenly cut short.

"Great Lord Hippocrates! It's you. Get in. Quick, will you—before the mare pulls my arms from their sockets." Tulloch wrapped the rug about his passenger; proceeded without questions; he knew the virtue of a healing silence.

By half-past ten Francis was drinking hot broth before the fire in the doctor's living room, now bereft of its occupants and so unnaturally still the cat slept peacefully on the hearth-rug. A moment later Mrs. Tulloch came in, her hair in plaits, her quilted dressing gown open above her nightgown. She stood with her husband studying the dead-beat boy, who seemed unconscious of their presence, their murmured converse, wrapped in a curious apathy. Though he tried to smile, he could not when the doctor came forward, producing his stethoscope with a jocular air: "I'll bet my boots that cough of yours is a put-up job." But he submitted, opening his shirt, letting the doctor tap, and listen to, his chest.

Tulloch's saturnine face wore a queer expression as he straightened himself. His fund of humour had surprisingly dried up. He darted a look at his wife, bit his full lip, and suddenly kicked the cat.

"Damn it to hell!" he cried. "We use our children to build our battleships. We sweat them in our coal mines and our cotton-mills. We're a Christian country. Well! I'm proud to be a pagan." He turned brusquely, quite fiercely, to Francis. "Look here, boy, who are these folks you knew in Tynecastle? What's that—Bannon, eh? The Union Tavern. Get away home now and into bed unless you want treble pneumonia."

Francis went home, resistance crushed in him. All the next week Mrs. Glennie wore a martyred frown and Malcom a new checked waistcoat: price half a sovereign at the stores.

It was a dire week for Francis. His left side hurt him, especially when he coughed; he had to drag himself to work. He was aware, dimly, that his grandfather fought a battle for him. But Daniel was beaten down, defeated. All the little baker could do was to offer, humbly, some cherry cakes that Francis could not eat.

When Saturday afternoon came round he had not the strength to go out. He lay upstairs in his bedroom gazing in hopeless lethargy through the window.

Suddenly he started, his heart gave a great and unbelieving bound. In the street below, slowly approaching, like a barque navigating strange and dangerous waters, was a hat, a thing of memory, unique, unmistakable. Yes, yes: and the gold-handled umbrella, tightly rolled, the short sealskin jacket with the braided buttons. He cried out weakly, with pale lips: "Aunt Polly."

The shop door pinged below. Dithering to his feet, he crept downstairs, poised himself, trembling, behind the half-glazed door.

Polly was standing, very erect, in the centre of the floor, her lips pursed, her gaze sweeping the shop, as though amusedly inspecting it. Mrs. Glennie had half-risen, to confront her. Lounging against the counter, his mouth half-open, gaping from one to the other, was Malcom.

Aunt Polly's vision came to rest above the baker's wife. "Mrs. Glennie, if I remember right!"

Mrs. Glennie was at her worst: still unchanged, wearing her dirty forenoon wrapper, her blouse open at the neck, a loose tape hanging from her waist. "What do you want?"

Aunt Polly raised her eyebrows. "I have come to see Francis Chisholm." "He's out."

"Indeed! Then I'll wait till he comes in." Polly arranged herself on the chair by the counter as though prepared to remain all day.

There was a pause. Mrs. Glennie's face had turned a dirty red. She remarked, aside: "Malcom! Run round to the bakehouse and fetch your father."

Malcom answered shortly: "He went to the Hall five minutes ago. He won't be back till tea."

Polly removed her gaze from the ceiling, brought it critically to bear on Malcom. She smiled slightly when he flushed, then, entertained, she glanced away.

For the first time Mrs. Glennie showed signs of uneasiness. She burst out angrily: "We're busy people here, we can't sit about all day. I've told you the boy is out. Like enough he won't be back till all hours—with the company he keeps. He's a regular worry with his late hours and bad habits. Isn't that so, Malcom?"

Malcom nodded sulkily.

"You see!" Mrs. Glennie rushed on. "If I was to tell you everything you'd be amazed. But it makes no difference, we're Christian people here, we look after him. You have my word for it—he's perfectly well and happy."

"I'm glad to hear it," Polly spoke primly, politely stifling a slight yawn with her glove, "for I've come to take him away."

"What!" Taken aback, Mrs. Glennie fumbled at the neck of her blouse, the colour flooding, then fading from, her face.

"I have a doctor's certificate," Aunt Polly enunciated, almost masticated, the formidable phrase with a deadly relish, "that the boy is underfed, overworked and threatened with a pleurisy."

"It's not true."

Polly pulled a letter from her muff and tapped it significantly with the head of her umbrella. "Can you read the Queen's English?"

"It's a lie, a wicked lie. He's as fat and well fed as my own son!"

There was an interruption. Francis, flat against the door, following the scene in an agony of suspense, leaned too heavily against the ricketty catch. The door flew open, he shot into the middle of the shop. There was a silence.

Aunt Polly's preternatural calm had deepened. "Come over, boy. And stop shaking. Do you want to stay here?"

"No, I don't."

Polly threw a look of justification towards the ceiling. "Then go and pack your things."

"I haven't anything to pack."

Polly stood up slowly, pulling on her gloves. "There's nothing to keep us."

Mrs. Glennie took a step forward, white with fury. "You can't walk over me. I'll have the law on you."

"Go ahead, my woman." Polly meaningly restored the letter to her muff. "Then maybe we'll find out how much of the money that came from the sale of poor Elizabeth's furniture has been spent on her son and how much on yours."

Again there was a shattered silence. The baker's wife stood, pale, malignant and defeated, one hand clutching at her bosom.

"Oh, let him go, Mother," Malcom whined. "It'll be good riddance."

Aunt Polly, cradling her umbrella, examined him from top to toe. "Young man, you're a fool!" She swung round towards Mrs. Glennie. "As for you, woman," looking straight over her head, "you're another!"

Taking Francis triumphantly by the shoulder, she propelled him, bare-headed, from the shop.

They proceeded in this fashion towards the station, her glove grasping the fabric of his jacket firmly, as though he were some rare and captive creature who might at any moment escape. Outside the station she bought him, without comment, a bag of Abernethy biscuits, some cough drops, and a brand-new bowler hat. Seated opposite him in the train, serene, singular, erect, observing him moisten the dry biscuits with tears of thankfulness, extinguished almost by his new hat which enveloped him to the ears, she remarked with half-closed, judicial eyes:—

"I always knew that creature was no lady, I could see it in her face. You made an awful mistake letting her get hold of you, Francis dear. The next thing we'll do is get your hair cut!"

3

IT WAS wonderful these frosty mornings to lie warm in bed until Aunt Polly brought his breakfast, a great plate of bacon and eggs still sizzling, boiling black tea and a pile of hot toast, all on an oval metal tray stamped *Allgood's Old Ale*. Sometimes he woke early, in an agony of apprehension; then came the blessed knowledge that he need no longer fear the hooter. With a sob of relief he burrowed more deeply into his thick yellow blankets, in his cosy bedroom with its paper of climbing sweet peas, its stained boards and wool-work rug, a lithograph of Allgood's Prize Brewery Dray Horse on one wall, of Pope Gregory on another, and a little china holy-water font with a sprig of Easter palm stuck sideways in it by the door. The pain in his side was gone, he seldom coughed, his cheeks were filling out. The novelty of leisure was like a strange caress and, though the uncertainty of his future still troubled him, he received it gratefully.

On this fine morning of the last day of October, Aunt Polly sat on the edge of his bed exhorting him to eat. "Lay in, boy! That'll stick to your ribs!" There were three eggs on the plate, the bacon was crisp and streaky, he had forgotten that food could taste so good.

As he balanced the tray on his knees, he sensed an unusual festivity in her manner. And soon she gave him one of her profound nods.

"I've news for you today, young man—if you can stand it."

"News, Aunt Polly?"

"A little excitement to cheer you up—after your dull month with Ned and me." She smiled dryly at the quick protest in his warm brown eyes. "Can't you guess what it is?"

He studied her with the deep affection which her unceasing kindness had awakened in him. The homely angular face—poor-complexioned, the long upper lip downed with hair, a tufted blemish at the angle of the cheek—was now familiar and beautiful.

"I can't think, Aunt Polly."

She was moved to her short rare laugh, a little snort of satisfaction at her success in provoking his curiosity.

"What's happened to your wits, boy? I believe too much sleep has addled them."

He smiled happily in sympathy. It was true that the routine of his convalescence had hitherto been tranquil. Encouraged by Polly, who had feared for his lungs,—she had a dread of "consumption," which "ran" in her family,—he had usually lain abed until ten. Dressed, he accompanied her on her shopping, a stately progress through the main streets of Tynecastle which, since Ned ate largely and nothing but the best, demanded great prodding of poultry and sniffing of steak. These excursions were revealing. He could see that it pleased Aunt Polly to be "known," deferred to, in the best stores. She would wait, aloof and prim, until her favourite shopman was free to serve her. Above all, she was ladylike. That word was her touchstone, the criterion of her actions, even of her dresses, made by the local milliner in such dreadful taste they sometimes evoked a covert snigger from the vulgar. In the street she had a graduated series of bows. To be recognized, greeted by some local personage—the surveyor, the sanitary inspector or the chief constable—afforded her a joy which, though sternly concealed, was very great. Erect, the bird in her hat atwitter, she would murmur to Francis: "That was Mr. Austin, the tramway manager . . . a friend of your uncle's . . . a fine man." The height of her gratification was reached when Father Gerald Fitzgerald, the handsome portly priest of St. Dominic's, gave her in passing his gracious and slightly condescending smile. Every forenoon they would stop in at the church and, kneeling, Francis would be conscious of Polly's intent profile, the lips moving silently, above her rough chapped reverent hands. Afterwards she bought him something for himself, a stout pair of shoes, a book, a bag of aniseed drops. When he protested, often with tears in his eyes, as she opened her worn purse, she would simply press his arm and shake her head. "Your uncle won't take 'no.'" She was touchingly proud of her relationship with Ned, her association with the Union Tavern.

The Union stood near the docks at the corner of Canal and Dyke Streets, with an excellent view of the adjacent tenements, of coal barges, and the terminus of the new horse tramway. The brown painted stucco building was of two stories, and the Bannons lived above the tavern. Every morning at half-past seven Maggie Magoon, the scrubwoman, opened the saloon and began, talking to herself, to clean it. At eight precisely Ned Bannon came down, in his braces, but closely shaved, with his forelock oiled, and strewed the floor with fresh sawdust from the box behind the bar. It was unnecessary: a kind of ritual. Next, he inspected the morning, took in the milk and crossed the back yard to feed his whippets. He kept thirteen—to prove that he was not superstitious.

Soon the first of the regulars began to drop in, Scanty Magoon always in the van, hobbling on his leather padded stumps to his favourite corner, followed by a few dockers, a tram driver or two, returning from the night shift. These workmen did not stop: only long enough to down their half of spirits and chase it with a glass, a schooner, or a pint of beer. But Scanty was a permanent, a kind of faithful watchdog, gazing propitiatingly at Ned as he stood bland, unconscious, behind the bar with its sombre woodwork and the framed notice: GENTLEMEN BEHAVE OTHERS MUST.

Ned, at fifty, was a big thick figure of a man. His face was full and yellowish, with prominent eyes, very solemn in repose, matching his dark clothes. He was neither genial nor flashy, the qualities popularly attributed to a publican. He had a kind of solemn, bilious dignity. He was proud of his reputation, his establishment. His parents had been driven out of Ireland by the potato famine, he had known poverty and starvation as a boy, but he had succeeded against inconceivable odds. He had a "free" house, stood well with the licencing authorities and the brewers, had many influential friends. He said, in effect, The drink trade is respectable and I prove it. He set his face against young men drinking and refused rudely to serve any woman under forty: there was no *Family Department* in the Union Tavern. He hated disorder, at the first sound of it he would rap crossly with an old shoe—maintained handy for that purpose—on the bar, and keep rapping till the discord ceased. Though a heavy drinker himself he was never seen the worse for it. Perhaps his grin was loose, his eye inclined to wander on those rare evenings which he deemed "an occasion," such as St. Patrick's night, Halloween, Hogmanay, or after a day's dog racing when one of his whippets had added another medal to the galaxy on the heavy watch-chain that spanned his stomach. At any rate, on the following day he would wear a sheepish air and send Scanty up for Father Clancy, the curate at St. Dominic's. When he had made his confession he rose heavily, dusting his knees, from the boards of the back room and pressed a sovereign for the poor-box into the young priest's hand. He had a healthy respect for the clergy. For Father Fitzgerald, the parish priest, he had, indeed, considerable awe.

Ned was reputed "comfortable," he ate well, gave freely and, distrusting stocks and shares, had money invested in "bricks and mortar." Since Polly had a competence of her own, inherited from Michael, the dead brother, he had no anxiety on her account.

Though slow to form an affection, Ned was, in his own cautious word, "taken" with Francis. He liked the boy's unobtrusiveness, the sparseness of his speech, the quiet way he held himself, his silent gratitude. The sombreness of the young face, caught unguarded, in repose, made him frown dumbly, and scratch his head.

In the afternoon Francis would sit with him in the half-empty bar, drowsy with food, the sunlight slanting churchwise through the musty air, listening with Scanty to Ned's genial talk. Scanty Magoon, husband and encumbrance of the worthy witless Maggie, was so named because there was not enough of him, only in fact a torso. He had lost his legs from gangrene caused by some obscure disorder of the circulation. Capitalizing on his complaint, he had promptly "sold himself to the doctors," signing a document which would deliver his body to the dissecting slab on his demise. Once the purchase price was drunk, a sinister aura settled on the bleary, loquacious, wily, unfortunate old scamp. An object now of popular awe, in his cups he indignantly declared himself defrauded. "I never got enough for myself. Them bloody scalpers! But they'll never get ahold of me poor old Adam! God damn the fear! I'll enlist for a sailor and drown myself."

Occasionally Ned would let Francis draw a beer for Scanty, partly for charity, partly to give the boy the thrill of the "engine." As the ivory-handled pull came back, filling the mug—Scanty prompting anxiously, "Get a head on her, boy!"—the foamy brew smelled so nutty and good Francis wanted to taste it. Ned nodded permission, then smiled in slow delight at the wryness of his nephew's face. "It's a acquired taste," he gravely asserted. He had a number of such clichés, from "Women and beer don't mix," to "A man's best friend is his own pound note," which, through frequency and profundity of utterance, had been hallowed into epigrams.

Ned's gravest, most tender affection was reserved for Nora, daughter of Michael Bannon. He was devoted to his niece who when three had lost her brother from tuberculosis, and her father through that same murderous malady, so fatal to the Celtic race, two years later. Ned had brought her up, sent her off at the age of thirteen to St. Elizabeth's, the best convent boarding school in Northumberland. It was a genuine pleasure for him to pay the heavy fees. He watched her progress with a fond indulgent eye. When she came home for the holidays he was a new man: spryer, never seen in braces, ponderously devising excursions and amusements and, lest anything should offend her, much stricter in the bar.

"Well—" Aunt Polly was gazing half-reproachfully across the breakfast tray at Francis. "I see I'll have to tell you what it's all about. In the first place your uncle's decided to give a party tonight to celebrate Halloween . . . and"—momentarily she dropped her eyes—"for another reason. We'll have a goose, a four-pound black bun, raisins for the snapdragon, and of course the apples—your uncle gets special ones at Lang's market garden in Gosforth. Maybe you'll go over for them this afternoon. It's a nice walk."

"Certainly, Aunt Polly. Only, I'm not quite sure of where it is."

"Someone'll show you the way." Polly composedly produced her main surprise. "Someone who's coming home from her school to spend a long weekend with us."

"Nora!" he exclaimed abruptly.

"The same." She nodded, took up his tray and rose. "Your uncle's pleased as punch she's got leave. Hurry up and dress now, like a good boy. We're all going to the station to meet the little monkey at eleven."

When she had gone Francis lay staring in front of him with a queer perplexity. This unexpected announcement of Nora's arrival had taken him aback, and strangely thrilled him. He had always liked her, of course. But now he faced the prospect of meeting her again with an odd new feeling, between diffidence and eagerness. To his surprise and confusion he suddenly found himself reddening to the roots of his hair. He jumped up hurriedly and began to pull on his clothes.

Francis and Nora started off, at two o'clock, on their excursion, taking the tram across the city to the suburb of Clermont, then walking across country toward Gosforth, each with a hand on the big wicker basket, swinging it between them.

It was four years since Francis had seen Nora and, stupidly tongue-tied all through lunch, when Ned had surpassed himself in massive playfulness, he was still painfully shy of her. He remembered her as a child. Now she was nearly fifteen and, in her modestly long navy-blue skirt and bodice, she seemed quite grown-up, more elusive and unreadable than ever before. She had small hands and feet and a small, alert provoking face, which could be brave or suddenly timid. Though she was tall and awkward from her growth her bones were fine and slender. Her eyes were teasing, darkly blue against her pale skin. The cold made them sparkle, made her little nostrils pink.

Occasionally, across the basket handle, his fingers touched Nora's. The sensation was remarkable: sweet and warmly confusing. Her hands were the nicest things to touch that he had ever known. He could not speak, did not dare look at her, though from time to time he felt her looking at him and smiling. Though the golden blaze of the autumn was past, the woods still glowed with bright red embers. To Francis the colours of the trees, of the fields and sky, had never appeared more vivid. They were like a singing in his ears.

Suddenly she laughed outright and, tossing back her hair, began to run. Attached to her by the basket he raced like the wind alongside until she drew up, gasping, her eyes sparkling like frost on a sunny morning.

"Don't mind me, Francis. I get wild sometimes. I can't help it. It's being out of school, perhaps."

"Don't you like it there?"

"I do and I don't. It's funny and strict. Could you believe it?" She laughed, with a little rush of disconcerting innocence. "They make us wear our night-gowns when we take a bath! Tell me, did you ever think of me all the time you were away?"

"Yes." He stumbled out the answer.

"I'm glad . . . I thought of you." She threw him a swift glance, made as though to speak, and was silent.

Presently they reached the Gosforth market garden. Geordie Lang, Ned's good friend and the owner of the garden, was in the orchard, among the half-denuded trees, burning leaves. He gave them a friendly nod, an invitation to join him. They raked the crackling brown and yellow leaves towards the great smouldering cone he had already built, until the smell of the leaf smoke impregnated their clothing. It was not work but glorious sport. They forgot their earlier embarrassment, competed as to who should rake the most. When he had raked a great pile for himself Nora mischievously despoiled it. Their laughter rang in the high clear air. Geordie Lang grinned in broad sympathy. "That's women, lad. Take your pile and laugh at ye."

At last Lang waved them towards the apple shed, a wooden erection at the end of the orchard.

"You've earned your keep. Go and help yourself!" he called after them. "And give my best respects to Mr. Bannon. Tell him I'll look in for my drop of spirits sometime this week."

The apple shed was soft with crepuscular twilight. They climbed the ladder to the loft where, spaced out on straw, not touching, were rows and rows of the Ribston Pippins for which the garden was renowned. While Francis filled the basket, crouching under the low roof, Nora sat cross-legged on the straw, picked an apple, shone it on her bony hip and began to eat.

"Oh, my, it's good," she said. "Have one, Francis?"

He sat down opposite, took the apple she held out to him. The taste was delicious. They watched each other eating. When her small teeth bit through the amber skin into the crisp white flesh, little spurts of juice ran down her chin. He did not feel so shy in the dark little loft, but dreamy and warm, suffused with the joy of living. He had never liked anything so much as being here, in the garden, eating the apple she had given him. Their eyes, meeting frequently, smiled; but she had a half-smile, strange and inward, that seemed entirely for herself.

"I dare you to eat the seeds," she teased suddenly; then added quickly: "No, don't, Francis! Sister Margaret Mary says they give you colic. Besides a new apple tree will grow from each of those seeds. Isn't it funny! Listen, Francis . . . you're fond of Polly and Ned?"

"Very." He stared. "Aren't you?"

"Of course . . . except when Polly coddles me every time I get a cough . . . and when Ned pets me on his knee—I hate that."

She hesitated, lowered her gaze for the first time. "Oh, it's nothing, I shouldn't, Sister Margaret Mary thinks I'm impudent, do you?"

He glanced away awkwardly, his passionate repudiation of the charge condensed in a clumsy: "No!"

She smiled almost timidly. "We're friends, Francis, so I will say it, and spite old Margaret Mary. When you're a man what are you going to be?"

Startled, he stared at her. "I don't know. Why?"

She picked with sudden nervousness at the serge of her dress. "Oh, nothing . . . only, well . . . I like you. I've always liked you. All those years I've thought of you a lot and it wouldn't be nice if you . . . sort of disappeared again."

"Why should I disappear?" He laughed.

"You'd be surprised!" Her eyes, still childish, were wide and wise. "I know Aunt Polly . . . I heard her again today. She'd give anything to see you made a priest. Then you'd have to give up everything, even me." Before he could reply she jumped up, shaking herself, with a great show of animation. "Come on, don't be silly, sitting here all day. It's ridiculous with the sun shining outside, and the party tonight." He made to rise. "No, wait a minute. Shut your eyes and you might get a present."

Even before he thought of complying she darted over and gave him a hurried little kiss on the cheek. The quick warm contact, the touch of her breath, the closeness of her thin face with the tiny brown mole on the cheekbone, stunned him. Blushing deeply, unexpectedly she slipped down the ladder and ran out of the shed. He followed slowly, darkly red, rubbing the small moist spot upon his cheek as though it were a wound. His heart was pounding.

That night the Halloween party began at seven o'clock. Ned, with a sultan's privilege, closed the bar at five minutes to the hour. All but a few favoured patrons were politely asked to leave. The guests assembled upstairs, in the parlour, with its glass cases of wax fruit, the picture of Parnell above the blue-glass lustres, the velvet-framed photograph of Ned and Polly at the Giant's Causeway, the bog oak jaunting car,—a present from Killarney,—the aspidistra, the varnished shillelagh hung on the wall with green ribbon, the heavy padded furniture which emitted a puff of dust when heavily sat upon. The mahogany table was fully extended, with legs like a dropsical woman, and set for twenty. The coal fire, banked halfway up the chimney, would have prostrated an African explorer. The smell, off, was of rich basting birds. Maggie Magoon, in cap and apron, ran about like a maniac. In the crowded room were the young curate, Father Clancy, Thaddeus Gilfoyle, several of the neighbouring tradesmen, Mr. Austin the manager of the tramways, his wife and three children, and, of course, Ned, Polly, Nora and Francis.

Amidst the din, with beaming benevolence and a sixpenny cigar, Ned stood laying down the law to his friend Gilfoyle. A pale, prosaic and slightly catarrhal young man of thirty was Thaddeus Gilfoyle, clerk at the gasworks, —who in his spare time collected the rents of Ned's property in Varrell Street, was a sidesman at St. Dominic's, a steady-going chap who could always be relied on to do an odd job, to fill the breach, to "come forward," as Ned phrased it,—who never had two words to rub against one another nor a single idea that might be called his own, yet who somehow managed to be there, hanging around, on the spot when he was wanted, dull and dependable, nodding in agreement, blowing his nose, fingering his confraternity badge, fish-eyed, flat-footed, solemn, safe.

"You'll be for making a speech tonight?" he now inquired of Ned, in a tone which implied that if Ned did not make a speech the world would be desolate.

"Ah, I don't know now." Modestly yet profoundly, Ned considered the end of his cigar.

"Ah, you will now, Ned!"

"They'll not expect it."

"Pardon me, Ned, if I beg to differ."

"Ye think I should?"

With solemnity, "Ned, ye both should and would!"

"Ye mean . . . I ought to?"

"You must, Ned, and you will."

Delighted, Ned rolled the cigar across his mouth. "As a matter of fact, Thad," he cocked his eye, significantly, "I have a announcement . . . a important announcement I want to make. I'll say a few words later, since you press me."

Led by Polly as a kind of overture to the main event, the children began to play Halloween games—first snapdragon, scrambling for the flat blue raisins, ablaze with spirit, on a big china dish, then duck-apple, dropping a fork from between the teeth over the back of a chair into a tub of swimming apples.

At seven o'clock the "gowks" came in: working lads from the neighbourhood, with soot-blackened faces and grotesque attire, mumming their way around the district, singing for sixpences, in the strange tradition of All Hallows Eve. They knew how to please Ned. They sang "Dear Little Shamrock," "Kathleen Mavourneen," and "Maggie Murphy's Home." Largesse was distributed. They clattered out. "Thank you, Mr. Bannon! Up the Union! Good night, Ned!"

"Good lads. Good lads all of them!" Ned rubbed his hands, his eye still moist with Celtic sentiment. "Now, Polly, our friends' stomachs will be thinking their throats is cut."

The company sat down at table, Father Clancy said grace, and Maggie Magoon staggered in with the largest goose in Tynecastle. Francis had never tasted such a goose—it dissolved, in rich flavours, upon the tongue. His body glowed from the long excursion in the keen air and from a strange interior joy. Now and then his eyes met Nora's across the table, shyly, with exquisite understanding. Though he was so quiet her gaiety thrilled him. The wonder of this happy day, of the secret bond which lay between them, was like a pain.

When the repast was over Ned got up slowly, amidst applause. He struck an oratorical attitude, one thumb in his armpit. He was absurdly nervous.

"Your Reverence, Ladies and Gentlemen, I thank you one and all. I'm a man of a few words,"—a cry of "No, No" from Thaddeus Gilfoyle,—"I say what I mean, and I mean what I say!" A short pause while Ned struggled for more confidence. "I like to see my friends happy and contented round about me—good company and good beer never hurt any man." Interruption at the doorway from Scanty Magoon, who had sneaked in with the gowks and contrived to remain. "God save you, Mr. Bannon!"—brandishing a drumstick of the goose. "You're a fine man!" Ned remained unperturbable—every great man has his sycophants. "As I was remarkin' when Mrs. Magoon's husband flung a brick at me . . ." Laughter. ". . . I favour the social occasion. I'm sure we're proud and pleased, every mother's son of us,—and daughter,—to welcome into our midst my poor wife's brother's boy!" Loud applause and Polly's voice: "Take a bow, Francis." "I'm not going into recent history. Let the past bury its dead, I say. But I say and say it I will, Look at him now, I say, and when he came!" Applause and Scanty's voice in the corridor: "Maggie, for the love of God, will ye bring some more of the goose!" "Now, I'm not one to blow my own trumpet! I try to do fair between God and man and beast. Look at my whippets if ye don't believe me." Gilfoyle's voice: "The best dogs in Tynecastle!" A longer pause, during which Ned lost the thread of his speech. "Where am I?" "Francis!" Polly prompted quickly. "Ah, yes." Ned raised his voice. "When Francis came, I said to myself, says I, here's a boy that might be useful. Shove him behind the bar and let him earn his keep? No, by God—Saving your presence, Father Clancy—that's not us. We talk it over, Polly and me. The boy's young, the boy's been ill-treated, the boy has a future before him, the boy's my poor dead wife's brother's boy. Let's send him to college, we say; we can manage it between us." Ned paused. "Your Reverence, Ladies and Gentlemen, I'm pleased and proud to announce that next month Francis starts off for Holywell!" Making the name the triumphant keystone of his peroration, Ned sat down, perspiring, amidst loud applause.

4

THOUGH the elm shadows were long upon the cropped lawns of Holywell, the northern June evening was still light as noon. The darkness would come late, so close to dawn the aurora borealis would but briefly glitter across the high pale heavens. As Francis sat at the open window of the high little study which he shared, since his election to the "Philosophers," with Laurence Hudson and Anselm Mealey, he felt his attention wander from the notebook, drawn, almost sadly, with a sense of the transience of beauty, to the lovely scene before him.

From the steep angle of his vision he could see the school, a noble grey granite baronial mansion, built for Sir Archibald Frazer in 1609, and en-

dowed, this century, as a Catholic College. The chapel, styled in the same
severity, lay at right angles, linked by a cloister, to the library, enclosing a
quadrangle of historic turf. Beyond were the fives and handball courts, the
playing fields, the end of a game still in progress, wide reaches of pasture
threaded by the Stinchar River with stumpy black Polled Angus cattle grazing
stolidly, woods of beech and oak and rowan clustering the lodge, and in the
ultimate distance the backdrop, blue, faintly serrated, of the Aberdeenshire
Grampians.

Without knowing, Francis sighed. It seemed only yesterday that he had
landed at Doune, the draughty northern junction, a new boy, scared out of
his wits, facing the unknown and that first frightful interview with the Headmaster, Father Hamish MacNabb. He remembered how "Rusty Mac," great
little Highland gentleman, blood cousin to MacNabb of the Isles, had
crouched at his desk beneath his tartan cape, peering from bushy red eyebrows, dreadfully formidable.

"Well, boy, what can you do?"

"Please, sir . . . nothing."

"Nothing! Can't you dance the Highland Fling?"

"No, sir."

"What! With a grand name like Chisholm?"

"I'm sorry, sir."

"Humph! There's not much profit in you, is there boy?"

"No, sir, except sir . . ." Trembling: ". . . Maybe I can fish."

"Maybe, eh?" A slow dry smile. "Then maybe we'll be friends." The smile
deepened. "The clans of Chisholm and MacNabb fished together, ay, and
fought together, before you or I were thought of. Run now, before I cane ye."

And now, in one more term, he would be leaving Holywell. Again his gaze
slanted down to the little groups promenading to and fro on the gravelled
terraces beside the fountain. A seminary custom! Well, what of it? Most of
them would go from here to the Seminary of San Morales in Spain. He
discerned his room-mates walking together: Anselm, as usual, extrovert in his
affections, one arm tenderly linking his companion's, the other gesticulating,
but nicely, as befitted the outright winner of the Frazer Good Fellowship
Prize! Behind the two, surrounded by his coterie, paced Father Tarrant—
tall, dark, thin . . . intense yet sardonic . . . classically remote.

At the sight of the youngish priest Francis' expression tightened oddly. He
viewed the open notebook before him on the window ledge with distaste,
picked up his pen and began, after a moment, his imposition. His frown of
resolution did not mar the clean brown moulding of his cheek or the sombre
clearness of his hazel eyes. Now, at eighteen, his body had a wiry grace. The
chaste light heightened absurdly his physical attractiveness, that air, unspoiled
and touching, which—inescapable—so often humiliated him.

"*June 14th, 1887.* Today there occurred an incident of such phenomenal
and thrilling impropriety I must revenge myself on this beastly diary, and

Father Tarrant, by recording it. I oughtn't really to waste this hour before vespers—afterwards I shall be dutifully cornered by Anselm to play handball— I should jot down *Ascension Thursday: Fine day; memorable adventure with Rusty Mac*, and leave it. But even our incisive Administrator of Studies admitted the virtue of my breed—conscientiousness—when he said to me, after his lecture: 'Chisholm! I suggest you keep a diary. Not of course for publication,'—his confounded satire flashed out,—'as a form of examen. You suffer, Chisholm, inordinately, from a kind of spiritual obstinacy. By writing your inmost heart out . . . if you could . . . you might possibly reduce it.'

"I blushed, of course, like a fool, as my wretched temper flared. 'Do you mean I don't do what I'm told, Father Tarrant?'

"He barely looked at me, hands tucked away in the sleeves of his habit, thin, dark, pinched in at the nostrils and oh, so unanswerably clever. As he tried to conceal his dislike of me, I had a sharp awareness of his hard shirt, of the iron discipline I know he uses unsparingly upon himself. He said vaguely: 'There is a mental disobedience . . .' and walked away.

"Is it conceit to imagine he has his knife in me because I do not model myself upon him? Most of us do. Since he came here two years ago he has led quite a cult of which Anselm is deacon. Perhaps he cannot forget the occasion when, at his instruction to us upon the 'one, true, and apostolic religion' I suddenly remarked: 'Surely, sir, creed is such an accident of birth God can't set an exclusive value on it.' In the shocked hush which followed he stood nonplussed, but icy cold. 'What an admirable heretic you would have made, my good Chisholm.'

"At least we have one point in common: agreement that I shall never have a vocation.

"I'm writing ridiculously pompously for a callow youth of eighteen. Perhaps it is what is named the affectation of my age. But I'm worried . . . about several things. Firstly, I'm terribly, probably absurdly, worried about Tyne-castle. I suppose it's inevitable that one should lose touch, when one's 'home-leave' is limited to four short summer weeks. This brief annual vacation, Holywell's only rigour, may serve its purpose of keeping vocations firm, but it also strains the imagination. Ned never writes. His correspondence during my three years at Holywell has been effected through the medium of sudden and fantastic gifts of food: that colossal sack of walnuts for instance, from the docks, in my first winter, and last spring, the crate of bananas, three quarters of which were over-ripe and created an undignified epidemic amongst the 'clergy and laity' here.

"But even in Ned's silence there's something queer. And Aunt Polly's letters make me more apprehensive. Her dear inimitable gossip about paro-chial events has been replaced by a meagre catalogue of, mainly, meteorologi-cal facts. And this change in tone arrived so suddenly. Naturally Nora hasn't helped me. She is the original postcard girl, who scribbles off her obligations in five minutes, once a year, at the seaside. It seems, however, centuries since her last brilliant 'Sunset from Scarborough Pier' and two letters of mine have failed even to produce a 'Moon over Whitley Bay.' Dear Nora! I shall never forget your Evelike gesture in the apple loft. It's because of you that I anticipate these coming holidays so eagerly. Shall we walk again, I wonder, to Gosforth? I have watched you grow, holding my breath—seen your character —by which I mean your contradictions—develop. I know you as someone quick, shy, bold, sensitive and gay, a little spoiled by flattery, full of innocence and fun. Even now, I see your impudent sharp little face, lit up from within, as you indulge your amazing gift of mimicry—'taking off' Aunt Polly . . . or me—your skinny arms akimbo, blue eyes provoking, reckless, ending by flinging yourself into a dance of gleeful malice. Everything about you is so—human and alive, and—even those flashes of petulance and fits of temper which shake your delicate physique and end in such tremendous weepings. And I know, despite your faults, how warm and impulsive is your nature, making you run, with a quick and shamefaced blush, towards someone you have hurt . . . unconsciously. I lie awake thinking of you, of the look in your eyes, the tender pathos of your collar bones above your small round breasts . . ."

Francis broke off here, and with a sudden flush scored out the last line he had written. Then, conscientiously, he resumed.

"Secondly, I am selfishly concerned about my future. I'm now educated above—here again Fr. Tarrant would agree—my station. I've only another term at Holywell. Am I to return gracefully to the beer-pulls of the Union? I can't continue to be a charge on Ned—or more justly Polly, since I recently ascertained quite by accident that my fees have been discharged, out of her modest income, by that wonderful woman! My ambitions are so muddled. My fondness for Aunt Polly, my overbrimming gratitude make me long to repay her. And it is her dearest wish to see me ordained. Again, in a place like this, where three quarters of the students and most of one's friends are predestined for the priesthood, it is hard to escape the inevitable pull of sympathy. One wants to line up in the ranks. Tarrant apart, Father MacNabb thinks I should make a good priest—I can feel it in his shrewd, friendly provocativeness, his almost Godlike sense of waiting. And as Principal of this College he should know something about vocations.

"Naturally I'm impetuous and hot-tempered; and my mixed upbringing has left me with a schismatic quirk. I can't pretend to be one of these consecrated youths—our college library teems with them—who lisp prayers throughout their infancy, make boyish shrines in the woods and sweetly rebuke the little girls who jostle them at the village fair. 'Keep away, Thérèse and Annabelle, I am not for thee.'

"Yet who can describe those moments that come to one suddenly: alone upon the back road to Doune, waking in the darkness in one's silent room, remaining behind, quite solitary, when the scraping, coughing, whispering mob has gone in the empty yet breathing church. Moments of strange apprehension, of intuition. Not that sentimental ecstasy which is as loathsome to me as ever—Query: why do I want to vomit when I see rapture on the Master of Novices' face?—but a sense of consolation, of hope.

"I'm distressed to find myself writing like this—though it is for no other eye than mine. One's private ardours make chilling stuff on paper. Yet I must record this inescapable sense of belonging to God which strikes at me through the darkness, the deep conviction, under the measured, arranged, implacable movement of the universe, that man does not emerge from, or vanish into, nothing. And here—is it not strange?—I feel the influence of Daniel Glennie, dear, cracked Holy Dan, feel his warm unearthly gaze upon me. . . .

"Confound it! And Tarrant! I *am* literally pouring out my heart. If I am such a Holy Willie why don't I set out and do something for God, attack the great mass of indifference, of sneering materialism in the world today . . . in short, become a priest? Well . . . I must be honest. I think it is because of Nora. The beauty and tenderness of my feeling for her overfills my heart. The vision of her face, with its light and sweetness, is before me even when I am praying to Our Lady in church. Dear, dear Nora. You are the real reason why I don't take my ticket on the celestial express for San Morales!"

He stopped writing and let his gaze travel into the distance, a faint frown on his brow, but his lips smiling. With an effort, he again collected himself.

"I must, I must get back to this morning and Rusty Mac. This being a holiday of obligation, I had the forenoon on my hands. On my way down to post a letter at the lodge I ran into the Headmaster coming up from the Stinchar with his rod and without fish. He stopped, supporting his short burly form on the gaff, his ruddy face screwed up, rather put out, beneath his blaze of red hair. I do love Rusty Mac. I think he has some fondness for me and perhaps the simplest explanation is that we are so dourly Scottish and both of us fishers . . . the only two in the school. When Lady Frazer endowed the College from her Stinchar properties, Rusty claimed the river as his own. The jingo in the *Holywell Monitor* beginning,

> I'll not have my pools
> Whipped to ribbons by fools . . .

neatly takes off his attitude—for he's a mad fisher. There's a story of him, in the middle of mass at Frazer Castle, which Holywell serves, when his staunch friend, the Presbyterian Gillie, stuck his head through the window of the oratory, bursting with suppressed excitement. 'Your Reverence! They're rising like fury in Lochaber Pool!' Never was a mass more quickly completed. The stupefied congregation, including Her Ladyship, was pattered over, blessed at breakneck speed; then a dark streak, not unlike the local concept of the Devil, was seen flying from the sacristy. 'Jock! Jock! What flee are they taking?'

"Now, he looked at me disgustedly. 'Not a fish in sight. Just when I wanted one for the notables!' The Bishop of the diocese and the retiring principal of our English Seminary at San Morales were coming to lunch at Holywell that day.

"I said, 'There's a fish in the Glebe Pool, sir.'

"'There's no fish in the river at all, not even a grilse . . . I've been out since six.'

"'It's a big one.'

"'Imaginary!'

"'I saw it there yesterday, under the weir, but of course I didn't dare try for it.'

"From beneath his sandy brows he gave me his dour smile. 'You're a perverse demon, Chisholm. If you want to waste your time—you've my dispensation.' He handed me his rod and walked off.

"I went down to the Glebe Pool, my heart leaping as it always does at the sound of running water. The fly on the leader was a Silver Doctor, perfect for the size and colour of the river. I began to fish the pool. I fished it for an hour. Salmon are painfully scarce this season. Once I thought I saw the movement of a dark fin in the shadows of the opposite bank. But I touched nothing. Suddenly I heard a discreet cough. I swung round. Rusty Mac, dressed in his best blacks, wearing gloves and his ceremonial top hat, had stopped, on his way to meet his guests at Doune Station, to condole with me.

"'It's these large ones, Chisholm—' he said with a sepulchral grin—'they're always the hardest!'

"As he spoke, I made a final cast thirty yards across the pool. The fly fell exactly on the spume eddying beneath the far edge of the weir. The next instant I felt the fish, struck, and was fast in it.

"'Ye have one!' Rusty cried. Then the salmon jumped—four feet in the air. Though for my own part I nearly dropped, the effect on Rusty was stupendous. I could feel him stiffen beside me. 'In the name of God!' he muttered in stricken awe. The salmon was the biggest I had ever seen, here, in the Stinchar, or in my father's Tweedside bothy. 'Keep his head up!' Rusty suddenly shouted. 'Man, man—give him the butt!'

"I was doing my best. But now the fish was in control. It set off, downstream, in a mad tearing rush. I followed. And Rusty followed me.

"The Stinchar, at Holywell, is not like the Tweed. It runs in a brown torrent through pines and gorges, making not inconsiderable somersaults over slippery boulders and high shaley ledges. At the end of ten minutes, Rusty Mac and I were half a mile downstream, somewhat the worse for wear. But we still stayed with the fish.

"'Hold him, hold him!' Mac was hoarse from shouting. 'You fool, you fool, don't let him get in that slack!' The brute, of course, was already in the slack, sulking in a deep hole, with the leader ensnared in a mess of sunken roots.

"'Ease him, ease him!' Mac hopped in anguish. 'Just ease him while I give him a stone.'

"Gingerly, breathlessly, he began flipping stones, trying to start out the fish without snapping the cast. The game continued for an agony of time. Then *whirr!*—off went the fish, to the scream of the reel. And off again went Rusty and I.

"An hour later, or thereabouts, in the slow wide flats opposite Doune village, the salmon at last showed signs of defeat. Exhausted, panting, torn by a hundred agonizing and entrancing hazards, Rusty gave a final command.

" 'Now, now! On this sand!' He croaked: 'We've no gaff. If he takes you down farther, he's gone for good.'

"My mouth was gulpy and dry. Nervously, I stood the fish close. It came, quiet, then suddenly made a last frantic scuttle. Rusty let out a hollow groan. 'Lightly . . . lightly! If you lose him now I'll never forgive you!'

"In the shallows the fish seemed incredible. I could see the frayed gut of the leader. If I lost him!—an icy lump came under my shirt. I slid him gently to the little flat of sand. In an absolute tense silence Mac bent over, whipped his hand in the gills and heaved the fish, monstrous, onto the grass.

"It made a noble sight on the green meadow, a fish of over forty pounds, run so freshly the sea lice still were on its arching back.

" 'A record, a record!' Mac chanted, swept, as was I, by a wave of heavenly joy. We had joined hands and were dancing the fandango. 'Forty-two pounds if it's an ounce . . . we'll put it in the book.' He actually embraced me. 'Man, man—You're a bonny, bonny fisher.'

"At that moment, from the single railway line across the river, came the faint whistle of an engine. Rusty paused, gazed in bewildered fashion at the plume of smoke, at the toylike red-and-white signal which had suddenly dipped over Doune village station. Recollection flooded him. He dug in consternation for his watch. 'Good Heavens, Chisholm!' His tone was that of the Holywell Headmaster. 'That's the Bishop's train.'

"His dilemma was apparent: he had five minutes to meet his distinguished visitors and five miles of roundabout road to reach the station—visible, only two fields away, across the Stinchar.

"I could see him slowly make up his mind. 'Take the fish back, Chisholm, and have them boil it whole for luncheon. Go quickly now. And remember Lot's wife and the pillar of salt. Whatever you do, *don't look back!*'

"I couldn't help it. Once I reached the first bend of the stream, from behind a bush, I risked a salty ending. Father Mac had already stripped to the buff and tied his clothing in a bundle. Wearing his top hat firmly on his head, with the bundle uplifted like a crozier, he stepped stark naked into the river. Wading and swimming, he reached the other side, scrambled into his suit and sprinted manfully towards the approaching train.

"I lay on the grass, rolling, in a kind of ecstasy. It was not the vision—which would live with me forever—of the top hat planted dauntlessly upon the nubile brow, but the moral pluck which lay behind the escapade. I thought: He too must hate our pious prudery, which shudders at the sight of human flesh, and cloaks the female form as though it were an infamy."

A sound outside made Francis pause and he ceased writing as the door opened. Hudson and Anselm Mealey came into the room. Hudson, a dark quiet youth, sat down and began to change his shoes. Anselm had the evening mail in his hand.

"Letter for you, Francis," he said effusively.

Mealey had grown into a fine pink-and-white young man. His cheek had the smoothness of perfect health. His eye was soft and limpid, his smile ready. Always eager, busy, smiling: without question he was the most popular student in the school. Though his work was never brilliant, the masters liked him—his name was usually on the prize list. He was good at fives and racquets and all the less rough games. And he had a genius for procedure. He ran half a dozen clubs—from the Philatelists to the Philosophers. He knew, and glibly employed, such words as "quorum," "minutes" and "Mr. Chair." Whenever a new society was proposed, Anselm's advice was sure to be invoked—automatically he became its president. In praise of the clerical life he was lyrical. His only cross was this singular paradox: the Headmaster and a few odd lonely souls cordially disliked him. To the rest he was a hero, and he bore his successes with open smiling modesty.

Now, as he handed Francis the letter, he gave him that warm disarming smile. "Hope it's full of good news, dear fellow."

Francis opened the letter. Undated, it was written in pencil upon an invoice headed:

Dr. to Edward Bannon
Union Tavern,
Corner Dyke and Canal Streets,
Tynecastle.

Dear Francis,

I hope this finds you well as it leaves me. Also please excuse pencil. We are all upset. It grieves me to tell you Francis you won't be able to come home this holiday. No one is more sick and sorry than me about it not having seen you since last summer and all. But believe me it is impossible and we must bow to the will of God. I know you are not one to take no for an answer but this time you must the B.V.M. be my witness. I won't disguise we have trouble as you must guess but it is nothing you can help or hinder. It is not money nor sickness so do not worry. And it will all pass by the help of God and be forgotten. You can easy arrange to stay the holidays at the college. Ned will pay all extras. You'll have your books and your nice surroundings and all. Maybe we'll fix for you to come down at Christmas, so don't fret. Ned has sold his whippets but not for the money. Mr. Gilfoyle is a comfort to all. You are not missing much in the weather, it has been terrible wet. Now don't forget Francis we have people in the house, there isn't no room, you are not [underlined twice] to come.

Bless you my dear boy and excuse haste.

Yours affectionately,

POLLY BANNON

At the window, Francis read the letter several times: though its purpose was plain, its meaning remained troubling and inscrutable. With a strained look he folded the sheet and placed it in his pocket.

"Nothing wrong I hope?" Mealey had been studying his face solicitously. Francis, uncomfortably silent, hardly knew what to say.

"My dear fellow, I am sorry." Anselm took a step forward, placed his arm lightly, comfortingly, around the other's shoulders. "If there's anything I can do for mercy's sake let me know. Perhaps,"—he paused earnestly,—"perhaps you don't feel like handball tonight?"

"No," Francis mumbled. "I believe I'd rather not."

"Quite all right, my dear Francis!" The vespers bell rang. "I can see there is something bothering you. I'll remember you tonight in my prayers."

All through vespers Francis worried about Polly's incomprehensible letter. When the service was over he had a sudden impulse to take his trouble to Rusty Mac. He went slowly up the wide staircase.

As he entered the study he became aware that the Headmaster was not alone, Father Tarrant sat with him, behind a pile of papers; and from the odd sudden silence his appearance provoked, Francis had the extraordinary feeling that the two had been discussing him.

"I'm sorry, sir." He cast an embarrassed glance towards Rusty Mac. "I didn't know you were engaged."

"That's all right, Chisholm. Sit down."

The quick warmth of the tone compelled Francis, already half-turned towards the door, into the wicker chair beside the desk. With slow movements of his stubby fingers Rusty went on stuffing shag into his corroded briar pipe. "Well! What can we do for you, my good man?"

Francis coloured. "I . . . I rather thought you'd be alone."

For some queer reason the Headmaster avoided his appealing gaze. "You don't mind Father Tarrant? What is it?"

There was no escape. Without guile to invent further excuse Francis stumbled out: "It's a letter I've had . . . from home." He had meant to show Polly's note to Rusty Mac but, in Tarrant's presence, his pride restrained him. "For some obscure reason they don't seem to want me back for the vacation."

"Oh!" Was he mistaken: was there again swift interchange between the two? "That must be something of a disappointment."

"It is, sir. And I feel worried. I was wondering . . . in fact I came to ask you what I should do."

Silence. Father MacNabb himself sank more deeply into his old cape, still fumbling at his pipe. He had known many boys, known them inside-out; yet there was about this youth who sat beside him a fineness, beauty, and dogged honesty which lit a fire in his heart. "We all have our disappointments, Francis." His meditative voice was sad, more than unusually mild. "Father Tarrant and I have suffered one today. Retirements are the order of the day at our Seminary in Spain." He paused. "We are appointed there, I as Rector, Father Tarrant as my Administrator of Studies."

Francis stammered a reply. San Morales was, indeed, a coveted advancement, next step to a bishopric; but whatever Tarrant's reaction—Francis shot a quick glance at the expressionless profile—MacNabb would not so regard it. The dry Aragon plains would be alien for a man who loved the green woods and rushing waters of Holywell with all his soul. Rusty Mac smiled gently. "I had my heart set on staying here. You had set yours on going away. What d'you say? Shall we both agree to take a beating from Almighty God?"

Francis strove to pluck the proper phrase from his confusion. "It's just . . . being anxious . . . I wondered if I shouldn't find out what's wrong and try to help?"

"I question if I should." Father MacNabb answered quickly. "What would you say, Father Tarrant?"

In the shadow, the younger master stirred. "Troubles resolve themselves best, in my experience, without outside interference."

There appeared nothing more to be said. The Headmaster turned up his desk lamp which, while it brightened the dark study, seemed to terminate the interview. Francis got up. Though he faced them both, haltingly, from his heart, he spoke to Rusty Mac.

"I can't say how sorry I am that you are leaving for Spain. The school . . . I . . . I shall miss you."

"Perhaps we shall see you there?" There was hope, quiet affection in the voice.

Francis did not answer. As he stood there, indecisively, hardly knowing what to say, torn by conflicting difficulties, his downcast gaze struck suddenly upon a letter, lying open on the desk. It was not so much the letter—illegible at that distance—as the letter's bright blue-stamped heading which caught his eye. Quickly he glanced away. But not before he had read *St. Dominic's Presbytery, Tynecastle.*

A shiver went through him. Something was wrong at home. Now he was sure. His face revealed nothing, remained impassive. Neither of the two masters was aware of his discovery. But as he moved towards the door he knew, despite all persuasion to the contrary, that one course at least was clear before him.

5

THE train arrived at two o'clock that sultry June afternoon. Carrying his handbag, Francis walked rapidly from the station, his heart beating faster as he approached the familiar quarter of the city.

A queer air of quiet hung outside the tavern. Thinking to take Aunt Polly by surprise, he ran lightly up the side stairs and entered the house. Here, too, it was quiet and oddly dim after the glare of the dusty pavements; no one in the lobby or the kitchen, no sound but the thunderous ticking of a clock. He went into the parlour.

Ned was seated at the table, both elbows on the red drugget cover, gazing endlessly at the opposite blank wall. Not the attitude alone, but the alteration in the man himself, drew from Francis a stifled exclamation. Ned had lost three stone in weight, his clothes hung upon him, the rotund beaming face had turned dreary and cadaverous.

"Ned!" Francis held out his hand.

There was a pause, then Ned sluggishly slewed round, perception slowly dawning through his settled wretchedness.

"It's you, Francis." His smile was bewitching, evasive. "I'd no idea you were expected."

"I'm not really, Ned." Through his anxiety Francis essayed a laugh. "But the minute we broke up I simply couldn't wait. Where's Aunt Polly?"

"She's away. . . . Yes . . . Polly's away for a couple of days to Whitley Bay."

"When'll she be back?"

"Like enough . . . tomorrow."

"And where's Nora?"

"Nora!" Ned's tone was flat. "She's away with Aunt Polly."

"I see." Francis was conscious of a throb of relief. "That's why she didn't answer my wire. But Ned . . . you . . . you're well yourself, I hope?"

"I'm all right, Francis. A trifle under the weather maybe . . . but the like of me'll come to no harm." His chest took a sudden grotesque heave. Francis was horrified to see tears run down the egg-shaped face. "Away now and get yourself a bite. There'll be plenty in the cupboard. Thad'll get you anything you want. He's below in the bar. A great help he's been to us, has Thad." Ned's gaze wavered, then wandered back to the opposite wall.

In a daze, Francis turned, put his bag in his own small room. As he came along the passage the door of Nora's room was open: the neat white privacy caused him to withdraw his eyes in sudden confusion. He hastened downstairs.

The saloon was empty, even Scanty vanished, his vacant corner arresting, unbelievable, like a gap blown through the solid structure of the wall. But behind the bar, in his shirt sleeves, smugly drying glasses, was Thaddeus Gilfoyle.

Thad stopped his silent whistle as Francis entered. Slightly taken aback, an instant elapsed before he offered a welcome with his limp and dampish hand.

"Well, well!" he exclaimed. "Here's a sight for sore eyes."

Gilfoyle's air of proprietorship was hateful. But Francis, now thoroughly alarmed, succeeded in affecting indifference. He said lightly: "I'm surprised to see you here, Thad? What's happened to the gasworks?"

"I've give up the office," Thad answered composedly.

"What for?"

"To be here. Permanent." He picked up a glass and eyed it professionally, breathed on it softly, and began to polish. "When they asked me to come forward . . . I couldn't do more!"

Francis felt his nerves tighten beyond endurance. "In the name of heaven, what's all this about, Gilfoyle?"

"*Mister* Gilfoyle, if you don't mind, Francis!" Thad rolled his tongue smugly around the reproach. "It heartbreaks Ned not to see me get my place. He's not the same man, Francis. I doubt he'll ever be himself again."

"What's happened to him? You talk as if he were out of his mind!"

"He was, Francis, he was . . ." Gilfoyle groaned, "but he's come to senses now, poor man." His eye watchful, he stopped Francis' angry interruption with a whine. "Now don't take on that way with me. I'm the one that's doin' right. Ask Father Fitzgerald if you disbelieve me. I know you've never liked me much. I've seen ye on vacations making sport of me as you growed up. I've the best intentions towards you, Francis. We ought to pull together . . . now, especially."

"Why now especially?" Francis gritted his teeth.

"Oh, yes, yes . . . you wouldn't know . . . to be sure." Thad darted a fearful smirk. "The banns was only put up for the first time last Sunday. You see, Francis, me and Nora's going to be wed!"

Aunt Polly and Nora returned late the following evening. Francis, sick with apprehension, with his failure to penetrate Gilfoyle's fishlike secrecy, had awaited their arrival in an agony of impatience. He tried immediately to corner Polly.

But Polly, after her first start, her wail of recognition,—"Francis, I told you not to come,"—had fled upstairs with Nora, her ears closed to his importunities, reiterating the formula, "Nora's not well . . . she's sick I tell you . . . get out of my road . . . I've got to tend to her."

Rebuffed, he climbed sombrely to his room, chilled by the mounting premonitions of this unknown dread. Nora, having scarcely given him a look, had gone immediately to bed. And for an hour he heard Polly, scurrying with trays and hot-water bottles, entreating Nora in a low voice, persecuting her with agitated attentions. Nora, thin as a wand, and pale, somehow had the air of sick-rooms. Polly, worn and harassed, even more negligent in her dress, had acquired a new gesture—a quick pressing of her hand against her brow. Late into the night, from her adjoining room, he heard the mutter of her prayers. Torn by the enigma, Francis bit his lip, turning restlessly between his sheets.

Next morning dawned clear. He rose and, according to his habit, went out to early mass. When he returned he found Nora seated outside on the back-yard steps warming herself in a patch of sunshine while at her feet some chickens cheeped and scuttled. She made no move to let him pass, but when he had stood a moment, she raised her head contemplatively.

"It's the holy man . . . been out already, saving his soul!"

He reddened at her tone, so unexpected, so quietly bitter.

"Did the Very Reverend Fitzgerald officiate?"

"No. It was the curate."

"The dumb ox in the stall! Ah, well, at least he's harmless."

Her head drooped, she stared at the chickens, propping her thin chin upon a thinner wrist. Though she had always been slight he was startled to discover this almost childish fragility which matched so ill the sullen maturity in her eyes, and the new grey dress, womanly and costly, which stiffly adorned her. His heart melted, his breast was filled with a white fire, an unsupportable pain. Her hurt plucked at the chords of his soul. He hesitated, his gaze averted. His voice was low.

"Have you had breakfast?"

She nodded. "Polly shoved it down my throat. God! If she'd only leave me be!"

"What are you doing today?"

"Nothing."

He paused again, then blurted out, all his feeling for her flooding through the anxiety in his eyes, "Why don't we go for a walk, Nora? Like we used to. It's so glorious a day!"

She did not move. Yet a faint tinge of animation seemed to penetrate her hollow, shadowed cheek.

"I can't be bothered," she said heavily. "I'm tired!"

"Oh, come on, Nora . . . please."

A dull pause. "All right."

His heart gave another great painful thud. He hurried into the kitchen and cut, with nervous haste, some sandwiches and cake, wrapped them clumsily into a packet. There was no sign of Polly and now, indeed, he was eager to avoid her. In ten minutes Nora and he sat in the red tram, clanging across the city. Within the hour, they tramped side by side, unspeaking, towards the Gosforth Hills.

He wondered at the impulse which had sent him to this familiar stretch. Today the burgeoning countryside was lovely; but its very loveliness was tremulous, unbearable. As they came upon Lang's orchard, now foamy with blossom, he paused, tried to break the steely silence which lay between them.

"Look, Nora! Let's take a stroll round. And have a word with Lang."

She threw one glance at the orchard, the trees standing spaced and stiff, like chessmen, around the apple shed. She said rudely, bitterly: "I don't want to. I hate that place!"

He did not answer. Dimly he knew her bitterness was not towards him.

By one o'clock they reached the summit of Gosforth Beacon. He could see that she was tired and, without consulting her, stopped under a tall beech, for lunch. The day was unusually warm and clear. In the flat distance beneath them, sparkling with golden light, lay the city, domed and spired, and from afar, ineffably beautiful.

She scarcely touched the sandwiches he produced and, remembering Polly's demonstrative tyranny, he did not press her. The shade was soothing. Overhead the new green flickering leaves sent quiet patterns chasing across the

moss, carpeted with dry beechnuts, on which they sat. There was a smell of
flowing sap; the throaty call of a thrush came from a high twig overhead.

After a few moments she leaned back against the bole of the tree, tilted
her head, and closed her eyes.

Her relaxation seemed somehow the greatest tribute she could pay him.
He considered her with a deeper surge of tenderness, stirred to undreamed-of
compassion by the arch of her neck, so thin and unprotected. The welling
tenderness within him made him strangely protective. When her head slipped
a little from the tree he scarcely dared touch her. Yet, fancying her asleep,
he moved his arm instinctively to support her. The next instant she wrenched
herself free, struck him repeatedly on the face and chest with her clenched
knuckles, hysterically breathless.

"Leave me alone! You brute! You beast!"

"Nora, Nora! What's the matter?"

Panting, she drew back, her face quivering, distorted. "Don't try to get
round me that way. You're all the same. Every one of you!"

"Nora!" He pleaded with her desperately. "For pity's sake . . . let's get
this straight."

"Get what straight?"

"Everything . . . why you're going on like this . . . why you're marrying
Gilfoyle."

"Why shouldn't I marry him?" She threw the question at him, with a
bitter defensiveness.

His lips were dry, he could scarcely speak. "But Nora, he's such a poor
creature . . . he's not your sort."

"He's as good as anybody. Haven't I said you're all the same? At least
I'll keep him in his place."

Confounded, he stared at her with a pale and stricken face. And there
was that in his unbelieving eyes which cut her so cruelly, she more cruelly
cut back.

"Perhaps you think I should be marrying you . . . the bright-eyed altar boy
. . . the half-baked carpet priest!" Her lip twitched with the bitterness of
her sneer. "Let me tell you this. I think you're a joke . . . a sanctimonious
scream. Go on, turn up your blessed eyes. You don't know how funny you
are . . . you holy pater noster. Why if you were the last man in the world
I wouldn't . . ." She choked and shuddered violently, tried, painfully, use-
lessly, to check her tears with the back of her hand and then, sobbing, flung
her head upon his breast. "Oh, Francis, Francis, dear, I'm sorry! You know
I've always loved you. Kill me if you want to . . . I don't care."

While he quieted her, clumsily, stroking her brow, he felt himself trembling as much as she. The racking violence of her sobs diminished gradually.
She was like a wounded bird in his arms. She lay, spent and passive, her face
hidden against his coat. Then slowly she straightened herself. With averted
eyes, she took her handkerchief, rubbed her ravaged, tear-stained face,

straightened her hat, then said, in an exhausted neutral tone: "We'd better get home."

"Look at me, Nora?"

But she would not, only remarking in that same odd monotone: "Say what you want to say."

"I will then, Nora." His youthful vehemence overcame him. "I'm not going to stand this! I can see there's something behind it. But I'll get to the bottom of it. You're not going to marry that fool Gilfoyle. I love you, Nora. I'll stand by you."

There was a pitiful stillness.

"Dear Francis," she said, with an oddly hollow smile. "You make me feel as though I'd lived a million years." And rising, she bent and kissed him, as she had kissed him once before, upon the cheek. As they went down the hill the thrush had ceased its singing in the high tree.

That evening, with fixed intention, Francis set out for the dockside tenement inhabited by the Magoons. He found the banished Scanty alone, since Maggie was still out charring, squatting by a spark of fire in the single "back to back" apartment, glumly working a wool-rug shuttle by the light of a tallow dip. As he recognized his visitor there was no mistaking the pleasure in the exile's bleary eye, a gleam that heightened when Francis uncovered the gill bottle of spirits he had privily removed from the bar. Quickly, Scanty produced a chipped delft cup, solemnly toasted his benefactor.

"Ah, that's the stuff!" he muttered, across the back of his ragged sleeve. "Devil the sup have I had since that skinflint Gilfoyle took over the bar."

Francis drew up the backless wooden chair. He spoke with dark intensity, the shadows heavy beneath his eyes.

"Scanty! What's happened at the Union—to Nora, Polly, Ned? I've been back three days and I'm still no wiser. You've got to tell me!"

A look of alarm invaded Scanty's expression. He glanced from Francis to the bottle—from the bottle to Francis.

"Ah! How would I know?"

"You do know! I can see it in your face."

"Didn't Ned say nothing?"

"Ned! He's like a deaf-mute these days!"

"Poor ould Ned!" Scanty groaned, blessed himself, and poured out more whiskey. "God save us! Who would ever have dreamed it. Sure there's bad in the best of us." With a sudden hoarse emphasis: "I couldn't tell ye, Francis, it's a shame to remember, it don't do no good."

"It will do good, Scanty," Francis urged. "If I know, I can do something."

"Ye mean, Gilfoyle . . ." With head cocked, Scanty considered, then he nodded slowly. He took another tot to stiffen himself, his battered face oddly sober, his tone subdued. "I'll tell you then, Francis, if you swear to keep it dark. The truth of it is . . . God pity us . . . that Nora's had a baby."

Silence: long enough for Scanty to take another drink. Francis said: "When?"

"Six weeks ago. She went down to Whitley Bay. The woman there has the child . . . a daughter. . . . Nora can't bear the sight of it."

Cold, rigid, Francis struggled with the tumult in his breast. He made himself ask: "Then Gilfoyle is the father?"

"That gutless fish!" Hatred overcame Scanty's caution. "No, no, he's the one that came forward, as he's pleased to call it, to give the little one a name, and get his foot in the Union to the bargain, the bla'g'ard! Father Fitzgerald's behind him, Francis. It's all settin' pretty as a pictur', the way they've pulled it. Marriage lines in the drawer, not a soul the wiser, and the daughter brought here later on, as it were, at the end of a long vaycation. God strike me down dead, if it don't turn the stomach of a pig!"

A band, an insupportable constriction, girded Francis' heart. He fought to keep his voice from breaking.

"I never knew Nora was in love with anyone? Scanty . . . Do you know who it was . . . I mean . . . the father of her child?"

"Before God I don't!" The blood rushed to Scanty's forehead as he thumped the floor boards in vociferous denial. "I don't know nothing about that at all. How should a poor creature like me! And Ned don't either, that's gospel truth! Ned always treated me right, a fine generous upstanding man, except for occasions, like when Polly was away, and the drink took hold of him. No, no. Francis, take it from me, there's not a hope of findin' the man!"

Again a silence, frozen, prolonged. A film clouded Francis' eyes. He felt deathly sick. At last, with a great effort he got up.

"Thank you, Scanty, for telling me."

He quitted the room, went giddily down the bare flights of tenement stairs. His brow, the palms of his hands, were bedewed with icy sweat. A vision haunted, tormented him: the trim neatness of Nora's bedroom, white and undisturbed. He had no hatred, only a searing pity, a dreadful convulsion of his soul. Outside in the squalid courtyard he leaned, suddenly overcome, against the single lamp-post and retched his heart out, into the gutter.

Now he felt cold, but firmer in his intention. He set out resolutely in the direction of St. Dominic's.

The housekeeper at St. Dominic's admitted him with that noiseless discretion which typified the Presbytery. In a minute, she glided back to the half-lit hall, where she had left him, and for the first time faintly smiled at him. "You're fortunate, Francis. His Reverence is free to see you."

Snuff-box in hand, Father Gerald Fitzgerald rose as Francis entered, his manner a mixture of cordiality and inquiry, his fine handsome presence matching the French furniture, the antique prie-dieu, the choice copies of Italian primitives upon the walls, the vase of lilies on the escritoire, scenting the tasteful room.

"Well young man, I thought you were up North? Sit down! How are all my good friends in Holywell?" As he paused to take snuff, his eye touched upon the College tie, which Francis wore, with affectionate approval. "I was there myself, you know, before I went to the Holy City . . . a grand gentlemanly place. Dear old MacNabb. And Father Tarrant. A classmate of mine at the English College in Rome. There's a fine, a coming man! Well now, Francis." He paused, his needled glance sheathed by a courtier's suavity. "What can we do for you?"

Painfully distressed, breathing quickly, Francis kept his eyes down. "I came to see you about Nora."

The stammered remark rent the room's serenity, its note of mannered ease. "And what about Nora, pray?"

"Her marriage with Gilfoyle . . . She doesn't want to go through with it . . . she's miserable . . . it seems so stupid and unjust . . . such a needless and horrible affair."

"What do you know about the horrible affair?"

"Well . . . everything . . . that she wasn't to blame."

There was a pause. Fitzgerald's fine brow expressed annoyance, yet he gazed at the distraught youth before him with a kind of stately pity.

"My dear young man, if you enter the priesthood, as I trust you will, and gain even half the experience which unhappily is mine, you will comprehend that certain social disorders demand equally specific remedies. You are staggered by this—" He returned the phrase with an inclination of his head—"horrible affair. I am not. I even anticipated it. I know and abominate the whiskey trade for its effect upon the brute mentality of the clods who constitute this parish. You and I may sit down and quietly enjoy our Lachryma Christi, like gentlemen. Not so Mr. Edward Bannon. Enough! I make no allegations. I merely say, we have a problem, unhappily not unique to those of us who spend drab hours in the confessional." Fitzgerald paused to take snuff, with a distinguished wrist. "What are we to do with it? I will tell you. First, legitimize and baptize the offspring. Secondly, marry the mother if we can, to as decent a man as will have her. We must regularize, regularize. Make a good Catholic home out of the mess. Weave the loose ends into our sound social fabric. Believe me, Nora Bannon is highly fortunate to get Gilfoyle. He's not so bright, but he's steady. In a couple of years you'll see her at mass with her husband and family . . . perfectly happy."

"No, no." The interruption was wrenched from Francis' shut lips. "She'll never be happy—only broken and miserable."

Fitzgerald's head was a trifle higher. "And is happiness the ultimate objective of our earthly life?"

"She'll do something desperate. You can't compel Nora. I know her better than you."

"You seem to know her intimately." Fitzgerald smiled with withering suavity. "I hope you have no physical interest in the lady yourself."

A dark red spot burned on Francis' pale cheek. He muttered: "I am very fond of Nora. But if I love her—it's nothing that would make your confessional more drab. I beg you—" His voice held a low, desperate entreaty.

"Don't force her into this marriage. She's not common clay . . . she's a bright sweet spirit. You can't thrust a child upon her bosom and a husband into her arms—because—in her innocence, she's been . . ."

Stung to the quick, Fitzgerald banged his snuff-box on the table.

"Don't preach at me, sir!"

"I'm sorry. You can see I don't know what I'm saying. I'm trying to beg you to use your power." Francis mustered his flagging forces in a final effort. "At least give her a little time."

"That is enough, Francis!"

The parish priest, too much master of himself, and of others, to lose his temper or his countenance for long, rose abruptly from his chair and looked at his flat gold watch. "I have a confraternity meeting at eight. You must excuse me." As Francis got up, he patted him reproachfully on the back. "My dear boy, you are very immature. Might I even say a little foolish? But thank God you have a wise old mother in Holy Church. Don't run your head against the walls, Francis. They've stood for generations—against stronger batterings than yours. But there now—I know you're a good lad. Come up and have a chat about Holywell when the wedding's over. And meanwhile—as a little act of reparation for your rudeness will you say the Salve Regina for my intention?"

A pause. It was useless, quite useless. "Yes, Father."

"Good night then, my son . . . and God bless you!"

The night air was raw and chill. Defeated, crushed by the impotence of his youth, Francis dragged himself away from the Presbytery. His footsteps echoed dully on the paved pathway. As he passed the chapel steps, the sacristan was closing the side doors. When the last chink of light was gone, Francis stood, hatless, in the darkness, his eyes fixed on the wraithlike windows of the clerestory. He blurted out, in a kind of final desperation: "Oh, God! Do what's best for all of us."

As the wedding day approached, consuming Francis with a deadly, sleepless fever, the atmosphere of the tavern seemed insensibly to settle, like a stagnant pool. Nora was quiet, Polly vaguely hopeful; and though Ned still cringed in solitude, the muddled terror in his eyes was less. The ceremony would, of course, be private. But no restraint need operate upon the trousseau, the dowry, the elaborate honeymoon to Killarney. The house was littered with robes and rich materials. Polly, beseeching another "try-on," with a mouthful of pins, waded through bales of cloth and linen, enveloped in merciful fog.

Gilfoyle, smugly observant, smoking the Union's best cigars, would occasionally hold conference, upon matters of finance, with Ned. There was a deed of partnership, duly signed, and great talk of building, to accommodate the new ménage. Already Thad's numerous poor relatives hung about the house, sycophantic yet assertive. His married sister, Mrs. Neily, and her daughter Charlotte, were perhaps the worst.

Nora had little enough to say. Once, meeting Francis in the passage, she stopped.

"You know . . . don't you?"

His heart was breaking, he dared not meet her eye. "Yes, I know."

There was a suffocating pause. He could not sustain the torture in his breast. Incoherently he burst out, boyish tears starting in his eyes: "Nora . . . We can't let this happen. If you knew how I've felt for you . . . I could look after you—work for you. Nora . . . let me take you away."

She considered him with that strange and pitying tenderness. "Where would we go?"

"Anywhere." He spoke wildly, his cheek wet and shining.

She did not answer. She pressed his hand without speaking, then went on, quickly, to be fitted for a dress.

On the day before the wedding, she unbent a little, losing something of her marble acquiescence. Suddenly, over one of those cups of tea which Polly inflicted upon her, she declared: "I believe I'd like to go to Whitley Bay today."

Astounded, Polly echoed: "Whitley Bay?"—then added in a flutter, "I'll come with you."

"There's no need." Nora paused, gently stirring her cup. "But of course if you want to . . ."

"I do indeed, my dear!"

Reassured by that lightness in Nora's manner,—as though a bar of that old mischievous gaiety re-echoed, like distant music, in her being,—Polly came to view the excursion without disfavour. She had a gratified, bewildered idea that Nora was "coming round." As she finished her tea she discoursed upon the beautiful Lake of Killarney, which she had once visited as a girl. The boatmen there had been most amusing.

The two women, dressed for the expedition, left for the station after the dinner hour. As she turned the corner, Nora looked up towards the window where Francis stood. She seemed to linger for a second, smiled gravely, and waved her hand. Then she was gone.

News of the accident reached the district even before Aunt Polly was brought home, in a state of collapse, in a cab. The sensation throughout the city was impressive. Popular interest could never have been so stirred by the mere stupidity of a young woman stumbling between a platform and a moving train. It was the prenuptial timing which made the thing so exquisite. Around the docks women ran out of their doorways, gathering in groups, beshawled, arms akimbo. Blame for the tragedy was finally pinned upon the victim's new shoes. There was enormous sympathy for Thaddeus Gilfoyle, for the family, for all young women about to be married and under the necessity of travelling by train. There was talk of a public funeral—with the confraternity band—for the mangled remains.

Late that night, how he knew not, Francis found himself in St. Dominic's church. It was quite deserted. The flickering wick of the sanctuary lamp drew his haggard eyes, a feeble beacon. Kneeling, stiff and pale, he felt, like an embrace, the remorseless foreclosure of his destiny. Never had he known such a moment of desolation, of abandonment. He could not weep. His lips, cold and stricken, could not move in prayer. But from his tortured mind there soared an offering of anguished thought. First his parents; and now Nora. He could no longer ignore these testaments from above. He would go away . . . he must go . . . to Father MacNabb . . . to San Morales. He would give himself entirely to God. He must become a priest.

6

DURING Easter, in the year 1892, an event occurred in the English Seminary of San Morales which set the place humming with a note of consternation. One of the students, in the subdiaconate, disappeared completely for the space of four entire days.

Naturally the Seminary had witnessed other seditions since its foundation in these Aragon uplands fifty years before. Students had mutinied for an hour or so, skulking to the *posada* outside the walls, hurriedly deranging conscience and digestion with long *cigarros* and the local *aguardiente*. Once or twice it had been necessary to drag some tottering recusant by the ears from the dingy parlours of the Via Amorosa in the town. But this—for a student to march out through the open gates in broad daylight and, half a week later, by the same gates, in even brighter light of day, to limp in again, dusty, unshaven, dishevelled, offering every evidence of horrible dissipation, and then, with no other excuse than "I've been for a walk!" to fling himself upon his bed and sleep the clock round—it was apostasy.

At the recreation the students discussed it in awed tones—little groups of dark figures on the sunny slopes, between the bright green copperas-sprayed vineyards, with the Seminary, white and gleaming against the pale pink earth, beneath them.

It was agreed that Chisholm would undoubtedly be expelled.

The Committee of Examination had immediately been constituted. According to precedent, as in all grave breaches of discipline it was composed of the Rector, the Administrator, the Director of Novices and the Head Seminarian. After some preliminary discussion, the tribunal opened its proceedings, in the theological atrium, on the day following the runagate's return.

Outside the *solano* was blowing. The ripe black olives fell from the blade-leafed trees and burst beneath the sun. A scent of orange flowers swept across from the grove above the infirmary. The baked earth crackled with the heat. As Francis entered the white and lofty-pillared room, its polished empty benches cool and dark, he had a quiet air. The black alpaca soutane stressed the thinness of his figure. His hair, cropped and tonsured, gave tautness to his face-bones, intensified the darkness of his eyes, his dark contained reserve. There was an odd tranquillity about his hands.

Before him, on the platform reserved for protagonists in debate, were four desks, already occupied by Father Tarrant, Monsignor MacNabb, Father Gomez and Deacon Mealey. Conscious of a mingling of displeasure and concern in the united gaze now upon him, Francis hung his head, while in a rapid voice Gomez, Director of Novices, read out the accusation.

There was a silence. Then Father Tarrant spoke.

"What is your explanation?"

Despite the quietness which enclosed him Francis suddenly began to flush. He kept his head down.

"I went for a walk!" The words resounded lamely.

"That is sufficiently apparent. We use our legs whether our intentions are good or bad. Apart from the obvious sin of leaving the Seminary without permission, were your intentions bad?"

"No."

"During your absence did you indulge in alcoholic liquor?"

"No."

"Did you visit the bullfight, the fair, the casino?"

"No."

"Did you consort with women of ill fame?"

"No."

"Then what did you do?"

Silence again, then the muttered inarticulate reply. "I've told you. You wouldn't understand. I . . . I went for a walk!"

Father Tarrant smiled thinly. "Do you wish us to believe that you spent these entire four days ceaselessly perambulating the countryside?"

"Well . . . practically."

"What destination did you reach eventually?"

"I—I got to Cossa!"

"Cossa! But that is fifty miles away!"

"Yes, I suppose so."

"You were there for some specific purpose?"

"No."

Father Tarrant bit his thin lip. He could not brook obstruction. He had a sudden wild longing for the rack, the boot, the wheel. Small wonder the mediævalists had recourse to such instruments! There were circumstances which fully justified them.

"I believe you are lying, Chisholm."

"Why should I lie—to you?"

A muffled exclamation came from Deacon Mealey. His presence was purely formal. As the chief prefect he sat there as a symbol, perhaps a cipher, expressive of the student body. Yet he could not restrain his earnest pleading.

"Please, Francis! For the sake of all of the students . . . all of us who love you . . . I . . . I implore you to own up."

As Francis remained silent, Father Gomez, the young Spanish novice master, inclined his head and murmured to Tarrant: "I've had no evidence . . . none whatever, from the town. But we might write to the priest at Cossa."

Tarrant shot a swift glance at the Spaniard's subtle face.

"Yes. That is decidedly an idea."

Meanwhile the Rector had taken advantage of the lull. Older, slower than at Holywell, he leaned forward. He spoke slowly and kindly.

"Of course, you must realize, Francis, that in the circumstances, so general an explanation is barely adequate. After all, it is a serious matter to play truant—not merely the breaking of the Seminary rule—the disobedience—but rather the underlying motive which prompted you. Tell me! Are you not happy here?"

"Yes, I am happy."

"Good! And you've no reason to doubt your vocation?"

"No! I want more than ever to try to do some good in the world."

"That pleases me greatly. You don't wish to be sent away?"

"No!"

"Then tell us in your own words how you came to—to take your remarkable adventure."

At the quiet encouragement, Francis raised his head. He made a great effort, his eyes remote, his face troubled.

"I . . . I had just been to the chapel. But I couldn't pray, I couldn't seem to settle. I was restless. The *solano* was blowing—the hot wind seemed to make me more restless, the routine of the Seminary suddenly seemed petty and vexatious. Suddenly, I saw the road outside the gates, white and soft with dust. I couldn't help myself. I was on the road, walking. I walked all night, miles and miles. I walked—"

"All the next day." Father Tarrant bit out the satiric interruption. "And the next!"

"That's what I did."

"I never heard such a pack of rubbish in my life! It is an insult to the intelligence of the Committee."

The Rector, with frowning resolution, suddenly straightened himself in his chair.

"I propose that we temporarily adjourn." While the two priests stared at him in surprise, he said decisively to Francis: "You may go for the present. If we think it necessary we will recall you."

Francis left the room in a dead silence. Only then did the Rector turn to the others. He declared coldly: "I assure you that bullying will do no good. We must go carefully. There is more in this than meets the eye."

Smarting under the interference, Father Tarrant moved fretfully.

"It is the culmination of an unruly career."

"Not at all." The Rector demurred. "He's been eager and persevering ever since he came here. There is nothing damaging in his record, Father Gomez?"

Gomez turned the pages, on the desk, before him.

"No." He spoke slowly, reading from the record. "A few practical jokes. Last winter he set fire to the English newspaper when Father Despard was perusing it in the common room. Asked why . . . he laughed and answered, 'The Devil finds work for idle hands!' "

"Never mind that." The Rector spoke sharply. "We all know Father Despard corners every paper that comes into this Seminary."

"Then," Gomez resumed, "when deputed to read aloud in the refectory he smuggled in and substituted for *The Life of St. Peter of Alcantara* a C. R. S. tract entitled *When Eva Stole the Sugar* which—until he was stopped —induced much unseemly hilarity."

"Harmless mischief."

"Again . . ." Gomez turned another page. "In the comical procession the students got up, representing the Sacraments—you may remember, one dressed up as a baby representing Baptism, two others were got up as Matrimony, and so on—it was all done with permission of course. But," Gomez shot a dubious glance at Tarrant, "on the back of the corpse carried in for Extreme Unction, Chisholm pinned a card:

> "Here lies Father Tarrant
> I've gladly signed his warrant.
> If ever—"

"That's enough." Tarrant broke in sharply. "We've more to concern us than these absurd lampoons."

The Rector nodded. "Absurd, yes. But not malicious. I like a young man who can knock some fun out of life. We cannot ignore the fact that Chisholm is an unusual character—most unusual. He has great depth and fire. He's sensitive, inclined to fits of melancholy. He conceals it behind these high spirits. You see, he's a fighter, he'll never give in. He's a queer mixture of childlike simplicity and logical directness. And, above all, he's a complete individualist!"

"Individualism is rather a dangerous quality in a theologian," Tarrant interposed acidly. "It gave us the Reformation."

"And the Reformation gave us a better-behaved Catholic Church." The Rector smiled mildly at the ceiling. "But we're getting from the point. I don't deny there's been a gross breach of discipline. It must be punished. But the punishment cannot be rushed. I can't expel a student of Chisholm's quality without first knowing positively that he deserves expulsion. Therefore, let us wait a few days." He rose, innocently. "I'm sure you all agree."

As the three priests left the platform, Gomez and Tarrant went off together.

During the next two days an air of suspended doom overhung the unhappy Francis. He was not restrained. No apparent ban was placed upon his studies. But wherever he went—to the library, refectory or common room—an unnatural silence struck his fellows, followed swiftly by an exaggerated casualness which deceived no one. The knowledge that he was the universal topic gave him a guilty look. His Holywell companion, Hudson, also in the subdiaconate, pursued him with affectionate attentions and a worried frown. Anselm Mealey led another faction which clearly felt itself outraged. At recreation they consulted, approached the solitary figure. Mealey was the spokesman.

"We don't want to hit you when you're down, Francis. But this touches all of us. It's a slur upon the student body as a whole. We feel that it would be so much finer and manlier if you would make a clean breast and own up to it."

"Own up to what?"

Mealey shrugged his shoulders. There was a silence. What more could he do? As he turned away with the others he said:—

"We've decided to make a novena for you. I feel it worse than the others. I hoped you were my best friend."

Francis found it harder to maintain his pretence of normality. He would start off to walk in the Seminary grounds, then stop, sharply, recollecting that walking had been his ruin. He drifted about, aware that for Tarrant and the other professors he had ceased to exist. At the lectures he found he was not listening. The summons to the Rector he half hoped for did not come.

His sense of personal stress increased. He failed to understand himself. He was a purposeless enigma. He brooded over the justification of those who had predicted that he had no vocation. He had wild conceptions of setting out as a lay brother to some dangerous and distant mission. He began to haunt the church—but secretly. Above all there existed the necessity of putting on a face to meet his little world.

It was on the morning of the third day, Wednesday, that Father Gomez received the letter. Shocked but deeply gratified, his resourcefulness confirmed, he ran with it to the Administrator's office. He stood, while Father Tarrant read the note, like an intelligent dog awaiting its reward, a kind word or a bone.

Mi Amigo,

In reply to your honoured communication of Whit-Sunday, I deeply regret to inform you that inquiries have elicited the fact that a Seminarian, of such bearing, height and colour as you define, was observed in Cossa on April 14th. He was seen to enter the house of one Rosa Oyarzabal late that evening and to leave early the following morning. The woman in question lives alone, is of a known character, and has not frequented the altar rails for seven years.

I have the honour to remain, dear Padre,

Your devoted brother in Jesus Christus,

SALVADOR BOLAS
P. P. Cossa

Gomez murmured: "Don't you agree it was good strategy?"

"Yes, yes!" With a brow of thunder Tarrant brushed the Spaniard aside. Bearing the letter like something obscene, he strode into the Rector's room at the end of the corridor. But the Rector was saying his mass. He would be occupied for half an hour.

Father Tarrant could not wait. He crossed the courtyard like a whirlwind and, without knocking, burst into Francis' room. It was empty.

Checked, realizing that Francis must also be at mass, he struggled with his fury as an ungovernable horse might fight its bit. He sat down, abruptly, forcing himself to wait, his dark thin figure charged with lightning.

The cell was barer even than others of its kind, its inventory a bed, a chest, a table, the chair he occupied. Upon the chest stood one faded photograph, an angular woman in a frightful hat holding the hand of a white-clad little girl: *Love from Aunt Polly and Nora.*

Tarrant repressed his sneer. But his lip curled at the single picture on the whitewashed walls, a tiny replica of the Sistine Madonna, Our Lady of Chastity.

Suddenly, upon the table, he saw an open notebook: a diary. Again he started, like a nervous horse, his nostrils dilated, a dark red fire in his eye. For a moment he sat, battling his scruples, then rose and went slowly towards the book. He was a gentleman. It was repugnant to pry like a vulgar chambermaid, into another's privacy. But it was his duty. Who could guess what further iniquities this scroll contained? With relentless austerity upon his face, he picked up the written page.

". . . was it Saint Anthony who spoke of his 'ill-judged, obstinate and perverse behaviour'? I must console myself in the greatest despondency I have ever known, with that single thought! If they send me away from here my life will be broken. I'm a miserable crooked character, I don't think straight like the others, I cannot train myself to run with the pack. But with my whole soul I desire passionately to work for God. In our Father's house there are many mansions! There was room for such diversities as Joan of Arc and . . . well, Blessed Benedict Labre who let even the lice run over him. Surely there is room for me!

"They ask me to explain to them. How can one explain nothing—or what is so obvious as to be shameful? Francis de Sales said: 'I will be ground to powder rather than break a rule.' But when I walked out of the Seminary I did not think of rules, or of breaking them. Certain impulses are unconscious.

"It helps me to write this down: it gives my transgression the semblance of reason.

"For weeks I had been sleeping badly, tossing through these hot nights in a fever of unrest. Perhaps it is harder for me here than for the others—judged at least by the voluminous literature on the subject, wherein the steps to the priesthood are represented as sweet untroubled joys, piled one upon another. If our beloved laity knew how one has to fight!

"Here my greatest difficulty has been the sense of confinement, of physical inaction—what a bad mystic I should make!—always aggravated by echoes, stray sounds, penetrating inwards from the outer world. Then I realize that I am twenty-three, that I have done nothing yet to help a single living soul, and I am fevered with unrest.

"Willie Tulloch's letters provide—in Father Gomez' phrase—the most per-nicious stimuli. Now that Willie is a qualified doctor and his sister Jean a certified nurse, both working for the Tynecastle Poor Law Board and enjoying many thrilling, if verminous, adventures in the slums, I feel that I should be out and fighting too.

"Of course I shall, one day. . . . I must be patient. But my present ferment seems heightened by the news of Ned and Polly. I was happy when they decided to remove from above the tavern and have Judy, the child, to live with them in the little flat which Polly had taken at Clermont, on the out-skirts of the city. But Ned has been ill, Judy troublesome, and Gilfoyle—left to manage Union Tavern—a most unsatisfactory business partner. Ned, in fact, has gone to pieces, refuses to go out, sees no one. That one impulse of blind unthinkable stupidity has finished him. A baser man would have survived it.

"The pattern of life sometimes demands great faith. Dear Nora! That tender platitude conceals a thousand avenues of thought and feeling. When Father Tarrant gave us that practical talk—*agendo contra*—he said most truly: 'Some temptations cannot be fought—one must close one's mind and fly from them!' My excursion to Cossa must have been that kind of flight.

"At first, though walking fast, I did not mean to go far when I passed through the Seminary gates. But the relief, the sense of escape from myself which the violent exercise afforded, drove me on. I sweated gloriously, like a peasant in the fields—that salty running sweat which seems to purge one of human dross. My mind lifted, my heart began to sing. I wanted to go on and on until I dropped!

"I walked all day without food or drink. I covered a great distance, for, when evening drew near, I could smell the sea. And as the stars broke out in the pale sky, I came over the hill and found Cossa at my feet. The village, harboured on a sheltered creek where the sea barely lapped, with blossoming acacia trees lining its single street, had an almost heavenly beauty. I was dead with tiredness. There was an enormous blister on my heel. But as I came down the hill the place welcomed me with its quiet pulse of life.

"In the little square the villagers were enjoying the cool air, scented with acacia flowers, the dusk made dimmer by the lamps of the little inn, where at an open doorway stood two pine benches. Before the benches in the soft dust some old men were playing bowls with wooden balls. From the creek came the booming of frogs. Children laughed and ran. It was simple and beautiful. Though I now realized that I had not a peseta in my pocket, I seated myself on one of the benches outside the door. How good it was to rest. I was stupid with fatigue. Suddenly, in the quiet darkness beneath the trees, the sound of Catalan pipes rang out. Not loud—low, attuned to the night. If one has not heard these reeds, or the shrill, sweet native tunes, one cannot fully estimate the gladness of that moment. I was enchanted. I sup-pose, as a Scot, I've the lilt of the pipes in my blood. I sat as though drugged by the music, the darkness, the beauty of the night, my utter weakness.

"I had resolved to sleep out on the beach. But presently, as I thought to move there, a mist rolled in from the sea. It fell like a mystery upon the village. In five minutes the square was choked with twisting vapour, the trees dripping, and everybody going home. I had reached the conclusion, unwillingly, that I must go to the local priest, 'give myself up,' and get a bed, when a woman seated on the other bench suddenly spoke to me. For some time I had felt her gazing at me with that mixture of pity and contempt which the mere sight of a religious seems to provoke in Christian countries. Now, as if she read my thoughts, she said: 'They are tight people there. They will not take you in.'

"She was about thirty years of age, dressed quietly in black, with a pale face, dark eyes and a thickened figure. She continued indifferently:

" 'There is a bed in my house if you wish to sleep in it.'

" 'I have no money to pay for a lodging.'

"She laughed scornfully. 'You can pay me with your prayers.'

"It had now begun to rain. They had closed the *fonda*. We both sat on the wet benches under the dripping acacia trees in the deserted square. The absurdity of this seemed to strike her. She rose.

" 'I am going home. If you are not a fool you will accept my hospitality.'

"My thin soutane was soaked. I had begun to shiver. I reflected that I could send her money for my room on my return to the Seminary. I got up and walked with her down the narrow street.

"Her house was halfway down the row. We descended two steps into the kitchen. When she had lit the lamp, she threw off the black shawl, put a pot of chocolate on the fire and took a new loaf from the oven. She spread a red-checked tablecloth. Bubbling chocolate and hot bread made a good smell in the small clean room.

"As she poured the chocolate into thick cups she looked at me across the table. 'You had better say grace. That improves the flavour!' Though now there was no mistaking the irony in her voice, I said grace. We began to eat and drink. The flavour needed no improvement.

"She kept watching me. She had once been a very pretty woman, but the remnants of her beauty made her dark-eyed olive face seem hard. Her small ears were close to her head and pierced with heavy gold rings. Her hands were plump like the hands of a Rubens Madonna.

" 'Well, little padre, you are lucky to be here. I have no liking for the priests. In Barcelona, when I pass them I break into open laughter!'

"I couldn't help smiling. 'You don't surprise me. It's the first thing we learn—to be laughed at. The best man I ever knew used to preach in the open air. The whole town turned out to laugh at him. They named him, in mockery, Holy Daniel. You see, there's so little doubt nowadays that anyone who believes in God is a hypocrite or a fool!'

"She took a slow drink of chocolate, watching me over her cup. 'You are no fool. Tell me, do I please you?'

" 'I think you are charming and kind.'

" 'It is my nature to be kind. I've had a sad life. My father was a Castilian noble who was dispossessed by the Madrid Government. My husband commanded a great ship in the Navy. He was lost at sea. I myself am an actress —living quietly here at present until my father's estate is recovered. Of course you understand that I am lying.'

" 'Perfectly!'

"She didn't take this as a joke as I had hoped. She reddened slightly. 'You are too clever. But I know why you are here, my runaway priestling; you are all the same.' She got over her fit of pique, and mocked: 'You forsake Mother Church for Mother Eve.'

"I was puzzled, then her meaning dawned on me. It was so absurd I wanted to laugh. But it was annoying too—I supposed I'd have to clear out. I had finished my bread and chocolate. I rose and took my hat. 'Thank you exceedingly for my supper. It was excellent.'

"Her expression changed, all the malice driven out of it by surprise. 'So you are a hypocrite then.' She bit her lip sulkily. As I went to the door she said suddenly: 'Don't go!'

"A silence. She said defiantly:—

" 'Don't look at me like that. I'm entitled to do as I choose. I enjoy myself. You should see me Saturday evenings, sitting in the Cava at Barcelona—more fun than ever you'll have in your miserable little life. Go upstairs and sleep.'

"There was a pause. Her attitude now seemed reasonable; and I could hear the rain outside. I hesitated, then moved towards the narrow stairs. My feet were swollen and smarting. I must have limped badly, for she exclaimed suddenly, coldly: 'What is the matter with your precious foot?'

" 'It's nothing . . . only blistered.'

"She studied me with those strange unfathomable eyes.

" 'I will bathe it for you.'

"In spite of all my protests she made me sit down. When she had filled a basin with warm water she knelt and took off my boot. My sock was sticking to the raw flesh. She softened it with water and drew it off. Her unexpected kindness embarrassed me. She bathed both my feet and put some ointment on them. Then she stood up.

" 'That should feel better. Your socks will be ready for you in the morning.'

" 'How can I thank you?'

"She said unexpectedly in an odd dull tone: 'What does one do with a life like mine!' Before I could answer she raised the pitcher in her right hand. 'Do not preach at me or I will break your head. Your bed is on the second landing. Good night.'

"She turned away towards the fire. I went upstairs, found a small room beneath the skylight. I slept as though stunned.

"Next morning when I came down, she was moving about the kitchen, making coffee. She gave me breakfast. As I took my leave I tried to express my gratitude. But she cut me short. She gave me her sad peculiar smile. 'You are too innocent to be a priest. You will be a great failure.'

"I started back for San Morales. I was lame and rather scared of my reception. I was afraid. I took my time."

Father Tarrant remained motionless at the window for a long moment, then quietly replaced the diary upon the table, reminded by a glint of recollection that it was he who had first asked Francis to keep it. Methodically he tore the Spanish priest's letter into fragments. The expression on his face was quite remarkable. For once it lacked its bleakness, that iron austerity seared into every feature by pitiless self-mortification. It became a young face, flooded with generosity and thoughtfulness. With his clenched hand still holding the pieces of the letter, slowly, almost unconsciously, he struck his breast three times. Then he spun round and left the room.

As he descended the broad staircase Anselm Mealey's solid head came up and around the spiral balustrade. Observing Father Tarrant, the model seminarian dared to pause. He admired the Administrator to excess. To be noticed by him was a heavenly joy. He ventured modestly:—

"Excuse me, sir. We are all very anxious. I am wondering if there is any more news . . . concerning Chisholm?"

"What news?"

"Well . . . of his leaving."

Tarrant contemplated his creature with remote distaste. "Chisholm is not leaving." He added, with sudden violence, "You fool!"

That evening as Francis sat in his study, dizzy and unbelieving under the miracle of his redemption, one of the college servants silently handed in a packet. It contained a superb figure of the Virgin of Montserrat carved in ebony, a tiny masterpiece of fifteenth-century Spanish craftsmanship. No message accompanied the exquisite thing. Not a word of explanation. Suddenly, with a wild consuming thought, Francis remembered he had seen it above the prie-dieu in Father Tarrant's room.

It was the Rector, meeting Francis at the end of the week, who put his finger on the manifest inconsistency. "It strikes me, young sir, that you have escaped gey lightly, through a sinister screen of sanctity. In my young days playing truant—'plunking' we called it—was a punishable crime." He fixed on Francis his shrewd and twinkling gaze. "As a penance you might write me an essay—two thousand words—on 'The Virtue of Walking.'"

In the small universe of a seminary the very walls have ears, the keyholes diabolic vision. The story of Francis' escapade came gradually to light, was fitted, piece by piece, together. It grew, gained indeed, as it passed from lip to ear. Assuming the facets of the finished gem, it seemed likely to descend—a classic in the Seminary's history. When Father Gomez had the final details, he wrote fully to his friend the parish priest of Cossa. Father Bolas was much impressed. He wrote back, a glowing five-page letter, of which, perhaps, the final paragraph merits quotation:—

Naturally, the pinnacle of achievement would have been the conversion of the woman, Rosa Oyarzabal. How wonderful it would have been had she come to me and wept, on her knees, in true contrition, as the result of our young apostle's visitation! But alas! She has gone into partnership with another madam and opened a brothel in Barcelona, which I grieve to report is flourishing.

III

AN UNSUCCESSFUL CURATE

1

It was raining steadily, early that Saturday evening in January when Francis arrived at Shalesley, on the branch line, some forty miles from Tynecastle. But nothing could damp the eagerness, the burning of his spirit. While the train disappeared into the mist, he stood expectantly on the wet open platform, his alert eyes sweeping its dreary vacancy. No one had come to meet him. Undismayed, he picked up his bag and swung into the main street of the colliery village. The Church of the Redeemer should not be hard to find.

It was his first appointment, his first curacy. He could scarcely believe it. His heart sang . . . at last, at last, newly ordained, he had his chance to get into the battle and fight for human souls.

Though he had been forewarned, Francis had never seen greater ugliness than that which now surrounded him. Shalesley consisted of long grey rows of houses and poor cheap shops, interspaced with plots of waste land, slag heaps,—smoking even in the rain,—a refuse dump, several taverns and chapels, all dominated by the high black headstocks of the Renshaw Colliery. But he told himself gaily that his interest lay in the people, not the place.

The Catholic church stood on the east side of the village, adjacent to the colliery, harmonizing with the scene. It was a big erection of raw red brick with Gothic blue-stained windows, a dark red corrugated iron roof, and a sawed-off rusty spire. The school lay on one side; the Presbytery, fronted by a weedy plot and girded by a broken-toothed fence, upon the other.

With a deep, excited breath, Francis approached the small, ramshackle house and pulled the bell. After some delay, when he was about to ring again, the door was opened by a stout woman in a blue striped apron. Inspecting him, she nodded.

"It'll be yourself, Father! His Reverence is expecting you. In there!" She pointed with privileged good nature to the parlour door. "What weather to be sure. I'll away and put on the kippers."

Francis sturdily entered the room. Already seated at a table covered with a white cloth and laid for a repast, a thickset priest of about fifty stopped his impatient knife-tapping to greet his new curate.

"You're here at last. Come in."

Francis extended his hand. "Father Kezer, I imagine?"

"That's right. Who did you expect? King William of Orange? Well, you're just in time for supper. Trust you!" Tilting back, he called to the adjoining kitchen. "Miss Cafferty! Are you going to be all night?" Then, to Francis: "Sit down and stop looking like the lost chord. I hope you play cribbage. I like a game of an evening."

Francis took a chair at the table and soon Miss Cafferty hurried in with a large covered dish of kippers and poached eggs. As Father Kezer helped himself to two eggs and a brace of kippers she laid another place for Francis. Then Father Kezer passed over the dish, his mouth full.

"Go ahead and help yourself. Don't stint. You'll have to work hard here so you'd better eat."

He himself ate rapidly, his strong crunching jaws and capable hands, felted with black hairs, never at rest. He was burly, with a round cropped head, and a tight mouth. His nose was flat, with wide nostrils out of which sprouted two dark snuff-stained tufts. He conveyed the impression of strength, of authority. Every movement was a masterpiece of unconscious self-assertion. As he cut an egg in two and slipped one half into his mouth his little eyes watched, formed an opinion of Francis, as a butcher might weigh the merits of a steer.

"You don't look too hardy. Under eleven stone, eh? I don't know what you curates are coming to. My last was a weak-kneed effort! Should have called himself flea—not Lee—he hadn't the guts of one. It's this Continental la-de-da that ruins you. In my time—well, the fellows that came out of Maynooth with me were men."

"I think you'll find me sound in wind and limb." Francis smiled.

"We'll soon see." Father Kezer grunted. "Go in and hear confessions when you've finished. I'll be in later. There won't be many tonight though . . . seeing it's wet. Give them an excuse! They're bone lazy—my beautiful lot!"

Upstairs, in his thin-walled room, massively furnished with a heavy bed and an enormous Victorian wardrobe, Francis washed his hands and face at the stained washstand. Then he hastened down towards the church. The impression Father Kezer had given him was not favourable, but he told himself he must be fair: immediate judgements were so often unjust. He sat for a long time in the cold confessional box,—still marked with the name of his predecessor, Fr. Lee,—hearing the drumming of the rain on the tin roof. At last he came out and wandered round the empty church. It was a depressing spectacle—bare as a barn and not very clean. An unhappy attempt had been made to marble the nave with dark green paint. The statue of Saint Joseph had lost a hand and been clumsily repaired. The stations of the cross were sad little daubs. On the altar some gaudy paper flowers, in vases of tarnished brass, hit the eye like an affront. But these little shortcomings only made his opportunity the greater. The tabernacle was there. And Francis knelt before it, with throbbing fervour, dedicating his life anew.

Habituated to the cultured atmosphere of San Morales, a half-way house for scholars and preachers, men of breeding and distinction moving between London, Madrid and Rome, Francis found the next few days increasingly difficult. Father Kezer was not an easy man. Naturally irascible and inclined to surliness, age, experience, and failure to win affection from his flock had made him hard as nails.

At one time he had held an excellent parish in the seaside resort of East-cliffe. He had proved himself so disagreeable that important people in the town had petitioned the Bishop to remove him. The incident, at first bitterly resented, had been hallowed by time into an act of personal sacrifice. He would remark, soulfully: "Of my own free will I stepped from the throne to the footstool . . . but, ah! . . . those were the days."

Miss Cafferty, his cook and housekeeper combined, alone stood by him. She had been with him for years. She understood him, she was of his own kidney, she could take his slangings and heartily slang him back. The two respected each other. When he departed on his annual six weeks' holiday to Harrogate he allowed her to go home for her own vacation.

In his personal habits he had scant refinement. He stamped around his bedroom, opened and slammed the single bathroom door. The matchboard house reverberated with his wind.

Unwittingly, he had reduced his religion to a formula—with no conception of interior meanings, of the unsubstantial, no elasticity of outlook. "Do this or be damned" was imprinted on his heart. There were certain things to be accomplished with words, water, oil and salt. Without them, hell was ready, hot and gaping. He was deeply prejudiced, loudly voicing his detestation of every other denomination in the village—an attitude which did little to gain him friends.

Even in his relations with his own congregation he was not at peace. The parish was a poor one with a heavy debt upon the church and despite a stringent economy he was often desperately pressed to make ends meet. He had a legitimate case to place before his people. But his natural ire was a poor substitute for tact. In his sermons, planted solidly on his feet, head thrust aggressively forward, he lashed the sparse congregation for its neglect.

"How do you expect me to pay the rent, and the taxes, and the insurance? And keep the church roof over your heads? You're not giving it to me, you're giving it to Almighty God. Now listen to me, every man and woman of ye. It's silver I want to see in the plate, not your miserable brass farthings. You're most of you in work you men, thanks to the generosity of Sir George Renshaw. You've no excuse! As for the wimmen of the parish—if they'd put more in the offertory and less on their backs it would fit them better." He thundered on, then took up the collection himself, glaring accusingly at each of his parishioners as he shoved the plate beneath their noses.

His demands had provoked a feud, a bitter vendetta between himself and his parishioners. The more he berated them the less they gave. Enraged, he devised schemes, took to distributing little buff envelopes. When they left the empty envelopes behind he went round the church after the service, gathering up the litter and muttering furiously: "That's how they treat Almighty God!"

In this gloomy financial sky there was one bright sun.

Sir George Renshaw, who owned the Shalesley colliery, with, indeed, fifteen other coal mines in the county, was not only a man of immense resources and a Catholic but an inveterate philanthropist. Though his country seat, Renshaw Hall, was seventy miles away, on the other side of the shire, the Church of the Redeemer had somehow gained a place upon his list. Every Christmas, with the utmost regularity, a cheque for one hundred guineas reached the parish priest. "Guineas, mind ye!" Father Kezer anointed the word. "Not just measly pounds. Ah! There's a gentleman for ye!" He had seen Sir George only twice, at public gatherings in Tynecastle many years before, but he spoke of him with reverence and awe. He had a lurking fear that, through no fault of his, the magnate might discontinue the charity.

By the end of his first month at Shalesley, close association with Father Kezer began to take effect on Francis. He was continually on edge. No wonder young Father Lee had had such a bad nervous breakdown. His spiritual life became overcast, his sense of values confused. He found himself regarding Father Kezer with growing hostility. Then he would recollect himself with an inward groan, and strive wildly for obedience, for humility.

His parochial work was desperately hard, particularly in this wintry weather. Three times a week he had to bicycle to Broughton and Glenburn, two distant wretched hamlets, to say mass, hear confessions, and take the catechism class in the local town hall. The lack of response amongst his people increased his difficulties. The very children were lethargic, shuffling. There was much poverty, heartrending destitution; the whole parish seemed steeped in apathy, savourless and stale. Passionately he told himself he would not surrender to routine. Conscious of his clumsiness and inefficiency, he had a burning desire to reach these poor hearts, to succour and revive them. He would kindle a spark, blaze the dead ashes into life, if it were the last thing he did.

What made it worse was the fact that the parish priest, astute and watchful, seemed to sense, with a kind of grim humour, the difficulties his curate was experiencing, and to anticipate slyly a readjustment of the other's idealism to his own practical common sense. Once when Francis came in, tired and wet, having bicycled ten miles through wind and rain to an outlying sick call at Broughton, Father Kezer compressed his attitude into a single jibe. "Handing out halos isn't what you thought it was—eh?" He added, naturally: "A good-for-nothing lot."

Francis flushed hotly. "Christ died for a good-for-nothing lot."

Deeply upset, Francis began to mortify himself. At meals he ate sparingly, often only a cup of tea and some toast. Frequently, when he woke up in the middle of the night, tortured by misgivings, he would steal down to the church. Shadowed and silent, washed in pale moonlight, the bare edifice lost its distracting crudity. He flung himself down on his knees, begging for courage to embrace the tribulations of this beginning, praying with impetuous violence. At last, as he gazed at the wounded figure on the cross, patient, gentle, suffering, peace would fill his soul.

One night, shortly after midnight, when he had made a visit of this nature and was tiptoeing upstairs, he found Father Kezer waiting on him. Wearing his nightshirt and an overcoat, a candle in his hand, the parish priest planted his thick hairy legs on the top landing, angrily barred the way.

"What d'you think you're doing?"

"Going to my room."

"Where have you been?"

"To the church."

"What! At this time of night!"

"Why not?" Francis forced a smile. "Do you think I might wake our Lord up?"

"No, but you might wake me up." Father Kezer lost his temper. "I won't have it. I never heard such nonsense in my life. I'm running a parish, not a religious order. You can pray all you want in the day, but while you're under my orders you'll sleep at night."

Francis suppressed the hot answer on his tongue. He walked to his bedroom in silence. He must curb himself, make a great effort to get on with his superior, if he were to do any good in the parish at all. He tried to concentrate on Father Kezer's good points: his frankness and courage, his odd jocularity, his adamantine chastity.

A few days later, choosing a moment which he thought propitious, he diplomatically approached the older priest.

"I've been wondering, Father . . . we've such a scattered district, so out of the way, with no proper places of amusement . . . wondering if we couldn't have a club for the youngsters of the parish."

"Aha!" Father Kezer was in his jocular mood. "So you're out for popularity, my lad!"

"Good gracious, no." Francis took up an equal heartiness, so intent was he on winning his point. "I don't want to presume. But a club might take the young people off the streets—and the older ones out of the pubs. Develop them physically and socially." He smiled. "Even make them want to come to church."

"Ho, ho!" Father Kezer guffawed. "It's well you're young. I believe you're worse than Lee. Well, go ahead if you want to. But you'll get all your thanks in one basket from the good-for-nothing crowd that hangs out here."

"Thank you, thank you. I only wanted your permission."

With thrilling eagerness Francis immediately began to carry out his plan. Donald Kyle, the manager at Renshaw Colliery, was a Scot and a steady Catholic who had showed signs of goodwill. Two other officials at the pit, Morrison the check-weigher, whose wife occasionally came in to help at the Presbytery, and Creeden, the head shot-firer, were also members of the church. Through the manager, Francis received permission to use the colliery first-aid hall three nights a week. With the help of the other two he set out to stir up interest in the proposed club. His own money, added up, made less than two pounds, and he would have died sooner than ask assistance from the parish. But he wrote to Willie Tulloch—whose work brought him into touch with the Tynecastle Corporation Recreation Centres—begging him to send along some old and cast-off athletic gear.

Puzzling how he might best launch the venture, he decided that nothing could draw the young people better than a dance. There was a piano in the room and Creeden was a first-rate performer on the fiddle. He posted up a notice on the Red Cross door, and when Thursday arrived, he expended his capital on a buffet of cakes, fruit and lemonade.

The success of the evening, after a stiff start, surpassed his wildest expectations: so many turned out they managed eight sets of lancers. Most of the lads had no shoes, they danced in their pit boots. Between the dances they sat on the benches round the room, red-faced and happy, while the girls went to the buffet to find them refreshment. When they waltzed they all sang the words of the refrain. A little group of pitmen going off shift gathered at the entrance, the gaslight showing their teeth white against their grimed faces. Towards the end they joined in the singing, and one or two of the brighter sparks amongst them nipped in and stole a dance. It was a merry evening.

As he stood at the door, with their good nights ringing in his ears, Francis thought with a surge of trembling joy: "They've begun to come alive. Dear God, I've made a start."

Next morning Father Kezer came in to breakfast in a towering rage.

"What's this I hear? A fine to-do! A right royal example. You ought to be ashamed of yourself."

Francis looked up in amazement. "What on earth do you mean?"

"You know what I mean! That infernal stew you put on last night."

"You gave me permission—only a week ago."

Father Kezer snarled: "I didn't give you permission to start a promiscuous rigadoon on the very doorstep of my church. I've had trouble enough to keep my young girls pure without your introducin' your immodest pawing and prancing!"

"The entire evening was perfectly innocent."

"Innocent!—As God is above us!" Father Kezer was dark red with anger. "Don't you know what that sort of gallantry leads to—you poor dolt—clutching and clasping and bodies and legs together? It starts bad thoughts working in these young folks' minds. It leads to concupiscence, carnality and lusts of the flesh."

Francis was very pale, his eyes were blazing with indignation.

"Aren't you confusing lust with sex?"

"Holy St. Joseph! What's the difference?"

"As much as there is between disease and health."

Father Kezer's hands made a convulsive gesture. "What in the foul fiend's name are you talking about?"

The pent-up bitterness of the past two months broke over Francis in a tempestuous wave. "You can't suppress nature. If you do it'll turn on you and rend you. It's perfectly natural and good for young men and women to mix together, to dance together. It's a natural prelude to courtship and marriage. You can't keep sex under a dirty sheet like a stinking corpse. That's what starts the sly laugh, the prurient sneer. We must learn to educate and transmute sex, not choke it as though it were an adder. If you try that you'll fail, besides making something filthy out of what is clean and fine!"

A horrible silence. The veins in Father Kezer's neck were swollen, purple. "You blasphemous pup! I'll not have my young folks couplin' in your dance halls!"

"Then you'll drive them to couple—as you call it—in the dark lanes and fields."

"You lie," Father Kezer stuttered. "I'll keep the maidenhood of this parish undeflowered. I know what I'm about."

"No doubt," Francis answered bitterly. "But the fact remains that statistics show the Shalesley illegitimacy rate to be the highest in the diocese."

For a moment it seemed as though the parish priest must have a fit. His hands clenched and unclenched, as though seeking something to strangle. Rocking slightly on his feet, he raised his finger and levelled it at Francis. "Statistics'll show another thing. And that is there's no club within five miles of this spot I'm standing on. Your fine plan is finished, smashed, done for. I say that! And in this case *my* word is final!" He flung himself down at the table and furiously began his breakfast.

Francis finished quickly and went upstairs to his room, pale and shaken. Through the dusty panes he could see the first-aid room, with the packing case of boxing gloves and Indian clubs outside, which had arrived yesterday from Tulloch, all useless now, forbidden. A terrible emotion rose up in him. He thought rigidly: I cannot continue to submit, God cannot demand such subservience, I must fight, fight, on Father Kezer's level, fight, not for myself, but for this pitiful, broken-winded parish. He was rent by an overflowing love, an undreamed-of longing to help these poor people, his first charge from God.

During the next few days, as he went through the routine of the parish, he sought feverishly for some means of lifting the ban upon his club. Somehow the club had become the symbol of the parish's emancipation. But the more he dwelt upon it the more unassailable Father Kezer's position appeared.

Drawing his own conclusions from Francis' quietness the older priest showed an ill-concealed jubilation. He was the one to tame them, to bring these young pups to heel. The Bishop must know how good he was to send him so many, one after the other. His sour grin broadened.

Quite suddenly, Francis had an idea. It struck him with overwhelming force, a slender chance, perhaps, yet one which might succeed. His pale face coloured slightly, he almost cried out loud. With a great effort, he calmed himself. He thought: I'll try, I must try . . . whenever Aunt Polly's visit is over.

He had arranged for Aunt Polly and Judy to come to Shalesley for a holiday during the last week in June. Shalesley, it is true, was not a health resort. But it stood high, the air was good. The fresh green of spring had touched its bleakness with a transient beauty. And Francis was particularly anxious that Polly should have the rest she so richly deserved.

The winter had been hard for her, physically and financially. Thaddeus Gilfoyle was, in her own phrase, "ruining" the Union, drinking more than he sold, failing to show receipts, trying to get the remnants of the business into his own hands. Ned's chronic illness had taken a peculiar turn, for twelve months now he had lost the power of his legs and was quite beyond business. Confined to a wheeled chair, he had lately become irresponsible and irrational. He had absurd delusions, spoke to the smirking, toadying Thaddeus of his steam yacht, his private brewery in Dublin. One day he had escaped her care and attended by Scanty—a grotesque spectacle of motion—had propelled himself to the Clermont shops and ordered himself two dozen hats. Dr. Tulloch, called in at Francis' request, had pronounced Ned's condition no stroke, but a tumour of the brain. It was he who had procured the male nurse who was now relieving Polly.

Francis would have greatly preferred Judy and Aunt Polly to occupy the guest room at the Presbytery—indeed, one of his dreams was a parish of his own where Polly would be his housekeeper and Judy his particular charge. But Father Kezer's attitude made a request for hospitality out of the question. Francis found a comfortable lodging for them at Mrs. Morrison's. And on June 21st, Aunt Polly and Judy arrived.

Welcoming them at the station, he felt a sudden pain in his heart. Polly, a stiff valiant figure, advanced from the train, leading by the hand, as she had led Nora, the small, dark, glossy-haired child.

"Polly. Dear Polly." He spoke as to himself. She was little changed, a trifle shabbier perhaps, her gaunt cheeks more drawn. She had the same short coat, gloves, and hat. She never spent a penny on herself, always on others. She had cared for Nora and himself, for Ned and now for Judy. She was so utterly selfless, his breast filled. He stepped forward and hugged her.

"Polly, I'm so glad to see you . . . you're . . . you're eternal."

"Oh, dear." She fumbled in her bag for her handkerchief. "It's windy here. And there's something in my eye."

He took her arm and Judy's, and escorted them to their rooms.

He did his utmost to give them a happy time. In the evenings he had long talks with Polly. Her pride in him, in what he had become, was touching. She made light of her troubles.

But she admitted one anxiety—Judy was a problem.

The child, now ten years of age and attending the day school at Clermont, was a queer mixture. Superficially she had an engaging frankness, but beneath she was suspicious and secretive. She hoarded all sorts of odds and ends in her bedroom, and would shake with temper if they were disturbed. She had wild enthusiasms which quickly faded. In other moods she was timid and uncertain. She could not bear to admit a fault and would wander glibly from the truth to hide it. The hint that she was lying brought floods of indignant tears.

With this before him Francis made every effort to win her confidence. He had her frequently to the Presbytery where, with the complete unconsciousness of the young, she made herself at home, often wandering off into Father Kezer's room, climbing on his sofa, fingering his pipes and paperweights. It was embarrassing, but since the parish priest made no protest, Francis did not restrain the child.

On the last day of their short holiday, when Aunt Polly had gone for a final walk and Judy had at length come to rest with a picture book in the corner of Francis' room, a knock sounded on the door. It was Miss Cafferty. She addressed Francis.

"His Reverence wants to see you immediately."

Francis' brows lifted at the unexpected request. There was something ominous in the housekeeper's words. He rose, slowly.

Father Kezer stood waiting in his own room. For the first time in weeks he looked straight at Francis.

"That child is a thief."

Francis said nothing. But he felt a sudden hollow in his stomach.

"I trusted her. I let her play about the place. I thought she was a nice little thing even though—" Kezer broke off angrily.

"What has she taken?" Francis said. His lips were stiff.

"What do thieves usually take?" Father Kezer swung round to the mantelpiece where a row of little pillars stood, each made up of twelve pennies, wrapped in white paper by his own careful hands. He picked one up. "She's stolen from the collection money. It's worse than thievery. It's simony. Look at this."

Francis examined the packet. It had been opened and clumsily retwisted at the top. Three of the pennies were missing.

"What makes you think Judy did this?"

"I'm not a fool," Father Kezer snapped. "I've been missing pennies all week. Every copper in these packets is marked."

Without a word Francis turned towards his own room. The parish priest followed him.

"Judy. Show me your purse."

Judy looked as though she had been struck. But she recovered quickly. She smiled innocently.

"I left it at Mrs. Morrison's."

"No, here it is." Francis bent forward and took the purse from the outside patch pocket of her dress. It was a new little strap purse which Aunt Polly had given her before the holiday. Francis opened it with a sinking heart. There were three pennies inside. Each had a cross scratched on the back.

Father Kezer's scowl was both outraged and triumphant. "What did I tell you? Ah! You wicked little brat, stealing from God!" He glared at Francis. "She ought to be prosecuted for this. If she were my responsibility I'd march her straight down to the police."

"No, no." Judy burst into tears. "I meant to put it back, truly I did."

Francis was very pale. The situation was horrible for him. He took his courage in both hands.

"Very well," he said quietly. "We'll go down to the police station and charge her before Sergeant Hamilton straightaway."

Judy's grief became hysterical. Father Kezer, taken aback, sneered: "I'd like to see you."

Francis picked up his hat and took Judy's hand.

"Come along, Judy. You must be brave. We're going down to Sergeant Hamilton to tell him Father Kezer charges you with stealing three pennies."

As Francis led the child towards the door, confusion, then positive apprehension, flared up in Father Kezer's eyes. He had let his tongue run away with him. Sergeant Hamilton, an Orangeman, was no friend of his: they had often clashed bitterly in the past. And now . . . this trivial charge . . . he saw himself jeered at all over the village. He mumbled suddenly:—

"Ye needn't go!"

Francis did not seem to hear.

"Stop!" Father Kezer shouted. He fought down his temper, choked out: "We'll . . . we'll forget about it. Talk to her yourself."

He walked out of the room seething with rage.

When Aunt Polly and Judy returned to Tynecastle, Francis had a quick revulsion: he wanted to explain, to express his regret for Judy's petty pilfering. But Father Kezer froze him. A sense of being balked had further embittered the older man. Besides, he was shortly leaving on his vacation. He wanted to put the curate thoroughly in his place before he left.

He ignored Francis with tight-mouthed surliness. By arrangement with Miss Cafferty he took his meals alone, before the junior priest was served. On the Sunday before his departure, he preached a violent sermon, every word aimed at Francis, on the seventh commandment: "Thou shalt not steal."

The sermon decided Francis. Immediately the service was over he went direct to Donald Kyle's house, took the manager aside, and talked to him with restrained intensity. Gradually a light broke over Kyle's face, still dubious perhaps, but hopeful, aroused. He muttered, finally: "I doubt if we can do it! But I'm with ye all the way." The two men shook hands.

On Monday morning Father Kezer left for Harrogate where, for the next six weeks, he would drink the waters. That evening Miss Cafferty went off to her native Rosslare. And on Tuesday, early, Francis met Donald Kyle by appointment at the station. Kyle carried a portfolio of papers and a glossy new brochure recently issued by a large rival coal combine in Nottingham. He wore his best clothes and an air only slightly less resolved than Francis'. They took the eleven o'clock train from Shalesley.

The long day passed slowly, they did not return until late evening. They came up the road together in silence; each looked straight ahead. Francis seemed tired, his expression revealed nothing. It was perhaps significant that the colliery manager smiled with grim solemnity as they said "Good night."

The next four days passed normally. Then, without warning, there began a period of strange activity.

The activity seemed centred upon the colliery, not unnaturally, since the colliery was the centre of the district. Francis was there a good deal between the works of the parish, consulting with Donald Kyle, studying the architect's blue prints, watching the squads of men at work. It was remarkable how quickly the new building grew. In a fortnight it had risen above the adjoining aid-room, in a month the structure was complete. Then the carpenters and plasterers came in. The sound of hammering fell exquisitely on Francis' ears. He sniffed the aroma of fresh wood shavings. Occasionally he set to and did a job with the men. They liked him. He had inherited from his father a fondness for working with his hands.

Alone in the Presbytery, except for the unobtrusive daily visits of Mrs. Morrison, his temporary housekeeper, free of the nagging of his superior, his fervour knew no limits, a pure white glow pervaded him. He felt himself getting close to the people, breaking down suspicion, gradually entering their dulled lives, bringing to hidden stolid eyes a sudden startled gleam. It was a glorious sensation, a mingling of purpose and achievement, as though, embracing the poverty and wretchedness about him, he drew near in pity and soaring tenderness to the threshold of the unseen God.

Five days before Father Kezer's return, Francis sat down and wrote a letter. It ran as follows:—

                                                Shalesley,
                                                September 15th, 1897.
Dear Sir George,

The new recreation centre which you have so generously donated to Shalesley Village is now practically complete. It should prove a tremendous boon, not only to your own colliery workers and their families, but to everyone else in this scattered industrial district, irrespective of class or creed. A non-partisan committee has already been formed and a syllabus drawn up on the lines we discussed. From the copy I enclose you will see how comprehensive is our winter programme: boxing and singlestick classes, physical culture, first-aid instruction and a weekly dance every Thursday.

When I consider the unhesitating liberality with which you met the diffident and perhaps unwarranted approach of Mr. Kyle and myself I am quite overwhelmed. Any words of gratitude which I might use would be hopelessly inadequate. Your real thanks will come from the happiness which you bring to the working people of Shalesley and from the good which must undoubtedly result from their increased social unity.

We propose holding a gala opening night on September 21st. If you would consent to honour us with your presence our gratification would be complete.

                                        Believe me,
                                                Yours most sincerely,
                                                FRANCIS CHISHOLM
                                        Curate of the Church of the Redeemer

He posted the letter with a strange taut smile. His words were heartfelt, burningly sincere. But his legs were trembling.

At midday on the nineteenth, one day after his housekeeper's return, Father Kezer reappeared. Fortified by the saline waters, he was bursting with energy—in his own phrase: fair itching to get his fingers on the reins. Reinfusing the Presbytery with his loud, black, hairy essence, with his shouted greeting to Miss Cafferty, his demand for substantial food, he ran through his correspondence. Then he bustled into lunch, rubbing his hands. On his plate lay an envelope. He ripped it open, drew out the printed card.

"What's this?"

Francis moistened his dry lips, mustered all his courage. "It appears to be an invitation to the opening night of the new Shalesley Athletic and Recreation Club. I've had one too."

"Recreation Club. What's that to us!" Holding it at arm's length, he glared redly at the card. "What is it?"

"A fine new centre. You can see it from the window." Francis added, with a tremor: "The gift of Sir George Renshaw."

"Sir George . . ." Kezer broke off, stupefied, then stamped to the window. He gazed through the window, a long time, at the impressive proportions of the new erection. Then he returned, sat down and slowly began his lunch. His appetite was scarcely that of a man with a purified liver. He kept darting glances at Francis out of his small, lowering eyes. His silence blasted the room.

At length Francis spoke—awkwardly, with tense simplicity. "You must decide, Father. You've put a ban on dancing and all mixed recreation. On the other hand if our people don't co-operate, ostracize the club, and stop away from the dances, Sir George will feel himself mortally insulted." Francis kept his eyes on his plate. "He's coming down, in person, on Thursday, for the opening."

Father Kezer could eat no more. The thick and juicy beefsteak on his plate might have been dishcloth. He rose abruptly, crushing the card in his hairy fist with sudden, dreadful violence. "We'll not go to the foul fiends' opening! We'll not. Do you hear me? Once and for all, I've said it!" He rampaged out of the room.

On the Thursday evening, freshly shaved, in clean linen and his best black, his face a dreadful compromise of gaiety and gloom, Father Kezer stalked over to the ceremony. Francis followed behind him.

The new hall was warm with lights and excitement, filled to capacity with the working people of the community. On the raised platform a number of the local notables were seated, Donald Kyle and his wife, the colliery doctor, the council schoolmaster, and two other ministers of religion. As Francis and Father Kezer took their seats there was prolonged cheering, then a few cat-calls and loud laughter. Father Kezer's jaws snapped sourly together.

The sound of a car arriving outside heightened the expectation and a minute later, amidst a great ovation, Sir George appeared on the platform. He was a medium-sized man of about sixty with a shining bald head fringed with white hair. His moustache was silvery also, and his cheeks were brightly coloured. He had that remarkably fresh pink-and-whiteness achieved by some fair-haired persons in their declining years. It seemed preposterous that one so quiet in his dress and manner should command such enormous power.

He listened agreeably while the ceremony proceeded, sustained the address of welcome from Mr. Kyle, then delivered a few remarks himself. He concluded amiably:—

"I should like in fairness to state that the first suggestion of this very worthy project came directly from the vision and broadmindedness of Father Francis Chisholm."

The applause was deafening and Francis flushed, his eyes, pleading and remorseful, bent on his superior.

Father Kezer raised his hands automatically, brought them soundlessly together twice, with a grin of sickly martyrdom. Later, when the impromptu dance started, he stood watching Sir George swing round the hall with young Nancy Kyle. Then he faded into the night. The music of the fiddlers followed him.

When Francis returned, late, he found the parish priest sitting up in the parlour, with no fire, his hands on his knees.

Father Kezer seemed oddly inert. All the fight had gone out of him. In the last ten years he had knocked out more curates than Henry VIII had wives. And now a curate had knocked him out. He said tonelessly:—

"I'll have to report you to the Bishop!"

Francis felt his heart turn over in his breast. But he did not flinch. No matter what happened to him, Father Kezer's authority was shaken. The older priest continued glumly: "Perhaps you'd be the better of a change. The Bishop can decide. Dean Fitzgerald needs another curate in Tynecastle . . . your friend Mealey's there, isn't he?"

Francis was silent. He did not wish to leave this now faintly stirring parish. Yet even if he were forced to do so things would be easier for his successor. The club would continue. It was a beginning. Other changes would come. He had no personal exultation, but a quiet, almost visionary, hope. He said in a low voice: "I'm sorry if I have upset you, Father. Believe me, I was only trying to help . . . our good-for-nothing lot."

The eyes of the two priests met. Father Kezer's fell first.

2

ONE Friday towards the end of Lent, in the dining room of St. Dominic's Presbytery, Francis and Father Slukas were already seated at the meagre midday repast of boiled stock-fish and butterless brown toast served on Victorian silver and fine blue Worcester china, when Father Mealey returned from an early sick call. From the suppression of his manner, his indifferent mode of helping himself, Francis was immediately aware that Anselm had something on his mind. Dean Fitzgerald dined upstairs at this season of the

Church and the three junior priests were alone. But Father Mealey, munching without taste, a faint colour beneath his skin, kept silence till the end of the meal. Only when the Lithuanian had brushed the crumbs from his beard, risen, bowed, and departed, did his tension relax. He drew a long pressing breath.

"Francis! I want you to come with me this afternoon. You've no engagements?"

"No . . . I'm free till four o'clock."

"Then you must come. I'd like you as my friend, as my fellow priest, to be the first . . ." He broke off, would say no more to lift the heavy mystery of his words.

For two years Francis had been the second curate at St. Dominic's, where Gerald Fitzgerald, now Dean Fitzgerald, still remained, with Anselm his senior assistant and Slukas, the Lithuanian Father, a necessary encumbrance on account of the many Polish immigrants who kept crowding into Tynecastle.

The change from the backwoods of Shalesley to this familiar city parish where the services went like clockwork and the church was elegantly perfect had left a curious mark on Francis. He was happy to be near Aunt Polly, to maintain an eye on Ned and Judy, to see the Tullochs, Willie and his sister, once or twice a week. He had a queer consolation, a sense of indefinable support, in the recent elevation of Monsignor MacNabb from San Morales to be Bishop of the diocese. Yet his new air of maturity, the lines about his steady eyes, the spareness of his frame, gave silent indications that the transition had not been easy.

Dean Fitzgerald, refined and fastidious, priding himself on being a gentleman, stood at the opposite pole from Father Kezer. Yet, though he strove to be impartial, the Dean was not without a certain lofty prejudice. While he warmly approved Anselm—now his prime favourite—and blankly ignored Father Slukas,—whose broken English and table habits, a napkin tucked beneath the beard at every meal, coupled with a strange predilection for wearing a derby hat with his soutane, placed him far beyond the pale,—towards his other curate he had a strange wariness. Francis soon realized that his humble birth, his association with the Union Tavern, with, indeed, the whole stark Bannon tragedy, must prove a handicap he could not lightly overcome.

And he had made such a bad beginning! Tired of the shopworn platitudes, the same old parrot sermons that came, almost by rote, on the appointed Sundays of the year, Francis had ventured, soon after his arrival, to preach a simple homily, fresh and original, his own thoughts, on the subject of personal integrity. Alas, Dean Fitzgerald had cuttingly condemned the dangerous innovation. Next Sunday, at his behest, Anselm had mounted the pulpit and given forth the antidote: a magnificent peroration on The Star of the Sea, in which harts panted for the water and barques came safe across the bar; ending dramatically with arms outstretched, a handsome suppliant for Love, on the admonition: "Come!" All the women of the congregation were in tears, and afterwards, as Anselm ate a hearty breakfast of mutton chops, the Dean pointedly congratulated him. "That!—Father Mealey—was eloquent. I heard our late Bishop deliver practically the same sermon twenty years ago."

Perhaps these opposite orations set their courses: as the months passed Francis could not but dejectedly compare his own indifferent showing with Anselm's remarkable success. Father Mealey was a figure in the parish, always cheerful, even gay, with a ready laugh and a comforting pat on the back for anyone in trouble. He worked hard and with great earnestness, carrying a little book full of his engagements in his waistcoat pocket, never refusing an invitation to address a meeting or make an after-dinner speech. He edited the *St. Dominic's Gazette*: a newsy and often humorous little sheet. He went out a good deal and, though no one could call him a snob, took tea at all the best houses. Whenever an eminent cleric came to preach in the city, Anselm was sure to meet him and to sit admiringly at his feet. Later he would send a letter, beautifully composed, expressing ardently the spiritual benefit he had derived from the encounter. He had made many influential friends through this sincerity.

Naturally there were limits to his capacity for work. While he vigorously assumed the post of secretary to the new Diocesan Foreign Missionary Centre in Tynecastle—a cherished project of the Bishop—and worked unremittingly to please His Grace, he had been obliged reluctantly to decline, and depute to Francis, the management of the Working Boy's Club in Shand Street.

The property round Shand Street was the worst in the city, tall tenements and lodging houses, a network of slums, and this, properly enough, had come to be regarded as Francis' district. Here, though his results seemed trivial and meaningless, he found plenty to do. He had to train himself to look destitution in the eye, to view without shrinking the sorrow and the shame of life, the eternal irony of poverty. It was not a communion of saints that grew about him but a communion of sinners, rousing such pity in him it brought him sometimes to the brink of tears.

"Don't say you're taking forty winks," said Anselm reproachfully.

Almost with a start Francis came out of his reverie to find Father Mealey, waiting on him, hat and stick in hand, beside the lunch table. He smiled and rose in acquiescence.

Outside, the afternoon was fresh and fine, with a rousing, bustling breeze, and Anselm strode along with a brisk swing, clean, honest and healthy, greeting his parishioners bluffly. His popularity at St. Dominic's had not spoiled him. To his many admirers his most engaging characteristic was the way in which he deprecated his achievements.

Soon Francis saw that they were making for the new suburb recently added to the parish. Beyond the city boundary, a housing development was in progress, on the parklands of an old country property. Workmen were moving with hods and barrows. Francis subconsciously noted a big white board: *Hollis Estate, Apply Malcom Glennie, Solicitor.* But Anselm was pushing on, over the hill, past some green fields, then down a wooded pathway to the left. It was a pleasant rural stretch to be so near the chimney-pots.

Suddenly Father Mealey halted, with the still excitement of a pointing hound.

"You know where we are, Francis? You've heard of this place?"

"Of course."

Francis had often passed it: a little hollow of lichened rocks, screened with yellow broom and enclosed by an oval copse of copper beeches. It was the prettiest spot for miles around. He had often wondered why it was known as "The Well" and sometimes, indeed, as "Marywell." The basin had been dry for fifty years.

"Look!" Clutching his arm, Father Mealey led him forward. From the dry rocks gushed a crystal spring. There was an odd silence, then, stooping with cupped hands, Mealey took an almost sacramental drink.

"Taste it, Francis. We ought to be grateful for the privilege of being among the first."

Francis bent and drank. The water was sweet and cold. He smiled. "It tastes good."

Mealey regarded him with wise indulgence, not without its tinge of patronage. "My dear fellow, I could call it a heavenly taste."

"Has it been flowing long?"

"It began yesterday afternoon at sundown."

Francis laughed. "Really, Anselm, you're a Delphic oracle today—full of signs and portents. Come on, give me the whole story. Who told you about this?"

Father Mealey shook his head. "I can't . . . yet."

"But you've made me so confoundedly curious."

Pleased, Anselm smiled. Then his expression regained its solemnity. "I can't break the seal yet, Francis. I must go to Dean Fitzgerald. He's the one who must deal with this. Meantime, of course, I trust you . . . I know you will respect my confidence."

Francis knew his companion too well to press him further.

On their return to Tynecastle, Francis parted from his fellow curate and went on to Glanville Street to make a sick call. One of his club members, a boy named Owen Warren, had been kicked on the leg in a football game some weeks before. The youngster was poor and undernourished and heedless of the injury. When the Poor Law doctor was eventually called in, the condition had developed into an ugly ulcer of the shin.

The affair had upset Francis—the more so since Dr. Tulloch seemed dubious of the prognosis. And this evening, in his endeavour to bring some comfort to Owen and his worried mother, the peculiar and inconclusive excursion of the afternoon was driven completely from his mind.

Next morning, however, loud and minatory sounds emerging from Dean Gerald Fitzgerald's room brought it back before him.

Lent was a deadly penance for the Dean. He was a just man, and he fasted. But fasting did not suit his full elegant body, well habituated to the stimuli of rich and nourishing juices. Sorely tried in health and temper, he kept to himself, walked the Presbytery with no recognition in his hooded eye, and each night marked another cross upon the calendar.

Although Father Mealey stood so high in Fitzgerald's favour it demanded considerable resourcefulness to approach him at such a time, and Francis heard Anselm's voice fall, persuasive and pleading, across the Dean's irascible abruptness. In the end the softer voice triumphed—like drops of water, Francis reflected, wearing out granite through sheer persistence.

An hour later, with a very bad grace, the Dean came out of his room. Father Mealey was waiting on him in the vestibule. They departed together in a cab in the direction of the centre of the town. They were absent three hours. It was lunchtime when they returned and for once the Dean broke his rule. He sat down at the curate's table. Though he would eat nothing he ordered a large pot of French coffee, his one luxury in a desert of self-denial. Sitting sideways, his legs crossed, a handsome elegant figure, sipping the black and aromatic brew, he diffused an air of warmth, almost of comradeship, as though a little taken out of himself by an inner, thrilling exaltation. He said, meditatively, to Francis and the Polish priest—it was notable that he included Slukas in his friendly glance:—

"Well, we may thank Father Mealey for his persistence . . . in the face of my somewhat violent disbelief. Naturally it is my duty to maintain the utmost scepticism towards certain . . . phenomena. But I have never seen, I had never hoped to see, such a manifestation, in my own parish—" He broke off and, taking up his coffee cup, made a generous gesture of renunciation towards the senior curate. "Let it be your privilege to tell them, Father."

That faint excited colour persisted in Father Mealey's cheek. He cleared his throat and began, readily and earnestly, as though the incident he related demanded his most formal eloquence:—

"One of our parishioners, a young woman, who has been delicate for a considerable time, was out walking on Monday of this week. The date, since we wish above everything to be precise, was March fifteenth, and the time, half-past three in the afternoon. The reason for her excursion was no idle one —this girl is a devout and fervent soul not given to giddiness or loitering. She was walking in accordance with her doctor's instructions—to get some fresh air—the medical man being Dr. William Brine of 42 Boyle Crescent, whom we all know as a physician of unimpeachable, I might say, of the highest, integrity. Well!" Father Mealey took a tense gulp of water and went on. "As she was returning from her walk, murmuring a prayer, she chanced to pass the place which we know as Mary's Well. It was twilight, the last rays of the sun lingering in pure radiance upon the lovely scene. This young girl stopped to gaze and admire when suddenly to her wonder and surprise she saw standing before her a lady in a white robe and a blue cape with a diadem of stars upon her forehead. Guided by holy instinct our Catholic girl immediately fell upon her knees. The lady smiled to her with ineffable tenderness and said: 'My child, sickly though you are, you are the one to be chosen!' Then, half-turning, still addressing the awestruck yet comprehending girl: 'Is it not sad that this Well which bears my name is dry? Remember! It is for you and those like you that this shall happen.' With a last beautiful smile she disappeared. At that instant a fount of exquisite water sprang from the barren rock."

There was a silence when Father Mealey concluded.

Then the Dean resumed: "As I have said, our approach to this delicate matter was made in the frankest incredulity. We don't expect miracles to grow on every gooseberry bush. Young girls are notoriously romantic. And the starting of the spring might have been a sheer coincidence. However—" His tone took on a deeper gratification. "I've just completed a long interrogation of the girl in question with Father Mealey and Dr. Brine. As you may imagine, the solemn experience of her vision was a great shock to her. She went to bed immediately after it and has remained there ever since." The voice became slower, fraught with immense significance. "Though she is happy, normal and physically well-nourished, in these five days she has touched neither food nor drink." He gave the amazing fact its due weight in silence. "Moreover . . . moreover, I say, she shows plainly, unmistakably and irrefutably, the blessed stigmata!" He went on triumphantly: "While it is too early to speak yet, while final evidence must be collected, I have the strongest premonition, amounting almost to conviction, that we in this parish have been privileged by Almighty God to participate in a miracle comparable to, and perhaps far-reaching as, those which gave our holy religion the new-found Grotto at Digby and the older and more historic Shrine at Lourdes."

It was impossible not to be affected by the nobility of his peroration.

"Who is the girl?" Francis asked.

"She is Charlotte Neily!"

Francis stared at the Dean. He opened his lips and closed them again. The silence remained impressive.

The next few days brought a growing excitement to the Presbytery. No one could have been better equipped to deal with the crisis than Dean Gerald Fitzgerald. A man of sincere devotion, he was wise also in worldly ways. Long and hard-won experience on the local school board and urban councils gave him an astute approach to temporal affairs. No news of the event was permitted to escape, not a whisper, even, in the parochial halls. The Dean had everything under his own hand. He would raise his hand only when he was ready.

The incident, so miraculously unexpected, was a breath of new life to him. Not for many years had he known such inner satisfaction: both spiritual and material. He was a strange mixture of piety and ambition. His exceptional attributes of mind and body had seemed to destine him, automatically, for advancement in the Church. And he longed passionately for that advancement as much, perhaps, as he longed for the advancement of Holy Church herself. A keen student of contemporary history, he likened himself often in his own mind to Newman. He merited equal eminence. Yet he remained, becalmed, at St. Dominic's. The only preferment they had given him, the reward of twenty distinguished years, was this petty elevation to the rank of Dean, an infrequent title in the Catholic Church and one which often embarrassed him on his journeying beyond the city, causing him to be mistaken for an Anglican clergyman, an inference he most cordially resented.

Perhaps he realized that while he was admired he was not liked. With the passage of each day he was growing more and more a disappointed man. He strove for resignation. Yet when he bent his head and said "O Lord, Thy will be done!" deep down beneath his humility was the burning thought: "By this time they should have given me my mozzetta."

Now everything was changed. Let them keep him at St. Dominic's. He would make St. Dominic's a shrine of light. Lourdes was his exemplar and, nearer in time and space, the recent striking instance of Digby in the Midlands, where the foundation of a miraculous grotto, with many authenticated cures, had transformed the dreary hamlet into a thriving town, and elevated, at the same time, an unknown but resourceful parish priest to the status of a national figure.

The Dean sank into a splendid vision of a new city, a great basilica, a solemn triduum, himself enthroned in stiff vestments . . . then sharply took himself in hand and scrutinized the draft contracts. His first action had been to place immediately a Dominican nun, Sister Teresa, trustworthy and discreet, in Charlotte Neily's home. Reassured by her impeccable reports he had taken to the law.

It was fortunate that Marywell and all the land adjacent formed the estate of the old and wealthy Hollis family. Though not a Catholic, Captain Hollis had married one, Sir George Renshaw's sister. He was friendly and welldisposed. He and his solicitor, Malcom Glennie, were closeted with the Dean upon successive days, holding long conferences over sherry and biscuits. A fair and amicable arrangement was at length worked out. The Dean had no personal interest in money. He regarded it contemptuously as so much dross. But the things that money could purchase were important and he must ensure the future of his shining project. No one but a fool could fail to realize that the value of the land would rocket to the sky.

On the last day of the negotiations Francis ran into Glennie in the upper corridor. Frankly, he was surprised to find Malcom dealing with the Hollis affairs. But the solicitor, when articled, had shrewdly bought himself into an old established firm with his wife's money, and quietly succeeded to some first-rate practice.

"Well, Malcom!" Francis held out his hand. "Glad to see you again."

Glennie shook hands with damp effusiveness.

"But I'm amazed," Francis smiled, "to find you in the house of the Scarlet Woman!"

The solicitor's answering smile was thin. He mumbled: "I'm a liberal man, Francis . . . besides being obliged to chase the pennies."

There was a silence. Francis had often thought to restore his relationship with the Glennies. But news of the death of Daniel had dissuaded him—and a chance encounter with Mrs. Glennie in Tynecastle when, as he crossed the street to greet her, she had sighted him from the corner of her eye, and shied away, as though she spied the Devil.

He said: "It made me very sad to hear of your father's death."

"Ay, ay! We miss him of course. But the old man was such a failure."

"It's no great failure to get into heaven," Francis joked.

"Well, yes, I suppose he's there." Glennie vaguely twisted the emblem on his watch-chain. He was already tending towards an early middle age, his figure slack, shoulders and stomach pendulous, his thin hair plastered in streaks over his bare scalp. But his eye, though palely evasive, was gimlet sharp. As he moved towards the stairs he threw off a tepid invitation.

"Look us up when you have time. I'm married, as you know—two of a family—but Mother still lives with us."

Malcom Glennie had his own peculiar interest in the beatific vision of Charlotte Neily. Since his early youth he had been patiently seeking an opportunity to acquire wealth. He inherited from his mother a burning avarice and something of her long-nosed cunning. He smelled money in this ridiculous Romish scheme. Its very uniqueness convinced him of its possibilities. His opportunity was here, dangling like a ripe fruit. It would never occur again, never in a lifetime.

Working disingenuously for his client, Malcom remembered what everyone else had forgotten. Secretly, and at considerable expense, he had a geological survey carried out. Then he was sure of what he had already suspected. The flow of water to the property came exclusively through an upper tract of heath land, above and remote from the estate.

Malcom was not rich. Not yet. But by taking all his savings, by mortgaging his house and business, he had just enough to execute a three months' option on this land. He knew what an artesian bore would do. That bore would never be driven. But a bargain would be driven, later, on the threat of that bore, which would make Malcom Glennie a landed gentleman.

Meanwhile the water still gushed clear and sweet. Charlotte Neily still maintained her rapture and her stigmata, still existed without sustenance. And Francis still prayed, broodingly, for the gift of faith.

If only he could believe like Anselm who, without a struggle, blandly, smilingly, accepted everything from Adam's rib to the less probable details of Jonah's sojourn in the whale! He did believe, he did, he did . . . but not in the shallows, only in the depths . . . only by an effort of love, by keeping his nose to the grindstone in the slums, when shaking the fleas from his clothing into the empty bath . . . never, never easily . . . except when he sat with the sick, the crippled, those of stricken, ashen countenance. The cruelty of this present test, its unfairness, was wrecking his nerves, withering in him the joy of prayer.

It was the girl herself who disturbed him. Doubtless he was prejudiced: he could not overlook the fact that Charlotte's mother was Thaddeus Gilfoyle's sister. And her father was a vague and windy character, pious yet lazy, who stole away from his small chandler's premises every day, to light candles before the side altar for success in his neglected business. Charlotte had all her father's fondness for the Church. But Francis had a worried suspicion that the incidentals drew her, the smell of incense and of candle grease, that the darkness of the confessional struck overtures upon her nerves. He did not deny her unblemished goodness, the regularity with which she carried out her duties. As against that, she washed sketchily, and her breath was rancid.

On the following Saturday as Francis walked down Glanville Street, feeling absurdly depressed, he observed Dr. Tulloch come out of Number 143, the house of Owen Warren. He called, the doctor turned, stopped, then fell into step beside his friend.

Willie had broadened with the years, but had otherwise changed little. Slow, tenacious and canny, loyal to his friends, hostile to his enemies, he had, in manhood, all his father's honesty, but little of his charm and nothing of his looks. His blunt-nosed face was red and stolid, topped by a shock of unmanageable hair. He had an air of plodding decency. His medical career had not been brilliant, but he was sound and enjoyed his work. He was quite contemptuous of all orthodox ambitions. Though he spoke occasionally of "seeing the world," of pursuing adventure in far-off romantic lands, he remained in his Poor Law appointment—which demanded no hateful bedside falsities and enabled him at most times to speak his mind—anchored by the humdrum, by his matter-of-fact capacity of living from day to day. Besides, he never could save money. His salary was not large; and much of it was spent on whiskey.

Always careless of his appearance, this morning he had not shaved. And his deepset eyes were sombre, his expression unusually put out: as though today he had a grudge against the world. He indicated briefly that the Warren boy was worse. He had been in to take a shred of tissue for pathological examination.

They continued along the street, linked by one of their peculiar silences. Suddenly, on an unaccountable impulse, Francis divulged the story of Charlotte Neily.

Tulloch's face did not change, he trudged along, fists in his deep coat pockets, collar up, head down.

"Yes," he said at last. "A little bird told me."

"What do you think of it?"

"Why ask me?"

"At least you're honest."

Tulloch looked oddly at Francis. For one so modest, so conscious of his mental limitations, the doctor's rejection of the myth of God was strangely positive. "Religion isn't my province, I inherited a most satisfying atheism . . . which the anatomy room confirmed. But if you want it straight—in my old dad's words, I have my doubts. See here, though! Why don't we take a look at her? We're not far from the house. We'll go in together."

"Won't that get you into trouble with Dr. Brine?"

"No. I can square it with Salty tomorrow. In dealing with my colleagues I find it pays to act first and apologize afterwards." He threw Francis a singular smile. "Unless you're afraid of the hierarchy?"

Francis flushed but controlled his answer. He said a minute later: "Yes, I'm afraid, but we'll go in."

It proved surprisingly easy to effect an entrance. Mrs. Neily, worn-out by a night of watching, was asleep. Neily, for once, was at his business. Sister Teresa, short, quiet and amiable, opened the door. Since she came from a distant section of Tynecastle she had no knowledge of Tulloch, but she knew and recognized Francis, at once. She admitted them to the polished, immaculately tidy room where Charlotte lay on spotless pillows, washed and clothed in a high white nightgown, the brasses of the bedstead shining. Sister Teresa bent over the girl, not a little proud of her stainless handiwork.

"Charlotte, dear. Father Chisholm has come to see you. And brought a doctor who is a great friend of Dr. Brine."

Charlotte Neily smiled. The smile was conscious, vaguely languid, yet charged with curious rapture. It lit up the pale, already luminous face, motionless upon the pillow. It was deeply impressive. Francis felt a stir of genuine compunction. There was no doubt that something existed, here, in this still white room, outside the bonds of natural experience.

"You don't mind if I examine you, Charlotte?" Tulloch spoke kindly.

At his tone, her smile lingered. She did not move. She had the cushioned repose of one who is watched, who knows that she is watched, yet is undisturbed, rather exalted, by such watching: a consciousness of inner power, a mollification, a dreamy and elevated awareness of the deference and reverence evoked amongst the watchers. Her pale eyelids fluttered. Her voice was untroubled, remote.

"Why should I mind, doctor? I'm only too glad. I'm not worthy to be chosen as God's vessel . . . but since I am chosen I can only joyfully submit."

She allowed the respectful Tulloch to examine her.

"You don't eat anything, Charlotte?"

"No, doctor."

"You've no appetite?"

"I never think of food. I just seem sustained by an inner grace."

Sister Teresa said quietly: "I can assure you she hasn't put a bite in her mouth since I came into this house."

A silence fell in the hushed white room. Dr. Tulloch straightened himself, pushing back his unruly hair. He said simply:—

"Thank you, Charlotte. Thank you, Sister Teresa. I'm much indebted to you for your kindness." He went towards the bedroom door.

As Francis made to follow the doctor a shadow fluttered over Charlotte's face.

"Don't you want to see too, Father? Look . . . my hands! My feet are just the same."

She extended both her arms, gently, sacrificially. Upon both her pale palms, unmistakably, were the blood-stained marks of nails.

Outside, Dr. Tulloch maintained his attitude of reserve. He kept his lips shut until they reached the end of the street. Then, at the point where their ways diverged, he spoke rapidly. "You want my opinion I suppose. Here it is. A borderline case—or just over: manic depressive in the exalted stage. Certainly a hysteric bleeder. If she steers clear of the asylum, she'll probably be canonized!" His composure, his perfect manner left him. His red plain face became congested. His words choked him. "Damn it to hell! When I think of her trigged up there in her simpering holiness, like an anæmic angel in a flour bag—and little Owney Warren, stuck in a dirty garret, with worse pain than your hellfire in his gangrenous leg, and the threat of malignant sarcoma over him, I could just about explode. Bite on that when you say your prayers. You're probably going back to say them now. Well, I'm going home to have a drink." He walked rapidly away before Francis could reply.

That same evening when Francis returned from Tenebrae an urgent summons awaited him, written on the slate which hung in the Presbytery vestibule. With a premonition of misfortune, he went upstairs to the study. The Dean was wearing out his temper and his carpet with short exasperated paces.

"Father Chisholm! I am both amazed and indignant. Really, I expected better of you than this. To think that you should bring in—from the streets— an atheistic doctor—I resent it violently!"

"I'm sorry." Francis answered heavily. "It's just—oh, well, he happens to be my friend."

"That in itself is highly reprehensible. I find it wildly improper that one of my curates should associate with a character like Dr. Tulloch."

"We . . . we were boys together."

"That is no excuse. I'm hurt and disappointed. I'm thoroughly and justifiably incensed. From the very beginning your attitude towards this great event has been cold and unsympathetic. I daresay you are jealous that the honour of the discovery should have fallen to the senior curate. Or is there some deeper motive behind your manifest antagonism?"

A sense of wretchedness flowed over Francis. He felt that the Dean was right. He mumbled:—

"I'm terribly sorry. I'm not disloyal. That's the last in the world I'd want to be. But I admit I've been lukewarm. It's because I've been troubled. That's why I took Tulloch in today. I have such doubts—"

"Doubts! Do you deny the miracles of Lourdes?"

"No, no. They're unimpeachable. Authenticated by doctors of all creeds."

"Then why deny us the opportunity to create another monument of faith —here—in our very midst?" The Dean's brow darkened. "If you disregard the spiritual implications, at least respect the physical." He sneered. "Do you fondly imagine that a young girl can go nine days without food or drink—and remain well and perfectly nourished—unless she is receiving other sustenance?"

"What sustenance?"

"Spiritual sustenance." The Dean fumed. "Didn't Saint Catherine of Siena receive a spiritual mystic drink which supplanted all earthly food? Such insufferable doubting! Can you wonder that I lose my temper?"

Francis hung his head. "Saint Thomas doubted. In the presence of all the disciples. Even to putting his fingers in our Lord's side. But no one lost their temper."

There was a sudden shocked pause. The Dean paled, then recovered himself. He bent over his desk, fumbling at some papers, not looking at Francis. He said in a restrained tone:—

"This is not the first time you have proved obstructive. You are getting yourself into very bad odour in the diocese. You may go."

Francis left the room with a dreadful sense of his own deficiencies. He had a sudden overwhelming impulse to take his troubles to Bishop MacNabb. But he suppressed it. Rusty Mac seemed no longer approachable. He would be too fully occupied by his new high office to concern himself with the worries of a wretched curate.

Next day, Sunday, at the eleven o'clock high mass, Dean Fitzgerald broke the news in the finest sermon he had ever preached.

The sensation was immediate and tremendous. The entire congregation stood outside the church talking in hushed voices, unwilling to go home. A spontaneous procession formed up and departed, under the leadership of Father Mealey, for Marywell. In the afternoon crowds collected outside the Neily home. A band of young women of the confraternity, to which Charlotte belonged, knelt in the street reciting the rosary.

In the evening the Dean consented to be interviewed by a highly curious press. He conducted himself with dignity and restraint. Already esteemed in the city, rated as a public-spirited clergyman, he produced a most favourable impression. Next morning the newspapers gave him generously of their space. He was on the front page of the *Tribune*, had a eulogistic double spread inside the *Globe*. "Another Digby," proclaimed the *Northumberland Herald*. Said the *Yorkshire Echo*, "Miraculous Grotto Brings Hope to Thousands." The *Weekly High Anglican* hedged, rather cattily, "We await further evidence." But the London *Times* was superb with a scholarly article from its theological correspondent tracing the history of the Well back to Aidan and Saint Ethelwulf. The Dean flushed with gratification. Father Mealey could eat no breakfast, and Malcom Glennie was beside himself with joy.

Eight days later Francis paid an evening visit to Polly's little flat in Clermont, at the north end of the city. He was tired, after a long day's visiting in the dingy tenements of his district, and most desperately depressed. That afternoon a note had come round from Dr. Tulloch which curtly signed young Warren's death warrant. The condition had been revealed as malignant sarcoma of the leg. There was no hope whatsoever for the boy: he was dying and might not last the month.

At Clermont, Polly was her indomitable self, Ned, perhaps, a trifle more trying than usual. Hunched in his wheeled chair, a blanket wrapped about his knees, he talked much and rather foolishly. Some sort of final settlement had at last been squeezed out of Gilfoyle on account of the remnants of

Ned's interest in the Union Tavern. A pitiful sum. But Ned had boasted as though it were a fortune. As the result of his complaint his tongue seemed too large for his mouth, he was distressingly inarticulate.

Judy was already asleep when Francis arrived, and although Polly said nothing there was a hint in her manner that the child had misbehaved and been sent off early. The thought saddened him further.

Eleven o'clock was striking when he left the flat. The last tram to Tynecastle had gone. Tramping home, his shoulders drooping slightly under this final discomfiture, he entered Glanville Street. As he drew opposite the Neily home he observed that the double window on the ground floor, which marked Charlotte's room, was still illuminated. He made out the movements of figures, vague shadows on the yellow blind.

A rush of contrition overcame him. Oppressed by the realization of his obduracy, he had a sudden desire to see the Neilys and make amends. The instinct of reparation was strong within him as he crossed the street and went up the three front steps. He raised his hand towards the knocker, altered his mind and turned the old-fashioned handle of the door. He had acquired that facility, common to priests and physicians, of making his sick visits unannounced.

The bedroom, opening off the small lobby, projected a wide slant of gaslight. He tapped gently on the lintel and entered the room. Then he stood, suddenly transformed to stone.

Charlotte, propped up in bed, with an oval tray before her laden with breast of chicken and a custard, was stuffing herself with food. Mrs. Neily, wrapped in a faded blue dressing gown, bent with solicitude, was noiselessly decanting stout.

It was the mother who saw Francis first. Arrested, she gave a neighing cry of terror. Her hand flew to her throat, dropping the glass, spilling the stout upon the bed.

Charlotte raised her gaze from the tray. Her pale eyes dilated. She gazed at her mother, her mouth opened, she began to whimper. She slid down on the bed, shielding her face. The tray crashed on to the floor. No one had spoken. Mrs. Neily's throat worked convulsively. She made a stupid, feeble effort to secrete the bottle in her dressing gown. At last she gasped: "I've got to keep her strength up somehow . . . all she's been through . . . it's invalid's stout!"

Her look of frightened guilt revealed everything. It sickened him. He felt debased and humiliated. He had difficulty in finding words.

"I suppose you've given her food every night . . . when Sister left her, thinking she was asleep?"

"No, Father! As God is my witness!" She made a last desperate attempt at denial, then broke down, lost her head completely. "What if I did? I couldn't see my poor child starve, not for nobody. But dear Saint Joseph . . . I'd never have let her do it if I'd known it would mean so much . . . with the crowds . . . and the papers . . . I'm glad to be through with it. . . . Don't . . . don't be hard on us, Father."

He said in a low voice: "I'm not going to judge you, Mrs. Neily."

She wept.

He waited patiently until her sobs subsided, seated on a chair at the door, gazing at his hat, between his hands. The folly of what she had done, the folly, at that moment, of all human life, appalled him. When the two were quieter he said: "Tell me about it."

The story came, gulped out, mostly by Charlotte.

She had read such a nice book, from the church library, about Blessed Bernadette. One day when she was passing Marywell, it was her favourite walk, she noticed the water running. That's funny, she thought. Then the coincidence struck her, between the water, Bernadette and herself. It was a shock. She had almost, in a sort of way, fancied she saw the Blessed Virgin. When she got home, the more she thought of it the surer she became. It gave her quite a turn. She was all white and trembling, she had to take to her bed and send for Father Mealey. And before she knew where she was, she was telling him the whole story.

All that night she'd lain in a kind of ecstasy, her body seemed to go rigid, stiff as a board. Next morning, when she woke up, the marks were there. She'd always bruised terrible but these were different.

Well, that convinced her. All that day, when food came, she refused it, just waved it away. She was too happy, too excited to eat. Besides, lots of Saints had lived without food. That idea fixed itself on her, too. When Father Mealey and the Dean heard she was living on Grace—and perhaps she was too—it was a glorious feeling. The attention she had, it was like she was a bride. But of course, after a bit, she got dreadfully hungry. She couldn't disappoint Father Mealey and the Dean: the way she was looked up to by Father Mealey especially. She just told her mother. And things had gone so far her mother had to help her. She had a big meal, sometimes two, every night.

But then, oh, dear, things had gone even further. "At first, as I told you, Father, it was wonderful. The best of all was the confraternity girls praying to me outside the window!" But when the newspapers started and all that, she got really frightened. She wished to God she had never done it. Sister Teresa was harder to pull the wool over. The marks on her hands were getting faint, instead of being all lifted up and excited she was turning low, depressed . . .

A fresh burst of sobbing terminated the pitiful revelation—tawdry as an illiterate scrawl upon a wall. Yet tragic, somehow, with the idiocy of all humanity.

The mother interposed.

"You won't tell Dean Fitzgerald on us, will you, Father?"

Francis was no longer angry, only sad and strangely merciful. If only the wretched business had not gone so far. He sighed.

"I won't tell him, Mrs. Neily, I won't say a word. But—" He paused. "I'm afraid you must."

Terror leaped again in her eyes. "No, no . . . for pity's sake no, Father."

He began, quietly, to explain why they must confess, how the scheme which the Dean contemplated could not be built upon a lie, especially one which must soon be palpable. He comforted them with the thought that the nine days' wonder would soon subside and be forgotten.

He left them an hour later, somewhat appeased, and with their faithful promise that they would follow out his advice. But as he directed his echoing footsteps homewards through the empty streets his heart ached for Dean Gerald Fitzgerald.

The next day passed. He was out visiting most of the time, and did not see the Dean. But a curious hollowness, a kind of suspended animation, seemed to float within the Presbytery. He was sensitive to atmosphere. He felt this strongly.

At eleven o'clock on the following forenoon, Malcom Glennie broke into his room.

"Francis! You've got to help me. He's not going on with it. For God's sake, come in and talk to him."

Glennie was painfully distressed. He was pale, his lips worked, there was a wildness in his eye. He stuttered:—

"I don't know what's taken him. He must be out of his mind. It's such a beautiful scheme. It'll do so much good—"

"I have no influence with him."

"But you have—he thinks the world of you. And you're a priest. You owe it to your flock. It'll be good for the Catholics—"

"That hardly interests you, Malcom."

"But it does," Glennie babbled. "I'm a liberal man. I admire the Catholics. It's a beautiful religion. I often wish— Oh, for God's sake, Francis, come in, quick, before it's too late."

"I'm sorry, Malcom. It's disappointing for all of us." He turned away towards the window.

At that Glennie lost all control of himself. He caught hold of Francis' arm. He snivelled abjectly.

"Don't turn me down, Francis. You owe everything to us. I've bought a little bit of land, put all my savings in it, it's worthless if the scheme falls through. Don't see my poor family ruined. My poor old mother! Think of how she brought you up, Francis. Please, please persuade him. I'd do anything in the world. I'll even turn a Catholic for you!"

Francis kept staring out of the window, his hand gripping the curtain, his eyes fixed on the church gable, pointed with a grey stone cross. A dull thought crossed his mind. What would mankind do for money? Everything. Even to selling its immortal soul.

Glennie exhausted himself at last. Convinced, finally, that nothing could be gained from Francis, he struggled for the remnants of his dignity. His manner altered.

"So you won't help me. Well, I'll remember you for this." He moved towards the door. "I'll get even with you all. If it's the last thing I do."

He paused on his way out, his pallid face contorted with malice. "I should have known you'd bite the hand that fed you. What else could you expect from a lot of dirty papists!"

He slammed the door behind him.

The hollowness continued within the Presbytery: that kind of vacuum in which people lose their clear outlines, become unsubstantial, transitory. The servants moved on tiptoe, as though it were a house of death. The Lithuanian Father wore a look of sheer bewilderment. Father Mealey went about with his eyes cast down. He had received a grave hurt. But he kept silence, which in one so naturally effusive was a singular grace. When he spoke it was of other matters. He distracted himself, passionately, with his work at the Foreign Missions office.

For more than a week after Glennie's outburst Francis had no encounter with Fitzgerald. Then, one morning, as he entered the sacristy, he found the Dean unvesting. The altar boys had gone; the two were alone.

Whatever his personal humiliation, the Dean's control of the disaster had been consummate. Indeed, in his hands it ceased to be disaster. Captain Hollis had willingly torn up the contracts. An occupation had been found for Neily in a distant town: the first step towards discreet withdrawal of the family. The clangour in the journals was tactfully stilled. Then, on Sunday, the Dean climbed again into the pulpit. Facing the hushed congregation, he gave the text: "O Ye of Little Faith!"

Quietly, with still intensity, he developed his thesis: What need had the Church of additional miracles? Had she not fully justified herself, miraculously, already? Her foundations were planted deep, foursquare, upon the miracles of Christ. It was pleasant, no doubt exciting, to meet a manifestation like that of Marywell. They had all, himself included, been carried away with it. But on sober reflection, why all this outcry about a single blossom, when the very flower of heaven bloomed here in the church, before their eyes? Were they so weak, so pusillanimous in their faith they needed further material evidence? Had they forgotten the solemn words: "Blessed are they that have not seen, and have believed"? It was a superb feat of oratory. It surpassed his triumph of the previous Sunday. Gerald Fitzgerald, still a Dean, alone knew what it cost him.

At first, in the sacristy, the Dean seemed about to maintain his inflexible reserve. But, when ready to leave, with his black coat cast about his shoulders, he suddenly swung round. In the clear light of the sacristy Francis was shocked to see the deep lines on the handsome face, the weariness in the full grey eyes.

"Not one lie, Father, but a tissue of lies. Well! God's will be done!" He paused. "You're a good fellow, Chisholm. It's a pity you and I are incompatible." He went out of the sacristy, erect.

By the end of Easter the event had almost been forgotten. The neat white railing which had been erected round the Well in the Dean's first ardour still stood; but the little entrance gate remained unlocked, swinging, rather pathetically, in the light spring air. A few good souls went occasionally to pray and bless themselves with the sparkling, ever-gushing water.

Francis, caught by a spurt of parish work, rejoiced in his own forgetfulness. The smear of the experience was gradually wearing off. What remained was only a faint ugliness at the back of his mind, which he quickly suppressed and would soon bury completely. His idea of a new playing field for the boys and young men of the parish had taken tangible form. He had been offered the use of a strip of the Public Park by the local council. Dean Fitzgerald had given his consent. He was now immersed in a pile of catalogues.

On the eve of Ascension Day he received an urgent call to visit Owen Warren. His face clouded. He rose immediately, the cricket folder falling from his knee. Though he had expected this summons for many weeks, he dreaded it. He went quickly to the church and, with the viaticum upon his person, hurried through the crowded town to Glanville Street.

His expression was fixed and sad as he saw Dr. Tulloch pacing restlessly outside the Warren home. Tulloch was attached to Owen too. He looked deeply upset as Francis approached.

"Has it come at last?" Francis said.

"Yes, it's come!" As an afterthought: "Yesterday the main artery thrombosed. It wasn't any use—even to amputate."

"Am I too late?"

"No." Tulloch's manner held a subdued violence. He shouldered roughly past Francis. "But I've been in three times at the boy while you've been strolling along. Come in, damn it . . . if you're coming in at all."

Francis followed the other up the steps. Mrs. Warren opened the door. She was a spare woman of fifty, worn out by the weeks of anxiety, plainly dressed in grey. He saw that her face was wet with tears. He pressed her hand in sympathy.

"I'm so sorry, Mrs. Warren."

She laughed—weakly, chokingly.

"Go into the room, Father!"

He was shocked. He thought that grief had momentarily turned her mind. He went into the room.

Owen was lying on the counterpane of his bed. His lower limbs were unbandaged, bare. They were rather thin, showing the wasting of disease. Both were sound, unblemished.

Dazed, Francis watched Dr. Tulloch lift up the right leg and run his hand firmly down the sound straight shin which yesterday had been a festering malignant mass. Finding no answer in the doctor's challenging eyes, he turned giddily to Mrs. Warren, saw that her tears were tears of joy. She nodded blindly, through these tears.

"I bundled him up warm in the old gocar' this morning before anybody was about. We wouldn't give up, Owney and me. He had always believed . . . if he could only get up there to the Well . . . We prayed and dipped his leg in the water. . . . When we got back . . . Owney . . . took the bandage off himself!"

The stillness in the room was absolute. It was Owen who finally broke it. "Don't forget to put me down for your new cricket team, Father."

In the street, outside, Willie Tulloch stared doggedly at his friend.

"There's bound to be a scientific explanation beyond the scope of our present knowledge. An intense desire for recovery—psychological regeneration of the cells." He stopped short, his big hand trembling on Francis' arm. "Oh, God!—if there is a God!—let's all keep our bloody mouths shut about it!"

That night Francis could not rest. He stared with sleepless eyes into the blackness above his head. The miracle of faith. Yes, faith itself was the miracle. The waters of Jordan, Lourdes, or Marywell—they mattered not a jot. Any muddy pool would answer, if it were the mirror of God's face.

Momentarily, the seismograph of his mind faintly registered the shock: a glimmering of the knowledge of the incomprehensibility of God. He prayed fervently. O dear God, we don't even know the beginning. We are like tiny ants in a bottomless abyss, covered with a million layers of cotton wool, striving . . . striving to see the sky. O God . . . dear God, give me humility . . . and give me faith!

3

IT was three months later when the Bishop's summons arrived. Francis had expected it for some time now, yet its actual arrival somewhat dismayed him. Heavy rain began as he walked up the hill towards the palace; only by racing the intervening distance did he avoid a thorough drenching. Out of breath, wet and splashed with mud, he felt his arrival somewhat lacking in dignity. Insensibly his anxiety increased as he sat, slightly shivering, in the formal parlour, gazing at his mired boots, so incongruous upon the red pile carpet.

At last the Bishop's secretary appeared, ushered him up a shallow flight of marble stairs, and silently indicated a dark mahogany door. Francis knocked and went in.

His Lordship was at his desk, not bent at work but resting, his cheek against his hand, elbow on the arm of his leather chair. The fading light, striking sideways through the velvet pelmets of the tall window, enriched the violet of his biretta but found his face in shadow.

Francis paused uncertainly, disconcerted by the impassive figure, asking himself if this were really his old friend of Holywell and San Morales. There was no sound but the faint ticking of the Buhl clock on the mantelpiece. Then a severe voice said:—

"Well, Father, any miracles to report tonight? And by the by, before I forget, how is the dance-hall business doing now?"

Francis felt a thickness in his throat, he could have cried for sheer relief. His Lordship continued his scrutiny of the figure marooned on the wide rug. "I must confess it affords some relief to my old eyes to see a priest so manifestly unprosperous as you. Usually they come in here looking like successful

undertakers. That's an abominable suit you're wearing—and dreadful boots!"
He rose slowly, and advanced towards Francis. "My dear boy, I am delighted
to see you. But you're horribly thin." He placed his hand on the other's
shoulder. "And good gracious, horribly wet, too!"

"I got caught in the rain, your Grace."

"What! No umbrella! Come over to the fire. We must get you something
warm." Leaving Francis, he went to a small escritoire and produced a decanter
and two liqueur glasses. "I am not yet properly acclimatized to my new dignity. I ought to ring and command some of these fine vintages used by all the
Bishops one reads about. This is only Glenlivet, but it's fit tipple for two
Scots." He handed Francis a tiny glassful of the neat spirit, watched him
drink it, then drank his own. He sat down on the other side of the fireplace.
"Speaking of dignity, do not look so scared of me. I'm bedizened now—I
admit. But underneath is the same clumsy anatomy you saw wading through
the Stinchar!"

Francis reddened. "Yes, your Grace."

There was a pause, then His Lordship said, directly and quietly: "You've
had a pretty thin time, I imagine, since you left San Morales."

Francis answered in a low voice. "I've been a pretty good failure."

"Indeed?"

"Yes, I felt this coming . . . this disciplinary interview. I knew I wasn't
pleasing Dean Fitzgerald lately."

"Just pleasing Almighty God, eh?"

"No, no. I'm really ashamed, dissatisfied with myself. It's my incorrigibly
rebellious nature." A pause.

"Your culminating iniquity seems to be that you failed to attend a banquet
in honour of Alderman Shand . . . who has just made a magnificent donation
of five hundred pounds to the new high altar fund. Can it be that you disap-
prove of the good Alderman—who, I am told, is slightly less pious in his
dealings with the tenants of his slum property in Shand Street?"

"Well . . ." Francis halted in confusion. "I don't know. I was wrong not
to go. Dean Fitzgerald specially advised us we must attend . . . he attached
great importance to it. But something else cropped up . . ."

"Oh?" The Bishop waited.

"I was called to see someone that afternoon." Francis spoke with great
reluctance. "You may remember . . . Edward Bannon . . . though he's unrecognizable now, in his illness, paralyzed, drooling, a caricature of God-made
man. When it was time for me to go he clutched my hand, implored me not
to leave him. I couldn't help myself . . . or restrain a terrible sick pity for
this . . . grotesque, dying outcast. He fell asleep mumbling, 'John the Father,
John the Son, John the Holy Ghost,' saliva running down his grey unshaven
chin, holding my hand. . . . I remained with him till morning."

A longer pause. "No wonder the Dean was annoyed that you preferred the
sinner to the saint."

Francis hung his head. "I am annoyed with myself. I keep trying to do better. It's strange—when I was a boy I had the conviction that priests were all quite infallibly good . . ."

"And now you are discovering how terribly human we are. Yes, it's unholy that your 'rebellious nature' should fill me with joy, but I find it a wonderful antidote to the monotonous piety I am subjected to. You are the stray cat, Francis, who comes stalking up the aisle when everyone is yawning their head off at a dull sermon. That's not a bad metaphor—for you *are* in the church even if you don't match up with those who find it all by the well-known rule. I am not flattering myself, when I say that I am probably the only cleric in this diocese who really understands you. It's fortunate I am now your Bishop."

"I know that, your Grace."

"To me," His Lordship meditated, "you are not a failure, but a howling success. You can do with a little cheering up—so I'll risk giving you a swelled head. You've got inquisitiveness and tenderness. You're sensible of the distinction between thinking and doubting. You're not one of our ecclesiastical milliners who must have everything stitched up in neat little packets—convenient for handing out. And quite the nicest thing about you, my dear boy, is this—you haven't got that bumptious security which springs from dogma rather than from faith."

There was a silence. Francis felt his heart melt towards the old man. He kept his eyes cast down. The quiet voice went on.

"Of course, unless we do something about it you're going to get hurt. If we go on with cudgels there'll be too many bloody heads—including your own! Oh, yes, I know—you're not afraid. But I am. You're too valuable to be fed to the lions. That's why I have something to put before you."

Francis raised his head quickly, met His Lordship's wise and affectionate gaze. The Bishop smiled.

"You don't imagine I'd be treating you as a boon companion if I didn't want you to do something for me!"

"Anything . . ." Francis stumbled on the words.

There was a long pause. The Bishop's face was gravely chiselled. "It's a big thing to ask . . . a great change to suggest . . . if it is too much . . . you must tell me. But I think it is the very life for you." Again a pause. "Our Foreign Missions Society has at last been promised a vicariate in China. When all the formalities are completed, and you've had some preparation, will you go there as our first unprincipled adventurer?"

Francis remained completely still, numb with surprise. The walls seemed to crumble about him. The request was so unexpected, so tremendous, it took his breath away. To leave home, his friends, and move into a great unknown void . . . He could not think. But slowly, mysteriously, a strange animation filled his being. He answered haltingly: "Yes . . . I will go."

Rusty Mac leaned over and took Francis' hand in his. His eyes were moist and had a poignant fixity. "I thought you would, dear boy. And I know you'll do me credit. But you'll get no salmon fishing there, I warn you."

IV

THE CHINA INCIDENT

1

EARLY in the year 1902 a lopsided junk making dilatory passage up the endless yellow reaches of the Ta-Hwang River in the province of Chek-kow, not less than one thousand miles inland from Tientsin, bore a somewhat unusual figurehead in the shape of a medium-sized Catholic priest wearing list slippers and an already wilted topee. With his legs astride the stubby bowsprit and his breviary balanced on one knee, Francis ceased momentarily his vocal combat with the Chinese tongue, in which every syllable seemed to his exhausted larynx to have as many inflections as a chromatic scale, and let his gaze rest on the drifting brown-and-ochre landscape. Fatigued after his tenth night in the three-foot den between-decks which was his cabin, he had, in the hope of a breath of air, forced himself forward into the bows through the packed welter of his fellow passengers: farm labourers, basket and leather workers from Sen-siang, bandits and fishermen, soldiers and merchants on their way to Pai-tan, squatting elbow to elbow, smoking, talking and tending their cooking pots amongst the crates of ducks, the pigpens and the heaving net which held the solitary but fractious goat.

Although Francis had vowed not to be fastidious the sounds, sights and smells of this final yet interminable stage of his journey had tried him severely. He thanked God and Saint Andrew that tonight, short of further delay, he would at last reach Pai-tan.

Even yet he could not believe himself a part of this new fantastic world, so remote and alien, so incredibly divorced from all that he had known, or hoped to know. He felt as if his life had suddenly been bent, grotesquely, away from its natural form. He checked his sigh. Others lived to a smooth and normal pattern. He was the oddity, the misfit, the little crooked man.

It had been hard to say good-bye to those at home. Ned, mercifully, had passed away three months ago, a blessed ending to that grotesque and pitiful epilogue of life. But Polly . . . he hoped, he prayed he might see Polly in the future. There was consolation in the fact that Judy had been accepted as a shorthand-typist in the Tynecastle Council offices—a post which offered security and good chances of promotion.

As if to steel himself anew he pulled from his inside pocket the final letter relating to his appointment. It was from Father Mealey, now relieved of his parish duties at St. Dominic's to devote himself exclusively to the F.M.S. Administration.

Addressed to him at Liverpool University, where for the past twelve months he had hammered out his language course, the letter ran:—

My dear Francis,

I am overjoyed to be the bearer of glad tidings! We have just received news that Pai-tan, in the Vicariate of Chek-kow, which, as you well know, was presented to us by the A.F.M.S. in December, has now been ratified by the Congregation of Propaganda. It was decided at our meeting held at the F.M.S. in Tynecastle tonight that nothing need delay your departure. At last, at last, I am able to speed you on your glorious mission to the Orient.

So far as I can ascertain Pai-tan is a delightful spot, some miles inland, but on a pleasant river, a thriving city specializing in the manufacture of baskets, with an abundance of cereal, meat, poultry, and tropical fruits. But the supremely important, the blessed fact is that the mission itself, while somewhat remote and for the past twelve months unfortunately without a priest, is in a highly flourishing condition. I'm sorry we have no photographs but I can assure you the layout is most satisfactory: comprising chapel, priest's house and compound. (What an exciting sound that word "compound" has! Don't you remember as boys when we played Indians? Forgive my enthusiasms.)

But *la crème de la crème* lies in our proved statistics. Enclosed you will find the annual report of the late incumbent, Father Lawler, who, a year ago, returned to San Francisco. I don't propose to analyze this for you since you will indubitably con it over, nay, digest it in the wee small hours. Nevertheless I may stress these figures: that although established only three years ago the Pai-tan mission can boast of four hundred communicants and over one thousand baptisms, only a third of which were *in articulo mortis*. Is it not gratifying, Francis? An example of how the dear old grace of God leavens even heathen hearts amidst pagan temple bells.

My dear fellow, I rejoice that this prize is to be yours. And I have no doubt that by your labours in the field you will materially increase the vineyard's crop. I look forward to your first report. I feel that you have at last found your métier and that the little eccentricities of tongue and temper which have been your trouble in the past will no longer be part and parcel of your daily life. Humility, Francis, is the life blood of God's Saints. I pray for you every night.

I will be writing you later. Meanwhile don't neglect your outfit. Get good strong durable soutanes. Short drawers are the best and I advise a body belt. Go to Hanson & Son; they are sound people; and cousins of the organist at the Cathedral.

It is just possible I may be seeing you sooner than you imagine. My new post may make me quite a globe trotter. Wouldn't it be grand if we met in the shady compound of Pai-tan?

Again my congratulations and with every good wish,

I remain, your devoted brother in J. C.

ANSELM MEALEY
Secretary to the Foreign Missions Society,
Diocese of Tynecastle.

Towards sundown a heightening of the commotion in the junk indicated the imminence of their arrival. As the vessel yawed round a bend into a great bight of dirty water, mobbed by a pack of sampans, Francis eagerly scanned the low tiered reaches of the town. It seemed like a great low hive, humming with sound and yellow light, fronted by the reedy mud flats with their flotsam of rafts and boats, backed distantly by mountains, pink and of a pearly translucency.

He had hoped the mission might send a boat for him but the only private wherry was for Mr. Chia, merchant and wealthy resident of Pai-tan, who now emerged for the first time, silent and satin-clad, from the recesses of the junk.

This personage was about thirty-five, but of such composure he looked older, with a supple golden skin and hair so black it seemed moist. He stood with leisurely indifference while the kapong fussed around him. Though his lashes did not once flicker in the direction of the priest, Francis had the odd conviction he was being taken in minutely.

Owing to the preoccupation of the purser, some time elapsed before the new missioner secured passage for himself and his japanned tin trunk. As he stepped down to the sampan he clutched his large silk umbrella, a glorious thing covered in Chisholm tartan which Bishop MacNabb had pressed upon him as a parting gift.

His excitement rose when, nearing the bank, he saw a great press of people on the landing steps. Was it a welcome from his congregation? What a splendid thought for the end of his long, long journey! His heart began to beat almost painfully, with happy expectation. But alas, when he landed he saw he was mistaken. No one greeted him. He had to push his way through the staring yet incurious throng.

At the end of the steps, however, he stopped short. Before him, smiling happily, dressed in neat blue and bearing, as a symbol of their credentials, a brightly coloured picture of the Holy Family, were a Chinese man and woman. As he stood, the two small figures approached him, their smile deepening, overjoyed to see him, bowing and zealously blessing themselves.

Introductions began—less difficult than he had supposed. He asked warmly:—

"Who are you?"

"We are Hosannah and Philomena Wang—your beloved catechists, Father."

"From the mission?"

"Yes, yes, Father Lawler made a most excellent mission, Father."

"You will conduct me to the mission?"

"By all means, let us go. But perhaps Father will honour us and come first to our humble abode."

"Thank you. But I am eager to reach the mission."

"Of course. We will go to the mission. We have bearers and a chair for Father."

"You are very kind, but I would prefer to walk."

Still smiling, though less perceptibly, Hosannah turned and in a rapid unintelligible exchange, which had some semblance of an argument, dismissed the sedan chair and the string of porters which he had in tow. Two coolies remained: one shouldered the trunk, the other the umbrella, and the party set off on foot.

Even in the tortuous and dirty streets it was agreeable for Francis to stretch his legs, cramped from confinement in the junk. A quick fervour stirred his blood. Amidst the strangeness he could feel the pulse of humanity. Here were hearts to be won, souls to be saved!

He became aware of one of the Wangs, pausing, to address him.

"There is an agreeable dwelling in the Street of the Netmakers . . . only five taels by the month . . . where Father might wish to spend the night."

Francis looked down in amused surprise. "No, no, Hosannah. Onwards to the mission!"

There was a pause. Philomena coughed. Francis realized that they were standing still. Hosannah politely smiled.

"Here, Father, is the mission."

At first he did not fully understand.

Before them on the riverbank was an acre of deserted earth, sun-scorched, gullied by the rains, encircled by a tramped-down piece of kaolin. At one end stood the remnants of a mud-brick chapel, the roof blown off, one wall collapsed, the others crumbling. Alongside lay a mass of caved-in rubble which might once have been a house. Tall feathery weeds were sprouting there. A single meagre shell remained, amidst the ruins, leaning yet still straw-roofed —the stable.

For three minutes Francis stood in a kind of stupor, then he slowly turned to the Wangs, who were close together, watching him, neat, unfathomable, similar as Siamese twins.

"Why has this taken place?"

"It was a beautiful mission, Father. It cost much—and we made many financial arrangements for its building. But alas, the good Father Lawler placed it near the river. And the Devil sent much wicked rain."

"Then where are the people of the congregation?"

"They are wicked people without belief in the Lord of Heaven." The two spoke more rapidly now, helping each other, gesticulating. "Father must understand how much depends upon his catechists. Alas! Since the good Father Lawler has gone away we have not been paid our lawful stipend of fifteen taels each month. It has been impossible to keep these wicked people properly instructed."

Crushed and devastated, Father Chisholm removed his gaze. This was his mission, these two his sole parishioners. The recollection of the letter within his pocket sent a sudden upsurge of passion over him. He clenched his hands, stood thinking, rigidly.

The Wangs were still talking fluently, trying to persuade him to return to the town. With an effort he rid himself of their importunities, their unctuous presence. It was, at least, a relief to be alone.

Determinedly, he carried his box into the stable. At one time a stable had been good enough for Christ. Gazing round he saw that some straw still littered the earthen floor. Though he had neither food nor water, at least he had a bed. He unpacked his blankets, began to make the place as habitable as he could. Suddenly a gong sounded. He ran out of the stable. Across the decapitated fence, outside the nearest of the temples which stippled the adjacent hill, stood an aged bonze wearing thick stockings and a quilted yellow robe, beating his metal plaque into the short unheeding twilight with measured boredom. The two priests—of Buddha and of Christ—inspected each other in silence; then the old man turned, expressionless, mounted the steps and vanished.

Night fell with the swiftness of a blow. Francis knelt down in the darkness of the devastated compound and lifted his eyes to the dawning constellations. He prayed with fierce, with terrible intensity. Dear God, you wish me to begin from nothing. This is the answer to my vanity, my stubborn human arrogance. It's better so! I'll work, I'll fight for you. I'll never give up . . . never . . . never!

Back in the stable, trying to rest, while the shrill ping of mosquitoes and the crack of flying beetles split the sweltering air, he forced himself to smile. He did not feel heroic, but a dreadful fool. Saint Teresa had likened life to a night in a hotel. This one they had sent him to was not the Ritz!

Morning came at last. He rose. Taking his chalice from its cedar box, he made an altar of his trunk and offered up his mass, kneeling on the stable floor. He felt refreshed, happy and strong. The arrival of Hosannah Wang failed to discompose him.

"Father should have let me serve his mass. That is always included in our pay. And now—shall we find a room in the Street of the Netmakers?"

Francis reflected. Though he had stubbornly made up his mind to live here till the situation cleared, it was true that he must find a more fitting center for his ministrations. He said: "Let us go there now."

The streets were already thronged. Dogs raced between their legs, pigs were rooting for garbage in the gutter. Children followed them, jeering and shouting. Beggars wailed with importunate palms. An old man setting out his wares, in the Street of the Lanternmakers, spat sullenly across the foreign devil's feet. Outside the yamen of justice, a peripatetic barber stood twanging his long tongs. There were many poor, many crippled, and some, blinded by smallpox, who tapped their way forward with a long bamboo and a queer high whistle.

It was an upper room Wang brought him to, clumsily partitioned with paper and bamboo, but sufficient for any service he would conduct. From his small store of money he paid a month's rent to the shopkeeper, named Hung, and began to set out his crucifix and solitary altar cloth. His lack of vestments, of altar furnishings, fretted him. Led to expect a full equipment at the "flourishing" mission, he had brought little. But his standard, at least, was planted.

Wang had preceded him to the shop below and as he turned to descend he observed Hung take two of the silver taels which he had given him and pass them, with a bow, to Wang. Though he had early guessed the worth of Father Lawler's legacy Francis was conscious of a sudden mounting of his blood. Outside, in the street, he turned quietly to Wang.

"I regret, Hosannah, I cannot pay your stipend of fifteen taels a month."

"Father Lawler could pay. Why cannot the Father pay?"

"I am poor, Hosannah. Just as poor as was my Master."

"How much will the Father pay?"

"Nothing, Hosannah! Even as I am paid nothing. It is the good Lord of Heaven who will reward us!"

Wang's smile did not falter. "Perhaps Hosannah and Philomena must go where they are appreciated. At Sen-siang the Methodys pay sixteen taels for highly respected catechists. But doubtless the good Father will change his mind. There is much animosity in Pai-tan. The people consider the *feng shua* of the city—the Laws of Wind and Order—destroyed by the intrusion of the missionary."

He waited for the priest's reply. But Francis did not speak. There was a strained pause. Then Wang bowed politely and departed.

A coldness settled upon Francis as he watched the other disappear. Had he done right in alienating the friendly Wangs? The answer was that the Wangs were not his friends, but lick-spittle opportunists who believed in the Christian God because of Christian money. And yet . . . his one contact with the community was severed. He had a sudden, frightening sense of being alone.

As the days passed this horrible loneliness increased, coupled with a paralyzing impotence. Lawler, his predecessor, had built upon sand. Incompetent, credulous, and supplied with ample funds, he had rushed about, giving money and taking names, baptizing promiscuously, acquiring a string of "rice-Christians," filling long reports, unconsciously the victim of a hundred subtle squeezes, sanguine, bombastic, gloriously triumphant. He had not even scratched the surface. Of his work nothing remained except perhaps—in the city's official circles—a lingering contempt for such lamentable foreign folly.

Beyond a small sum set for his living expenses, and a five-pound note pressed into his hand by Polly on his departure, Francis had no money whatsoever. He had been warned, too, on the futility of requesting grants from the new society at home. Sickened by Lawler's example, he rejoiced in his poverty. He swore, with a feverish intensity, that he would not hire his congregation. What must be done would be done with God's help and his own two hands.

Yet so far he had done nothing. He hung a sign outside his makeshift chapel; it made no difference: none appeared to hear his mass. The Wangs had spread a wide report that he was destitute, with nothing to distribute but bitter words.

He attempted an open-air meeting outside the courts of justice. He was laughed at, then ignored. His failure humiliated him. A Chinese laundryman preaching Confucianism in pigeon-English in the streets of Liverpool would have met with more success. Wildly he fought that insidious demon, the inner whisper of his own incompetence.

He prayed, he prayed most desperately. He ardently believed in the efficacy of prayer. "Oh God, you've helped me in the past. Help me now, for God's sake, please."

He had hours of raging fury. Why had they sent him, with plausible assurances, to this outlandish hole? The task was beyond any man, beyond God Himself! Cut from all communications, buried in the hinterland, with the nearest missioner, Father Thibodeau, at Sen-siang, four hundred miles away, the place was quite untenable.

Fostered by the Wangs, the popular hostility towards him increased. He was used to the jeers of the children. Now, on his passage through the town, a crowd of young coolies followed, throwing out insults. When he stopped a member of the gang would advance and perform his natural functions in the vicinity. One night, as he returned to the stable, a stone sailed out of the darkness and struck him on the brow.

All Francis' combativeness rose hotly in response. As he bandaged his broken head, his own wound gave him a wild idea, making him pause, rigid and intent. Yes . . . he must . . . he must get closer to the people . . . and this . . . no matter how primitive . . . this new endeavour might help him to that end.

Next morning, for two extra taels a month, he rented the lower back room of the shop from Hung and opened a public dispensary. He was no expert—God knew. But he had his St. John's certificate, and his long acquaintance with Dr. Tulloch had grounded him soundly in hygiene.

At first no one ventured near him; and he sweated with despair. But gradually, drawn by curiosity, one or two came in. There was always sickness in the city and the methods of the native doctors were barbaric. He had some success. He exacted nothing in money or devotion. Slowly his clientèle grew. He wrote urgently to Dr. Tulloch, enclosing Polly's five pounds, clamouring for an additional supply of dressings, bandages, and simple drugs. While the chapel remained empty the dispensary was often full.

At night, he brooded frantically amongst the ruins of the mission. He could never rebuild on that eroded site. And he gazed across the way in fierce desire at the pleasant Hill of Brilliant Green Jade where, above the scattered temples, a lovely slope extended, sheltered by a grove of cedars. What a noble situation for a monument to God!

The owner of this property, a civil judge named Pao, member of that inner intermarried community of merchants and magistrates who controlled the city's affairs, was rarely to be seen. But on most afternoons, his cousin, a tall dignified mandarin of forty, who managed the estate for Mr. Pao, came to inspect and to pay the labourers who worked the clay-pits in the cedar grove.

Worn by weeks of solitude, desolate and persecuted, Francis was undoubtedly a little mad. He had nothing; he was nothing. Yet one day, on an impulse, he stopped the tall mandarin as he crossed the road towards his chair. He did not understand the impropriety of this direct approach. In fact he knew little of what he did: he had not been eating properly, and was light-headed from a touch of fever.

"I have often admired this beautiful property which you so wisely administer."

Taken wholly by surprise, Mr. Pao's cousin formally viewed the short alien figure with its burning eyes, and the soiled bandage on its forehead. In frigid politeness he bore with the priest's continued assaults upon the syntax, briefly deprecated himself, his family, his miserable possessions, remarked on the weather, the crops, and the difficulty the city had experienced last year in buying off the Wai-Chu bandits; then pointedly opened the door of his chair. When Francis, with swimming head, strove to return the conversation to the Green Jade land, he smiled coldly.

"The Green Jade property is a pearl without price, in extent more than sixty mous . . . shade, water, pasture . . . in addition a rich and extraordinary clay-pit for the purpose of tiles, pottery and bricks. Mr. Pao has no desire to sell. Already, for the estate, he has refused . . . fifteen thousand silver dollars."

At the price, ten times greater than his most fearful estimate, Francis' legs shook. The fever left him, he suddenly felt weak and giddy, ashamed at the absurdity into which his dreams had led him. With splitting head, he thanked Mr. Pao's cousin, muttered a confused apology.

Observing the priest's disappointed sadness, the lean, middle-aged, cultured Chinese allowed a flicker of disdain to escape his watchful secrecy.

"Why does the Shang-Foo come here? Are there no wicked men to regenerate in his own land? For we are not wicked people. We have our own religion. Our own gods are older than his. The other Shang-Foo made many Christians by pouring water from a little bottle upon dying men and singing 'Ya . . . ya!' Also, by giving food and clothing, to many more who would sing any tune to have their skins covered and their bellies full. Does the Shang-Foo wish to do this also?"

Francis gazed at the other in silence. His thin face had a worn pallor, there were deep shadows beneath his eyes. He said quietly: "Do you think that is my wish?"

There was a strange pause. All at once, Mr. Pao's cousin dropped his eyes. "Forgive me," he said, in a low tone. "I did not understand. You are a good man." A vague friendliness tinctured his compunction. "I regret that my cousin's land is not available. Perhaps in some other manner I may assist you?"

Mr. Pao's cousin waited with a new courtesy, as if anxious to make amends.

Francis thought for a moment, then asked heavily: "Tell me, since we are being honest. . . . Are there no true Christians here?"

Mr. Pao's cousin answered slowly: "Perhaps. But I should not seek them in Pai-tan." He paused. "I have heard, however, of a village in the Kwang Mountains." He made a vague gesture towards the distant peaks. "A village Christian for many years . . . but it is far away, many many li from here."

A gleam of light shot into the haggard gloom of Francis' mind. "That interests me deeply. Can you give me further information?"

The other shook his head regretfully. "It is a small place on the uplands— almost unknown. My cousin only learned of it from his trade in sheepskins."

Francis' eagerness sustained him. "Could you ask him? Could you procure directions for me . . . perhaps a map?"

Mr. Pao's cousin reflected, then nodded gravely. "It should be possible. I shall ask Mr. Pao. Moreover I shall be careful to inform him that you have spoken with me in a most honourable fashion."

He bowed and went away.

Overwhelmed with this wholly unexpected hope, Francis returned to the ruined compound where, with some blankets, a water-skin and the few utensils purchased in the town, he had made his primitive encampment. As he prepared himself a simple meal of rice, his hands trembled, as from shock. A Christian village! He must find it—at all costs. It was his first sense of guidance, of divine inspiration, in all these weary, fruitless months.

As he sat tensely thinking in the dusk he was disturbed by a hoarse barking of crows, fighting and tearing at some carrion by the water's edge. He went over at length, to drive them off. And there, as the great ugly birds flapped and squawked at him, he saw their prey to be the body of a newly born female child.

Shuddering, he took up the infant's torn body from the river, saw it to be asphyxiated, thrown in and drowned. He wrapped the little thing in linen, buried it in a corner of the compound. And as he prayed he thought: yes, despite my doubts, there is need for me, in this strange land, after all.

2

Two weeks later, when the early summer burgeoned, he was ready. Placing a painted notice of temporary closure on his premises in Netmaker Street, he strapped a pack of blankets and food upon his back, took up his umbrella and set off briskly on foot.

The map given him by Mr. Pao's cousin was beautifully executed, with wind-belching dragons in the corners and a wealth of topographic detail as far as the mountains. Beyond it was sketchy, with little drawings of animals instead of place names. But from their conversations and his own sense of direction Francis had in his head a fair notion of his route. He set his face towards the Kwang Gap.

For two days his journey lay through easy country, the green wet rice fields giving place to woods of spruce, where the fallen needles made a soft resilient carpet for his feet. Immediately below the Kwangs he traversed a sheltered valley aflame with wild rhododendrons, and later, that same dreamy afternoon, a glade of flowering apricots whose perfume pricked the nostrils like the fume of sparkling wine. Then he began the steep ascent of the ravine.

It grew colder with every step up the narrow stony track. At night he folded himself under the shelter of a rock, hearing the whistle of the wind, the thunder of snow-water in the gorge. In the daytime, the cold blazing whiteness of the higher peaks burned his eyes. The thin iced air was painful to his lungs.

On the fifth day he crossed the summit of the ridge, a frozen wilderness of glacier and rock, and thankfully descended the other side. The pass led him to a wide plateau, beneath the snowline, green with verdure, melting into softly rounded hills. These were the grasslands of which Mr. Pao's cousin had spoken.

Thus far the sheer mountains had defined his twisted course. Now he must rely on Providence, a compass and his good Scots sense. He struck out directly towards the west. The country was like the uplands of his home. He came on great herds of stoic grazing goats and mountain sheep that streamed off wildly at his approach. He caught the fleeting image of a gazelle. From the bunch-grass of a vast dun marsh thousands of nesting ducks rose screaming, darkening the sky. Since his food was running low, he filled his satchel gratefully with the warm eggs.

It was trackless, treeless plain: he began to despair of stumbling on the village. But early on the ninth day when he felt he must soon turn back, he sighted a shepherd's hut, the first sign of habitation since he'd left the southern slopes. He hastened eagerly towards it. The door was sealed with mud, there was no one inside. But as he swung round, his eyes sharp with disappointment, he saw a boy approaching over the hill behind his flock.

The young shepherd was about seventeen, small and wiry, like his sheep, with a cheerful and intelligent face now caught between wonderment and laughter. He wore short sheepskin trousers and a woollen cape. Round his neck was a small bronze Yuan cross, wafer-thin with age, and roughly scratched with the symbol of a dove. Father Chisholm gazed from the boy's open face to the antique cross in silence. At last he found his voice and greeted him, asking if he were from the Liu village.

The lad smiled. "I am from the Christian village. I am Liu-Ta. My father is the village priest." He added, not to be thought boasting, "One of the village priests!"

Again, there was a silence. Father Chisholm thought better of questioning the boy further. He said: "I have come a long distance, and I too am a priest. I should be grateful if you would take me to your home."

The village lay in an undulating valley five li farther to the westward, a cluster of some thirty houses, tucked away in this fold of the uplands, surrounded by little stone-walled fields of grain. Prominent, upon a central hillock, behind a queer conical mound of stones shaded by a ginkgo tree, was a small stone church.

As he entered the village the entire community immediately surrounded him, men, women, children and dogs, all crowding round in curiosity and excited welcome, pulling at his sleeves, touching his boots, examining his umbrella with cries of admiration, while Ta threw off a rapid explanation in a dialect he could not understand. There were perhaps sixty persons in the throng, primitive and healthy, with naïve, friendly eyes and features that bore the imprint of their common family. Presently, with a proprietary smile, Ta brought forward his father Liu-Chi, a short and sturdy man of fifty with a small grey beard, simple and dignified in his manner.

Speaking slowly, to make himself understood, Liu-Chi said: "We welcome you with joy, Father. Come to my house and rest a little before prayer."

He led the way to the largest house, built on a stone foundation next the church, and showed Father Chisholm, with courteous urbanity, into a low cool room. At the end of the room stood a mahogany spinet and a Portuguese wheel clock. Bewildered, lost in wonder, Francis stared at the clock. The brass dial was engraved: *Lisbon 1632.*

He had no time for closer inspection, Liu-Chi was addressing him again. "Is it your wish to offer mass, Father? Or shall I?"

As in a dream Father Chisholm nodded his head towards the other. Something within him answered: "You . . . please!" He was groping in a great confusion. He knew he could not rudely break this mystery with speech. He must penetrate it graciously, in patience, with his eyes.

Half an hour later they were all within the church. Though small it had been built with taste in a style that showed the Moorish influence on the Renaissance. There were three simple arcades, beautifully fluted. The doorway and the windows were supported by flat pilasters. On the walls, partly incomplete, free mosaics had been traced.

He sat in the front row of an attentive congregation. Every one had ceremonially washed his hands before entering. Most of the men and a few of the women wore praying caps upon their heads. Suddenly a tongueless bell was struck and Liu-Chi approached the altar, wearing a faded yellow alb and supported by two young men. Turning, he bowed ceremoniously to Father Chisholm and the congregation. Then the service began.

Father Chisholm watched, kneeling erect, spellbound, like a man beholding the slow enactment of a dream. He saw now that the ceremony was a strange survival, a touching relic of the mass. Liu-Chi must know no Latin, for he prayed in Chinese. First came the confiteor, then the creed. When he ascended the altar and opened the parchment missal on its wooden rest, Francis clearly heard a portion of the gospel solemnly intoned in the native tongue. An original translation. . . . He drew a quick breath of awe.

The whole congregation advanced to take communion. Even children at the breast were carried to the altar steps. Liu-Chi descended, bearing a chalice of rice wine. Moistening his forefinger he placed a drop upon the lips of each.

Before leaving the church, the congregation gathered at the Statue of the Saviour, placing lighted joss-sticks on the heavy candelabrum before the feet. Then each person made three prostrations and reverently withdrew.

Father Chisholm remained behind, his eyes moist, his heart wrung by the simple childish piety—the same piety, the same simplicity he had so often witnessed in peasant Spain. Of course this ceremony was not valid—he smiled faintly, visualizing Father Tarrant's horror at the spectacle—but he had no doubt it was pleasing to God Almighty none the less.

Liu-Chi was waiting outside to conduct him to the house. There a meal awaited them. Famished, Father Chisholm did full justice to the stew of mountain mutton—little savoury balls floating in cabbage soup—and the strange dish of rice and wild honey which followed. He had never tasted such a delicious sweet in all his life.

When they had both finished, he began tactfully to question Liu-Chi. He would have bitten out his tongue rather than give offence. The gentle old man answered trustingly. His beliefs were Christian, quite childlike and curiously mingled with the traditions of Tâo-tê. Perhaps, thought Father Chisholm, with an inward smile, a touch of Nestorianism thrown in for value. . . .

Chi explained that the faith had been handed down from father to son through many generations. The village was not dramatically isolated from the world. But it was sufficiently remote; and so small, so integrated in its family life, that strangers rarely troubled it. They were one great family. Existence was purely pastoral and self-supporting. They had grain and mutton in plenty even through the hardest times; cheese, which they sealed in the stomach of a sheep, and two kinds of butter, red and black, both made from beans and named *chiang*. For clothing they had home-carded wool, sheepskins for extra warmth. They beat a special parchment from the skins that was much prized in Pekin. There were many wild ponies on the uplands. Rarely, a member of the family went out with a ponyload of vellum.

In the little tribe there were three Fathers, each chosen for this honoured position while still in infancy. For certain religious offices a fee of rice was paid. They had a special devotion to the Three Precious Ones—the Trinity. Within living memory they had never seen an ordained priest.

Father Chisholm had listened with rapt attention and now he put the question uppermost in his mind.

"You have not told me how it first began!"

Liu-Chi looked at his visitor with final appraisal. Then with a faint reassured smile he got up and went into the adjoining room. When he returned he bore under his arm a sheepskin-covered bundle. He handed it over silently, watched Father Chisholm open it, then, as the priest's absorption became apparent, silently withdrew.

It was the journal of Father Ribiero, written in Portuguese, brown, stained and tattered, but mostly legible. From his knowledge of Spanish, Francis was able slowly to decipher it. The fascinating interest of the document made the labour as nothing. It held him riveted. He remained motionless, except for the slow movement of his hand turning, at intervals, a heavy page. Time flew back three hundred years: the old stopped clock took up its measured tick.

Manoel Ribiero was a missioner of Lisbon who came to Pekin in 1625. Francis saw the Portuguese vividly before him: a young man of twenty-nine, spare, olive-skinned, a little fiery, his swart eyes ardent yet humble. In Pekin the young missionary had been fortunate in his friendship with Father Adam Schall, the great German Jesuit, missionary, courtier, astronomer, trusted friend and canon founder extraordinary to the Emperor Tchoun-Tchin. For several years Father Ribiero shared a little of the glory of this astounding man who moved untouched through the seething intrigues of the Courts of Heaven, advancing the Christian Faith, even in the celestial harem, confounding virulent hatreds with his accurate predictions of comets and eclipses, compiling a new calendar, winning friendship and illustrious titles for himself and all his ancestors.

Then the Portuguese had pressed to be sent on a distant mission to the Royal Court of Tartary. Adam Schall had granted his request. A caravan was sumptuously equipped and formidably armed. It started from Pekin on the Feast of the Assumption, 1629.

But the caravan had failed to reach the Tartar Royal Courts. Ambushed by a horde of barbarians on the northern slopes of the Kwang Mountains the formidable defenders dropped their arms and fled. The valuable caravan was plundered. Father Ribiero escaped, desperately wounded by flint arrows, with only his personal belongings and the least of his ecclesiastical equipment. Benighted in the snow, he thought his last hour had come and offered himself, bleeding, to God. But the cold froze his wounds. He dragged himself next morning to a shepherd's hut, where he lay for six months neither dead nor alive. Meanwhile an authentic report reached Pekin that Father Ribiero was massacred. No expedition was sent out to search for him.

When the Portuguese decided he might live, he made plans to return to Adam Schall. But time went on and he still remained. In these wide grasslands, he gained a new sense of values, a new habit of contemplation. Besides, he was three thousand li from Pekin, a forbidding distance, even to his intrepid spirit. Quietly he took his decision. He collected the handful of shepherds into one small settlement. He built a church. He became friend and pastor—not to the King of Tartary but to this humble little flock.

With a strange sigh Francis put down the journal. In the failing light he sat thinking, thinking, and seeing many things. Then he rose and went out to the great mound of stones beside the church. Kneeling, he prayed at Father Ribiero's tomb.

He remained at the Liu village for a week. Persuasively, in a manner to hurt no one, he suggested a ratification of all baptisms and marriages. He said mass. Gently he dropped a hint, now here, now there, suggesting an emendation of certain practices. It would take a long time to regularize the village to hidebound orthodoxy: months—no, years. What did that matter? He was content to go slowly. The little community was as clean and sound as a good apple.

He spoke to them of many things. In the evenings a fire would be lit outside Liu-Chi's house, and when they had all seated themselves about it, he would rest himself on the doorstep and talk to the silent, flame-lit circle. Best of all they liked to hear of the presence of their own religion in the great outside world. He drew no captious differences. It enthralled them when he spoke of the churches of Europe, the great cathedrals, the thousands of worshippers flocking to St. Peter's, great kings and princes, statesmen and nobles, all prostrating themselves before the Lord of Heaven, that same Lord of Heaven whom they worshipped here, their master too, their friend. This sense of unity, hitherto but dimly surmised, gave them a joyful pride.

As the intent faces, flickering with light and shadow, gazed up at him in happy wonderment, he felt Father Ribiero at his elbow smiling a little, darkly, not displeased with him. At such moments he had a terrible impulse to throw up Pai-tan and devote himself entirely to these simple people. How happy he could be here! How lovingly he would tend and polish this jewel he had found so unexpectedly in the wilderness! But no, the village was too small, and too remote. He could never make it a centre for true missionary work. Resolutely, he put the temptation away from him.

The boy Ta had become his constant follower. Now he no longer called him Ta but Joseph, for that was the name the youngster had demanded at his conditional baptism. Fortified by the new name, he had begged permission to serve Father Chisholm's mass; and though he naturally knew not a shred of Latin, the priest had smilingly consented. On the eve of his departure Father Chisholm was seated at the doorway of the house when Joseph appeared, his usually cheerful features set and woebegone, the first arrival for the final lecture. Studying the boy the priest had an intuition of his regret, followed by a sudden happy thought.

"Joseph! Would it please you to come with me—if your father would permit it? There are many things you might do to help me."

The boy jumped up with a cry of joy, fell before the priest and kissed his hand.

"Master, I have waited for you to ask me. My father is willing. I will serve you with all my heart."

"There may be many rough roads, Joseph."

"We shall travel them together, Master."

Father Chisholm raised the young man to his feet. He was moved and pleased. He knew he had done a wise thing.

Next morning the preparations for departure were completed.

Scrubbed and smiling, Joseph stood with the bundles, beside the two shaggy mountain ponies he had rounded up at dawn. A small group of younger boys surrounded him, already he was awing his companions with the wonders of the world. In the church Father Chisholm was finishing his thanksgiving. As he rose, Liu-Chi beckoned him to the cryptlike sanctuary. From a cedar chest he drew an embroidered cope, an exquisite thing, stiff with gold. In parts the satin had rubbed paper-thin but the vestment was intact, usable and priceless. The old man smiled at the expression on Francis' face.

"This poor thing pleases you?"

"It is beautiful."

"Take it. It is yours!"

No protestations could prevent Liu-Chi from making the superb gift. It was folded, wrapped in clean flax-cloth, and placed in Joseph's pack.

At last Francis had to bid them all farewell. He blessed them, gave repeated assurances that he would return within six months. It would be easier next time, mounted, and with Joseph as his guide. Then the two departed, together, their ponies nodding neck-to-neck, climbing to the uplands. The eyes of the little village followed them with affection.

With Joseph beside him, Father Chisholm set a good round pace. He felt his faith restored, gloriously fortified. His breast throbbed with fresh hope.

3

THE summer which followed their return to Pai-tan had passed. And now the cold season fell upon the land. With Joseph's help he made the stable snug, patching the cracks with fresh mud and kaolin. Two wooden bunks now buttressed the weakest wall and a flat iron brazier made a hearth upon the beaten earth floor. Joseph, whose appetite was healthy, had already acquired an interesting collection of cooking pots. The boy, now less angelic, improved upon acquaintance: he was a great prattler, loved to be praised and could be wilful at times, with a naïve facility for abstracting ripe musk melons from the market garden down the way.

Francis was still determined not to quit their lowly shelter until he saw his course ahead. Gradually a few timid souls were creeping to his chapel room in Netmaker Street, the first an old woman, ragged and ashamed, furtively pulling her beads from the sacking which served her for a coat, looking as though a single word would send her scurrying. Firmly, he restrained himself, pretended not to notice her. Next morning she returned with her daughter.

The pitiful sparsity of his followers did not discourage him. His resolve neither to cajole nor to buy his converts was tempered, like fine steel.

His dispensary was going with a swing. Apparently his absence from the little clinic had been regretted. On his return he found a nondescript assembly awaiting him outside Hung's premises. With practice, his judgement, and indeed his skill, increased. All sorts of conditions came his way: skin diseases, colics and coughs, enteritis, dreadful suppurations of the eyes and ears; and most were the result of dirt and overcrowding. It was amazing what cleanliness and a simple bitter tonic did for them. A grain of potassium permanganate was worth its weight in gold.

When his meagre supplies threatened to run out, an answer came to his supplication to Dr. Tulloch—a big nailed-up box of lint, wool and gauze, iodine and antiseptics, castor oil and chlorodyne, with a scrawled torn-off prescription sheet crumpled at the foot.

"Your Holiness: I thought I was the one to go doctoring in the tropics! And where is your degree? Never mind—cure what you can and kill what you can't. Here is a little bag of tricks to help you."

It was a neatly packed first-aid case of lancet, scissors, and forceps. A postscript added: "For your information, I am reporting you to the B.M.A., the Pope and Chung-lung-soo."

Francis smiled at the irrepressible facetiousness. But his throat was tight with gratitude. With this stimulation of his own endeavour and the comfort of Joseph's companionship, he felt a new and thrilling exaltation. He had never worked harder, nor slept sounder, in his life.

But one night in November his sleep was light and troubled and after midnight he suddenly awoke. It was piercing cold. In the still darkness he could hear Joseph's deep and peaceful breathing. He lay for a moment, trying to reason away his vague distress. But he could not. He got up, cautiously, so that he might not wake the sleeping boy, and slipped out of the stable into the compound. The frozen night stabbed him: the air was razor-edged with cold, each breath a cutting pain. There were no stars, but from the frosted snow came a strange and luminous whiteness. The silence seemed to reach a hundred miles. It was terrifying.

Suddenly, through that stillness, he fancied he heard a faint and uncertain cry. He knew he was mistaken, listened, and heard no more. But as he turned to re-enter the stable the sound was repeated, like the feeble squawking of a dying bird. He stood indecisively, then slowly crunched his way across the crusted snow, towards the sound.

Outside the compound, fifty paces down the path, he stumbled on a stiff dark shadow: the prostrate form of a woman, her face sunk into the snow, starkly frozen. She was quite dead, but under her, in the garments about her bosom, he saw the feeble writhings of a child.

He stooped and lifted up the tiny thing, cold as a fish, but soft. His heart was beating like a drum. He ran back, slipping, almost falling, to the stable, calling in a loud voice to Joseph.

When the brazier was blazing with fresh wood, throwing out light and heat, the priest and his servant bent over the child. It was not more than twelve months old. Its eyes were dark and wild, unbelieving towards the warmth of the fire. From time to time it whimpered.

"It is hungry," Joseph said in a wise tone.

They warmed some milk and poured it into an altar vial. Father Chisholm then tore a strip of clean linen and coaxed it, like a wick, into the flask's narrow neck. The child sucked greedily. In five minutes the milk was finished and the child asleep. The priest wrapped it in a blanket from his own bed.

He was deeply moved. The strangeness of his premonition, the simplicity of the coming of the little thing, into the stable, out of the cold nothingness, was like a sign from God. There was nothing upon the mother's body to tell who she might be, but her features, worn by hardship and poverty, had a thin, fine Tartar cast. A band of nomads had passed through the day before: perhaps she had been overcome by cold, had fallen behind to die. He sought in his mind for a name for the child. It was the feast day of Saint Anna. Yes, he would name her Anna.

"Tomorrow, Joseph, we shall find a woman to take care of this gift from heaven."

Joseph shrugged. "Master, you cannot give away a female child."

"I shall not give the child away," Father Chisholm said sternly.

His purpose was already clear and fixed. This babe, sent to him by God, would be his first foundling—yes, the foundation of his children's home . . . that dream he had cherished since his arrival in Pai-tan. He would need help of course, the Sisters must one day come—it was all a long way off. But, seated on the earth floor, by the dark red embers, gazing upon the sleeping infant, he felt it was a pledge from heaven that he would, in the end, succeed.

It was Joseph, the prize gossip, who first told Father Chisholm that Mr. Chia's son was sick. The cold season was late in breaking, the Kwang Mountains were still deep in snow; and the cheerful Joseph blew upon his nipped fingers as he chattered away after mass, assisting the priest to put away his vestments. "*Tch!* My hand is as useless as that of the little Chia-Yu."

Chia-Yu had scratched his thumb upon no one knew what; but in consequence, his five elements had been disturbed and the lower humours had gained ascendency, flowing entirely into one arm, distending it, leaving the boy's body burning and wasted. The three highest physicians of the city were in attendance and the most costly remedies had been applied. Now a messenger had been despatched to Sen-siang for the *elixir vitae*: a priceless extract of frog's eyes, obtained only in the circle of the Dragon's moon.

"He will recover," Joseph concluded, showing his white teeth in a sanguine smile. "This *hao kao* never fails . . . which is important for Mr. Chia, since Yu is his only son."

Four days later, at the same hour, two closed chairs, one of which was empty, drew up outside the chapel shop in the Street of the Netmakers, and a moment later the tall figure of Mr. Pao's cousin, wrapped in a cotton-padded tunic, gravely confronted Father Chisholm. He apologized for his unseemly intrusion. He asked the priest to accompany him to Mr. Chia's house.

Stunned by the implication of the invitation, Francis hesitated. Close relationship, through business and marriage ties, existed between the Paos and the Chias, both were highly influential families. Since his return from the Liu village he had not infrequently encountered the lean, aloof, and pleasantly cynical cousin of Mr. Pao, who was, indeed, also first cousin to Mr. Chia. He had some evidence of the tall mandarin's regard. But this abrupt call, this sponsorship, was different. As he turned silently to get his hat and coat, he felt a sudden hollow fear.

The Chia house was very quiet, the trellised verandahs empty, the fish pond brittle with a film of ice. Their steps rang softly, but with a momentous air, upon the paved, deserted courtyards. Two flanking jasmine trees, swathed in sacking, lolled like sleeping giants, against the tented, red-gold gateway. From the women's quarters across the terraces came the strangled sound of weeping.

It was darkish in the sick-chamber, where Chia-Yu lay upon a heated *kang*, watched by the three bearded physicians in long full robes seated upon fresh rush matting. From time to time one of the physicians bent forward and placed a charcoal lump beneath the boxlike *kang*. In the corner of the room, a Taoist priest in a slate-coloured robe was mumbling, exorcising, to the accompaniment of flutes behind the bamboo partition.

Yu had been a pretty child of six, with soft cream colouring and sloe-black eyes, reared in the strictest traditions of parental respect, idolized, yet unspoiled. Now, consumed by remorseless fever and the terrible novelty of pain, he was stretched upon his back, his bones sticking through his skin, his dry lips twisting, his gaze upon the ceiling, motionless. His right arm, livid, swollen out of recognition, was encased in a horrible plaster of dirt mixed with little printed paper scraps.

When Mr. Pao's cousin entered with Father Chisholm there was a tiny stillness; then the Taoist mumbling was resumed, while the three physicians, more strictly immobilized, maintained their vigil by the *kang*.

Bent over the unconscious child, his hand upon the burning brow, Father Chisholm knew the full import of that limpid and passionless restraint. His present troubles would be as nothing to the persecution which must follow a futile intervention. But the desperate sickness of the boy and this noxious pretence of treatment whipped his blood. He began, quickly yet gently, to remove from the infected arm the *hao kao*, that filthy dressing he had so often met with in his little dispensary.

At last the arm was free, washed in warm water. It floated almost, a bladder of corruption, with a shiny greenish skin. Though now his heart was thudding in his side Francis went on steadfastly, drew from his pocket the little leather case which Tulloch had given him, took from that case the single lancet. He knew his inexperience. He knew also that if he did not incise the arm the child, already moribund, would die. He felt every unwatching eye upon him, sensed the terrible anxiety, the growing doubt gripping Mr. Pao's cousin as he stood motionless behind him. He made an ejaculation to Saint Andrew. He steeled himself to cut, to cut deep, deep and long.

A great gush of putrid matter came heaving through the wound, flowing and bubbling into the earthenware bowl beneath. The stench was dreadful, evil. In all his life Francis had never savoured anything so gratefully. As he pressed, with both his hands, on either side of the wound, encouraging the exudation, seeing the limb collapse to half its size, a great relief surged through him, leaving him weak.

When, at last, he straightened up, having packed the wound with clean wet linen, he heard himself murmur, foolishly, in English: "I think he'll do now, with a little luck!" It was old Dr. Tulloch's famous phrase: it demonstrated the tension of his nerves. Yet on his way out he strove to maintain an attitude of cheerful unconcern, declaring to the completely silent cousin of Mr. Pao, who accompanied him to his chair: "Give him nourishing soup if he wakes up. And no more *hao kao*. I will come tomorrow."

On the next day little Yu was greatly better. His fever was almost gone, he had slept naturally and drunk several cups of chicken broth. Without the miracle of the shining lancet he would almost certainly have been dead.

"Continue to nourish him." Father Chisholm genuinely smiled as he took his departure. "I shall call again tomorrow!"

"Thank you." Mr. Pao's cousin cleared his throat. "It is not necessary." There was an awkward pause. "We are deeply grateful. Mr. Chia has been prostrate with grief. Now that his son is recovering he also is recovering. Soon he may be able to present himself in public!" The mandarin bowed, hands discreetly in his sleeves, and was gone.

Father Chisholm strode down the street—he had angrily refused the chair —fighting a dark and bitter indignation. This was gratitude. To be thrown out, without a word, when he had saved the child's life, at the risk, perhaps, of his own . . . From first to last he had not even seen the wretched Mr. Chia, who, even on the junk, that day of his arrival, had not deigned to glance at him. He clenched his fists, fighting his familiar demon: "O God, let me be calm! Don't let this cursed sin of anger master me again. Let me be meek and patient of heart. Give me humility, dear Lord. After all it was Thy merciful goodness, Thy divine providence, which saved the little boy. Do with me what Thou wilt, dear Lord. You see, I am resigned. But, O God!" —with sudden heat: "You must admit it was such damned ingratitude after all!"

During the next few days Francis rigorously shunned the merchant's quarter of the city. More than his pride had been hurt. He listened in silence while Joseph gossiped of the remarkable progress of little Yu, of the largesse distributed by Mr. Chia to the wise physicians, the donation to the Temple of Lao-tzŭ, for the exorcising of the demon which had troubled his beloved son. "Is it not truly remarkable, dear Father, how many sources have benefited by the mandarin's noble generosity?"

"Truly remarkable," said Father Chisholm dryly, but wincing.

A week later, when about to close his dispensary after a stale and profitless afternoon, he suddenly observed, across the flask of permanganate he had been mixing, the discreet apparition of Mr. Chia.

He started hotly, but said nothing. The merchant wore his finest clothes: a rich black satin robe with yellow jacket, embroidered velvet boots in one of which was thrust the ceremonial fan, a fine flat satin cap, and an expression both formal and dignified. His too-long fingernails were protected by gold metal cases. He had an air of culture and intelligence, his manners expressed perfect breeding. There was a gentle, enlightened melancholy on his brow.

"I have come," he said.

"Indeed!" Francis' tone was not encouraging. He went on stirring with his glass rod, mixing the mauve solution.

"There have been many matters to attend to, much business to settle. But now,"—a resigned bow,—"I am here."

"Why?" Shortly, from Francis.

Mr. Chia's face indicated mild surprise. "Naturally . . . to become a Christian."

There was a moment of dead silence—a moment which, traditionally, should have marked the climax of these meagre toiling months, the thrilling first fruits of the missionary's achievement: here, the leading savage, bowing the head for baptism. But there was little exultation in Father Chisholm's face. He chewed his lip crossly, then he said slowly: "Do you believe?"

"No!" Sadly.

"Are you prepared to be instructed?"

"I have not time to be instructed." A subdued bow. "I am only eager to become a Christian."

"Eager? You mean you want to?"

Mr. Chia smiled wanly. "Is it not apparent—my wish to profess your faith?"

"No, it is not apparent. And you have not the slightest wish to profess my faith. Why are you doing this?" The priest's colour was high.

"To repay you," Mr. Chia said simply. "You have done the greatest good to me. I must do the greatest good for you."

Father Chisholm moved irritably. Because the temptation was so alluring, because he wished to yield and could not, his temper flared. "It is not good. It is bad. You have neither inclination nor belief. My acceptance of you would be a forgery for God. You owe me nothing. Now please go!"

At first Mr. Chia did not believe his ears.

"You mean you reject me?"

"That is putting it politely," growled Father Chisholm.

The change in the merchant was seraphic. His eyes brightened, glistened, his melancholy dropped from him like a shroud. He had to struggle to contain himself; but although he had the semblance of desiring to leap into the air he did contain himself. Formally, he made the kowtow three times. He succeeded in mastering his voice.

"I regret that I am not acceptable. I am of course most unworthy. Nevertheless, perhaps in some slight manner . . ." He broke off, again he made the kowtow three times and, moving backwards, went out.

That evening, as Father Chisholm sat by the brazier with a sternness of countenance which caused Joseph, who was cooking tasty river mussels in his rice, to gaze at him timidly, there came the sudden sound of firecrackers.

Six of Mr. Chia's servants were exploding them, ceremoniously, in the road outside. Then Mr. Pao's cousin advanced, bowed, handed Father Chisholm a parchment wrapped in vermilion paper.

"Mr. Chia begs that you will honour him by accepting this most unworthy gift—the deeds of the Brilliant Green Jade property with all land and water rights and the rights to the crimson clay-pit. The property is yours, without restraint, forever. Mr. Chia further begs that you accept the help of twenty of his workmen till any building you may wish to carry out is fully accomplished."

So completely taken aback was Francis he could not speak a word. He watched the retreating figure of the cousin of Mr. Pao, and of Mr. Chia, with a strange still tensity. Then he wildly scanned the title deeds and cried out joyfully, "Joseph! Joseph!"

Joseph came hurrying, fearing another misfortune had befallen them. His master's expression reassured him. They went together to the Hill of Brilliant Green Jade and there, standing under the moon amidst the tall cedars, they sang aloud the Magnificat.

Francis remained bare-headed, seeing in a vision what he would create on this noble brow of land. He had prayed with faith, and his prayer had been answered.

Joseph, made hungry by the keen wind, waited uncomplainingly, finding his own vision in the priest's rapt face, glad he had shown the presence of mind to take his rice-pot from the fire.

4

EIGHTEEN months later, in the month of May, when all Chek-kow province lay basking in that span of short perfection between the winter snows and the swelterings of summer, Father Chisholm crossed the paved courtyard of his new Mission of St. Andrew.

Never, perhaps, had such a sense of quiet contentment suffused him. The crystal air, where a cloud of white pigeons wheeled, was sweet and sparkling. As he reached the great banyan tree which, through his design, now shaded the forecourt of the mission, he threw a look across his shoulder, partly of pride, part in wry wonderment, as though still apprehensive of a mirage which might vanish overnight.

But it was there, shining and splendid: the slender church sentineled between the cedars, his house, vivid with scarlet lattices, adjoining the little schoolroom, the snug dispensary opening through the outer wall, and a further dwelling screened by the foliage of pawpaw and catalpa, which sheltered his freshly planted garden. He sighed, his lips smiling, blessing the miracle of the fruitful clay-pit which had yielded, through many blendings and experimental bakings, bricks of a lovely soft pale rose, making his mission a symphony in cinnabar. He blessed, indeed, each subsequent wonder: the implacable kindness of Mr. Chia; the skilful patience of his workers; the incorruptibility—almost complete—of his sturdy foreman; even the weather, this recent brilliant spell, which had made his opening ceremony, held last week and politely attended by the Chia and Pao families, a notable success.

For the sole purpose of viewing the empty classroom he took the long way round: peering, like a schoolboy, through the window at the brand-new pictures upon the whitewashed wall, at the shining benches which, like the blackboard, he had carpentered himself. The knowledge that his handiwork was in that particular room lay warmly round his heart. But recollection of the task he had in mind drove him to the end of the garden where, near the lower gate, and beside his private workshop, was a small brick kiln.

Happily, he jettisoned his old soutane and, in stained denim trousers, shirt sleeves and suspenders, he took a wooden spade and began to puddle-up some clay.

Tomorrow the three Sisters would arrive. Their house was ready—cool, curtained, already smelling of beeswax. But his final conceit, a secluded loggia in which they might rest and meditate, was not quite finished, demanding at least another batch of bricks from his own especial oven. As he shaped the marl he shaped the future in his mind.

Nothing was more vital than the advent of these nuns. He had seen this from the outset, he had worked and prayed for it, sending letter upon letter to Father Mealey and even to the Bishop, while the mission slowly rose before his eyes. Conversion of the Chinese adult was, he felt, a labour for archangels. Race, illiteracy, the tug of an older faith—these were formidable barriers to break down honestly, and one knew that the Almighty hated being asked to do conjuring tricks with each individual case. True, now that he was sustained in "face" by his fine new church, increasing numbers of repentant souls were adventuring to mass. He had some sixty persons in his congregation. As their pious cadences ascended at the Kyrie it sounded quite a multitude.

Nevertheless, his vision was focussed, brightly, on the children. Here, quite literally, children went two a penny. Famine, grinding poverty, and the Confucianism of masculine perpetuation made female infants, at least, a drug upon the market. In no time at all he would have a schoolful of children, fed and cared for by the Sisters, here in the mission, spinning their hoops, making the place gay with laughter, learning their letters and their catechism. The future belonged to the children: and the children . . . his children . . . would belong to God!

He smiled self-consciously at his thoughts as he shoved the moulds into the oven. He could not call himself, precisely, a ladies' man. Yet he had hungered, these long months, amidst this alien race, for the comfort of intercourse with his own kind. Mother Maria-Veronica, though Bavarian by birth, had spent the past five years with the Bon Secours in London. And the two whom she led, the French Sister Clotilde and Sister Martha, a Belgian, had equal experience in Liverpool. Coming direct from England they would bring him, at least, a friendly breath of home.

A trifle anxiously—for he had taken enormous trouble—he reviewed his preparations for their arrival on the following day: A few fireworks in the best Chinese style, but not enough to alarm the ladies, at the river landing stage, where the three best chairs in Pai-tan would await them. Tea served immediately they reached the mission. A short rest followed by benediction—he hoped they would like the flowers—and then, a special supper.

He almost chuckled as he conned, in his mind's eye, the menu of that supper. Well . . . they'd get down to hard-tack soon enough, poor things! His own appetite was scandalously meagre. During the building of the mission he had subsisted abstractedly, standing on scaffolds, or fingering a plan with Mr. Chia's foreman, upon rice and bean curd. But now he had sent Joseph scouring the city for mangos, chowchow and, rarest delicacy of all, fresh bustard from Shon-see in the North.

Suddenly, across his meditation, came the sound of footsteps. He lifted his head. As he turned, the gate was thrown open. Signed forward by their guide, a ragged riverside coolie, three nuns appeared. They were travel-stained, with a vague uneasiness in their uncertain glances. They hesitated, then advanced wearily up the garden path. The foremost, about forty years of age, had both dignity and beauty. There was high breeding in the fine bones of her face and in her wide heavy blue eyes. Pale with fatigue, impelled by a kind of inward fire, she forced herself on. Barely looking at Francis, she addressed him in fair Chinese.

"Please take us immediately to the mission Father."

Dreadfully put out at their obvious distress, he answered in the same tongue.

"You were not expected till tomorrow."

"Are we to return to that dreadful ship?" She shivered with contained indignation. "Take us to your master at once."

He said slowly, in English: "I am Father Chisholm."

Her eyes, which had been searching the mission buildings, returned incredulously to his short shirt-sleeved figure. She stared with growing dismay at his working clothes, dirty hands and caked boots, the smear of mud across his cheek. He murmured awkwardly: "I'm sorry . . . most distressed you weren't met."

For a moment her resentment mastered her. "One might have supposed some welcome at the end of six thousand miles."

"But you see . . . the letter said quite definitely—"

She cut him short with a repressed gesture.

"Perhaps you will show us to our quarters. My companions"—with a proud negation of her own exhaustion—"are completely worn-out."

He was about to make a final explanation, but the sight of the two other Sisters, staring and very frightened, restrained him. He led the way in painful silence to their house. Here he stopped.

"I hope you will be comfortable. I will send for your baggage. Perhaps . . . perhaps you will dine with me tonight."

"Thank you. It is impossible." Her tone was cold. Once again her eyes, holding back haughty tears, touched his disreputable garments. "But if we could be spared some milk and fruit . . . tomorrow we shall be fit for work."

Subdued and mortified, he returned slowly to his house, bathed and changed. From amongst his papers he found and carefully examined the letter from Tientsin. The date given was May 19th, which, as he had said, was tomorrow. He tore the letter into little pieces. He thought of that fine, that foolish bustard. He flushed. Downstairs he was confronted by Joseph, bubbling with spirits, his arms full of purchases.

"Joseph! Carry the fruit you have bought to the Sisters' house. Take everything else and distribute it to the poor."

"But, Master. . . ." Stupefied at the tone of the command, the expression on the priest's face, Joseph swallowed rapidly; then, his jubilation gone, he gulped: "Yes, Master."

Francis went towards the church, his lips compressed as though they sealed an unexpected hurt.

Next morning the three Sisters heard his mass. And he hurried, unconsciously, through his thanksgiving, hoping to find Mother Maria-Veronica awaiting him outside. She was not there. Nor did she come, for her instructions, to his house. An hour later he found her writing in the schoolroom. She rose quietly.

"Please sit down, Reverend Mother."

"Thank you." She spoke pleasantly. Yet she continued to stand, pen in hand, notepaper before her on the desk. "I have been waiting on my pupils."

"You shall have twenty by this afternoon. I've been picking them for many weeks." He strove to make his tone light and agreeable. "They seem intelligent little things."

She smiled gravely. "We shall do our utmost for them."

"Then there is the dispensary. I am hoping you will assist me there. I've very little knowledge—but it's amazing what even a little does here."

"If you will tell me the dispensary hours I shall be there."

A brief silence. Through her quiet civility, he felt her reserve deeply. His gaze, downcast, moving awkwardly, lit suddenly upon a small framed photograph which she had already established on the desk.

"What a beautiful scene!" He spoke at random, striving to break the impersonal barrier between them.

"Yes, it is beautiful." Her heavy eyes followed his to the picture of a fine old house, white and castellated against a dark wall of mountain pines, with a sweep of terraces and gardens running down towards the lake. "It is the Schloss Anheim."

"I have heard that name before. It is historic, surely. Is it near your home?"

She looked at him for the first time straight in the face. Her expression was completely colourless. "Quite near," she said.

Her tone absolutely closed the subject. She seemed to wait for him to speak, and when he did not she said, rather quickly:—

"The Sisters and I . . . we are most earnest in our desire to work for the success of the mission. You have only to mention your wishes and they will be carried out. At the same time—" Her voice chilled slightly. "I trust you will afford us a certain freedom of action."

He stared at her oddly. "What do you mean?"

"You know our rule is partly contemplative. We should like to enjoy as much privacy as possible." She gazed straight in front of her. "Take our meals alone . . . maintain our separate establishment."

He flushed. "I never dreamed of anything else. Your little house is your convent."

"Then you permit me to manage all our convent affairs."

Her meaning was quite plain to him. It settled like a weight upon his heart. He smiled, unexpectedly, rather sadly.

"By all means. Only be careful about money. We are very poor."

"My order has made itself responsible for our support."

He could not resist the question. "Does not your order enforce holy poverty?"

"Yes," she gave back swiftly, "but not meanness."

There was a pause. They remained standing side by side. She had broken off sharply, with a catch in her breath, her fingers tight upon the pen. His own face was burning; he had a strange reluctance to look at her.

"I will send Joseph with a note of the dispensary hours . . . and of church services. Good morning, Sister."

When he had gone she sat down, slowly, at the desk, her gaze still fixed ahead, her expression proudly unreadable. Then a single tear broke and rolled mysteriously down her cheek. Her worst forebodings were justified. Passionately, almost, she dipped her pen in the inkwell and resumed her letter.

". . . It has happened, already, as I feared, my dear, dear brother, and I have sinned again in my dreadful . . . my ineradicable Hohenlohe pride. Yet who could blame me? He has just been here, washed free of earth and approximately shaved—I could see the scrubby razor cuts upon his chin—and armed with such a dumb authority. I saw instantly, yesterday, what a little bourgeois it was. This morning he surpassed himself. Were you aware, dear count, that Anheim was historic? I almost laughed as his eyes fumbled at the photograph: you remember the one I took from the boathouse that day we went sailing with Mother on the lake—it's gone with me everywhere—my sole temporal treasure. He said, in effect, 'Which Cook's tour did you take to view it?' I felt like saying, 'I was born there!' My pride restrained me. Yet had I done so he would probably have kept on gazing at his boots, still creviced with mud, where he had failed to clean them—and muttered: 'Oh, indeed! Our blessed Lord was born in a stable.'

"You see, there is something about him which strikes at one. Do you recollect Herr Spinner, our first tutor . . . we were such brutes to him . . . and the way he had of looking up suddenly with such hurt, yet humble restraint? His eyes, here, are the same. Probably his father was a woodcutter like Herr Spinner's, and he too has struggled up, precariously, with dogged humility. But, dear Ernst, it is the future that I dread, shut up in this strange and isolated spot which intensifies every aspect of the situation. The danger is a lowering of one's inborn standards, yielding to a kind of mental intimacy with a person one instinctively despises. That odious familiar cheerfulness! I must drop a hint to Martha and Clotilde—who has been such a poor sick calf all the way from Liverpool. I am resolved to be pleasant and to work myself to the bone. But only complete detachment, an absolute reserve, will . . ."

She broke off, gazing again, remote and troubled, through the window.

Father Chisholm soon perceived that the two under Sisters went out of their way to avoid him.

Clotilde was not yet thirty, flat-bosomed and delicate, with bloodless lips and a nervous smile. She was very devout and when she prayed, with her head inclined to one side, tears would gush from her pale green eyes. Martha was a different person: past forty, stocky and strong, a peasant type, dark-complexioned and with a net of wrinkles round her eyes. Bustling and outspoken, a trifle coarse in manner, she looked as though she would be immediately at home in a kitchen or a farmyard.

When by chance he met them in the garden the Belgian sister would drop a quick curtsey while Clotilde's sallow face flushed nervously as she smiled and fluttered on. He knew himself to be the subject of their whisperings. He had the impulse, often, to stop them violently. "Don't be so scared of me. We've made a stupid beginning. But I'm a much better fellow than I look."

He restrained himself. He had no grounds whatsoever for complaint. Their work was executed scrupulously, with minute perfection of purpose. New altar linen, exquisitely stitched, appeared in the sacristy; and an embroidered stole which must have taken days of patient labour. Bandages and dressings, rolled, cut to all sizes, filled the store-cupboard in the surgery.

The children had come and were comfortably housed in the big ground-floor dormitory of the Sisters' house. And presently the schoolroom hummed with little voices, or with the chanted rhythm of a much-repeated lesson. He would stand outside, open breviary in hand, sheltered by the bushes, listening. It meant so much to him, this tiny school, he had so joyfully anticipated its opening. Now he rarely went in; and never without a sense of his intrusion. He withdrew into himself, accepting the situation with a sombre logic. It was very simple. Mother Maria-Veronica was a good woman, fine, fastidious, devoted to her work. Yet from the first she had conceived a natural aversion to him. Such things cannot be overcome. After all, he was not a prepossessing character, he had been right when he judged himself no squire of dames. It was a sad disappointment, nevertheless.

The dispensary brought them together on three afternoons each week when, for four hours at a stretch, Maria-Veronica worked close beside him.

He could see that she was interested, often so deeply as to forget her aversion. Though they spoke little he had on such occasions a strange sense of comradeship with her.

One day, a month after her arrival, as he finished dressing a severe whitlow, she exclaimed, involuntarily: "You would have made a surgeon."

He flushed. "I've always liked working with my hands."

"That is because you are clever with them."

He was ridiculously pleased. Her manner was friendlier than it had ever been. At the end of the clinic, as he put away his simple medicines, she gazed at him questioningly. "I've been meaning to ask you . . . Sister Clotilde has had too much to do lately, preparing the children's meals with Martha in the kitchen. She isn't strong and I'm afraid it is too much for her. If you have no objection I would like to get some help."

"But of course." He agreed at once—even happier that she should have asked his permission. "Shall I find you a servant?"

"No thank you. I already have a good couple in mind!"

Next morning when crossing the compound, he observed on the convent balcony, airing and brushing the matting, the unmistakable figures of Hosannah and Philomena Wang. He stopped short, his face darkening, then he took immediate steps towards the Sisters' house.

He found Maria-Veronica in the linen room checking over the sheets. He spoke hurriedly: "I'm sorry to disturb you. But—these new servants—I'm afraid you won't find them satisfactory."

She turned slowly from the cupboard, sudden displeasure in her face. "Surely I am the best judge of that?"

"I don't want you to think I'm interfering. But I'm bound to warn you that they are far from reliable characters."

Her lip curled. "Is that your Christian charity?"

He paled. She was placing him in a horrible position. But he went on determinedly. "I am obliged to be practical. I am thinking of the mission. And of you."

"Please do not trouble about me." Her smile was icy. "I am quite capable of looking after myself."

"I tell you these Wangs are a really bad lot."

She answered with peculiar emphasis: "I know they've had a really bad time. They told me."

His temper flared. "I advise you to get rid of them."

"I won't get rid of them!" Her voice was cold as steel. She had always suspected him, and now she knew. Because she had relaxed her vigilance yesterday, for a moment, in the dispensary, he had rushed to interfere, to show his authority, on this frivolous pretext. Never, never would she be weak with him again. "You already agreed that I am not responsible to you for the administration of my house. I must ask you to keep your word."

He was silent. There was nothing more that he could say. He had meant to help her. But he had made a bad mistake. As he turned away he knew that their relationship, which he had thought to be improving, was now worse than it had been before.

The situation began to affect him seriously. It was hard to keep his expression unruffled when the Wangs passed him, with an air of muted triumph, many times a day. One morning, towards the end of July, Joseph brought him his breakfast of fruit and tea with swollen knuckles and a sheepish air—part triumphant, part subdued.

"Master, I am sorry. I have had to give that rascal Wang a beating."

Father Chisholm sat up sharply, his eye stern: "Why so, Joseph?"

Joseph hung his head. "He says many unkind words about us. That Reverend Mother is a great lady and we are simply dust."

"We all are dust, Joseph." The priest's smile was faint.

"He says harder words than that."

"We can put up with hard words."

"It is more than words, Master. He has become puffed-up beyond measure. And all the time he is making a bad squeeze on the Sisters' housekeeping."

It was quite true. Because of his opposition, the Reverend Mother was indulgent towards the Wangs. Hosannah was now the major-domo of the Sisters' house while Philomena departed, every day, with a basket on her arm, to do the shopping as if she owned the place. At the end of each month, when Martha paid the bills with the roll of notes which the Reverend Mother gave her, the precious pair would depart for the town, in their best clothes, to collect a staggering commission from the tradesmen. It was barefaced robbery, anathema to Francis' Scottish thrift.

Gazing at Joseph he said grimly: "I hope you did not hurt Wang much."

"Alas! I fear I hurt him greatly, Master."

"I am cross with you, Joseph. As a punishment you shall have a holiday tomorrow. And that new suit you have long been asking of me."

That afternoon, in the dispensary, Maria-Veronica broke her rule of silence. Before the patients were admitted she said to Francis:

"So you have chosen to victimize poor Wang again?"

He answered bluntly: "On the contrary. It is he who is victimizing you."

"I do not understand you."

"He is robbing you. The man is a born thief and you are encouraging him."

She bit her lip fiercely. "I do not believe you. I am accustomed to trust my servants."

"Very well then, we shall see." He dismissed the matter quietly.

In the next few weeks his silent face showed deeper lines of strain. It was dreadful to live in close community with a person who detested, despised, him—and to be responsible for that person's spiritual welfare. Maria-Veronica's confessions, which contained nothing, were torture to him. And he judged they were equal torture for her. When he placed the sacred wafer between her lips while her long delicate fingers upheld the altar cloth in the still and pallid dawn of each new day, her upturned pale face, with eyelids veined and tremulous, seemed still to scorn him. He began to rest badly and to walk in the garden at night. So far, their disagreement had been limited to the sphere of her authority. Constrained, more silent than ever, he waited for the moment when he must enforce his will.

It was autumn when that necessity arose, quite simply, out of her inexperience. Yet he could not pass it by. He sighed as he walked over to the Sisters' house.

"Reverend Mother . . ." To his annoyance he found himself trembling. He stood before her, his eyes upon those memorable boots. "You have been going into the city these last few afternoons with Sister Clotilde?"

She looked surprised. "Yes, that is true."

There was a pause.

On guard, she inquired with irony: "Are you curious to know what we are doing?"

"I already know." He spoke as mildly as he could. "You go to visit the sick poor of the city. As far away as the Manchu Bridge. It is commendable. But I'm afraid it must cease."

"May I ask why?" She tried to match his quietness but did not quite succeed.

"Really, I'd rather not tell you."

Her fine nostrils were tense. "If you are prohibiting my acts of charity . . . I have a right . . . I insist on knowing."

"Joseph tells me there are bandits in the city. Wai-Chu has begun fighting again. His soldiers are dangerous."

She laughed outright proudly, contemptuously.

"I am not afraid. The men in my family have always been soldiers."

"That is most interesting." He gazed at her steadily. "But you are not a man, nor is Sister Clotilde. And Wai-Chu's soldiers are not exactly the kid-gloved cavalry officers infallibly found in the best Bavarian families."

He had never used that tone with her before. She reddened, then paled. Her features, her whole figure seemed to contract. "Your outlook is common and cowardly. You forget that I have given myself to God. I came here prepared for anything—sickness, accident, disaster, if necessary death—but not to listen to a lot of cheap sensational rubbish."

His eyes remained fixed on her, so that they burned her, like points of light. He said unconditionally: "Then we will cease to be sensational. It would, as you infer, be a small matter if you were captured and carried off. But there is a stronger reason why you should restrain your charitable promenades. The position of women in China is very different from that to which you are accustomed. In China women have been rigidly excluded from society for centuries. You give grave offence by walking openly in the streets. From a religious standpoint it is highly damaging to the work of the mission. For that reason I forbid you, absolutely, to enter Pai-tan unescorted, without my permission."

She flushed, as though he had struck her in the face. There was a mortal stillness. She had nothing whatever to say.

He was about to leave her when there came a sudden scud of footsteps in the passage and Sister Martha bundled into the room. Her agitation was so great she did not observe Francis, half-hidden by the shadow of the door. Nor did she guess the tension of the moment. Her gaze, distraught beneath her rumpled wimple, was bent on Maria-Veronica. Wringing her hands, she lamented wildly:—

"They've run away . . . taken everything . . . the ninety dollars you gave me yesterday to pay the bills . . . the silver . . . even Sister Clotilde's ivory crucifix . . . they've gone, gone . . ."

"Who has gone?" The words came, with a dreadful effort, from Maria-Veronica's stiff lips.

"The Wangs, of course . . . the low, dirty thieves. I always knew they were a pair of rogues and hypocrites."

Francis did not dare to look at the Mother Superior. She stood there, motionless. He felt a strange pity for her. He made his way clumsily from the room.

5

As FATHER CHISHOLM returned to his own house he became aware, through the strained preoccupation of his mind, of Mr. Chia and his son, standing by the fish pond, watching the carp, with a quiet air of waiting. Both figures were warmly padded against the chill,—it was a "six-coat cold day,"—the boy's hand was in his father's, and the slow dusk, stealing from the shadows of the banyan tree, seemed reluctant to envelop them, and to efface a charming picture.

The two were frequent visitors to the mission and perfectly at home there; they smiled, as Father Chisholm hurried over, greeted him with courteous formality. But Mr. Chia, for once, gently turned aside the priest's invitation to enter his house.

"We come instead to bid you to our house. Yes, tonight, we are leaving for our mountain retreat. It would afford me the greatest happiness if you would accompany us."

Francis stood amazed. "But we are entering upon winter!"

"It is true, my friend, that I and my unworthy family have hitherto ventured to our secluded villa in the Kwangs only during the inclement heat of summer." Mr. Chia paused blandly. "Now we make an innovation which may be even more agreeable. We have many cords of wood and much store of food. Do you not think, Father, it would be edifying to meditate, a little, amongst these snowy peaks?"

Searching the maze of circumlocution with a puzzled frown, Father Chisholm shot a swift glance of interrogation at the merchant.

"Is Wai-Chu about to loot the town?"

Mr. Chia's shoulders mildly deprecated the directness of the query but his expression did not falter. "On the contrary, I myself have paid Wai considerable tribute and billeted him comfortably. I trust he will remain in Pai-tan for many days."

A silence. Father Chisholm's brows were drawn in complete perplexity.

"However, my dear friend, there are other matters which occasionally make the wise man seek the solitudes. I beg of you to come."

The priest shook his head slowly. "I am sorry, Mr. Chia—I am too busy in the mission. . . . How could I leave this noble place which you have so generously given me?"

Mr. Chia smiled amiably. "It is most salubrious here at present. If you change your mind do not fail to inform me. Come, Yu . . . the waggons will be loaded now. Give your hand to the holy Father in the English fashion."

Father Chisholm shook hands with the little wrapped-up boy. Then he blessed them both. The air of restrained regret in Mr. Chia's manner disturbed him. His heart was strangely heavy as he watched them go.

The next two days passed in a queer atmosphere of stress. He saw little of the Sisters. The weather turned worse. Great flocks of birds were seen flying to the South. The sky darkened and lay like lead upon all living things. But except for a few flurries no snow came. Even the cheerful Joseph showed unusual signs of grievance, coming to the priest and expressing his desire to go home.

"It is a long time since I have seen my parents. It is fitting for me to visit them."

When questioned, he waved his hand around vaguely, grumbling that there were rumours in Pai-tan of evil things travelling from the North, the East, the West.

"Wait till the evil spirits come, Joseph, before you run away." Father Chisholm tried to rally his servant's spirits. And his own.

Next morning, after early mass, he went down to the town, alone, in determined quest of news. The streets were teeming, life apparently pulsed undisturbed, but a hush hung about the larger dwellings and many of the shops were closed. In the Street of the Netmakers, he found Hung boarding up his windows with unobtrusive urgency.

"There is no denying it, Shang-Foo!" The old shopkeeper paused to give the Father a calamitous glance over his small pebble spectacles. "It is sickness . . . the great coughing sickness which they name the Black Death. Already six provinces are stricken. People are fleeing with the wind. The first came last night to Pai-tan. And one of the women fell dead inside the Manchu Gate. A wise man knows what that portends. Ay, ay, when there is famine we march and when there is pestilence we march again. Life is not easy when the gods show their wrath."

Father Chisholm climbed the hill to the mission with a shadow upon his face. He seemed already to smell the sickness in the air.

Suddenly he drew up. Outside the mission wall, and directly in his path, lay three dead rats. Judging by the priest's expression there was, in this stiff trinity, a dire foreboding. He shivered unexpectedly, thinking of his children. He went himself for kerosene, and poured it on the corpses of the rats, ignited the oil, and watched their slow cremation. Hurriedly, he took up the remains with tongs and buried them.

He stood thinking deeply. He was five hundred miles from the nearest telegraph terminal. To send a messenger to Sen-siang by sampan, even by the fastest pony, might take at least six days. And yet he must at all costs establish some contact with the outer world.

Suddenly his expression lifted. He found Joseph and led him quickly by the arm to his room. His face was set with gravity as he addressed the boy.

"Joseph! I am sending you on an errand of the first importance. You will take Mr. Chia's new launch. Tell the kapong you have Mr. Chia's permission and mine. I even command you to steal the launch if it is necessary. Do you understand?"

"Yes, Father." Joseph's eyes flashed. "It will not be a sin."

"When you have the boat, proceed with all speed to Sen-siang. There you will go to Father Thibodeau at the mission. If he is away go to the offices of the American oil company. Find someone in authority. Tell him the plague is upon us, that we need immediately medicine, supplies, and doctors. Then go to the telegraph company, send these two messages I have written for you. See . . . take the papers . . . the first to the Vicariate at Pekin, the second to the Union General Hospital at Nankin. Here is money. Do not fail me, Joseph. Now go . . . go. And the good God go with you!"

He felt better an hour later as the lad went padding down the hill, his blue bundle bobbing on his back, his intelligent features screwed to a staunch tenacity. The better to view the departure of the launch, the priest hastened to the belfry tower. But here, as he perched himself against the pediment, his eye darkened. On the vast plain before him he saw two thinly moving streams of beasts and straggling humans, reduced, alike, by distance to the size of little ants—two moving streams, the one approaching, the other departing from the city.

He could not wait; but, descending, crossed immediately to the school. In the wooden corridor Sister Martha was on her knees scrubbing the boards. He stopped.

"Where is Reverend Mother?"

She raised a damp hand to straighten her wimple. "In the class-room." She added, in a sibilant, confederate's whisper: "And lately much disarranged."

He went into the class-room, which, at his entry, fell immediately to silence. The rows of bright childish faces gave him, suddenly, a gripping pang. Quickly, quickly, he fought back that unbearable fear.

Maria-Veronica had turned towards him with a pale, unreadable brow. He approached and addressed her in an undertone.

"There are signs of an epidemic in the city. I am afraid it may be plague. If so, it is important for us to be prepared." He paused, under her silence, then went on. "At all costs we must try to keep the sickness from the children.

That means isolating the school and the Sisters' house. I shall arrange at once for some kind of barrier to be put up. The children and all three Sisters should remain inside, with one Sister always on duty at the entrance." He paused again, forcing himself to be calm. "Don't you think that wise?"

She faced him, cold and undismayed. "Profoundly wise."

"Are there any details we might discuss?"

She answered bitterly: "You have already familiarized us with the principle of segregation."

He took no notice. "You know how the contagion is spread?"

"Yes."

There was a silence. He turned towards the door, sombre from her fixed refusal to make peace. "If God sends this great trouble upon us, we must work hard together. Let us try to forget our personal relations."

"They are best forgotten." She spoke in her most frigid tone, submissive upon the surface, yet charged, beneath, with high disdainful breeding.

He left the class-room. He could not but admire her courage. The news he had conveyed to her would have terrified most women. He reflected tensely that they might need all their spirit before the month was past.

Convinced of the need of haste, he recrossed the compound and despatched the gardener for Mr. Chia's foreman and six of the men who had worked on the church. Immediately, when these arrived, he set them to build a thick fence of kaolin on the boundary he had marked off. The dried stalks of maize made an excellent barricade. While it rose under his anxious eyes, girding the school and convent house, he trenched a narrow ditch around the base. This could be flooded with disinfectant if the need arose.

The work went on all day and was not completed until late at night. Even after the men had gone he could not rest, a mounting tide of dread was in his blood. He took most of his stores into the enclosure, carrying sacks of potatoes and flour on his shoulders, butter, bacon, condensed milk, and all the tinned goods of the mission. His small stock of medicines he likewise transferred. Only then did he feel some degree of relief. He looked at his watch: three o'clock in the morning. It was not worth while to go to bed. He went into the church and spent the hours remaining until dawn in prayer.

When it was light, before the mission was astir he set out for the yamen of the Chief Magistrate. At the Manchu Gate fugitives from the stricken provinces were still crowding unhindered into the city. Scores had taken up their lodging beneath the stars, in the lee of the Great Wall. As he passed the silent figures, huddled under sacking, half-frozen by the bitter wind, he heard the racking sound of coughing. His heart flowed out towards these poor exhausted creatures, many already stricken, enduring humbly, suffering without hope; and a burning, impetuous desire to help them suffused his soul. One old man lay dead and naked, stripped of the garments he no longer needed. His wrinkled toothless face was upturned towards the sky.

Spurred by the pity in his breast, Francis reached the yamen of justice. But here a blow awaited him. Mr. Pao's cousin was gone. All the Paos had departed, the closed shutters of their house stared back at him like sightless eyes.

He took a swift and painful breath and turned, chafing, into the courts. The passages were deserted, the main chamber a vault of echoing emptiness. He could see no one, except a few clerks scurrying with a furtive air. From one of these he learned that the Chief Magistrate had been called away to the obsequies of a distant relative in Tchientin, eight hundred li due south. It was plain to the harassed priest that all but the lowest court officials had been "summoned" from Pai-tan. The civil administration of the city had ceased to exist.

The furrow between Francis' eyes was deeply cut, a haggard wound. Only one course lay open to him now. And he knew that it was futile. Nevertheless, he turned and made his way rapidly to the cantonment.

With the bandit Wai-Chu complete overlord of the province, ferociously exacting voluntary gifts, the position of the regular military forces was academic. They dissolved or seceded as a matter of routine on the bandit's periodic visits to the town. Now, as Francis reached the barracks, a bare dozen soldiers hung about, conspicuously without arms, in dirty grey-cotton tunics.

They stopped him at the gate. But nothing could withstand the fire which now consumed him. He forced his way to an inner chamber, where a young lieutenant in a clean and elegant uniform lounged by the paper-latticed window, reflectively polishing his white teeth with a willow twig.

Lieutenant Shon and the priest inspected one another, the young dandy with polite guardedness, his visitor with all the dark and hopeless ardour of his purpose.

"The city is threatened by a great sickness." Francis fought to inject his tone with deliberate restraint. "I am seeking for someone with courage and authority, to combat the grave danger."

Shon continued dispassionately to consider the priest. "General Wai-Chu has the monopoly of authority. And he is leaving for Tou-en-lai tomorrow."

"That will make it easier for those who remain. I beg of you to help me."

Shon shrugged his shoulders virtuously. "Nothing would afford me greater satisfaction than to work with the Shang-Foo entirely without prospect of reward, for the supreme benefit of suffering mankind. But I have no more than fifty soldiers. And no supplies."

"I have sent to Sen-siang for supplies." Francis spoke more rapidly. "They will arrive soon. But meanwhile we must do all in our command to quarantine the refugees and prevent the pestilence from starting in the city."

"It has already started." Shon answered coolly. "In the Street of the Basketmakers there are more than sixty cases. Many dead. The rest dying."

A terrible urgency tautened the priest's nerves, a surge of protest, a burning refusal to accept defeat. He took a quick step forward.

"I am going to aid these people. If you do not come I shall go alone. But I am perfectly assured that you are coming."

For the first time the Lieutenant looked uncomfortable. He was a bold youngster, despite his foppish air, with ideas of his own advancement and a sense of personal integrity which had caused him to reject the price offered him by Wai-Chu, as dishonourably inadequate. Without the slightest interest in the fate of his fellow citizens, he had been, on the priest's arrival, idly debating the advisability of joining his few remaining men in the Street of the Stolen Hours. Now, he was disagreeably embarrassed and reluctantly impressed. Like a man moving against his own will, he rose, threw away his twig and slowly buckled on his revolver.

"This does not shoot well. But as a symbol it encourages the unswerving obedience of my most trusted followers."

They went out together into the cold grey day.

From the Street of the Stolen Hours they routed some thirty soldiers and marched to the teeming warrens of the basket-weavers' quarters by the river. Here the plague had already settled, with the instinct of a dunghill fly. The river dwellings, tiers of cardboard hovels, leaning one on top of another, against the high mud bank, were festering with dirt, vermin, and the disease. Francis saw that unless immediate measures were taken the contagion would spread in this congestion like a raging conflagration.

He said to the Lieutenant, as they emerged, bent double, from the end hovel of the row:—

"We must find some place to house the sick."

Shon reflected. He was enjoying himself more than he had expected. This foreign priest had shown much "face" in stooping close to the stricken persons. He admired "face" greatly.

"We shall commandeer the yamen of the *yu shih*—the imperial recorder." For many months Shon had been at violent enmity with this official, who had defrauded him of his share of the salt tax. "I am confident that my absent friend's abode will make a pleasing hospital."

They went immediately to the recorder's yamen. It was large and richly furnished, situated in the best part of the city. Shon effected entry by the simple expedient of breaking down the door. While Francis remained with half a dozen men to make some preparations for receiving the sick, he departed with the remainder. Presently the first cases arrived in litters and were arranged in rows on quilted mats upon the floor.

That night, as Francis went up the hill towards the mission, tired from his long day's work, he heard above the faint incessant death music the shouts of wild carousing and sporadic rifle shots. Behind him, Wai-Chu's irregulars were looting the shuttered shops. But presently the city fell again to silence. In the still moonlight he could see the bandits, streaming from the Eastern Gate, spurring their stolen ponies across the plains. He was glad to see them go.

At the summit of the hill the moon suddenly was dimmed. It began at last to snow. When he drew near the gateway in the kaolin fence the air was alive and fluttering. Soft dry blinding flakes came whirling out of the darkness, settling on eyes and brow, entering his lips like tiny hosts, whirling so dense and thick that in a minute the ground was carpeted in white. He stood outside, in the white coldness, rent by anxiety, and called in a low voice. Immediately Mother Maria-Veronica came to the gate, holding up a lantern which cast a beam of spectral brightness on the snow.

He scarcely dared to put the question. "Are you all well?"

"Yes."

His heart stopped pounding in sheer relief. He waited, suddenly conscious of his fatigue and the fact that he had not eaten all that day. Then he said: "We have established a hospital in the town . . . not much . . . but the best we could do." Again he waited, as if for her to speak, deeply sensible of the difficulty of his position, and the greatness of the favour he must ask. "If one of the Sisters could be spared . . . would volunteer to come . . . to help us with the nursing . . . I should be most grateful."

There was a pause. He could almost see her lips shape themselves to answer coldly: "You ordered us to remain in here. You forbade us to enter the town." Perhaps the sight of his face, worn, drawn and heavy-eyed, through the maze of snowflakes, restrained her. She said: "I will come."

His heart lifted. Despite her fixed antagonism towards him she was incomparably more efficient than Martha or Clotilde. "It means moving your quarters to the yamen. Wrap up warmly. And take all you need."

Ten minutes later he took her bag; they went down to the yamen together in silence. The dark lines of their footprints in the fresh snow were far apart.

Next morning sixteen of those admitted to the yamen were dead. But three times that number were coming in. It was pneumonic plague and its virulence surpassed the fiercest venom. People dropped with it as if bludgeoned and were dead before the next dawn. It seemed to congeal the blood, to rot the lungs, which threw up a thin white speckled sputum, swarming with lethal germs. Often one hour spaced the interval between a man's heedless laugh and the grin that was his death-mask.

The three physicians of Pai-tan had failed to arrest the epidemic by the method of acupuncture. On the second day they ceased prickling the limbs of their patients with needles, and discreetly withdrew to a more salubrious practice.

By the end of that week the city was riddled from end to end. A wave of panic struck through the apathy of the people. The southern exits of the city were choked with carts, chairs, overburdened mules and a struggling, hysterical populace.

The cold intensified. A great blight seemed to lie on the afflicted land, here and beyond. Dazed with overwork and lack of sleep, Francis nevertheless dimly sensed the calamity at Pai-tan to be but a portion of the major tragedy. He had no news. He did not grasp the immensity of the disaster: a hundred thousand miles of territory stricken, and half a million dead beneath the snow. Nor could he know that the eyes of the civilized world were bent in sympathy on China, that expeditions quickly organized in America and Britain had arrived to combat the disease.

His torturing suspense deepened daily. There was still no sign of Joseph's return. Would help never reach them from Sen-siang? A dozen times each day he plodded to the wharfside for the sight of the up-coming boat.

Then, at the beginning of the second week, Joseph suddenly appeared, weary and spent, but with a pale smile of achievement. He had encountered every obstacle. The countryside was in a ferment, Sen-siang a place of torment, the mission there ravaged by the disease. But he had persisted. He had sent his telegrams and bravely waited, hiding in his launch in a creek of the river. Now he had a letter. He produced it with a grimed and shaking hand. More: a doctor who knew the Father, an old and respected friend of the Father, would arrive on the supply boat!

With beating excitement, and a strange wild premonition, Father Chisholm took the letter from Joseph, opened it and read:—

> *Lord Leighton Relief Expedition*
> *Chek-kow*

Dear Francis,

I have been in China five weeks now with the Leighton expedition. This should not surprise you if you remember my youthful longings for the decks of ocean-going freighters and the exotic jungles that lay beyond. Quite truly, I thought I had forgotten all that nonsense myself. But at home, when they began asking for volunteers for the relief party, I suddenly surprised myself by joining up. It certainly was not the desire to become a National Hero which prompted the absurd impulse. Probably a reaction, long deferred, against my humdrum life in Tynecastle. And perhaps, if I may say it, a very real hope of seeing you.

Anyhow, ever since we arrived, I've been working my way up-country, trying to push myself into your sacred presence. Your telegram to Nankin was turned over to our headquarters there and word of it reached me at Hai-chang next day. I immediately asked Leighton, who is a very decent fellow, despite his title, if I might push off to give you a hand. He agreed and even let me have one of our few remaining power boats. I've just reached Sen-siang and am collecting supplies. I will be along full steam ahead, probably arriving twenty-four hours behind your servant. Take care of yourself till then. All my news later.

> In haste,
> Yours,

> WILLIE TULLOCH

The priest smiled, slowly, for the first time in many days, and with a deep and secret warmth. He felt no great amazement; it was so typical of Tulloch to sponsor such a cause. He was braced, fortified by the unexpected fortune of his friend's arrival.

It was difficult to hold his eagerness in check. Next day when the relief boat was sighted he hastened to the wharf. Even before the launch drew alongside Tulloch had stepped ashore, older, stouter, yet unchangeably the same dour quiet Scot, careless as ever in his dress, shy, strong and prejudiced as a Highland steer, as plain and honest as homespun tweed.

The priest's vision was absurdly blurred.

"Man, Francis, it's you!" Willie could say no more. He kept on shaking hands, confused by his emotion, debarred by his Northern blood from more overt demonstration. At last he muttered, as if conscious of the need of speech: "When we walked down Darrow High Street we never dreamed we'd forgather in a place like this." He tried a half-laugh, but with little success. "Where's your coat and gumboots? You can't stroll through the pest in these shoes. It's high time I kept an eye on you."

"And on our hospital." Francis smiled.

"What!" The doctor's sandy eyebrows lifted. "You have a hospital of sorts? Let's see it."

"As soon as you are ready."

Instructing the crew of the launch to follow him with the supplies, Tulloch set off, at the priest's side, agile despite his increased girth, his eyes intent in his red hard-wearing face, his thinned hair showing a mass of freckles on his ruddy scalp as he punctuated his friend's brief report with comprehending nods.

At the end of it, as they reached the yamen, he remarked with a dry twinkle: "You might have done worse. Is this your centre?" Across his shoulder he told his bearers to bring in the cases.

Inside the hospital he made a quick inspection, his eyes darting right, left, and with an odd curiosity towards Mother Maria-Veronica, who now accompanied them. He took a swift glance at Shon, when the young dandy came in, then firmly shook hands with him. Finally as they stood, all four, at the entrance to the long suite of rooms which formed the main ward, he addressed them quietly.

"I think you have done wonders. And I hope you don't expect melodramatic miracles from me. Forget all your preconceived ideas and face the truth—I'm not the dark handsome doctor with the portable laboratory. I'm here to work with you, like one of yourselves, which means . . . flatly . . . like a navvy. I haven't a drop of vaccine in my bag—in the first place because it isn't one damn bit of good outside the story-books. And in the second because every flask we brought to China was used up in a week. Ye'll note," he inserted mildly, "it didn't check the epidemic. Remember! This is practically a fatal disease once it gets you. In such circumstances, as my old dad used to say," he smiled faintly, " 'an ounce of prevention is better than a ton of cure.' That's why, if you don't mind, we'll turn our attention—not to the living—but to the dead."

There was a silence while they slowly grasped his meaning. Lieutenant Shon smiled.

"Cadavers are accumulating in the side streets at a disconcerting rate. It is discouraging to stumble in the darkness and fall into the arms of an unresponsive corpse."

Francis shot a quick glance at Maria-Veronica's expressionless face. Sometimes the young Lieutenant was a little indiscreet.

The doctor had moved to the nearest crate and, with stolid competence, was prying off the lid.

"The first thing we do is fit you out properly. Oh! I know you two believe in God. And the Lieutenant in Confucius." He bent and produced rubber boots from the case. "But I believe in prophylaxis."

He completed the unpacking of his supplies, fitting white overalls and goggles upon them, berating their negligence of their own safety. His remarks ran on, matter-of-fact, composed. "Don't you realize, you confounded innocents . . . one cough in your eye and you're done for . . . penetration of the cornea. They knew that even in the fourteenth century . . . they wore vizors of isinglass against this thing . . . it was brought down from Siberia by a band of marmoset hunters. Well, now, I'll come back later, Sister, and have a real look at your patients. But first of all, Shon, the Reverend and myself will take a peek round."

In his stress of mind, Francis had overlooked the grim necessity of swift interment before the germ-infested bodies were attacked by rats. Individual burial was impossible in that iron ground and the supply of coffins had run out long ago. All the fuel in China would not have burned the bodies—for as Shon again remarked, nothing is less inflammable than frozen human flesh. One practical solution remained. They dug a great pit outside the walls, lined it with quicklime, and requisitioned carts. The loaded carts, driven by Shon's men, bumped through the streets and shot their cargo into this common grave.

Three days later, when the city was cleared and the stray carcasses, half-devoured and dragged away by dogs, collected from the ice-encrusted fields, stricter measures were enforced. Afraid lest the spirits of their ancestors be defiled by an unholy tomb, people were hiding the bodies of their relatives, storing scores of infected corpses under the floor boards of their houses and in the kaolin roofs.

At the doctor's suggestion Lieutenant Shon promulgated an edict that all such hoarders would be shot. When the death carts rumbled through the city his soldiers shouted: "Bring out your dead. Or you yourselves will die."

Meanwhile, they were ruthlessly destroying certain properties which Tulloch had marked as breeding grounds of the disease. Experience and dire necessity made the doctor vengefully efficient. They entered, cleared the rooms, demolished the bamboo partitions with axes, spread kerosene, and made a pyre for the rats.

The Street of the Basket-makers was the first they razed. Returning, scorched and grimed, a hatchet still in his hand, Tulloch cast a queer glance at the priest, walking wearily beside him through the deserted streets. He said, in sudden compunction:—

"This isn't your job, Francis. And you're worn so fine you're just about to drop. Why don't you get up the hill for a few days, back to those kids you're worrying yourself stiff over?"

"That would be a pretty sight. The man of God taking his ease while the city burns."

"Who is there to see you in this out-of-the-way hole?"

Francis smiled strangely. "We are not unseen."

Tulloch dropped the matter abruptly. Outside the yamen he swung round, gazing glumly at the redness still smouldering in the low dim sky. "The fire of London was a logical necessity." Suddenly his nerves rasped. "Damn it, Francis, kill yourself if you want to. But keep your motives to yourself."

The strain was telling on them. For ten days Francis had not been out of his clothes, they were stiff with frozen sweat. Occasionally he dragged his boots off, obeyed Tulloch's command to rub his feet with colza oil—even so his right great toe was inflamed with agonizing frostbite. He was dead with fatigue, but always there was more . . . more to be done.

They had no water, only melted snow, the wells were solid ice. Cooking was near impossible. Yet every day, Tulloch insisted that they all meet to have their midday meal together, to counteract the growing nightmare of their lives. At this hour, doggedly, he exerted himself to be cheerful, occasionally giving them Edison Bell selections on the phonograph he had brought out with him. He had a fund of North Country anecdotes, stories of the Tyne-castle "Georgies," which he drew on freely. Sometimes he had the triumph of bringing a pale smile to Maria-Veronica's lips. Lieutenant Shon could never understand the jokes, though he listened politely while they were explained to him. Sometimes Shon was a little late in coming to the meal. Though they guessed that he was solacing some pretty lady who still, like themselves, survived, the empty chair took an unsuspected toll upon their nerves.

As the third week began Maria-Veronica showed signs of breaking down. Tulloch was bewailing the lack of floor space in the yamen, when she remarked: "If we took hammocks from the Street of the Netmakers we could house double our number of patients . . . more comfortably, too."

The doctor paused, gazed at her with grim approbation. "Why didn't I think of that before? It's a grand suggestion."

She coloured deeply under his praise, cast down her eyes and tried to go on with her dish of rice. But she could not. Her arm began to shake. It shook so violently the food dropped off her fork. She could not raise a grain of rice towards her lips. Her flush deepened, spread into her neck. Several times she repeated the attempt and failed. She sat with bent head, enduring the absurd humiliation. Then she rose without a word and left the table.

Later, Father Chisholm found her at work in the women's ward. He had never known such calm and pitiless self-sacrifice. She performed the most hateful duties for the sick, work which the lowest Chinese sweeper would have spurned. He dared not look at her, so unbearable had their relationship become. He had not addressed her directly for many days.

"Reverend Mother, Dr. Tulloch thinks . . . we all think you have been doing too much . . . that Sister Martha should come down to relieve you."

She had regained only a vestige of her cold aloofness. His suggestion disturbed her anew. She drew herself up. "You mean that I am not doing enough?"

"Far from it. Your work is magnificent."

"Then why attempt to keep me from it?" Her lips were trembling.

He said clumsily, "We are considering you."

His tone seemed to sting her to the quick. Holding back her tears, she answered passionately: "Do not consider me. The more work you give me . . . and the less sympathy . . . the better I shall like it."

He had to leave it at that. He raised his eyes to look at her but her gaze was fixedly averted. He sadly turned away.

The snow which had held off for a week suddenly began again. It fell and fell unendingly. Francis had never seen such snow, the flakes so large and soft. Each added snowflake made an added silence. Houses were walled up in the silent whiteness. The streets were choked with drifts, hindering their work, increasing the sufferings of the sick. His heart was wrung again . . . again. In the endless days he lost all sense of time and place and fear. As he bent over the dying, succouring them with deep compassion in his eyes, stray thoughts swam through his dizzy brain. . . . Christ promised us suffering . . . this life was given us only as a preparation for the next . . . when God will wipe all sorrow from our eyes, weeping and mourning shall be no more.

Now they were halting all nomads outside the walls, disinfecting and holding them in quarantine until assured of their freedom from the disease. As they came back from the isolation huts they had thrown up, Tulloch inquired of him, overtaxed, frayed to a raw anger:—

"Is hell any worse than this?"

He answered, through the fog of his fatigue, blundering forward, unheroic, yet undismayed: "Hell is that state where one has ceased to hope."

None of them knew when the epidemic eased. There was no climax of achievement, no operatic crowning of their efforts. Visible evidence of death no longer lingered in the streets. The worst slums lay as dirty ashes on the snow. The mass flight from the Northern Provinces gradually ceased. It was as if a great dark cloud, immovably above them, were at last rolling slowly to the southwards.

Tulloch expressed his feelings in a single dazed and jaded phrase. "Your God alone knows if we've done anything, Francis . . . I think . . ." He broke off, haggard, limp, and for the first time seemed about to break. He swore. "The admissions are down again today . . . let's take time off or I'll go mad."

That evening the two took a brief respite, for the first time, from the hospital and climbed to the mission to spend the night at the priest's house. It was after ten o'clock and a few stars were faintly visible in the dark bowl of sky.

The doctor paused on the brow of the snow-embowered hill, which they had ascended with great effort, studying the soft outlines of the mission, lit by the whiteness of the earth. He spoke with unusual quietness: "It's a bonny place you've made, Francis. I don't wonder you've fought so hard to keep your little brats safe. Well, if I've helped at all, I'm mortal glad." His lips twitched. "It must be pleasant to spend your days here with a fine-looking woman like Maria-Veronica."

The priest knew his friend too well to take offence. But he answered, with a strained and wounded smile:—

"I'm afraid she does not find it agreeable."

"No?"

"You must have seen that she loathes me."

There was a pause. Tulloch gave the priest a queer glance.

"Your most endearing virtue, my holy man, has always been your painful lack of vanity." He moved on. "Let's go in and have some toddy. It's something to have worked through this scourge and to have the end of it in sight. It sort of lifts one up above the level of the brutes. But don't try to use that on me as an argument to prove the existence of the soul."

Seated in Francis' room they knew a moment of exhausted exaltation, talked of home late into the night. Briefly, Tulloch satirized his own career. He had done nothing, acquired nothing but a taste for whiskey. But now, in his sentimental middle age, aware of his limitations, having proved the fallacy of the world's wide-open spaces, he was hankering for his home in Darrow and the greater adventure of matrimony. He excused himself with a shamed smile.

"My dad wants me in the practice. Wants to see me raise a brood of young Ingersolls. Dear old boy, he never fails to mention you, Francis . . . his Roman Voltaire."

He spoke with rare affection of his sister Jean, now married and comfortably settled in Tynecastle. He said, oddly, not looking at Francis:—

"It took her a long time to reconcile herself to the celibacy of the clergy."

His silence on the subject of Judy was strangely suspect. But he could not speak enough of Polly. He had met her six months ago in Tynecastle, still going strong. "What a woman!" He nodded across his glass. "Mark my words, she may astound you one day. Polly is, was, and always will be a holy trump." They slept in their chairs.

By the end of that week the epidemic showed further indications of abatement. Now the death carts seldom rattled through the streets, vultures ceased to swoop from the horizon and snow no longer fell.

On the following Saturday Father Chisholm stood again on his balcony at the mission, inhaling the ice-cold air, with a deep and blessed thankfulness. From his vantage he could see the children playing in complete unconsciousness behind the tall kaolin fence. He felt like a man towards whom sweet daylight slowly filters after a long and dreadful dream.

Suddenly his gaze was caught by a figure of a soldier, dark against the snowbanks, moving rapidly up the road towards the mission. At first he took the man for one of the Lieutenant's followers. Then, with some surprise, he saw that it was Shon himself.

This was the first time the young officer had visited him. A puzzled light hovered about Francis' eyes as he turned and went down the stairs to meet him.

On the doorstep, the sight of Shon's face stopped the welcome on his lips. It was lemon pale, tight-drawn, and of a mortal gravity. A faint dew of perspiration on the brow bespoke his haste, as did the half-unbuttoned tunic, an unbelievable laxity in one so precise.

The Lieutenant wasted no time. "Please come to the yamen at once. Your friend the doctor is taken ill."

Francis felt a great coldness, a cold shock, like the impact of a frigid blast. He shivered. He gazed back at Shon. After what seemed a long time he heard himself say: "He has been working too much. He has collapsed."

Shon's hard dark eyes winced imperceptibly. "Yes, he has collapsed."

There was another pause. Then Francis knew it was the worst. He turned pale. He set out, as he was, with the Lieutenant.

They walked half the way in complete silence. Then Shon, with a military precision that suppressed all feeling, revealed briefly what had occurred. Dr. Tulloch had come in with a tired air and gone to take a drink. While he poured the drink he had coughed explosively, and steadied himself against the bamboo table, his face a dingy grey, except for the prune-juice froth upon his lips. As Maria-Veronica ran to help him, he gave her before he collapsed a weak, peculiar smile: "Now is the time to send for the priest."

When they reached the yamen a soft grey mist was drooping, like a tired cloud, across the snow-banked roofs. They entered quickly. Tulloch lay in the small end room, on his narrow camp bed, covered with a quilted mat of purple silk. The rich deep colour of the quilt intensified his dreadful pallor, threw a livid shadow upon his face. It was agony for Francis to see how swiftly the fever had struck. Willie might have been a different man. He was shrunken, unbelievably, as though after weeks of wasting. His tongue and lips were swollen, his eyeballs glazed and shot with blood.

Beside the bed Maria-Veronica was kneeling, replenishing the pack of snow upon the sick man's forehead. She held herself erect—tensely, her expression rigid in its fixed control. She rose as Francis and the Lieutenant entered. She did not speak.

Francis went over to the bedside. A great fear was in his heart. Death had walked with them these past few weeks, familiar and casual, a dreadful commonplace. But now that death's shadow lay upon his friend, the pain that struck at him was strange and terrible.

Tulloch was still conscious, the light of recognition remained in his congested gaze. "I came out for adventure." He tried to smile. "I seem to have got it." A moment later, he added, half-closing his eyes, as a kind of afterthought: "Man, I'm weak as a cat."

Francis sat down on the low stool at the head of the bed. Shon and Maria-Veronica were at the end of the room.

The stillness, the painful sense of waiting, was insupportable, growing, alike, with a frightful feeling of intrusion upon the privacy of things unknown.

"Are you quite comfortable?"

"I might be worse. Spare me a drop of that Japanese whiskey. It'll help me along. Man, it's an awful conventional thing to die like this . . . me that damned the story-books."

When Francis had given him a sip of spirits he closed his eyes and seemed to rest. But soon he lapsed into a low delirium.

"Another drink, lad. Bless you, that's the stuff! I've drunk plenty in my time, round the slums of Tynecastle. And now I'm away home to dear old Darrow. On the banks of Allan Water, when the sweet springtime had fled. D'you mind that one, Francis . . . it's a bonny song. Sing it Jean. Come on, louder, louder . . . I cannot hear you in the dark." Francis gritted his teeth, fighting the tumult in his breast. "That's right, Your Reverence. I'll keep quiet and save my strength . . . It's a queer business . . . altogether . . . we've all got to toe the line sometime." Muttering, he sank into unconsciousness.

The priest knelt in prayer by the bedside. He prayed for help, for inspiration. But he was strangely dumb, gripped by a kind of stupor. The city outside was ghostly in its silence. Twilight came. Maria-Veronica rose to light the lamp, then returned to the far corner of the room outside the beam of lamplight, her lips unmoving, silent, but her fingers steadily enumerating the beads beneath her gown.

Tulloch was getting worse: his tongue black, his throat so swollen his bouts of vomiting were an agony to watch.

But suddenly he seemed to rally; he dimly opened his eyes.

"What o'clock is it?" His voice crouped huskily. "Near five . . . at home . . . that's when we had our tea. D'you mind, Francis, the crowd of us at the big round table . . . ?" A longer pause . . . "Ye'll write the old man and tell him that his son died game. Funny . . . I still can't believe in God."

"Does that matter now?" What was he saying? Francis did not know. He was crying and, in the stupid humiliation of his weakness, the words came from him, in blind confusion. "He believes in you."

"Don't delude yourself . . . I'm not repentant."

"All human suffering is an act of repentance."

There was a silence. The priest said no more. Weakly, Tulloch reached out his hand and let it fall on Francis' arm.

"Man, I've never loved ye so much as I do now . . . for not trying to bully me to heaven. Ye see—" His lids dropped wearily. "I've such an awful headache."

His voice failed. He lay on his back, exhausted, his breathing quick and shallow, his gaze upturned as though fixed far beyond the ceiling. His throat was closed, he could not even cough.

The end was near. Maria-Veronica was kneeling now, at the window, her back towards them, her gaze directed fixedly into the darkness. Shon stood at the foot of the bed. His face was set immovably.

Suddenly Willie moved his eyes, in which a lingering spark still flickered. Francis saw that he was trying, vainly, to whisper. He knelt, slipped his arm about the dying man's neck, brought his cheek close to the other's breath. At first he could hear nothing. Then weakly came the words: "Our fight . . . Francis . . . more than sixpence to get my sins forgiven."

The sockets of Tulloch's eyes filled up with shadow. He yielded to an unaccountable weariness. The priest felt rather than heard the last faint sigh. The room was suddenly more quiet. Still holding the body, as a mother might hold her child, he began blindly, in a low and strangled voice, the De Profundis.

"Out of the depths have I cried unto thee, O Lord. Lord, hear my voice . . . because with the Lord there is mercy: and with him plentiful redemption."

He rose at last, closed the eyes, composed the limp hands.

As he went out of the room he saw Sister Maria-Veronica still bowed at the window. As though still within a dream he gazed at the Lieutenant. He saw, in a kind of dim surprise, that Shon's shoulders were shaking convulsively.

6

THE plague had passed, but a great apathy gripped the snowbound land. In the country the rice fields were frozen lakes. The few remaining peasants could not work a soil so mercilessly entombed. There was no sign of life. In the town survivors emerged as from a painful hibernation, began dully to gather up their daily lives. The merchants and magistrates had not yet returned. It was said that many distant roads were quite impassable. None could remember such evil weather. All the passes were reported blocked and avalanches hurtled down the distant Kwangs like puffs of pure white smoke. The river, in its upper reaches, was frozen solid, a great grey wasteland over which the wind drove powder snow, in blinding desolation. Lower down there was a channel. Huge lumps of ice crashed and pounded in the current under the Manchu Bridge. Hardship was in every home and famine lurked not far behind.

One boat had risked the jagged floes and steamed up-river from Sen-siang, bringing food and medical comforts from the Leighton Expedition, and a long-delayed packet of letters. After a brief stay it had cast off, taking the remaining members of Dr. Tulloch's party back to Nankin.

In the mail which arrived one communication surpassed the others in importance. As Father Chisholm came slowly up from the end of the mission garden where a small wooden cross marked Dr. Tulloch's grave, he bore this letter in his hand and his thoughts were busy with the visit it announced.

He hoped his work was satisfactory—the mission was surely worthy of his pride in it. If only the weather would break—thaw quickly—in the next two weeks!

When he reached the church Mother Maria-Veronica was coming down the steps. He must tell her—though he had come to dread these rare occasions when official business forced him to break the silence which lay between them.

"Reverend Mother . . . the provincial administrator of our Foreign Missions Society, Canon Mealey, is making a tour of inspection of the Chinese missions. He sailed five weeks ago. He will arrive in about a month's time . . . to visit us." He paused. "I thought you'd like to have notice . . . in case there is anything you wish to put before him."

Muffled against the cold, she raised her gaze, impenetrable, behind the rimed vapour of her breath. Yet she started faintly. Now she so seldom saw him closely, the change which those last weeks had brought was strikingly manifest. He was thin, quite emaciated. The bones of his face had become prominent, the skin drawn tighter, cheeks slightly sunken, so that his eyes seemed larger and oddly luminous. A terrible impulse took possession of her.

"There is only one thing I wish to put before him." She spoke instinctively, the sudden news lifting from the recesses of her soul a deeply buried thought. "I shall ask to be transferred to another mission."

There was a long pause. Though not wholly taken by surprise, he felt chilled, defeated. He sighed. "You are unhappy here?"

"Happiness has nothing to do with it. As I told you, when I entered the religious life I prepared myself to endure everything."

"Even the enforced association of someone whom you despise?"

She coloured with a proud defiance. That deep throbbing in her bosom drove her to continue. "You mistake me completely. It is obvious. It is something deeper . . . spiritual."

"Spiritual? Will you try to tell me?"

"I feel"—she took a quick breath—"that you are upsetting me . . . in my inner life . . . my spiritual beliefs."

"That is a serious matter." He stared at the letter unseeingly, twisting it in his bony hands. "It hurts me . . . as much, I am sure, as it hurts you to say it. But perhaps you have misunderstood me. To what do you refer?"

"Do you think I have prepared a list?" Despite her control she felt her agitation rising. "It is your attitude . . . For instance, some remarks you made when Dr. Tulloch was dying . . . and afterwards, when he was dead."

"Please go on."

"He was an atheist, and yet you virtually promised he would have his eternal reward . . . he who didn't believe . . ."

He said quickly: "God judges us not only by what we believe . . . but by what we do."

"He was not a Catholic . . . not even a Christian!"

"How do you define a Christian? One who goes to church one day of the seven and lies, slanders, cheats his fellow men the other six?" He smiled faintly. "Dr. Tulloch didn't live like that. And he died—helping others . . . like Christ himself."

She repeated stubbornly: "He was a free-thinker."

"My child, our Lord's contemporaries thought him a dreadful free-thinker . . . that's why they killed him."

She was pale now, quite distraught. "It is inexcusable to make such a comparison—outrageous!"

"I wonder! . . . Christ was a very tolerant man—and humble."

A rush of colour again flooded her cheek. "He made certain rules. Your Dr. Tulloch did not obey them. You know that. Why, when he was unconscious, at the end, you did not even administer extreme unction."

"No, I didn't! And perhaps I should have." He stood, thinking worriedly, rather depressed. Then he seemed to cheer up. "But the good God may forgive him none the less." He paused, with simple frankness. "Didn't you love him too?"

She hesitated, lowered her eyes. "Yes . . . Who could help that?"

"Then don't let us make his memory the occasion of a quarrel. There is one thing we most of us forget. Christ taught it. The Church teaches it . . . though you wouldn't think so to hear a great many of us today. No one in good faith can ever be lost. No one. Buddhists, Mohammedans, Taoists . . . the blackest cannibals who ever devoured a missionary . . . If they are sincere, according to their own lights, they will be saved. That is the splendid mercy of God. So why shouldn't He enjoy confronting a decent agnostic at the Judgement Seat with a twinkle in his eye: 'I'm here you see, in spite of all they brought you up to believe. Enter the Kingdom which you honestly denied.'" He made to smile, then, seeing her expression, sighed and shook his head. "I'm truly sorry you feel as you do. I know I'm hard to get on with, and perhaps a little odd in my beliefs. But you've worked so wonderfully here . . . the children love you . . . and during the plague . . ." He broke off. "I know we haven't got on very well . . . but the mission would suffer terribly if you should go."

He gazed at her with a queer intentness, a sort of strained humility. He waited for her to speak. Then, as she did not, he slowly took his leave.

She continued on her way to the refectory where she superintended the serving of the children's dinner. Later, in her own bare room, she paced up and down in a strange continuance of her agitation. Suddenly, with a gesture of despair, she sat down and set herself to complete a further passage in another of those lengthy letters in which, from day to day, as the outlet for her emotions, a penance and a consolation, she compiled the record of her doings for her brother.

Pen in hand, she seemed calmer; the act of writing seemed to tranquillize her.

"I have just told him I must ask to be transferred. It came suddenly, a sort of climax to all I have suppressed, and something of a threat as well. I was amazed at myself, startled by the words issuing from my lips. Yet when the opportunity presented itself I could not resist, I wanted instantly to startle, to hurt him. But, my dear dear Ernst, I am no happier. . . . After that second of triumph when I saw dismay cloud his face I am even more restless and distressed. I look out at the vast desolation of these grey wastes—so different from our cosy winter landscape with its golden air, its sleighbells and clustered chalet roofs—and I want to cry . . . as if my heart would break.

"It is his silence which defeats me—that stoic quality of enduring, and of fighting, all without speech. I've told you of his work during the plague, when he went about amongst foul sickness and sudden repulsive death as carelessly as if he were walking down the main street of his dreadful Scottish village. Well, it wasn't merely his courage, but the muteness of that courage, which was so unbelievably heroic. When his friend, the doctor, died, he held him in his arms, unmindful of the contagion, of that final cough which spattered his cheek with clotted blood. And the look upon his face . . . in its compassion and utter selflessness . . . it pierced my heart. Only my pride saved me the humiliation of weeping in his sight! Then I became angry. What irks me most of all is that I once wrote you that he was despicable. Ernst, I was wrong,—what an admission from your stubborn sister!—I can no longer despise him. Instead I despise myself. But I detest him. And I won't, I won't let him beat me down to his level of harrowing simplicity.

"The two others here have both been conquered. They love him—that is another mortification I must sustain. Martha, the stolid peasant, with bunions but no brains, is prepared to adore anything in a cassock. But Clotilde, shy and timid, flushing on the slightest provocation, a gently sweet and sensitive creature, has become a perfect devotee. During her enforced quarantine she worked him a thick quilted bed-mat, soft and warm, really beautiful. She took it to Joseph, his servant, with instructions to place it on the Father's bed—she is much too modest even to whisper the word 'bed' in his hearing. Joseph smiled: 'I am sorry, Sister, there is no bed!' It appears he sleeps upon the bare floor, with no covering but his overcoat, a greenish garment of uncertain age, which he is fond of, and of which, caressing the frayed and threadbare sleeves, he says proudly, 'Actually! I had it when I was a student at Holywell!'

"Martha and Clotilde have been making inquiries in his kitchen, nervous and perturbed, convinced that he does not look after himself. Their expressions, like shocked tabbies, almost made me laugh as they told me what I already knew, that he eats nothing but black bread, potatoes and bean curd.

" 'Joseph has instructions to boil a pot of potatoes and place them in a wicker basket,' Clotilde mewed. 'He eats one cold when he is hungry, dipping it in bean curd. Often they are quite musty before the basketful is finished.'

" 'Isn't it dreadful?' I answered curtly. 'But then some stomachs have never known a good cuisine—it is not hardship for them to do without it.'

" 'Yes, Reverend Mother,' murmured Clotilde, blushing, and retreating.

"She would do penance for a week to come and see him eat one nice hot meal. Oh, Ernst, you know how I abominate the sedulous and fawning nun who in the presence of a priest exposes the whites of her eyes and dissolves in obsequious rapture. Never, never, will I descend to such a level. I vowed it at Coblenz when I took the veil, and again at Liverpool . . . and will keep that vow . . . even in Pai-tan. But bean curd! *You* will not encounter it. A thin pinkish paste tasting of stagnant water and chewed wood!" She raised her head at an unexpected sound. "Ernst . . . It is unbelievable . . . it is raining . . ." She stopped writing, as if unable to continue, and slowly laid down her pen. With dark and self-distrustful eyes she sat watching the novelty of the rain, which trickled down the pane like heavy tears.

A fortnight later it was still raining. The skies, dull as tallow, were open sluices from which a steady deluge fell. The drops were large, pitting the upper crust of yellowish snow. It seemed everlasting . . . the snow. Great frozen slabs of it still came sliding from the church roof, with unpremeditated acceleration, landing soddenly upon the slushy snow beneath. Rivulets of rain went rushing across the dun-coloured sludge, channeling, undercutting the banks, which toppled with a slow splash into the stream beneath. The mission was a quagmire of slush.

Then the first patch of brown earth appeared, momentous as the tip of Ararat. Further patches sprouted and coalesced, forming a landscape of bleached grass and scabby desert all fissured and cratered with the flood. And still the rain continued. The mission roofs broke down at last and leaked incessantly. Water came in cataracts from the eaves. The children sat, green and miserable, in the class-room, while Sister Martha placed pails for the larger drips. Sister Clotilde had a dreadful cold and took lessons at her desk beneath Reverend Mother's umbrella.

The light soil of the mission garden could not withstand the scouring fusion of rain and thaw. It swept down the hill in a yellow turbulence on which floated uptorn sareta plants and oleander shrubs. Carp from the fish pond darted frightened, through the flood. The trees were slowly undermined. For a painful day the lychees and catalpas stood upright on their naked roots, which groped like pallid tentacles, then slowly toppled. The young white mulberries followed next, then the lovely row of flowering plum, these on the day that the lower wall was washed away. Only the toughened cedars stood, with the giant banyan, amidst the muddied desolation.

On the afternoon before Canon Mealey's arrival Father Chisholm heavily surveyed the dreary havoc, on his way to children's benediction. He turned to Fu, the gardener, who stood beside him.

"I wished for a thaw. The good God has punished me by sending one."

Fu, like most gardeners, was not a cheerful man. "The great Shang-Foo who arrives from across the seas will think much ill of us. Ah! If only he had seen my bloom of lilies last spring!"

"Let us be of good heart, Fu. The damage is not irreparable."

"My plantings are lost." Fu gloomed. "We shall have to begin all over again."

"That is life . . . to begin again when everything is lost!"

Despite his exhortation, Francis was deeply depressed as he went into the church. Kneeling before the lighted altar, while the rain still drummed upon the roof, he seemed to hear, above the childish treble of the Tantum Ergo, a liquid murmuring beneath him. But the sound of flowing water had long been echoing in his ears. His mind was burdened by the wretched appearance which the mission must present to his visitor upon the following day. He put the thing away as an obsession.

When the service was over and Joseph had snuffed the candles and left the sacristy he came slowly down the aisle. A dank vapour hung about the white-washed nave. Sister Martha had taken the children across the compound for their supper. But still in prayer upon the damp boards were Reverend Mother and Sister Clotilde. He passed them in silence; then suddenly stopped short. Clotilde's running head catarrh made her a spectacle of woe and Maria-Veronica's lips were drawn with cold. He had an extraordinary inner conviction that they should neither of them be allowed to remain.

He stepped back to them and said: "I am sorry, I'm going to close the church now."

There was a pause. This interference was unlike him. They seemed surprised. But they rose obediently, in silence, and preceded him to the porch. He locked the front doors and followed them through the streaming dusk.

A moment later the sound broke upon them. A low rumble, swelling to a roll of subterranean thunder. As Sister Clotilde screamed, Francis swung round to see the slender structure of his church in motion. Glistening, wetly luminous, it swayed gracefully in the fading light; then, like a reluctant woman, yielded. His heart stood still in horror. With a rending crash, the undermined foundations broke. One side caved in, the roof's spire snapped, the rest was a blinding vision of torn timbers and shattered glass. Then his church, his lovely church, lay dissolved into nothing, at his feet.

He stood rooted, for an instant, in a daze of pain, then ran towards the wreckage. But the altar lay smashed to rubble, the tabernacle crushed to splinters beneath a beam. He could not even save the sacred species. And his vestments, the precious Ribiero relic, these were in shreds. Standing there, bare-headed in the teeming rain, he was conscious, amidst the frightened babble which now surrounded him, of Sister Martha's lamentation.

"Why . . . why . . . why has this come on us?" She was moaning, wringing her hands. "Dear God! What worse could you have done to us?"

He muttered, not moving, desperately sustaining his own faith rather than hers:—

"Ten minutes sooner . . . we should every one of us have been killed."

There was nothing to be done. They left the fallen wreckage to the darkness and the rain.

Next day, at three o'clock punctually, Canon Mealey arrived. Because of the turbulence of the flooded river, his junk had dropped anchor in a backwater five li below Pai-tan. There were no chairs available: only some wheelbarrows, long-shafted like ploughs, with solid wooden wheels which, since the plague, were used by the few remaining runners to transport their passengers. The situation was difficult for a man of dignity. But there was no alternative. The Canon, mud-spattered and with dangling legs, reached the mission in a wheelbarrow.

The modest reception rehearsed by Sister Clotilde—a song of welcome, with waving of little flags, by the children—had been abandoned. Watching from his balcony, Father Chisholm hurried to the gate to meet his visitor.

"My dear Father!" cried Mealey, stiffly straightening himself and warmly grasping both Francis' hands. "This is the happiest day in many months—to see you again. I told you I should one day run the gamut of the Orient. With the interest of the world centred upon suffering China it was inevitable my resolve should crystallize to action!" He broke off, his eyes bulging across the other's shoulder at the scene of desolation. "Why . . . I don't understand. Where is the church?"

"You see all that is left of it."

"But this mess . . . You reported a splendid establishment."

"We have had some reverses." Francis spoke quietly.

"Why, really, it's incomprehensible . . . most disturbing."

Francis intervened with a hospitable smile. "When you have had a hot bath and a change I will tell you."

An hour later, pink from his tub, in a new tussore suit, Anselm sat stirring his hot soup, with an aggrieved expression.

"I must confess this is the greatest disappointment of my life . . . to come here, to the very outposts . . ." He took a mouthful of soup, meeting the spoon with plump, pursed lips. He had filled out in these last years. He was big now, full-shouldered and stately, still smooth-skinned and clear-eyed, with big palps of hands, hearty or pontifical at will. "I had set my heart on celebrating high mass in your church, Francis. These foundations must have been badly laid."

"It is a wonder they were laid at all."

"Nonsense! You've had lots of time to establish yourself. What in heaven's name am I to tell them at home?" He laughed shortly, dolefully. "I even promised a lecture at London Headquarters of the F.M.S.—'St. Andrew's: or God in Darkest China.' I'd brought my quarter-plate Zeiss to get lantern slides. It places me . . . all of us . . . in a most awkward position."

There was a silence.

"Of course I know you've had your difficulties," Mealey continued between annoyance and compunction. "But who hasn't? I assure you we've had ours. Especially lately since we merged the two divisions . . . after Bishop Mac-Nabb's death!"

Father Chisholm stiffened, as in pain.

"He's dead?"

"Yes, yes, the old man went at last. Pneumonia—this March. He was past his best, very muddled and queer, quite a relief to all of us when he went, very peacefully. The coadjutor, Bishop Tarrant, succeeded him. A great success."

Again a silence fell. Father Chisholm raised his hand to shield his eyes. Rusty Mac gone . . . A rush of unbearable recollection swept him: that day by the Stinchar, the glorious salmon, those kind wise peering eyes and the warmth of them when he was worried at Holywell; the quiet voice in the study at Tynecastle before he sailed, "Keep fighting, Francis, for God and good old Scotland."

Anselm was reflecting, with friendly generosity: "Well, well! We must face things, I suppose. Now that I'm here I'll do my best to get things straight for you. I've a great deal of organizing experience. It may interest you, some day, to hear how I have put the Society on its feet. In my personal appeals, delivered in London, Liverpool and Tynecastle, I raised thirty thousand pounds—and that is only the beginning." He showed his sound teeth in a competent smile. "Don't be so depressed, my dear fellow. I'm not unduly censorious . . . the first thing we'll do is have Reverend Mother over to lunch —she seems an able woman—and have a real round-table parochial conference!"

With an effort Francis pulled himself back from the dear forgotten days. "Reverend Mother doesn't care to take her meals outside the Sisters' house."

"You haven't asked her properly." Mealey gazed at the other's spare figure with a hearty, pitying kindliness. "Poor Francis! I'd hardly expect you to understand women. She'll come all right . . . just leave it to me!"

On the following day, Maria-Veronica did, in fact, present herself for lunch. Anselm was in high spirits after an excellent night's rest and an energetic morning of inspection. Still benevolent from his visit to the schoolroom, he greeted the Reverend Mother, though he had parted from her only five minutes before, with effusive dignity.

"This, Reverend Mother, is indeed an honour. A glass of sherry? No? I assure you it is fine—pale Amontillado. A little travelled perhaps," he beamed, "since it came with me from home. Coddlesome, maybe . . . but a palate, acquired in Spain, is hard to deny."

They sat down at table.

"Now, Francis, what are you giving us? No Chinese mysteries, I trust, no birds'-nest soup or purée of chopsticks. Ha! Ha!" Mealey laughed heartily as he helped himself to boiled chicken. "Though I must confess I am somewhat enamoured of the Oriental cuisine. Coming over on the boat—a stormy passage, incidentally; for four days no one appeared at the skipper's table but your humble servant—we were served with a quite delicious Chinese dish, chow mein."

Mother Maria-Veronica raised her eyes from the tablecloth. "Is chow mein a Chinese dish? Or an American edition of the Chinese custom of collecting scraps?"

He stared at her, mouth slightly agape. "My dear Reverend Mother! Chow mein! Why . . ." He glanced at Francis for support, found none, and laughed again. "At any rate, I assure you, I chewed mine! Ha! Ha!"

Swinging round, for better access to the dish of salad which Joseph was presenting, he ran on: "Food apart, the lure of the Orient is immensely fascinating! We Occidentals are too apt to condemn the Chinese as a greatly inferior race. Now I for one will shake hands with any Chinaman, provided he believes in God and . . ." he bubbled . . . "carbolic soap!"

Father Chisholm shot a quick glance at Joseph's face, which, though expressionless, showed a faint tightening of the nostrils.

"And now," Mealey paused suddenly, his manner dropping to pontifical solemnity. "We have important business on our agenda. As a boy, Reverend Mother, our good mission father was always leading me into scrapes. Now it's my task to get him out of this one!"

Nothing definite emerged from the conference. Except, perhaps, a modest summary of Anselm's achievements at home.

Free of the limitations of a parish, he had set himself wholeheartedly to work for the missions, mindful that the Holy Father was especially devoted to the Propagation of the Faith and eager to encourage the workers who so selflessly espoused his favourite cause.

It had not been long before he won recognition. He began to move about the country, to preach sermons of impassioned eloquence in the great English cities. Through his genius for collecting friends, no contact of any consequence was ever thrown away. On his return from Manchester, or Birmingham, he would sit down and write a score of charming letters, thanking this person for a delightful lunch, the next for a generous donation to the Foreign Mission Fund. Soon his correspondence was voluminous, and employed a whole-time secretary.

Presently, London acknowledged him as a distinguished visitor. His debut, in the pulpit of Westminster, was spectacular. Women had always idolized him. Now he was adopted by the wealthy coterie of Cathedral spinsters who collected cats and clergymen in their rich mansions south of the Park. His manners had always been engaging. That same year he became a country member of the Athenæum. And the sudden engorgement of the F.M. moneybags evoked a most gracious token of appreciation, direct from Rome.

When he became the youngest canon in the Northern Diocese, few grudged him the success. Even the cynics who traced his exuberant rise to an overactive thyroid gland admitted his business acumen. For all his gush he was no fool. He had a level head for figures and could manage money. In five years he had founded two fresh missions in Japan and a native seminary in Nankin. The new F.M.S. offices in Tynecastle were imposing, efficient and completely free of debt.

In brief, Anselm had made a fine thing of his life. With Bishop Tarrant at his elbow there was every chance that his most admirable work would continue to expand.

Two days after his official meeting with Francis and Reverend Mother, the rain ceased and a watery sun sent pale feelers towards the forgotten earth. Mealey's spirits bounded. He joked to Francis.

"I've brought fine weather with me. Some people follow the sun around. But the sun follows me."

He unlimbered his camera and began to take countless photographs. His energy was tremendous. He bounded out of bed in the morning shouting "Boy! Boy!" for Joseph to get his bath. He said mass in the schoolroom. After a hearty breakfast he departed in his solar topee, a stout stick in hand, the camera swinging on his hip.

He made many excursions, even poking discreetly for souvenirs amongst the ashes of Pai-tan's plague-spots. At each scene of blackened desolation he murmured reverently: "The hand of God!" He would stop suddenly, at a city gate, arresting his companion with a dramatic gesture. "Wait! I must get this one. The light is perfect."

On Sunday, he came in to lunch greatly elated. "It's just struck me, I can still give that lecture. Treat it from the angle of Dangers and Difficulties in the Mission Field. Work in the plague and the flood. This morning I got a glorious view of the ruins of the church. What a slide it will make, titled 'God Chastiseth His Own'! Isn't that magnificent?"

But on the eve of his departure Anselm's manner altered and his tone, as he sat with the mission priest on the balcony after supper, was grave.

"I have to thank you for extending hospitality to a wanderer, Francis. But I am not happy about you. I can't see how you are going to rebuild the church. The Society cannot let you have the money."

"I haven't asked for it." The strain of the past two weeks was beginning to tell on Francis, his stern self-discipline was wearing thin.

Mealey threw his companion a sharp glance. "If only you had been more successful with some of the better-class Chinese, the rich merchants. If only your friend Mr. Chia had seen the light."

"He hasn't." Father Chisholm spoke with unusual shortness. "And he has given munificently. I shall not ask him for another tael."

Anselm shrugged his shoulders, annoyed. "Of course that's your affair. But I must tell you, frankly, I'm sadly disappointed in your conduct of this mission. Take your convert rate. It doesn't compare with our other statistics. We run them as a graph at headquarters, and you're the lowest in the whole chart."

Father Chisholm gazed straight ahead, his lips firmly compressed. He answered with unusual irony: "I suppose missionaries differ in their individual capabilities."

"And in their enthusiasm." Anselm, sensitive to satire, was now justly incensed. "Why do you persist in refusing to employ catechists? It's the universal custom. If you had even three active men, at forty taels a month, why, one thousand baptisms would only cost you fifteen hundred Chinese dollars!"

Francis did not answer. He was praying desperately that he might control his temper, suffer this humiliation as something he deserved.

"You're not getting behind your work here," Mealey went on. "You live, personally, in such poor style. You ought to impress the natives, keep a chair, servants, make more of a show."

"You are mistaken." Francis spoke steadily. "The Chinese hate ostentation. They call it *ti-mien*. And priests who practice it are regarded as dishonourable."

Anselm flushed angrily. "You're referring to their own low heathen priests, I presume."

"Does it matter?" Father Chisholm smiled palely. "Many of these priests are good and noble men."

There was a strained silence. Anselm drew his coat about him with a shocked finality.

"After that, of course, there is nothing to be said. I must confess your attitude pains me deeply. Even Reverend Mother is embarrassed by it. Ever since I arrived it has been plain how much she is at variance with you." He got up and went into his own room.

Francis remained a long time in the gathering mist. That last remark had cut him worst of all: the stab of a premonition confirmed. Now he had no doubt that Maria-Veronica had submitted her request to be transferred.

Next morning Canon Mealey took his departure. He was returning to Nankin to spend a week at the Vicariate and would go from there to Nagasaki to inspect six missions in Japan. His bags were packed, a chair waited to bear him to the junk, he had taken his farewells of the Sisters and the children. Now, dressed for the journey, wearing sun-glasses, his topee draped with green gauze, he stood in final conversation with Father Chisholm in the hall.

"Well, Francis!" Mealey extended his hand in grudging forgiveness. "We must part friends. The gift of tongues is not given to all of us. I suppose you are a well-meaning fellow at heart." He threw out his chest. "Strange! I'm itching to be off. I have travel in my blood. Good-bye. *Au revoir. Auf Wiedersehen.* And last but not least—God bless you!"

Dropping the mosquito veil he stepped into his chair. The runners groaningly bent their shoulders, supported him and shuffled off. At the sagging mission gates he leaned through the window of the chair, fluttered his white handkerchief in farewell.

At sundown, when he took his evening walk, his beloved hour of stealing twilight and far-off echoing stillness, Father Chisholm found himself meditating, amongst the débris of the church. He seated himself upon a lump of rubble, thinking of his old Headmaster—somehow he always saw Rusty Mac with schoolboy's eyes—and of his exhortation to courage. There was little courage in him now. These last two weeks, the perpetual effort to sustain his visitor's patronizing tone, had left him void. Yet perhaps Anselm was justified. Was he not a failure, in God's sight and in man's? He had done so little. And that little, so laboured and inadequate, was almost undone. How was he to proceed? A weary hopelessness of spirit took hold of him.

Resting there, with bent head, he did not hear a footstep behind him. Mother Maria-Veronica was compelled to make her presence known to him.

"Am I disturbing you?"

He glanced up, quite startled. "No . . . no. As you observe,"—he could not suppress a wincing smile,—"I am doing nothing."

There was a pause. In the indistinctness her face had a swimming pallor. He could not see the nerve twitching in her cheek yet he sensed in her figure a strange rigidity.

Her voice was colourless. "I have something to say to you. I—"

"Yes?"

"This is no doubt humiliating for you. But I am obliged to tell you. I—I am sorry." The words, torn from her, gained momentum, then came in a tumbled flood. "I am most bitterly and grievously sorry for my conduct towards you. From our first meeting I have behaved shamefully, sinfully. The devil of pride was in me. It's always been in me, ever since I was a little child and flung things at my nurse's head. I have known now for weeks that I wanted to come to you . . . to tell you . . . but my pride, my stubborn malice restrained me. These past ten days, in my heart, I have wept for you . . . the slights and humiliations you have endured from that gross and worldly priest, who is unworthy to untie your shoe. Father, I hate myself— forgive me, forgive me . . ." Her voice was lost, she crouched, sobbing into her hands, before him.

The sky was strained of all colour, except the greenish afterglow behind the peaks. This faded swiftly and the kind dusk enfolded her. An interval of time, in which a single tear fell upon her cheek. . . .

"So now you will not leave the mission?"

"No, no . . ." Her heart was breaking. "If you will let me stay. I have never known anyone whom I wished so much to serve . . . Yours is the best . . . the finest spirit I have ever known."

"Hush, my child. I am a poor and insignificant creature . . . you were right . . . a common man . . ."

"Father, pity me." Her sobs went choking into the earth.

"And you are a great lady. But in God's sight we are both of us children. If we may work together . . . help each other . . ."

"I will help with all my power. One thing at least I can do. It is so easy to write to my brother. He will rebuild the church . . . restore the mission. He has great possessions, he will do it gladly. If only you will help me . . . help me to defeat my pride."

There was a long silence. She sobbed more softly. A great warmth filled his heart. He took her arm to raise her but she would not rise. So he knelt beside her and gazed, without praying, into the pure and peaceful night where, across the ages, among the shadows of a garden, another poor and common man also knelt and watched them both.

7

ONE sunny forenoon in the year 1912 Father Chisholm was separating bees-wax from his season's yield of honey. His workshop, built in Bavarian style, at the end of the kitchen garden—trim, practical, with a pedal lathe and tools neatly racked, as much a source of delight to him as on the day Mother Maria-Veronica had handed him the key—was sweet with the fume of melted sugar. A great bowl of cool yellow honey stood among fresh shavings upon the floor. On the bench, setting, was the flat copper pan of tawny wax from which, tomorrow, he would make his candles. And such candles—smooth-burning and sweet-scented; even in St. Peter's one would not find the like!

With a sigh of contentment, he wiped his brow, his short fingernails blobbed with the rich wax. Then, shouldering the big honey jar, he pulled the door behind him and set off through the mission grounds. He was happy. Waking in the morning with the starlings chattering in the eaves, and the coolness of the dawn still dewed upon the grass, his second thought was that there could be no greater happiness than to work—much with his hands, a little with his head, but mostly with his heart—and to live, simply, like this, close to the earth which, to him, never seemed far from heaven.

The province was prospering and the people, forgetting flood, pestilence and famine, were at peace. In the five years which had elapsed since its reconstruction, through the generosity of Count Ernst von Hohenlohe, the mission had flourished in a quiet fashion. The church was bigger, stouter than the first. He had built it solidly, with grim compunction, using neither plaster nor stucco, after the monastic model which Queen Margaret had introduced to Scotland centuries before. Classic and severe, with a simple bell-tower, and aisles supported by groined arches, its plainness grew on him until he preferred it to the other. And it was safe.

The school had been enlarged, a new children's home added to the building. And the purchase of the two adjoining irrigated fields provided a model home farm with pigpen, byre, and a chicken run down which Martha stalked, thin-shanked, in wooden shoes and kilted habit, casting corn and clucking joyously in Flemish.

Now his congregation comprised two hundred faithful souls, not one of whom knelt under duress before his altar. The orphanage had trebled in size and was beginning to bear the first fruits of his patient foresight. The older girls helped the Sisters with the little ones, some were already novices, others would soon be going into the world. Why, last Christmas he had married the eldest, at nineteen, to a young farmer from the Liu village. He smiled ruefully at the implications of his cunning. At his recent pastoral visit to Liu—a happy and successful expedition from which he had returned only last week—the young wife had hung her head and told him he must return presently to perform another baptism.

As he shifted the heavy honey to his other shoulder, a bent little man of forty-three, growing bald, with rheumatism already nibbling at his joints, a bough of jessamine flailed him on the cheek. The garden had seldom been so lovely: that, also, he owed to Maria-Veronica. Admitting some adroitness with his hands, he could not remotely claim to have green fingers. But Reverend Mother had revealed an unsuspected skill in growing things. Seeds had arrived from her home in Germany, bundles of shoots wrapped tenderly in sacking. Her letters, begging for this cutting and for that, had sped to famous gardens in Canton and Pekin—like his own swift white doves, importunate and homing. This beauty which now surrounded him, this sun-shot sanctuary, alive with twittering hum, was her work.

Their comradeship was not unlike this precious garden. Here, indeed, when he took his evening walk, he would find her, intent, coarsely gloved, cutting the full white peonies that grew so freely, training a stray clematis, watering the golden azaleas. There they would briefly discuss the business of the day. Sometimes they did not speak. When the fireflies flitted in the garden they had gone their separate ways.

As he approached the upper gate he saw the children march in twos across the compound. Dinner. He smiled and hastened. They were seated at the long low table in the new annex to the dormitory, twoscore little blue-black polls and shining yellow faces, with Maria-Veronica at one end, Clotilde at the other. Martha, aided by the Chinese novices, was ladling steaming rice broth into a battery of blue bowls. Anna, his foundling of the snow, now a handsome girl, handed round the bowls with her usual air of dark and frowning reserve.

The clamour stilled upon his entry. He shot a shamed boyish look at the Reverend Mother, craving indulgence, and placed the honey jar triumphantly on the table.

"Fresh honey today, children! It is a great pity. I am sure no one wishes it!"

Shrill, immediate denial rose like the chatter of little monkeys. Suppressing his smile, he shook his head dolefully at the youngest, a solemn mandarin of three who sat swallowing his spoon, swaying dreamily, his soft small buttocks unstable on the bench.

"I cannot believe a good child could enjoy such monstrous depravity! Tell me, Symphorien—" It was dreadful the way in which new converts chose the most resounding saint names for their children—"Tell me, Symphorien . . . would you not rather learn nice catechism than eat honey?"

"Honey!" answered Symphorien dreamily. He stared at the lined brown face above him. Then, surprised by his own temerity, he burst into tears and fell off the bench.

Laughing, Father Chisholm picked up the child. "There, there! You are a good boy, Symphorien. God loves you. And for speaking the truth you shall have double honey."

He felt Maria-Veronica's reproving gaze upon him. She would presently follow him to the door and murmur: "Father . . . we must consider discipline!" But today—it seemed so long since he stood outside the buzzing classroom, troubled and unhappy, afraid to penetrate the chill unfriendly air —nothing could restrain his manner with the children. His fondness towards them had always been absurd, it was what he named his patriarchal privilege.

As he expected, Maria-Veronica accompanied him from the room but, though her brow seemed unusually clouded, she did not even mildly rebuke him. Instead, after some hesitation, she remarked: "Joseph had a strange story this morning."

"Yes. The rascal wants to get married . . . naturally. But he is deafening me with the beauties and convenience of a lodge . . . to be built at the mission gate . . . not, of course, for Joseph or for Joseph's wife . . . but solely for the benefit of the mission."

"No, it isn't the lodge." Unsmiling, she bit her lip. "The building is taking place elsewhere, in the Street of the Lanterns—you know that splendid central site—and on a grander scale, much grander than anything we have accomplished here." Her tone was strangely bitter. "Scores of workmen have arrived, barges of white stone from Sen-siang. Everything. I assure you money is being spent as only American millionaires can spend it. Soon we shall have the finest establishment in Pai-tan, with schools, for both boys and girls, a playground, public rice kitchen, free dispensary, and a hospital with resident doctor!" She broke off, gazing at him with tears in her troubled eyes.

"What establishment?" He spoke automatically, stunned by a presage of her answer.

"Another mission. Protestant. The American Methodists."

There was a long pause. Secure in the remoteness of his situation, he had never contemplated even the possibility of such intrusion. Reverend Mother, recalled to the refectory by Clotilde, left him in painful silence.

He walked slowly towards his house, all the brightness of the morning dimmed. Where was his mediæval fortress now? In a quick throwback to his childhood, he had the same sensation of injustice as when, out berry-picking, another boy had encroached upon a secret bush of his own discovery and rudely begun to strip it of its fruit. He knew the hatreds which developed between rival missions, the ugly jealousies, above all, the bickerings on points of doctrine, the charge and countercharge, the raucous denunciation which made the Christian faith appear, to the tolerant Chinese mind, an infernal tower of Babel where all shouted at lung-pitch: "Behold, it is here! Here! Here!" But where? Alas! When one looked, there was nothing but rage and sound and execration.

At his house he found Joseph, duster in hand, idling about the hall, in pretence of work, waiting to bemoan the news.

"Has the Father heard of the hateful coming of these Americans who worship the false God?"

"Be silent, Joseph!" The priest answered harshly. "They do not worship the false God, but the same true God as we. If you speak such words again you will never get your gate-house!"

Joseph edged away, grumbling beneath his breath.

In the afternoon Father Chisholm went down to Pai-tan and, in the Street of the Lanterns, received the fateful confirmation of his eyes. Yes, the new mission was begun—was rising rapidly under the hands of many squads of masons, carpenters, and coolies. He watched a string of labourers, swaying along a strip of planking, bearing baskets of the finest Soochin glaze. He saw that the scale of operations was princely.

As he lingered there, with his thoughts for company, he suddenly discovered Mr. Chia at his elbow. He greeted his old friend quietly.

As they talked of the fineness of the weather and the general excellence of trade, Francis sensed more than usual kindness in the merchant's manner.

Suddenly, having appeased the proprieties, Mr. Chia guilelessly remarked: "It is pleasant to observe the excess growth of goodness, though many would consider it a superfluity. For myself I much enjoy walking in other mission gardens. Moreover, when the Father came here many years ago he received much ill-usage." A gentle and suggestive pause. "It seems highly probable, even to such an uninfluential and lowly-placed citizen as I, that the new missioners could receive such execrable treatment on their arrival that they might be most regretfully forced to depart."

A shiver passed over Father Chisholm as an unbelievable temptation assailed him. The ambiguity, the forced understatement, of the merchant's remark was more significant than the direst threat. Mr. Chia, in many subtle and subterranean ways, wielded the greatest power in the district. Francis knew that he need only answer, gazing into space: "It would certainly be a great misfortune if disaster befell the coming missioners . . . But then, who can prevent the will of heaven?" to foredoom the threatened invasion of his pastorate. But he recoiled, abhorring himself for the thought. Conscious of a cold perspiration on his brow, he replied as calmly as he could:—

"There are many gates to heaven. We enter by one, these new preachers by another. How can we deny them the right to practice virtue in their own way? If they desire it, then they must come."

He did not observe that spark of singular regard which for once irradiated in Mr. Chia's placid eye. Still deeply disturbed, he parted from his friend and walked homeward up the hill. He entered the church and seated himself, for he was tired, before the crucifix on the side altar. Gazing at the face, haloed with thorns, he prayed, in his mind, for endurance, wisdom, and forbearance.

By the end of June the Methodist mission was near completion. For all his fortitude, Father Chisholm had not brought himself to view the successive stages of construction; he had sombrely avoided the Street of the Lanterns. But when Joseph, who had not failed as a baleful informant, brought news that the two foreign devils had arrived, the little priest sighed, put on his one good suit, took his tartan umbrella, and steeled himself to call.

When he rang the door-bell the sound echoed emptily into the new smell of paint and plaster. But after waiting indeterminately for a minute under the green-glass portico, he heard hastening steps within, and the door was opened by a small faded middle-aged woman in a grey alpaca skirt and high-necked blouse.

"Good afternoon. I am Father Chisholm. I took the liberty of calling to welcome you to Pai-tan."

She started nervously and a look of quick apprehension flooded her pale blue eyes.

"Oh, yes. Please come in. I am Mrs. Fiske. Wilbur . . . my husband . . . Dr. Fiske . . . he's upstairs. I'm afraid we are all alone, and not quite settled yet!" Hurriedly, she silenced his regretful protest. "No, no . . . you must step in."

He followed her upstairs to a cool, lofty room, where a man of forty, clean-shaven, with a short-cropped moustache, and of her own diminutive size, was perched on a stepladder methodically arranging books upon the shelves. He wore strong glasses over his intelligent, apologetic, short-sighted eyes. His baggy cotton knickers gave his thin little calves an indescribable pathos. Descending the ladder, he stumbled, almost fell.

"Do be careful, Wilbur!" Her hands fluttered protectively. She introduced the two men. "Now let's sit down . . . if we can." She unsuccessfully attempted a smile. "It's too bad not having our furniture . . . but then one gets used to anything in China."

They sat down. Father Chisholm said pleasantly:—

"You have a magnificent building here."

"Yes." Dr. Fiske deprecated. "We're very lucky. Mr. Chandler, the oil magnate, is most generous with us."

A strained silence. They so little fulfilled the priest's uneasy expectations, he felt taken unawares. He could not claim gigantic stature, yet the Fiskes, by the very sparseness of their physical economy, silenced the merest whisper of aggression. The little doctor was mild, with a bookish, even timid air, and a smile, deprecating, about his lips, as though afraid to settle. His wife, more clearly distinguishable in this good light, was a gentle, steadfast creature, her blue eyes easily receptive of tears, her hands alternating between her thin gold locket chain and a frizzy pad of rich, net-enclosed, brown hair which, with a slight shock, Francis perceived to be a wig.

Suddenly Dr. Fiske cleared his throat. He said, simply: "How you must hate our coming here!"

"Oh, no . . . not at all." It was the priest's turn to look awkward.

"We had the same experience once. We were up-country in the Lan-hi province, a lovely place. I wish you'd seen our peach trees. We had it all to ourselves for nine years. Then another missionary came. Not," he inserted swiftly, "a Catholic priest. But, well . . . We did resent it, didn't we, Agnes?"

"We did, dear." She nodded tremulously. "Still . . . we got over it. We are old campaigners, Father."

"Have you been long in China?"

"Over twenty years! We came as an insanely young couple the day we were married. We have given our lives to it." The moisture in her eyes receded before a bright and eager smile. "Wilbur! I must show Father Chisholm John's photograph." She rose, proudly took a silver-framed portrait from the bare mantelpiece. "This is our boy, taken when he was at Harvard, before he went as Rhodes Scholar to Oxford. Yes, he's still in England . . . working in our dockland settlement in Tynecastle."

The name shattered his strained politeness. "Tynecastle!" He smiled. "That is very near my home."

She gazed at him, enchanted, smiling back, holding the photograph to her bosom with tender hands.

"Isn't that amazing? The world is such a small place after all." Briskly she replaced the photograph on the mantel. "Now I'm going to bring in coffee, and some of my very own doughnuts . . . a family receipt." Again she silenced his protests. "It's no trouble. I always make Wilbur take a little refreshment at this hour. He has had some bother with his duodenum. If I didn't look after him who would?"

He had meant to stay for five minutes; he remained for more than an hour.

They were New England people, natives of the town of Biddeford, in Maine, born, reared and married in the tenets of their own strict faith. As they spoke of their youth he had a swift and strangely sympathetic vision of a cold crisp countryside, of great salty rivers flowing between wands of silver birches to the misty sea, past white wooden houses amidst the wine of maples, and sumac, velvet-red in winter, a thin white steeple above the village, with bells and dark silent figures in the frosted street, following their quiet destiny.

But the Fiskes had chosen another and harder path. They had suffered. Both had almost died of cholera. During the Boxer rebellion, when many of their fellow missioners were massacred, they had spent six months in a filthy prison under daily threat of execution. Their devotion to each other, and to their son, was touching. She had, for all her tremulousness, an indomitable maternal solicitude towards her two men.

Despite her antecedents, Agnes Fiske was a pure romantic whose life was written in the host of tender souvenirs she so carefully preserved. Soon she was showing Francis a letter of her dear mother's, a quarter of a century old, with the formula for these doughnuts, and a curl from John's head worn within her locket. Upstairs in her drawer were many more such tokens: bundles of yellowing correspondence, her withered bridal bouquet, a front tooth her son had shed, the ribbon she had worn at her first Biddeford Church Social. . . .

Her health was frail and presently, once this new venture was established, she was leaving for a six months' vacation which she would spend in England with her son. Already, with an earnestness that presaged her goodwill, she pressed Father Chisholm to entrust her with any commissions he might wish executed at home.

When, at last, he took his leave, she escorted him beyond the portico, where Dr. Fiske stood, to the outer gate. Her eyes filled up with tears. "I can't tell you how relieved, how glad I am at your kindness, your friendliness in calling . . . especially for Wilbur's sake. At our last station he had such a painful experience . . . hatreds stirred up, frightful bigotry. It got so bad, latterly, when he went out to see a sick man he was struck and knocked senseless by a young brute of a . . . a missionary who accused him of stealing the man's immortal soul." She suppressed her emotion. "Let us help one another. Wilbur is such a clever doctor. Call on him any time you wish." She pressed his hand quickly and turned away.

Father Chisholm went home in a curious state of mind. For the next few days he had no news of the Fiskes. But on Saturday a batch of home-baked cookies arrived at St. Andrew's. As he took them, still warm and wrapped in the white napkin, to the children's refectory, Sister Martha scowled.

"Does she think we cannot bake here—this new woman?"

"She is trying to be kind, Martha. And we also must try."

For several months Sister Clotilde had suffered from a painful irritation of her skin. All sorts of lotions had been used, from calamine to carbolic, but without success. So distressing was the affliction, she made a special novena for a cure. The following week Father Chisholm saw her rubbing her red excoriated hands in a torment of itching. He frowned and, fighting his own reluctance, sent a note to Dr. Fiske.

The doctor arrived within half an hour, quietly examined the patient in Reverend Mother's presence, used no resounding words, praised the treatment that had been given and, having mixed a special physic to be taken internally every three hours, unobtrusively departed. In ten days the ugly rash had vanished and Sister Clotilde was a new woman. But after the first radiance she brought a troubling scruple to her confession.

"Father . . . I prayed to God so earnestly . . . and . . ."

"It was the Protestant missionary who cured you?"

"Yes, Father."

"My child . . . don't let your faith be troubled. God did answer your prayer. We are his instruments . . . every one of us." He smiled suddenly. "Don't forget what old Lao-tzŭ said—'Religions are many, reason is one, we are all brothers.'"

That same evening as he walked in the garden Maria-Veronica said to him, almost unwillingly:—

"This American . . . he is a good doctor."

He nodded. "And a good man."

The work of the two missions marched forward without conflict. There was room for both in Pai-tan, and each was careful not to give offence. The wisdom of Father Chisholm's determination to have no rice-Christians in his flock was now apparent. Only one of his congregation betook himself to Lantern Street, and he was returned with a brief note: "Dear Chisholm, The bearer is a bad Catholic but would be a worse Methodist. Ever, Your friend in the Universal God, Wilbur Fiske, M.D. *P.S.* If any of your people need hospitalization send them along. They'll receive no dark hints on the fallibility of the Borgias!"

The priest's heart glowed. Dear Lord, he thought, kindness and toleration —with these two virtues how wonderful Thy earth would be!

Fiske's accomplishments were not worn on his sleeve: he was revealed gradually as an archeologist and Chinese scholar of the first order. He contributed abstruse articles to the archives of obscure societies at home. His hobby was Chien-lung porcelain and his collection of eighteenth-century *famille noire*, picked up with unobtrusive guile, was genuinely fine. Like most small men ruled by their wives, he loved an argument, and it was not long before Francis and he were friends enough to debate, warily, with cunning on both sides, and sometimes, alas, with rising heat, certain points which separated their respective creeds. Occasionally, carried away by the fervour of their opposite views, they parted with a certain tightness of the lips—for the pedantic little doctor could be querulous when roused. But it soon passed.

Once, after such a disagreement, Fiske met the mission priest. He stopped abruptly. "My dear Chisholm, I have been reflecting on a sermon which I once heard from the lips of Dr. Elder Cummings, our eminent divine, in which he declared: 'The greatest evil of today is the growth of the Romish Church through the nefarious and diabolical intrigues of its priests.' I should like you to know that since I have had the honour of your acquaintance I believe the Reverend Cummings to have been talking through his hat."

Francis, smiling grimly, consulted his theological books and ten days later formally bowed.

"My dear Fiske, in Cardinal Cuesta's catechism I find, plainly printed, this illuminating phrase: 'Protestantism is an immoral practice which blasphemes God, degrades man, and endangers society.' I should like you to know, my dear Fiske, that even before I had the honour of your acquaintance I considered the Cardinal unpardonable!" Raising his hat he solemnly marched off.

Neighbouring Chinese thought the "doubled-up-with-laughter small-foreign-devil Methody" had completely lost his reason.

One gusty day towards the end of October Father Chisholm met the doctor's good lady on the Manchu Bridge. Mrs. Fiske was returning from marketing, one hand holding a net bag, the other clasping her hat securely to her head.

"Goodness!" she exclaimed cheerfully. "Isn't this a gale? It does blow the dust into my hair. I shall have to shampoo it again tonight!"

Familiar now with this one eccentricity, this single blot upon a blameless soul, Francis did not smile. Upon every possible occasion she guilelessly assumed her dreadful toupee to be a perfect mane of hair. His heart went out to her for the gentle little lie.

"I hope you are all well."

She smiled, head inclined, being very careful of her hat. "I am in rude health. But Wilbur is sulking—because I am off tomorrow. He will be so lonely, poor fellow. But then you are always lonely—what a solitary life you have!" She paused. "Do tell me, now that I am going to England, if there is anything I can do for you. I am bringing Wilbur back some new winter underwear—there's no place like Britain for woollens. Shall I do the same for you?"

He shook his head, smiling; then an odd thought struck him. "If you have nothing better to do one day . . . look up a dear old aunt of mine in Tyne-castle. Miss Polly Bannon is the name. Wait, I'll write down her address."

He scribbled the address with a stub of pencil on a scrap of paper torn from a package in her shopping bag. She tucked it into her glove.

"Shall I give her any message?"

"Tell her how well and happy I am . . . and what a grand place this is. Tell her I'm—next to your husband—the most important man in China."

Her eyes were bright and warm towards him. "Perhaps I shall tell her more than you think. Women have a way of talking when they get together. Good-bye. See that you look in on Wilbur occasionally. And do take care of yourself."

She shook hands and went off, a poor weak woman with a will of iron.

He promised himself he would call on Dr. Fiske. But as the weeks slipped past he seemed never to have an hour of leisure. There was the matter of Joseph's house to be arranged, and, when the little lodge was nicely built, the marriage ceremony itself, a full nuptial mass with six of the youngest children as train-bearers. Once Joseph and his bride were suitably installed, he returned to the Liu village with Joseph's father and brothers. He had long cherished the dream of an outpost, a small secondary mission at Liu. There was talk of a great trade route being constructed through the Kwangs. At some future date he might well have a younger priest to help him, one who might operate from this new centre in the hills. He had a strange impulse to set his plans in motion by increasing the area of the village grain-fields, arranging with his friends in Liu to clear, plough and sow an additional sixty mu of arable upland.

These affairs offered a genuine excuse, yet he experienced a sharp twinge of self-reproach as, some five months later, he unexpectedly encountered Fiske. The doctor, however, was in good spirits, lit by a guarded, oddly jocose animation, which permitted only one deduction.

"Yes." He chuckled, then corrected himself to a fitting gravity. "You're quite right. Mrs. Fiske rejoins me at the beginning of next month."

"I'm glad. It has been a long journey for her to take alone."

"She was fortunate in finding a most congenial fellow-passenger."

"Your wife is a very friendly person."

"And with a great talent," Dr. Fiske seemed to suppress a preposterous tendency to giggle, "for not minding her own business. You must come and dine with us when she arrives."

Father Chisholm rarely went out, his mode of life did not permit it, but now compunction drove him to accept. "Thank you, I will."

Three weeks later he was reminded of his commitment, not altogether willingly, by a copper-plate note from the Street of the Lanterns: "Tonight, without fail, seven-thirty."

It was inconvenient, when he had arranged for vespers at seven o'clock. But he advanced the service by half an hour, sent Joseph to procure a chair, and that evening set out in formal style.

The Methodist mission was brightly illuminated, exuding an unusual air of festivity. As he stepped out into the courtyard he hoped it would not be a large or lengthy affair. He was not antisocial, but his life had grown increasingly interior in these last years and that strain of Scots reserve, inherited from his father, had deepened into an odd guardedness towards strangers.

He was relieved, on entering the upper room, now gay with flowers and festoons of coloured paper, to find only his host and hostess, standing together on the hearth-rug, rather flushed from the warm room, like children before a party. While the doctor's thick lenses scintillated rays of welcome, Mrs. Fiske came quickly forward and took his hand.

"I am so glad to see you again, my poor neglected and misguided creature."

There was no mistaking the warmth of her greeting. She seemed quite taken out of herself. "You're happy to be back anyway. But I'm sure you've had a wonderful trip."

"Yes, yes, a wonderful trip. Our dear son is doing splendidly. How I wish he were with us tonight." She rattled on, ingenuous as a girl, her eyes bright with excitement. "Such things I have to tell you. But you'll hear . . . indeed, you'll hear . . . when our other guest comes in."

He could not prevent a questioning elevation of his brows.

"Yes, we are four tonight. A lady . . . in spite of our different viewpoints . . . now a most particular friend of mine. She is here on a visit." She stumbled, aware of his amazement, then faltered nervously. "My dear good Father, you are not to be cross with me." She faced the door and clapped her hands, in prearranged signal.

The door opened and Aunt Polly came into the room.

8

In the convent kitchen on that September day of 1914 neither Polly nor Sister Martha gave the slightest heed to the faint familiar sound of rifle-fire in the hills. While Martha cooked the dinner, using her spotless battery of copper pans, Polly stood by the window ironing a pile of linen wimples. In three months the two had become as inseparable as two brown hens in a strange farmyard. They respected each other's qualities. Martha had acclaimed Polly's crochet as the finest she had ever seen while Polly, after fingering Martha's cross-stitch, admitted her own inferior for the first time in her life. And they had, of course, a topic which never failed them.

Now, as Polly damped the linen and raised the iron expertly to her cheek to test its heat, she complained: "He is looking very poorly again." With one hand Martha put some more wood into the stove while she stirred the soup reflectively with the other. "What would one expect? He eats nothing."

"When he was a young man he had a good appetite."

The Belgian Sister shrugged her shoulders in exasperation. "He is the worst feeder of all the priests I have known. Ah! I have known some great feeders. There was our abbé at Metiers—six courses of fish in Lent. Of course I have a theory. When one eats little the stomach contracts. Thereafter it becomes impossible."

Polly shook her head in mild disagreement. "Yesterday when I took him some new baked scones he looked at them and said, 'How can one eat when thousands are hungry, within sight of this room?'"

"Bah! They are always hungry. In this country it is customary to eat grass."

"But now he says it will be worse because of all this fighting that is going on."

Sister Martha tasted the soup, her famous *pot-au-feu*, and her face registered critical approval. But as she turned to Polly she made a grimace. "There is always fighting. Just as there is always starving. We have bandits with our coffee in Pai-tan. They pop a few guns—like you hear now. Then the city buys them off and they go home. Tell me, did he eat my scones?"

"He ate one. Yes, and said it was excellent. Then he told me to give the set to Reverend Mother for our poor."

"That good Father will drive me to distraction." Though Sister Martha was, outside her kitchen, as mild as mother's milk, she scowled as if she were a creature of splendid rages. "Give, give, give! Until one's skin cracks with the strain. Shall I tell you what occurred last winter? One day in the town when it was snowing he took his coat off, his fine new coat that we sisters had made for him of best imported wool cloth, and gave it to some already half-frozen good-for-nothing. I would have let him have a tonguing, I assure you. But Mother Superior chose to correct him. He looked at her with those surprised eyes which hurt you deep inside. 'But why not? What's the use of preaching Christianity if we don't live as Christians? The great Christ would have given that beggar his coat. Why shouldn't I?' When Reverend Mother answered very crossly that the coat was a gift from us he smiled, standing there, shivering with cold. 'Then you are the good Christians—not I.' Was not that incredible? You wouldn't believe it, if like me you were brought up in a country where thrift is inculcated. Enough! Let us sit and drink our soup. If we wait until these greedy children have done we may faint for weakness."

Walking past the uncurtained window on his way back from the town Father Chisholm caught a glimpse of the two seated at their early lunch. The deep shadow of anxiety lifted momentarily from his face, his lips faintly smiled.

Despite his first premonitions, the accident of Polly's visit was an immense success; she fitted miraculously into the frame of the mission, and was enjoying herself with the same placidity that she would have displayed during a short week-end at Blackpool. Undismayed by clime or season, she would stalk silently to her seat in the kitchen garden and knit for hours among the cabbages with shoulders squared, elbows angled, and needles flashing, her mouth slightly pursed, her eyes remotely complacent, the yellow mission cat purring like mad, crouched half beneath her skirts. She was the closest crony of old Fu and became a hub round which the gloomy gardener revolved, exhibiting prodigious vegetables for her approval and prognosticating the weather with signs and baleful portents.

In her contact with the Sisters she never interfered, never assumed a privilege. Her tact was instinctive and beautiful, springing from her gift of silence, from the prosaic simplicity of her life. She had never been happier. She was realizing her cherished longing to see Francis at his missionary work, a priest of God, helped, perhaps, to the worthy end—though she would never have dreamed of voicing such a thought—by her own humble effort. The length of her stay, set primarily at two months, had been extended until January.

Her one regret, naïvely expressed, was that she had been unable to take this trip earlier in her life. Though she had served Ned hand and foot so long, his death had not freed her from responsibility. Judy remained, a constant anxiety, with her whims and giddiness, her capricious inconstancy of purpose. From her first employment with the Tynecastle Council she had passed through half a dozen secretarial positions, each acclaimed as perfect in the beginning, then presently thrown up in disgust. From a business career she had turned to pupil-teaching, but her course at the Normal College soon bored her, and she vaguely entertained the idea of entering a convent. At this stage, when twenty-seven years of age, she had suddenly discovered that her true vocation was to become a nurse and had joined the staff of the Northumberland General Hospital as a probationer. This was the circumstance which had provided Polly with her present opportunity—a freedom which, alas, seemed only momentary. Already, after four short months, the hardships of the probationer's life were discouraging Judy, and letters kept coming, full of petulance and grievance, hinting that Aunt Polly must return soon to look after her poor neglected niece.

As Francis pieced together the pattern of Polly's life at home—gradually, for she was never garrulous—he came to see her as a saint. Yet her fixity was not that of a plaster image. She had her foibles, and her genius for the malapropos still remained. For instance, with remarkable initiative, and a loyal desire to aid Francis in his work, she had practically reconverted two errant souls, who on one of her staid excursions through Pai-tan obsequiously attached themselves to her person and her purse. It had cost Francis some trouble to rid her of Hosannah and Philomena Wang.

If only for the consolation of their daily conversations, he had reason to value this amazing woman. Now, in the trials which had suddenly confronted him, he clung to her common sense.

As he reached his house, there, awaiting him on the porch verandah, stood

Sister Clotilde and Anna. He sighed. Was he never to have peace to consider the disquieting news he had received?

Clotilde's sallow face wore a nervous flush. She stood close to the girl, almost like a gaoler, restraining her with a freshly bandaged hand. Anna's eyes were dark with defiance. She also smelled of perfume.

Under his interrogating gaze Clotilde took a quick breath. "I had to ask Reverend Mother to let me bring Anna over. After all, in the basket workroom, she's under my special charge."

"Yes, Sister?" Father Chisholm forced himself to speak patiently. Sister Clotilde was quivering with hysterical indignation.

"I've put up with so much from her. Insolence and disobedience and laziness. Watching her upset the other girls. Yes, and steal! Why, even now she's reeking of Miss Bannon's Eau-de-Cologne. But this last—"

"Yes, Sister?"

Sister Clotilde reddened more deeply. It was a greater ordeal for her than for the graceless Anna.

"She's taken to going out at night. You know the place is infested with soldiers just now. She was out all last night with one of Wai-Chu's men, her bed not even slept in. And when I reasoned with her this morning, she struggled with me and bit me."

Father Chisholm turned his eyes on Anna. It seemed incredible that the little child he had held in his arms that winter night, who had come to him like a gift from heaven, should now confront him as a sulky and unruly young woman. In her teens, she was quite mature, with a full bosom, heavy eyes, and a plummy ripeness on her lips. She had always been different from the other children: uncaring, bold, never submissive. He thought: For once the copy-books are wrong—Anna has turned out no angel.

The heavy burden upon his mind made his voice mild. "Have you anything to say, Anna?"

"No."

"No, Father," Sister Clotilde hissed. Anna gave her a sullen glance of hatred.

"It seems a pity, after all we've tried to do for you, Anna, that you should repay us like this. Aren't you happy here?"

"No, I am not."

"Why?"

"I didn't ask to come to the convent. You didn't even buy me. I came for nothing. And I am tired of praying."

"But you don't pray all the time. You've got your work."

"I don't want to make baskets."

"Then we'll find something else for you to do."

"What else? Sewing? Am I to go on sewing all my life?"

Father Chisholm forced a smile. "Of course not. When you've learned all those useful things, one of our young men will want to marry you."

She gave him a sullen sneer, which said plainly: "I want something more exciting than your nice young men."

He was silent; then he said, somewhat bitterly, for her lack of gratitude hurt him: "No one wishes to keep you against your will. But until the district is more settled you must remain. Great trouble may be coming to the town. Indeed, great trouble may be coming to the world. While you are here you are safe. But you must keep the rule. Now go with Sister and obey her. If I find that you do not I shall be very angry."

He dismissed them both, then as Clotilde turned he said: "Ask Reverend Mother to come and see me, Sister." He watched them cross the compound, then went slowly to his room. As if he had not enough to weigh him down!

Five minutes later when Maria-Veronica entered he stood at the window viewing the city below. He let her join him there, keeping silent. At last he said: "My dear friend, I have two bad pieces of news for you, and the first is that we are likely to have a war here—before the year is out."

She gazed at him calmly, waiting. He swung round and faced her.

"I have just come from Mr. Chia. It is inevitable. For years the province has been dominated by Wai-Chu. As you know, he has bled the peasants to death with taxation and forced levies. If they didn't pay, their villages were destroyed—whole families slaughtered. But—brute though he is—the merchants of Pai-tan have always managed to buy him off." He paused. "Now another war lord is moving into the district—General Naian, from the lower Yangtze. He's reported to be not so bad as Wai—in fact our old friend Shon has gone over to him. But he wants Wai's province, that is, the privilege of squeezing the people there. He will march into Pai-tan. It is impossible to buy off both leaders. Only the victor can be bought off. So this time they must fight it out."

She smiled slightly. "I knew most of this before. Why are you so ominous today?"

"Perhaps because war is in the air." He gave her a queer strained glance. "Besides, it will be a bitter battle."

Her smile deepened. "Neither you nor I are afraid of a battle."

There was a silence. He glanced away. "Of course, I am thinking of ourselves, exposed here outside the city walls—if Wai attacks Pai-tan we shall be in the middle of it. But I am thinking more of the people—so poor, so helpless and so hungry. I have come to love them here with all my heart. They only beg to be left in peace, to get a simple living from the soil, to live in their homes quietly with their families. For years they've been oppressed by one tyrant. Now, because another appears on the scene, guns are being thrust into their hands, yes, into the hands of the men of our congregation, flags are being waved, the usual cries are already raised—Freedom and Liberty. Hatreds are being worked up. Then, because two dictators wish it, these poor creatures will fall upon one another. And to what purpose? After the slaughter, when the smoke and the shooting have cleared away, there will be more taxation, more oppression, a heavier yoke than before." He sighed, "Can one help feeling sad for poor mankind?"

She moved somewhat restively. "You have not a great opinion of war. Surely some wars can be just and glorious? History proves it. My family has fought in many such."

He did not answer for a long time. When at last he turned to her the lines about his eyes had deepened. He spoke slowly, heavily. "It is strange you should say that at this moment." He paused, averting his eyes. "Our little trouble here is only the echo of a greater disorder." He found it difficult, most difficult, to continue. But he forced himself on. "Mr. Chia has had word by special courier from his business associates in Sen-siang. Germany has invaded Belgium and is at war with France and Britain."

There was a short pause. Her face altered, she did not speak, but stood silent, her head immobile, unnaturally arrested.

At length he said: "The others will soon know. But we must not let it make any difference to us at the mission."

"No, we must not." She answered mechanically, as though her gaze were fixed thousands of miles away.

The first sign came some days later: a small Belgian flag, sewn hurriedly with coloured threads upon a square of silk, and placed prominently in Sister Martha's bedroom window. That same day, indeed, Martha scurried in early to the Sisters' house from the dispensary, with her new eagerness, then gave a cluck of nervous satisfaction. They had come—what she looked forward to with all her soul: the newspapers. It was the *Intelligence*, an American daily published in Shanghai, and it arrived, in batches, erratically, about once a month. Hurriedly, her fingers trembling between expectation and apprehension, she undid the wrappers at the window.

For a minute she turned the pages, hastily. Then she gave an outraged cry. "What monsters! Oh my God, it is insupportable!" She beckoned urgently, not lifting her head, to Clotilde, who had come quickly into the room, drawn by the same magnetic force. "Look, Sister! They are in Louvain—the Cathedral is in ruins—shelled to pieces. And Metrieux—ten kilometers from my home—destroyed to the ground. Oh, dear God! Such a fine and prosperous town!"

Linked by common calamity, the two Sisters bent over the sheets, punctuating their reading with exclamations of horror.

"The very altar blown to pieces!" Martha wrung her hands. "Metrieux! I drove there with my father in the high cart when I was a little thing of seven. Such a market! We bought twelve grey geese that day . . . so fat and beautiful . . . and now . . ."

Clotilde, with dilated eyes, was reading of the battle of the Marne. "They are slaughtering our brave people. Such butchery, such vileness!"

Though Reverend Mother had entered and seated herself quietly at the table, Clotilde remained unconscious of her presence. But Martha saw her, from the corner of her eye, and Martha was beside herself.

Suffused with indignation, her voice shaking, she pointed her finger to a paragraph. "Consider this, Sister Clotilde. 'It is reliably reported that the convent of Louvain was violated by the German invaders. Unimpeachable sources confirm the fact that many innocent children have been mercilessly butchered.'"

Clotilde was pale as ivory. "In the Franco-Prussian War it was the same. They are inhuman. No wonder, in this good American journal, they already call them Huns." She hissed the word.

"I cannot allow you to speak in such terms of my people."

Clotilde spun round, supporting herself on the window frame, taken aback. But Martha was prepared.

"Your people, Reverend Mother? I would not be so proud to own them if I were you. Brutal barbarians. Murderers of women and little children."

"The German Army is comprised of gentlemen. I do not believe that vulgar sheet. It is not true."

Martha spread her hands on her hips; her harsh peasant voice grated with resentment. "Is it true when the vulgar sheet reports the ruthless invasion of a little peaceful country by your gentlemanly army?"

Reverend Mother was paler now than Clotilde.

"Germany must have her place in the sun."

"So she kills and plunders, blows up cathedrals, and the market place I went to as a girl, because she wants the sun and the moon, the greedy swine—"

"Sister!" Dignified even in her agitation, Reverend Mother rose up. "There is such a thing as justice in this world. Germany and Austria have never had justice. And do not forget that my brother is fighting even now to forge the new Teutonic destiny. Therefore I forbid you both, as your superior, to speak any such slanders as have just defiled your lips."

There was an intolerable pause, then she turned to leave the room. As she reached the door Martha cried: "Your famous destiny isn't forged yet. The Allies will win the war."

Maria-Veronica gave her a cold and pitying smile. She went out.

The feud intensified, fanned by the stray news that filtered to the far-off mission itself under threat of war. Though the French Sister and the Belgian had never greatly liked each other, now they were linked in bosom friendship. Martha was protective towards the weaker Clotilde, solicitous for her health, dosing her troublesome cough, giving her choice pieces from every dish. Together, openly, they knitted mittens and socks to be sent to the brave *blessés*. They would talk of their beloved countries, over Reverend Mother's head, with many sighs and innuendoes—careful, oh so careful to give no offence. Then Martha with a strange significance would remark: "Let us go over a moment to pray for our intention."

Maria-Veronica endured it all with a proud silence. She, too, prayed for victory. Father Chisholm could see the three faces in a row, beatifically up-turned, praying for opposing victories while he, careworn and harassed, watch-ing Wai's forces march and countermarch amongst the hills, hearing of Naian's final mobilization, prayed for peace . . . safety for his people . . . and enough food for the children.

Presently Sister Clotilde began to teach her class the *Marseillaise*. She did it secretly, when Reverend Mother was engaged in the basket room at the other end of the mission. The class, being imitative, picked it up quickly. Then, one forenoon as Maria-Veronica came slowly across the compound, her air fatigued and noticeably constrained, there burst, through the open windows of Clotilde's class-room, to the accompaniment of a thumped piano, the full-throated blast of the French national anthem.

"Allons, enfants de la patrie . . ."

For an instant Maria-Veronica's step faltered; then her figure, which showed signs of softening, became steeled. All her fortitude was summoned to sustain her. She walked on with her head high.

One afternoon towards the end of the month, Clotilde was again in her schoolroom. The class, having given its daily rendering of the *Marseillaise*, had now concluded its catechism lesson. And Sister Clotilde, following her recently instituted custom, remarked:—

"Kneel down, dear children, and we will say a little prayer for the brave French soldiers."

The children knelt down obediently and repeated the three Hail Marys after her.

Clotilde was about to signal them to rise when, with a slight shock, she became aware of Reverend Mother standing behind her. Maria-Veronica was calm and pleasant. Gazing across Sister Clotilde's shoulder she addressed the class.

"And now, children, it is only right that you should say the same prayer for the brave German soldiers."

Clotilde turned a dirty green. Her breath seemed to choke her.

"This is my class-room, Reverend Mother."

Maria-Veronica ignored her. "Come now, dear children, for the brave Germans, 'Hail Mary full of Grace . . .'"

Clotilde's breast heaved, her pale lips retracted from her narrow teeth. Convulsively, she drew back her hand and slapped her superior on the face.

There was a terrified hush. Then Clotilde burst into tears and ran sobbing from the room.

Maria-Veronica moved not a muscle. With that same agreeable smile she said to the children:—

"Sister Clotilde is unwell. You see how she knocked against me. I will finish the class. But first, children, three Hail Marys for the good German soldiers."

When the prayer concluded she seated herself, unruffled, at the high desk and opened the book.

That evening, entering the dispensary unexpectedly, Father Chisholm surprised Sister Clotilde measuring herself a liberal dose of chlorodyne. She whipped round at his step and almost dropped the full minim glass, her cheek flooded by a painful flush. The episode in the class-room had strung her to breaking pitch.

She stammered: "I take a little for my stomach. We have so much to worry us these days." He knew, from the measure and her manner, that she was using the drug as a sedative.

"I wouldn't take it too often, Sister. It contains a good deal of morphine."

When she had gone he locked the bottle in the poison cupboard. As he stood in the empty dispensary, torn by the anxiety of their danger here, weighed down by the sheer futility of that far-off, awful war, he felt a slow surge of anger at the senseless rancour of these women. He had hoped it would settle. But it had not settled. He compressed his lips in sudden resolution.

After school that day he sent for the three Sisters. He made them stand before his desk, his face unusually stern, choosing his words, almost with bitterness.

"Your behaviour at a time like this is greatly distressing me. It must cease. You have no justification for it whatsoever."

There was a short pause. Clotilde was shaking with contention. "But we have justification." She fumbled in the pocket of her robe and agitatedly thrust into his hand a much-creased, cut-out section of newsprint. "Read this, I beg of you. From a prince of the Church."

He scanned the cutting, slowly read it aloud. It was the report of a pronouncement by Cardinal Amette, from the pulpit of the Cathedral of Notre Dame in Paris. " 'Beloved Brethren, Comrades in Arms of France and her Glorious Allies, Almighty God is upon our side. God has helped us to our greatness in the past. He will help us once again in our hour of need. God stands beside our brave soldiers in the battlefield, strengthening their arms, girding them against the enemy. God protects his own. God will give us victory . . .' "

He broke off, he would go no further.

A rigid silence followed. Clotilde's head trembled with nervous triumph and Martha's face was dogged with vindication. But Maria-Veronica remained undefeated. Stiffly, from the black cloth bag she wore upon her girdle, she unfolded a neat square clipping.

"I know nothing of the prejudiced opinion of any French Cardinal. But here is the joint statement to the German people of the Archbishops of Cologne, Munich and Essen." In a cold and haughty voice she read: " 'Beloved People of the Fatherland, God is with us in this most righteous struggle which has been forced upon us. Therefore we command you in God's name to fight to the last drop of your blood for the honour and glory of our country.

God knows in his wisdom and justice that we are in the right and God will give us . . .' "

"That is enough."

Francis stopped her, struggling for self-control, his soul suffused by wave upon wave of anger and despair. Here, before him, was the essence of man's malice and hypocrisy. The senselessness of life seemed suddenly to overwhelm him. Its hopelessness crushed him.

He remained with his head resting upon his hand, then in a low voice he said: "God knows God must get sick of all this crying out to God!"

Mastered by his emotion he rose abruptly and began to pace the room. "I can't refute the contradictions of cardinals and archbishops with still more contradictions. I wouldn't presume to. I'm nobody—an insignificant Scottish priest stuck in the wilds of China on the edge of a bandit's war. But don't you see the folly and the baseness of the whole transaction? We, the Holy Catholic Church—yes, all the great Churches of Christendom—condone this world war. We go further—we sanctify it. We send millions of our faithful sons to be maimed and slaughtered, to be mangled in their bodies and their souls, to kill and destroy one another, with a hypocritical smile, an apostolic blessing. Die for your country and all will be forgiven you. Patriotism! King and Emperor! From ten thousand smug pulpits: 'Render to Cæsar the things that are Cæsar's . . .' " He broke off, hands clenched, eyes remotely burning. "There is no Cæsar nowadays—only financiers and statesmen who want diamond mines in Africa and rubber in the slave-driven Congo. Christ preached everlasting love. He preached the brotherhood of man. He did not climb the mountain and shout, 'Kill! kill! Go forth in hatred and plunge a bayonet into thy brother's belly!' It isn't His voice that resounds in the churches and high cathedrals of Christendom today—but the voice of time-servers and cowards." His lips quivered. "How in the name of the God we serve can we come to these foreign lands, the lands we call pagan, presuming to convert the people to a doctrine we give the lie to by our every deed? Small wonder they jeer at us. Christianity—the religion of lies! Of class and money and national hatreds! Of wicked wars!" He stopped short, perspiration beading his brow, his eyes dark with anguish. "Why doesn't the Church seize her opportunity? What a chance to justify herself as the Living Bride of Christ! Instead of preaching hatred and incitement, to cry, in every land, with the tongues of her pontiff and all her priests: 'Throw down your weapons. Thou shalt not kill. We command you *not* to fight.' Yes, there would be persecutions and many executions. But these would be martyrdoms—not murders. The dead would decorate, not desecrate, our altars." His voice dropped, his attitude was calmer, strangely prophetic. "The Church will suffer for its cowardice. A viper nourished in one's bosom will one day strike that bosom. To sanction the might of arms is to invite destruction. The day may come when great military forces will break loose and turn upon the Church, corrupting millions of her children, sending her down again—a timid shadow—into the Catacombs."

There was a strained stillness when he concluded. Martha and Clotilde hung their heads, as though touched, against their will. But Maria-Veronica, with something of the arrogance that marked those early days of strife, faced him with a cold clear gaze, hardened by a glint of mockery.

"That was most impressive, Father . . . worthy of these cathedrals you decry. . . . But aren't your words rather empty if you don't live up to them . . . here in Pai-tan?"

The blood rushed to his brow, then quickly ebbed. He answered without anger.

"I have solemnly forbidden every man in my congregation to fight in this wicked conflict which threatens us. I have made them swear to come with their families inside the mission gates, when trouble breaks. Whatever the consequences I shall be responsible."

All three Sisters looked at him. A faint tremor passed over Maria-Veronica's cold still face. Yet, as they filed from the room, he could see they were not reconciled. He suddenly felt a shiver of unnameable fear. He had the strange sensation that time swung suspended, balanced in fateful expectation of what might come to pass.

9

On a Sunday morning, he was awakened by a sound which he had dreaded for many days—the dull concussion of artillery in action. He jumped up and hurried to the window. On the western hills, a few miles distant, six light field-pieces had begun to shell the city. He dressed rapidly and went downstairs. At the same moment Joseph came running from the porch.

"It has begun, Master. Last night General Naian marched into Pai-tan and the Wai forces are attacking him. Already our people are arriving at the gates."

He glanced swiftly over Joseph's shoulder. "Admit them at once."

While his servant went back to unlock the gates he hastened over to the home. The children were collected at breakfast and amazingly undisturbed. One or two of the smaller girls whimpered at the sudden distant banging. He went round the long tables, forcing himself to smile. "It is only firecrackers, children. For a few days we are going to have big ones."

The three Sisters stood apart at the head of the refectory. Maria-Veronica was calm as marble but he saw at once that Clotilde was upset. She seemed to hold herself in, and her hands were clenched in her long sleeves. Every time the guns went off she paled. Nodding towards the children, he joked expressly for her. "If only we could keep them eating all the time!"

Sister Martha cackled too quickly: "Yes, yes, then it would be easy." As Clotilde's stiff face made the effort to smile the far-off guns rolled again.

After a moment he left the refectory and pressed on to the lodge where Joseph and Fu stood at the wide-open gates. His people were pouring in with their belongings, young and old, poor humble illiterate creatures, frightened, eager for safety, the very substance of suffering mortality. His heart swelled as he thought of the sanctuary he was giving them. The good brick walls would afford them sound protection. He blessed the vanity which had made him build them high. With a queer tenderness, he watched one aged ragged dame, whose withered face bespoke a patient resignation to a long life of privation, stumble in with her bundle, establish herself quietly in a corner of the crowded compound, and painstakingly begin to cook a handful of beans in an old condensed-milk can.

At his side, Fu was imperturbable but Joseph, the valiant, showed a slight variation of his normal colour. Marriage had altered him, he was no longer a careless youth, but a husband and a father, with all the responsibilities of a man of property.

"They should hurry," he muttered restively. "We must lock and barricade the gates."

Father Chisholm put his hand on his servant's shoulder. "Only when they are all inside, Joseph."

"We are going to have trouble," Joseph answered with a shrug. "Some of our men who have come in were conscripted by Wai. He will not be pleased when he finds they prefer to be here rather than to fight."

"Nevertheless they will not fight." The priest answered firmly. "Come, now, don't be despondent. Run up our flag, while I watch at the gate."

Joseph departed, grumbling, and in a few minutes the mission flag, of pale blue silk with a deeper blue St. Andrew's cross, broke and fluttered on the flagstaff. Father Chisholm's heart gave an added bound of pride, his breast was filled with a quick elation. That flag stood for peace and goodwill to all men, a neutral flag, the flag of universal love.

When the last straggler had entered they locked the gates provisionally. At that moment Fu drew the priest's attention to the cedar grove, some three hundred yards to the left, on their own Jade hillside. In this clump of trees a long gun had unexpectedly appeared. Indistinctly, between the branches, he could see the quick movements of soldiers, in Wai green tunics, trenching and fortifying the position. Though he knew little of such matters the gun seemed a far more powerful weapon than the ordinary field-pieces now in action. And even as he gazed there came a swift flash, followed instantly by a terrifying concussion and the wild scream of the shell overhead.

The change was devastating. As the new heavy gun deafeningly pounded the city, it was answered by a Naian battery of ineffectual range. Small shells, falling short of the cedar grove, rained about the mission. One plunged into the kitchen garden, erupting a shower of earth. Immediately a cry of terror rose in the crowded compound and Francis ran to shepherd his congregation from the open into the greater safety of the church.

The noise and confusion increased. In the class-room the children were in a milling stampede. It was Reverend Mother who stemmed the panic. Calm and smiling, but shouting above the bursting shells, she drew the children round her, made them close their ears with their fingers and sing at the pitch of their lungs. When they became calmer they were herded quickly across the courtyard into the cellars of the convent. Joseph's wife and the two children were already there. It was strange to see all these small yellow faces, in the half-light, amongst stores of oil and candles and sweet potatoes, below the long shelves on which stood Sister Martha's preserves. The screaming of the shells was less down below. But from time to time there was a heavy shock, the building shook to its foundations.

While Polly remained below with the children, Martha and Clotilde scurried to fetch them lunch. Clotilde, always highly strung, was now almost out of her wits. As she crossed the compound a spent piece of metal struck her lightly on her cheek.

"Oh, God!" she cried, sinking down. "I'm killed!" Pale as death she began to make an act of contrition.

"Don't be a fool." Martha shook her fiercely by the shoulder. "Come and get these wretched brats some porridge."

Father Chisholm had been called by Joseph to the dispensary. One of the women had been slightly wounded in the hand. When the bleeding was controlled and the wound bandaged, the priest sent both Joseph and the patient over to the church, then hurried to the window, anxiously gauging the effects of the bursts, damaging puffs of débris, as the shells from the Wai gun exploded in Pai-tan. Sworn to neutrality, he could not repress a terrible desire, surging and devastating, that Wai, the unspeakable, might be defeated.

Suddenly, as he stood there, he saw a detachment of Naian soldiers strike out from the Manchu Gate. They flowed out like a stream of grey ants, perhaps two hundred of them, and began in a ragged line to mount the hill.

He watched them with a dreadful fascination. They came quickly, at first, in little sudden rushes. He could see them vividly against the untroubled green of the hillside. Bent double, each man bolted forward, carrying his rifle, for a dozen yards, then flung himself, desperately, upon the earth.

The Wai gun continued firing into the city. The grey figures drew nearer. They were crawling now, flat on their stomachs, completing their toiling ascent in that blazing sun. At a distance of a hundred paces from the cypress grove they paused, hugging the slope, for a full three minutes. Then their leader gave a sign. With a shout they jumped erect and rushed on the emplacement.

They covered half the distance rapidly. A few seconds and they would have reached their objective. Then the harsh vibration of machine guns resounded in the brilliant air.

There were three, manned and waiting, in the cypress grove. At their jarring impact the rushing grey figures seemed to stop, to fall in sheer bewilderment. Some fell forwards, others on their backs, some for a moment upon their knees, as though in prayer. They fell all ways, comically, then lay still, in the sunshine. At that, the rattling of the Maxims ceased. All was stillness, warm and quiet, until the heavy concussion of the big gun boomed again, reawakening everything to life—all but those quiet little figures on the green hillside.

Father Chisholm stood rigid, consumed by the torment of his mind. This was war. This toylike pantomime of destruction, magnified a million times, was what was happening now on the fertile plains of France. He shuddered, and prayed passionately: O Lord, let me live and die for peace.

Suddenly his haggard eye picked up a sign of movement on the hill. One of the Naian soldiers was not dead. Slowly and painfully, he was dragging himself down the slope in the direction of the mission. It was possible to observe the ebbing of his strength in the gradual slowing of his progress. Finally he came to rest, utterly spent, lying on his side, some sixty yards from the upper gate.

Francis thought, He is dead . . . this is no time for mock-heroics, if I go out there I will get a bullet in my head . . . I must not do it. But he found himself leaving the dispensary and moving towards the upper gate. He had a shamed consciousness as he opened the gate: fortunately no one was watching from the mission. He walked out into the bright sunshine upon the hillside.

His short black figure and long black shadow were shockingly obvious. If the mission windows were blank he felt many eyes upon him from the cypress grove. He dared not hurry.

The wounded soldier was breathing in sobbing gasps. Both hands were pressed weakly against his lacerated belly. His human eyes gazed back at Francis with an anguished interrogation.

Francis lifted him on his back and carried him into the mission. He propped him up while he relocked the gate. Then he pulled him gently into shelter. When he had given him a drink of water he found Maria-Veronica and told her she must prepare a cot in the dispensary.

That afternoon another unsuccessful raid was made on the gun position. And when night fell Father Chisholm and Joseph brought in five more wounded men. The dispensary assumed the appearance of a hospital.

Next morning the shelling continued without interruption. The noise was interminable. The city took severe punishment, and it looked as if a breach were being driven in the western wall. Suddenly, at the angle of the Western Gate, about a mile away, Francis saw the main body of the Wai forces bearing in upon the broken parapet. He thought with a sinking heart, They are in the city. But he could not judge.

The remainder of the day passed in a state of sick uncertainty. In the late afternoon he liberated the children from the cellar and his congregation from the church to let them have a breath of air. At least they were unharmed. As he went among them, heartening them, he buoyed himself with this simple fact.

Then, as he finished his round, he found Joseph at his side, wearing for the first time a look of unmistakable fear.

"Master, a messenger has come over from the Wai gun in the cedar grove."

At the main gate three Wai soldiers were peering between the bars while an officer, whom Father Chisholm took to be the captain of the gun crew, stood by. Without hesitation Francis unlocked the gate and went outside.

"What do you wish of me?"

The officer was short, thickset and middle-aged, with a heavy face and thick mulish lips. He breathed through his mouth, which hung open, showing his stained upper teeth. He wore the usual peaked cap and green uniform with a leather belt, bearing a green tassel. His puttees ended in a pair of broken canvas plimsolls.

"General Wai favours you with several requests. In the first place you are to cease sheltering the enemy wounded."

Francis flushed sharply, nervously. "The wounded are doing no harm. They are beyond fighting."

The other took no notice of this protest. "Secondly, General Wai affords you the privilege of contributing to his commissariat. Your first donation will be eight hundred pounds of rice and all American canned goods in your storerooms."

"We are already short of food." Despite his resolution, Francis felt his temper rise; he spoke heatedly. "You cannot rob us in this fashion."

As before, the gun captain let the argument pass unheeded. He had a way of standing sideways, with his feet apart, delivering each word across his shoulder, like an insult.

"Thirdly, it is essential that you clear your compound of all whom you are protecting there. General Wai believes you are harbouring deserters from his forces. If this is so they will be shot. All other able-bodied men must enlist immediately in the Wai army."

This time Father Chisholm made no protest. He stood tense and pale, his hands clenched, his eyes blazing with indignation. The air before him vibrated on a red haze. "Suppose I refuse to comply with these most moderate solicitations?"

The obstinate face before him almost smiled. "That, I assure you, would be a mistake. I should then most reluctantly turn our gun upon you and in five minutes reduce your mission, and all within, to an inconsiderable powder."

There was a silence. The three soldiers were grimacing, making signs to some of the younger women in the compound. Francis saw the situation as cold and clear-cut as a picture etched on steel. He must yield, under threat of annihilation, to these inhuman demands. And that yielding would be but the prelude to greater and still greater demands. A dreadful sweep of anger conquered him. His mouth went dry, he kept his burning eyes on the ground.

"General Wai must realize that it will take some hours to make ready these stores for him . . . and to prepare my people . . . for their departure. How much time does he afford me?"

"Until tomorrow." The officer answered promptly. "Provided you deliver to me before midnight at my gun position a personal offering of tinned goods together with sufficient valuables to constitute a suitable present."

Again there was a silence. Francis felt a dark choking swelling of his heart.

He lied in a suppressed voice: "I agree. I have no alternative. I will bring you your gift tonight."

"I commend your wisdom. I shall expect you. And I advise you not to fail." The captain's tone held a heavy irony. He bowed to the priest, shouted a command to his men, and marched off squatly towards the cedar grove.

Francis re-entered the mission in a trembling fury. The clang of the heavy iron gate behind him set a chain of febrile echoes ringing through his brain. What a fool he had been, in his fatuous elation, to imagine he could escape this trial. He . . . the dove-like pacifist. He gritted his teeth as wave after wave of pitiless self-anger assailed him. Abruptly, he rid himself of Joseph and of the silent gathering who timidly searched his face for the answer to their fears.

Usually he took his troubles to the Church, but now he could not bow his head and tamely murmur: Lord, I will suffer and submit. He went to his room and flung himself violently into the wicker chair. His thoughts for once ran riot, without the rein of meekness or forbearance. He groaned as he thought of his pretty gospel of peace. What was to happen to his fine words now? What was to happen to them all?

Another barb struck him—the needlessness, the crass inanity of Polly's presence in the mission at such a time. Under his breath he cursed Mrs. Fiske for the interfering officiousness which had subjected his poor old aunt to this fantastic tribulation. God! He seemed to have the cares of all the world upon his bent incompetent shoulders. He jumped up. He could not, he would not, yield, weakly, to the maddening menace of Wai's threat and the deadlier menace of that gun which grew in his feverish imagination, swelled to such gigantic size it became the symbol of all wars, and of every brutal weapon built by man for the slaughter of mankind.

As he paced his room, tense and sweating, there came a mild knock at his door. Polly entered the room.

"I don't like to disturb you, Francis . . . but if you have a minute to spare. . . ." She smiled remotely, using the privilege of her affection to disturb his privacy.

"What is it, Aunt Polly?" He composed his features with a great effort. Perhaps she had further news, another message from Wai.

"I'd be glad if you'd try on this comforter, Francis. I don't want to get it too large. It should keep you nice and warm in the winter." Under his bloodshot gaze she produced a woollen Balaclava helmet she was knitting him.

He scarcely knew whether to weep or laugh. It was so like Polly. When the crack of doom resounded she would no doubt pause to offer him a cup of tea. There was nothing for it but to comply. He stood and let her fit the half-finished capote upon his head.

"It looks all right," she murmured critically. "Maybe a trifle wide about the neck." With her head on one side and her long wrinkled upper lip pursed, she counted the stitches with her bone knitting-needle. "Sixty-eight. I'll take it in four. Thank you, Francis. I hope I haven't troubled you."

Tears started to his eyes. He had an almost irresistible desire to put his head on her hard shoulder and cry brokenly, outrageously: "Aunt Polly! I'm in such a mess. What in God's name am I to do?"

As it was, he gazed at her a long time. He muttered: "Don't you worry, Polly, about the danger we're all in here?"

She smiled faintly. "Worry killed the cat. Besides . . . aren't you looking after us?"

Her ineradicable belief in him was like a breath of pure cold air. He watched her wrap up her work, skewer it with needles and, giving her competent nod, silently withdraw. Somehow, beneath her casualness, her air of commonplace, there lay a hint of deeper knowledge. He had no doubts now as to what he must do. He took his hat and coat, made his way secretly towards the lower gate.

Outside the mission the deep darkness blindfolded him. But he went down the Brilliant Green Jade road towards the city, rapidly, heedless of any obstacle.

At the Manchu Gate he was sharply halted and a lantern thrust close against his face, while the sentries scrutinized him. He had counted on being recognized—he was, after all, a familiar figure in the city—yet his luck went further still. One of the three soldiers was a follower of Shon who had worked all through the plague epidemic. The man vouched for him immediately and after a short exchange with his companions agreed to take him at once to the Lieutenant.

The streets were deserted, choked in parts with rubble and ominously silent. From the distant eastern section there came occasional bursts of firing. As the priest followed the quick padding footsteps of his guide he had a strange exhilarating sense of guilt.

Shon was in his old quarters at the cantonment, snatching a short rest, fully dressed, on that same camp bed which had been Dr. Tulloch's. He was unshaven, his puttees white with mud, and there were dark shadows of fatigue beneath his eyes. He propped himself upon his elbow as Francis entered.

"Well!" he said slowly. "I have been dreaming about you, my friend, and your excellent establishment on the hill."

He slid from the bed, turned up the lamp and sat down at the table. "You do not want some tea? No more do I. But I am glad to see you. I regret I cannot present you to General Naian. He is leading an attack on the East section . . . or perhaps executing some spies. He is a most enlightened man."

Francis sat down at the table, still in silence. He knew Shon well enough to let him talk himself out. And tonight the other had less to say than usual. He glanced guardedly at the priest. "Why don't you ask it, my friend? You are here for help which I cannot give. We should have been in your mission two days ago except that then we should merely have been blown to pieces together by that infamous Sorana."

"You mean the gun?"

"Yes, the gun," Shon answered with polite irony. "I have known it too well for a period of years . . . It came originally from a French gunboat. General Hsiah had it first. Twice I took it from him with great trouble, but each time he bought it back from my commandant. Then Wai had a concubine from Pekin who cost him twenty thousand silver dollars. She was an Armenian lady, very beautiful, named Sorana. When he ceased to regard her with affection he exchanged her to Hsiah for the gun. You saw us try to capture it yesterday. It is not possible. . . . Fortified . . . Across that open country . . . with only our *piff-paff* battery to protect us. Perhaps it is going to lose us our war . . . just when I am making a great personal advancement with General Naian."

There was a pause. The priest said stiffly: "Suppose it were possible to capture the gun?"

"No. Do not entice me." Shon shook his head with concealed bitterness. "But if ever I get near that dishonourable weapon I shall finish it for good."

"We can get very near the gun."

Shon raised his head deliberately, sounding Francis with his eyes. A glint of excitement enlivened him. He waited.

Father Chisholm leaned forward, his lips making a tight line. "This evening under threat of shelling the mission, the Wai officer who commands the gun crew ordered me to bring food and money to him before midnight . . ."

He went on, gazing at Shon, then abruptly broke off, conscious that he need say no more. For a full minute nothing was said. Shon was thinking, behind his careless brow. At last he smiled—at least the muscles of his face went through the act of smiling, but there was nothing of humour in his eyes.

"My friend, I must continue to regard you as a gift from heaven."

A cloud passed over the priest's set face. "I have forgotten about heaven tonight."

Shon nodded, not thinking of that remark. "Now listen and I will tell you what we shall do."

An hour later Francis and Shon left the cantonment and made their way through the Manchu Gate towards the mission. Shon had changed his uniform for a worn blue blouse and a pair of coolie's slacks, rolled to the knee. A flat pleated hat covered his head. On his back he carried a large sack, tightly sewn with twine. Following silently, at a distance of some three hundred paces, were twenty of his men.

Halfway up the Brilliant Green Jade road Francis touched his companion on the arm. "Now it is my turn."

"It is not heavy." Shon shifted the bundle tenderly to his other shoulder. "And I am perhaps more used to it than you."

They reached the shelter of the mission walls. No lights were showing, the outline which compassed everything he loved lay shadowy and unprotected. The silence was absolute. Suddenly, from within the lodge, he heard the melodious strike of the American chiming clock he had given Joseph for a wedding present. He counted automatically. Eleven o'clock.

Shon had given the men a final word of instruction. One of them, squatting against the wall, suppressed a cough which seemed to echo out across the hill. Shon cursed him in a violent whisper. The men were not important. It was what Shon and he must do together that mattered. He felt his friend peering at him through the silent darkness.

"You know exactly what is going to occur?"

"Yes."

"When I fire into the can of gasoline it will ignite instantly and explode the cordite. But before that, even before I raise my revolver, you must begin to move away. You must be well away. The concussion will be extreme." He paused. "Let us go if you are ready. And for the love of your Lord of Heaven keep the torch away from the sack."

Nerving himself, Francis took matches from his pocket and let the split reed flare. Then, holding it up, he stepped from the cover of the mission wall and walked openly towards the cypress grove. Shon came behind him, like a servant, bearing the sack on his back, as if groaning beneath its weight, taking care to make a noise.

The distance was not great. At the edge of the grove he halted, called out into the watchful stillness of the invisible trees:—

"I have come as requested. Take me to your leader."

There was an interval of silence; then, close behind them, a sudden movement. Francis swung round and saw two of Wai's men standing in the pool of smoky glare.

"You are expected, Bewitcher. Proceed without undue fear."

They were escorted through a formidable maze of shallow trenches and sharp-ended bamboo stakes to the centre of the grove. Here the priest's heart sharply missed a beat. Behind a breastwork of earth and cedar branches, the crew dispersed in attitudes of care beside it, stood the long-muzzled gun.

"Have you brought all that was demanded of you?"

Francis recognized the voice of his visitor earlier that evening. He lied more readily this time.

"I have brought a great load of tinned goods . . . which will certainly please you."

Shon exhibited the sack, moving nearer, a trifle nearer, to the gun.

"It is not so great a load." The captain of the gun crew stepped into the light. "Have you brought money also?"

"Yes."

"Where is it?" The captain felt the neck of the sack.

"Not there." Francis spoke hurriedly, with a start. "I have the money in my purse."

The captain gazed at him, diverted from his examination of the sack, his expression lit by a sudden cupidity. A group of soldiers had collected, their staring faces all bent upon the priest.

"Listen, all of you." Francis held their attention, with a desperate intensity. He could see Shon edging imperceptibly into the fringe of shadow, closer, still closer to the gun. "I ask you—I beg you—to leave us unmolested in the mission."

Contempt showed in the captain's face. He smiled derisively. "You shall be unmolested . . . until tomorrow." Someone laughed in the background. "Then we shall protect your women."

Francis hardened his heart. Shon, as though exhausted, had unloaded the sack under the breech of the gun. Pretending to wipe the perspiration from his brow he came back a little towards the priest. The crowd of soldiers had increased and were growing impatient. Francis strove to gain one minute of extra time for Shon.

"I do not doubt your word but I should value some assurance from General Wai."

"General Wai is in the city. You will see him later."

The captain spoke curtly and stepped out to get the money. From the corner of his eye, Francis saw Shon's hand go beneath his blouse. It is coming now, he thought. In the same moment, he heard the loud report of the revolver shot and the impact of the bullet as it struck the oil tin inside the sack. Braced for the convulsion, he could not understand. There was no explosion. Shon in swift succession fired three further shots into the tin. Francis saw the gasoline flood all over the sacking. He thought, with a kind of sick disillusionment yet quicker than the thudding shots: Shon was mistaken, the bullets won't ignite the gasoline, or perhaps it is only kerosene they put inside the tin. He saw Shon shooting into the crowd now, struggling to free his gun, shouting hopelessly to his own men to rush in. He saw the captain and a dozen soldiers closing on him. It all happened as swiftly as his thought. He felt a final, devastating wave of anger and despair. Deliberately, as though casting with a salmon rod, he drew back his arm and threw his torch.

His accuracy was beautiful. The blazing flare arched like a comet through the night and hit the oil-soaked sacking squarely in the centre. Instantly a great sheet of sound and light struck at him. He no more than sensed the brilliant flash when the earth erupted and amidst a frightful detonation a blast of scorching air blew him backwards into crashing darkness. He had never lost consciousness before. He seemed falling, falling, into space and blackness, clutching for support and finding none, falling to annihilation, to oblivion.

When his senses returned he found himself stretched in the open, limp but unhurt, with Shon pulling his ear-lobes to bring him round. Dimly he saw the red sky above him. The whole cypress grove was ablaze, crackling and roaring like a pyre.

"Is the gun finished?"

Shon stopped the ear-tweaking and sat up, relieved.

"Yes, it is finished. And some thirty of Wai's soldiers blown to pieces with it." His teeth showed white in his scorched face. "My friend, I congratulate you. I have never seen such a lovely killing in my life. Another such and you may have me for a Christian."

The next few days brought a terrible confusion of mind and spirit to Father Chisholm. The physical reaction to his adventure almost prostrated him. He was no virile hero of romantic fiction but a stubby, short-winded little man well over forty. He felt shaken and dizzy. His head ached so persistently he had to drag himself to his room several times a day to plunge his splitting brow in the tepid water of his ewer. And through this bodily suffering ran the greater anguish of his soul, a chaotic mixture of triumph and remorse, a heavy and relentless wonder that he, a priest of God, should have raised his hand to slay his fellow men. He could barely find self-vindication in the safety of his people. His strangest torment lay in the stabbing recollection of his own unconsciousness under the shock of the explosion. Was death like that? A total oblivion . . .

No one but Polly suspected that he had left the mission grounds that night. He could feel her tranquil gaze travelling from his own silent and diminished form to the charred cedar stumps which marked the remnants of the gun emplacement. There was infinite understanding in the banal phrase she spoke to him:—

"Somebody has done us a good turn by getting that nuisance out of the way."

Fighting continued in the outskirts of the city and in the hills to the eastward. By the fourth day reports reaching the mission indicated that the struggle was turning against Wai.

The end of that week came grey and overcast, with heavy gathering clouds. On Saturday the firing in Pai-tan dwindled to a few spasmodic rattles. Watching from his balcony Father Chisholm saw strings of figures in the Wai green retreating from the Western Gate. Many of these had thrown away their arms in the fear of being captured and shot as rebels. This Francis knew to be an indication of Wai's reverses and of his inability to effect a compromise with General Naian.

Outside the mission, behind the upper wall where some bamboo canes screened them from observation from the city, a number of these scattered soldiers had collected. Their voices, indeterminate and plainly frightened, could be heard inside the mission.

Towards three o'clock in the afternoon Sister Clotilde came with renewed agitation to Father Chisholm as he paced the courtyard, too disturbed to rest.

"Anna is throwing food over the upper wall." She wailed out the complaint. "I am sure her soldier is there . . . they were talking together."

His own nerves were near to breaking point. "There is no harm in giving food to those who need it."

"But he is one of those dreadful cut-throats. Oh, dear, we shall all be murdered in our beds!"

"Don't think so much about your own throat." He flushed with annoyance. "Martyrdom is an easy way to heaven."

As twilight fell, masses of the beaten Wai forces poured from all the city gates. They came by the Manchu Bridge, swarming up the Brilliant Green Jade road past the mission, in great confusion. The dirty faces of the men were stamped with the urgency of flight.

The night that followed was one of darkness and disorder, filled with shouting and shots, with galloping horses and the flare of torches on the far-off plain below. The priest watched with a strange melancholy from the lower mission gate. Suddenly, as he stood there, he heard a cautious step behind him. He turned. As he had half-expected, it was Anna, her mission coat buttoned closely to her chin, a cloth-wrapped bundle in her hand.

"Where are you going, Anna?"

She drew back with a stifled cry, but immediately regained her sullen boldness.

"It is my own affair."

"You will not tell me?"

"No."

His mood had fallen to quieter key, his attitude was changed. What was the use of more compulsion here?

"You have made up your mind to leave us, Anna. That is evident. And nothing that I can say or do will change it."

She said bitterly: "You have caught me now. But the next time you will not do so."

"There need be no next time, Anna." He took the key from his pocket and unlocked the gate. "You are free to go."

He could feel her start in sheer amazement, feel the impact of those full sultry eyes. Then without a word of gratitude or farewell she gripped her bundle and darted through the opening. Her running form was lost in the crowded roadway.

He stood, bare-headed, while the rabble swept past him. Now the exodus had turned to a rout. Suddenly there was a louder shouting, and he saw in the bobbing glare of upheld torches a group of men on horses. They approached rapidly, beating their way through the slow unmounted stream that hindered them. As they reached the gate one of the riders wrenched his lathered pony to a stop. In the torchlight the priest had a vision of incredible evil, a death's-head face, with narrowed slits of eyes, and a low receding brow. The horseman shouted at him, an insult charged with hatred, then raised his hand with immediate deadly menace. Francis did not move. His perfect immobility, uncaring and resigned, seemed to disconcert the other. While he hesitated for an instant a pressing cry was raised from behind. "On, on, Wai . . . to Tou-en-lai . . . they are coming!"

Wai dropped his hand, holding the weapon, with a queer fatalism. As he spurred his beast forward he bent in the saddle and spat venomously in the priest's face. The night enclosed him.

Next morning, which dawned bright and sunny, the mission bells were ringing gaily. Fu, of his own accord, had clambered to the tower. He swung on the long rope, his thin beard wagging with delight. Most of the refugees were ready to go home, their faces jubilant, waiting only to have the mission Father's word before departing. All the children were in the compound, laughing and skipping, watched by Martha and Maria-Veronica, who had patched up their differences sufficiently to stand no more than six feet apart.

Even Clotilde was playing, the gayest of all, bouncing a ball, running with the little ones, giggling. Polly, upright in her favourite place in the vegetable garden, sat winding a new skein of wool as though life were nothing but a round of calm normality.

When Father Chisholm came slowly down the steps of his house Joseph met him joyfully, carrying his chubby infant on his arm. "It is over, Master. Victory for the Naians. The new general is truly great. No more war in Pai-tan. He promises it. Peace for all of us in our time." He bounced the baby tenderly, triumphantly. "No fighting for you my little Joshua, no more tears and blood. Peace! Peace!"

Inexplicably, a shaft of utter sadness pierced the priest's heart. He took the babe's tiny cheek, soft and golden, between his thumb and finger, caressingly. He stifled his sigh and smiled. They were all running towards him, his children, his people whom he loved—whom, at the cost of his dearest principle, he had saved.

10

THE end of January brought the first glorious fruits of victory to Pai-tan. And Francis felt relief that Aunt Polly was spared the sight of them. She had departed for England the week before, and although the parting had been difficult he knew in his heart that it was wiser for her to go.

This morning as he crossed to the dispensary he speculated on the length of the rice line. Yesterday it had stretched the whole length of the mission wall. Wai, in the fury of defeat, had burned every stalk of grain for miles around. The sweet potato crop was poor. The rice fields, tended only by the women, with men and water-oxen commandeered by the army, had produced less than half the usual yield. Everything was scarce and costly. In the city, the value of tinned goods had multiplied five times. Prices were soaring daily.

He hastened into the crowded building. All three Sisters were there, each with a wooden measure and a black japanned bin of rice, engaged in the interminable task of scooping three ounces of the grain, running it into the proffered bowls.

He stood watching. His people were patient, quite silent. But the motion of the dry kernels made a constant hissing in the room. He said in a low voice to Maria-Veronica: "We can't keep this up. Tomorrow we must cut the allowance in half."

"Very well." She made a gesture of acquiescence. The strain of the past weeks had taken toll of her, he thought her unusually pale. She kept her eyes on the bin.

He went to the outer door, once or twice, counting the numbers. At last, to his relief, the line began to thin. He recrossed the compound, and descended to the store-cellars, recasting the inventory of their supplies. Fortunately he had placed an order with Mr. Chia two months ago and it had been faithfully delivered. But the stock of rice and sweet potatoes, which they used in great quantity, was dangerously low.

He stood thinking. Though prices were exorbitant, food could still be purchased in Pai-tan. He took a sudden resolution and decided, for the first time in the mission's history, to cable the Society for an emergency grant.

A week later he received the answering cable:—

Quite impossible allocate any monies. Kindly remember we are at war. You are not and therefore extremely lucky. Am immersed Red Cross work. Best regards Anselm Mealey.

Francis crumpled the green slip with an expressionless face. That afternoon he mustered all the available financial resources of the mission and went to the town. But now it was too late—he could buy nothing. The grain market was closed. The principal shops showed only a minimum of perishable produce: some melons, radishes, and small-river fish.

Disturbed, he stopped at the Lantern Street mission, where he had a long conversation with Dr. Fiske. Then, on his way back, he visited Mr. Chia's house.

Mr. Chia made Francis welcome. They drank tea together in the latticed little office, smelling of spice and musk and cedar.

"Yes," Mr. Chia agreed gravely, when they had fully discussed the shortage. "It is a matter of some small concern. Mr. Pao has gone to Chek-kow to endeavour to procure certain assurances from the new government."

"With some chance of success?"

"With every chance." The mandarin added, with the nearest approach to cynicism Father Chisholm had heard from him: "But assurances are not supplies."

"It was reported that the granary held many tons of reserve grain."

"General Naian took every bushel for himself. He has gutted the city of food."

"But surely," the mission Father spoke frowningly, "he cannot see the people starve. He promised them great benefit if they fought for him."

"Now he has mildly expressed the belief that some slight depopulation might benefit the community."

There was a silence. Father Chisholm reflected. "At least it is a blessing that Dr. Fiske will have large supplies. He is promised three full junkloads from his headquarters in Pekin."

"Ah!"

Again the silence.

"You are dubious?"

Mr. Chia responded with his gentle smile. "It is two thousand li from Pekin to Pai-tan. And there are many hungry people on the way. In my unworthy opinion, my most esteemed friend, we must prepare for six months of greatest hardship. These things come to China. But what matter? We may go. China remains."

Next morning Father Chisholm was obliged to turn back the rice line. It cut him to the heart to do so, yet he had to close the doors. He instructed Joseph to paint a notice that cases of utter destitution might leave their names at the lodge. He would investigate them personally.

Back in his house he set himself to work out a plan for rationing the mission. And the following week he introduced it. As the scheme began to operate the children wondered, then passed through fretfulness into a kind of puzzled dullness. They were lethargic and they asked for more at every meal. The insufficiency of sugar and starchy stuffs seemed to cause them most discomfort. They were losing weight.

From the Methodist mission came no word of the relief stores. The junks were now nearly three weeks overdue, and Dr. Fiske's anxiety was too significant to be mistaken. His public rice-kitchen had been closed for more than a month. In Pai-tan the people had a sluggish air, a heavy apathy. There was no light upon their faces, no briskness in their movement.

Then it began and gradually gathered strength: the timeless transmigration, old as China itself, the silent departure of men and women with their children from the city towards the South.

When Father Chisholm saw this symptom his heart chilled. A horrible vision attacked him of his little community, emaciated, relaxed in the final debility of starvation. He drew the lesson, swiftly, from the slow procession now beginning before his eyes.

As in the days of plague, he summoned Joseph to him, spoke to him and sped him upon an urgent errand.

On the morning following Joseph's departure he came over to the refectory and ordered an extra portion of rice to be given to the children. One last box of figs remained in the larder. He went down the long table giving each child a sweet sticky mouthful.

This sign of better feeding made the community more cheerful. But Martha, with one eye on the almost empty store-cellar and the other upon Father Chisholm, muttered her perplexity.

"What is in the wind, Father? There's something . . . I'm sure."

"You shall know on Saturday, Martha. Meanwhile, please tell Reverend Mother we shall continue on the extra rice for the remainder of this week."

Martha went off to do his bidding but could not find Reverend Mother anywhere. It was strange.

All that afternoon Maria-Veronica did not appear. She failed to take her weaving class, which was always held on Wednesdays, in the basket room. At three o'clock she could not be found. Perhaps it was an oversight. Shortly after five, she came in for refectory duty as usual, pale and composed, offering no explanation of her absence. But that night in the convent both Clotilde and Martha were awakened by a startling sound which came, unmistakably, from Maria-Veronica's room.

Appalled, they talked of it next morning in whispers, in the corner of the laundry, watching Reverend Mother through the window as she crossed the courtyard, dignified and upright, yet much slower than before.

"She has broken at last." Martha's words seemed constricted in her throat. "Blessed Virgin, did you hear her weep last night?"

Clotilde stood twisting an end of linen in her hands. "Perhaps she has news of a great German defeat we have not heard of yet."

"Yes, yes . . . it is something terrible." Martha's face suddenly puckered up. "Truly, if she were not an accursed Boche I would feel almost sorry for her."

"I have never known her to weep before." Clotilde meditated, her fingers twisting indecisively. "She is a proud woman. That must make it doubly hard."

"Pride goeth before a fall. Would she have had sympathy for us if we had yielded first? Nevertheless I must admit—Bah! Let us continue with our ironing."

Early on Sunday morning a small cavalcade approached the mission, winding downwards from the mountains. Advised by Joseph of its arrival, Father Chisholm hastened to the lodge to welcome Liu-Chi and his three companions from the Liu village. He clasped the old shepherd's hands as though he would never let them go.

"This is true kindness. The good God will bless you for it."

Liu-Chi smiled, naïvely pleased by the warmth of his reception. "We would have come sooner. But we took much time to collect the ponies."

There were perhaps thirty of the short shaggy uplands ponies, bridled but unsaddled, with big double panniers strapped upon their backs. They were contentedly munching the swathes of dried grass strewn for them. The priest's heart lifted. He pressed the four men to the refreshments which Joseph's wife had already prepared in the lodge, told them they must rest when they had eaten.

He found Reverend Mother in the linen room silently passing out fresh white bundles of the week's requirements: tablecovers, sheets and towels, to Martha, Clotilde and one of the senior students. He no longer attempted to conceal his satisfaction.

"I must prepare you for a change. Because of the threat of famine we are moving to the Liu village. You'll find plenty there, I assure you." He smiled. "Sister Martha, you'll find many ways of cooking mountain mutton before you return. I know you will enjoy the experience. And for the children . . . it will be a fine holiday."

There was a moment's sheer surprise. Then Martha and Clotilde both smiled, conscious of a coming break in the monotony of life, already stirring to the excitement of the adventure.

"Doubtless you will expect us to be organized in five minutes," Martha grumbled amiably, casting her eye instructively, for the first time in many weeks, upon Reverend Mother, as if for her approval.

It was the first faint gesture of atonement. But Maria-Veronica, standing by, with a colourless face, gave no answering sign.

"Yes, you must look sharp." Father Chisholm spoke almost gaily. "The little ones will be packed into the panniers. The others must take turns of walking and riding. The nights are warm and fine. Liu-Chi will look after you. If you leave today you should reach the village in a week."

Clotilde giggled. "We shall be like one of the tribes of Egypt."

The priest nodded. "I am giving Joseph a basket of my fantails. Every evening he must release one to bring me a message of your progress."

"What!" Martha and Clotilde exclaimed together. "You are not coming with us?"

"I may follow at a later date." Francis felt happy that they should want him. "You see, someone must remain at the mission. Reverend Mother and you two will be the pioneers."

Maria-Veronica said slowly: "I cannot go."

There was a silence.

At first he thought it a continuation of her pique, a disinclination to accompany the other two, but one glance at her face told him otherwise.

He said persuasively: "It will be a pleasant trip. The change would do you good."

She shook her head slowly. "I shall be obliged to take a longer trip . . . quite soon."

There was a longer pause. Then standing very still, she spoke with a toneless lack of emotion. "I must return to Germany . . . to see about the disposal . . . to our order . . . of my estate." She gazed into the distance. "My brother has been killed in action."

The previous silence had been deep, but now there was a mortal stillness. It was Clotilde who burst into violent tears. Then Martha, as though trapped, like an animal, hung her head unwillingly, in sympathy. Father Chisholm glanced from one to the other in deep distress, then walked silently away.

A fortnight after the party had arrived at Liu the day of Maria-Veronica's departure was, incredibly, upon him. The latest information from the village, received by pigeon post, indicated that the children were primitively yet comfortably billeted, and wild with health in the keen high air. Father Chisholm had good reason to congratulate himself upon his own resourcefulness. Yet as he walked beside Maria-Veronica to the landing steps, preceded by two bearers with long poles, supporting her baggage upon their shoulders, he felt a desperate forlornness.

They stood on the jetty while the men placed the bundles in the sampan. Behind them the city lay, murmuring in still dejection. Before them, in midriver, lay the outgoing junk. The dun water which lapped its hull reached out to a grey horizon.

He could find no words to express himself. She had meant so much to him, this gracious and distinguished woman, with her help, encouragement, and comradeship. The future had stretched before them, indefinitely, a future filled with their work together. Now she was going, unexpectedly, almost furtively, it seemed, in a haze of darkness and confusion.

He sighed, at last, giving her his troubled smile. "Even if my country remains at war with yours . . . remember . . . I am not your enemy."

The understatement was so like him, and all that she admired in him, it shook her determination to be strong. As she gazed at his spare figure, gaunt face and thinning hair, tears clouded her beautiful eyes.

"My dear . . . dear friend . . . I will never forget you."

She gave him her warm firm clasp and stepped quickly into the little craft which would take her to the junk.

He stood there, leaning on his old tartan umbrella, his eyes screwed against the water's glitter, until the vessel was a speck, floating, vanishing beyond the rim of the sky.

Unknown to her, he had placed amongst her baggage the little antique figure of the Spanish Virgin which Father Tarrant had given him. It was his sole possession of any value. She had often admired it.

He turned and slowly plodded home. In the garden which she had made and loved so much, he paused, grateful for the silence and the peace there. The scent of lilies was in the air. Old Fu, the gardener, his sole companion in the deserted mission, was pruning the azalea bushes with gentle, inquiring hands. He felt worn-out by all that he had lately undergone. A chapter in his life was ended; for the first time, he dimly sensed that he was growing old. He seated himself on the bench beneath the banyan tree, rested his elbows on the pinewood table she had placed there. Old Fu, pruning the azaleas, pretended not to see him as, after a moment, he laid his head upon his arms.

11

THE broad leaves of the banyan tree still shaded him as he sat at the garden table turning the pages of his journal with hands which, as by some strange illusion, were veined and vaguely tremulous. Of course, old Fu no longer watched him, unless through a chink of heaven. Instead, two young gardeners bent by the azalea bed while Father Chou, his Chinese priest, small, gentle and demure, pacing with his breviary at a respectful distance, kept a warm brown filial eye upon him.

In the August sunshine the mission compound was aquiver with dry light, like the sparkle of a golden wine. From the playground the happy shouts of the children at their playtime told him the forenoon hour: eleven o'clock. His children, or rather, he corrected himself wryly, his children's children . . . How unfairly time had flashed across him, tumbling the years into his lap, one upon another, too fast for him to marshal them.

A jolly red face, plump and smiling, swam into his abstracted vision, above a tumblerful of milk. He forced a frown as Mother Mercy Mary drew near, annoyed to be reminded of his age by another of her coddling tricks. He was only sixty-seven . . . well, sixty-eight next month . . . a mere nothing . . . and fitter than any youngster.

"Haven't I told you not to bring me that stuff?"

She smiled soothingly—vigorous, bustling, and matronly. "You need it to-day, Father, if you will insist on taking that long unnecessary trip." She paused. "I don't see why Father Chou and Dr. Fiske couldn't go themselves?"

"Don't you?"

"No, indeed."

"Dear Sister, that's too bad. Your mind must be breaking up." She laughed indulgently and tried to coax him.

"Shall I tell Joshua you've decided not to go?"

"Tell him to have the ponies saddled in an hour."

He saw her depart, shaking her head reproachfully. He smiled again, with the dry triumph of a man who has had his way. Then, sipping his milk, without, now that she was gone, the necessity of a grimace, he resumed his leisured perusal of the diary before him. It was a habit into which he had lately fallen, a kind of wilful retrospection, evoked by turning the frayed and dog-eared pages at random.

This morning it opened, strangely, first at the date *October* 1917.

"Despite the improving conditions in Pai-tan, the good rice crop and the safe homecoming of my little ones from Liu, I have been downcast lately; yet today a simple incident gave me preposterous happiness.

"I had been away for four days at the annual conference which the Prefect Apostolic has thought fit to institute at Sen-siang. As the farthest outpost of the Vicariate I had fancied myself immune from such junketings. Indeed, we missioners are so widely scattered and so few—only Father Surette, poor Thibodeau's successor, the three Chek-kow Chinese priests and Father Van Dwyn the Dutchman from Rakai—that the occasion seemed scarcely worth the long river journey. But there we were 'exchanging viewpoints.' And natu-rally I talked indiscreetly against 'aggressive Christianizing methods,' got hot under the collar and quoted Mr. Pao's cousin: 'You missionaries walk in with your Gospel and walk off with our land.' I fell into disgrace with Father Surette, a bustling Father who rejoices in his muscles, which he has used to destroy all the pleasant little Buddhist wayside shrines within twenty li of Sen-siang, and who in addition claims the amazing record of 50,000 pious ejaculations in one day.

"On my return trip I was overcome with remorse. How often have I had to write in this journal: 'Failed again. Dear Lord, help me restrain my tongue!' And they thought me such a queer fish at Sen-siang!

"To mortify myself I had dispensed with a cabin on the boat. Next to me on deck was a man with a cage of prime rats which he dined on, progressively, under my jaundiced eye. In addition it rained hard, blew down streams and I was, as I deserved to be, extremely sick.

"Then, as I stepped off the vessel at Pai-tan, more dead than alive, I found an old woman waiting for me on the drenched, deserted jetty. As she approached I saw her to be my friend, old mother Hsu, she who cooked beans in the milk-can in the compound. She is the poorest, the lowest person in my parish.

"To my amazement her face was illuminated at the sight of me. Quickly she told me she had missed me so much she had stood there in the rain these past three afternoons, waiting my arrival. She produced six little ceremonial cakes of rice flour and sugar, not for eating—the kind they place before the images of Buddha—the same images that Father Surette knocks down. A comic gesture . . . But the joy of knowing that to one person at least one is dear . . . and indispensable . . .

"*May 1918.* This lovely morning my first batch of young settlers departed for Liu, twenty-four in all,—I might discreetly add, twelve of each kind,— amidst great enthusiasm and many knowing nods and practical admonitions from our good Reverend Mother Mercy Mary. Though I resented her coming intensely—weighing her sulkily against the memory of Maria-Veronica—she is a fine, capable, cheerful person, and for a holy nun she has an amazing insight into the exigencies of the marriage bed.

"Old Meg Paxton, the Cannelgate fishwife, used to reassure me that I wasn't such a fool as I looked; and I'm quite proud of my inspiration to colonize Liu—with the finest produce of this mission of St. Andrew's. There simply aren't enough jobs here for my growing-up young people. It would seem the worst kind of stupidity, having pulled them out of the gutter, to throw them back again, benevolently, now they are educated. And Liu itself will profit by an infusion of fresh blood. There is ample land, a stirring climate. Once the numbers are adequate I shall establish a young priest there. Anselm must send me one, until he does so I shall deafen him with my importunities. . . .

"I am tired tonight from the excitement and the ceremonies—these mass marriages are no joke, and Chinese ceremonial oratory leaves the vocal cords in ruins. Perhaps my depression is reactionary, perhaps physical. I do need a holiday quite badly, I am a little stale. The Fiskes have gone off for their routine six months' rest, to visit their son, now established in Virginia. I miss them. Their relief, the Reverend Ezra Salkins, makes me realize how fortunate I am to have such sweet and gentle neighbours. Shang-Foo Ezra is neither—a big man with a fixed beam, a Rotarian handshake, and a smile like melting lard. He boomed at me as he cracked my finger-bones: 'Anything I can do to help you, brother, anything at all.'

"The Fiskes would be my honoured guests at Liu. But to Ezra I am dumb. In just sixty seconds he would have Father Ribiero's tomb plastered with bill-heads: *Brother are you saved?* Oh, blow! I am crabbed and sour, it's that plum pie Mercy Mary made me eat at the wedding breakfast. . . .

"I have been made truly happy by a long letter dated June 10th, 1922 from Mother Maria-Veronica. After many vicissitudes, the trials of the war and the humiliations of the armistice, she has at last been rewarded by her appointment as Superior of the Sistine Convent in Rome. This is the mother house of her order, a fine old foundation on the high slopes between the Corso and the Quirinal overlooking the Saporelli and the lovely church of Santi Apostoli. It is an office of the first importance but no more than she deserves. She seems contented . . . at peace. Her letter brings me such a fragrance of the Holy City—that might be one of Anselm's phrases!—always the object of my tender longings, I have dared to make a plan. When my sick-leave, already twice postponed, does arrive, what is to prevent my visiting Rome, wearing my boots out on the mosaics of St. Peter's, and seeing Mother Maria-Veronica in the bargain? When I wrote in April congratulating Anselm on his appointment as Rector of the Tynecastle Cathedral Church he assured me, in his reply, that I should have an assistant priest within six months and my 'much-needed vacation' before the year was out.

"An absurd thrill pervades my sun-bleached bones when I think that such happiness may be in store for me. Enough! I must start to save to buy myself a suit of clothes. What would the good Abbess of Santi Apostoli think if the little bricklayer who claimed her acquaintance turned out to have a patch on the backside of his pants. . . .

"*September 17th, 1923.* Breathless excitement! Today, my new priest arrived, at last I have a colleague, and it seems almost too good to be true.

"Although, at first, Anselm's voluminous hieratics gave me hope of a stout young Scot, preferably with freckles and sandy hair, later advices had prepared me for a native Father from the College at Pekin. It was like my perverted humour to tell the Sisters nothing of the coming dénouement. For weeks they had been gathering themselves to coddle the young missioner from home —Clotilde and Martha wanted something Gallic with a beard, but poor Mother Mercy Mary had made a very special novena for an Irish one. The look on her honest Hibernian face as she burst into my room, purple with tragedy! 'The new Father is a Chinese!'

"But Father Chou seems a splendid little fellow, not only quiet and amiable, but conveying a deep sense of that extraordinary interior life which is such an admirable characteristic of the Chinese. I have met several native priests on my infrequent pilgrimages to Sen-siang and I have always been impressed. If I wished to be pompous I should say that the good ones appear to combine the wisdom of Confucius with the virtue of Christ.

"And now I am off to Rome, next month . . . my first holiday in nineteen years. I am like a Holywell schoolboy, at the end of term, banging his desk and chanting:—

'Two more weeks and I shall be,
Outside the gates of mis-er-ee.'

"I wonder if Mother Maria-Veronica has lost her taste for fine stem ginger. I shall take her a jar and risk being told she has turned to macaroni. Heigh-ho! This life is most jolly. Through my window I see the young cedars swaying in the wind with a wild joy. I must write now to Shanghai for my tickets. Hurrah!

"*October 1923.* Yesterday the cable came cancelling my trip to Rome and I have just returned from my evening walk by the riverbank where I stood a long time in a soft mist watching the cormorant fishers. It is a sad way of catching fish, or perhaps I had a sad way of looking at it. The great birds are ringed by the neck to prevent their swallowing the fish. They crouch indolently on the gunwale of the boat as though dreadfully bored with the whole proceeding. Suddenly there is a dip and a splutter and up comes the great bill, pouched with fish, a tail wriggling at the tip. An embarrassing undulation of the neck follows next. When relieved of their catch the birds shake their heads, disconsolate, yet as though experience had taught them nothing. Then they squat again, brooding blackly, recuperating for a fresh defeat.

"My own mood was dark and defeated enough, God knows. As I stood by the slaty water, from which the night wind threw waves upon the weed coiled like hair upon the shore, my thoughts, strangely, were not of Rome but of the streams of Tweedside, with myself, barefoot in the rippling crystal, casting a withy rod for trout.

"More and more of late I find myself living in the memory of my childhood, recollected so vividly it might be yesterday—a sure symptom of approaching age! . . . I even dream, tenderly, wistfully—isn't this unbelievable?—of my boyish love: my own dear Nora.

"You see, I have reached the sentimental stage of disappointment, which is next to getting over it, but when the telegram arrived, in old Meg's words, 'it was hard to thole.'

"Now I am almost resigned to the utter finality of my exile. The principle is probably correct that a return to Europe unsettles the missionary priest. After all, we give ourselves entirely, there is no retreat. I am here for life. And I'll lay myself, at last, in that little piece of Scotland where Willie Tulloch rests.

"Moreover, it is certainly logical and just that Anselm's trip to Rome is more necessary than mine. The funds of the Society cannot sustain two such excursions. And he can better tell the Holy Father of the advances of 'his troops'—as he calls us. Where my tongue would be stiff and clumsy his will captivate—garner funds and support for all the F. S. missions. He has promised to write me fully of his doings. I must enjoy Rome vicariously, have my audience in imagination, meet Maria-Veronica in spirit. I could not bring myself to accept Anselm's suggestion of a short vacation in Manila. Its gaiety would have troubled me, I should have laughed at the solitary little man, poking round the harbour, fancying himself on the Pontine Hill. . . .

"A *month later.* . . . Father Chou is nicely established in the Liu village and our pigeons pass one another at celestial speed. What a joy that my scheme is working so beautifully. I wonder if Anselm will mention it, perhaps, when he sees the Holy Father, just a word of that tiny jewel, set in the great wilderness, once forgotten . . . by all but God. . . .

"*22d November, 1928.* How can one compass a sublime experience in mere words—in one bald and arid phrase? Last night Sister Clotilde died. Death is a topic I have not often dwelt upon in this sketchy record of my own imperfect life.

"Thus, twelve months ago when Aunt Polly passed away in her sleep at Tynecastle, uneventfully and of pure goodness and old age, and the news reached me in Judy's tear-smudged letter, I made no comment here beyond the simple entry: '*Polly died, 17th October, 1927.*' There is an inevitability in the death of those whom we know to be good. But there are others . . . sometimes we tough old priests are staggered, as by a revelation.

"Clotilde had been ailing, slightly it seemed, for several days. When they called me just after midnight I was shocked to see the change in her. I sent at once to tell Joshua, Joseph's eldest boy—to run for Dr. Fiske. But Clotilde, with a strange expression, restrained me. She indicated, with a peculiar smile, that Joshua might spare himself the journey. She said very little; but enough.

"When I recollected how, years ago, I tartly reproached her for that inexplicable recourse to chlorodyne, I could have wept for my stupidity. I had never thought enough of Clotilde: the tension of her manner, which she could not help, her morbid dread of flushing, of people, of her own overcharged nerves, made her superficially unattractive, even ridiculous. One should have reflected on the struggles of such a nature to overcome itself, one should have thought of the invisible victories. Instead, one thought only of the visible defeats.

"For eighteen months she had been suffering from a growth of the stomach arising out of a chronic ulcer. When she learned from Dr. Fiske that nothing could be done she pledged him to secrecy and set herself to fight an unsung battle. Before I was called the first bad hæmorrhage had prostrated her. At six next morning she had the second and succumbed quite quietly. Between, we talked . . . but I dare not make a record of that conversation. Broken and disjointed, it would seem meaningless . . . a prey for easy sneers . . . and alas, the world cannot be reformed by a sneer . . .

"We are all much upset, Martha especially. She is like me, strong as a mule, and will go on forever. Poor Clotilde! I think of her as a gentle creature so strung to sacrifice that sometimes she vibrated harshly. To see a face become at peace, a quiet acceptance of death, without fear . . . it ennobles the heart of man.

"*November 30th, 1929.* Today Joseph's fifth child was born. How life flies on! Who would have dreamed that my shy, grave, garrulous, touchy youngster had in him the makings of a patriarch? Perhaps his early fondness for sugar should have warned me! Really, he is quite a personage now—officious, uxorious, a little pompous, very curt to callers he thinks I should not see—I am rather scared of him myself. . . .

"A *week later*. More local news . . . Mr. Chia's dress boots have been hung up at the Manchu Gate. This is a tremendous honour here . . . and I rejoice for my old friend, whose ascetic, contemplative, generous nature has always been devoted to the reasonable and the beautiful, to that which is eternal.

"Yesterday the mail came in. Even without the presage of his immense success in Rome, I had long realized that Anselm must achieve high honour in the Church. And at last his work for the foreign missions has earned him a fitting reward from the Vatican. He is the new Bishop of Tynecastle. Perhaps the greatest strain is thrown upon our moral vision by the spectacle of another's success. The dazzle hurts us. But now, in my approaching old age, I'm short-sighted. I don't mind Anselm's lustre, I'm rather glad, because I know that he will be supremely glad himself. Jealousy is so hateful a quality. One should remember that the defeated still have everything if they still have God.

"I wish I might take credit for my magnanimity. But this is not magnanimity, merely an awareness of the difference between Anselm and myself . . . of the ridiculous presumption of myself aspiring to the crozier. Though we started from the same mark Anselm has far outstripped me. He has developed his talents to the full, is now, I observe from the *Tynecastle Chronicle*, 'an accomplished linguist, a notable musician, a patron of arts and science in the diocese, with a vast circle of influential friends.' How lucky! I have had no more than six friends in my uneventful life, and all except one were humble folk. I must write to Anselm to congratulate him, making it clear, however, that I do not presume upon our friendship and have no intention of asking for preferment. *Viva Anselmo!* I am sad when I think how much you have made of your life and how little I have made of mine. I have bumped my head so often . . . and so hard, in my strivings after God.

"*December 30, 1929*. I have not written in this journal for almost a month . . . not since the news of Judy arrived. I still find it difficult to set down even the barest outline of what has taken place at home . . . and here, within myself.

"I flattered myself I had achieved a beatific resignation towards the finality of my exile. Two weeks ago today, I was remarkably complacent. Having made a survey of my recent additions to the mission, the four rice fields by the river which I bought last year, the enlarged stockyard beyond the white mulberry grove, and the new pony farm, I came into the church to help the children make the Christmas crib. This is a job I particularly enjoy, partly from that lamentable obsession which has stuck to me all my life, I suppose the ribald would call it a suppressed paternal instinct: a love of children—from the dear Christ child down to the meanest little yellow waif who ever crawled into this mission of St. Andrew's.

"We had made a splendid manger with a snowy roof of real cotton wool and were arranging the ox and ass in their stall behind. I had all sorts of things up my sleeve too, coloured lights, and a fine crystal star to hang on the spruce-branched sky. As I saw the shining faces about me and listened to the excited chatter—this is one of the occasions when distractions are permissible in church—I had a wonderful sense of lightness, a vision of all the Christmas cribs in all the Christian churches of the world, dignifying this sweet festival of the Nativity, which, even to those who cannot believe, must at least be beautiful as the feast of all motherhood.

"At that moment one of the bigger boys, sent by Mother Mercy Mary, hurried in with the cablegram. Surely ill-tidings come fast enough without flashing them round the earth. As I read my expression must have changed. One of the smallest girls began to cry. The brightness in my breast was quenched.

"Perhaps I might be judged absurd for taking this so much to heart. I lost Judy when in her teens, on my departure for Pai-tan. But I have lived her life with her in thought. The infrequency of her letters made them stand out like beads upon a chain.

"The hand of heredity propelled Judy forward without mercy. She never quite knew what she wanted or where she was going. But so long as Polly stood beside her she could not become the victim of her own caprice. All through the war she prospered, like many other young women, working for high wages in a munitions factory. She bought a fur coat and a piano—how well I recollect the letter in which the joyful information reached me—and was keyed to sustain her effort by the sense of emergency in the air. This was her heyday. When the war ended, she was over thirty, opportunities were scarce, she gradually abandoned all thought of a career and lapsed into a quiet life with Polly, sharing the small flat in Tynecastle and gaining, one hoped, with maturity, an added balance.

"Judy seemed always to have a queer suspicion towards the other sex and had never been attracted by the thought of marriage. She was forty when Polly died and one never dreamed that she would change her single state. Nevertheless, within eight months of the funeral, Judy was married . . . and later deserted.

"One does not disguise the brutal fact that women do strange things before the climacteric. But this was not the explanation of the pitiful comedy. Polly's legacy to Judy was some two thousand pounds, enough to provide a modest annual competence. Not until Judy's letter arrived did I guess how she had been persuaded to realize her capital, to transfer it to her sober, upright and gentlemanly husband whom she had first met, apparently, in a boarding house at Scarborough.

"No doubt whole volumes might be written on this basic mundane theme . . . dramatic . . . analytical . . . in the grand Victorian manner . . . perhaps with that sly smirk which sees a rich deep humour in the gullibility of our human nature. But the epilogue was briefly written in ten words on the telegraph form that I held in my hands before the Christmas crib. A child had been born to Judy of this belated, transitory union. And she had died in bearing it.

"Now I reflect there had always been a dark thread running through the flimsy fabric of Judy's inconsequential life. She was the visible evidence, not of sin—how I detest and distrust that word!—but of man's weakness and stupidity. She was the reason, the explanation of our presence here on earth, the tragic evidence of our common mortality. And now, differently, yet with the same essential sadness, that mortal tragedy is again perpetuated.

"I cannot bring myself to contemplate the fate of this unlucky infant, with no one to look after it but the woman who attended Judy—she who has now sent me the news. It is easy to fit her to the pattern of events: one of those handywives who take in expectant mothers, in straitened, slightly dubious circumstances. I must reply to her at once . . . send some money, what little I have. When we bind ourselves to holy poverty we are strangely selfish, forgetful of the awful obligations which life may place upon us. Poor Nora . . . poor Judy . . . poor unnamed little child . . .

"*June 19th, 1930.* A grand day of early summer sunshine and my heart is lighter for the letter received this afternoon. The child is baptized Andrew, after this same infamous mission, and the news makes me chuckle with senile vanity, as though I, myself, were the little wretch's grandfather. Perhaps, whether I wish it or not, this relationship will devolve on me. The father has vanished and we shall make no attempt to trace him. But if I send a certain sum each month, this woman, Mrs. Stevens, who seems a worthy creature, will care for Andrew. Again I can't help smiling . . . my priestly career has been a hotch-potch of peculiarities . . . to rear an infant at a distance of eight thousand miles will be its crowning oddity!

"Wait a moment! I've flicked myself on the raw with that phrase: 'my priestly career.' The other day, during one of our friendly tiffs, on Purgatory I think it was, Fiske declared—heatedly, for I was getting the better of him: 'You argue like a mixed Convention of Holy Rollers and High Anglicans!'

"That brought me up short. I daresay my upbringing, and that early bit of the uncalculable influence of dear old Daniel Glennie, shaped me towards undue liberality. I love my religion, into which I was born, which I have taught, as best I could, for over thirty years, and which has led me unfailingly to the source of all joy, of everlasting sweetness. Yet in my isolation here my outlook has simplified, clarified with my advancing years. I've tied up, and neatly tucked away, all the complex, pettifogging little quirks of doctrine. Frankly, I can't believe that any of God's creatures will grill for all Eternity because of eating a mutton chop on Friday. If we have the fundamentals—love for God and our neighbour—surely we're all right? And isn't it time for the churches of the world to cease hating one another . . . and unite? The world is one living, breathing body, dependent for its health on the billions of cells which comprise it . . . and each tiny cell is the heart of man . . .

"*December 15th, 1932.* Today the new patron saint of this mission was three years old. I hope he had a pleasant birthday and didn't eat too much of the toffee I wrote Burley's, in Tweedside, to send him.

"*September 1st, 1935.* Oh Lord, don't let me be a silly old man . . . this journal is becoming more and more the fatuous record of a child I have not seen and shall never see. I cannot return and he cannot come here. Even my obstinacy balks at that absurdity . . . though I did in fact inquire of Dr. Fiske, who told me that the climate would be deadly for an English child of such tender years.

"Yet I must confess I'm troubled. Reading between her letters it would seem as though Mrs. Stevens had lately come down a little in her luck. She has moved to Kirkbridge, which, as I remember it, is a cotton town, not prepossessing, near Manchester. Her tone has altered, too, and I am beginning to wonder if she is more interested in the money she receives than in Andrew. Yet her parish priest gave her an excellent character. And hitherto she has been admirable.

"Of course, it's all my own fault. I could have secured Andrew's future, after a fashion, by turning him over to one of our excellent Catholic institutions. But somehow . . . he's my one 'blood relation,' a living memento of my dear lost Nora . . . I can't and I won't be so impersonal . . . it's my inveterate crankiness, I suppose, which makes me fight against officialdom. Well . . . if that is so . . . I . . . and Andrew . . . must take the consequences . . . we are in God's hands and he will . . ."

Here, as Father Chisholm turned another page, his concentration was disturbed by the sound of ponies stamping in the compound. He hesitated, listening, half unwilling to relinquish his mood of precious reverie. But the sound increased, mingled with brisk voices. His lips drew together in acceptance. He turned to the last entry in the journal and, taking his pen, added a paragraph.

"*April 30th, 1936.* I am on the point of leaving for the Liu settlement with Father Chou and the Fiskes. Yesterday Father Chou came in, anxious for my advice about a young herdsman he had isolated at the settlement, fearing he might have the smallpox. I decided to go back with him myself—with our good ponies and the new trail, it is only a two days' journey. Then I amplified the idea. Since I have repeatedly promised to show Dr. and Mrs. Fiske our model village, I decided we might all four take the trip. It will be my last opportunity to fulfill my long-outstanding pledge to the doctor and his wife. They are returning home to America at the end of this month. I hear them

calling now. They are looking forward to the excursion . . . I'll tackle Fiske
en route on his confounded impudence . . . Holy Roller, indeed! . . ."

12

THE sun was already dropping towards the bare rim of the hills which enclosed the narrow valley. Riding ahead of the returning party, occupied by
thoughts of Liu, where they had left Father Chou with medicine for the
sick herdsman, Father Chisholm had resigned himself to another night encampment before reaching the mission when, at a bend of the road, he met
three men in dirty cotton uniforms slouching head-down with rifles on their
hips.

It was a familiar sight: the province was swarming with irregulars, dis-
banded soldiers with smuggled weapons who had formed themselves into
roving gangs. He passed them with a muttered, "Peace be with you," and
slowed down till the others of the party made up to him. But as he turned
he was surprised to see terror on the faces of the two porters from the
Methodist mission and a sudden anxiety in his own servant's eyes.

"These look like followers of Wai." Joshua made a gesture towards the
road ahead. "And there are others."

The priest swung round stiffly. About twenty of the grey-green figures were
approaching down the path kicking up a cloud of slow white dust. On the
shadowed hill, straggling in a winding line, were at least another score. He
exchanged a glance with Fiske.

"Let's push on."

The two parties met a moment later. Father Chisholm, smiling, with his
usual greeting, kept his beast moving steadily down the middle of the path.
The soldiers, gaping stupidly, gave way automatically. The only mounted
man, a youngster with a broken peaked cap and some air of authority, en-
hanced by a corporal's stripe misplaced upon his cuff, halted his shaggy pony
indecisively.

"Who are you? And whither are you going?"

"We are missionaries, returning to Pai-tan." Father Chisholm gave the
answer calmly across his shoulder, still leading the others forward. They were
now almost through the dirty, puzzled, staring mob: Mrs. Fiske and the doctor behind him, followed by Joshua and the two bearers.

The corporal was uncertain but partly satisfied. The encounter was robbed
of danger, reduced to commonplace, when suddenly the elder of the two
porters lost his head. Prodded by a rifle butt in his passage between the men,
he dropped his bundle with a screech of panic and bolted for the cover of
the brushwood on the hill.

Father Chisholm suppressed a bitter exclamation. In the gathering twilight, there was a second's dubious immobility. Then a shot rang out, another, and another. The echoes went volleying down the hills. As the blue
figure of the bearer, bent double, vanished into the bushes, a loud defrauded

outcry broke amongst the soldiers. No longer dumbly wondering, they crowded round the missionaries, in furious, chattering resentment.

"You must come with us." As Father Chisholm had foreseen, the corporal's reaction was immediate.

"We are only missionaries," Dr. Fiske protested heatedly. "We have no possessions. We are honest people."

"Honest people do not run away. You must come to our leader, Wai."

"I assure you—"

"Wilbur!" Mrs. Fiske interposed quietly. "You'll only make it worse. Save your breath."

Bundled about, surrounded by the soldiers, they were roughly pushed along the path which they had recently traversed. About five li back, the young officer turned west into a dry watercourse which took a tortuous and stony course into the hills. At the head of the gully the company halted.

Here perhaps a hundred ill-conditioned soldiers were scattered about in postures of ease—smoking, chewing betel nut, scraping lice from their armpits and caked mud from between their bare toes. On a flat stone, cross-legged, eating his evening meal before a small dung fire, with his back against the wall of the ravine, was Wai-Chu.

Wai was now about fifty-five, gross but full-bellied, with a greater and more evil immobility. His ghee-oiled hair, worn long and parted in the middle, fell over a forehead so drawn down by a perpetual frown as to narrow the oblique eyes to slits. Three years before, a bullet had sheared away his front teeth and upper lip. The scar was horrible. Despite it, Francis plainly recognized the horseman who had spat into his face at the mission gate that night of the retreat. Hitherto he had sustained their detention with composure. But now, under that hidden, subhuman gaze, charged beneath its blankness with an answering recognition, the priest was conscious of a sharp constriction of his heart.

While the corporal volubly related the circumstances of the capture, Wai continued unfathomably to eat, the twin sticks sending a stream of liquid rice and pork lumps into his gullet from the bowl pressed beneath his chin. Suddenly two soldiers broke up the ravine at the double, dragging the fugitive bearer between them. With a final heave they threw him into the circle of fire-glow. The unhappy man fell on his knees close to Wai, his arms skewered behind him, panting and gibbering, in an ecstasy of fear.

Wai continued to eat. Then, casually, he pulled his revolver from his belt and fired it. Caught in the act of supplication, the porter fell forward, his body still jerking against the ground. A creamy pinkish pulp oozed from his blasted skull. Before the stunning reverberations of the report had died Wai had resumed his meal.

Mrs. Fiske had screamed faintly. But beyond a momentary lifting of their heads, the resting soldiers took no notice of the incident. The two who had brought in the bearer now pulled his corpse away and systematically dispossessed it of boots, clothing, and a string of copper cash. Numb and sick, the priest muttered to Dr. Fiske, who stood, very pale, beside him.

"Keep calm . . . show nothing . . . or it is hopeless for all of us."

They waited. The cold and senseless murder had charged the air with horror. At a sign from Wai the second bearer was driven forward and flung upon his knees. The priest felt his stomach turn with a dreadful premonition. But Wai merely said, addressing them all, impersonally:—

"This man, your servant, will leave immediately for Pai-tan and inform your friends that you are temporarily in my care. For such hospitality a voluntary gift is customary. At noon on the day following tomorrow two of my men will await him, half a li outside the Manchu Gate. He will advance, quite alone." Wai paused blankly. "It is to be hoped he will bring the voluntary gift."

"There is little profit in making us your guests." Dr. Fiske spoke with a throb of indignation. "I have already indicated that we are without worldly goods."

"For each person five thousand dollars is requested. No more."

Fiske breathed more easily. The sum, though large, was not impossible to a mission as wealthy as his own.

"Then permit my wife to return with the messenger. She will ensure that the money is paid."

Wai gave no sign of having heard. For one apprehensive moment the priest thought his overwrought companion was about to make a scene. But Fiske stumbled back to his wife's side. The messenger was despatched, sent bounding down the ravine with a last forceful injunction from the corporal. Wai then rose and, while his men made preparations for departure, walked forward to his tethered pony, so casually that the dead man's bare upturned feet, protruding from an arbutus bush, struck the eye like a hallucination.

The missionaries' ponies were now brought up, the four prisoners forced to mount, then roped together by long hemp cords. The cavalcade moved off into the gathering night.

Conversation was impossible at this bumping gallop. Father Chisholm was left to the mercy of his thoughts, which centred on the man now holding them for ransom.

Lately Wai's waning power had driven him to many excesses. From a traditional war lord, dominating the Chek-kow district of the province with his army of three thousand men, bought off by the various townships, levying taxes and imposts, living in feudal luxury in his walled fortress at Tou-en-lai, he had slowly fallen to ruinous days. At the height of his notoriety he had paid fifty thousand taels for a concubine from Pekin. Now he lived from hand to mouth by petty forays. Beaten decisively in two pitched battles with neighbouring mercenaries, he had thrown in his lot first with the *Min-tuan*, then, in a fit of malice, with the opposing faction, the *Yu-chi-tui*. The truth was that neither desired his doubtful aid. Degenerate, vicious, he fought solely for his own hand. His men were steadily deserting. As the scale of his operations dwindled his ferocity intensified. When he reached the humiliation of a bare two hundred followers, his round of pillage and burnings stood as a dreadful theme of terror. A fallen Lucifer, his hatreds fed on the glories he had lost, he was at enmity with mankind.

The night was interminable. They crossed a low range of hills, forded two rivulets, spattered for an hour through low-lying swamplands. Beyond that, and his conjecture from the pole star that they were travelling due west, Father Chisholm had no knowledge of the terrain they traversed. At his age, used to the quiet amble of his beast, the rapid jolting shook his bones until they rattled. But he reflected, with commiseration, that the Fiskes, too, were enduring the bone-shaking, for the good God's sake. And Joshua, poor lad, though supple enough, was so young he must be sadly frightened. The priest told himself that on the return to the mission he would assuredly give the boy the roan pony he had coveted, silently, these past six months. Closing his eyes, he said a short prayer for the safety of their little party.

Dawn found them in a wilderness of rock and windblown sand, quite uninhabited, with no vegetation but scattered clumps of yellowish tuft grass. But within an hour, the sound of rushing water reached them and there, behind an escarpment, was the ruined citadel of Tou-en-lai, a huddle of ancient mud-brick houses on the cliff slope, surrounded by a crenellated wall, scarred and scorched by many sieges, the old glazed pillars of a Buddhist temple standing roofless, by the riverside.

Within the walls, the party dismounted, and Wai, without a word, entered his house, the only habitable dwelling. The morning air was raw. As the missionaries stood shivering on the hard mud courtyard, still roped together, a number of women and older men came crowding from the little caves which honeycombed the cliff and joined the soldiers in a chattering inspection of the captives.

"We should be grateful for food and rest." Father Chisholm addressed the company at large.

"Food and rest." The words were repeated, passed from mouth to mouth, amongst the onlookers, as an amusing curiosity.

The priest proceeded patiently. "You observe how weary is the missionary woman." Mrs. Fiske was, indeed, half-fainting, on her feet. "Perhaps some well-disposed person would offer her hot tea."

"Tea . . . hot tea," echoed the mob, crowding closer.

They were now within touching distance of the missionaries and suddenly, with a simian acquisitiveness, an old man in the front rank snatched at the doctor's watch-chain. It was the signal for a general spoliation—money, breviary, Bible, wedding ring, the priest's old silver pencil—in three minutes the little group stood divested of everything except their boots and clothing.

As the scramble ended, a woman's eye was caught by the dull sparkle of a jet buckle on the band of Mrs. Fiske's hat. Immediately, she clutched at it. Aware, desperately, of her awful hazard, Mrs. Fiske struggled, with a shrill defensive cry. But in vain. Buckle, hat and wig came off together in her assailant's tenacious grasp. In a flash her bald head gleamed, like a bladder of lard, with grotesque and terrible nakedness, in the remorseless air.

There was a hush. Then a babble of derision broke, a paroxysm of shrieking mockery. Mrs. Fiske covered her face with her hands and burst into scalding tears. The doctor, attempting tremulously to cover his wife's scalp with his handkerchief, saw the coloured silk snatched away. Poor woman, Father Chisholm thought, compassionately averting his eyes.

The sudden arrival of the corporal ended the hilarity as quickly as it had begun. The crowd scattered as the missionaries were led into one of the caves, which possessed the distinction of a hatch. This heavy-ribbed door was slammed and fastened. They were left alone.

"Well," said Father Chisholm after a pause, "at least we have this to ourselves."

There was a longer silence. The little doctor, seated on the earth floor with his arm about his weeping wife, said dully: "It was scarlet fever. She caught it the first year we were in China. She was so sensitive about it. We took such pains never to let a soul know."

"And no one will know," the priest lied swiftly. "Joshua and I are silent as the grave. When we return to Pai-tan the—the damage can be repaired."

"You hear that, Agnes, dear? Pray stop crying, my dearest love."

A slackening, then cessation of the muffled sobs. Mrs. Fiske slowly raised her tear-stained eyes, red-rimmed in that ostrich orb.

"You are very kind," she choked.

"Meanwhile, they seem to have left me with this. If it can be of any service." Father Chisholm produced a large maroon bandana from his inner pocket.

She took it humbly, gratefully; tied it, like a mob-cap, with a butterfly knot behind her ear.

"There now, my dear." Fiske patted her on the back. "Why, you look quite captivating again."

"Do I, dear?" She smiled wanly, coquettishly. Her spirits lifted. "Now let's see what we can do to put this wretched yao-fang in order."

There was little they could do: the cave, no more than nine feet deep, held nothing but some broken crockery and its own dank gloom. The only light and air came from chinks in the barricaded entry. It was cheerless as a tomb. But they were worn-out. They stretched themselves on the floor. They slept.

It was afternoon when they were wakened by the creak of the opening hatch. A shaft of fantastic sunshine penetrated the yao-fang, then a middle-aged woman entered with a pitcher of hot water and two loaves of black bread. She stood watching as Father Chisholm handed one loaf to Dr. Fiske, then silently broke the other between Joshua and himself. Something in her attitude, in her dark and rather sullen face, caused the priest to gaze at her attentively.

"Why!" He gave a start of recognition. "You are Anna!" She did not answer. After sustaining his gaze, boldly, she turned and went out.

"Do you know that woman?" Fiske asked quickly.

"I am not sure. But yes, I am sure. She was a girl at the mission who . . . who ran away."

"Not a great tribute to your teaching." For the first time Fiske spoke acidly.

"We shall see."

That night they all slept badly. The discomforts of their confinement grew hourly. They took turns lying next to the hatch, for the privilege of breathing in the damp moist air. The little doctor kept groaning: "That awful bread! Dear heaven, it's tied my duodenum in a knot."

At noon, the next day, Anna came again with more hot water and a bowl of millet. Father Chisholm knew better than to address her by name.

"How long are we to be kept here?"

At first it seemed as though she would make no reply, then she said, indifferently:—

"The two men have departed for Pai-tan. When they return you will be free."

Dr. Fiske interposed restively: "Cannot you procure better food for us and blankets? We will pay."

She shook her head, scared off. But when she had retreated and let down the hatch she said, through the bars: "Pay me if you wish. It is not long to wait. It is nothing."

"Nothing." Fiske groaned again when she had gone. "I wish she had my insides."

"Don't give way, Wilbur." From the darkness beyond Mrs. Fiske exhorted him. "Remember, we've been through this before."

"We were young, then. Not old crocks on the verge of going home. And this Wai . . . he's got his knife in us missionaries especially . . . for changing his good old order when crime paid."

She persisted: "We must all keep cheerful. Look, we've got to distract ourselves. Not talk—or you two will start quarrelling about religion. A game. The silliest we can think of! We'll play 'animal, vegetable or mineral.' Joshua, are you awake? Good. Now listen and I'll explain how it goes."

They played the guessing game with heroic vigour. Joshua showed surprising aptitude. Then Mrs. Fiske's bright laugh cracked suddenly. They all fell very quiet. A dragging apathy succeeded; snatches of fitful sleep; uneasy, restless movements.

"Dear God, they must surely be back by now." All next day that phrase fell incessantly from Fiske's lips. His face and hands were hot to the touch. Lack of sleep and air had made him feverish. But it was evening before a loud shouting and the barking of dogs gave indication of a late arrival. The silence which followed was oppressive.

At last, footsteps approached and the hatch was flung open. On being commanded, they scrambled out on their hands and knees. The freshness of the night air, the sense of space and freedom, induced a delirium, almost, of relief.

"Thank heaven!" Fiske cried. "We're all right now."

An escort of soldiers took them to Wai-Chu.

He was seated, in his dwelling, on a coir mat, a lamp and a long pipe beside him, the lofty dilapidated room impregnated with the faintly bitter reek of poppy. Beside him was a soldier with a soiled blood-stained rag tied round his forearm. Five others of his troop, including the corporal, stood by the walls with rattans in their hands.

A penetrating silence followed the introduction of the prisoners. Wai studied them with deep and meditative cruelty. It was a hidden cruelty, sensed rather than seen, behind the mask of his face.

"The voluntary gift has not been paid." His voice was flat, unemotional. "When my men advanced to the city to receive it one was killed and the other wounded."

A shiver passed over Father Chisholm. What he had dreaded had come to pass. He said:—

"Probably the message was never delivered. The bearer was afraid and ran away to his home in Shansee without going to Pai-tan."

"You are too talkative. Ten strokes on the legs."

The priest had expected this. The punishment was severe, the edge of the long square rod, wielded by one of the soldiers, lacerating his shins and thighs.

"The messenger was our servant." Mrs. Fiske spoke with suppressed indignation, a high spot of colour burning on her pale cheek. "It is not the Shang-Foo's fault if he ran away."

"You are also too talkative. Twenty slaps on the face."

She was beaten hard with the open palm on both cheeks while the doctor trembled and struggled beside her.

"Tell me, since you are so wise. If your servant ran away why should my emissaries be waited upon and ambushed?"

Father Chisholm wished to say that, in these times, the Pai-tan garrison was perpetually on the alert and would shoot any of Wai's men on sight. He knew this to be the explanation. He judged it wiser to hold his tongue.

"Now you are not so talkative. Ten strokes on the shoulders for keeping unnatural silence."

He was beaten again.

"Let us return to our missions." Fiske threw out his hands, gesticulating, like an agitated woman. "I assure you on my solemn oath that you will be paid without the slightest hesitation."

"I am not a fool!"

"Then send another of your soldiers to Lantern Street with a message which I will write. Send him now, immediately."

"And have him slaughtered also? Fifteen blows for assuming that I am a fool."

Under the blows the doctor burst into tears. "You are to be pitied," he blubbered. "I forgive you but I pity, I pity you."

There was a pause. It was almost possible to observe the dull flicker of gratification in Wai's contracted pupils. He turned to Joshua. The lad was healthy and strong. He desperately needed recruits.

"Tell me. Are you prepared to make atonement by enlisting under my banner?"

"I am sensible of the honour." Joshua spoke steadily. "But it is impossible."

"Renounce your foreign devil god and you will be spared."

Father Chisholm endured an instant of cruel suspense, preparing himself for the pain and humiliation of the boy's surrender.

"I will die gladly for the true Lord of Heaven."

"Thirty blows for being a contumacious wretch."

Joshua did not utter a cry. He took the punishment with eyes cast down. Not a moan escaped him. But every blow made Father Chisholm wince.

"Now will you advise your servant to repent?"

"Never." The priest answered firmly, his soul illuminated by the boy's courage.

"Twenty blows on the legs for reprehensible obduracy."

At the twelfth blow, delivered on the front of his shins, there was a sharp brittle crack. An agonizing pain shot through the broken limb. Oh Lord, thought Francis, that's the worst of old bones.

Wai considered them with an air of finality. "I cannot continue to shield you. If the money does not arrive tomorrow I have a foreboding that some evil may befall you."

He dismissed them blankly. Father Chisholm could barely limp across the courtyard. Back in the *yao-fang* Mrs. Fiske made him sit down and, kneeling beside him, stripped off his boot and sock. The doctor, somewhat recovered, then set the broken limb.

"I've no splint . . . nothing but these rags." His voice had a high and tremulous ring. "It's a nasty fracture. If you don't rest it'll turn compound. Feel how my hands are shaking. Help us, dear Lord! We're going home next month. We're not so—"

"Please, Wilbur." She soothed him with a quiet touch. He completed dressing the injury in silence. Then she added: "We must try to keep our spirits up. If we give in now, what's going to happen to us tomorrow?"

Perhaps it was well that she prepared them.

In the morning the four were led out into the courtyard, which was lined with the population of Tou-en-lai, and humming with the promise of a spectacle. Their hands were tied behind their backs and a bamboo pole passed between their arms. Two soldiers then seized the ends of each spit and, raising the prisoners, marched them in procession round the arena six times, in narrowing circles, bringing up before the bullet-pocked façade of the house where Wai was seated.

Sick with the pain of his broken leg, Father Chisholm felt, through the stupid ignominy, a terrible dejection, amounting to despair, that the creatures of God's hand should make a careless festival out of the blood and tears of others. He had to still the dreadful whisper that God could never fashion men like this . . . that God did not exist.

He saw that several of the soldiers had their rifles, he hoped that a merciful end was near. But after a pause, at a sign from Wai, they were turned about and frog-marched down the steep path, past some beached sampans on a narrow spit of shingle, to the river. Here, before the reassembled crowd, they were dragged through the shallows and each secured with cord to a mooring stake in five feet of running water.

The switch from the threat of sudden execution was so unexpected, the contrast to the filthy squalour of the cave so profound, it was impossible to escape a sensation of relief. The shock of the water restored them. It was cold from mountain springs, and clear as crystal. The priest's leg ceased to pain him. Mrs. Fiske smiled feebly. Her courage was heartrending.

Her lips shaped the words: "At least we shall get clean."

But after half an hour a change set in. Father Chisholm dared not look at his companions. The river, at first so refreshing, gradually grew colder, colder, losing its gentle numbness, compressing their bodies and lower limbs in an algid vice. Each heartbeat, straining to force the blood through frozen arteries, was a throb of pulsing agony. The head, engorged, floated disembodied, in a reddish haze. With his swimming senses the priest still strove to find the reason of this torture, which now he dimly recollected as "the water ordeal," an intermittent sadism, hallowed by tradition, first conceived by the tyrant Tchang. It was a punishment well suited to Wai's purpose, since it probably expressed his lingering hope that the ransom might still be paid. Francis suppressed a groan. If this were true, their sufferings were not yet over.

"It's remarkable." With chattering teeth the doctor tried to talk. "This pain . . . perfect demonstration of angina pectoris . . . intermittent blood supply through constricted vascular system. O blessed Jesus!" He began to whimper. "O Lord God of Hosts—why hast thou forsaken us? My poor wife . . . thank God she has fainted. Where am I? . . . Agnes . . . Agnes . . ." He was unconscious.

The priest painfully turned his eyes towards Joshua. The boy's head, barely visible to his congested gaze, seemed decapitated, the head of a young Saint John the Baptist on a streaming charger. Poor Joshua—and poor Joseph! How he would miss his eldest-born. Francis said gently:—

"My son, your courage and your faith—they are very pleasing to me."

"It is nothing, Master."

A pause. The priest, deeply moved, made a great effort to stem the torpor stealing over him.

"I meant to tell you, Joshua. You shall have the roan pony when we return to the mission."

"Does the Master think we shall ever return to the mission?"

"If not, Joshua, the good God will give you a finer pony to ride in heaven."

Another pause. Joshua said faintly:—

"I think, Father, I should prefer the little pony at the mission."

A great surging flowed into Francis' ears, ending their conversation with waves of darkness. When the priest came to himself again they were all back in the cave, flung together in a sodden heap. As he lay a moment, gathering his senses, he heard Fiske talking to his wife, in that querulous plaint to which his speech had fallen.

"At least we are out of it . . . that dreadful river."

"Yes, Wilbur dear, we are out of it. But unless I mistake that ruffian, to-morrow we shall be into it again." Her tone was quite practical as though she were discussing the menu for his dinner. "Don't let's delude ourselves, dearest. If he keeps us alive it's only because he means to kill us as horribly as possible."

"Aren't you . . . afraid, Agnes?"

"Not in the least, and you mustn't be either. You must show these poor pagans . . . and the Father . . . how good New England Christians die."

"Agnes dear . . . you're a brave woman."

The priest could feel the pressure of her arm about her husband. He was greatly stirred, reshaken by a passionate concern for his companions, these three people, so different, yet each so dear to him. Was there no way of escape? He thought deeply, with gritted teeth, his brow pressed against the earth.

An hour later when the woman entered with a dish of rice he placed himself between her and the door.

"Anna! Do not deny that you are Anna! Have you no gratitude for all that was done for you at the mission? No—" She tried to push past him. "I shall not let you go until you listen. You are still a child of God. You cannot see us slowly murdered. I command you in His name to help us."

"I can do nothing." In the darkness of the cave it was impossible to see her face. But her voice, though sullen, was subdued.

"You can do much. Leave the hatch unfastened. No one will think to blame you."

"To what purpose? All the ponies are guarded."

"We need no ponies, Anna."

A spark of inquiry flashed in her lowering gaze. "If you leave Tou-en-lai on foot you will be retaken next day."

"We shall leave by sampan . . . and float down-river."

"Impossible." She shook her head with vehemence. "The rapids are too strong."

"Better to drown in the rapids than here."

"It is not my business where you drown." She answered with sudden passion: "Nor to help you in any manner whatsoever."

Unexpectedly, Dr. Fiske reached out in the darkness and gripped her hand. "Look, Anna, take my fingers and give heed. You must make it your business. Do you understand? Leave the door free tonight."

There was a pause.

"No." She hesitated, slowly withdrew her hand. "I cannot tonight."

"You must."

"I will do it tomorrow . . . tomorrow . . . tomorrow." With an odd change of manner, a sudden wildness, she bent her head and darted from the cave. The hatch closed behind her with a heavy slam.

And a heavier silence settled upon the cave. No one believed that the woman would keep her word. Even if she meant it, her promise was a feeble thing to weigh against the prospects of the coming day.

"I'm a sick man," Fiske muttered peevishly, laying his head against his wife's shoulder. In the darkness they could hear him percussing his own chest. "My clothes are still sopping. D'you hear that . . . it's quite dull . . . lobar consolidation. Oh, God, I thought the tortures of the inquisition were matchless."

Somehow the night passed. The morning was cold and grey. As the light filtered through and sounds were heard in the courtyard, Mrs. Fiske straightened herself with a look of sublime resolution on her peaked and pallid face, still girded by the shrunken headdress. "Father Chisholm, you are the senior clergyman here. I ask you to say a prayer before we go out to what may be our martyrdom."

He knelt down beside her. They all joined hands. He prayed, as best he could, better than he had prayed in all his life. Then the soldiers came for them.

Weakened as they were, the river seemed colder than before. Fiske shouted hysterically as they drove him in. To Father Chisholm it now became a hazy vision.

Immersion, his thoughts ran mazily, purification by water, one drop and you were saved. How many drops were here? Millions and millions . . . four hundred million Chinese all waiting to be saved, each with a drop of water. . . .

"Father! Dear good Father Chisholm!" Mrs. Fiske was calling him, her eyes glassy with a sudden feverish gaiety. "They are all watching us from the bank. Let us show them. An example. Let us sing. What hymn have we in common? The Christmas Hymn, of course. A sweet refrain. Come, Joshua . . . Wilbur . . . all of us."

She struck up, in a high quavering pipe:—

"Oh, come, all ye faithful,
Joyful and triumphant . . ."

He joined with the others:—

"Oh, come ye, oh, come ye, to Bethlehem."

Late afternoon. They were back in the cave again. The doctor lay on his side. His breath came raspingly. He spoke with an air of triumph.

"Lobar pneumonia. I knew it yesterday. Apical dullness and crepitations. I'm sorry, Agnes, but . . . I'm rather glad."

No one said anything. She began to stroke his hot forehead with her bleached sodden fingers. She was still stroking when Anna came to the cave. This time, however, the woman brought no food with her.

She did no more than stand in the entrance staring at them with a kind of grudging sullenness. At last she said:—

"I have given the men your supper. They think it is a great joke. Go quickly before they discover their mistake."

There was an absolute silence. Father Chisholm felt his heart bound in his racked, exhausted body. It seemed impossible that they might leave the cave of their own free will. He said: "God will bless you, Anna. You have not forgotten Him and He has not forgotten you."

She gave no answer. She stared at him with her darkly inscrutable eyes which he had never read, even on that first night amidst the snow. Yet it gave him a burning satisfaction that she should justify his teaching, openly, before Dr. Fiske. She stood for a moment, then glided silently away.

Outside the cave it was dark. He could hear laughter and low voices from the neighbouring *yao-fang*. Across the courtyard there was a light in Wai's house. The adjacent stables and soldiers' quarters showed a feeble illumination. The sudden barking of a dog sent a shock through his tortured nerves. This slender hope was like a new pain, suffocating in its intensity.

Cautiously, he tried to stand upon his feet. But it was impossible, he fell heavily, beads of perspiration breaking on his brow. His leg, swollen to three times its natural size, was quite unusable.

In a whisper he told Joshua to take the half-unconscious doctor on his back and carry him very quietly to the sampans. He saw them go off, accompanied by Mrs. Fiske, Joshua bent under his sacklike burden, keeping cleverly to the dense shadows of the rocks. The faint clatter of a loose stone came back to him, so loud it seemed to wake the dead. He breathed again; no one had heard it but himself. In five minutes Joshua returned. Leaning on the boy's shoulder, he dragged slowly and painfully down the path.

Fiske was already stretched out on the bottom of the sampan with his wife crouched beside him. The priest seated himself in the stern. Lifting his useless leg with both hands he arranged it out of the way, like a piece of timber, then propped himself against the gunwale with his elbow. As Joshua climbed into the bow and began to untie the mooring rope he seized the single stern oar in readiness to push off.

Suddenly a shout rang out from the top of the cliff, followed by another and the sound of running. A loud commotion broke, dogs set up a violent barking. Then two torches flared in the upper darkness and came rapidly, amidst shrill voices and excited, clattering footsteps, down the river path.

The priest's lips moved, in the anguished immobility of his body. But he remained silent. Joshua, fumbling and tearing at the matted rope, knew the danger, without the added confusion of a command.

At last, with a wild gasp, the boy pulled the rope loose, falling backwards against the thwarts. Instantly, Father Chisholm felt the sampan float free and with all his remaining strength he fended it into the current. Out of the slack water, they spun aimlessly, then began to slide downstream. Across and behind them, the flares now showed a group of running figures on the bank. A rifle-shot cracked, followed by an irregular volley. The lead skipped the water with a twanging hum. They were sliding faster now, much faster; they were almost out of range. Father Chisholm was staring into the dark wall ahead with almost feverish relief when suddenly, amidst the scattered shooting, a great weight struck at him out of the night. His head rocked under the impact of what seemed a heavy flying stone. Beyond the crashing blow he had no pain. He raised his hand to his wet face. The bullet had smashed through his upper jaw, torn out by his right cheek. He kept silent. The firing ceased. No one else was hit.

The river now moved them forward at intimidating speed. He was quite sure in his own mind that it must ultimately join the Hwang—no other outlet was possible. He leaned forward towards Fiske and, seeing him conscious, made an effort to cheer him.

"How do you feel?"

"Pretty comfortable, considering I'm dying." He repressed a short cough. "I'm sorry I've been such an old woman, Agnes."

"Please don't talk, dear."

The priest straightened himself, sadly. Fiske's life was ebbing away. His own resistance was almost gone. He had to fight an almost irresistible impulse to weep.

Presently an increase in the volume of the river's sound heralded their approach to broken water. The noise seemed to blot out what vision was left him. He could see nothing. With his single oar he pulled the sampan straight with the current. As they shot down, he commended their souls to God.

He was beyond caring, beyond realizing how the craft lived in that unseen thunder. The roar dulled him into stupor. He clung to the useless oar as they lurched and plunged, invisibly. At times they seemed to drop through empty space, as if the bottom had fallen from the boat. When a splintering crash arrested their momentum, he thought numbly that they must founder. But they plunged off again, the boiling water surging in on them as they whirled, down, down. Whenever he felt they must be free, a new roaring reared itself ahead, reached out, engulfed them. At a narrow bend they hit the rocky bank with stunning force, ripping low branches from overhanging trees, then bounced, spun, crashed on again. His brain was caught in the swirl, battered and jarred, down, down, down.

The peace of the quiet water, far below, brought him feebly to his senses. A faint streak of dawn lay ahead of them, limning a broad expanse of gentle pastoral waters. He could not guess what distance they had come, though dimly he surmised it must be many li. All he knew was this: they had reached the Hwang and were floating calmly on its bosom towards Pai-tan.

He tried to move, but could not, his weakness held him fettered. His damaged limb felt heavier than lead, the pain of his smashed face was like a raging toothache. But with incredible effort he turned and pulled himself slowly down the boat with his hands. The light increased. Joshua was huddled in the bow, his body limp, but breathing. He was asleep. In the bottom of the sampan Fiske and his wife lay together, her arm supporting his head, her body shielding him from the water they had shipped. She was awake and calmly reasonable. The priest was conscious of a great wonder as he gazed at her. She had shown the highest endurance of them all. Her eyes answered his unspoken inquiry with a wan negation. He could see that her husband was almost gone.

Fiske was breathing in little staccato spasms, with intervals when he did not breathe at all. He muttered constantly but his eyes, though fixed, were open. And, suddenly, there appeared in them a vague, uncertain light of recognition. The shadow of a movement crossed his lips—nothing, yet in that nothingness hovered the suggestion of a smile. His muttering took on coherent form.

"Don't pride yourself . . . dear fellow . . . on Anna." A little gasp of breathing. "Not so much your teaching as—" Another spasm. "I bribed her." Weakly, the flutter of a laugh. "With the fifty-dollar bill I always carried in my shoe." A feeble triumphant pause. "But God bless you, dear fellow, all the same."

He seemed happier now he had scored his final point. He closed his eyes. As the sun rose in a flood of sudden light they saw that he was gone.

Back in the stern Father Chisholm watched Mrs. Fiske compose the dead man's hands. He looked dizzily at his own hands. The backs of both his wrists were covered peculiarly with raised red spots. When he touched them they rolled like buckshot beneath his skin. He thought, Some insect has bitten me while I slept.

Later, through the rising morning vapours, he saw down-river, in the distance, the flat boats of cormorant fishers. He closed his throbbing eyes. The sampan was drifting . . . drifting in the golden haze, towards them.

13

ONE afternoon six months later the two new missionary priests, Father Stephen Munsey, M.B. and Father Jerome Craig, were earnestly discussing the arrangements over coffee and cigarettes.

"Everything has got to be perfect. Thank God the weather looks good."

"And settled." Father Jerome nodded. "It's a blessing we have the band."

They were young, healthy, full of vitality, with an immense belief in themselves and God. Father Munsey, the American priest, with a medical degree from Baltimore, was slightly the taller of the two, a fine six-footer, but Father Craig's shoulders had gained him a place in the Holywell boxing team. Though Craig was British he had a pleasant touch of American keenness, for he had taken a two years' missionary preparatory course at the College of St. Michael's in San Francisco. Here, indeed, he had met Father Munsey.

The two had felt, instinctively, a mutual attraction, had soon become, affectionately, "Steve" and "Jerry" to each other—except on those occasions when a burst of self-conscious dignity induced a more formal tone. "Say, Jerry, old boy, are you playing basketball this afternoon?— And oh, er, by the way, Father, what time is your mass tomorrow?" To be sent to Pai-tan together had set the seal upon their friendship.

"I asked Mother Mercy Mary to look in." Father Steve poured himself fresh coffee. He was clean-cut and virile, two years senior to Craig, admittedly the leader of the partnership. "Just to discuss the final touches. She's so cheery and obliging. She's going to be a great help to us."

"Yes, she's a grand person. Honestly, Jerry, we'll make things hum here when we have it to ourselves."

"Hist! Don't talk so loud," Father Steve warned. "The old boy's not so deaf as you'd think."

"He's a case." Father Jerry's blunt features melted to a reminiscent smile. "Of course I know you pulled him through. But at his age to shake off a broken leg, a smashed jaw, and the smallpox on top of it—well!—it says something for his pluck."

"He's terribly feeble though." Munsey spoke seriously. "It's quite finished him. I'm hoping the long voyage home'll do him good."

"He's a funny old devil—sorry, Father, I mean fogy. D'you remember, when he was so sick and Mrs. Fiske sent up the four-poster bed before she left for home? The awful trouble we had to get him into it? Remember how he kept saying 'How can I rest if I'm comfortable?' " Jerry laughed.

"And that other time he threw the beef tea at Mother Mercy Mary's head—" Father Steve stifled his grin. "No, no, Father, we mustn't let our tongues get the better of us. After all he's not so bad if you take him the right way. Anybody would get a bit queer in the topknot after being over thirty years out here alone. Thank God we're a pair. Come in."

Mother Mercy Mary entered, smiling, red-cheeked, her eyes friendly and merry. She was very happy with her new priests, whom she thought of, instinctively, as two nice boys. She would mother them. It was good for the mission to have this infusion of young blood. It would be more human for her to have a proper priest's laundry to oversee, decent thick underwear to darn.

"Afternoon, Reverend Mother. Can we tempt you to the cup that cheers but doesn't inebriate? Good. Two lumps? We'll have to watch that sweet tooth of yours in Lent. Well now, about tomorrow's farewell ceremonies for Father Chisholm."

They talked together, amicably and earnestly, for half an hour. Then Mother Mercy Mary seemed to prick up her ears. Her expression of maternal protectiveness deepened. Listening acutely, she sounded a note of concern with her tongue.

"Do you hear him about? I don't. God bless my soul, I'm sure he's away out without telling us." She rose. "Excuse me, Fathers. I'll have to find out what he's up to. If he goes and gets his feet wet it'll ruin everything."

Leaning on his old rolled umbrella, Father Chisholm had made a last pilgrimage of his mission of St. Andrew's. The slight exertion fatigued him absurdly; he realized, with an inward sigh, how sadly useless his long illness had left him. He was an old man. The thought was quite staggering—he felt so little different, within his heart, so unchanged. And tomorrow he must leave Pai-tan. Incredible! When he had made up his mind to lay his bones at the foot of the mission garden alongside Willie Tulloch. Phrases in the Bishop's letter recurred to him: ". . . not up to it, solicitous your health, deeply appreciative, end your labours in the foreign mission field." Well, God's will be done!

He was standing, now, in the little churchyard, swept by a flood of tender, ghostly memories, noting the wooden crosses—Willie's, Sister Clotilde's, the gardener Fu's, a dozen more, each an end and a beginning, the milestones of their common pilgrimage.

He shook his head like an old horse amidst a hum of insects in a sunny field: really he must not yield to reverie. He fixed his gaze across the low wall in the new pasture field. Joshua was putting the roan pony through its paces while four of his younger brothers watched admiringly. Joseph himself was not far off. Fat, complacent and forty-five, shepherding the remainder of his nine children back from their afternoon stroll, he slowly pushed a wicker perambulator towards the lodge. What richer instance, thought the priest with a faint slow smile, of the subjugation of the noble male?

He had made the grand tour, as unobtrusively as possible, for he guessed what lay in store for him tomorrow. School, dormitory, refectory, the lace and mat-making workrooms, the little annex he had opened last year to teach basket-weaving to the blind children. Well . . . why continue the meagre tally? In the past he had judged it some small achievement. In his present mood of gentle melancholy he measured it as nothing. He swung round stiffly. From the new hall came the ominous stertor of wind on brass. Again he suppressed a crooked smile, or was it perhaps a frown? These young curates with their explosive ideas! Only last night, when he was trying—vainly, of course—to instruct them in the topography of the parish, the doctor one had whispered: *Aeroplane*. What were things coming to! Two hours by air to the Liu village. And his first trip had taken him two weeks on foot!

He ought not to go farther, for the afternoon was turning chill. But, though he knew his disobedience would earn a merited scolding, he pressed harder on his umbrella and went slowly down the Hill of Brilliant Green Jade towards the deserted site of the first forgotten mission. Though the compound was now rank with bamboo, the lower edge eroded to a muddy swamp, the mud-brick stable still remained.

He bowed his head and passed under the sagging roof, assailed, immediately, by another host of recollections, seeing a young priest, dark, eager and intent, crouched before a brazier, his sole companion a Chinese boy. That first mass he had celebrated here, on his japanned tin trunk without bell or server, no one but himself—how sharply it struck the taut chords of his memory. Clumsily, a stiff ungainly figure, he knelt down, and begged God to judge him less by his deeds than by his intention.

Back at the mission he let himself in by the side porch and went softly upstairs. He was fortunate; no one saw him come in. He did not wish "the grand slam," as he had come to call it, a flurry of feet and doors, with hot-water bottles and solicitous profferings of soup. But, as he opened the door of his room, he was surprised to find Mr. Chia inside. His disfigured face, now grey with cold, lit up to a sudden warmth. Heedless of formality, he took his old friend's hand and pressed it.

"I hoped you would come."

"How could I refrain from coming?" Mr. Chia spoke in a sad and strangely troubled voice. "My dear Father, I need not tell you how deeply I regret your departure. Our long friendship has meant much to me."

The priest answered quietly: "I, too, shall miss you much. Your kindness and benefactions have overwhelmed me."

"It is less than nothing," Mr. Chia waved the gratitude away, "beside your inestimable service to me. And have I not always enjoyed the peace and beauty of your mission garden? Without you, the garden will hold a great sadness." His tone lifted to a fitful gleam. "But then . . . perhaps, on your recovery . . . you may return to Pai-tan?"

"Never." The priest paused, with the suspicion of a smile. "We must look forward to our meeting in the celestial hereafter."

An odd silence fell. Mr. Chia broke it with constraint. "Since our time together is limited it might not be unfitting if we talked a moment regarding the hereafter."

"All my time is dedicated to such talk."

Mr. Chia hesitated, beset by unusual awkwardness. "I have never pondered deeply on what state lies beyond this life. But if such a state exists it would be very agreeable for me to enjoy your friendship there."

Despite his long experience, Father Chisholm did not grasp the import of the remark. He smiled but did not answer. And Mr. Chia was forced in great embarrassment to be direct.

"My friend, I have often said: There are many religions and each has its gate to heaven." A faint colour crept beneath his dark skin. "Now it would appear that I have the extraordinary desire to enter by your gate."

Dead silence. Father Chisholm's bent figure was immobilized, rigid.

"I cannot believe that you are serious."

"Once, many years ago, when you cured my son, I was not serious. But then I was unaware of the nature of your life . . . of its patience, quietness and courage. The goodness of a religion is best judged by the goodness of its adherents. My friend . . . you have conquered me by example."

Father Chisholm raised his hand to his forehead, that familiar sign of hidden emotion. His conscience had often reproached him for his initial refusal to accept Mr. Chia, even without a true intention. He spoke slowly. "All day long my mouth has been bitter with the ashes of failure. Your words have rekindled the fires in my heart. Because of this one moment I feel that my work has not been worthless. In spite of that I say to you . . . don't do this for friendship—only if you have belief."

Mr. Chia answered firmly. "My mind is made up. I do it for friendship and belief. We are as brothers, you and I. Your Lord must also be mine. Then, even though you must depart tomorrow, I shall be content, knowing that in our Master's garden our spirits will one day meet."

At first the priest was unable to speak. He fought to conceal the depth of his feeling. He reached out his hand to Mr. Chia. In a low uncertain tone he said:—

"Let us go down to the church." . . .

Next morning broke warm and clear. Father Chisholm, awakened by the sound of singing, escaped from the sheets of Mrs. Fiske's bed and stumbled to the open window. Beneath his balcony twenty little girls from the junior school, none more than nine years of age, dressed in white and blue sashes, were serenading him: *Hail, Smiling Morn* . . . He grimaced at them. At the end of the tenth verse he called down:—

"That's enough. Go and get your breakfast."

They stopped, smiled up at him, holding their music sheets. "Do you like it, Father?"

"No . . . Yes. But it's time for breakfast."

They started off again from the beginning and sang it all through with extra verses while he was shaving. At the words "on thy fresh cheek" he cut himself. Peering into the minute mirror at his own reflection, pocked and cicatrized, and now gory, he thought mildly, Dear me, what a dreadful-looking ruffian I've become, I really must behave myself today.

The breakfast gong sounded. Father Munsey and Father Craig were both waiting on him, alert, deferential, smiling—the one rushing to pull out his chair, the other to lift the cover from the kedgeree. They were so anxious to please they could scarcely sit still. He scowled.

"Will you young idiots kindly stop treating me like your great-grandmother on her hundredth birthday?"

Must humour the old boy, thought Father Jerry. He smiled tenderly. "Why, Father, we're just treating you like one of ourselves. Of course you can't escape the honour due to a pioneer who blazed the first trails. You don't want to, either. It's your natural reward and don't you have any doubt about it."

"I have a great many doubts."

Father Steve said heartily: "Don't you worry, Father. I know how you feel, but we won't let you down. Why, Jerry—I mean Father Craig and I have schemes in hand for doubling the size and efficiency of St. Andrew's. We're going to have twenty catechists—pay them good wages too—start a rice-kitchen in Lantern Street, right opposite your Methodist pals there. We'll poke them in the eye all right." He laughed good-naturedly, reassuringly. "It's going to be downright, honest, foursquare Catholicism. Wait till we get our plane! Wait till we start sending you our conversion graphs. Wait till—"

"The cows come home," said Father Chisholm dreamily.

The two young priests exchanged a sympathetic glance. Father Steve said kindly:—

"You won't forget to take your medicine in the trip home, Father? One tablespoonful *ex aqua*, three times a day. There's a big bottle in your bag."

"No, there isn't. I threw it out before I came down." Suddenly Father Chisholm began to laugh. He laughed until he shook. "My dear boys, don't mind me. I'm a cantankerous scoundrel. You'll do grandly here if you're not too cocksure . . . if you're kind and tolerant, and especially if you don't try to teach every old Chinaman how to suck eggs."

"Why . . . yes . . . yes, of course, Father."

"Look! I have no aeroplanes to spare but I'd like to leave you a useful little souvenir. It was given me by an old priest. It's been with me on most of my travels." He left the table, handed them from the corner of the room the tartan umbrella Rusty Mac had given him. "It has a certain status amongst the state umbrellas of Pai-tan. It may bring you luck."

Father Jerry took it gingerly as though it were a sort of a relic.

"Thank you, thank you, Father. What pretty colours. Are they Chinese?"

"Much worse, I'm afraid." The old priest smiled and shook his head. He would say no more.

Father Munsey put down his napkin with a surreptitious signal to his colleague. There was an organizing glitter in his eye. He rose.

"Well, Father, if you'll excuse Father Craig and myself. Time is getting on, and we're expecting Father Chou any moment now . . ."

They departed briskly.

He was due to leave at eleven o'clock. He returned to his room. When he had completed his modest packing he had still an hour in which to wander round. He descended, drawn instinctively towards the church. There, outside his house, he drew up, genuinely touched. His entire congregation, nearly five hundred, stood awaiting him, orderly and silent, in the courtyard. The contingent from the Liu village, under Father Chou, stood on one flank, the older girls and handicraft workers upon the other, with his beloved children, shepherded by Mother Mercy Mary, Martha, and the four Chinese Sisters, in front. There was something in the mass attention of their eyes, all bent affectionately upon his insignificant form, which gripped him with a sudden pang.

A deeper hush. From his nervousness it was clear that Joseph had been entrusted with the honour of the address. Two chairs were produced like a conjuring trick. When the old Father was seated in one, Joseph mounted unsteadily upon the other, almost overbalancing, and unrolled the vermilion scroll.

"Most Reverend and Worthy Disciple of the Lord of Heaven, it is with the utmost anguish that we, thy children, witness thy departure across the broad oceans . . ."

The address was no different from a hundred other eulogies suffered in the past except that it was lachrymose. Despite a score of secret rehearsals before his wife, Joseph's delivery was vanquished by the open courtyard. He began to sweat and his paunch quivered like a jelly. Poor dear Joseph, thought the priest, staring at his boots and thinking of a slim young boy running, unfaltering, at his bridle rein thirty years ago.

When it was over the entire congregation sang the *Gloria laus* quite beautifully. Still looking at his boots, as the clear voices ascended, the priest felt a melting of his old bones. "Dear God," he prayed, "don't let me make a fool of myself."

For the presentation, they had chosen the youngest girl in the basket-weaving centre for the blind. She came forward, in her black skirt and white blouse, uncertain yet sure, guided by her instinct and Mother Mercy Mary's whispered instructions. As she knelt before him, holding out the ornate gilt chalice of execrable design, bought by mail order from Nankin, his eyes were sightless as her own. "Bless you, bless you, my child," he muttered. He could say no more.

Mr. Chia's number-one chair now swam into the orbit of his hazy vision. Disembodied hands helped him into it. The procession formed and set off amidst the popping of firecrackers and a sudden burst of Sousa from the new school band.

As he swayed slowly down the hill, borne pontifically on the shoulders of the men, he tried to rivet his consciousness upon the gimcrack comedy of the band: twenty schoolboys in sky-blue uniforms, blowing their cheeks out, preceded by a Chinese majorette aged eight in fleecy shako and high white boots, strutting, twirling a cane, kicking up her knees. But somehow, his sense of the ridiculous had ceased to function. In the town the doorways were crowded with friendly faces. More firecrackers welcomed him at every street crossing. As he neared the landing stage flowers were cast before him.

Mr. Chia's launch lay waiting at the steps, the engines quietly running. The chair was lowered, he stepped out. It had come at last. They were surrounding him bidding him farewell: the two young priests, Father Chou, Reverend Mother, Martha, Mr. Chia, Joseph, Joshua . . . all of them, some of the women of the congregation weeping, kneeling to kiss his hand. He had meant to say something. He could not mumble one incoherent word. His breast was overflowing.

Blindly, he boarded the launch. As he turned again to face them there fell a bar of silence. At a prearranged signal, the children's choir began his favourite hymn: the *Veni Creator*. They had saved it till the last.

> "Come, Holy Spirit, Creator, come,
> From thy bright heav'nly throne."

He had always loved these noble words, written by the great Charlemagne in the ninth century, the loveliest hymn of the Church. Everyone on the landing was singing now.

> "Take possession of our souls,
> And make them all thy own."

Oh, dear, he thought, yielding at last, that's kind, that's sweet of them . . . but oh, how wickedly unfair! A convulsive movement passed over his face.

As the launch moved away from the stage and he raised his hand to bless them, tears were streaming down his battered face.

V

THE RETURN

1

His Grace Bishop Mealey was extremely late. Twice a nice young priest of the household had peeped round the parlour door to explain that His Lordship and His Lordship's secretary were detained, unavoidably, at a Convocation. Father Chisholm blinked formidably over his copy of the *Tablet*.

"Punctuality is the politeness of prelates!"

"His Lordship is a very busy man." With an uncertain smile, the young priest withdrew, not quite sure of this old boy from China, half-wondering if he could be trusted with the silver. The appointment had been for eleven. Now the clock showed half-past twelve.

It was the same room in which he had awaited his interview with Rusty Mac. How long ago? Good heavens . . . thirty-six years! He shook his head dolefully. It had amused him to intimidate the pretty stripling, but his mood was far from combative. He felt rather shaky this morning, and desperately nervous. He wanted something from the Bishop. He hated asking favours, yet he must ask this one, and his heart had jumped when the summons to the interview arrived at the modest hotel where he had been staying since the ship unloaded him at Liverpool.

Valiantly, he straightened his wrinkled vest, spruced up his tired collar. He was not really old. There was plenty of go in him yet. Now that it was well past noon, Anselm would undoubtedly ask him to remain to luncheon. He would be spry, curb his outrageous tongue, listen to Anselm's stories, laugh at his jokes, not be above a little, or perhaps a lot of, flattery. He hoped to God the nerve wouldn't start twitching in his damaged cheek. That made him look a perfect lunatic!

It was ten minutes to one. At last there came a commotion of importance in the corridor outside and, decisively, Bishop Mealey entered the room. Perhaps he had been hurrying; his manner was brisk, his eye beaming towards Francis, not unconscious of the clock.

"My dear Francis. It's splendid to see you again. You must pardon this little delay. No, don't get up, I beg of you. We'll talk here. It's . . . it's more intimate than in my room."

Briskly, he pulled out a chair and seated himself with an easy grace beside Father Chisholm at the table. As he rested his fleshy, well-tended hand affectionately upon the other's sleeve, he thought: Good heavens, how old and feeble he has become!

"And how is dear Pai-tan? Not unflourishing, Monsignor Sleeth tells me. I vividly remember when I stood in that stricken city, amidst deadly plague and desolation. Truly the hand of God lay upon it. Ah, those were my pioneering days, Francis. I pine for them sometimes. Now," he smiled, "I'm only a Bishop. Do you see much change in me since we parted on that Orient strand?"

Francis studied his old friend with an odd admiration. There was no doubt of it—the years had improved Anselm Mealey. Maturity had come late to him. His office had given him dignity, toned his early effusiveness to suavity. He had a fine presence and held his head high. The soft full ecclesiastic face was lit by the same velvety eye. He was well preserved, still had his own teeth, and a supple vigorous skin.

Francis said simply, "I've never seen you look better."

The Bishop inclined his head, pleased. "*O tempora! O mores!* We're neither of us so young as we were. But I don't wear too badly. Frankly, I find perfect health essential to efficiency. If you knew what I have to cope with! They've put me on a balanced diet. And I have a masseur, a husky Swede, who literally pummels the fear of God into me. . . . I'm afraid," with a sudden genuine solicitude, "you've been very careless of yourself."

"I feel like an old ragman beside you, Anselm, and that is God's truth. . . . But I keep young in heart . . . or try to. And there's still some service left in me. I . . . I hope you're not altogether dissatisfied with my work in Pai-tan."

"My dear Father, your efforts were heroic. Naturally we're a little disappointed in the figures. Monsignor Sleeth was showing me only yesterday . . ." The voice was quite benevolent. ". . . In all your thirty-six years you made less conversions than Father Lawler made in five. Please don't think I'm reproaching you—that would be too unkind. Someday when you have leisure we'll discuss it thoroughly. Meanwhile—" His eye was hovering round the clock. "Is there anything we can do for you?"

There was a pause; then, in a low tone, Francis answered: "Yes . . . There is, your Grace . . . I want a parish."

The Bishop almost started out of his benign, affectionate composure. He slowly raised his brows as Father Chisholm continued, with that quiet intensity: "Give me Tweedside, Anselm. There's a vacancy at Renton . . . a bigger, better parish. Promote the Tweedside priest to Renton. And let me . . . Let me go home."

The Bishop's smile had become fixed, rather less easy, upon his handsome face. "My dear Francis, you seem to wish to administer my diocese."

"I have a special reason for asking you. I would be so very grateful . . ." To his horror Father Chisholm found his voice out of control. He broke off, then added huskily: "Bishop MacNabb promised I should have a parish if ever I came home." He began to fumble in his inside pocket. "I have his letter . . ."

Anselm raised his hand. "I can't be expected to honour the posthumous letters of my predecessor." A silence; then, with kindly urbanity, His Lordship continued: "Naturally, I will bear your request in mind. But I cannot promise. Tweedside has always been very dear to me. When the weight of the pro-cathedral is off my shoulders I had thought of building myself a retreat there—a little Castle Gondolfo." He paused—his ear, still keen, picking up the sound of an arriving car, followed by voices in the hall outside. Diplomatically his eye sought the clock. His pleasant manner quickened. "Well . . . It is all in God's hands. We shall see, we shall see."

"If you would let me explain—" Francis protested humbly. "I'm . . . rather anxious to make a home . . . for someone."

"You must tell me some other time." Another car outside and more voices. The Bishop gathered up his violet cassock, his tone honeyed with regret. "It is quite a calamity, Francis, that I must slip away, just as I was looking forward to our long and interesting talk. I have an official luncheon at one. The Lord Mayor and City Council are my guests. More politics, alas . . . school board, water board, finance . . . a *quid pro quo* . . . I have to be a stockbroker these days . . . But I like it Francis, I like it!"

"I wouldn't take more than a minute . . ." Francis stopped short, dropped his gaze to the floor.

The Bishop had risen blandly. With his arm lightly on Father Chisholm's shoulder he aided him affectionately to the door. "I can't express what a great joy it has been for me to welcome you home. We will keep in touch with you, never fear. And now, I must leave you. Good-bye, Francis . . . and bless you."

Outside, a stream of large dark limousines flowed up the drive towards the high portico of the palace. The old priest had a vision of a purple face beneath a beaver hat, of more faces, hard and bloated, of miniver, gold chains of office. A wet wind was blowing and it cut his old bones, used to sunshine and covered only by his thin tropic suit. As he moved away a carwheel churned near the curb and a spurt of mud flew up and hit him in the eye. He wiped it off with his hand, gazing down the arches of the years, reflecting, with a faint grim smile: Anselm's mud bath is avenged.

His breast was cold, yet through his disappointment, his sinking weakness, a white flame burned, unquenchably. He must find a church at once. Across the street the great domed bulk of the new cathedral loomed, a million pounds in sterling, transmuted to massive stone and marble. He limped urgently towards it.

He reached the broad entrance steps, mounted them, then suddenly drew up. Before him, on the wet stone of the topmost step, a ragged cripple crouched in the wind, with a card pinned upon his chest: *Old Soldier, Please Help.*

Francis contemplated the broken figure. He pulled out the solitary shilling from his pocket, placed it in the tin cup. The two unwanted soldiers gazed at each other in silence, then each gazed away.

He entered the pro-cathedral, an echoing vastness of beauty and silence, pillared in marble, rich in oak and bronze, a temple of towering and intricate design, in which his mission chapel would have stood unnoticed, forgotten, in a corner of the transept. Undaunted, he marched towards the high altar. There he knelt and fiercely, with unshaken valour, prayed.

"Oh, Lord, for once—not Thy will, but mine, be done."

2

FIVE weeks later Father Chisholm made his expedition, long deferred, to Kirkbridge. As he left the railway station the cotton-thread mills of that large industrial centre were disgorging their workers for the dinner hour. Hundreds of women with shawls wrapped about their heads went hurrying through the drenching rain, yielding only to an occasional tram clanging over the greasy cobbles.

At the end of the main street he inquired his way, then took to the right, past an enormous statue erected to a local thread magnate, and entered a poorer locality: a squalid square imprisoned by high tenements. He crossed the square and plunged into a narrow alley, fetid with smells, so dark that, on the brightest day, no gleam of sun could penetrate. Despite his joy, his high excitement, the priest's heart sank. He had expected poverty but not this. . . . He thought: What have I done in my stupidity and neglect! Here, it was like being at the bottom of a well.

He inspected the numbers on the tenement entrances, singled out the right one, and began to climb the stairs, which were without light or air, the windows foul, the gas brackets plugged. A cracked soil pipe had drenched one landing.

Three flights up he stumbled and almost fell. A child was seated upon the stairs, a boy. The priest stared through the foggy gloom at the small rachitic figure, supporting his heavy head with one hand, bracing his sharp elbow against his bony knee. His skin was the colour of candle tallow. He was almost transparent. He looked like a tired old man. He might have been seven years of age.

Suddenly the boy lifted his head so that a shaft from the broken skylight fell upon him. For the first time Francis saw the child's face. He gave a stifled exclamation and a heavy wave of terrible emotion broke over him, he felt it as a ship might feel the buffet of a heavy wave. That pallid upturned face was unmistakable in its likeness to Nora's face. The eyes, especially, enormous in the pinched skin, could never be denied.

"What is your name?"

A pause. The boy answered: "Andrew."

Behind the landing door there was a single room where, cross-legged on a dirty mattress stretched on the bare boards, a woman stitched rapidly, her needle flying with deadly, automatic speed. Beside her, on an upturned egg-box, was a bottle. There was no furniture, only a kettle, some sacking, and a cracked jug. Across the egg-box lay a pile of half-finished coarse serge trousers.

Torn by his distress, Francis could barely speak. "You are Mrs. Stevens?" She nodded. "I came . . . about the boy."

She let her work fall nervously into her lap: a poor creature, not old, nor vicious, yet worn-out by adversity, sodden through and through. "Yes, I had your letter." She began to whimper out an explanation of her circumstances, to exonerate herself, to produce irrelevant evidence proving how misfortune had lowered her to this.

He stopped her quietly; the story was written in her face. He said: "I'll take him back with me today."

At this quietness, she dropped her eyes to her swollen hands, the fingers blue-stippled by countless needle-pricks. Though she made an effort to conceal it, his attitude agitated her more than any rebuke. She began to weep. "Don't think I'm not fond of him. He helps me in a heap of ways. I've treated him well enough. But it's been a sore struggle." She looked up with sudden defiance, silent.

Ten minutes later he left the house. Beside him, clutching a paper bundle to his pigeon chest, was Andrew. The priest's feelings were deep and complex. He sensed the child's dumb alarm at the unprecedented excursion, yet felt he could best reassure him by silence. He thought, with a slow deep joy: God gave me my life, brought me from China . . . for this!

They walked to the railway station without a word between them. In the train, Andrew sat staring out of the window, hardly moving, his legs dangling over the edge of the seat. He was very dirty, grime was ingrained into his thin pallid neck. Once or twice he glanced sideways at Francis, then immediately he glanced away again. It was impossible to guess his thoughts, but in the depths of his eyes there lurked a dark glimmer of fear and suspicion.

"Don't be afraid."

"I'm not afraid." The boy's underlip quivered.

Once the train had quitted the smoke of Kirkbridge it sped across the country and down the riverside. A look of wonder dawned slowly on the boy's face. He had never dreamed that colours could be so bright, so different from the leaden squalor of the slums. The open fields and farmlands gave place to a wilder scene, where woods sprang up about them, rich with green bracken and the part's-tongue fern, where the glint of rushing water showed in little glens.

"Is this where we are going?"

"Yes, we're nearly there."

They ran into Tweedside towards three in the afternoon. The old town, clustered on the riverbank, so unchanged he might have left it only yesterday, lay basking in brilliant sunshine. As the familiar landmarks swam into his gaze Francis' throat constricted with a painful joy. They left the little station and walked to St. Columba's Presbytery together.

VI

END OF THE BEGINNING

1

FROM the window of his room Monsignor Sleeth frowned down towards the garden where Miss Moffat, basket in hand, stood with Andrew and Father Chisholm, watching Dougal fork up the dinner vegetables. The tacit air of companionship surrounding the little group heightened his fretful feeling of exclusion, hardened his resolution. On the table behind him, typed on his portable machine, lay his finished report—a terse and lucid document, crammed with hanging evidence. He was leaving for Tynecastle in an hour. It would be in the Bishop's hands this evening.

Despite the keen, incisive satisfaction of accomplishment it was undeniable that the past week at St. Columba's had been trying. He had found much to annoy, even to confuse him. Except for a group centred round the pious yet obese Mrs. Glendenning, the people of the parish had some regard, he might even say affection, for their eccentric pastor. Yesterday, he had been obliged to deal severely with the delegation that waited on him to protest their loyalty to the parish priest. As if he didn't know that every native son must have his claque! The height of his exasperation was touched that same evening when the local Presbyterian minister dropped in and, after hemming and hawing, ventured to hope that Father Chisholm was not "leaving them"—the "feeling" in the town had lately been so admirable. . . . Admirable—indeed!

While he meditated, the group beneath his eye broke up and Andrew ran to the summerhouse to get his kite. The old man had a mania for making kites, great paper things with waving tails, which flew—Sleeth grudgingly admitted—like monster birds. On Tuesday, coming upon the two breezily attached to the clouds by humming twine, he had ventured to remonstrate.

"Really, Father. Do you think this pastime dignified?"

The old man had smiled—confound it, he was never rebellious: always that quiet, maddeningly gentle smile.

"The Chinese do. And they're a dignified people."

"It's one of their pagan customs, I presume."

"Ah, well! Surely a very innocent one!"

He remained aloof, his nose turning blue in the sharp wind, watching them. It appeared that the old priest was merging pleasure with instruction. From time to time, while he held the string, the boy would sit in the summerhouse taking down dictation on strips of paper. Completed, these laboured scrawls were threaded on the string, sent soaring to the sky, amidst joint jubilation.

An impulse of curiosity had mastered him. He took the latest missive from the boy's excited hands. It was clearly written and not ill-spelled. He read: "I faithfully promise to oppose bravely all that is stupid and bigoted and cruel. Signed, ANDREW. P.S. Toleration is the highest virtue. Humility comes next."

He looked at it bleakly, for a long time, before surrendering it. He even waited with a chilled face until the next was prepared. "Our bones may moulder and become the earth of the fields but the Spirit issues forth and lives on high in a condition of glorious brightness. God is the common Father of all mankind."

Mollified, Sleeth looked at Father Chisholm. "Excellent. Didn't Saint Paul say that?"

"No." The old man shook his head apologetically. "It was Confucius."

Sleeth was staggered. He walked away without a word.

That night he misguidedly began an argument, which the old man evaded with disconcerting ease. At the end he burst out, provoked:—

"Your notion of God is a strange one."

"Which of us has any notion of God?" Father Chisholm smiled. "Our word 'God' is a human word . . . expressing reverence for our Creator. If we have that reverence, we shall see God . . . never fear."

To his annoyance, Sleeth had found himself flushing. "You seem to have a very slight regard for Holy Church."

"On the contrary . . . all my life I have rejoiced to feel her arms about me. The Church is our great mother, leading us forward . . . a band of pilgrims, through the night. But perhaps there are other mothers. And perhaps even some poor solitary pilgrims who stumble home alone."

The scene, of which this was a fragment, seriously disconcerted Sleeth and gave him, when he returned that night, a shockingly distorted nightmare. He dreamed that while the house slept his guardian angel and Father Chisholm's knocked off for an hour and went down to the living room for a drink. Chisholm's angel was a slight cherubic creature, but his own was an elderly angel with discontented eyes and a ruffled angry plumage. As they sipped their drink, wings at rest on the elbows of their chairs, they discussed their present charges. Chisholm, although indicted as a sentimentalist, escaped lightly. But he . . . he was torn to shreds. He sweated in his sleep as he heard his angel dismiss him with a final malediction. "One of the worst I ever had . . . prejudiced, pedantic, over-ambitious, and worst of all, a bore."

Sleeth wakened with a start in the darkness of his room. What a hateful, disgusting dream. He shivered. His head ached. He knew better than to give credence to such nightmares, no more than odious distortions of one's waking thoughts, altogether different from the good, authentic scriptural dreams, that of Pharaoh's wife, for instance. He dismissed his dream violently, like an impure thought. But it nagged him now, as he stood at the window: *Prejudiced, pedantic, over-ambitious, and worst of all, a bore.*

Apparently he had misjudged Andrew, for the child emerged from the summerhouse bearing, not his kite, but a large wicker trug into which, with Dougal's aid, he began to place some fresh-picked plums and pears. When the task was accomplished the boy moved towards the house, carrying the long basket on his arm.

Sleeth had an inexplicable impulse to retreat. He sensed that the gift was for him. He resented it, was vaguely, absurdly disconcerted. The knock on his door made him pull his scattered wits together.

"Come in."

Andrew entered the room and put the fruits upon the chest of drawers. With the shamed consciousness of one who knows himself suspected he delivered his message, memorized all the way upstairs. "Father Chisholm hopes you will take these with you—the plums are very sweet—and the pears are the very last we'll get."

Monsignor Sleeth looked sharply at the boy, wondering if a double meaning were intended in that final simple phrase.

"Where is Father Chisholm?"

"Downstairs. Waiting on you."

"And my car?"

"Dougal has just brought it round for you to the front door."

There was a pause. Andrew began, hesitantly, to move away.

"Wait!" Sleeth drew up. "Don't you think it would be more convenient . . . altogether politer . . . if you carried down the fruit and put it in my car?"

The boy coloured nervously and turned to obey. As he lifted the basket from the chest one of the plums fell off and rolled below the bed. Darkly red, he stooped and clumsily retrieved it, its smooth skin burst, a trickle of juice upon his fingers. Sleeth watched him with a cold smile.

"That one won't be much good . . . will it?"

No answer.

"I said, will it?"

"No, sir."

Sleeth's strange pale smile deepened. "You are a remarkably stubborn child. I've been watching you all the week. Stubborn and ill-bred. Why don't you look at me?"

With a tremendous effort the boy wrenched his eyes from the floor. He was trembling, like a nervous foal, as he met Sleeth's gaze.

"It is the sign of a guilty conscience not to look straight at a person. Besides being bad manners. They'll have to teach you better at Ralstone."

Another silence. The boy's face was white. Monsignor Sleeth still smiled. He moistened his lips.

"Why don't you answer? Is it because you do not wish to go to the Home?"

The boy faltered: "I don't want to go."

"Ah! But you want to do what is right, don't you?"

"Yes, sir."

"Then you will go. In fact, I may tell you that you are going very soon. Now you may put the fruit in the car. If you can do so without dropping all of it."

When the boy had gone, Monsignor Sleeth remained motionless, the contour of his lips fixed into a stiff, straight mould. His arms stretched down at his sides. His hands were clenched.

With that same stiff look upon his face he moved to the table. He could not have believed himself capable of such sadism. But that very cruelty had purged the darkness from his soul. Without hesitation, inevitably, he took up his compiled report, and tore it into shreds. His fingers ripped the sheets with methodical violence. He threw the torn and twisted fragments from him, scattered them irrevocably on the floor. Then he groaned and sank upon his knees.

"Oh, Lord." His voice was simple and pleading. "Let me learn something from this old man. And dear Lord . . . Don't let me be a bore."

That same afternoon, when Monsignor Sleeth had gone, Father Chisholm and Andrew came guardedly through the back door of the house. Though the boy's eyes were still swollen, their brightness was that of expectation, his face, at last, was reassured.

"Be careful of the nasturtiums, laddie." Francis urged the boy forward with a conspirator's whisper. "Heaven knows we've had enough trouble in one day without Dougal starting on us."

While Andrew dug the worms in the flower-bed the old man went to the toolshed, brought out their trout rods, and stood waiting at the gate. When the child arrived, breathless, with a wriggling tinful, he chuckled.

"Aren't you the lucky boy to be going trouting with the best fisher in all Tweedside? The good God made the little fishes, Andrew . . . and sent us here to catch them."

Their two figures, hand in hand, dwindled and disappeared, down the pathway, to the river.